When Life Gives You Werewolves

Also by Aeron Dusk

*The Mark of Amulii*
*The Varcross Key*

www.theliteratebeast.com

# When Life Gives You Werewolves

## AERON DUSK

Publisher's Note:
This is a work of fiction. Names, characters, places, and incidents are a product of the author's imagination. Locales and public names are sometimes used for atmospheric purposes. Any resemblance to actual people, living or dead, or to businesses, companies, events, institutions, or locales is completely coincidental.

Ordering Information:
Quantity sales. Special discounts are available on quantity purchases by corporations, associations, and others.

Cover Design and Artwork: Kusunagi
patreon.com/Kusunagi

Internal Design: Henrik Strömberg
strmberg.se

Line Editor: Holly Atkinson
reedsy.com/atkinson-holly

Proof Reader: Eddie Joo

Audiobook Narration: Skuru
musky.dog

When Life Gives You Werewolves/Aeron Dusk. -- 1st ed.
ISBN (Paperback) 978-1-7378433-6-8
ISBN (Hardcover) 978-1-7378433-7-5
ISBN (EBook) 978-1-7378433-8-2

# When Life Gives You Lemons...

That was a proverb my mother used to use often when I was younger, and I hated it. Whenever I was going through tough times—which was often—we'd talk on the phone, and she'd say those words. Then one day, I never heard her say those words again. It's funny how the stuff that makes us angry in the moment are the things we need to hear the most.

One of my mother's favorite movies was *It's a Wonderful Life*, and she'd make my brother and I watch it every Christmas or New Year's Eve. We hated that tradition... until it was gone. Now I have written a story inspired by those annoying things my mother did or watched, wishing I could have just one more lecture about lemons.

I wanted this book to be more than just a spicy monster romance novel. This book is an amalgamation of things I'd either gone through or observed in the forty-two years I've been alive. *When Life Gives You Werewolves* draws a lot of inspiration from my mother's favorite movie, but it also gets a bit of inspiration from somewhere else.

Years ago, I was riding with a friend to Cocoa Beach when I lived in Merritt Island Florida, and we saw a car with a bumper sticker that I'll never forget. "Only when it's darkest can you truly see the stars." I remember how much that meant to both of us, since we were both going through some very heavy stuff at the time. That quote got me through a lot over the next decade.

The year 2024 would be the year it rained lemons. I had a terrible breakup, which ended a close friendship. To make matters worse, a few weeks later, I was then laid off from the job I'd been working at for over a decade. And finally, both of my dogs got sick. I ended up losing them within four months of each other. But even after all that, there was always a tiny spark of hope deep in my mind, even when I'd ask myself, "Why am I still here?"

Then came the lemonade. I met new friends, and my writing career took off. I got a new, better job, and I still live in one of the most beautiful places in the world. I couldn't just roll over and do nothing. It was hard, and there were times when I'd think about how much I just didn't want to exist anymore, but I made lemonade.

I'm thankful to my supporters who played a pivotal role in shaping this story and all my stories. Many were beta readers, artists, designers, youtubers, and writers themselves who helped me along the way. Those that stuck with me through it all, words cannot express my gratitude.

This story is for those that are going through it. If you're at a point where you just can't see the light at the end of the tunnel, know that we've all been there. It doesn't matter the circumstances because we're all meant to learn different lessons in life. The bad times come and go, but they make us appreciate the good times more. They make us appreciate the time we spend with those we love, and the lessons we've learned from those we've lost.

Here's to a beautiful life...

# Chapter 1

# When It Rains

The interview lasted ten minutes, a whole five minutes longer than usual. I was a lot more prepared this time—that was, until the suspicious marketing manager started drilling. That was the moment I knew the jig was up. I waded too far into a morass of half-truths and outright embellishments with each 'updated' resume, and it had finally caught up with me. I looked down at the now-wrinkled clear binder I'd been clutching like a lifeline with every question that soared over my head.

At least my picture looked good. I didn't have enough money for a professional portrait, so I had to settle for a slightly grainy smart phone image of me in a dark blue collared shirt. My brown hair had been combed neatly enough they wouldn't be able to tell it hadn't been cut in several months. It was probably one of the better pictures of me, but the closer I examined it, the stranger I looked. Over the last year, my eyes had changed color from dark brown to a gross yellowy green. I'd wanted to go to an optometrist to see if it was something serious, but I didn't have insurance.

For the most part, I was healthy. In fact, aside from emotional exhaustion, I'd felt more energetic than I had in years. Despite having the diet of a six-year-old, I was actually gaining some lean muscle. Perhaps it was all those late nights carrying drinks and food to all the drunk college gays for hours on end. Or maybe it was all the walking from one company to the next, hoping to get my foot in the door.

Everyone I worked with carried on as if it was life as usual, but there was always this hint of desperation coupled with the smaller tips and orders. The economy was getting worse, and internships were practically non-existent. I needed just one chance to work in a place that wasn't a bar or a restaurant; somewhere that paid just enough to keep me off the streets.

"Fake it 'til you make it," I whispered through my teeth, pushing open heavy glass doors while shrugging off humiliation and failure. Oh well, no use crying. The worst was over, and it was almost time for work. It had stormed while I was inside, and the scent of steam from the hot asphalt overpowered the exhaust that wafted onto the sidewalk from the busy downtown traffic. Everything in this miserable city smelled terrible, but the odors seemed to get worse over the last few months.

My watch read twenty minutes until one, and my stomach began to complain. I was down to one small meal a day, surviving on greasy discounted food from the city's seediest gay bar, Bottom's Up. I hated wearing the logoed shirts, and while the pay sucked, at least it was a fun place to work. And I had been getting slightly more tips lately.

I stood at the bus stop, holding the cane-end of an umbrella with my right hand, not daring to sit on the bench. Everything was covered in piss, and the homeless werewolves that often occupied them harassed anyone unfortunate enough to wander too close. The monsters looked dangerous, most being well over seven feet tall with sharp teeth and claws, but they were harmless, for the most part. That didn't mean they weren't a nuisance, always asking for money or making creepy advances toward anyone walking by. Despite that, their cheesy pickup lines and overly confident flirting paid off a lot more than I would have expected.

Thinking I was in the clear, I moved closer to the shelter as a few drops of rain fell onto my dress shirt. The hair on my neck stood straight when a huge gray werewolf in a ripped orange hoodie stumbled toward me from an alley close by.

"Hey bud," he said with a deep grunt.

I did what I normally did in these situations. I ignored the beast, knowing he would get the hint and annoy someone else. Unfortunately for me, though, there wasn't anyone else at the bus stop. The werewolves had been pestering me more than usual lately. Sometimes they'd try to get money from passersby, but once they spotted me, they would drop everything and rush over. It was getting so bad that I didn't want to leave the apartment.

"Got any spare change?" He gave the air next to me a deep sniff. "Damn, you smell good. Just get out of church or somethin'?"

This was going to be difficult, but if I held my ground and ignored him long enough, he'd leave—eventually. I glanced at my watch again, struggling to avoid making eye contact. "Where's that damn bus?"

The werewolf moseyed next to me, giving me a better view. I flushed when I noticed he wasn't wearing any pants. Most did, but some didn't. Even though there was a thick patch of fur covering his crotch, this was still considered indecent exposure, even if law enforcement rarely bothered with citations anymore.

"C'mon. Ya got any? I'm sure you got some money lookin' all fancy."

"No," I said, side-stepping to avoid the stench of vodka and wet dog. "Leave me alone."

"All right." Even as he spoke, he stepped closer, leaning until his snout was next to my ear. "If you get me some booze, I'll suck yer dick."

I groaned before seeing my salvation in the form of the A-line bus. "My ride's here. You'll have to save such a tempting offer for someone else," I muttered.

The dirty werewolf watched the incoming transport and grinned. "Hey, looks like we were waitin' for the same bus."

I closed my eyes and let out a frustrated sigh. "Yeah. What a coincidence."

The bar was ten blocks away, and I would have walked, but the rain sprinkling on my face made me reconsider.

"What's yer name, bud?" His deep voice vibrated the air.

"Why are you still talking to me? I don't have any money. Do you think if I did, I'd be taking the bus?"

"Ah, I see why yer all dressed up," the werewolf said, letting out a loud belch while tapping the resume in my hand. "You got a job now? Wanna buy me some lunch to celebrate?"

This one was audacious. My blood started to boil, and all I could do was clench my jaw shut until the bus got there.

"Well, I guess if you don't got any money, I'll just skip lunch."

I looked down at his protruding gut and rolled my eyes. "You should probably skip a few more."

He wasn't fat by normal means. Werewolves rarely were, and the beast still had a lot of natural muscle to offset his beer belly. If he were human, I'd have probably found him even grosser, but oddly, this seemed to work for him. It wasn't like he was ugly, either. They all had an alluring charm, otherwise they wouldn't have as much luck getting laid as they often did.

The bus finally slowed to a stop, and I ran up the steps before swiping my pass. The werewolf followed, feeling around the side pockets of his hoodie.

"Aw damn. Forgot my bus pass," he said with a flirty wink to the bus driver.

The large woman sighed. "Just get on the damn bus, Roscoe."

He smiled and patted the driver on the shoulder. "I owe you another good time."

"You're a real piece of work, and you owe the city thirty bucks." She looked up at him and lowered her voice. "Tomorrow, six-thirty. Don't be late again, bastard."

I tried to scrub that exchange from my brain before taking a seat by the window, but to my abject horror, the beast decided to squeeze in next to me, the seat way too small to accommodate him.

"The werewolf section, Roscoe," the bus driver called back. "Stop harassing people."

"Aw come on, Patty." He put his heavy arm around my neck and yanked me close. My nose was practically in his armpit. "He's a good friend of mine."

"Let me go," I whispered just loud enough to not make any more of a scene as the other passengers gawked at us. The bus began to move, and Roscoe released me.

"What's yer name, bud?"

"None of your business," I said, staring out the window. "And I'm not your bud, so stop talking to me."

I could still see him staring from my peripheral vision. When he tilted his face downward, I pulled the resume to my other side.

"Dakota." The werewolf snorted. "What a queermo name, Dakota." He enunciated it slower, in a nasally tone. "Daaaa-ko-daaaaah."

"Dude, your name is Roscoe. I'm surprised anyone would find you remotely fuckable."

"Ouch," he said, his tail wagging for some reason. "Little twink's got some sass to him."

"Do not call me that."

"What, Dacooter?"

I bit my lower lip and looked away from him again. "I think I know your game now. You're just going to keep following me and annoying me until I give you money." I reached into my pocket and pulled out a five-dollar bill. "Here." I threw it into his lap. "Now get lost."

"Gee thanks, bud." He folded the money in his palm. "So, where're ya headed?"

I tilted my head back against the seat and let out a groan. "Okay, see this is how it's supposed to work. I give you money, and you leave me alone. Why are you still talking?"

"'Cause you gave me money," Roscoe said, still grinning like an asshole. "Gotta complete the transaction, ya know. So what'ya want? Want me to suck yer dick?"

My face got hot as every passenger in earshot turned toward us in unison.

"I'm done with this." The bus stopped a few blocks from the bar, and I stood, squeezing by him as I made my way down the aisle.

"I can eat yer ass too," he called after me, even louder. "You got a nice one, and I got a good tongue for it."

The bus driver looked back at me with an expression I could only assume was pity as I picked up the pace and practically jumped off the bus. When it pulled away, what was once a drizzle earlier turned into a thunderous deluge, and in my desperate attempt to escape, I'd left my umbrella behind.

I wanted to kill that werewolf.

"Whoa! What happened to you?" Rob hopped the bar and ran to me as I dripped on the floor, my shoes making squishing sounds with every step. "Did you miss the bus?"

"I don't want to talk about it," I said, still fuming from my earlier encounter before throwing my now-ruined resume into the garbage. "I'm going to need a uniform. I forgot mine."

"Okay, you're not going to like this."

I glared at him.

"This is all we have. I mean, you could just march that hot ass out there naked and everyone would be throwing their money at you."

"I know you have normal clothes back there."

"Those are for the shop. Gays come from all around just to get a Bottom's Up t-shirt." He paused and gave me a more concerned look. "How's the job hunt going?"

My stomach knotted at that question.

"I haven't been—"

"Oh stop the act." He flamboyantly flicked his wrist and smiled. "You're too smart for this place. You think I didn't know?"

"I guess. I'll let you know when I have an interview that doesn't end with security practically shoving me out the door." I walked into the back storage room with Rob following close behind. After removing my sopping wet shirt, I hung it to drip dry on a wooden chair. "I think I speak for a quarter of my generation when I say college is a fucking scam."

"At least you're trying. If you're that hard up for cash, I have a buddy who owns a bar on Ruskin."

"I'm not dealing with any more werewolves," I snapped, slipping off my nice shoes and dress pants.

"Okay, calm down. It was just a suggestion. They aren't all bums, and the half-turns pay pretty well since they get all that government money."

"Freeloading pieces of shit. What are they going to tip me with at that bar? IOUs? Food stamps? I hate them all."

"Yikes. My friend who owns the bar is a werewolf, so... this is awkward."

I gritted my teeth while wondering how I'd walk back that statement. "I'm sure he's a nice guy."

"You need to be a little more understanding and a little less judgy. If you think it's tough for you to find a good job in this economy, just imagine trying to find any job that wants a werewolf. And if you're a half-turn, forget it. You're too much of a liability."

"I still don't understand that. I thought half-turns were mostly human."

"They're unpredictable and kind of dangerous. But at least they qualify for government assistance and housing, which is why you always see a werewolf living with one." Rob tossed me the skimpy *uniform* I dreaded wearing—blue jorts and a black tank top with the 'Bottom's Up' logo printed on it. It wouldn't have been so bad if the B wasn't a giant, hairy ass sporting a snug g-string.

"I suppose this isn't the most embarrassing thing to happen to me today." Stepping behind a stack of boxes, I removed my briefs and slipped the short denim over my bare skin, taking care to make sure everything was tucked and nothing peeked through the bottom. After slipping on the tank top, I emerged. "Well?"

Rob put his hand over his mouth, pretending to rub his chin while stifling a laugh. "Good lord…"

I held up my hand. "I'm going to need a couple shots to get through this shift."

"I'm imagining what kind of reaction your mother would have."

"She'd have to be sober for that," I muttered while walking out into the hallway. "So, if you have all these werewolf friends, why don't *you* hire any?"

"The same reason I don't let them drink here. Can't afford the insurance."

"Are you for real?"

"It's shitty, but if a werewolf hurts someone in my bar, it's my ass that foots the bill. I mean, I feel bad, but… you just never know when alcohol's involved."

We stepped back into the empty bar, house music playing at low volume. It typically didn't pick up until around seven, and my shift didn't technically start until four. However, being there with friends and around people was less depressing than sitting on a beanbag chair in a bare studio apartment watching old sitcoms.

"It's not like every werewolf has a problem controlling themselves. Ever been to White Dunes?"

"I barely have enough time or money to go to the shitty park downtown. How am I supposed to get to the beach?"

"Well, if you ever do go, there's a werewolf lifeguard that's kind of famous. Met him once, and he's a cool guy. Always makes people laugh with stories about his sharkman boyfriend who can't swim."

I narrowed my eyes. "A sharkman?"

Rob shrugged. "He gets high and makes up shit like that all the time. But my point is, the issue with fully turned werewolves is mostly overblown. You just need to get to know some of them before you judge."

He made a good point; I also didn't want to bring up my earlier encounter. It would just make me look like an asshole, considering Roscoe hadn't actually done anything more than annoy me. Well, that coupled with sexual harassment.

"Okay," I replied, brushing off the suggestion.

That night's shift ended up being the best I'd had in a while, which kind of irritated me because I knew why. I wasn't comfortable wearing revealing clothing or pretending to be interested in some random guy's weird kinks. I was cripplingly introverted, and all these clothes did was throw me into a world I wasn't ready for.

Walking around homeless encampments with three hundred dollars in tips in my pockets at two in the morning had me looking over my shoulders every few seconds. My normal clothes were still damp, balled up in a plastic bag, which made the walk home even more unnerving. As much as I hated the city, it did have a bit of beauty to it, especially when countless skyscraper windows reflected in the mirror-like puddles from the rain earlier.

My watch read two thirty, but it sure didn't feel like it. I couldn't recall the last time I had so much energy after work, and I wasn't even in a particularly good mood.

"Hey! It's Dakooootah!"

I shuddered. Was this another *happy coincidence*, or had he been trailing me?

"Go away," I said, turning to glare at the half-clothed werewolf leaning against a brick alley wall with his arms crossed. His hood was up, and an unnerving shadow covered most of his face. The only features I could make out were two blood-orange dots leering from the darkness. "I thought I made it clear I'm not interested."

He emerged from the alleyway holding my umbrella in his giant hand, the streetlights giving form to his wolfy face. "Well, okay then. If you don't want it, I'll take it."

"Gimme that." I snatched the umbrella away. "You could have said something before I got off the bus."

"I thought I did. I said a couple things, if I remember."

"You're fucking disgusting." I turned and walked away from him, but his wet footsteps followed me.

"Hey," Roscoe called out, catching my arm, the sudden movement freaking me out more. He let go and shoved both hands into the pockets of his hoodie as if fishing for something. "Aw shit. What the hell did I spend it on?" He scratched behind his ears. "Well, I was gonna give you yer money back, but... it's the thought that counts, right?"

I rolled my eyes and resumed walking home, but Roscoe kept following close.

"Shiiiit. You look real hot in that."

"Dude, no." I didn't turn around this time. "I don't know how to make this any clearer. I'm not interested."

"Dakota," he said, earnestly this time.

I stopped and turned again to see a different expression on his face. His eyes were big, and even though they had a creepy orange glow to them, his pathetic body language made me think of a hungry stray dog.

"What?"

"Listen... I don't got a place to sleep tonight, and I was wondering..."

"Fuck. No."

With his tail tucked between his legs, he got down on his knees, looking up at me with even sadder eyes.

"I'll do anything, and it don't got to be sexual. What do you want? Breakfast in bed? Want me to do some housework? Rub yer feet?"

Nothing about this felt good, but he was just going to keep following me. Even if I refused, he'd probably pester me all the way home. It was one night, and the guy did seem friendly. There was a weird cuteness to his face when he wasn't being a complete troll.

I let out a heavy breath, knowing I was probably going to regret this decision. "Your dirty ass sleeps on the floor—after I put some towels down so you don't ruin the carpet. Werewolves aren't allowed in my apartment complex, so if anyone catches you, you're shit out of luck. Capiche?"

His tail wagged. "You ain't gotta worry about that. No one'll even know I'm there."

"This is going to be a mistake. I just know it."

"Nah." There was that shitty grin again. "Tonight's gonna be fun. Got any booze?"

And with that question, regret came crashing down on my head like a cartoon safe.

I opened the door to my cramped studio apartment, and the werewolf and I walked inside.

"Aw damn. Did you get robbed? Where's all yer stuff?"

"This *is* all my stuff," I muttered, tossing the bag of wet clothes on the floor.

"Shit. If I'd known you were this poor, I wouldn't have spent yer five dollars."

"At least you ate."

His stomach growled in response to that.

"You did eat, right?"

"I had more of a liquid lunch."

"Of course you did," I said, washing a bit of dirt from Roscoe off my hands in the kitchen sink. Since I had some extra cash, I wanted to order something to eat, but there probably wasn't anything open at this hour, and deliveries were too expensive anyways. After opening a few cabinets and grabbing anything edible, I laid it all out on the counter. I was going to save it all for a rare lunch tomorrow, but there was a hungry werewolf in my living room, for some absurd reason. "I've got canned tuna and bread."

"Hell yeah. Whip that shit up," he said, leaning over the counter. His excitement quickly turned to flat-eared disappointment. "Where's the mayo?"

"What do you think this is, Benihana? I told you, I have tuna and bread. Do you want it or not?"

"I really shouldn't have spent that money," he muttered, looking at the can and half a loaf of white bread. "All right. I'll have one of yer sad tuna sandwiches."

"You know what's even sadder? No sandwiches," I said, pulling out my can opener before getting to work on the meal. "Why are you homeless? Couldn't get a real job?"

"Oh, I got a job," he said.

I stopped opening the can at the halfway point and glared at him.

"I work as a bouncer at The Booby Trap. The girlfriend kicked me out, so I didn't have a place to stay."

"Get the fuck out of my apartment!"

"What? I wasn't lyin' or nothin'. The bitch took all my money, and I don't get paid 'til Thursday. I just needed a place to crash while things cool."

"I'm such a gullible idiot."

Roscoe looked down at the can, tapping his fingers against the counter. "You gonna finish opening that?"

I had never felt the kind of rage that was brewing in my chest, but being around this werewolf brought me to entirely new levels. Part of me wanted to wrap my hands around his neck and squeeze until he stopped breathing, but he'd probably end up laughing it off.

"Yer face is kind of red. You gettin' sick or something?"

"Something like that," I grumbled, draining the can before spreading the tuna on two pieces of bread.

"You gonna put a couple more pieces on that?"

I picked up the tuna-covered bread, folded it in half and shoved it in his face. "No. I'm saving that bread for toast tomorrow."

He stuffed the entire thing into his mouth. "You gonna actually butter it, or will it be another disappointing culinary experience like this one?" he said with his mouth full.

"You've got one hell of a set of balls on you to be complaining."

"I mean, mayo cost like, what? A couple bucks?"

"I hate you so much."

Roscoe grinned with chunks of food in his teeth, folded the other sandwich, and took it all in one bite.

"I need to grab some towels for you to sleep on," I said, walking into the bathroom linen closet. "Don't touch anything."

"I'll try not to touch any of the three things you got in this place."

I heard something open from the kitchen. "What did I just say?"

"I'm thirsty. Hope you don't mind."

"Roscoe! Drink water," I said, grabbing as many towels as I could before running back into the room. I threw them onto the floor and tried to take the bottle of wine from him, but he lifted it out of my reach. "Give me that, now!"

"How 'bout we both get a little drunk?"

"I was saving those."

"For what? Company? With yer personality, they'd just sit there and go bad."

"Funny." I grabbed a glass. "I guess since you opened it..."

"Don't be a sissy." He took a few hearty gulps of the wine before shoving the bottle into my hands. "Drink it like that."

"You got your slobber all over it!"

"There's a fair bit of backwash in there too."

"Ugh," I groaned, passing him back the bottle.

"I'm kidding. Just drink it."

The ceiling got farther away as I leaned back in the beanbag chair, drunker than I'd been in a while. Roscoe and I finished off both bottles, and he wasn't even remotely tipsy.

"So yer parents are druggies. You got a useless degree, and you can't land a good job." He sat upright on the towels I laid out for him, smirking. "Yer hot and young. Just get yourself an old rich homo to shack up with and yer money troubles go away. Don't know why the hell you try so hard."

"I'd rather not end up a worthless bum like you."

He grinned wider. "I get by just fine."

"You're in *my* house, eating *my* food, and drinking *my* wine. You're only getting by because you leech off other people."

"I think I need to correct you a little here. *You* let me follow you home. *You* made me dinner without me asking, and I got you to drink with me. That all took persistence and effort, buddy. And I've been perfecting my injured dog face for added effect. You fell hard for it."

He was so beyond audacious that I couldn't even be mad at him anymore.

"I don't understand. You stink, you're a slob, and you use people. How do you even have a girlfriend?"

"Because I'm confident and hung and I know how to fuck humans real good."

The wine must have clouded my judgment because I actually found I was turned on. God, I felt so gross.

"You know, the offer's still on the table," he said, crawling closer to me.

"I'll pass."

His hand landed on my crotch, startling me for a second.

"How many times do I have to say no to you?"

"If you think about it, you haven't really said no to me yet." He rubbed his thumb against the seam of my jean shorts. "Yer dick sure doesn't agree with you."

"If you actually applied yourself, you'd make a decent used car salesman."

He pulled the zipper down and unbuttoned my shorts.

"I'm going to let you do this, aren't I?"

"Sure are," he said, pulling the thick fabric all the way off. "Damn, look at that. The twink's packin'."

"I told you not to call me that."

His massive, slobbery tongue caressed my balls. The heat of his mouth soon enveloped my cock, and despite his sharp teeth, I barely felt them graze me.

"Well fuck," I said with a half-sigh, half-moan as his mouth went from my crotch to my ass. "Whoa! What the hell are you doing?"

"Gotta eat something good tonight."

I didn't know when I passed out, but things started becoming clear as different smells assaulted my nose. Alcohol, wet fur, sweat, and semen mixed together in one angry, almost scolding odor. When I looked at the satisfied werewolf snoring with his tongue lolling out of his mouth, I'd never felt more ashamed than I did at that moment.

"Goddamn it," I whispered, shoving Roscoe hard until he snorted awake. "I didn't say you could sleep on my bed."

"What, are you gonna kick me out?" He wrapped his arms around me, shoving his damp crotch into my back. "I'd like to see you try."

I wasn't sure if I had become a victim or if I'd gotten lucky, because even though I was hazy and sore, my reality was undeniable. It was clear as crystal why these werewolves' cringey ways worked so well, especially if they were all that good in bed. One thing was for certain—absolutely no one could ever know about this.

"Just shut up and go to sleep. I'll have to deal with you tomorrow."

"Ooo..." Roscoe's ears perked up.

"Not like that."

His ears flattened against his head. "Aww..."

# Chapter 2

# Angry Afterglow

One of my eyes opened slowly as a bassy voice belted out the lyrics to "Doctor Jones," which played obnoxiously loud from my television. I was way too tired to move, but when I heard the fridge open and close, a rush of panic made me snap my eyes all the way open. I jumped out of the bed and threw on some clean shorts before making a mad dash to the kitchen.

"What the—" I froze as plates of fried eggs, bacon, biscuits, sausage, pancakes and a half-eaten rib eye steak lay spread along the counter in front of me. "Where the hell did you get all this?"

"I found some money in yer pocket, so I got ya some groceries."

My mouth dropped open. "WHAT?"

"You had like three hundred bucks in there, buddy." He held up an open jar of mayonnaise. "Yer welcome."

"Where the fuck is my money, Roscoe?" I asked through my teeth, balling my fists.

"Relax. I didn't spend too much." He pointed to a wad of cash on the counter, and I ran over to count it.

"You spent one hundred and fifty dollars!"

"Yeah, and look." He opened the fridge, now full of food—and, of course—a few cases of beer. "You can thank me later with that ass again." He gave me a slap from behind, and I reached for his neck.

"I'm going to kill—"

"You didn't have no food," he interrupted, holding me back with one arm.

"I eat at work," I shouted, pointing to the banquet on the counter. "I have rent due in a week, and I'm barely scraping by as it is."

"Don't worry about it. I get paid on Thursday, and I'll help with the rent." He winked, which infuriated me even more. "Gotta get to work at six today, so I'll be home late, babe."

I paused and cocked my head. "Dude, this was a one-night thing. You're not staying here."

He turned off the stove and moved the skillet to the side before strutting over to me. "I know the way to yer heart." He pulled me into him, squeezing my rear end with both hands as he laid into me with a deep-tongue kiss.

The building resentment was about to boil over into homicidal rage, but I took a deep breath and pushed him away. "Get the hell off me. Aren't you more into women?"

"Psh, nah. Can't get a man pregnant—at least I don't think so." He winked at me again. "I just get my dick wet with the ladies sometimes until they kick me out."

"I can't have a werewolf living with me." I looked at the food on the counter again. "Did anyone see you this morning?"

"Nah. I'm good with disguises. No one would even know."

"Everyone on this end of the complex probably knows after last night."

"Yeah, you loved it."

"Don't change the subject!"

He grinned, baring those dangerous canines before handing me a plate of food. "I made you breakfast. Don't normally do that with hookups, you know."

"How romantic. I bet you say that to all the people you steal money from." I snatched the plate from him. "I have to get ready for an interview in two hours." I took a forkful of grits and eggs into my mouth, intending to swallow it down quickly, but the unexpected flavor made me stop chewing.

"Hmm? What was that?" he asked, stabbing the steak with a knife before fitting the rest of it into his maw.

"What was what?"

"Can I shack up with you or not?"

I started chewing again, contemplating the question. If he was true to his word and had a job, having someone else help with the rent and utilities could take some of the burden off me, but there was no way in hell I could trust this guy after he spent my money.

"You're definitely not worth the frustration."

He sat his fork on the counter, and with a cocky stride, slid behind me and wrapped his arms around my waist, playfully biting my neck. "C'mon. I can make you make those noises again."

His stiffening cock pressed against my lower back, and my throat went dry as I swallowed my remaining food. This sucked, but no amount of denial would change what happened. The regret came rushing back.

"Good sex doesn't pay the bills," I said, now facing him. "This was a one-time thing."

Roscoe didn't say anything. Instead, he grabbed my hand and forced his dick into it.

"I mean it," I said, swatting him away, but he caught my arm and pushed me against the counter. It was going to happen again, and I loathed myself for actually liking it.

"God, I hate you," I hissed, fisting the longer fur on his chest and pulling him in for a kiss.

"This has got to stop," I muttered under my breath, still glaring at the werewolf snoring loudly next to me. His long tongue hung off to the side as usual, this time, leaving a shallow puddle of drool on my once clean pillow. Even in his sleep he looked smug. Was I really so touch-starved that I was simping for *this*? I never really understood the saying until now, but good dick is a prison.

My muscles ached from the waist down, and the whole apartment smelled like werewolf and spunk. I wasn't even sure how long we'd been going at it until I noticed the time glowing blue on the digital alarm clock next to me. Less than an hour to get ready and catch a bus for my next interview. As I stood and limped across the room, the consequence of my lack of self-control trickled down my inner thigh and then onto the carpet. Were all werewolves like this? I wasn't even sure how he'd managed to get something that large all the way inside of me but far be it from me to question what obviously worked.

There was still food all over the place, and I wanted to eat as much as I could before leaving. Though I was furious at Roscoe for spending my money, I would have probably spent half that on takeout, and none of it would have lasted. Still, his rifling through my pockets made me nervous about leaving him here.

After finishing a plate of pancakes, I hobbled my way to the shower then donned fresh clothes. Dishes clattered from the kitchen, and closing cabinet doors rattled the thin walls. I brushed my hair, pulling it back into a ponytail before stepping out into the room.

"Make sure you get all the grease off that stove," I said, plopping down onto my beanbag chair.

He turned the water off and gave me an expectant stare. "Did you make up yer mind?"

I didn't respond. Instead, I groaned and leaned further back while staring at the ceiling.

"C'mon. I made you come like three times, and I'm doing dishes. What more's a guy gotta do?"

"*You're* the one who messed up the dishes. And just because you're a good lay doesn't mean you're a good person to live with. Which reminds me. Why did your *girlfriend* kick you out anyways?"

"Women are complicated. They want shit like commitment and love and all that. I just want a place to live, a hole to fuck, and a buddy to play video games with. So, hell, I thought, why not just fuck guys?"

"You're a real Casanova," I said, rolling my eyes. "Just get your own damn apartment and stop leeching off of other people."

Roscoe opened his mouth but didn't say anything as he shifted his eyes to the side.

"You do have a job, right?"

"Of course I do," he said, a little quieter. "I just, uh, can't seem to hold on to 'em down for long."

"Ah! There it is," I said, pointing at him. "I can barely afford to feed myself, let alone a five-hundred-pound monster."

"Four hundred and forty pounds!" He looked down and patted his gut. "Damn, how'd I get so fat?"

"Gee, I don't know," I said sarcastically before scooting off the chair to a stand. "Couldn't possibly be the fried steaks, pancakes, sausage and eggs you horked down earlier." I walked by him and opened the fridge. "Where are the leftovers?"

Roscoe answered that question with a gurgled belch. "Well..."

Air hissed through my teeth, and I let the fridge door shut on its own.

"I had to refuel after bein' a good lay and all."

I grabbed my backpack off the floor, making certain I had my money with me this time. "I'll have to finish cleaning the kitchen later. Get out."

Roscoe's ears fell, and his watery eyes went wide. "So, I take it yer not gonna let me stay?"

"Hell no. And that stupid face isn't going to work this time. When I get through this interview, I'll meet up with you later, and we'll discuss... something."

His tail wagged.

"That wasn't a yes, Roscoe."

The energetic appendage slowed before hanging limp between his legs.

I was still in shock. The interviewer must have thought I was nuts after I asked her for the third time if she was for real. I actually got a job. A real job. It paid like shit, of course, but there was a future.

It was hard to suppress the desire to dance out of that office, but I did whisper an excited, "Yes!" when I hurried out the front door. Persistence, it seemed, had finally paid off, and it couldn't have happened at a more crucial time.

"Look at you all chipper." Roscoe's voice boomed from behind as I rounded a corner.

"I thought you were going to work."

"I don't work 'til six, remember? And you locked me out of yer house. Where else am I supposed to go?"

"Do you have to walk so damn close? I don't want people getting the wrong idea."

He laughed and turned to a man in a suit who walked past us on the right. "Hey dude, I'm bangin' this guy."

"Shut the fuck up," I hissed, walking faster, but his longer strides made it hard to put a reasonable distance between us.

"C'mon, no one cares," he belted out as I made a sharp right turn into an alleyway. "You gonna tell me how yer job interview went?"

"I got it."

His flirty grin faded. "Ah, that's... That's real good."

"Why did you say it like that?"

He patted me on the back and turned away. "I'mma head to work early. You want to meet up later for some fun?"

"Whatever," I said, more annoyed by the reaction than I should have been. Why did it even matter?

"All right," he grunted, not bothering to look back.

The way he left didn't sit right, but I wouldn't let it bother me. Things were starting to finally look up, and I was going to celebrate tonight.

"That's great news," Rob shouted over the loud music while mixing another cocktail. "It's not gonna to be the same without you, though."

"You know I just love working here and all—"

"Eh, cut the bullshit. A piece of your soul dies every time you take an order for fried pickles."

"Well, maybe if I didn't have to say, 'Hope this tickles your pickle' every time I serve them, I wouldn't seem so soulless." We looked at each other for a moment and laughed. "Plus, being a server in a gay dive bar isn't exactly paying the bills."

"You know I'd pay you more, but I'm struggling to keep this place open as it is."

I carried a tray of beer and aforementioned fried pickles to a corner table illuminated by the orange, green and purple neon letters on the wall. Seated were five partially drunk college guys, all obnoxiously talking over each other.

"Here's your order." I placed the food and drinks in the center of the table before letting out a sigh. "Hope it... tickles your pickles," I muttered the last part.

"How about you tickle *my* pickle?" the taller guy on the far end of the table asked with a ridiculous grin. It made me cringe a little, but I didn't mind the extra attention as long as it came with amazing tips.

"Tempting," I said with a flirty inflection, walking my fingers over the table before grabbing his hand. "But there are just so many guys that need service tonight."

That felt as gross as it sounded.

He pulled out a pen and scribbled his number on the back of a beer-stained napkin. "Well, if you're not too tired for another service call, here's my number."

And just like that, I was now a pretend hooker. I grabbed the napkin and slid it into my pocket. "I might take you up on that some time," I said with a slight wink before turning away. For some reason, I could still hear their conversation, even though I should have been out of earshot.

"What is it with you and really hairy guys?"

When I got to the bar, I set the serving tray down and tried to examine myself when another man called to me, pulling my attention to a table with three men in their mid-thirties. They were regulars, but I never could remember their names. The bar was getting harder to handle, and the music was louder—so much louder. The strobe lights in the dark, stuffy room were also starting to hurt my eyes.

"Hey you," I said, forcing a smile, while trying to push away the throbbing in my head. "What can I get you guys?"

"We'll take whatever's on tap tonight."

"Anything else?"

"Got a boyfriend?" one of the other men asked.

I was used to the attention, but never like this. Sure, people got drunk and would sometimes hit on me, but I started to feel like I was standing naked in the middle of a crowded room under a spotlight. And none of these guys ever showed interest before.

"Unfortunately, I do," I shouted over the deafening music.

"You smell amazing," another man said, and I backed away, trying to maintain a smile. "What cologne is that?"

"Thanks. I uh, always try to smell my best," I said awkwardly as I backed toward the bar. The confidence I'd exuded earlier drained as quickly as it had come. I wasn't even wearing cologne.

"Are you okay?" Rob asked.

"Not really," I said, pointing to a pitcher. "Could I get one of those filled?"

"Why don't you go home? I'll call in Zack. He's been pestering me for more hours."

"Are you sure? It'll be overtime for him."

"Yeah, it'll be fine." He handed a drink to one of the guys sitting at the bar before staring at me again. "Did you get a haircut or something?"

"No," I replied, as I stepped behind the bar, grabbing my bag. "I'll call you later."

"All right," he shouted, his attention pulled back to the bar as he filled another order.

I stepped out the front door, slipping through groups of people crowding along the sidewalks of downtown. Everyone was so loud, and there were so many strong smells, which only further exacerbated my pounding headache.

I arrived at the bus stop and noted a pair of glowing eyes leering at me from the blackened alley across the street. The clock on my phone read a quarter to ten; I'd have at least twenty minutes to kill until the next bus arrived. It was unbearable. Every car driving by left a trail of noxious exhaust that had me in coughing fits, and the drunk people stumbling along the walkways were even more unpleasant.

Sitting on the bench, I slumped over, resting my head in my hands. A large body sat next to me, and I got a whiff of a familiar dog-like odor. It was another werewolf—brown this time, wearing a pair of ragged, frayed jeans and nothing more.

"I remember my first night," he said, pointing up at the full moon peeking between the skyscrapers. "I didn't know what was happening, and I wanted to rip everyone's heads off just to make the world shut up."

"Huh?"

"I don't think like that anymore since hitting my full-turn, but everything was a little harder to control back then."

"Why are you telling me this?"

The werewolf paused and narrowed his eyes. "Are you looking for a roommate?" He reached into his pocket, grabbing a wrinkled piece of paper.

I put up my hand to stop him. "Not really, no."

"You sure? It's hard for us to live alone. I—don't have a job right now, but I can pay you in other ways. I can get you a nice-looking kuu, too."

I stood and slipped into the straps of my backpack. That last part confused me, but I wasn't about to ask. I just wanted to get away from him. "Sorry, no."

"Did another one beat me to it already?" He clicked his tongue, sighed, then stood and walked away, his tail tucked.

"What the hell was that about?"

I awoke to the sound of loud knocking, having fallen asleep minutes after arriving at the apartment. My body ached even more, and I was running a slight fever. Of all the weeks I could have gotten the flu...

With a groan, I dragged myself out of bed and hobbled across the room before squinting through the peephole of the front door. I couldn't see much other than what looked like a sheet over a huge standing lamp.

"Who's out there?"

"Roscoe," he grunted. "Hurry up and let me in before someone gets suspicious."

I opened the door, revealing the ridiculous disguise. The grimy sheet he wore barely covered anything, just his head and most of his upper body. His tail and furry legs still showed. This was how he planned on not drawing attention to himself?

"What the hell is this?" I asked as Roscoe tried to push his way past me, but I shoved him back. "Did you walk all the way here like that? How can you see anything?"

He removed the sheet and held up a plastic freezer bag full of what I suspected was weed. "Of course I didn't. That would have been stupid," he said, pointing to his snout. "Plus, I don't need to see nothin' when this works just fine."

"When you said you were good with disguises, I thought you'd actually put some effort into them."

A man walked alongside the building at the other end of the hall toward my unit, so I pulled Roscoe inside and slammed the door before locking the deadbolt.

"The last thing I need right now is the police showing up," I shouted.

"You know what you need?" he asked, tossing me the small plastic bag he carried.

"I don't smoke," I said, handing the bag back to him.

He crossed his arms. "C'mon. It's good shit, and there's a prize at the bottom."

I narrowed my eyes while staring down at the now open bag. After feeling around, I pulled out a roll of cash secured with a rubber band.

"What's this?"

"The deed to my beach house," Roscoe replied before making his way to the fridge.

I began counting the money. "This is fifty dollars more than you took. I thought you didn't get paid until Thursday."

"I forgot about the OnlyStans payout this month."

"*You* have an OnlyStans?"

"Sure do. Just don't make much money off of it."

"Surprising," I said, following him. "Can't imagine why."

Roscoe continued rifling through the fridge. "Hey, it's a saturated market. Just about every werewolf's got a big dick, so it ain't like I'm anything special."

"I'm going to regret asking this, but... what exactly do you do on that app?"

"Sometimes I jack off."

I waited as he turned and leaned against the countertop, popping open a can of beer.

"And?"

Roscoe took a few gulps before responding. "And what?"

"Sometimes I wonder how you get up the motivation to keep breathing," I muttered, stuffing the money into my pocket, though not before setting the extra fifty on the counter. "It's not even like you have to put in that much effort. It's OnlyStans. Get some mood lighting, wear a harness, and shove a huge dildo up your lazy ass."

"Sounds like you know what yer doing," he said, eyeing the money. "That's yers, by the way."

"No, it's not. You need to find your own place to live."

"Dude..." The werewolf trailed off and took another sip of beer.

"I gave it some thought, and the whole thing doesn't sit well with me. I don't know you, and you're being a little too pushy about this. It's like you're hiding something."

"I ain't hidin' nothing," Roscoe snapped, his ears lowering against his head. "And you knew me well enough to let me fuck you... twice."

"That's just a hookup, remember?"

Roscoe crinkled the empty can before tossing it into the garbage. "I'll pay half the rent. Hell, I'll even buy the groceries. Come on, that's a good deal. Think of all the money you'll save."

"I'll be making enough money with my new job—oh." The events from earlier made more sense. "Now I know why you had a shitty attitude."

"I didn't have a shitty attitude. I was happy for ya."

"Uh huh," I muttered. "It's nothing against you. I just don't want a roommate."

"You mean, you don't want a *werewolf* roommate," he corrected, grabbing another beer from the fridge. "Sounds like someone's a little racist."

"Nice try, Roscoe. You sound about as white and southern as Jimmy Dean. Also, you were the one just wearing a white sheet over your head."

He wrinkled his nose, seemingly trying to come up with something else to make me feel sorry for him.

"Listen, I get it. It ain't the first time I've heard that," he said walking over to me before setting the open can on the counter. Roscoe was so close, he was practically pushing against me as my back hit the wall. "Look me in the eyes and tell me you don't feel nothin' for me."

This werewolf was a lot more dangerous than I'd suspected, and not because he had sharp teeth, claws, and deadly body odor. He knew how to manipulate people, and for some fucked up reason, it was kind of hard to resist.

I stared at the floor and remained silent.

"Dakota," he said, his tone uncharacteristically soft.

"Call me Cody. Dakota pisses me off."

"Cody." He stood over me a little longer before sighing and taking a step back. "Can I at least stay until next week?"

I had to look away from him because he was making that face again.

"Come on, Cody," he prodded, a little whinier than before.

"God damn it! Fine. Just promise you won't get me kicked out." I walked over to the bed and sat on the mattress. "Ugh, I feel like shit. I don't even want to argue anymore."

"Wanna hear a story?" Roscoe asked, picking up the bag of weed and walking to the other side of the bed. The covers hadn't been washed yet, so I didn't object this time.

"You're gonna smoke that in here?"

"We are," he said, leaning back against the wall. He pulled a lighter and a small pack of cigarette paper from the bag.

"I don't smoke."

He ignored me and rolled the joint anyway.

"I grew up in bumfuck nowhere Arkansas, and my parents were, uh... missing a lot of the time. When I was about seventeen, I never stayed at home. At night I'd sleep in barns, and during the day, I'd dig ditches or whatever else people wanted me to do to make a little money. It was pure shit, but when I went half-turn, that's when things really got bad." He took a drag of the joint before passing it to me.

"So, what happened?" I put the joint to my lips and took in a deeper drag than I intended. Roscoe slapped my back as I choked.

"Good shit, ain't it?" he asked, gently taking the joint from my fingers.

"My lungs are on fire."

He let out a deep laugh before resuming his story. "When you go half-turn, you get really horny. I mean, so horny it starts to hurt unless you got a werewolf to fuck ya. When the town found out what I was, they nearly ran me out with shotguns thinkin' I was gonna start knocking up their daughters with werewolf babies."

"Well, they had a point," I said, feeling a little light-headed, but calmer. "When did all this happen?"

Roscoe took another puff before scratching his head. "The twenties? Thirties? Somewhere in that time. Hell, I don't even remember if this is really my story."

My eyes widened. "How old are you?"

He shrugged. "I did a lot of heavy drugs for a long time. I couldn't remember if I tried. Maybe a hundred? Seventy?"

"You're old enough to be my great grandfather," I said, sounding more disgusted than I was. "Was your dad a werewolf?"

"Don't know. He died in some war, I think. My momma said I must have gotten it from dad's dad. Apparently, he was a huge Sicilian alpha. He ran the mafia before mafias were a thing."

I eyed him suspiciously. "You're Italian?"

"Uh, sure. Yeah."

"So, if your grandfather had it, your dad probably did too, right?"

"I don't think that's how it works, kid. Most people who go half-turn have no idea they got the unlucky gene until it happens in their teens." He passed me the joint again. "Curious. How old are you?"

"Twenty-two," I said, and took a lighter drag. "So, did they end up running your ass out of town?"

"Didn't need to. No one would hire me to do anymore work, so I had to find a place that was a little more progressive. You know, it's funny. They were so worried about me fucking their daughters, they had no idea what I was doing to their sons. That was kinda how I survived for a little while. In exchange for not telling anyone they were sucking half-turned werewolf dick, they gave me food and hush-money until I had enough to hop a train and head up north. The rest is just a mess of hard drugs, psychedelics, weed and lots and lots of great sex."

"Doesn't sound like you really minded being a werewolf."

"I wouldn't have if society didn't completely fuck me over after turnin'. It's a lot harder than you think. You call me lazy, but I wasn't always this way. I just stopped giving a fuck because anything I'd do never mattered. No one wants to hire a werewolf for the good jobs, so they make us do all the shit humans don't want to." He took one long drag until the joint almost disappeared. "And I say, fuck that."

Even though his mood had shifted, he was being a lot more sincere.

"Why are you telling me this? Another werewolf said something similar on my way home, and he asked if I had a roommate."

He snapped his head back to me. "You told him you did, right?"

"What does it matter?"

"Because now that yer makin' the change, yer gonna get a lot more unwanted attention."

"Yeah, it is a big change, but just because I have a job doesn't mean I want werewolf roommates."

"Ya need a werewolf, Cody. No one's gonna look out for us, so we gotta make our own way."

"What the hell are you talking about?"

"You bein' a half-turn."

I gave him a silent and bewildered stare.

"Shit, I thought you knew. I mean, have you looked in the mirror lately?" He stopped himself and cleared his throat.

"What... the fuck did you do to me, Roscoe?" I looked down at my arms, which were hairier than before. "I thought it was genetic! I'm way too old for this."

Roscoe shrugged and picked the bag of weed up off the nightstand before rolling another joint. "I didn't do nothin'. You obviously got the werewolf gene, so let's celebrate."

I felt like throwing up.

He nudged my arm with his elbow and passed me the joint. "You need to take a few more hits of this and calm down."

# An Enchanting Agreement

I sat alone on a weathered wooden bench outside of a run-down café, the morning sun partially obscured by clouds. Or maybe it was smog. I wasn't sure. This was a part of the city I never wanted to end up in, but if this was going to be my life, then I had to find places that would accept a half-turn.

Part of me wanted to break down crying, but the rest was still catching up to my new reality. It was like coming out of the closet all over again, only this time I had no control over it.

Even though my affliction wasn't obvious yet, I still felt embarrassed enough to hide. My black hoodie and mirrored aviator sunglasses did a good job hiding the thicker body hair and weird orange tint to my irises. My shoes had grown a bit tighter, but thankfully everything else still fit.

I didn't wake Roscoe before leaving, and I didn't care anymore if he stayed in my apartment alone. In fact, it became increasingly harder to care about anything. It wouldn't be long before I was the smelly, vodka-soaked monster at the bus stop, pestering strangers for money.

"Are you gonna come in and order something?" a deep voice called out from inside the building. The door had been propped open with a small trash can that hadn't been emptied. For a place that served food, it should have been a turn-off, but the werewolves didn't seem to care.

The last few years of being forced into frugality caused me to hesitate, but what was the point of holding back? I wasn't about to waste what little money I had left on bills like rent. The moment the property managers found out about this, I'd be gone. They also wouldn't be legally required to return the rest of my rent or any deposit I'd made.

Flashes ripped through my mind like red lightning as my landlord's head rolled across the floor, blood dripping from my claws. The scary thing was, I felt like I'd probably do it.

"Fuck it," I whispered before finally pushing myself off the bench. Every muscle in my body complained at once. Even the walk up here was more exhausting and painful than usual.

As I made my way toward the café counter, several werewolves eyed me, most notably the barista who was tall, silver and surprisingly well-dressed and clean.

"Could I get..." I glanced at the menu on the wall, not knowing the difference between an americano and a cappuccino, but I had always wanted to try something that sounded bougie. "A mocha latte?"

"How do you want it?"

"I don't know. Mocha-y? Surprise me," I muttered, trying to stifle my irrational animosity the more I stared at him. It wasn't as though I hated werewolves, but I wasn't ready to look my future in the face yet.

The barista got to work on the beverage, and I shuffled to an empty table at the far end of the café, hiding my hands in my pockets and averting my eyes. The place wasn't as run-down as it looked from outside; in fact, it was kind of cozy. The walls were brick, purposely half-finished with cracked Tuscan stucco, giving the inside a bit of old-world charm. The chairs were antique and solid oak with decades of scratches and wear, while the tabletops had been recently polished.

I lost myself for a moment in the steady, low-fi music trickling through the speakers overhead while staring out the window at the werewolves strolling by. There wasn't a single car on the road; I started to wonder if I was even in the city anymore. It was like I had walked into a portal where everything smelled better and there weren't many loud noises.

A cup of hot, foamy liquid slid in front of me, pulling my attention back. The silver-furred barista gave a warm, toothy smile before nodding.

"Thanks," I said, looking back down at the cup.

"Can I get you something else?" His tail swayed softly behind him. "Maybe something to eat?"

"Um, one sec," I said before taking out my wallet to make sure Roscoe hadn't decided to help himself to the cash he'd returned last night.

The werewolf grabbed my hand, stopping me. "You don't pay."

"Excuse me?"

"It's free," he replied before pointing to my hoodie. "It's a little hot in here for that, isn't it?"

The werewolves sitting at the other tables stared at me while occasionally glancing at each other, each one rigid as if waiting. The classical ambiance of the room suddenly shifted to a bunch of crinkling papers.

"What's the catch?" I asked, narrowing my eyes. After my last encounter with a werewolf—who was now sleeping in my bed—I couldn't help but be suspicious.

"New half-turns don't pay. That's the policy."

"Oh," I said, my face growing hot. "Do I look worse now?"

"It's not how you look," he said, pointing to his nose. "You may as well take the coat off. It's just making you sweat more."

Another rush of embarrassment hit me as I slowly removed the coat and sunglasses. The barista gave a nod before walking away, disappearing into the back room. When he was out of sight, a different werewolf approached, nervously holding a wrinkled sheet of paper. Three more got up from their tables and rushed over to me, holding similar sheets.

"What's your name?" a tall, black werewolf asked. The shorter brown one next to him let out a growl before a gray one cut in front. The mood of the place shifted to what I could only describe as polite aggression.

"Cody," I answered, growing more nervous as the atmosphere of the room grew tense.

"Need a roommate?" the brown one asked.

Before I could answer, all of them slid their papers in front of me and stood waiting, their ears sticking straight up.

"I've got a job," the brown one said with a proud, toothy smirk.

The gray werewolf pushed brown to the side. "He works one day a week at the quarry, and he doesn't bathe. I don't have a job, but I'm clean, and I'll do anything you want. Nothing's off-limits."

When the larger black werewolf shoved them both, and they fell into the third, things started getting violent. Snarls tore through the cafe as punches and claws splattered blood, some getting on my shirt. As the noise in the café grew louder, the door to the back room swung open, and the barista ran out, banging a pan with a wooden spoon.

"Knock it off!"

Each werewolf went still and silent, turning their attention back to me.

"I've got a roommate," I said, clearing my throat as they each took a seat at the table. I looked down at the papers they placed in front of me earlier. "What's all this?"

"Stuff about us," the black werewolf said. "You're going to need a werewolf roommate."

"Why?" I asked, picking up one of the wrinkled papers. It was like reading poorly written resumes. There was everything from detailed—and at times graphic—physical descriptions as well as what they did for fun, and it was typed in small, bulleted font. I looked at the others. Each of these profile sheets followed the same template. "I already have a werewolf roommate."

"It's too early to make a decision like that," the barista said, setting a plate of hot apple turnovers in front of me, way more than I could eat alone. "You should at least review a list of candidates first."

"What are you talking about?"

"Whenever there's a new half-turn in this part of town, he gets handed these." The barista pointed at the papers. "You just go through them and pick out which one you like best."

"You guys... just carry these on you all the time?"

The four werewolves nodded in unison.

"Never know when we'll get lucky. So, hopefully you'll choose me," the gray werewolf said, flashing his eyebrows. "I put a little something in mine that might spark your interest."

I looked down and read until I got to the bold print. "Dude. That's kinda gross."

"I'll do it, if you want."

I folded the paper and tossed it with the others. "I'm not interested. Plus, I have a roommate already, like I said."

They all stared in silence, and I had a feeling they knew I was lying since I hadn't completely made up my mind about the Roscoe situation.

"That sounds kind of suspicious," the barista muttered in a contemplative tone. "You might have gotten yourself into a bad situation."

"What do you mean?" I asked, and took a bite of one of the turnovers.

Before the werewolf could answer, another half-turn entered the cafe with a cocky stride, thankfully taking some of the attention off me. He wore a black tank top and torn, brown cargo shorts. Something thicker than body hair covered his arms and chest—like short, peppery fur—though there were places where his dark bare skin showed. The guy looked a little younger than me, his jawline sharp and hair styled in unruly dreads.

"Perfect timing," the barista said, waving the guy over.

"What?" he grunted before glaring at me.

"Adam, this is..." The barista trailed off. "What's your name again?"

"Cody," I said, extending my hand toward the half-turn.

He didn't take it. Instead, he eyed the turnovers before snatching one. "Don't care."

I opened my mouth to speak, but the barista cut me off. "Don't be rude, you little shit. He's about to go half-turn." He smacked the guy on the back of the head. "And those are for him. You owe me two bucks."

"Aw come on. He's not gonna eat all these." The half-turn glanced at the folded sheets of paper in front of me. "Want some advice? Be picky as hell when you decide to let one of these dirty fuckers live with you."

"Show him your kuu," the barista said, pointing to a dark, metal choker around Adam's neck.

"Ah yeah, the trap," he said, tugging at the choker. It shimmered a little more than it should have in the dim, natural light of the café. He glared at the barista again. "Once you get one of these, you've gotta pay for your pastries."

"Why's it a trap?" I asked.

"It's not. He's being dramatic," the barista said. "You get one of these from your chosen werewolf, and once you wear it, everyone will know you're not looking. But—"

"It's a fucking trap," Adam repeated.

"Stop scaring him. You're just upset because you were thinking with your dick when you chose your werewolf."

Adam picked up the folded papers off the table and waved them in my face. "Read. These. Carefully." He turned and glared at the other werewolves. "Don't put up with their shit, and don't let one try to sweet-talk you. They're good at that because they only want to use you."

He just described Roscoe to a T, and I started to feel stupid again. Of course he'd left out all this weird kuu shit.

"Why don't you just take it off and find another one?" I asked, pointing to the choker. "And why should I even accept one?"

"If I could take it off, I'd have done it already, dumbass." Adam leaned in closer. "Welcome to werewolf hell." He pulled up a chair and took his place next to me. "This thing is supposed to help with the homeless werewolf problem, but it's just exploitation through magic."

"Magic?" I rolled my eyes. "Would you stop with this crap?"

"Sounds stupid, but I'm telling the truth. You're about to see a lot of fucked up shit, man."

"Let me explain this a little better." The barista slapped the back of Adam's head again. "We're kind of pigeonholed into doing shitty jobs the humans don't want to do, and these *jobs* don't offer any kind of livable wage. Most werewolves would rather just be homeless rather than work for slave wages. In this part of town, all businesses are werewolf-owned, and most houses are designated Section-L for half-turns. They're tiny little shit-boxes that only have enough space for two, so in response, our community took matters into its own hands by gaming the system, so to speak.

"When you start to shift into a half-turn, you're eligible for government assistance and housing. It's also an unspoken rule that you will have to choose a werewolf to live with until you make the full shift, and you'll be required to donate half the money you get from the government to the settlement project. The kuu is a way to ensure you comply with this. After it's over, you'll get to live at a werewolf commune, not governed by humans. It's guaranteed housing and actual career opportunities for both you and your chosen werewolf."

"Once it's finished? So, I'll just be homeless until a commune is ready? *And* they're gonna take half my money? What is this commie bullshit?"

"Commie? You're getting money from the government. What did you expect?" Adam snapped. "It's really the only good deal there is—if you can find a werewolf to live with that isn't a useless piece of shit."

He grabbed another turnover, but the barista slapped it out of his hand. "Stop being a nazi. He's not going to eat six of these things."

I tore off a corner of one and held it to my mouth. "If it's a good deal, why has this been going on for years? It's not like a commune takes all that long to build."

"Well, it's a new system, and it's not entirely legal—yet," the brown werewolf said. "The communes are still off the government radar, and it takes time and money to build enough housing. We're essentially stealing from the government to do this. Half-turns that contributed and their chosen werewolves have first dibs on everything. These communes will spread all over until they are towns big enough to incorporate, and since every werewolf still has the right to vote, we'll gain real power in the government for once. Werewolf mayors, werewolf commissioners. Maybe one day we'll have a werewolf governor."

"This sounds a little sketchy. Has anyone actually seen these places?" I asked.

"Well, not exactly, but—"

"It sounds like someone's getting their palms greased while giving everyone false hope," I said, interrupting the barista. "I'd want to see these places for myself before giving money to anything." I looked around, noting the mood shift. "Hasn't anyone actually questioned this?"

"I may not have seen the communes, but I have seen towns that have become much more werewolf-friendly," the barista answered. "Plus, you have to get the kuu, which means you don't really have a choice. They will take a portion of your money."

"I don't have to do anything. I don't need to live with a werewolf, and I don't need whatever the hell a kuu is. I'll just save all the money I get and—"

"And what? Buy a house?" Adam shot me a smug grin. "Who's gonna sell it to you?"

"It's a necessary evil, man," the brown werewolf cut in again. "Even if the communes are just bullshit, the idea's gaining traction. Those werewolf towns exist, and they wouldn't have just ten years ago. Sometimes just the idea is enough to spark change."

I glanced at the chain Adam wore around his neck. "What exactly is a kuu?"

"It's a piece of enchanted jewelry your chosen werewolf picks out," the barista replied.

"Why can't I pick it out?"

"Half-turns aren't allowed to buy them. They have to be ritualistically attuned to the werewolf before you put it on. The jewelry he picks out needs to be enchanted on the phase of the moon it corresponds with. I don't know all the details, but I do know that it helps calm the unpredictable urges and violence that will come with the transformation. One of the elders will collect blood from the werewolf and it all happens behind closed doors. All you have to do is wear it and the government won't throw you in a cell."

"So, no one questions any of this shit? What happens if I lose this thing?"

Adam grabbed my hand and placed it on his necklace. "Try to pull this off."

"I don't want to break it."

He laughed. "If only."

I gripped the chain and tried to find the fastener, but there wasn't one. After I gave it a firm tug, the metal seemed to come to life in my hand, shrinking a bit as I let it go. It really looked like magic—or maybe something secretly high tech that no one was allowed to understand.

"It won't come off until he's a full werewolf," the barista said. "That's when the contract ends."

It was around noon when I finally made it home, having spent an extra hour or so fending off unwanted attention. Desperate werewolves from all over Ruskin bombarded me with their weird resumes, some of which looked like they had been carried around for months. The whole song and dance was a terrible reminder of my months searching for a job, but now I was the one with the power to decide whether someone had a home or remained on the streets. It was so easy to put emotional distance between me and them when I was human, but those days were quickly drawing to a close.

The apartment was dark and quiet, save for snoring coming from a giant lump on my bed. How long was he going to sleep? I removed my hoodie and tossed it to the floor before collapsing onto the beanbag chair. With a remote in hand, I flipped on the television for background noise while shuffling through the folded sheets of paper.

Roscoe groaned repeatedly, as the commotion had finally woken him up, but I ignored him. He groaned louder, and I cranked the volume until the duvet flew off the bed, and he jumped out, baring his teeth.

"I'm tryin' to sleep!"

I muted the television and glared at him. "It's noon. Wake the hell up."

Roscoe yawned and scratched his head. "Really?" He trudged unsteadily toward the window and peeked through the blinds. "Well shit. Why didn't you wake me up?"

"I just did," I muttered, unmuting the TV and skimming the next resume for anything interesting. "Why does every werewolf open with how big his dick is?"

"Wait a minute." Roscoe walked toward me, his eyes wide. "What's all that?"

"Details of sexual positions and dick sizes, apparently." I folded the paper and set it aside. "They're werewolf roommate candidates."

"Aw, come on, Dakota!"

I glared at him again.

"I mean, Cody. Yer still on the fence with me? Even after our heart-to-heart last night?"

I fanned the stack of papers at him. "You've been trying to pull one over on me since we met. Apparently, there's a procedure you have to follow for this stuff." I dropped the stack in front of me. "You conveniently left out the whole kuu thing."

"Not entirely. I did tell ya I'd get you a nice one last night," Roscoe said, clearing his throat and sauntering toward the kitchen. "Want something to eat?"

I pushed myself up and stomped into the kitchen, now even more annoyed. "That's all you said. You didn't mention that I'd have to wear cursed jewelry that doesn't come off!"

"It can come off, if you wanna break the contract. It's not like you die or nothin'. You just lose out on a place to live and we both get a scarlet letter. You can be a homeless werewolf with me. How's that sound?" He turned back and gave me a half grin.

A familiar pang of rage raced through my head as I pushed past him toward the fridge. To my surprise, there was a pitcher of iced tea on the top shelf.

"You said you liked tea with lemon, so I made some." He leaned in and sniffed my neck. "See? I remember things you tell me. I'd make a good kuu mate."

I shut the refrigerator door before grabbing a handful of Roscoe's chest fluff. "When were you going to tell me about all of this weird shit?"

"After I got them."

"Them?"

Roscoe brushed my hand away and backed up. "I was thinkin' you'd look pretty hot in a pair of earrings."

"I don't have pierced ears, and I don't want any."

"Yet," he said, his tail fanning behind him. "I know a guy—"

"No."

"C'mon. You ever see a half-turn's ears? You'd look really good."

"I said no." As I turned away, he caught my chin.

"Didn't know you were such a nerd."

"This isn't high school you idiot. That shit's not going to work," I said, pretending to be unfazed. "I met a half-turn today, and he didn't have earrings."

"So?" Roscoe's warm tongue traced my neck. "Live a little, Cody. Yer about to go half-turn, and you need to learn how to not be such a tightass or yer gonna get aggressive."

"Bodily mutilation is not something that will make me less of a *tightass*."

"Mutilation? It's just a goddamn hole in your ear." His gut shook as he laughed. "Yer not just a nerd. Yer a fuckin' square."

"A square? What is this, the 1950s?" I broke away and calmly made my way toward the beanbag chair before picking up the stack of roommate candidates I'd thrown on the floor.

"Did I say square? I meant yer pretty damn cool for standin' up for what you believe in," he said, fumbling through his words while following me. "I'm just poking fun. That's what buddies do."

"Yeah, okay." I looked down at the resume on top. "I bet Dallas here with his—" I looked closer at some of the text that had smeared. "Fourteen-inch dick and charming personality wouldn't think I'm a nerd."

"Yes, he would." He snatched the papers out of my hand.

"Give those back!"

"Listen, you don't gotta wear earrings. I can have them make something else. What do you want?"

"A necklace is fine."

"What about a collar?"

"A necklace."

"A cock ring?"

I shot him a confused look. "Why the fuck would anyone wear a cock ring that doesn't come off? Are you insane?"

"It was a joke. Why are you so damn boring?"

"You're really new to this whole ass kissing thing, aren't you?"

Roscoe tossed the papers into the trash can and leaned against the counter. "You think any of those guys I just threw away are gonna be real with you? No, they're gonna pretend, put on their little shows, and then yer stuck with them. I don't pretend to be someone I'm not. I'm too old for that shit. Hell, I don't even wear pants. I like being able to scratch my balls wherever and give my fingers a good sniff afterwards."

I gave him an openmouthed, disgusted look, dumbfounded but not at all surprised.

"Oh, don't pretend you don't do it."

I let out a sigh. "I guess you have a point."

"Wait, I was right? You scratch and sniff too?"

"About the roommate you moron!" I threw my hands up and walked back toward the TV. "God, you're so gross."

"Are you sure this time? I swear yer giving me anxiety."

"Do we have any more of that weed?" I asked, eyeing the nightstand next to my bed.

"You sure you want some? I mean, if yer scared of two little holes in yer ear..."

"I'll kill you in your sleep, I swear to God," I muttered under my breath.

"While yer at it, maybe you should stop drinkin' booze, too. Yer *mutilating* your liver, ya know."

I slammed my hand on the counter. "Fine, I'll get my damn ears pierced!"

"You don't got to. I'm just messin'."

"Good, because I don't like needles."

"Don't be such a pussy. You take monster dicks up yer ass like it's nothin', but one little poke in the ear'll make you cry. Nerd."

My vision turned red, and a startlingly realistic vision of me jumping onto his back while choking the life out of him played out in my head. "Get the hell out of my house!"

"Lighten up, Cody-boy. I'm just messin' again." The werewolf flashed his brows before grabbing my cell phone off the counter, and to my horror, he managed to unlock it. "Want me to make the appointment?"

"How the fuck did you get my pin?" I asked, trying to snatch the phone away, but he kept it just out of reach.

"You told me when you were drunk."

I gave up when I heard a light tone through the speaker. "You already dialed the number, didn't you?"

He gave a trollish grin in response while holding the phone to his ear.

### The Next Day

I waited in the tall, sunlit lobby, fidgeting with the aglets dangling from the drawstrings of my hoodie. This was even more nerve wracking than my interview two days ago. Perhaps if I had enough experience to be invaluable, the company would work with me—and even that was a long shot.

"Cody," the receptionist called out as she hung up the phone. I shot up from the chair. "Ms. Williams is in conference room three, down the hall to the right, last door on the left." She stared at me, perhaps noticing the creepy color of my eyes. They had turned an even darker shade of orange, and my sclera were already darkening.

"Thanks," I said as she nervously pressed a button to unlock the main doors. Despite how high tech and corporate the building looked, the environment was surprisingly laid back. I made my way down the hall, each office open and bright as employees talked amongst themselves, often laughing or collaborating around a whiteboard or giant flat screens mounted to the walls. I'd always dreamed of starting a career in a place like this. Unfortunately, after today, a dream was all it would ever be.

I wanted to curse whatever god was in charge of my life. If given the chance, I could have climbed the corporate ladder. I had ambition and discipline and a strong work ethic, but I wondered if all that would change once I turned into one of *them*. What Roscoe said earlier about me being a homeless bum with him haunted my thoughts even more.

*Later that night*

I was stupid and left the front door unlocked, and Roscoe burst into the apartment wearing the creepiest human latex mask I'd ever seen. It had wiry black hair with random bald spots and deep wrinkles around the eyes and mouth. What made it even more horrifying was the fake nose protruding well past what the material was meant to handle, giving the 'human' face an overexaggerated caricature quality. He'd covered the rest of himself in stitched-together potato sacks which did little to conceal his monstrous shape—oh, and his tail was still out and wagging away.

"What the fuck?" I yelled out, running over to the door as an older, white-haired woman ambled unsteadily through the narrow, outside corridor of the complex. She pointed and let out a scream.

"Jesus, lady—" Before he could finish, I slammed the door shut.

"I don't even know where to begin with this," I said, my tone exhausted. "Every time I think you can't get any dumber, you prove me wrong."

"You like it? The community theater was just throwin' it away." He held his arms to the side, his right hand closed as though holding something. "Give me one of them black frocks and a yamaka, and I could give a Derashah at the synagogue downtown."

My mouth hung open.

"It was a joke. You know, my grandma was Jewish."

"I thought you said you were Italian."

"I did?" He scratched his head. "Yeah, okay, that sounds right."

"You're not Italian, are you?"

He took my hand and placed something metallic into it before backing away and letting the nightmare fuel he wore fall to the floor in the corner.

I looked down at solid gold hoop earrings. "Oh, come on. You couldn't have gotten something a little less... *this*?"

"They're perfect."

"They're hideous." I picked them up with my fingers, and they began to glow. "This is so creepy."

"Yer gonna look so damn hot." Roscoe walked over to the fridge and grabbed a bottle of beer. "My buddy said to bring you down to his place ASAP before you get too wolfy."

"I thought we'd do it next week."

"Can't. If we wait too long, you'll heal too fast, and he says it's too much of a pain in the ass then. He can't put studs in like normal, so he's gotta put yer kuu on directly."

"I don't know what any of that means," I said, my stomach knotting. "I really think I should look at more werewolves."

"Here." Roscoe grabbed his dirty, orange hoodie off the floor in the corner of the room and pulled a folded sheet of paper from the pocket. "Since yer so damn anal about everything, I made one." He handed it to me, and I dropped the kuu earrings on the countertop.

"All right, let's see how you measure up." My eyes rolled the moment I started reading the sloppily written profile.

*Dick reeeeal huge. Like bigger than everyone else.*

*I like food, beer & sex. Prefer to have them all at the same time.*

*I jerk off in front of someone else's phone every month, and I kick annoying drunks out of bars for money.*

*I don't wear pants and never will.*

*My baked ziti will make you cum.*

I stopped reading. "Prove it."

"Prove what? You've already seen my dick."

"The baked ziti."

Roscoe flashed another grin, wagging his tail as he walked toward the kitchen. "You sure? Kuu signs are one thing, but this might actually make you fall in love with me."

"It's baked ziti, not ambrosia. Don't flatter yourself," I muttered before settling back onto my beanbag chair to start flipping through the channels.

# Chapter 4

# The Transition

*Later that evening*

I pulled the last corner of the fitted sheet snugly over the mattress before shoving my face into the warm, freshly laundered bedding. The overpowering floral scent of fabric softener might have been too much for my sensitive nose, but it was a welcome improvement over Roscoe's stink. Tonight, I'd put my foot down about the bed and bathing situation, and to make my point, I set up an inflatable mattress on the floor near the television.

I stopped by the bar to give everyone the bad news, with Rob being especially upset. He offered me more money on top of my last paycheck, but I nervously refused. Even though I could have used it, I wasn't the only one struggling, and my problems shouldn't fall on anyone else's shoulders. Legally, he couldn't continue employing me anyway, so thus ended my somewhat steady stream of income.

Being jobless wasn't all bad, and I got some grocery shopping done for Roscoe's 'better than sex' baked ziti while also getting a head start on packing. Rent was coming due soon, and it wouldn't be long before the eviction letters followed. Even though I was worried to the point of breaking, there wasn't anything I could do but let it happen.

The locked doorknob rattled moments before Roscoe rapped out a playful rhythm.

"Little piggy, let me in," he called out, his voice muffled.

"Oh. what plague have you brought upon me now," I muttered under my breath while twisting the deadbolt lock. When the door opened, Roscoe greeted me from inside of an old mattress with holes cut out for his legs and arms. He'd hidden his claws inside a pair of mismatched flannel oven mitts while black, heavy duty trash bags covered his feet. To add to the chaos, a grease-covered towel turban wrapped around a partially deflated volleyball, which was attached to the top of the mattress by what looked like Velcro. "God damn it."

"What?" He turned sideways and hobbled through the door. I glanced both ways to see if he'd drawn any attention to himself before shutting it.

"What the hell is this?"

"Ain't it obvious?" he asked, letting the oven mitts fall to the floor before struggling to point up at the turban. "I'm the Sultan of Serta."

I bit down hard on my lower lip and stared at him for a few moments, my vision turning red again.

"Get this nasty shit out of the apartment."

"It ain't that bad." Though I couldn't see his face, I could hear him inhale through his nose. "Smells a little like when I was helping one of my friends shoot a porno. We had an old mattress like this on the floor." He struggled a little, pulling both arms inside so he could unzip the bottom. Enough of the innards had been removed so he could fit while somehow keeping just enough stuffing to maintain its shape. Like a dog in an oversized E-collar, he struggled to slip out of the mattress, getting stuck halfway. "Uh... gonna need some help."

With a groan, I grabbed the top, which was slightly damp, and gave it a yank. "This is so disgusting." With one final pull, he slipped free—and then farted.

"Ahh, much better," he said, fanning the air behind him.

"You're a pig," I said, pointing to the back door leading to the balcony. "Put all this crap out there. It smells worse than you, if you can believe it."

He let out a laugh before dragging the nasty, mostly empty mattress to the door, shoving it outside. He rubbed his hands together, nudging me aside while sliding his dirty feet across the clean kitchen floor toward the fridge.

"I was thinking... maybe we should wait to do the piercings until next week. It's not a good time right now," I said, spraying air freshener around the living room.

"I told you, my buddy said we gotta get them in before you start healing too fast." The air mattress finally caught his eye. "You gonna sleep on that now?"

"No."

Roscoe cracked open a beer and let out a whine. "Aw, come on, Cody!"

"You're my roommate, not my boyfriend." I grabbed a bottle of werewolf shampoo sitting on the counter. "See this? Use it. You smell like Waffle House dumpster juice."

He snatched the bottle away and scowled. "You don't deserve my baked ziti." Roscoe gave me one more disgruntled growl before disappearing into the bathroom.

"Then I'll make it myself."

Roscoe popped his head out from around the corner, raising an eyebrow.

"It's not like it's that hard. Any idiot can dump noodles into sauce and bake it."

He slowly backed out of the bathroom, his expression growing concerned. "You really don't know how to cook, do you?"

I opened the pantry, grabbing a box of penne pasta and a couple jars of tomato sauce before laying them out on the counter.

"It's not organic chemistry." I picked up the box, pointing to the instructions. "If you can read, you can cook. It's why I'm surprised you can cook."

"I can fuckin' read!" His mouth hung open as he let out an overexaggerated gasp. Then he pointed at the counter. "What the hell is this? Jarred sauce? Did you seriously bring that shit into this house? The dumpster mattress was more appetizing."

"Then go chew on that." I said, flipping the jar to get a glimpse of the ingredients. "What the hell does it matter? Italian food is all just tomato sauce with different shaped noodles."

Roscoe wrinkled his nose but didn't respond.

"You know I'm right."

He grabbed his chest and looked up, muttering *"porca miseria"* in a surprisingly good Italian accent.

"What does that mean?"

He said nothing, his tail hanging between his legs as he slowly dragged himself to the bathroom and shut the door.

"You're such a drama queen."

I stared in amazement at a blackened red and brown mass that was somehow overcooked and undercooked at the same time. Squeaky shower handles silenced the running water in the bathroom, and I started to panic. Roscoe had been in there for over an hour, and I'd hoped the residual smoke billowing around the fluorescent lighting would have dissipated by now.

My attempt at baking a *simple* meal was a complete disaster, and I could practically hear Roscoe belching my words back into my face.

The blow dryer clicked on which meant I had a little more time. Perhaps I could let the ziti bake at a higher temperature to finish cooking the middle. After setting the oven to four hundred, I slid the pan back onto the center rack and waited.

Fifteen minutes later, the hair dryer cut off, and the bathroom door cracked open, Roscoe slithering out and sniffing the air.

"Smells like you've sure got things under control."

"Shut up," I muttered, opening the oven door for a moment to peek inside. Another puff of gray smoke rushed out. "It's almost done, I think."

"I think it was done before you even cooked it," he muttered, stepping into the living area. The werewolf eyed the air mattress with disdain before opting to sit on the beanbag chair. "When we move, I should bring my furniture."

"You have actual stuff?"

He nodded. "Well, yeah. It's in storage."

We both went quiet as he flipped through the channels. I turned back to the oven and opened the door again, this time letting out a puff of black smoke. The smoke alarm that I had taken off the wall earlier began to beep, so I threw it into a bottom cabinet.

"Oh boy. Sounds like dinner's ready," Roscoe said, running up to the counter.

"It's a little overdone, but I followed the instructions."

Roscoe scrutinized the pan, his expression darkening. "You need to be arrested for this."

"This is the first time I've ever made baked ziti. It's not that bad."

"You can't take a crispy dump in a pan, sprinkle it with cheese and call it baked ziti."

"Do you want to eat this or not?"

Roscoe scratched his head. "That's probably the toughest question I've ever been asked."

"Fine. Don't eat," I said, grabbing a metal spatula from the drawer. I stabbed at the overcooked meal from the edge, but the utinsil was rather difficult to push all the way through. This was going to require a knife and some elbow grease.

Roscoe stood patiently and watched.

"You smell good," I said, grabbing a butcher's knife.

"Does that mean I can sleep on the bed?"

"No." I sliced the rest of the way into the hard pasta, working toward the softer section. I'd never had this dish before, and in the pictures, they were able to spoon it onto a plate. Still, it couldn't be that bad, right? I lifted a hardened square with the spatula and tried to gently place it onto Roscoe's plate. However, it slid off and hit the ceramic with a loud clink.

The werewolf gave it another sniff, picking at it with his fork. "I think I'm gonna call the ASPCA. This is abuse."

"Just eat the damn shit!" I grabbed another plate and cut myself a piece. "It looks rough, but I'm sure it tastes fine."

"Is this... yer first time cooking anything?"

"It's not! It's just my first time ever using an oven."

"Christ almighty," he muttered, stabbing the pasta again, which had clumped together in a brown-colored mass instead of the usual red. He shoveled a forkful into his mouth and gagged. Leaning over the sink, he let the food fall from his long tongue and into the garbage disposal.

"Wow." I stuck my fork into the ziti and held it to my mouth. "You didn't even chew it."

"And break my precious teeth?" Roscoe heaved again, his ears pressing against the sides of his head.

"Stop being so dramatic." I took a bite and immediately regretted it. How in the hell did I manage to completely change the flavor profile of premade tomato sauce? The more I chewed, the more my body rejected it. There was no way I'd be able to swallow this along with my pride.

I ran over to the sink and spat everything out before rinsing my mouth with water.

The werewolf opened the refrigerator to grab another bottle of beer, remaining smugly quiet.

"What? You're not going to take a few more jabs? Kick me when I'm down?"

"I need a moment," Roscoe said, calmly composing himself. "What you just did to Italian cuisine brought my grandma back to life and killed her all over again."

I rolled my eyes. "I thought your grandma was Jewish."

"I had two, ya know." He took another sip of beer, swishing it around before swallowing. "I don't know how you did it. You made it taste so bad that even beer don't work."

I grabbed a frozen pizza from the freezer, but Roscoe snatched it out of my hand.

"No! You already raped my dead grandma, and I'm not letting you desecrate Mama Celeste." He pulled a pizza pan from the cabinet and frowned at the brick of ruined pasta sitting on top of the stove. "You were a victim of one man's hubris," he whispered, running his clawed fingers over burnt cheese.

I raised an eyebrow at that uncharacteristically articulate statement. "Are you done hamming it up for the Tony's?"

"Yeah, I think you get the point. Yer not allowed near a stove no more." Roscoe removed the pizza from the box and preheated the oven.

"It's my apartment!" I shouted as he shoved me out of the kitchen.

We ate in front of the television, him sitting on the air mattress and me on my beanbag chair, flipping through the channels. There hadn't been enough time lately to just sit down and watch something, so I wasn't even sure what basic cable had to offer.

"Hold up," Roscoe said with his mouth full. "Go back one."

I pressed the down arrow on the remote and recognized the show, but I was kind of surprised someone like Roscoe would be interested.

"*The Next Generation* was one of the good ones," he said, taking another bite. "They don't make *Star Trek* like this no more."

"Didn't peg you for a Trekkie."

"Get to know me, and I'll surprise ya." Despite him being an annoying piece of shit, I felt comfortable. He was like an ugly brown couch from the 80s that was held together by duct tape and smelled like farts, but was still the coziest thing in the room.

I caught his eye, so I turned back toward the TV and yawned. "I should probably get to bed soon."

"Wanna have some fun first?" His heavy tail pounded the mattress, and he shot me a jagged grin, a rope of drool hanging from an exposed canine.

"Not tonight. I haven't been feeling all that great."

Roscoe stood and stretched before plodding across the room. "Well, let's get to bed."

"You think you're so damn slick."

His ears fell, and his watery eyes widened.

"I'm immune now." I pointed at the air mattress. "If you want to act like a dog, then you'll get treated like one. So, go lay down."

A snarl replaced the puppy face. "Fine," he grumbled, lying back down on the inflatable bed, exaggerating his discomfort as he turned from side-to-side.

I hopped into my bed and shuffled under the clean covers while staring up at the shadows dancing from the glow of the television screen. My eyes got heavy before a *pop* followed by a rush of air had them snapping open.

"Oops," Roscoe said.

I threw the covers off and sat upright as Roscoe sank to the ground, the bed deflating under him.

"Roscoe!"

"It's yer fault," he said, slyly rolling off the ruined mattress. "You made a three-hundred-pound monster sleep on a flimsy inflatable bed. What the hell did you think was gonna happen?"

"You wish your fat ass was three hundred pounds. You did that on purpose!"

"Did not," he said calmly while walking over to my bed.

"No! Sleep on the floor."

Roscoe grinned before slipping under the covers. "What are you gonna do? Make me?"

I ground my teeth and laid back down, facing away from the intruder.

"I'm not wearing those earrings."

Roscoe shuffled uncomfortably before sitting up against the headboard. "You're gonna have to learn to live with werewolves... and sleep with 'em."

"I shouldn't have to live with anyone if I don't want to. I could just live on my own, put all my money away and find a way to buy a house once I'm fully turned."

"Sounds like you've got it all figured out." Roscoe let out a sigh before lying back down.

I didn't respond, and he turned toward me before rubbing my head.

"You don't have a clue what's about to happen to you, but I've been there. The difference is, yer not gonna be alone."

A cold sweat woke me a little after midnight, and I rushed to the bathroom.

The bed creaked in the other room as Roscoe stirred. "You okay, bud?"

I didn't answer. Instead, I stared at the mirror while running my fingers through the thicker body hair covering my chest. My ears now tapered to a point, and the sclera around my orange irises was gray.

"Hey, look at this handsome fella," Roscoe said casually as he stepped behind me, his nostrils flaring while sniffing my neck. There was something off about his scent, something that was neither pleasant nor off-putting.

"What's wrong with my nose?" I inhaled deeply, and my brain was hit with what felt like a thousand zaps. "Everything smells funny."

Roscoe grabbed my arms and turned me around before lifting me onto the bathroom sink. He wasted no time pulling off my underwear, his warm tongue wrapping around my cock. I grabbed his mane with both hands, growling as he went to work. He seemed kind of worried, like his entire goal at the moment was to get me off as quickly as possible.

One more stroke of his tongue sent me into fits. I pushed my hips deeper against the wet warmth of his maw. I threw my head back and an involuntary, pathetic howl left my throat while the rest of my body trembled.

Roscoe hummed in satisfaction, his tongue the only part of his body moving.

"Shit," I cried out. More of my cum mixed with his saliva before roping along the corners of his mouth. I'd never felt such an intense desire to be ravaged before, but it was all I could think about. He ran his rough, slippery tongue along my shaft before working lower. I relented, not giving any resistance as the slender muscle prepared me for what was coming.

An increasingly violent Roscoe dug his claws into my arms, letting out a roar as he pulled me into the shower like a doll. The werewolf's gentle disposition shifted, and I responded as if some baser instinct had taken over. With his hefty, muscular body against my smaller frame, he pressed me against the wall, his tongue tracing along the crook of my neck.

A myriad of strange emotions had been building inside of me for days, but they threatened to turn to violent rage as my vision blurred red. Roscoe seemed to understand what was happening, and this felt like more than just sex. It was the only thing keeping me from losing my mind at that moment.

He quickly quelled any resistance my half-turned mind put up, each time restraining me with raw bestial strength. Roscoe was so lazy most of the time that this show of force startled me. The feeling of complete domination made my heart race and stomach knot as though I'd jumped from an airplane with no parachute.

As he pushed forward, the head of his cock sank into me. I thought since we'd done this a couple times, that I could handle him better. That wasn't the case at all as white-hot agony pulsed from below. I snarled, gritting my teeth while reaching back to stop him from going in deeper, but there was no slowing him down.

He gripped my shoulders tighter while lowering me onto his thick shaft. I tried pushing him out, clenching, anything, but all that did was allow him the freedom to delve deeper. Inch-by-painful-inch, he disappeared inside of me, and the slick squelching of the invader paired nicely with my moans as he began to thrust.

The way he snarled and clawed at my neck, giving little regard to my safety, somehow heightened the pleasure beyond anything I knew. I craved it. We both did. He was leaking so much into me that every time he pulled out a few inches, it would trickle down my inner thigh. The wet sounds and muffled thuds of his balls sent me into an almost trance-like state of ecstasy.

His tempo slowed, but the intensity increased. He would pull most of the way out before shoving himself back in with such aggression that my feet lifted from the tub. After a couple more minutes, he let out a moan so loud and deep it vibrated the tile walls. There wasn't any more pain as he sped up again.

The werewolf jackhammered faster than earlier, and I moaned more as he rubbed against my prostate in a rhythm that made me come again without touching myself.

"Roscoe," I yelled out, and he caught my neck with his hand, keeping me in place against the wall with my feet dangling several inches from the floor of the tub. A familiar heat spread inside, my abdomen gurgling with every pulse.

"Feel better now?" he asked, gently biting my neck.

Before I even could respond, his tongue met mine. Sex felt much more different this time. It wasn't just pleasure anymore. It was an urge, like my body would tear itself apart just to satisfy it.

The thought made me feel gross and kind of ashamed.

After finishing, Roscoe pulled away, his half-hard dick easily sliding out. As the passion cooled, an odd sensation covered my glans. I held my own cock in my hands, examining the foreskin that hadn't been there earlier.

"What the...?"

"Oh yeah," Roscoe said, his mouth right next to my ear. "It grows back. Looks like yer quick healing kicked in. Hopefully we can still get yer ears pierced."

I gently shoved him away. "I need a shower."

"I'm goin' back to bed." Roscoe stepped out of the tub, wiping the tip of his cock with the shower curtain.

"The towels are literally right in front of you!"

"Habit," he replied with his usual grin.

We left the apartment early that morning, making sure to stay out of sight of the other tenants. They might have already been suspicious that a werewolf was living with me, considering all the missed calls I received from the property manager. I didn't answer or check the voicemail because what I didn't hear I didn't have to deal with. It was like avoiding debt collectors, but sooner or later, I'd have to face it head-on.

The barred entrance of a seedy-looking tattoo parlor with a half-lit *open* sign stood before us, graffiti covering most of the cracking facade along the walls. I wouldn't have called it an eyesore considering how beautiful the artwork was. There was even some abstract painting near the roof that looked like a blocky werewolf and a topless woman with square tits holding hands on the beach.

"You okay?" Roscoe asked. There was actual concern in his voice which surprised me. I'd kind of expected him to be a little more relentless with his teasing considering how terrified I was.

"Let's just get this over with."

Roscoe grunted and pushed open the door.

"Well, look at this ugly bastard," a tall man at the counter said. He was older, perhaps in his late fifties, with peppered black and gray hair. Tattoos covered his body—some tasteful, others profanity-laden nudes of different women. He wore a skimpy leather vest with nothing underneath, revealing a pacemaker scar that had been decorated with an anatomically correct heart in a cage. "Finally snagged yourself a sucker, huh?"

Roscoe wrapped his arm playfully around my neck and pulled me close. "Cody, meet Brodie." He chuckled to himself before nudging me forward. "Yer in good hands—well, when he's sober."

I turned around, hoping to make a run for the door, but Roscoe caught me by the arm.

"He'd be in better hands had you gotten him here sooner," Brodie said, getting a closer look at my ears. "You got the kuu?"

Roscoe opened his hand, revealing the earrings. "Yup."

He took the jewelry and began walking to the back with us following close behind. "All right, let's get you pierced. It's gonna hurt like hell, though."

"Nope." I turned back to the door, but this time, Roscoe lifted me up like a child and carried me over his shoulder to the back room.

The piercing process didn't take quite as long as I thought it would, and it didn't hurt that much either, especially since I couldn't see what was going on. It was a good thing, too. He couldn't pierce my ears using the normal method of guiding a needle with a stud attached to the end. Apparently half-turns heal so rapidly that the needle could get stuck halfway if it's not done quickly enough. He ended up jamming it all the way before quickly guiding the earring through the hole. As soon as it was in, it wasn't coming out.

Roscoe and I walked back to the apartment, and every step seemed to tug at my lobes. The feeling of something dangling from my ears was going to take a while to get used to. Not only that, but I had felt something odd the moment both of them were secure—a sudden surge of warmth that pulsed through me before dissipating. After that, the eerie glow of the gold dulled and they looked like normal hoop earrings.

I looked up at Roscoe as he smiled, seemingly in relief, his tail swaying in time with his cocky stride.

"You got what you wanted, I guess," I mumbled as we passed people along the walkway. It felt like the whole world was staring at me now. There was no more blending into the background, no more hiding under hoodies and sunglasses. I was front and center, the side-show no one trusted.

"*We* got what *we* needed," Roscoe corrected as we began our ascent up the steps toward my apartment, a red envelope taped to the front door.

Roscoe and I glanced at one another, and I grabbed it before stepping inside.

"I guess I can't keep ignoring them." I opened the envelope which contained several security camera stills of Roscoe's idiotic costumes as well as him out of costume leaving my apartment. I began reading the letter, and there wasn't much to it, just some professionally worded sentences with some legal jargon.

"How long are they gonna give you?"

I sighed and tossed the envelope into the garbage. "Not long enough. I don't even know where I'm going to live yet."

"Tomorrow, we'll put yer stuff into my storage unit. Lucky you ain't got that much."

"Then what?"

"You like the beach?" he asked, stepping into the kitchen.

"I like having a roof over my head."

"I got a buddy that lives in a shack by the ocean. If we give him meat, beer and weed, he'll let us hang with him."

"A shack. By the ocean," I muttered before sitting on my bed. "Can't we just get a cheap motel near Ruskin Street?"

"You ain't gonna find a room. The whole reason I was on the streets was because I couldn't find any werewolf-friendly motels that weren't already full."

"How do you even know this buddy of yours is going to say yes?"

"In all the years I've known him, Darryl's had my back. I mean, the guy saves people for a living now."

I remembered something Rob mentioned last week. "This isn't the werewolf lifeguard at White Dunes by chance?"

"Ya heard of him, huh?" Roscoe popped open a bottle of beer. "He's a big fucker, too."

"He's one of my old boss's friends."

"Darryl's everybody's friend. Never met a nicer guy, but he fucks everything that moves."

"Shocking."

Roscoe let out a grunted laugh. "Okay I know what yer thinking, but Darryl's legendary. I don't know how he does it. He's even gotten with straight human guys. I wonder what he's up to lately."

"When's the last time you talked to him?"

"Uh..." Roscoe scratched his head. "Three years ago?"

"Well, call him and see if this is okay. You can't just drop in on someone unannounced like this."

"It worked with you. Plus, he doesn't have a phone." He swallowed the last of his beer and tossed the bottle into the trash can. "How about after I move yer stuff into my storage unit, we pay him a visit? I haven't been to the beach in years, and you need to get the hell away from this place."

"How are you going to move my stuff?"

"Let me worry about that."

# Beach Wolves

Roscoe and I sat in the back of the bus—in the designated werewolf section—with a few others from Ruskin Street. Though we'd left the apartment at six, it took us nearly four hours of bus-hopping to get to the beach.

"I didn't realize how far away this was," I whispered to Roscoe who was manspreading with his arms behind his head. While he had a lot of fur to hide his junk, everything was still partially visible, much to the horror of the humans sitting closer to the back. "I wish you'd wear some damn pants."

"They can't see nothin'," Roscoe muttered, crossing one leg over his knee. "You got the sausages?"

I held up my backpack. "Yeah, they're in here, but I don't know how much longer they're going to stay cool. Are you absolutely sure Darryl's not going to mind us dropping in like this?"

"Pssh, nah. He loves it when people visit him." Roscoe grabbed the case of beer on the floor in the aisle and set it in his lap as we approached the small beach town. "There's a little bodega on the way. We'll stop there and get some ice."

The brakes squealed, and the aging bus rolled to a stop. Most of the passengers stood, filing impatiently into the aisle with the humans getting off first. I slid my arms into the straps of my backpack and followed Roscoe as we side-stepped our way through, finally making it outside.

The atmosphere was definitely more pleasant here than in the city. The briny, cool seabreeze brushing against my face as we strolled along the sidewalk toward the sound of waves and shrieking gulls. I wore a white tank top, shorts and sandals, but covered my arms with a long-sleeved overshirt to hide my extra body hair. Thankfully, people here didn't seem to stare as much as they did in the city.

After grabbing a bag of ice from the bodega, we walked across the street toward a narrow boardwalk surrounded by thick palmettos. After about a quarter of a mile, the iconic white dunes appeared, and beyond the rolling sand was an endless blue with white capped waves breaking along the shore.

"This is pretty," I said, eyeing a huge, brown werewolf in the distance sitting high in a white wooden lifeguard chair, an orange rescue buoy loosely strapped to his back. He wore nothing else, and his tail swayed languidly as he leaned forward, keeping a close eye on three young teenagers swimming a little farther out than they should have been. His mane was trimmed shorter than Roscoe's, but it was still just as thick from behind. I wasn't able to get a look at his face from here, but he sure seemed handsome.

"Never seen the ocean?" Roscoe asked, slinging the dripping bag of ice over his shoulder.

"I've never had the time to come all the way out here."

Roscoe made a hard right turn as the werewolf lifeguard turned, pulling me with him.

"Shouldn't we say hi?"

"Not while he's workin'," Roscoe replied, pointing to a small beach house on stilts in the distance. "Looks bigger than it used to."

"You're not just going to walk into his house without asking."

"'Course not."

We approached the steps leading up to a wooden deck. There was a rusted steel barrel sitting in the corner, a charred, foil-covered grate over top. Old tiki torches surrounded the deck, and a large, wooden spool was used as a table with four mismatched lawn chairs. A faded orange parasol with a few frayed tears stuck out from a hole in the middle to give the deck some shade.

"He's gotten all fancy," Roscoe said. "Used to just sit on the sand around a fire at night and smoke weed while he played his guitar."

I placed my backpack on the spool table and sat in a green plastic chair, tipping it back until the top pressed against the wooden railing.

"Did you live around here?"

"Kinda." Roscoe grabbed an empty cooler that was sitting upside-down against the house. He filled it with ice before shoving bottles of beer into it. "Didn't really live anywhere back in those days. I'd just crash on couches until people kicked me out. Darryl and I had a lot of fun, especially when he'd bring home a human or half-turn to spit roast."

"Everyone's so classy," I whispered under my breath.

Roscoe tossed me a beer before cracking one open himself. "May have to get more beer. Darryl's probably not getting off until—" He stopped talking, his ears pointing toward the ocean. I heard it too, the sound of screaming, just loud enough to overtake the waves.

"Oh shit. They must have gotten pulled out too far," I said, watching two of the teenagers from earlier flail. Darryl immediately jumped from his chair and darted into the rough ocean.

The werewolf was an incredible swimmer, his powerful arms and legs allowing him to glide through the water like a fish. He grabbed the boy and pulled him onto his back before securing the girl onto the buoy, all while keeping both of them calm. He tugged them toward the shore, unimpeded by the strong current while swimming parallel to it.

"Look at him go," I said, unable to tear away from the rescue. As the waves carried all of them closer to shore, Darryl stumbled to his feet, shaking the excess water from his coarse fur, and I could finally see his face. His muzzle was broader than Roscoe's with a sharp, defined jawline. Below his lip was a little soul patch he'd left behind after trimming the rest of the thicker facial fur away. His furrowed brow and sly grin gave him a dangerously sexy look. He made sure the kids were okay while walking back to his post, but not before looking directly at Roscoe and me.

"Uh oh. Looks like he saw us," Roscoe said, his tone a little higher.

"Why did you say it like that?"

"Uh, no reason. Just wanted to surprise him later, is all."

I glared at him. "You were lying, weren't you?"

"'Course not!" He cleared his throat and changed the subject. "Darryl used to joke that during the full moon he turns into a shark, but when you watch him swim, you'd almost believe it. He's clumsy as hell on land, but right at home in the water."

To my relief, the huge werewolf in the distance smiled and waved up at us, and we waved back.

"I'm gonna go get more beer. One case ain't gonna be enough," Roscoe said as he closed the cooler. "Stay here and watch the goods."

I stood and reached into my backpack. "I can start grilling."

Roscoe snatched the backpack away from me. "I'm gonna hold onto these."

"I'm not an idiot, Roscoe."

"I've got brats and weisswurst in here. You'll just turn 'em into expensive charcoal." He slipped an arm through one of the straps. "I'll be back in a bit. I'm gonna get some buns, sauerkraut, and mustard."

"Get ketchup too," I added. Roscoe looked back and wrinkled his nose. "What the hell is wrong with ketchup?"

"You don't put ketchup on these."

"I hate sauerkraut and mustard," I said, looking beyond Roscoe at a human lifeguard talking with Darryl.

"Of course you do," Roscoe muttered as he turned away. "'Cause you've got the palate of a nine-year-old." He padded along the boardwalk before disappearing into the palmettos, and I took another sip of beer, turning my attention back to the water. Darryl wasn't in the seat, having been replaced by the human lifeguard.

I jumped when a contemplative hum growled from behind me.

"Roscoe snagged himself a half-turn," Darryl said, stumbling over the railing of the deck. Roscoe was right—he was kind of clumsy when he walked, which made sense considering the guy looked to be around nine feet tall. "Where'd he go, anyway?"

"He went to get more beer and gross condiments." I pointed to the cooler. "Want one, or do you have to go back to work?"

"Nah, I only filled in for someone this morning." The werewolf took two bottles in one massive hand and closed the lid before sitting at the table next to me. "You probably already know my name. What's yours?"

"Cody," I replied, now nervously gulping my beer, hoping to take some of the edge off.

He extended his hand. "You look like you're having a rough time."

"What?"

"Well, for one, you're with Roscoe. Plus, you just have a fresh look," he replied, opening a bottle with his claws. "Kind of confused, embarrassed, and a little worried. Like a baby deer."

I closed my overshirt a little more. "I've only been like this for a few days."

"We've all gone through it," he said with a sharp grin. "You're at the beach and it's a hot day. You should take your shirt off and enjoy it."

"I'm good. You know, you should probably wear some shorts if you're going to be right up on people when you rescue them."

"I swim better without them." Darryl took another drink. "Clothing on werewolves is kinda stupid, don't you think?" He pointed at his junk, which was mostly hidden by a thick patch of fur just like Roscoe's. "It's not like you can see everything."

"You know, that's something I've often wondered about. How the hell do you guys keep... things so hidden?"

"Let me show you something." Darryl grabbed what I thought was a tuft of fur, but it was actually a tube of fur-covered flesh. It kind of resembled a dog's but was longer and thicker, and blended in almost seamlessly as if it weren't there at all. "When we're in the mood, the skin slips up like this." He grabbed the glans of his dick and gently pushed the loose sheath toward his pelvis revealing a long, floppy, dark brown cock.

I glanced around to see if anyone was watching as the werewolf practically fondled himself. "Dude, there are people out here!"

"It's a lesson in anatomy."

"No, it's a possible felony. Put it away," I whispered sharply. Darryl let go of his dick and laughed at me. "At what point do you guys lose all sense of shame? Roscoe's the same way."

"Eventually, you've gotta stop giving a shit what other people think. We're not human anymore, and other humans either like us, hate us, or shit themselves when they see us. We either stop caring or it'll drive us nuts. The half-turn phase is important, and how you handle things now determines what kind of werewolf you'll turn out to be."

"I didn't know that."

Darryl reached for my head and ran his clawed fingers over my earrings.

"The kuu's not just for werewolves getting free places to live. Half-turns need werewolf companions, and these things help keep your urges and anger under control—or whatever."

"Speaking of," I said, wondering how I'd word this without him misinterpreting it. "I sometimes see red, like I'm gonna lose control or something. When I'm... *with* a werewolf, it goes away." This was an embarrassing topic for a complete stranger, but he was a werewolf, and he would probably give me better answers than Roscoe often did. "Is that normal?"

"Pretty much. Every time it happens, you get a little closer to being a werewolf."

"So, if I want to be a full werewolf, I just need to have more sex?"

Darryl scratched his head. "I don't really know how it all works, but I know it helps. It's why we're so damn horny all the time. I got fucked a lot as a half-turn. Like... *a lot.* Man, I was a huge slut." The werewolf smirked at me. "Still am."

Now I was starting to understand all the rumors about him. "How long have you been a lifeguard?"

"Couple decades. I did a lot of surfing when I was human and half-turn and just didn't feel right ever leaving the ocean. My life's here, and I wasn't gonna let being a werewolf determine where I'd end up. I bought this tiny chunk of beach, built a house on it, and now I live every day in paradise doing what I love." He raised his beer and drank the last of it. "You should strip naked tonight and come for a swim."

"I, uh... I don't know how to swim."

Using his pointer claw, he opened the other bottle he'd grabbed. "Well, you're in luck, bud! I give *adult* swimming lessons too."

"Adult?"

Darryl took another drink. "I've got a lesson plan with a one hundred percent success rate." He paused and let out a contemplative hum. "Okay, more like ninety-five percent. I got one guy who's a special case."

"That's tempting and all, but I don't think it's a good idea."

"You sure? It's a reeeeally good lesson plan, and everyone should learn how to swim."

I opened my mouth to respond but was interrupted by Roscoe calling from the boardwalk. He carried my backpack over one arm, which was so full he couldn't zip it all the way back up. He also carried four cases of beer, two in each hand and two under each arm.

"Daddy Darryl's drinkin' on the job?" Roscoe asked as he climbed up the deck steps. "I didn't think you did that anymore after you got in trouble that one time."

Darryl raised his bottle. "It's my day off. I was just filling in for someone earlier." He let out a sudden snarl, which startled me. "I also think you're misremembering who got in trouble."

   

Roscoe's ears fell as he cleared his throat again. "Gettin' to know my new roomie?" Roscoe sat the cases on the deck and began tearing into them, placing each bottle into the cooler.

"Roomie?" He glanced at my earrings. "Probably more like a mark. Didn't you say the whole kuu thing was dumb?"

"That was before they started promising houses. I'll get to sit in my own home and smoke as much weed as I want, and no one's sayin' shit!"

"You do realize they're probably going to make you get a job, right?" I said as Roscoe moved onto the sausages.

"We'll see about that. I'm pretty fuckin' useless." He smirked and closed the cooler lid. "And that's me not even trying. Just think of how useless I could be if I applied myself."

"When you apply yourself, things go missing," Darryl said, his eyes now aggressively wide as he stared Roscoe down. The atmosphere began to grow more uncomfortable, but the larger werewolf relaxed and looked back at me. "No one holds a candle to Roscoe when it comes to being useless," Darryl said in a tone that sounded like he was trying to hold back his anger. "I think he's been kicked out of every house he's ever lived in, including mine." He turned back to Roscoe, who was now in a more submissive posture. "Which brings me to my next question—why the fuck are you back?"

Roscoe scratched his head. "Uh, did you kick me out? I don't remember."

"Of course you don't remember. I'm surprised your brain still functions after all the drugs."

I glared at Roscoe.

"Oh," he said, letting out a nervous laugh. "Kinda forgot about that. I'm clean as a newborn now. I swear."

Darryl stood up, towering over Roscoe who was over a foot shorter than him. "You're not here to bribe me with beer and brats, are you?"

"And a bratty half-turn." He nodded to me with that shitty grin of his.

I shot up out of the chair. "Now wait just a minute!"

"Eh, you've been checkin' him out since we got here." Roscoe put his arm around my neck and looked over at Darryl. "I'll never forget the look on that one guy's face after you shot yer load in his ass. Fuck that was hot, but you sure messed him up."

The taller werewolf stroked the patch of fur on his chin while looking me over.

"You're a real piece of shit," I said, shoving Roscoe away. "I regret this whole thing."

"Relax, you don't gotta do anything," Roscoe said. I glanced up in time to see him wink at Darryl. "The truth is, uh, we're gonna need a place to crash for a week or so until the government housing thing's finalized."

Darryl didn't respond.

"You don't wanna see this poor guy out in the cold, do ya?" He wrapped his arm around my neck, pulling me close. My vision started turning red again, and I think Darryl noticed. His disposition changed from aggressive to something a lot gentler.

"I hate your guts, but Cody seems pretty cool. Just bought a California king, so we got enough room. I just got one condition," Darryl said, turning toward me again.

"I can keep the house clean," I said, trying not to sound desperate. "I can pay my fair share once the money comes in, too."

"Relax. You don't have to do any of that, but you do have to take swimming lessons, *and* you have to swim naked in the ocean at least once."

That wasn't quite what I expected him to say, but at least he was pretty laid back now and not ready to rip Roscoe's head off.

"Sure, okay," I said, relieved as I sat back down on the chair.

"We'll start tonight," Darryl said, pulling out a package of bratwurst before tossing it to Roscoe. "I'm hungry. Work your magic, chef."

Roscoe's tail wagged as he pulled an old apron from my backpack, shook it out, and put it on. It had the words *kiss the cook* in bold capital letters, only the 'o' next to the 'k' had been purposely scratched out to look like a 'c.'

"You just keep getting classier," I muttered before turning my attention back to Darryl. "Why tonight?"

"I wanna get to know you a little better."

"I don't know about this," I said, looking down at the empty pool illuminated by a glowing light down at the deep end. The pool belonged to the condo nearby, but Darryl somehow had the keys. "What if someone comes out here?"

"It's empty," Darryl replied. "No one's gonna see, so go ahead and strip."

Roscoe watched us while laying on a lounge chair next to the pool. I didn't expect to actually swim, so I didn't bring a suit. After removing my shirt, I kicked off my sandals and pulled off my shorts and underwear.

"Damn," Darryl said, sucking back the drool that had roped along the corners of his mouth.

"You're just teaching me how to swim, right?"

"Yeah, sure." The tall werewolf prodded me toward the steps going down into the pool. "We'll start out in the shallow end."

I stepped down into the surprisingly warm water and waded into it, keeping my feet on the rough bottom. Darryl followed, getting uncomfortably close.

"All right. First thing you're gonna learn is how to float," he said in his deep tone before placing one hand on my back, supporting me as he pushed me flat with the other.

I panicked for a moment as my feet left the bottom of the pool, and I thrashed around.

"Relax. I'm not gonna let you sink. Just imagine yourself as a piece of driftwood."

My entire body tensed as I struggled to keep calm, but as soon as I was oriented, I allowed myself to loosen up. As long as I could feel his arms supporting my back, I was okay. He grabbed a pool noodle floating behind him and placed it under my neck to keep my head from sinking.

"See? Like a duck to water," he said, gently stroking my chest. He removed one of his hands from my back but the other still supported my rear. The noodle kept my upper body from sinking, but I also couldn't move much or I'd start to panic. "Close your eyes and keep thinking of wood."

I raised an eyebrow at that.

"Driftwood," he added.

I did as he said.

"Now kick your feet a little bit."

There was something both comfortable and uncomfortable about the way he touched me, and I kind of knew what the werewolf was doing. As if sensing my unease, he chilled out on the physical contact and focused more on the lesson.

I kicked my feet, but each time I raised one leg, I'd sink. His large hand supported my back again, and I started to move.

"This is kinda fun," I said, now swimming without his support.

Roscoe snored, having fallen asleep while lying in the chair, and Darryl looked back for a moment before returning his attention to me.

"Okay, this is bothering the hell out of me. How did someone like you end up with *that* trainwreck?"

I maneuvered myself upright and waded to the steps before sitting, still halfway submerged in the warm water. Darryl took his place next to me.

"To be honest? It all happened so fast, I still don't know. He told me you both were friends, and now I feel like shit for intruding."

"Dude, you're not intruding, and you don't seem like the type to take advantage of people." He smiled and patted me on the back. "So, why the hell did you take a kuu from Roscoe, of all people?"

"I don't know. Maybe I'm stupid, but there's something about him." I looked back at the now drooling werewolf, his tongue hanging out of his mouth as he snored louder. "Maybe it's because he's so fucking repulsive, and for some reason, it turns me on. I'm a neat freak, and my idea of fun is a quiet evening doing a crossword puzzle." I'd never actually admitted that to anyone before, but it felt good to get it off my chest. "I wasn't always like this, but that's a boring story. Roscoe's the complete opposite, so he kind of forces me to not be that way all the time."

"Aw man, I'm sorry. I was trying to put the moves on you, but I could tell you were really uncomfortable. Someone really fucked you up, huh?"

"Kind of, but I let him hurt me bad enough that I just stopped looking for a relationship. That's on me, though. Roscoe was a surprise. A really gross and annoying surprise, and I'm still not sure what the hell I'm even doing. We literally met a few days ago."

"Dude... that's not long enough to be accepting a kuu. You don't even know what kind of person he is."

"Well, it's not like it's permanent. I just have to hold out until I'm a werewolf."

"And that can take a few years." He sighed and nodded. "But I get it. You seem like the type of person that's not gonna take his shit, and who knows? That might be good for him."

"What's the history between you two?" I asked but regretted it when the scowl returned to his face. "You don't have to answer that."

"Sorry. Just thinking about it puts me in a bad mood. Maybe some other time. It was a long time ago, and he seems sober."

"Roscoe? Sober? I don't think I've ever seen him in that condition."

"Naw. It was way worse when he was on pills. This is just booze."

"Great. I'm stuck with an addict."

"Good news is he's definitely clean. I've seen him when he's not. We might be strangers, but if he ever starts back up on that shit, you come here. Got it?"

Darryl really sounded genuine, which made me smile.

"You're pretty grounded. You've got a stable job and a house. I didn't think that was possible for a werewolf."

"Cody, what you've seen in that city isn't reality. That kind of poverty is what happens when you drain the hope and ambition from an entire demographic while giving them just enough of a handout to be dependent and desperate." He stood up and stretched before reaching for my hand. "It's all by design. I'll give you the best advice you'll ever receive in your life. Get the hell out of that place as soon as you can." He looked back at Roscoe, this time with more sympathy in his silvery eyes. "It'll suck away your soul until there's nothing good left."

Darryl broke his well-worn facade of a simple beach wolf that night, revealing something almost regal. I couldn't help but admire whatever that was.

The midnight moon's reflection danced over the calmer ocean as I sat cross-legged in the warm sand. Both werewolves had fallen asleep in Darryl's bed, but the house had no air conditioning and sleep wasn't going to come easy. I was still thinking about the earlier conversation, and I wondered if I had made a huge mistake.

"Hey," Roscoe whispered from behind. "What're you doin' out here, bud?"

"Can't sleep."

He sat next to me in the sand. "I think I realized something earlier."

"What's that?"

Roscoe smiled, his orange eyes reflecting the moon. "I'm not young no more. Hell, I'm not even close to the same person I was three years ago."

"From what I've heard, that's a good thing."

He nodded but slumped forward a little as if embarrassed. That was an expression I hadn't seen him make yet. "Back in the day, Darryl and I would've fucked through a dozen half-turns and humans all night long and wanted more. Wouldn't have felt anything for anyone. It was just all good times."

A larger wave crashed into shore before the ocean quieted again.

I kept my eyes on the water while trying to think of what to say. "It seems like everyone gets to enjoy being young, and I'm the one that got old before my time."

"Most half-turns usually go through this phase when they're younger. Yer kinda in a weird situation, but I guess that's what makes you different—but in a good way."

"What do you mean?"

Roscoe paused for a moment. "I dunno." He let out a sigh before laying back in the sand, his hands folded behind his head. "Nothin' feels like it used to. It ain't a bad thing. I mean, this is the first time in years I've been sober. I guess you being a tight ass is rubbin' off on me a little bit."

"I think that's just called being an adult." I laid next to him, his arm supporting my head. "It's nice out here."

"Yeah, it is."

"Darryl's a great guy, and he seems like a good friend."

"He was a great friend. I wasn't, though." He sighed and shuffled a bit next to me. "It seems like a lifetime ago, but it hasn't been that long."

I wondered if he'd overheard Darryl and me talking earlier and had just been pretending to be asleep. Maybe this wasn't a mistake, and Roscoe was actually a decent guy.

He snored lightly, having dozed off while looking up at the moon.

"Thank you for not leaving me alone," I whispered before closing my eyes, letting the waves lull me to sleep.

# A Business Proposition

Seagulls cried overhead as the tide rushed in. Gentle waves that had once been off in the distance now lapped at my bare feet. A moist, steady breeze brushed against my skin, which was more exposed than it had been yesterday since I'd gotten up the nerve to remove my overshirt. There weren't many people out here at this hour, and those that were said good morning before passing without a fuss.

It wasn't just a fluke. People really didn't seem to mind werewolves or half-turns on the beach, even though most of the population was human. I watched the older locals pass by Darryl, always nodding and waving, admiring their famous lifeguard. Who could blame them? There wasn't a soul out there swimming that didn't feel completely safe with him guarding their lives.

This town was my proof that we really could thrive when given the chance, and werewolves could have careers and jobs that weren't just mind-numbing manual labor. Perhaps one day I could be like Darryl. Confident, fun, responsible, and successful in my own way.

"Well, well, well," a flamboyant voice called out from a few feet away. I turned in time to get a face full of sand as Adam pranced around before sitting next to me.

"Dude, that got in my eyes!" I grabbed my water bottle, squirting some onto my face.

"My bad," the half-turn said in a mocking tone before snorting out a quiet laugh. "Whatcha doin'?"

"Trying to enjoy the ocean... with both eyes." After washing away as much sand as I could, I turned to him. "What are you doing here?"

"Swimming lessons." He eyed Darryl with a flirty grin. "Well, that and I heard you were here. Got yourself more hair, huh?"

"I feel like a freak," I muttered, looking down at a tuft of thick chest hair peeking from the collar of my tank top.

"Yeah, that doesn't really go away when you're half-turn."

"How did you know I was here?"

"You got your kuu, and Roscoe has a big mouth. I didn't know *he* was the werewolf you chose."

"You know Roscoe?"

Adam laughed. "Everyone knows Roscoe. He's legendary."

"Oh?"

"Not in a good way," he added.

"Oh..."

"I'm surprised out of anyone you could have chosen you picked the bummiest bum imaginable."

"He's... bad but he's not *that* bad." I smiled and looked back at the little beach house. Roscoe had gone inside to sleep after Darryl started his shift. "Sometimes he can surprise you."

We listened to the waves for an uncomfortable moment before I finally started in with the questions.

"Who's *your* werewolf?"

Adam frowned, letting out an almost disgusted groan. "Can we not ruin the morning? Thanks."

"Sorry. Just trying to get to know you."

"Small talk is fucking boring. Let's get into the dirty details. You know my name, and I've probably fucked every werewolf you've met—except Roscoe, because ew. Nice standards, by the way."

"This coming from a guy who just admitted to indiscriminately fucking everyone. If my standards are six feet under, yours must be in the pits of hell."

Adam opened his mouth but didn't respond right away. "You're a bitch," he finally said.

"Must be releasing all this bitchy energy I've been collecting since we met. What's your problem with me?"

He shoved my elbow playfully. "I didn't say I had a problem with you. I like your bitchiness."

"I swear to God, you're like Roscoe."

The look of pure horror on his face nearly had me on the ground. "Excuse me?"

"You both keep trying to get a rise out of me for some reason, and you seem to like it when I'm pissed off."

"That's because you're an easy mark." He picked up a broken shell and tossed it into the water. "And it's funny how your face gets all red. It must suck to be that white."

"You know, if I were to say that to you—"

"Probably not a good idea. I've got the card, you don't."

That time, I could really feel my face getting red. He shoved me again.

"Come on, I'm just kidding. We're both going to be fur-covered monsters soon, so it's not like skin color is going to be our defining feature anymore."

"So, do you actually do anything else other than fuck werewolves? Any hobbies? A job?"

"A job?" He broke into another fit of laughter. "I get free money from the government, *and* my family's rich. I'm happy just being a slut and playing video games."

"Is that really all you want out of life?"

"Uh, yeah," he said, rolling his eyes. "Once I'm a full werewolf, I'm just gonna party every day. I've earned it."

"Earned what?" I asked. "It doesn't sound like you've actually done anything." I knew why I was getting so angry. This was a kid who had life handed to him, and I had to bust my ass eating tuna without mayo.

"Don't sound all condescending. We're both earning it since we're forced to let werewolves live with us." He tugged at the chain around his neck. "These are the only things keeping us from going on killing rampages, and I'd rather spend a year or two living with a piece of shit than being locked up in a cage."

"Are these kuu a new thing? What did half-turns do before?"

"I don't know, man. I don't question it—I just deal with it." He sighed and leaned back on his arms. "Look. We're doing some good by getting werewolves off the streets while helping fund a future for all of us. It doesn't matter how much money you have when you're legally barred from spending it. Or in your case, *earning* it."

I glared at him again.

"Those earrings look really faggy, by the way. They look good on *you* though," he said, removing his shirt as he stood, brushing away the sand that had stuck to the backs of his legs. The obvious back-handed compliment annoyed me even more. "I'm going for a swim."

"I thought you were getting swimming lessons."

Adam gawked at the tall werewolf in the distance. "God, you're so clueless. No one actually goes to Darryl for swimming lessons."

The key slid into the door, and I heaved a sigh of relief. "Thank God."

"You've still got a day. Did you really think they were going to change the locks on you?" Roscoe asked, following me inside. "I wish we could take the AC with us."

"Maybe I can see how much a window unit costs. How much money do you have?"

"Enough for us to eat for a couple of days," Roscoe replied. His deep voice had a slight echo since the apartment was mostly empty, save for a few duffel bags full of clothes and toiletries. "Plus, Darryl hates air conditioning. It's only for a couple of weeks, anyway."

"I can't keep sleeping outside." I held up my arms, revealing several bug bites that, for some reason, hadn't completely healed yet. "I'm being eaten alive by whatever's on that beach."

Roscoe gently grabbed my arm and examined it. "Ah, I forgot about these. Dune fleas. Well, that ain't their actual names, but I know they bite the shit out of half-turns for some reason. They don't bother werewolves, though."

"I wish you hadn't destroyed my air mattress."

Roscoe grabbed the last two beers from the fridge and handed me one. "We'll figure something out."

I took a sip and looked out the only window with a view of the city and not a cracked brick facade. "Darryl was right about this place sucking your soul away. We've only been back in the city for an hour, and I already feel depressed."

"I never really put that together, but I think yer right." Roscoe set his beer on the counter and walked into the bathroom to pee with the door open. "I'm surprised Darryl couldn't sweet-talk his way into yer pants. He's sure changed a lot." He stopped peeing and walked back out into the room.

"Did you really not flush the toilet or wash your hands?"

"It's a surprise for the next tenant."

I folded my arms. "I wish I could quit you."

He let out a snort before walking back into the bathroom. "You really are a tight ass." The toilet flushed and the water in the sink came on. "Well, probably not anymore now that I've claimed it."

"That's really funny," I said as he padded back into the room, wiping his wet hands on his fur. "I still don't know how it all happened that first night."

"You may have looked human, but you were definitely half-turn, and half-turns are stretchy," Roscoe said while holding out his balled-up fist. "You heal so damn fast I could go full Caligula on you and you'd be just fine."

"Don't EVER do that," I shouted, swatting his fist away. "Are werewolves like that, too?"

"Well, yeah. That don't ever go away." He raised a brow. "Why? I didn't give you any ideas, did I?"

I cracked my knuckles. "I don't know. The Caligula thing sounds like it could be useful."

"I ain't letting you near my ass with yer nasty temper."

We both stared at one another before raising our beers.

"I can't believe I'm moving again already," I said before taking another sip. "Wasn't even in this place for more than a few months."

"Staying in one place too long gets boring. Think of this as an adventure. When you're with me, it's never gonna get boring."

"That's what I'm afraid of."

A loud knock sounded at the front door, startling me, but Roscoe remained calm as always.

"Expecting someone?" he asked.

"No," I said, hurrying to the front door. I peeked through the hole and saw two police officers accompanying a middle-aged man standing on the other side. "Well, this should be fun," I whispered, waving Roscoe away. "Stay out of sight."

He nodded, disappeared into the bathroom, and I opened the door.

"Hello?" I said as the man brushed by me.

"You were supposed to be out today," he said, looking around the apartment.

"No, the letter clearly stated tomorrow."

"Things have changed," he said, noticing the fur Roscoe had shed all over the carpet. "Having a werewolf live with you was one thing, but there is a strict ordinance against half-turns residing on this property."

"We'll be out today," I said, holding my hands up as one officer stepped closer.

Roscoe threw open the bathroom door, and the other cop pulled a taser out of its holster.

"Whoa there," Roscoe said, slowly pointing to the bags lined against the wall. "We're just gonna get our things and skedaddle." He froze, and that shitty grin inched up his maw as he eyed one of the officers. "Oh damn. It's Sergeant Buttercup!"

"You!" The officer grew more irritated at the sight of the werewolf. He looked to be in his mid-thirties but was built like he'd spent several hours a day in the gym. "Every time I'm called about werewolf disturbances, you're involved somehow."

Roscoe's tail wagged while he took a careful step closer. "If we keep meeting like this, we may as well start datin'."

"One day your luck's gonna run out, buddy. I want to be there when a judge finally puts your ass in werewolf prison."

"I didn't do nothin' wrong this time. I'm just helping the kid out."

"Yeah," he said, opening the front door. "Grab your shit and we'll escort you off the premises."

"I'll be mailing you the bill for the lease termination," the property manager said, opening the blinds before turning back to me.

"And I'll rub it against my sweaty taint as payment," Roscoe rebutted, grabbing four of the bags before leaning in close to the older man. "How's that sound?"

The man said nothing, visibly shaken by how close Roscoe's teeth were to his face.

The cop stomped his foot. "Roscoe! Out! Now!"

"Fine, whatever. Let's get the hell out of here," the werewolf grunted, pushing past the cops and walking outside with me close behind. As we got to the edge of the property, the officers stopped.

"If you come back, it's not going to end well for either of you, understand?"

I nodded, intending to leave it at that, but the temptation to be a complete idiot was too obviously much for Roscoe.

"I guess we'll have to put a pin in our plans to rob the place, huh?" There was an obvious air of sarcasm to his tone, but the cop that knew him furrowed his brows before leaning closer.

"Excuse me?"

"It's a joke, Deputy Donut. Lighten up a little."

The officer unsheathed the taser and fired it point blank into Roscoe's abdomen. He yelped, dropping the bags before collapsing onto the ground.

"Whoa! You can't just shoot people like that!" I shouted, and the officer turned his attention to me.

"You're not people," he said, his words dripping with disdain. Both men walked back to their patrol cars while bystanders gawked at the commotion, some recording on their smartphones.

I knelt next to Roscoe, who lay on the ground, holding his stomach. "Are you okay?"

"I think I pissed all over myself."

"You're a fucking moron," I hissed, grabbing his hand to help him into a sitting position. "You could have gotten us both in a lot of trouble."

He stumbled to his feet, winking at the cop car driving by. "Damn, if I had a dollar for every time I've been tasered."

"Are you a felon or something?"

He shrugged. "The past is the past."

"Roscoe, let's get one thing straight," I growled out, my vision turning red again. "I'm not going to jail because of you!"

"Stop worrying about it. I was just having some fun."

There was wet fur around Roscoe's crotch and a damp spot on the sidewalk where he had fallen. "Yeah, that looks like a real good time to me."

The slightly shaky werewolf picked up the bags and walked with me toward the bus stop. "You were worried about me, weren't you?"

"Yes," I said, annoyed by how nonchalant he was. I wasn't used to being treated like a criminal, especially since my only crime was existing in a place I no longer belonged. "If something happened to you, I'd have to carry all this myself."

"You really like me."

"I hate your guts, dude."

Roscoe put the bags on the ground before sitting on the bench as we waited for our ride. I sat next to him, the adrenaline rush from earlier finally settling.

"I just remembered something," Roscoe said, his ears lowering into a guilty, airplane position. "I, uh... may not have a job anymore. Kinda forgot to go back."

"Well, it's not like you can take four-hour-long bus rides every day. Just get another one at the beach."

When he slumped his shoulders forward and he let out a dog-like whine, I knew what was coming. "C'mon, Cody. We've got enough until yer money comes in."

"Yeah, *my* money, not *our* money. You're not going to leech off me and lay around the house doing nothing."

Roscoe continued with the act, his eyes growing big and watery.

"It didn't work before. What makes you think it's going to work now?"

He got on one knee and stared up, his nose nearly touching my face as his ears dropped to the sides of his head again.

"You're making an idiot of yourself," I whispered through my teeth.

He leaned back a bit. "Man, I must be losin' my touch."

"You never had a touch."

He made the face again, this time struggling to hold it. It was disturbing how easily he could do that. "Nothing? Really? Nary an ounce of pity?"

I glared at him.

"Eh, fine. I'll find a way to make some money."

"A *legal* way," I added.

"I wonder how many times people've called you a nerd," he muttered before sitting back on the bench. His tail wagged, which immediately set off alarm bells. "Hey, I've got an idea."

"Can't wait to hear it."

"You remember how I said I had an OnlyStans?"

"Yeah," I replied, growing more irritated by the second. "And three hundred dollars a month isn't going to cut it."

"Well, I could get more..." He flashed his brows. "If I had a nice half-turn to share the screen time with."

"No."

He playfully shoved me. "Werewolf accounts featuring half-turns are where the money's at. The nastier the sex, the more we make."

"I'm probably going to regret asking this. Why?"

"Cause half-turns look kind of human, and I could do stuff to you I can't with a regular guy, for obvious reasons. It's a fetish thing, and people love that shit."

"Absolutely disgusting."

"Don't pretend you didn't love what we did in that shower."

"That's different. It's not in front of a camera with a bunch of goons jerking off to it."

"Pretend the camera ain't there, and it's not like you're ever gonna see any of those people."

He had a point.

"So, hypothetically... how much could we make doing that?"

Roscoe's tail pounded the bench.

"Hypothetically," I repeated, a little sterner.

"Well, that depends. What are ya willing to do?"

"And with that question, I'm no longer interested."

His tail stopped wagging. "Okay, okay. We don't gotta do anything too gross, but it can't just be vanilla, either."

"It's your account. Come up with something interesting that doesn't make me want to vomit."

"All right, all right. Yer giving this consideration, so that's good at least." He grabbed the bags as the bus rolled to a stop in front of us. "You like bondage?"

I returned that question with another glare.

"I'll put that in my back pocket then." He walked up the steps of the bus with me following. "What about e-stim? Ever stuck an electric metal rod in your pee hole before?"

My face got hot as we walked down the aisle to the back of the bus, people staring.

"Can we not talk about this right now?" I whispered. "Idiot."

"Hey, if we're gonna go into business together, I gotta know what you like," he said, setting the bags down before taking his seat. "I think I've got a great idea."

"If the word *Caligula* leaves your mouth—"

"Costumes."

"Excuse me?"

"Think about it, Cody. We could do some dirty cosplay. People love that shit!" The fur on the back of his neck stood straight as he grinned. "I love Halloween, and it could be Halloween every week."

"This sounds like a lot of work. You've got to get the costumes, record us, edit the video, advertise somehow, and you have to upload often. Are you sure you're up for that much work?"

"Well, I was hoping you'd handle all the boring, non-sex stuff."

I sank my fingernails into his leg as I tried to not lose my temper.

"Ow ow ow," he said, prying my hand away.

"And what the hell are you going to do?"

"Well, I'll get the costumes and let you ride my dick."

His audacity once again left me speechless.

"Find an actual job, Roscoe."

"All right, I'll do the editing, but I don't got a computer." He paused and gave me a nudge. "Hey, you got a laptop, don't ya?"

"You're not editing porn on my computer." That was a little louder than I intended, and it garnered a few stares from humans sitting closer to us. I lowered my voice. "Sounds like you need to earn some money first to buy the equipment."

"Can't you just loan me the money?"

"What money, Roscoe? We need income now, and you're the only one who can walk into a business without getting thrown out."

"Damn, you *really* don't know me that well."

"Get a fucking job."

He let out a wistful whine. "I'll see if Darryl's company is hiring temporary lifeguards."

I poked Roscoe's protruding gut. "I don't think I've ever seen you so much as walk at a brisk pace. You're too fat to be a lifeguard."

"I'm a werewolf, and I'm buoyant," he grunted, flexing one arm while patting his stomach with the other. "I'm in the best shape of my life."

"I guess round could count as a shape."

Roscoe dropped his arms and laughed. "Okay, maybe a lifeguard is pushin' it a bit."

"Just find a little part-time gig so we can eat. Maybe once I start getting money, I'll give you a loan for a computer, and I'll dress up in your costumes. You're responsible for everything else."

A contemplative hum left his nose as he sat back in his seat, seeming to give my proposal some thought.

"I've never used a computer before."

"If you can use a smartphone, you can use a computer." I scratched my head. "Wait a minute, how do you have an OnlyStans account? I've never even seen you use a phone except for mine."

"Ah, see I got this buddy—"

"Never mind," I interrupted. "You're going to need to figure all this shit out, because I'll be busy trying not to kill you."

"All right. But I get most of the money."

"That's fair. You can cut me in for thirty-five percent."

"Thirty," he said.

"Thirty-six."

Roscoe held up a finger to negotiate further but cocked his head. "Wait, that's not how you do this. Yer supposed to go down until we meet in the middle."

"Now it's thirty-seven, because you're forgetting I have the golden ass."

After a moment of silence, he begrudgingly held out his hand. "Fine, thirty-five."

I grabbed hold and sighed. "All right. Let's make some porn, I guess."

I took a bite of leftover bratwurst while leaning back in the lounge chair, watching the sunset over the ocean waves, occasionally fending off hungry gulls. Roscoe sat next to me, and Darryl was inside working on something.

"It actually feels kind of nice outside with the sea breeze," I said, finishing the sausage before setting my plate on the sand next to me. "Maybe we should just find a place to live here."

"I don't think it works like that. You don't really have a choice where they put you. It'll probably be in the Ruskin area."

"God, I hope not. I also hope it's not a complete dump."

"It's government housing, Cody," Roscoe said, picking my plate off the ground before standing. "It's not going to be Shangri-La, but at least it's free." He stacked my plate on top of his. "Still hungry?"

"I'm good."

"One day, I'll make you my baked ziti. You like tiramisu?"

I looked up at him. "Were you some kind of chef or something?"

"Nah, I just really like food." He started walking back to the beach house. "It's nice to cook for someone else for a change."

"Hello? Why don't you do that for a job?"

Roscoe stopped and looked back at me, shaking his head. "No way. Once you start doin' something you like for money, it ruins it. Plus, I'm a walking health code violation."

"Wait a minute. You were just talking about having sex with me for money."

"Gotta get the dishes done before Darryl gets mad," he said, scrambling up the steps before disappearing inside.

"Since you get too hot sleeping in the bed with us, I think this is a good solution. What do you think?" Darryl asked while standing next to Roscoe.

I examined the mesh hammock Darryl set up between the two main support beams. It had a blanket and a pillow on top of it.

"I guess it matches the nautical theme, but I've never slept in one before."

"Try it out," the larger werewolf prodded. "We've still got to have our swimming lesson tonight."

I shot him a concerned glance.

"*Only* swimming, I swear."

After a moment of hesitation, I carefully positioned myself to sit on the swinging bed, but every time I'd try to sit, the hammock rocked too much.

"I don't know about this."

"I'd sleep in it myself and give you the bed, but I'm too heavy," Darryl said. "Just don't make any sudden movements."

"Don't make any sudden movements? This is supposed to be a bed. I'm not hiding from velociraptors," I said, my ass now making contact with the netting. When I leaned back slightly, the entire hammock flipped with me, the blanket, and pillow falling to the floor. "Damn it!" I shouted, rubbing the bump on my head.

"You okay?" Darryl asked, both werewolves snickering as they reached down to help me up.

"I could have broken my neck!"

"Yer a half-turn. You ain't gonna break nothin'," Roscoe said casually while helping me back onto the swinging bed.

This time, I crawled on top facing down until I was in position; however, I was now presented with a new dilemma. How would I turn onto my back without the bed flipping again?

Carefully, I repositioned my body while trying to keep the hammock stable. With every movement, it swung a little more until I was swinging so much the bed flipped again. This time my feet and arms remained tangled in the net, and I swung above the floor.

Darryl and Roscoe howled with laughter, and I was getting a lot more irritated as I let myself fall.

"I think I'd rather sleep with the fleas," I muttered, slapping both werewolves away as they tried to help me up again.

Darryl's front door swung open, and Adam strutted in as if he lived there.

"I thought you were going back home," Darryl said, slightly annoyed.

"I will, eventually." He glanced at Roscoe and then me. "What's going on here? Is this a sex thing?"

"No," I replied, trying to keep my cool. "Let's just get an air mattress."

Adam walked over and sat down on the hammock, effortlessly lying back while crossing his legs.

"I should get one of these," he said.

"How the hell did you do that?"

"How the hell did I do what? Lay down?" He rolled his eyes before looking over at Darryl. "You up for a swimming lesson?"

"Not tonight," Darryl replied. "Cody's on the schedule."

Adam looked me over and shrugged. "He's not exactly my type, but I could join in if I don't look at him too much."

"Sure, you can join us," I said, crossing my arms. "I think we left off on how to float. Face down. Without moving or coming up for air."

"That sounds kinda hot." He examined my face again and broke into laughter. "Wait, that wasn't innuendo? You really don't know how to swim?"

"Hey," Darryl cut in. "At least he's willing to learn something new. Not everyone's satisfied with mediocrity."

Adam sat up out of the hammock and snarled at the tall werewolf before storming out of the house.

"He's going to be really fun to talk to now," I said.

"I've known Adam for about a year, and the kid's got a shitty attitude. He's fun in the bedroom, but that's where the fun ends." He tossed a glance at Roscoe. "Maybe you should have a go at him."

"Well, I haven't gotten off today, so what the hell?"

"No, I mean *talk* to him. You've got plenty of experience being a shitty person, so maybe you could tell him what not to do with his life."

Roscoe didn't say anything.

"Just so you know, if Cody wasn't with you, I'd have beaten the shit out of you yesterday and told you to get lost."

The smaller werewolf stared at the floor, tail tucked between his legs. "I'm not that person no more."

"Yeah, I've heard that before." Darryl took a deep breath, forcing a smile. "While you're living here, you're gonna put that lazy ass to good use."

"Uh... sure. What do you want me to do?"

"You'll see." He turned his attention back to me. "Let's go have a swimming lesson."

# Chapter 7

# Night Out

**A**tall bonfire cast an orange glow on the beach in the distance as I sat on the deck, sipping a glass of cheap chardonnay. After that brief, uncomfortable exchange with Darryl last night, Roscoe hadn't been as talkative. In fact, I'd seen little of him and Adam today.

Darryl had to cut my swimming lesson short since the lifeguards needed him back on the beach, and he spent the rest of the evening entertaining friends around the fire with his guitar. I thought about joining, but I'd feel like the odd man out. Most of them were surfers or much older friends of his, and after getting lost in the lingo for several minutes with no one to talk to, I broke away to sit by myself. There had never been a moment in my life where social events with strangers weren't awkward and uncomfortable.

After a few more minutes, the music died and the crowd on the beach whittled to only Darryl and Adam. They seemed serious, but I was too far away to hear any of the conversation. The half-turn jumped to his feet and made a few angry gestures, but Darryl remained straight-faced. This seemed to upset Adam further, and he kicked sand at the huge werewolf before running toward town.

Darryl stared at the ocean, seemingly unfazed as he strummed a gentle tune while his tail swayed. The guy was hard to pin down. He was laid-back, funny, and talented, but at the same time, stern and honest with an almost sage-like quality. His own personality contradicted itself in such a way that it seemed to work in his favor with everyone else.

I stepped barefoot on the sand, which was still warm from the residual heat it absorbed from the afternoon sun. Though the confrontation wasn't any of my business, I wanted to make sure everything was okay. And since it was Adam, I had to admit a little gossip about him would be quite the pick-me-up. After approaching the crackling fire, I sat next to the huge werewolf playing the guitar with his eyes closed.

These weren't the folk songs he played earlier. This was classical and overly technical. Despite how large his fingers were, they effortlessly slid along the neck of the instrument with prodigy-like precision and emotion. Even as the music shifted from complex to gentle, his tranquil expression stayed the same until he was done.

"That was incredible," I whispered, staring up at Darryl as he breathed deeply through his nose and opened his eyes. He didn't look over at me, though a slightly toothy smile parted his lips.

"Thanks." He placed the guitar to the side. "My dad taught me."

"You're not classically trained?"

"I never said that." He let out a gentle laugh. "Sorry about our lesson earlier."

"That's fine. I needed to get all this housing stuff taken care of anyway."

"Have you heard anything?"

I shook my head. "I've been calling, and I keep getting the run-around. No one has a straight answer for me, and I'm starting to wonder if there really are any houses—or if any of this shit is real."

"You don't have to stress yourself out. My place might be small, but I don't mind you guys staying."

"That's not the kind of vibe I've been getting from you lately."

Darryl's smile faded. "Sorry."

"I know you don't like talking about it, but I have to know. What happened between you and Roscoe?"

The werewolf sighed and laid back on the sand, his hands cupped under his head. "I've known the guy since I was a half-turn." He shook his head. "Damn, that was like four decades ago. Time sure has a way of getting away from you the older you get."

"How old are you?"

"I'll be sixty in a month."

"Damn. I guess that's something neat to look forward to," I said. "I'll get to keep my boyish good looks for a while."

"I really hate that someone like you made a kuu with him," Darryl said abruptly. "It bothers me."

"Why do you care? Were you and Roscoe, like... *together*?"

"Oh, fuck no," he said with a laugh. "I'd probably end up killing him, for real. It's just... you remind me a little of myself. I was a late bloomer, too. Socially awkward as a kid. Spent a lot of time alone. It took going half-turn and meeting Roscoe to really break me out of my shell. I don't want him to betray you the way he betrayed me."

"When did you go half-turn?"

"Twenty-two. Everyone thought it was kinda weird me going through that being that old, but apparently, I was a special case. You might be, too."

"This really ruined my life. I've got a degree I can't even use now, and I'm in so much debt. Now I don't even know where I'm going to end up living in the long-term. It's not the first time in my life that I've been so scared, but I've never felt this hopeless."

"It's only hopeless if you're alone," he said, smiling at me before rubbing my head. "And you're not gonna be alone."

"You still haven't really answered my question. How did Roscoe betray you?"

"Well, I guess you need to know more than anyone what kind of asshole you're shacked up with." He let out a growled sigh before looking back over at me. "Roscoe and I were inseparable. We were best friends, and he taught me a lot about what to expect when I finally turned into this handsome beast. He also introduced me to a lot of drugs and shady people. It was fun at first, but I realized that we were way different people, and I started to see Roscoe for who he really was. I just never noticed until I stopped getting high."

"Maybe you guys need to talk it out now that he's sober." I lay back against the sand and turned to face him. "He's obviously changed since you last saw him, so maybe you can find some common ground?"

"That ship sailed years ago, Cody." The werewolf gritted his teeth for a moment before relaxing. "Just thinking about his face makes me want to rip something apart. But werewolves can't dwell on shit like that, or it gets dangerous. I put it out of my mind for so long, but then he showed up with you, and everything came flooding back." He shook his head, his smile a little sadder than before. "My dad was one hell of a musician when he was alive. There wasn't an instrument the man couldn't master, but the guitar was what he loved the most. Some of that musta rubbed off on me, because when I held his guitar, it felt like I was holding a piece of myself.

"My dad noticed and started teaching me when I was about seven. Mom died when I was a toddler, so I never really knew her—just have flashes of memories now and again. Dad was my world, and he taught me a lot about bein' a man. The guy was a chain smoker, but he wasn't a werewolf. It eventually caught up to him, and he died when I was seventeen. He left me a guitar that was passed down through generations, and was worth more than most luxury cars. That was the only thing of value he owned. Of course, I'd never sell it, and I kept it safe for years until I met Roscoe."

"Oh no." I whispered, already knowing where the story was going.

"One night while I was visiting the city with him, we were both fucked up pretty bad, and I woke up the next morning to a missing guitar and no Roscoe. I immediately put two and two together, and that was the first time I actually howled. It was the most painful feeling. Not only was I pretty hungover, but my best friend fucked me over, and I lost the only thing left of my dad. It was the second worst day of my life.

"I eventually tracked him down and beat the ever-living shit out of him. I'd never lost control like that, and I almost killed him. But he was so out of his head that nothing I did mattered—it was like hitting a ragdoll. He blacked out on the sidewalk and I left him there for good. I went to every pawnshop in the area looking for that guitar, and I did eventually find it." He shook his head. "The guy at that shop knew exactly what he had, and Roscoe practically gave the thing away. There was no way I could afford to buy it back, so I left it and left him in that shithole of a city. I hopped on a bus, came back here, and threw everything I had into surfing. Then I became a lifeguard, quit most of the drugs, and I have it pretty good now." He sat up and grabbed his guitar. "It's not Dad's, but I realized later on in life that I never lost the most valuable thing he left me." He strummed out a gorgeous riff, gently tapping the strings with his claws. "When I hit my full turn, it was harder to play with these hands, but I adapted a new way... the Darryl way."

"It's beautiful," I said, swaying in time with the music. "It seems like you've got a lot of friends now."

"I do. All walks of life, werewolf and human. I met a lot of people on this very beach, even met someone *really* special, but I'll save that for another time."

"Do you have someone?"

Darryl stopped playing and let out a deep laugh. "Sure do. He's not much of a swimmer, though."

"Lucky guy," I said, pushing myself to my feet. "You gonna stay out here for a while?"

"Yeah. Got a lot to think about. Looks like Roscoe's been gone all day."

"I don't know where he went. He didn't say anything to me."

"You're better off without him, but since he gave you the kuu—"

"We'll have a talk about things when he gets back," I interrupted, turning toward the direction of the small beach house. "If he ever starts back up old habits, I'll get out of this."

"If you need a place to stay, my house is always open."

I leaned over and gave him a hug. "Thanks, Darryl."

<br>

Sleep didn't come easy, and Roscoe still hadn't come back. I thought about what Darryl told me earlier, and despite it all, I wanted to believe Roscoe had changed. Given how I was still up, lying on the beach while worrying meant I actually cared about him.

"Yer gonna get fleas again," Roscoe said, his footsteps close enough that I could hear him kicking up sand.

I turned toward the lumbering werewolf, silhouetted by the moonlight overhead, his eyes glowing a fiery orange from inside the hood he had pulled up over his head.

"Where the hell have you been?"

"Out," he replied, sitting next to me. "Here." He took my hand and pressed a wad of cash into it.

"What's this?"

"You've really been helping me out, and I wanted you to have some spending money."

I glanced down at the wrinkled twenty-dollar bills, then up at him. "I like this Roscoe. Where the hell did he come from?"

"He was here. Ya just didn't notice him yet."

"We'll save this for groceries." I slipped the cash into my pocket and smiled at him.

"Nah, you'll use it for fun. Let me worry about the food."

"Where'd you get it?"

"Apparently, aside from Darryl, there ain't many werewolves in this town. Got offered a job at a nightclub nearby as a bouncer. The pay was nearly double what I made in the city, and they pay under the table, too. I love this little town."

"Damn, you actually got a job," I said, scooting closer to him. "You like it?"

"Eh, it's okay. Not as fun as my cosplay porn idea, though."

"Oh yeah. About that..."

"Don't tell me yer already gettin' cold feet."

"I'm not a camera person, and I don't like making private stuff public—especially my privates. You should ask Adam if he'll do it. Sounds like something he'd enjoy."

"Hell no. That prissy little shit would probably want more than half the profit." A jagged grin parted his thin black lips. "Plus, it's hotter with you."

I flushed and gave him a playful shove. "You're trying to butter me up to make cheap porn with you."

"Is it working?"

"Kinda."

His hand slipped around my waist. "Ever had sex on the beach?"

"No, and it sounds like an awful experience."

He pulled me closer to him, his warm tongue circling the crook of my neck. "It's fun."

"Someone's gonna see us."

"It's after two in the morning, Cody."

"Someone could still be walking around."

He pushed me against the sand before climbing on top, pulling down his hood. "If they're out this late, they're drunk and ain't gonna care." Roscoe's tongue slipped into my mouth, and his clawed finger hooked through the drawstring of my shorts, pulling the fabric away, leaving me exposed.

"Fine. Just try not to get sand in my ass."

A light drizzle pattered against the tin roof of the small beach house, and the three of us sat in front of the television scarfing down pizza. I was approaching my limit after the third slice, but Roscoe and Darryl were already halfway into their second pies, furiously smacking as drool roped from their mouths. I had to turn up the volume of whatever show was on just to cover up the unwanted ASMR.

"Can you guys eat a little quieter?"

"You try eating with a dog mouth and see how quiet you are," Roscoe said, sputtering some of the pizza he was in the middle of chewing.

"At least chew with your mouth closed."

"Can't," Darryl chimed in, taking another bite. "I've tried. It doesn't work out too well."

I tossed my crust into the box, and Roscoe immediately snatched it up before tossing it into his mouth.

"What are you, twelve?" he asked. "Want me to start cutting the crust off yer PB and J, too?"

"Pizza crust is just a handle for the edible parts," I said before leaning back against the couch. We were all sitting on the floor since Darryl didn't have a table inside. Lightning cracked the sky, pulling my attention to the window. "It's supposed to rain all week."

"It'd be perfect surfing weather if it weren't for the damn lightning," Darryl said, his lighter tone masking his irritation. He had been going stir crazy, sometimes going outside for a few minutes before coming back completely drenched.

"Why don't we do something tonight?" Roscoe said, closing the empty pizza box before leaning back to scratch his stomach. "Lots of bars downtown." He gave me a half grin, and his tail pounded the floor. "Lots of... *karaoke* bars."

"I don't sing in front of people," I said. "And I don't want to have to listen to you bark out more songs like you did the other morning."

"You heard Roscoe sing, huh?" Darryl asked.

"Yeah. He woke me up with it."

"Oh yeah." A smile finally replaced the scowl he had been wearing most of the day. "He used to do that to me, too. He's surprisingly good when he's not singing like shit to be annoying."

I looked back at Roscoe. "Why are you such a troll?"

"It's fun." He scooted closer, putting his arm around my neck. "C'mon. Let's get wasted and make fools of ourselves."

"Make a fool of yourself and leave me out of it." I turned to Darryl. "Do you sing too?"

"Oh fuck no. The guitar is the extent of my musical abilities."

"Remember when you used to play, and I'd—" Roscoe went rigid when Darryl bared his teeth.

"I think karaoke is a great idea," I cut in, trying to disperse the tension. "You guys wanna leave when the storm calms down?"

"Sounds good," Roscoe replied, giving a dangerously quiet Darryl a sideways glance. "Listen, buddy—"

"I'm not your buddy," the larger werewolf interrupted before climbing to his feet. He took a few steps toward the front door. "Karaoke's fine. I'll be back later."

With that, he disappeared outside, the door slamming shut behind him.

Roscoe stared down at the floor. "I'm sure he's had some nice things to say."

"Quite a bit, actually," I whispered, the tension tightening like a noose around us both. "I can't blame him for still being upset."

"I know. I searched for that damn guitar for years, even though I knew the thing was long gone. Part of me thought he'd moved on when I brought you here."

"Did you ever apologize?"

"Cody, what the hell am I supposed to say? 'Sorry I sold the most important thing in your life for smack'? That was my lowest point, and I still hate myself for it."

"You should open with that."

"I can barely look him in the eyes, and in case you haven't noticed, he's way bigger than me."

"Well, at least you heal fast."

"That ain't funny." His tone was a lot more serious than it had been. "He almost beat my brains out that morning. I'm actually kinda scared of him sometimes."

"Sorry."

"I fucked up, and I lost one of my best friends."

"I don't think you did." This was a good segue into what I really wanted to ask him. "You *are* clean, right?"

"Almost ten years," he said, his ears pointing a little higher.

"Then let that be the starting point. Find a way to make it up to him and apologize. If there wasn't a chance, he would have never let us stay here. The fact that you two can even sit in the same room together proves that."

"Let's see how tonight goes. It's up to him if he wants to hear me out."

"Just don't get too drunk, please."

Roscoe let out a whine. "But that's half the fun."

"Yeah, but it's not going to be much fun if you say something stupid and drunk Darryl gets your brain matter all over me."

"All right. I won't have that much, but you gotta sing a song with me."

"No. I don't know how many times I have to say it."

"It's gonna happen. I'll make you have some fun if it kills us both."

"Don't tempt fate, grandpa."

"I... can't believe it. He's actually good," I said, my eyes locked on Roscoe as he took command of the stage, his powerful voice effortlessly changing pitch while singing *Thriller*. He was so precise in his imitation that I thought he was lip syncing at first. Once more people started crowding in off the street to see the performance, I could have sworn I saw dollar signs flash in the owner's eyes. It really felt kind of odd envying Roscoe for once. I'd have given anything to have enough confidence to do that.

"The ham always knew how to work a crowd," Darryl said, taking another swig of beer. He'd been fending off friends all night just to keep me company. "You should have another drink."

"Am I that obvious?"

Darryl put his arm around me, patting me on the back. "You're a hell of a good-looking guy, and you're fun to talk to when you aren't shutting people out." He picked up a pitcher of pale-yellow ale and poured it into my glass.

"I'm just worried," I muttered, eyeing Roscoe before drinking half of the glass in one go. "He's got that look in his eyes. He's going to embarrass me; I just know it."

"Been thinking about him a lot today, and I've gotta try to let this shit go."

"He and I talked after you left, and he's scared."

"Well, I did knock all of his teeth out."

"Not of that... well, kind of that," I corrected. "He's scared of facing you and apologizing. Knowing you still hate him probably hurts him worse than any beating could. He knows he fucked up, but you have to hear it from him."

His eyes followed the singing werewolf as he began belting out the high notes of Bohemian Rhapsody. "He's really changed. Even though he could sing all those years ago, he'd slur and forget lyrics, usually making shit up on the spot. The old wolf's got more life in him now than he did decades ago." He looked back at me and took the beer out of my hand.

"Hey, I was about to drink that."

"It's *you*! Being all uptight and boring is making him a better person."

"I need alcohol, Darryl. He's looking at me again."

"There's a half-turn in here that's just itching to come sing," Roscoe barked through the microphone.

"Darryl, you need to kill him before he—" Roscoe's huge hand grabbed a hold of my arm, and he lifted me up on the stage. At first, I locked up, feeling like I was going to throw up at any moment. Then I saw the reassuring look on Darryl's face, and that no one in that noisy bar was paying much attention. "Roscoe, please," I whispered, trying to inch back off the stage, but the werewolf held me tight.

"What's a song you love to sing?"

"Let me go."

"Don't know that one. How 'bout some Aqua? You're Barbie and I'll be Ken."

"I swear to God," I said, keeping my voice low while covering the microphone. "Please don't make me do this."

He draped his heavy arm over my shoulders, leaning in close to whisper. "Everyone's here to have fun and pretend like they're famous. If you can sing, they cheer. If you can't, they cheer anyway, because fuck it, we're all drunk as hell."

I scanned the bar again, and he was right, everyone was having fun. They all seemed to like Roscoe, and tonight, he was a lot more than that bum I'd seen at the bus stop not too long ago.

"Fine. I've got a song."

 *Aeron Dusk*

The three of us staggered out of the bar, laughing with a few of Darryl's friends. I never thought I'd be able to find my voice in front of a crowd, but when Roscoe and I sang together, the chemistry was incredible.

"Wow," I said, tripping over my feet before Roscoe grabbed the collar of my shirt to keep me upright. "I actually had fun."

"I knew you would," Roscoe said, supporting me as we stumbled toward the beach house. "You sure as hell surprised me. I didn't know you could harmonize like that. I think I'm in love," he slurred, his tongue leaving a slobbery trail along my cheek.

I laughed and pushed him away.

"I bet you two could actually make a living doing that," Darryl chimed in. "I think we all needed this."

"This was a one-time thing," I said as we stepped up the wooden deck, Darryl leading the way. "Are you guys tired? Cuz I'm not."

"It's nice out now that it stopped raining," Darryl said. "Why don't we sit outside for a while? I'll light the tiki torches."

Roscoe stepped inside the house before peeking back out. "I'll get the beer."

"I really don't want anything else to drink," I said, laying a hand over my stomach.

Darryl and I sat on the mismatched patio furniture around the makeshift table, staring silently at one another.

"I'm glad you guys are here," he said, leaning back in the groaning chair.

"Me too. You really saved our asses. I definitely would not be having a good time out on the streets."

Roscoe stepped back outside, holding an armful of chilled bottles.

"I didn't expect the past to show back up at my front door," Darryl continued, and Roscoe tensed before setting the beer on the table. "Did you really think I forgot?"

The older werewolf shook his head and sat next to me. "Nah. I just kinda hoped all this time had fixed what I screwed up."

Darryl flicked the bottle cap off with his thumb claw and drank half of the beer in one gulp. "I always wondered how someone could hurt a best friend in such a terrible way, but I also knew you weren't the same while you were high on that shit."

"I tried for years to get that guitar back."

"You'd never be able to afford it."

"I'd find a way."

"It doesn't matter anymore," Darryl snapped. "I've got everything I want in life, and a missing guitar isn't going to erase memories of my dad."

"I couldn't apologize, even when I wanted to. They're just words, and you wouldn't have forgiven me even if I said 'em. You were the reason I got clean. I loved you like a brother, and when I hurt you, that was the last straw." Roscoe turned to me. "I may be a lot of things, but I'm not gonna be someone who hurts people no more."

"You better not be," Darryl said. "Because if Cody ever shows up on my doorstep as hurt as I was, I will break every last bone in your body." He held up his beer before finishing the rest of it. "The pack doesn't hurt its own."

"Losin' you as my family nearly killed me. I know it won't ever be the same between us, but I still wish we could be friends again."

Darryl grabbed another beer off the table and wiped away some of the condensation. "Well, I can tolerate being around you. That's a start."

"I'll take it."

"You sure will." Darryl set his beer down and looked at me, his eyes glowing that weird silver again. "You may wanna stay outside for a little while longer, unless you want to watch what I'm about to do to him."

Roscoe's ears hung off to the side, his eyes glowing an uncanny baby blue, his pupils seeming to disappear.

"Uh, what's going on here?"

Roscoe stumbled to his feet and slowly made his way inside, Darryl following before stopping at the door to answer.

"Remember a couple days ago when I told him he was going to put that lazy ass to good use? Tonight's the night he's gonna apologize to his alpha. The werewolf way." He stomped through the door and snarled Roscoe's name as the door gently rested against the frame.

# Chapter 8

# Uninvited Guests

"What do you mean, eight months?" I let out an involuntary growl, my hand shaking as I held the cellphone to my ear. "I was told it would be a few weeks, and that was a few weeks ago!"

"I don't make the zoning laws, Mr. Schultz. I just relay the information I've been given. The shortage is only in the tri-county area."

"So, you're saying there's a housing shortage in places people actually live. Got it," I said sarcastically, trying to keep my voice calm. "Is there anything in White Dunes?"

"I'm sorry, no."

"You didn't even look!"

"Don't take this personally, but White Dunes is for people of a certain means, and there's no public housing allowed."

It wasn't what he said, it was how he said it. This was a government agency specifically for finding housing for half-turns, but it was run by humans who obviously couldn't give a shit. The man on the other end didn't say anything else but he was typing loudly enough for the phone to pick it up.

"Would you be open to moving north?"

"That depends. Are we talking North Avenue or Greenland?"

The man stopped typing. "There's a little town in Clemson County called Norwich."

"Where is Clemson County?"

"It's on the border. About four hours from Sacramento."

I growled again. "The reason I chose this area was because the bus goes everywhere I need to go. There are enough vacant human apartments in the city. Do I really need to jump through all these hoops?"

"Again, you're trying to kill the messenger. Given your requirements, it's either Norwich or you'll have to relocate to another state, and I'll be frank with you—no bordering state is even going to let you drive through it in your current condition." He cleared his throat, his tone becoming more impatient. "Think it over, look up the town and call me back with your decision. By law, I have to tell you that it is illegal for a half-turn to live on the streets. If you don't find something suitable, you'll have to go to Stonebrook until you transition."

"What's that?"

The man paused again. "It's a place for adolescent half-turns that have nowhere to go."

"That sounds like an institution."

"It's a free place to live as a last resort."

"It sure as hell won't be *my* last resort!" With that, I ended the call and placed the phone face-down on the wooden spool table. The casual way he said that made me want to throw up. I had no idea they were locking half-turns away, and I still didn't understand why everyone thought we were so dangerous. Darryl and Roscoe could break me in half like a toothpick, but *they* were allowed in places like grocery stores at least. How was I the one who was a menace to society?

It was a little after seven in the morning, and I was outside as usual, sitting on a damp deck chair, watching low clouds overhead. Darryl had offered to let us stay until we found a place of our own, but eight months of the three of us living in this tiny place with no air conditioning was out of the question. I also hated sleeping on that hammock.

The door cracked open and Roscoe limped out onto the porch, holding werewolf-sized mugs of coffee in either hand, his head mane completely disheveled. It almost looked like something had buried him and dug him up. Stripes of dried blood clumped in the fur along his torso and legs, but there weren't any signs of injury. Whatever Darryl had done to him last night had healed up fast.

"You look like shit," I said, carefully grabbing the handle of the mug he gave me.

Roscoe snorted, but his eyes were still distant. "I ain't been fucked that hard in about ten years."

"What the hell did he do? Wrap you in barbed wire and rip it off?"

"You'll understand when you turn. We do things a lot differently. It's either rough and hard, rough and violent, rough and short, or rough and rougher." He ran his tongue along his sharp teeth, stopping where one of his canines was missing. "It ain't ever gentle though, especially when it comes with a lot of pent-up anger."

"Your tooth is gone."

"It'll grow back by tomorrow."

The door opened again, and Darryl strutted outside holding his own mug with an image of a surfboard and a red heart around it.

"Good morning," he said, taking in a deep sniff of fresh air, wagging his tail as if nothing at all had happened. "Looks like it's going to be a busy day."

"Why's that?" I asked.

Darryl gave a nod to the red flag above the lifeguard station in the distance then took a sip of coffee. "Rip currents. There's a storm off the coast that's making the water extra choppy, and people never pay attention to the warnings." He sat his mug on the table and grabbed Roscoe's muzzle, gently prying it open with his thumb. "Heh, I didn't know it actually fell out."

Roscoe pulled away and whistled through the empty cavity. "Wasn't paying attention when I landed on the floor. I'll look for it later and make a necklace for Cody."

"Aww. A necklace made from a tooth Darryl violently fucked loose. How romantic," I said, holding my hand up. "I'll pass."

"I'll take it." Darryl sat on the other side of the table and sipped his coffee. "It'll be a good conversation starter."

"Hey, uh, buddy," Roscoe said, his ears pulled back. "We good now?"

Darryl said nothing. Instead, he smiled while stroking the soul patch below his thin, black lips.

"I'll take that as a maybe."

The larger werewolf placed his rough hand on my shoulder, pulling my attention from the ocean. "You look more stressed out than usual, and that's saying something."

"Ever heard of a town called Norwich?"

Darryl shook his head, but Roscoe's face lit up.

"Norwich? Now that's a damn pretty place. What about it?"

"Apparently, it's the only halfway decent town where I can get housing. The problem is, it's like five hours away."

"So? What are you so afraid to leave behind? We ain't got nothin' here."

Roscoe actually made a good point. The only reason I'd moved to the city was to start a career, but that was out the window.

"Have you ever been there?"

Roscoe shook his head. "Nah, but I had a few friends that really loved it. That town's practically made for us. They got a healthy population of werewolves, and the humans are freaks. I'm talkin' occult type shit."

"You're sure as hell not selling me on this place," I said, typing the town's name into my phone's search engine.

"Think about it, Cody. It's practically Halloween every day! There's always something spooky goin' on, and the town's surrounded by woods people say is haunted. Plus, we ain't gonna be the only werewolves. The humans'll love us."

"Yeah, I bet they do. We'll be the most popular blood sacrifices to Satan next month. But that's fine, because it's cool and spooky."

"Aw come on. It ain't like that." Roscoe let out a loud laugh, but after a couple seconds, his face went straight. "I don't think it is, anyway."

"Sounds like a place for witches. I'd take Satan over those any day," Darryl said.

"Stop fucking with me, guys. I'm not stupid enough to believe this shit."

Darryl raised an eyebrow. "You think I'm stupid?"

"No. I think you're fucking with me."

"You better listen to Darryl. He was big into that shit back in the day."

I turned back to the larger werewolf, who gave a half grin. "Is he serious?"

"Nah, I just hung around with interesting people. And if I knew anyone that practiced *that* kind of magic, Roscoe's dick would have shriveled up and fallen off years ago."

"Oh hell naw," Roscoe shouted, the fur on his neck sticking straight up. "You really had 'em do spells 'n shit on me?"

"That was years ago, and last night, it looked like it was still all there."

"That ain't funny, man! You know about the rule of three, right?"

Darryl shrugged. "It's not like I did the rituals. What happened to all that excitement from earlier, hmm?"

"This is different." Roscoe looked down at his lap. "Now my dick hurts."

"Oh please," I said, shrugging off Roscoe's abrupt superstitious behavior. "You were fine before Darryl said anything. It's like voodoo. It only works if you really believe it does."

"My dick was hurtin' before."

I pointed to the dried blood along his torso and thighs. "You're right. There's no other explanation for that. It must be witchcraft." I continued scrolling through the internet search results. The town was just as rustic as Roscoe made it seem. The buildings and houses were old, and there was a lot of nature around the area. "I hope this place has decent internet."

"I hope they've got someone who gets rid of curses."

"You're fine, Roscoe. I didn't have anything of yours to use in the ritual." Darryl stood and calmly walked over to the door while Roscoe eyed him. "I just remembered something." He ran inside and slammed the door shut behind him.

Roscoe leaped out of his chair and dashed inside after him. It was probably the fastest I'd ever seen him run. "I rescind my offer! You ain't gettin' my tooth!"

I leaned back and shook my head while reading through more information on the town. The loud pounding of the floors and Roscoe yelling hysterically at Darryl lightened the mood a little bit. Maybe they were going to be okay after all, but I was still uncertain about *my* future. The last big move I'd made hadn't turned out so well, but I'd been younger then, and alone. This time I'd have someone to rely on—even if it was Roscoe.

His OnlyStans idea was actually pretty good, and despite my objections, it sounded like it could be fun if I hid my face. There was no way in hell I'd admit that to Roscoe.

Dark shades protected my eyes from the afternoon sun as I lay on the beach while reading a book I borrowed from Darryl's shelf. The supposed 'beach bum werewolf' was a surprisingly avid reader of epic fantasy. There were so many interesting layers to both him and Roscoe.

I'd managed to find a normal-sized book I'd thought was contemporary fiction, and I was half-right. It ended up being a fascinating read about the theorized origins of the werewolf condition. The book was science-y at first, but it quickly dove into the absurd and mystical, which made it even more fun.

Adam stopped in front of me and grabbed the book out of my hands. His hair style had changed since the last time I'd seen him—shaved on both sides, with the same long dreads in the middle. The thicker fur-like hair on his arms, chest, and legs dripped with sea water, and he wore only a pair of white swim trunks and sandals.

"Dude, c'mon."

"We need to talk." Adam glanced at the cover and rolled his eyes before plopping down next to me, tossing it back into my lap. "Are you and Roscoe gonna live with Darryl?"

"No, why?"

"That lying bastard. I'm not going to let him use that as an excuse next time I ask him if I can stay."

"Okay, I'm not sure if you know this or not, but usually when someone doesn't want you living with them, you don't keep asking." I picked the book back up then thumbed through the pages to find where I'd left off. "Don't you have a place of your own? And aren't your parents rich or something?"

He turned away and sifted sand through his fingers. "I'm not pathetic enough to live with them at this age."

"At this age? Aren't you like sixteen or something?"

"Hilarious." He threw the rest of the sand onto the ground and narrowed his eyes on me. "My living situation has changed."

"What do you mean? I thought you lived with your werewolf in an apartment?"

"I do, but… it's complicated. I had to keep him a secret for reasons. So, as far as the state knew, I was living by myself. I got a surprise audit a few days ago for the first time, and they're gonna kick me out."

"What about your werewolf?"

"He's the whole reason I'm in this mess, and he treats me like shit anyways. I'd rather break the kuu and live with Darryl."

"Is that why you both were arguing the other night?"

Adam groaned and rolled his eyes. "I wish I'd gotten the kuu from him. He keeps telling me he has a boyfriend and doesn't want to get involved with a half-turn, but I've never seen him serious with anyone. No one likes me."

"I like you," I said through my teeth, "when you aren't being a total prick."

"Sorry."

"If you get kicked out, what's going to happen?"

"They'll put me in Stonebrook, and I don't wanna go to that place. I heard they do weird experiments on half-turns."

"I'm sure they don't do that. That would be a violation of human rights."

"Yeah, *human* rights."

"We're still human... somewhat."

A huge, blond-furred werewolf with a lighter mane emerged from the ocean, shaking the excess water from his coat. Darryl glared at him for a moment before refocusing on the other swimmers.

"Damn it. I thought he wasn't going to come today."

"Who?"

Adam pointed, then tugged at the tight chain around his neck.

"Are you okay?"

Adam didn't respond as the werewolf stopped in front of us.

"Find us a new place yet?"

"Still looking," Adam replied quietly. There was something wrong with this dynamic, like all of Adam's personality had been sucked into a void.

"You're Adam's werewolf?" I asked.

"You've got that a little turned around," he said, flashing a toothy grin at Adam. "He's *my* half-turn. Isn't that right?"

"Yes sir," Adam whispered, his head down while the werewolf slipped a finger under the kuu before gently tracing along the underside.

"Were you in the army?" I asked, eyeing the embossed silver dog tags dangling from a chain around his neck.

The werewolf let go of Adam and sat cross-legged on the sand in front of us, snatching the jewelry before I could read the names. He hastily tucked them into the thicker fur of his mane.

"No! This is just some beach trash I picked up. Plus, it's none of your damn business."

"Wow, you're a real piece of shit," I said casually before setting the book aside.

Adam's eyes shifted nervously.

"And you're pretty bold," the werewolf replied, extending his hand. "Name's Austin."

"Cody," I replied, angrily returning the handshake. "So, about the piece of shit comment. That still stands. Any particular reason for the attitude?"

"Cody, stop," Adam whispered, jamming my ribs with an elbow as Austin leaned in close.

"You better listen to him. Looks like your werewolf never taught you your place."

Even though he made me nervous, I met his glare with my own. "And what place would that be? Last time I checked, we were the ones holding all the cards. It's our money and our housing. You're just leeching off it."

"Adam used to be a real smartass, too. You'll know who has all the power when the cravings hit and you're begging to be dicked down. That's all a half-turn is. A whore."

The more he spoke, the angrier I got. Everything in my vision turned the usual red.

Austin tugged at Adam's kuu chain. "I guess Darryl didn't fuck you yet, huh? You reek."

"He smells fine. What the hell is your problem?"

The thick, blond werewolf stood, pulling Adam's chain again until the half-turn was standing. Aside from Darryl, I hadn't seen another werewolf quite as large, and he was using that size to bully Adam and intimidate me.

"You're a new half-turn, aren't ya?" he asked.

"What does that have to do with anything?"

"You'll just have to wait and see." He gave me an intense stare while grabbing his crotch. "You're not my half-turn, but I got enough in the tank for two."

"You're also bold, I'll give you that." I picked up the book again. "Hard pass."

"Suit yourself." He let go of Adam's kuu before nodding toward Darryl's beach house. Adam led the way as Austin followed close, occasionally looking back as if something I'd said confused him.

The red hue faded from my vision when they disappeared into the house. I felt bad for Adam, but there wasn't anything I could really do at that moment. He was obviously in an abusive relationship, though I didn't know to what extent, and the kuu seemed to be making it worse. Adam never had any bruises or cuts, but he was also a rapidly healing half-turn. Regardless if it was physical or emotional, abuse was abuse, and I wasn't going to sit by and let it keep happening.

The sun was halfway below the endless blue horizon. Darryl and Roscoe were swimming in the ocean while I was jogging along the shore. They seemed to be playing around, but when Roscoe went under and Darryl disappeared after him, I grew concerned. I stopped running and waited for someone's head to pop back up. When neither emerged after a minute, the real panic sat in.

What was I going to do? I could barely swim in a pool of stagnant water, and now my werewolf was drowning. I paced back and forth, shouting their names over the crash of the waves, growing more hysterical by the minute.

Out of the corner of my eye, much farther out than before, both of them emerged, struggling to pull something along.

It took them a good five minutes before they were close enough to shore to be able to stand. Their disappearance made sense when Roscoe slung a heavy blue marlin over his shoulder and hobbled along, Darryl keeping him steady in the turbulent water.

"What the hell are you guys doing?" I asked, running closer to get a better look at the fish. There was a huge gash along the underside of its head where Roscoe or Darryl's powerful jaws made contact.

"Dinner's here," Roscoe said, giving the fish a slight shake. "Want some sushi?"

"You guys scared the hell out of me. I thought you were drowning."

Darryl threw his heavy, sodden arm over my shoulder. "No one's ever drowned on my beach, and Roscoe's an okay swimmer when food's involved."

"I'm so hungry, I could eat this whole thing," Roscoe said, drooling.

Darryl snatched the fish away and tripped Roscoe, who fell face-first onto the dry sand.

"Don't even think about it, fatty."

Roscoe climbed to his feet, shaking the sand out of his wet fur. "Oh, come on. When have I ever done that for real?"

"Christmas of '86, when we went camping, remember?"

Roscoe scratched his head. "Uh..."

"You volunteered to cook up that stag we killed that would have fed the ten of us, and everyone was so excited about it because you were the only one that knew how to actually cook."

Roscoe opened his mouth as if to object, but all that came out was a meek, "Ohh..."

"Yeah. And because you were *my* friend, we were both not invited to any more campouts. And need I bring up Thanksgiving at Jessie's?"

"All right, you made yer point. That was all in the 80s, and I'm just... hungry like the wolf."

"I'm honestly surprised you haven't gotten any fatter," Darryl added, poking Roscoe's muscle gut with his free hand. "If you weren't a werewolf, you'd probably be in one of those electric scooters, taking up an entire aisle at Walmart."

"You make it sound like it's a problem. We're big monsters with big appetites."

"Your *problem* is you take everything to excess." Darryl's tone went from scolding to lighthearted when he looked over at a frustrated Roscoe. "At least you're not as bad as you used to be."

We approached the porch, and Darryl slapped the fish into Roscoe's hands. "I've gotta build the fire in the barrel. Can I trust you to prepare this thing without it disappearing into your bottomless gut?"

"Of course! I bought the right spices and everything." Roscoe walked into the house but quickly reemerged. "You expecting company, Darryl?"

"Are they still in there?" I asked, looking up at the confused werewolf.

"I don't really wanna interrupt the fun." Roscoe looked down at his crotch. "Er, maybe I do."

Darryl threw open the door and stomped inside. "What the hell?" That was the last coherent thing I heard as the door slammed shut behind him.

"Four hours," I said, rather impressed and a bit worried for Adam.

Roscoe let the marlin fall to the table before sitting next to me.

"Well shoot, that got me in the mood. You wanna—"

"This is not exactly the time."

He shoved me with his elbow. "Hey. Wanna watch me fuck this fish?"

I shot the werewolf the most disgusted glance I could muster.

"What, you never looked at the StarKist tuna mascot and thought, 'yeah, I could fuck that'?" He stroked the dead fish seductively with his index finger.

"You're so nasty," I said, reluctantly cracking a smile before breaking into laughter. "God, what the hell is wrong with you?"

Roscoe pulled me closer. "I like it when you laugh."

We sat like that for a while longer, not saying anything as we listened to the angry commotion coming from the house. Moments like these made me realize how comfortable Roscoe made me. There was a charming guy in there, hiding underneath all the... other stuff. Perhaps the flaws were what attracted me the most to him. He was real, and he was funny, and he had those moments where he was sweet and caring.

The door slowly creaked open, and an embarrassed-looking Adam stepped outside with Austin following, a snarling scowl on his face.

"You could have at least let us finish," Austin said, turning back toward an equally angry Darryl. They were both about the same size and build. I wondered who would win if they started fighting.

"You finished enough. I've gotta sleep on that bed tonight, and your spunk is everywhere."

"Hell yeah," Roscoe chimed in. "Bet it smells great."

Everyone glared at him.

"What? Don't act like you guys don't like it."

"Hey, is that a blue?" Austin asked, looking down at the fish. "Who caught it?"

"I did," Roscoe said proudly. "Was just about to season this baby. You guys wanna join?" Roscoe's ears fell off to the side as he looked up at Darryl. "That is, if it's okay with you, buddy."

"Oh, why ask? Everyone invites themselves into my house and fucks on my bed. Why not stay for dinner, too?"

"Sounds like a yes to me," Austin said, eliciting an annoyed hiss from Darryl. "We're going to need another fish, though. I bet I can get a bigger one."

Roscoe stood up and playfully shoved the taller werewolf. "I bet it'll be smaller. Takes a lot of skill to catch these."

"You're on, shorty."

"Don't mess with the sharks," Darryl said. "I've got a soft spot for them."

Austin pouted as we all sat around the table eating slices of grilled marlin with a few smoked cods. It seemed the other werewolf couldn't live up to his boast after all.

"The cod's good," Darryl said patronizingly. "Can fit the whole thing in my mouth."

"Oh, shut up," Austin muttered, taking another bite of marlin steak. "Damn."

"Good, ain't it?" Roscoe put another piece of steak onto his plate.

"I've never met a werewolf chef before," he said, taking a much larger bite.

"There're two f's in life I love the most—food and fuckin'. May as well be good at both."

"I'll eat to that," Austin replied, patting a disgruntled Adam on the head, who looked more like a pissed-off wet cat than a half-turned werewolf. He hadn't said much since he walked out of the house. The dynamic playing out at the table wasn't at all what I'd expected. Austin and Roscoe seemed to hit it off pretty well; Darryl, on the other hand, was less than friendly.

"Do you and Austin know each other?" I asked, trying to strike up a conversation that would give me a bit more insight.

"Yes." Darryl's sharp, one-word response was a subtle hint not to press it further.

"I used to take swimming lessons from him when I was a half-turn," Austin chimed in. "Man, how long ago was that? Six years?"

"How old are you?" I asked.

"Twenty-four," he said. "How old are you? Like seventeen?"

"I'm twenty-two, asshole."

Adam snickered, likely remembering the jab I'd taken at him earlier for the same reason.

"For real? How the hell are you a twenty-two-year-old half-turn? Isn't that shit supposed to happen during puberty?" He let out a dickish chuckle. "You just now going through puberty?"

My face got hotter. "Fuck off."

"You look like you're still in high school."

"That's kinda hot." Roscoe shoved me playfully. "Gives me an idea for our little business."

"You're crossing a really creepy line right now," I said, scooting away.

"You're forgetting how puny you used to be," Darryl said, grabbing his scratched-up cell phone from the table. "He was the town twink. Let me see if I can find a picture."

Austin slammed his fist on the table. "I thought you fucking deleted that!"

Darryl kept scrolling, and his ears pressed against his head. "I may have, actually. Shit."

The other werewolf grinned smugly before leaning back in his chair. "I may have been puny, but the marines made a man out of me. Well, not exactly a man."

"Wait," I interrupted. "I thought you said you weren't in the military."

The werewolf went silent and continued eating.

"Way to blow your cover in the dumbest way possible," Adam said. "This is why we're being evicted, by the way."

"Why? Because he was in the marines?"

"No, because he went AWOL, and they've been looking for his ass. That's why I couldn't list him on the state contract. I didn't know that until after he gave me this stupid chain."

Darryl sighed. "How long do you have?"

"A week, maybe. I don't know what I'm going to do. If Austin and I get separated, I lose my chance to not end up a bum on the street when I turn."

"You're a trust fund kid, so what the fuck do you have to worry about?" Austin snapped. "I didn't get to make a kuu with a werewolf back then, and this is my last chance."

"That's not my fault."

"Why did you go AWOL?" I asked, breaking up their argument.

Austin sat back in his chair and slapped his chest. "You know what I enjoy doing the most in life? Living. That's why I left."

"But there aren't any wars right now."

"Listen. I don't wanna get into this shit but just know there's a reason werewolves shouldn't join the military. Lesson learned."

I turned to Adam. "Do you lose your income, too?"

"Thankfully, no."

"You guys should move in with us," Roscoe blurted.

"Brilliant idea. This way, we can also run into the exact same problem." I gave Roscoe a slap on the arm. "Do you even think before you speak? I can't just add more people to the list of roommates. I got so nervous that I listed you as my fiancé, and I have to keep the whole kuu thing secret, remember?"

Roscoe grinned. "Fiancé, huh? Sweet! May as well make it legal. What do you say?"

"Are you really proposing to me right now?"

"Yeah, what the hell? Let's do it."

"How romantic. How about hell no," I said sarcastically.

"It was worth a shot."

"You're going to die single. I just want you to know that."

Adam snapped his fingers. "Hey. About to be institutionalized here, which I think trumps... whatever the hell this is."

"Maybe Roscoe's onto something," I said.

Roscoe's ears perked up and his tail wagged, which meant he was about to say something stupid. "Fuck! I'm gettin' married! Too bad the folks are dead. Although, if they weren't dead by now, this'd probably do 'em in."

I said nothing for a moment, staring dead-eyed at Roscoe before continuing. "I have a feeling they audited you because they are trying to get werewolves and half-turns out of the city and into the surrounding counties. I wasn't able to find a house anywhere around here, and there were plenty a few weeks ago. Maybe call up the department and see if it would be legal for you to move there."

"I'd have to list Austin the same way you did for Roscoe, and I can't do that or they'll take him." He turned to the huge werewolf sitting next to him. "Then that's it for my future."

"*Your* future? Are you forgetting they'll probably kill me?" Austin shouted. "You know, in case for a moment you thought about anyone else but yourself."

"Oh, isn't that the pot calling the kettle black? The only thing you see me as is a fleshlight."

"What else are you good for?"

"All right, I'm getting pissed," Darryl said, turning toward Roscoe. "I thought you didn't have a social security number."

"I don't," Roscoe replied.

"Last name?"

"You know I forgot that years ago."

Darryl looked back at me. "How the hell did you put this guy on a state contract?"

"Well, I kind of made shit up."

"And they didn't say anything?"

"Not a thing."

Darryl and I both smiled and looked over at Austin and Adam.

"You mean to tell me all this time I could have just invented an identity and those idiots wouldn't have questioned it?" Austin asked, growing increasingly irritated.

"For housing? I guess so, but for anything else? Don't push your luck," I said. "They didn't seem particularly interested in knowing more about Roscoe. They just wanted us both out of the county."

"Well, a loophole's a loophole," Darryl said. "It's still a little risky. Call the auditor, tell them you're interested in moving to Norwich, list Austin under some bullshit name, and bam! Get a place to live."

"I don't know," Austin said, his ears off to the side. "What if Cody's was just a fluke, and they find out who I really am? They've got my picture in the system and everything."

"They didn't ask for a picture of Roscoe," I said.

"Yer sure this was the government you were talking to?" Roscoe asked. "This is starting to sound kind of—" He picked up a grilled cod's head and silently mouthed the word "fishy," which made everyone groan.

"Well, now I'm worried," I said, scrolling through the list of dialed numbers on my phone. I copied the one I called earlier and pasted it into my browser, relieved when the Southside Bureau of Nonhuman Housing and Development popped up. "Well, it's legit. I'll text you the number."

"I guess it couldn't hurt to ask," Adam said, holding up his phone.

Austin snatched the phone away. "Actually, it could. Never trust the government."

"No shit, but we don't have any other options. No one's gonna know it's you."

After a few moments of hesitation, Austin handed the phone back to Adam. "Fine. I'll tell you what name to use."

A subtle but mischievous smirk crept up Adam's face. "Yeah. I'll write it down."

# Chapter 9

# Lots of Potential

"This is bullshit," I said, furiously packing my belongings as Adam kept his gaze averted. "Why did you even bring it up to them?"

"Dude, I panicked. They said I couldn't qualify for another year if I couldn't find another half-turn to live with in Norwich. You know how convoluted the system is."

"And you brought me into it without asking if it was cool with me—which it's not! I spent weeks doing all that work, and with one stupid phone call, you threw everything into chaos."

"You're really gonna be selfish about it?"

My face grew hotter, and it took everything I had not to shove the half-turn through Darryl's window. "Selfish? I'll have you—"

"Okay, okay," Adam interrupted. "What else am I going to do, Cody? I need you. Please."

"Go live with your parents. Take Austin with you."

"I can't do that."

"Why not? Every time anyone brings up your money or your parents, you get all weird." I narrowed my eyes. "Did you get caught in another lie?"

Adam sighed. "Listen I—I may have embellished a few things."

"You mean your parents aren't rich?"

"It's complicated, and I don't want to talk about it."

"It's probably not that complicated. You're just being sleazy."

Adam bit his lower lip and looked away, and what I thought was an act turned into tears.

"I'm sorry," I said, now feeling terrible. That was a look I knew all too well when talking about parents. "So, there's no one you can live with or get assistance from?"

"If there was, the last place I'd live is in that roach-infested shithole apartment with that asshole." His mood shifted as he gave a sly smile, leaning in closer. "Which is why when I heard you were moving to a nice little town away from it all, I got kind of jealous. When the guy over the phone gave me that ultimatum, I knew you wouldn't say no. We're friends, right?"

"I barely know you." I folded a torn pair of briefs and shoved them into a suitcase. Most of my underwear bore the battle scars of Roscoe being a little too rough. "I don't understand why they make us jump through so many hoops."

"Half-turns, man. Humans don't want us around. We're always horny, and if we don't have sex, we get all ragey and stuff."

"I feel that kind of rage right now, actually," I half-joked, folding more of my clothes. The good thing about Roscoe not really wearing clothes was I didn't have to pack them. The only thing he really wore was that funk-covered orange hoodie, and I wasn't going to touch that thing.

"I'm serious. You haven't been half-turn long enough to know. I've been like this since I was sixteen, but the real shit only started happening like six months ago. It's making Austin act weird. He keeps sniffing me more, too. He says I reek, but he can't stop smelling me."

"What's with that? I catch Roscoe sniffing my dirty clothes all the time."

"We're like catnip to a werewolf. Wolfnip? Werewolfnip?" Adam snapped his fingers. "But getting back on topic here. Are you really gonna make me break my kuu and live in Stonebrook? I don't know what I'll do if that happens."

After a brief pause, I slumped forward.

"I really don't like you," I whispered, barely audible. "You're such a manipulative shit. No wonder you have Austin as a kuu mate."

"What was that?"

"Fine," I said. "It's going to be cramped with two werewolves, and I don't know what this place is gonna look like."

Adam looked around. "Dude, you're living in an unairconditioned shack with no rooms and two werewolves. I'm sure whatever they give us will be bigger than this."

"Yeah, but at least I can sit on the porch or on the beach, which makes it bearable. What am I going to do in Norwich?"

"Walk in the woods."

"You mean the supposedly haunted woods?"

Adam rolled his eyes. "I'm sure they're not really haunted."

"I'm being facetious. If you and Austin end up arguing all the time, take that shit outside. I don't want to listen to it."

The half-turn flinched before looking down at the floor. "We don't really argue. I usually just end up agreeing to anything, and Austin knows what he's doing to get his way. He's been getting me to do some weird shit, but every time he starts, I just let him do whatever he wants."

"That's really awful, man. Why the hell did you choose that guy anyway?"

"It's not like it'll last forever," Adam said. "And to answer your last question, let me show you something." He paced through the room and snatched his backpack from the corner, unzipped one of the front compartments, then pulled out a dirty, folded envelope. "I keep this to remind myself that he used to be kind of cute... and he played the dumb blond card really well." He pulled out a crumpled sheet of paper from the envelope and handed it to me. "Recognize this?"

"Oh lord." I began reading Austin's sex resume. "'Ex military can protect, am better than other *werewolfs*. Just look at me.'" We both broke into laughing fits. "Oh my God, it looks like a twelve-year-old wrote this."

"It gets better."

"'Can fuck you til you cum, ask for *demonstrashon*.'" I wiped a tear from my eye. "This poor guy."

"Read the bottom."

"'I'm a loner, have a past, don't ask about it.'"

Adam gave me a sad smile, and the atmosphere of the room turned somber. "He wanted me to ask about it." He grabbed the resume and held it up. "I don't know if it was a cry for some kind of attention, but I picked up on it. Maybe I shouldn't have. They really fucked him up in the marines, but I think there's more."

"What happened?"

"Werewolf things. Same story, just a different set of circumstances. They heal really fast, but they aren't immortal. Those evil assholes used Austin as a crash-test dummy, testing the effects of dirty

IEDs, chemical attacks, you name it. The poor guy was so toxic and radioactive sometimes that they'd have to put him in solitary confinement until they could decontaminate him.

"There aren't that many werewolves in the military, and the ones that are there usually join out of desperation and stick together like family. He was really close with the only other werewolves on base, but they disappeared one day. Austin doesn't know the details—or he doesn't want to tell them, but there were rumors of a new nerve agent that could kill werewolves and not humans. I guess they wanted to be prepared if a rogue country decided to weaponize us. He's convinced that's what happened to them."

"I'm surprised more countries aren't using werewolves as weapons."

"I'm not. They're dangerous and hard to control, and the world obviously thinks it's a terrible idea, hence the Petrone treaty. Austin was never going to war, and he kind of knew what he was getting himself into. He must have had a really fucked up past to think the marines was a good idea. But yeah, after his pack went missing, he packed a bag of stuff and peaced out. I don't think the government has actually been looking for him, because they would have found him by now. But Austin's always been really paranoid, and I don't blame him. So, I accepted his kuu more out of pity than anything, and the rest is history."

I gave him a doubtful stare.

"I have a thing for big hot blonds, okay?"

"Well, now I feel terrible for calling him a piece of shit."

"Don't. He's not a likeable person, but I thought I'd give you some context for the next time he does something shitty to me."

"That's not really an excuse," I said, sitting down on the couch a few steps from the hammock. "Just because he had something bad happen to him doesn't mean he gets a pass to make someone else's life miserable."

"I'll hold out until I turn, and then we'll both be free."

"Isn't there anything you guys like about each other?"

Adam hummed. "I mean, the sex is pretty good, even the kinkier stuff. He's huge, so he's pretty hung, and you know I like me some big werewolves." He looked away. "He also cries."

"What?"

"He doesn't know that I hear him, but he cries just about every night in his sleep. I'm torn because I feel sorry for him, but damn, he makes it so hard to even feel that lately. He's miserable, and I'm just an easy target."

I thought back to Austin and Roscoe the other day. Their rivalry was hard to pin down, but they both seemed to enjoy the others' company.

"Maybe this little fuck-up with the government might be a good thing," I said, zipping my bag closed. "The city is an awful place for us to live, and maybe Roscoe will be a good influence."

Adam laughed. "Are you serious?"

"Hey, don't write the guy off. He surprises me sometimes, and he treats me a hell of a lot better than Austin treats you."

Adam's laughter turned to stone silence.

"They both seem to like each other. At least I think they do."

"Darryl doesn't," Adam said. "I think it's more alpha mentality than personal. After he went full werewolf, Austin got huge and started fights with Darryl every chance he got. In case you haven't noticed, Darryl's pretty chill and super friendly, but you don't want to fuck with him. There's something weird about the guy. He has this gravity. I can't explain it."

"I really like Darryl."

"Stand in line. He's pretty cool, and I was really jealous that you were living here with him." Adam's smile shifted. "I should probably apologize to him for the other night."

"Being a half-turn sucks. I'm sure he understands."

"I want to be carefree like them," Adam said, plopping on the couch next to me.

"I just want to go back to being human," I said. "Who the hell starts turning at twenty-two? I thought my life was finally going somewhere."

"It is going somewhere." He placed his hand on my back. "To half-turn hell for a while."

"I wonder why some people turn while most don't. No one in my family was a werewolf as far as I know."

Adam shrugged and pointed to Darryl's bookshelf. "What's that book say about it?"

"Oh that?" I shook my head. "It was a bunch of nonsense about magic and curses and witches and demons. Oh, and aliens. That part was actually more plausible, if you can believe it."

"It's always aliens, isn't it?" We both sat in silent contemplation for a few moments. "I always had this dream that a portal would open up to a different world once a year some place up north, and that's where the werewolf curse came from. It's kind of fun to think about."

I turned to Adam, impressed there was actual depth to this conversation. "What do you mean?"

"Well, if we understood everything, it takes the mystery out of life. Demons, witches, aliens and gods are a lot more interesting than boring theories from nerds like you."

Well, I'd thought the conversation had depth. "The universe is pretty strange as it is, without all that stuff, and our understanding of science keeps changing."

Adam shook his head. "Again, let me reiterate. Nerd."

An old, unmarked truck slowly rolled onto the beach in front of Darryl's house, its brakes squealing when it stopped. Roscoe was driving, and Austin sat in the passenger seat. I ran up to the vehicle as the two hopped out.

"I thought you didn't have a license."

The werewolf's only response was his signature grin that would spark worry the moment it slithered up his face.

"Roscoe!"

"You wanna get to Norwich with all yer stuff, right?"

"Yeah, but it's not gonna matter if we get pulled over and arrested."

"Well, I'll just have to drive reeeal careful, won't I?"

"How'd you even rent this?"

"I got a friend that owed me a favor."

"After all the stories I've heard, I'm starting to have doubts about these so-called friends that owe *you* favors." I closed my eyes and rubbed my temples. "I might actually have a stroke in my twenties."

Roscoe laughed and slapped my back. "That'd be a first." He glanced over at Darryl in the distance, who was perched high in his chair, surveying the water. "Wonder if he's gonna see us off?"

"He's working. We should go say goodbye to him."

"You guys go do that. I'm gonna go wake Adam up," Austin muttered as he stomped toward the house.

"We don't have time for another four-hour fuck session in Darryl's bed, just so you know," I called after him.

He held up a middle finger without turning around.

"This is such an awful idea," I said under my breath. "Why did I agree to this?"

"Because yer helpin' out a friend, and there's nowhere else to go. Besides, Austin ain't bad. He's still a kid himself, and he's seen some shit."

"Yeah. So I've been told."

"Give him a chance. We'll have a good time if you know how to look at life a little better than you do." He wrapped his arm around me as we walked along the beach toward Darryl. "Stop worrying so much and enjoy being young for a change."

"How do you do it? How do you not give a shit about anything, even when you really should?"

"I'm old," he replied with a wily grin. "Drugs helped a lot back then, but now I just don't let things get to me. I ain't some fount of knowledge, but I've got a lot of experience. All those years, things always worked out somehow." He looked down at me. "Hell, even this worked out. I found a half-turn who's smart *and* hot... and didn't know about my history to refuse my kuu. What're the odds?"

We approached the high chair in front of the tower where the other lifeguards usually stayed.

"You guys heading out?" Darryl asked, still scanning the choppy water, his attention narrowing on a few children wading in waist-high surf.

"Yup. Gotta hit the road now if we want to get to Norwich before midnight," Roscoe said, pausing for a moment. "Thanks fer lettin' us stay here."

The huge werewolf didn't look down; instead, he nodded. "I'm actually going to miss having you guys around."

"Wish you could come with us," I said.

Darryl jumped down from the chair and pulled me into a hug. "You're a good kid, Cody. Just keep the old fart out of trouble." He let go and took a step back. "If you guys ever get the chance to come back to the beach, I'm not going anywhere."

Roscoe ran over and held his arms out. His tail wagged fast at first but slowed as Darryl stared him down.

"Eh, what the hell." Darryl wrapped his arms around Roscoe, and both of their tails swayed in time with one another. "I'm gonna miss pounding that ass into hamburger meat."

"Uh, yeah." Roscoe's tail lowered between his legs. "You gave the old hole an early retirement."

"Heh." Darryl pulled away and looked back out to the ocean, making sure the children were still safe. "These careless little turds have been turning my fur gray all morning." He turned back to us again. "Drive safe, okay?"

"You got it, bud." Roscoe slapped Darryl's arm and headed back toward the truck.

"I meant what I said, Cody. If you run into any problems out there, you've got my number." He stared at Roscoe who was now out of earshot. "I think you guys are going to be okay. All things considered, Roscoe's a nice guy, if he's not using. Just do me a favor and look after Adam."

"What's your take on Austin?"

Darryl paused, gritting his teeth. "He's fucked up in the head, but I feel sorry for him. When he was a half-turn, he was puny and had a big-dog complex. He hated himself, hated people, and hated life. I tried to help him, but sometimes you gotta let people make their own shitty choices. I'm still surprised he even managed to get Adam to like him."

That reminded me of something.

"Sorry to change the subject, but do you really have a boyfriend?"

Darryl's expression turned into what I could only describe as dreamy. "Sure do. He's the perfect guy."

"We've been here for about a month, and I've not seen any evidence of this. He's real, right?"

"He's shy. We meet in private a lot, but one day, hopefully he'll get up the nerve to live here." He scanned the ocean again. "There's a lot of weird and wonderful people in this world: human, werewolf..." He paused and took a deep breath through his nose. "Other."

"Other?"

"If you come back to my beach, I'll make sure you get to meet Bobby. He's the sweetest guy, and I love him as much as the ocean. Hell, he practically is the ocean."

"Is he really half shark?"

"How'd you hear about that?" Darryl let out a laugh. "He's the only one I've ever met, and the poor guy can't swim. He just sorta sinks. I don't know why he gets so hysterical. It's not like he'd drown."

"Okay, I'm still having a really hard time telling if you're fucking with me or not."

"Well, only one way to find out. Come back and see me, and you can meet him."

I thought for a moment about him and Roscoe, and even Austin's proposition earlier. "If you have a boyfriend, why do you sleep around?"

"It's a werewolf thing. But once relationships get really serious, we form strong bonds with one other person, and we stop sleeping around. Once I make that bond, it'll be the best day ever."

The hours passed at a snail's pace as Adam and I were crammed next to each other. Roscoe drove, and Austin sat on the other side by the window. Evening had arrived, and the sun was a sliver of fire over the hills. It was beautiful, but really out in the boonies. Every small town we passed had one gas station, and there were at least fifty miles or more between them.

Forests of tall evergreens dominated the landscape, and the weather was cooler and dryer out here, away from the coast. Roscoe was singing to the radio while Austin stared out the window, not having spoken much since we left White Dunes.

"I've never been this far before," Adam said, staring at the sky.

"Really?" I asked. "I used to live in Montana before I moved down here."

Roscoe stopped singing. "You never told me that. I heard it's real pretty up there."

"The west side is pretty. The rest of the state sucks."

"Why'd you move?" Austin asked.

"My parents were… not good people, but my aunt let me stay at her place until I graduated high school and had enough money to get out on my own. She was cool. Kind of the black sheep of the family, which is why we got along so well."

"That sucks," Austin grunted, turning back toward the window.

"It was a while ago."

"It's crazy that parents can just choose to abandon their kids," Adam said.

"You'd be surprised what bad parents can do," Austin muttered in almost a whisper before raising his voice again. "Stop talking about this stupid shit and grow up."

"How about we talk about whatever the hell we want to?" That redness returned to my vision. "And how about you stop being a miserable piece of shit?"

"You don't know anything about me."

"Well, take the stick out of your ass and actually talk about stuff instead of just bitching all the time."

Austin clicked his tongue but didn't raise his voice. "You've sure got a mouth on you for a little twerpy half-turn."

"C'mon guys," Roscoe said casually, turning the radio down. "We're all a little cranky and hungry, but we'll be there in a few hours."

"If we're all going to live together, I don't want to walk on eggshells in *my* house." I pulled a bottle of water out of my backpack and put it to my lips, hoping Austin caught the emphasis. "You should be kissing my ass instead of—"

"Austin, where're you from?" Roscoe interrupted.

The werewolf didn't say anything at first, but Adam shoved him with an elbow.

"Sweetwater, Arkansas," he growled.

Roscoe's face lit up. "Shit, no way. I'm from Black Springs."

"Where the hell's that?"

Roscoe scratched his head. "Don't really remember. I think it's a little town on the west side of the state."

"That would explain your dumb hillbilly accent." The larger werewolf cracked a toothy smile for the first time while fidgeting with the broken lock switch on the door. "I didn't live in that state for long, so I don't really know much about it."

"Did yer family do a lot of moving?"

"Fuck family." Austin's response came sharply before he went silent again.

Roscoe's ears fell to the side, and he turned up the radio, this time at a lower volume. I expected him to get angry, but that didn't happen. Roscoe was a smooth talker and obviously had a lot more patience than I did.

"How much longer?" Adam asked, squinting to get a better look at my phone's screen.

"Two hours and forty minutes," I replied. "I can't wait to sleep in my own bed again."

"I can't wait to sleep in yer bed again, either," Roscoe added, running his clawed hand along my inner thigh while keeping his eyes on the road.

I glared at him.

"Aw, don't look at me like that. Think of how warm you'll be when it starts gettin' colder. Remember when you fell asleep with my dick still in you? You looked so cute. It can be like that every night."

"Cute? I slipped into unconsciousness because I was exhausted." It was hard not to think about that night without smiling. He'd come into my life like a whirlwind, and just like that, we were about to start our lives in a whole new area. "Just don't piss me off, and I won't make you sleep on the floor... like a dog."

Roscoe's smile widened to a sinister grin.

"I mean it."

"Mm-hmm."

My threats didn't work on him anymore, and Adam's description of what was in store for this new body was all I could think about lately. Were the cravings really going to get worse than this? I'd gone from thinking I had control to knowing it was actually Roscoe who held the cards, similar to how Austin kept Adam coming back. There were major differences, and the more I thought about it, the more I may have lucked out.

The werewolf leaned in, and our lips met.

"God dammit! Keep your eyes on the road," Austin shouted, grabbing onto the 'oh shit' handle as the truck veered onto the rumble strips.

"I got it, I got it," Roscoe said, centering the vehicle again.

"It ain't terrible," Roscoe said while looking around the darkened living room. He flipped on the light switch, and a few roaches scattered into the cracks in the walls. "I've lived in worse."

Adam slipped into the hallway, turning on more lights. "Is it too late to get a hotel?"

I was in a strange state of mind—shocked at how awful the place looked, but too tired to react.

Austin ran his claws along the cracks in the paint. "Needs a little work, but at least it's roomy." I had expected him to complain the loudest, but he didn't seem fazed at all. When he opened the door to the garage, his tail went from limp to a rapid wag. "Hell yeah!"

"What?" Roscoe asked.

"Look at all this space. I can actually use my tools."

Adam peeked around the corner. "What tools?"

"I had to keep them in storage because we didn't have any room in that shitty little apartment."

The half-turn stomped on a small roach skittering past his foot. "Ugh. I can't live here."

"They're just bugs, damn. Try sharing a dumpster with rats some time," Austin said, closing the garage door. "This place can be a palace, especially if you've ever lived on the streets. Ain't that right?" He gave Roscoe a nudge.

"Palace it is." Roscoe peeked into both bedrooms before examining the one bathroom we'd all end up sharing. "Just needs some cleaning and a bit o' love." He looked over at me. "You okay?"

"I..." I trailed off, letting out a sigh before walking toward the door. "Let's just get our beds. We'll deal with this tomorrow."

*Later that night*

"Yer not seein' the possibilities," Roscoe whispered. "I bet we'll have this place looking like home in a few weeks."

"I'm almost afraid to look at the town now."

He tightened his arms around me. "It's an adventure, Cody. You gotta live in the moment and think about the cool shit we can do here." He leaned in, his cold, wet snout settling on the crook of my neck. "And yer lucky you ain't gotta go through the tough times alone. Having those two living with us is pretty lucky, too. We got two sources of income now. When you hit yer full turn, you want to be around other werewolves more, especially the older you get."

"When do you think I'll get to be a werewolf?"

"Hmm..." Roscoe slipped his hand under my pants, running his finger along the cleft of my ass. "You don't have a little tail, and there ain't a lot of fur, so it'll be a while. I know it ain't fun, and sometimes it can hurt, but try to enjoy the good parts." He pulled at the fabric until it ripped.

"Damn it, Roscoe. I'm running out of underwear." I pushed his hand away. "And I'm not in the mood."

"You'll feel better. Trust me." Roscoe's long tongue trailed along my neck. "When have I ever been wrong about this?" He lifted me on top of him before sliding my boxers off. There wasn't as much pain as the broad tip of his cock slipped inside.

The light flipped on, and Austin walked into the room, furiously sniffing the air.

"Looks fun. Got room for another?"

"Hell yeah," Roscoe said, catching himself as I grabbed a tuft of fur on his neck. "Uh, that's if it's okay with Cody."

"Get the hell out of here!" I shouted, throwing a pillow at the werewolf's head. Austin snorted and left the room, closing the door behind him.

"Is it too late to kick them out?"

Adam and I spent much of the morning cleaning the layers of grime and rust from the kitchen and bathroom, while Roscoe worked on the floors. Austin was busy patching the walls; he'd need to head into town later to buy paint and necessities with the little money we had left.

After tossing the scrub brush into a blue plastic bucket, I rinsed my hands and walked through the hallway out the back door. I hadn't really gotten a good look at the entire yard yet, but as the late morning sun unveiled what was hidden last night, a smile crossed my face.

The backyard was wild and overgrown but had a vine-covered firepit in the middle. Where the backyard ended, the woods began. It was pretty, and as Roscoe had said, I could kind of see the possibilities. Maybe I'd make a garden, and we could clean up the firepit. Perhaps we'd meet more people and invite them over for games and drinking.

"What's with that look?" Adam asked. I hadn't noticed him creeping up behind me.

"I haven't had a yard since I was a kid."

Adam kicked a small rotten log out of the way. "I want to go back to the city."

"Well, nothing's stopping you," I muttered, walking the perimeter of the property. Adam trailed behind.

"I bet there's not even a nightclub in this town. Just a bunch of old-people bars."

"You don't have to sell this town to me. I'm already liking it."

Adam huffed like a child throwing a tantrum.

"I'm just trying to look on the bright side for once, and you're not helping." I pointed to the woods. "You think it's really haunted?"

"Who cares?" Adam whined, looking back at the house. "I don't like the way it smells here."

"What are you talking about? It smells better than car exhaust and dumpsters."

"You don't smell it?"

I took a deep breath through my nose. "All I smell is bleach and window cleaner. I think I may have accidentally chlorine-gassed the entire house."

Adam shook his head. "It's not a scent I can describe. I don't know. I've been noticing weird shit like that lately. Nothing seems to smell good or bad, but it's different. Like information being shoved into my head that I can't understand."

I took in another whiff of air and shrugged. "I don't know what to tell you. I don't smell it."

We stopped at the edge of the woods.

"Austin's being weird again," Adam said, shifting the subject.

"Now what?"

"He's just weird."

"He seems to be his same unpleasant self to me."

"That's the weird thing. He's not. Last night, he was rough, but he wasn't mean about it. And he hasn't argued with me all day."

I shot the half-turn another confused look. "Why is this a bad thing?"

He ran his fingers through his dreadlocks, scratching the back of his head. "When he's quiet, it makes me more nervous than when he's angry. It usually means he'll be extra mean later."

"Roscoe and I will put a stop to it."

"How? You think Roscoe's gonna be able to take Austin?" Adam laughed. "The guy can't even fight his own appetite."

"He pretends to be stupid and passive, but he's pretty good at diffusing bad situations." I thought back to our unfortunate interaction with the police a couple of weeks ago. "Sometimes."

Adam turned toward the house. "We should probably finish cleaning this dump."

"It's not *that* bad."

"Fine. Let's finish cleaning this—how do real estate agents make shitty houses seem appealing in advertisements?"

"Adam."

"Oh yeah. Let's finish cleaning this quaint little bungalow with a lot of investment potential."

I opened the door, and we stepped inside, the sound of a disc sander whirring in the living room.

"I didn't know Austin had tools," Adam said, keeping his voice low. "I didn't even know he knew how to do anything other than lie around the house scratching his balls all day."

"Did you see him smile when he saw the garage?"

Adam muttered something I couldn't hear before speaking up. "Yeah. We'll see if it lasts."

# Halloween Town

It was around two when Roscoe and I left the house to pick up supplies, leaving Austin and Adam behind to finish unpacking. Downtown Norwich was within walking distance of our new place, and Roscoe was like a dog eager to go to the park.

Every house we passed looked like it had been built over a century ago, and just about every yard had pieces of occult symbolism hanging from trees. They weren't the cheesy decorations from department store clearance aisles, either. They were much creepier—Blair Witch creepy. Despite the seemingly hostile facade, the humans that were out in their yards seemed genuinely happy to see us, often waving or coming up to say hi. Even the children we encountered seemed more entertained by Roscoe's appearance than afraid.

"Ain't this place somethin'?" Roscoe said, pointing to a seven-foot-tall skeletal effigy in the center of a roundabout.

"It sure is," I replied, trying not to seem put-off by the haunting atmosphere. "Where are all the supposed werewolves?"

"You don't smell 'em?"

I glared at Roscoe.

"Really? Most half-turns can at least smell other werewolves." He scratched the messy mane on top of his head. "I don't remember much from when I was half-turn. Maybe you can only smell werewolves when yer really pent up." Roscoe gave me a sniff. "Half-turns give off a skunky smell when they need to be fucked. Sometimes you smell like really dank weed."

"What?" I sniffed my armpits. "Oh my God, are you for real? Have I stunk this whole time?"

"I just said you smelled good."

"You said I smelled skunky!" I took off my shirt and held it to my nose but couldn't smell anything aside from laundry detergent. "Do I need to take more showers?"

Roscoe wrapped an arm around my waist and pulled me into him. "It's a good smell, dude. It drives werewolves crazy."

"Do I stink now?"

He laughed. "Yer fine, jeez."

I slipped back into my T-shirt. "This is humiliating."

"Cody, you need to get used to smelling weird, and you can't do nothin' about it. It doesn't get much better when you turn." He held up an arm and leaned in, nearly engulfing my face in his armpit. I gagged and pushed him away.

"Jesus fuck! When's the last time you bathed?"

"Swimming in the ocean count?"

"You haven't been swimming in the ocean in about a week."

He grinned, exposing a sharp tooth. "Well, there's yer answer."

My usual response to him being gross was to shake my head and groan, but I found I'd grown rather numb to it.

"That's a good werewolf stink." He stepped closer again. "Admit it. You love it, don't you?"

When I'd first met Roscoe, I thought he smelled like dumpster juice mixed with wet dog, but there was *something* going on that I was subconsciously aware of. Sometime between the night I'd changed and now, I had actually grown comfortable with his smell. It wasn't a bouquet of roses by any means, but it kind of calmed me down.

Still, I really wanted him to start bathing more.

"You're a pig."

"Would ya look at that," Roscoe said abruptly, pointing to the group of people on the other side of main street. There were three younger human men, two women and one half-turn. He was tall and covered in thicker black body hair. Like Adam, he had a small tail jutting from the waistband of his sweatpants and the body of a jock. "He looks popular."

"He doesn't look like he has a kuu. How's he just allowed to hang out with humans?"

"This town probably has lots of werewolves at his beck and call. I'm sure he's doin' just fine keeping himself in check."

"We're just the sluttiest of sluts, aren't we?"

"*Yer* not, obviously."

"I guess I'm just weird then."

"Being weird ain't a bad thing, and neither is enjoying great sex with different people."

"I guess I was just brought up differently. You know, with morals and self-control."

"And a smug sense of superiority. Don't forget that."

I stopped and glared at him, but he just smiled. Every so often he'd hit me with a reality check, and it kind of pissed me off.

Roscoe sniffed the air, his stomach rumbling audibly as the scent of smoked meat wafted on the breeze. Hell, even I was starting to get hungry.

"Ooo," he said, making a sharp turn toward the origin like one of those cartoon characters smelling a pie on a windowsill.

"We don't have the money." I grabbed his arm and pulled him back. "Come on. We need to get paint and groceries."

Roscoe's ears fell. "We should get to work on that OnlyStans idea."

"That's *your* project, you know."

"Yeah, but I need *yer* help, remember? I don't know nothin' about computers." His face brightened for a second. "That reminds me. I was talkin' to Austin about our little idea—"

"Roscoe, I swear to God!"

"I was gonna talk to you first before agreeing to anything."

"If you want a three-way, talk to Adam. I'm sure he'll be more than happy."

Roscoe folded his arms. "Maybe I will. Yer holier-than-thou-ness."

"Whatever." I knew why this pissed me off, but even that annoyed me. I wanted it to be just me and him.

"I know that look." He gave me a shake, and I shrugged him off. "Yer mad at me again."

"Yo!" a male voice shouted. Roscoe and I turned to see a fit guy in jogging pants running toward us. He was human, but had different symbols tattooed on both arms, like some kind of Sanskrit surrounded by pentagrams. "New guys!"

"What's up?" Roscoe said, extending his hand. The man eagerly grabbed it and shook. "Just moved here. The name's Roscoe. This here's Cody."

He turned and grabbed my hand, shaking it more vigorously than he had Roscoe's.

"I'm Sean." He paused, the smile on his face widening. "Damn! We don't see many half-turns. You're the third one."

"Fourth," I corrected. "There's another one back home."

His expression became even more ecstatic, which startled me. Human reactions to seeing me were never this pleasant back in the city. Hell, even in White Dunes, people often kept their distance while walking by me on the beach.

"How many werewolves you got living here?" Roscoe asked, turning to look at a group of rowdy wolf-men scarfing down what looked like ribs on picnic tables outside a run-down barbeque restaurant.

"With you, that makes two hundred and forty-three." He turned toward me again. "What made you guys decide on Norwich?"

"Desperation," I muttered, catching myself as Roscoe shoved my arm. "And it seemed like a neat place."

"You guys are gonna love it here. Have you talked to the mayor for your orientation yet?"

I narrowed my eyes. "Why would we need to talk to the mayor?"

"I'd keep checking your mail if I were you because it's the law. Any non-human who moves to this town needs to know the rules."

Roscoe seemed more taken aback than I was. "Rules? I thought this place was cool."

"Trust me, Norwich is fucking awesome, but there's some really sketchy shit that goes on in the woods." Sean looked around before lowering his voice. "Between us, you guys should check out the mayor's wife, because holy shit."

"She a looker?"

I shoved Roscoe hard.

"What? I'm just askin'."

"Let's just say... she'll put a spell on you." He flashed his brows. "Once you get your letter, don't wait too long, because you don't want the mayor on your doorstep. A couple moved in a year ago and never went to their orientation. Ended up disappearing for a week, and after that, they fell in line quick."

"O-kay. What the hell did the mayor do to them?" I asked.

The human shrugged. "Don't let what I said freak you out. The mayor's great, but he's a hardass and a stickler for the rules when it comes to werewolves."

"Pfft. I ain't never been intimidated by authority. I'll tell a few dirty jokes with the guy and put a smile on his grumpy face."

The guy burst into nervous laughter. "I wish you luck, dude. I've never seen the guy so much as crack anything more than a frown in public. Mosavi knows how to run a town, but he's not exactly the baby-kissing type. Anyway, welcome to Norwich. We all just call it Halloween town."

Roscoe and I shook his hand. "It was nice meetin' ya, Sean. Maybe I'll see ya around."

"Likewise," he replied, giving us both a wave as he jogged toward the direction we'd just come from.

"That was the most bizarre welcome I've ever gotten," I said, looking around for the hardware store sign. "I'm starting to wonder if there are cameras everywhere, because that sounded kind of cult-like and rehearsed."

"Hmm," Roscoe grunted, scratching at his mane again.

"We can always take Darryl up on his offer and move back to White Sands."

"Nah, this place is gonna be great. You'll see." He grabbed my hand. "We already knew about the people before we came. It won't be so weird once we get to know everyone."

"I wonder what the sketchy shit is he was talking about in the woods."

"Yer overthinkin' again. Remember, you lived in a crack alley in the worst part of the city, and you felt fine enough to take the bus at night. Redneck sketchy isn't the same as the hood."

We passed a gnarled tree that closely resembled a monstrous claw with yellow leaves. "I've seen redneck, and this is definitely not it. It's like this place was teleported here from another world. Even the trees look fucked up."

"I think they look awesome." Roscoe stopped and began relieving himself on it.

I flushed and scanned our surroundings, moving as fast as I could away from the scene.

"Cody," Roscoe called after me, but I pretended to ignore him. "Hold up. There's still a little more."

I was at full sprint now, shelter from humiliation mere feet away at the store's entrance. The doors opened automatically, and I slipped inside as Roscoe continued shouting my name.

The hardware store wasn't as large as the ones in the city, and the shelves weren't stocked with much. I slowed my pace, reading the signs along the ends of aisles.

"You left me hangin'," Roscoe whispered from behind. It was startling how fast he could run. Even if he was on the porky side, he still had that werewolf speed.

"It's day one and you're already humiliating me."

"Cody, every werewolf in town's pissed on that tree. I was just adding my name to the roster."

"How do you know?"

Roscoe pointed to his nose.

"Gross."

"It's basically a community message board," he said, following closely.

I turned right, ambling along the paint aisle while feeling around my jean pockets. "Crap. I left the list at home. Do you remember what color Austin said we needed?"

"It's not rocket science. The walls are white, so just get white paint." Roscoe slowed, his ears dropping as he looked at the color swatches. "What the hell is Swiss Coffee? Why are there twenty different shades of white?"

"Maybe it was eggshell," I said, giving the swatch a closer look. "This looks pretty close, right?"

"You should probably call Austin."

"I don't have his number. Or Adam's."

Roscoe picked up a can of paint and shrugged. "Eggshell it is."

A sudden, uneasy sensation rattled me as a woman's chuckle echoed through the store, the lights dimming. I turned around just in time to see a flowing black dress disappear around the corner. The lights brightened, and Roscoe nudged my arm.

"You okay?"

"Wait, you didn't see that? Someone was laughing and the lights went out."

Roscoe looked around and narrowed his eyes. "I didn't see nothin'."

"The lights—and there was a woman." As his expression grew more concerned, I sighed and shook my head. "Never mind. Let's just buy this and go home."

"Without groceries? We don't got nothing to eat."

"We'll order a pizza or something."

"I thought you said—"

"I'll make Adam pay for it. He still owes me," I said, quickly making my way to the checkout line. "And he just got his check the other day."

"Sweeeeet," Roscoe whispered, licking some of the slobber away from his mouth. "Better yet, I could just go to the store and pick up some stuff to make pizza. I've been itching to cook fer a while."

"Maybe you should make your *amazing* baked ziti."

"Shit yeah!"

Other customers turned toward us as Roscoe's voice echoed through the store.

"Can you lower your voice?" I snatched the can of paint from Roscoe and set it on the counter. "I swear you're like a toddler."

"Did you find everything okay?" the cashier said, sliding the paint can in front of the scanner.

"Yes, thanks," I replied, reaching into my back pocket.

"That'll be forty-one even."

My stomach dropped. "Whoa! I thought it was fifteen."

"Fifteen for the quart-sized cans. That's the gallon."

"Uh, I didn't see nothin' smaller," Roscoe said.

"That's because we only carry the gallon."

"Then why do you have a price for a size you don't even carry?" I asked, growing frustrated as the line grew behind us.

"Must have been a mistake," the cashier said.

"Do you have anything cheaper?"

"Listen. You're not going to find paint any cheaper than that in this town."

I put my wallet away, but something inside snapped. Pins and needles pricked me from all over, the light in my vision turning that familiar red hue. Roscoe rested his hands on my shoulders, pushing me toward the door.

"Uh, it's a little out of our price range right now. We'll get it online," Roscoe said, before pulling me the rest of the way outside. "Cody, you need to calm the hell down."

"Why does this keep happening?"

"I dunno, but that was a dangerous look you gave." He examined me as we walked along main street. "Get mad at me all you want, that's fine. I love annoying the shit outta you, but the moment you feel yerself lose it in front of humans, you need to back away."

"Oh please. Do I look like I'm going to fight someone? The guy was obviously trying to rip us off, and I was about to go all Karen on his ass."

"No. I know that look well. You were ready to rip the guy to pieces, and I don't mean with yer words."

I rolled my eyes.

"I'm serious. Yer fur got thicker, and yer teeth and claws were growing. When a half-turn does that, it gets bad."

"I—that doesn't make any sense. We're not dangerous like werewolves."

"Where the hell'd you hear that?"

"Look at me! What am I going to do to someone? I'm just a glorified fleshlight."

"Jeez, Cody. The whole Austin and Adam thing ain't normal—usually. Is that what you think you are to me?"

I folded my arms but didn't respond.

"I think of you as my buddy. My best buddy," Roscoe continued, draping his arm over my shoulder. "We just also happen to fuck a lot. That's normal for us. It keeps you from gettin' all snarly."

"Am I dangerous? Is that why there are so many restrictions on half-turns?"

"Well, kinda, but not usually."

"Can you just tell me, please?"

Roscoe scratched his mane, cocking a grin. "Ever see a toddler throw a temper tantrum?"

"Excuse me? You're comparing *me* to a toddler?"

"I'm serious. The kid doesn't know why he's angry, and he doesn't know how to handle it other than crying, throwing things, and pitching a fit. Maybe break his toys. That's kinda like how half-turns are. They get all these new senses, emotions, abilities, and they get them really fast, but nothing's in sync yet. If I make you mad, I just work the ol' werewolf charm. If a human pisses you off and you don't know how to handle yerself, you could do some real damage. Yer probably the most repressed piece of work I've ever met, and yeah, that makes you really dangerous."

"Repressed?"

"You got all weird and embarrassed when I pissed on that tree. That's like... *our* thing. We pee on stuff." He grabbed my arm and pulled me toward one of those odd-looking gnarled trees that lined the walkway. "Here. Pee on it."

"I'm not peeing on a tree in front of the whole damn town," I hissed through my teeth.

"See? Uptight. Ashamed. Repressed. So worried about what everyone thinks."

"This is different. You know what they call guys that whip their dicks out in public?"

"You think that tree's gonna get all offended?" He laughed and patted the trunk. "Hell, look at it. It likes being peed on."

"Don't be a smart-ass. There are a lot of other trees in more private places. You don't have to make a show of it, and I know you do that shit on purpose."

"It's great bein' a werewolf, but it's also pretty sweet being a half-turn. We can get away with shit humans can't. If you wanna pee on this tree, no one's gonna care."

I began walking along the sidewalk again, with Roscoe following close. "Common decency," I said. "No one wants to see that shit."

"You'd be surprised."

"Not everyone wants to be fucked by you, Roscoe."

"Whoa. That came outta left field."

"Just drop it. I want to get home so I can listen to Austin bitch at us for not having paint."

Roscoe and I didn't speak for a few minutes before he finally spoke up.

"I'm glad I met you."

At first, I thought he was being sarcastic, but his face was sincere. "Huh?"

"I just thought you needed to hear that."

His tail wagged, which was usually an indicator he was going to say or do something that pissed me off. However, as another minute passed and nothing else was said, my annoyance faded away.

"I'm glad I met you, too. Even if you are annoying."

The two of us walked up the driveway as Austin watched from the front porch. He sat alone on the wooden steps, digging one of his claws into the weathered railing and wearing a frustrated grimace.

"Paint was too expensive," I said, making my way up the steps, brushing past the werewolf. "We'll have to get it online."

"Oh well," Austin muttered. "This house is gonna be a project, and we'll need money."

"You know we're only renting, right? I don't want to sink thousands of dollars into a place I don't even own."

"And I don't wanna live in a dump." Austin said. "Do we even know who the landlord is?"

"Everything is handled through the bureau. If we have complaints, I have to make them there and they'll work with the owner to make the repairs. I think."

"Forget it. Don't get 'em involved," Austin said, looking over at Roscoe. "That porn idea of yours... it's good money, right?"

"Uh—" Roscoe swayed nervously. "It can be. Depends on what yer willin' to do."

"I'm not doing shit. Not going to risk putting my face out on the internet, but Adam will do just about anything you want. I'll rent him out to you."

I was about to walk into the house, but stopped, slamming the door behind me. "You piece of—"

"Wait a minute now," Roscoe said calmly, putting up his hand. "That wasn't the deal. I'd only do it if Adam agreed to it."

"He'll agree to it."

"No, he won't," I interjected.

"Stay out of our business. What? Do you think you're better than the rest of us? We need money."

"Then grind your own ass for it. Adam's not your meal ticket."

Austin climbed to his feet and stood over me, but Roscoe pushed his way between us.

"Things are gettin' a little heated. Both of you need to calm down." He turned to Austin. "I've been trying to keep the peace, but we need to have a talk. Just the two of us."

The hackles on Austin's neck rose. "Is that a challenge? Are you challenging me, old man?"

"'Course not." Roscoe put his hand on the other werewolf's shoulder and nodded for me to go inside. "Just need to talk."

I allowed myself a moment to calm down before heading inside, letting the door rest quietly against the frame. Roscoe looked like he knew what he was doing, but I was a bit worried. I didn't know what

Austin was capable of; in fact, it probably wasn't wise of me to argue with him.

"Adam?" I called out, noticing the living room furniture neatly arranged, but the half-turn wasn't there. There wasn't a response, so I walked into the hall and opened their bedroom door. He wasn't there either.

As I made my way back, a soft snore reverberated from my bedroom. Adam was sound asleep on my side of the bed, wearing nothing but a pair of navy briefs with a hole in it for his little tail and a black tank top that had been shredded along the back.

It wasn't exactly a mystery whose claw marks those were.

I made a few creaky paces through the bedroom and sat on the mattress, giving him a light shake.

"Hey."

Adam groaned and turned away before falling back to sleep.

"Wake up," I said a little louder.

"Go away. I'm tired."

"It's my bed. I'll do what I want."

I climbed up and began jumping in an attempt to annoy him, but the cheap mattress was springier than I had anticipated. The force launched Adam about four feet into the air, and he shouted a curse word before coming to a hard rest on the floor.

"Oh my God! Are you okay?"

Adam moaned at first before the fur on his neck stuck straight out.

"Okay, I know you're pissed, but hear me out," I said, reaching down to help him off the floor.

Adam slapped my hand away. "Does it look like I'm in the mood to play around?"

"Does it ever?"

He glared at me, now sitting cross-legged on the floor.

"Did he hurt you?"

"He always hurts me," Adam said. "This is not news, Cody."

"All right, we need to do something about him, especially if he's physically abusing you."

Adam sighed. "He's not. He may be a monster, but he has his limits." He rubbed the bump on his head from the hard landing earlier. "It's weird. He always seems like he's going to cross that line, but he never does. He just likes to emotionally torment me."

"What happened?"

"Same shit, just in a new place. If I don't turn soon, I'm gonna break my kuu. I don't care about the future anymore because I can't keep living like this. What's more infuriating is he pretends to be somewhat decent toward me around you guys, but the moment you leave, he starts treating me like his chew toy."

"Roscoe's talking to him now."

"He's gonna get creamed if he pisses Austin off."

I shrugged. "Well, good thing werewolves heal fast then."

"Is it possible to hate and love someone at the same time?" Adam asked.

"I don't know. I would think not."

"Then I guess I'm an anomaly." He lifted his clawed hands in front of his face. "I want to wrap these around his neck sometimes. Darryl told me something a while ago that stuck with me. It made a lot of sense."

"What's that?"

Adam grinned. "Austin took on a role he wasn't meant for, and it makes him miserable. He wants to be this alpha male, but he knows he can't live up to that. So he overcompensates by picking fights with people for no reason. Darryl, though. He's a natural leader, and he makes people feel safe, not intimidated. That's what a real alpha is, and it pisses Austin off because he knows he could never be like that. So he makes me feel smaller so he can keep feeling big."

"Would *you* actually feel comfortable taking up that role?"

Adam climbed to his feet and sat next to me on the bed. "Right now? No. Darryl told me I'd know my role in werewolf society when I was close to going full-turn." His gaze went from sad to intense as he spoke. "I think it's gonna happen soon. I've never been more ready, but I've also never been sadder."

"Why's that?"

"I dunno. There's just something sad about knowing the person you were might change for good."

"But it'll be for *good*. I thought you wanted to leave Austin when you turned."

Adam shrugged. "I do, but I still love him. I don't know why. It's not like he has many redeeming qualities, but I get sick thinking about life without him. Isn't that fucked up?"

"I don't know. I'm not good at relationship stuff, but a lot of people have been in this position. If you're in love with someone, even if they're toxic, it's hard to change that."

"I'm gonna do something pretty risky the night I turn. I never told you what Darryl and I really fought about that night, but I did apologize... and I got some valuable information."

"Oh?" I waited for him to elaborate, but he simply smiled and stood up. "What, you're gonna leave me hanging? Why even bring it up?"

"It's painful, isn't it?" he said, rubbing the knot on his forehead. "Maybe next time you won't launch me off the bed."

He padded out of the bedroom.

"It was an accident!"

# The Forest's Secrets

Everyone always busted my chops for being uptight and moody, but Adam was a lot worse—at least in the moody department. We sat in front of my old television, and we didn't speak to one another. I didn't want to press him on what he told me earlier, but it was eating me alive. What did he have planned, and why was it risky?

The house was coming together, but it was still rough to look at. Even though I didn't like the guy, Austin was one hell of a handyman. He'd fixed the plumbing in the kitchen, patched the holes in the walls, tightened the loose boards on the porch, and replaced the wiring on a faulty outlet that nearly caught fire.

The front door squealed open, and both Roscoe and Austin padded inside.

"I gotta fix that," Austin said, examining the hinges.

Roscoe stepped up to me and held out his hand. "Could I get some cash?"

"How much?"

"How much you got?"

"Roscoe," I snapped, grabbing my wallet from my back pocket. "What are you going to get?"

"Groceries. Gotta get enough to last all of us the week."

I turned to Adam. "I don't have enough money to feed two werewolves for a week. Give Roscoe some of yours."

"Hell no. I've been waiting a whole month to get my check, and I've got shit to buy."

"You got fifteen hundred, right?"

"Why are you asking? You get the same amount I do."

"Good, the rent's due. That'll be seven hundred."

Adam shot off the couch. "You're outta your damn mind."

I jumped up and got as close to his face as I could without running into him. "No. I've been overly generous. Now pay the fuck up."

We both snarled, and I started seeing that red hue again.

"What the hell's goin' on with you guys?" Roscoe asked, pushing us apart before turning to Adam. "If you're gonna live here, you gotta contribute. Cody can't do everything by himself, and I don't got a job yet." His tail wagged. "And I know what I'm gonna cook tonight to put you grumps in a good mood."

"Seven hundred is too much," Adam said. "Four hundred."

"Seven hundred," I repeated.

"Five hundred."

"Seven hundred," I said slower, emphasizing each word. "And I'm about to go to eight if you keep being a cock about it."

After a brief pause, the half-turn finally relented, nearly tearing his pants as he jerked out his wallet. "I hate you."

"Keep pushing me, and you can find somewhere else to live."

Adam slapped the money into my hand before storming to his bedroom.

After licking a finger, I thumbed through three hundred dollars before stuffing the rest of the cash into my wallet. "Here," I said, handing the money to Roscoe. "This should be enough, right?"

Roscoe leaned in, whispering, "That was kinda hot."

I looked over at Austin, who seemed too preoccupied with the door to care about what was going on.

"What did you guys talk about?"

"Later," Roscoe said, rubbing my shoulders before heading toward the front door. "Still wanna come with?" he asked Austin.

"Yeah, sure."

The two pushed their way outside, closing the squeaky door behind them. Austin seemed calmer than usual, which made me even more curious about what Roscoe had said to him. Between that and Adam's secret, I needed something to occupy my mind before all of it drove me nuts.

The floorboards groaned under my feet as I walked down the hallway. Everything in this place seemed to make some kind of noise, even with the slightest agitation. It had been annoying at first, but the place was kind of growing on me. This was the first time I'd actually lived in a halfway decent house. Even as a kid, we just lived in run-down mobile homes, so I couldn't help but feel a sense of pride at how the place was shaping up.

I stepped into the backyard, and an idea hit. Since I didn't know much about fixing things to help out more, I did like to get things clean and orderly. Maybe the yard could be my project.

I cleared a path through the tall grasses and vines with a sickle from the shed. The tool worked surprisingly well, and the pendulous swinging was calming in its own way. Before I knew it, half an hour had passed and the entire backyard was a little less unruly. I'd already cleaned the weeds out of the pit, but I'd need to gather firewood if I was going to get any use out of it tonight.

There weren't any dead limbs in the yard, and I didn't have an axe. The only option was to take a little stroll through nature, but I had the herculean task of talking myself into it first. Any time I wandered too close to the trees, I'd think about all the rumors and warnings I'd heard. Was it ridiculous to believe the woods were haunted? Being a half-turn had opened up a new world I hadn't thought existed, and the kuu was proof of that. If magic existed in these earrings, it could exist in those trees.

After minutes of working up the nerve, I found my confidence and crossed the forest's edge. I was a goddamn werewolf—well, almost—and these were just trees. Half-turns could be just as dangerous, so what the hell was I afraid of?

My confidence evaporated as I hiked deeper into the dense brush. Something felt off; the farther I went, the darker it got. There weren't that many trees, and while it was only a little after five, it might as well have been dusk the way the canopy swallowed the sunlight.

"This was a really dumb idea," I whispered, turning to backtrack, but I didn't know which way I was going anymore. As a human, I had a terrible sense of direction. As a half-turn, I didn't even have a werewolf's sense of smell to guide me back.

Branches snapped in the distance and what little sunlight was left disappeared. Was this a repeat of what had happened at the hardware store? Maybe if I closed my eyes, everything would go back to normal.

"Hello?" I called, trying to keep my voice calm. A sharp, chilly breeze disrupted the stillness of the air, and a black shadow raced by me before disappearing into one of the many surrounding bushes.

Fear immediately settled into my chest—not a normal terror, either, rather something almost primal. I instinctively settled into something like a defensive stance, the red hue returning, giving a bit of light to the darkness. Maybe this was more than just an uncontrolled rage. Maybe it was a survival instinct.

The drive to fight suddenly faded as a dozen or so sets of glowing eyes closed in from the trees. Once again, my body behaved strangely, calming.

"Hello?" I said, quieter this time, my voice trembling as I stepped back.

Whatever creatures these were didn't make a sound at first, but furious sniffing broke the silence. Werewolves?

When my back hit something solid, I jumped and turned. A tall figure stared down at me with orange, glowing eyes. A werewolf, though he somehow looked more beastly. His feet were paw-like, and he wore a frayed leather rope around his waist from which hung about six fist-sized sacks. That was about all I could make out as my temporary night vision faded.

He held out his large hand, not breaking eye contact. Roscoe told me half-turns were like catnip to werewolves, and I wondered if I'd just run head-first into something I'd regret. Were these the feral werewolves I'd read about in Darryl's book?

"Can you talk?" I asked as more of these strange looking wolfmen emerged from the shadows. All I could make out were silhouettes and furry faces lit by glowing eyes of different colors. The taller among them, the one with the sacks tied to his waist, held up his hand and the pack dispersed back into the woods.

The werewolf reached into one of his sacks and pulled out a glowing prismatic stone resembling an opal. He blinked twice, grunting something resembling a word before taking my hand. He pressed the warm stone into my palm and pointed in what I assumed was the direction I'd come from. As I turned, he vanished without a sound, the dim light of the late afternoon rushing back into my vision.

I held my chest and took in a full breath of air for the first time in what seemed like hours, but the encounter had been brief. I shuffled the pretty stone between two fingers. Who were those creatures?

Perhaps the half-turn I'd seen earlier or one of the local werewolves would know.

I stuffed the stone into my pocket and made a mad dash toward the now-visible threshold leading to the backyard. The sky lightened even more until dappled sunlight warmed my skin. Every step I took toward the clearing, I felt a strange pull deep in my chest, almost beckoning me to turn away.

"Oh. The nerd's back," Adam said, startling me as he sat on one of the logs around the pit. "Why were you out there?"

"I was getting firewood."

His eyes narrowed. "Is it invisible?"

"I changed my mind," I said before making my way to the back door. Adam stood and ran over to me.

"You could have at least gotten something to burn."

"If you want to make a fire, go get the wood yourself."

Adam paused and then let out a sigh. "Why are we fighting?"

"You tell me. You're the one that's been shitty when all I've been trying to do is help and keep our heads above water."

Adam looked away, but I knew what this was about.

"I didn't take that money from you because I want to hoard our *riches*. Until we have income that's more than a monthly government check, we need to have emergency funds ready. We've got two werewolves that eat like horses, and we still have to pay the utilities and whatever other costs creep up."

"You do realize that werewolves hunt, right?" Adam asked.

I couldn't help but laugh at that as I entered the house. "I've never seen Roscoe hunt for anything other than the remote control."

"He caught that giant fish with his bare hands."

I'd forgotten about that.

"We're not going to starve. Austin and Roscoe can do things we can't, and if it came down to it, they'd get us food. There were times Austin and I had no money, and he would go out at night and hunt. The next morning, there was meat in the fridge." Adam's face twisted in disgust. "I don't know what kind of meat it was, but I try not to think too much about it. Werewolves seem to have a strong instinct to take care of half-turns. Even if some of them treat us like shit."

"I didn't know that. Why the hell are we wasting money on groceries when they could just go out there and get us something fresh?"

"Because we keep buying food. Werewolves get really lazy when they just get stuff without having to do anything for it."

"Well, the gravy train ends today."

Adam reached into his pocket and handed me a wad of cash. "You should control the money. You're more responsible than I am, plus Austin has a way of talking me into giving him extra cash."

I took the money and shoved it into my pocket with the rest. "How much money have you given him?"

"A lot. I don't know what he spends it on either."

"How much you wanna bet he's been holding out on us?"

"What do you mean?"

"He doesn't buy anything, right?"

"He apparently bought all those tools without me knowing."

I slowed my pace as we approached their bedroom.

"What are we doing?" Adam asked.

"If he's anything like me, he's got a stash somewhere."

"He's nothing like you." Adam pulled open a few drawers. "God, why do we have such a big dresser when I'm the only one that wears most of the clothes?"

After checking the nightstand drawer and finding nothing but one of Adam's dildos, I paused. "The bedroom's too obvious."

"You're giving him way too much credit."

"And you're underestimating him," I said, stepping back into the hallway. "He's been spending a lot of time on the porch."

"He's been fixing it. I'm surprised both of them haven't broken through the steps."

We walked outside onto the deck, and I looked around for anything out of place. "Keep an eye on the road. If you see them coming, say something."

"I feel like we're on a heist."

"We are. If Austin's been hoarding your money, I'm going to sniff it out."

"I swear, you must be Jewish or something."

My mouth fell open, and I crossed my arms. "That was incredibly insensitive."

"Sorry. I just thought since you were so good with money—" He paused and smiled, shoving me to the side. "You're Jewish, aren't you?"

"On my dad's side, yes. Let's drop this conversation before we both offend one another."

"Snowflakes aren't black."

I reached between a couple loose boards to see if one would pull away from the porch. It didn't. "I know he's hiding it."

"I'm telling you there's no stash. Your Jewy senses are malfunctioning."

Ignoring him, I pressed my heel against each floorboard, listening carefully. "Austin's ex-military, and he's really secretive. I know for a fact he's self-disciplined and paranoid enough to do this." One of the floorboards rattled and pulled away under my foot. "Bingo!"

Adam eyed me curiously as I pulled the board up. It was the last one closest to the edge, so chances of anyone stepping on it were slim to none.

"It's not like Austin to leave it like this, don't you think?" I said, reaching down into the crawlspace. My hand brushed against a tin box, so I removed it before replacing the board.

"Gee, I wonder what's in here," I said as I loosened the cover with a clawed fingernail. It popped open and several rolls of hundred-dollar bills lined the tin. I gave Adam an 'I told you so' look before putting the lid back on.

"That motherfucker."

I pulled the board back up and placed the tin back into the crawlspace.

"What are you doing? That's my money!" Adam shouted.

"And?" I said, making sure everything was the way I found it. "What are we gonna do? Take thousands of dollars away from a mentally unstable werewolf?"

"Okay, you have a point."

"I've got a better idea. I want to let him dig his own grave. From now on, give me any money you make, and I'll put it in my safe."

"That's going to really piss him off."

"Tell him I threatened to kick you guys out if you didn't."

"Dude, you need to be careful. He's never gotten physical with me, but I've also never talked to him the way you do."

"Well, if you're right about him, then I need to stand my ground. Otherwise, he's just going to treat me the way he treats you, and I don't have patience for that bullshit."

We entered the living room and sat on the sofa.

"This is turning into a dictatorship, just so you know," Adam grumbled.

"As long as I'm the dictator, I see nothing wrong with this. We're half-turns, Adam. We need to have some kind of control over them. When I found out how vulnerable we are, it scared the shit out of me, and I'm not going to let us end up in a hopeless situation."

Adam propped his feet on my lap and laid his head against the arm of the couch. "I guess I trust you more than anyone else."

"Well, Darryl told me to look after you, so I'll do that."

He kicked my leg. "I don't need to be looked after. I'm not a child."

"You literally just turned nineteen."

"And you're only three years older than me, so stop pretending you're a fucking sage."

"I've been told I'm an old soul."

"Yeah, and boring." Adam grabbed the remote and flipped on the television. "Did you know Austin wants Roscoe to fuck me in front of a camera? Like I'd ever be desperate enough to let that gross old werewolf put his dick in me." He looked over but didn't seem at all fazed by what he said. "No offense or anything."

"Yeah sure," I muttered. "Roscoe may not be the cleanest or the most well-spoken, but at least he's sincere and treats me like a friend."

"Sounds like you're in love."

"Sounds like you're jealous."

Adam didn't have a comeback aside from a sharp click of his tongue. He changed the channel.

"You want Roscoe, don't you?"

"Hell no!"

"Admit it. It's not like I'm gonna tell anyone." My grin widened. "That's why you're such a prick to him. You want him."

Adam kicked me again. "Shut the hell up!"

"He makes me come at least six times before blowing his load. He may be old, but he knows exactly what he's doing."

"Cody..." He paused and narrowed his eyes. "Seriously? Six times?"

"He's shockingly good."

"You're messing with me right now, aren't you?"

I shrugged. "Maybe, maybe not. It's not like you're gonna find out."

Adam glared at the television but didn't say anything else.

The front door opened and Roscoe walked in with several bags of groceries draped over each arm. Austin followed him, carrying the rest.

"Honey, I'm home, and I brought us some vittles," Roscoe said.

"Do you have to always talk like a dumbass hillbilly?" Adam stood and stomped into the bedroom.

"What the heck did I do?" Roscoe asked, setting some of the bags on the table.

"You turned him on," I said, grabbing some of the groceries before making my way into the kitchen. "What did you get?"

"Oh boy, yer in for a real treat tonight."

"Don't forget to put on your little boob dress while you're making us dinner," Austin said, reaching for the drill he set on the dining room table earlier.

"Apron!" Roscoe snapped, pulling out the folded fabric from one of the bags on the counter. With a flick of the wrist, he shook it out. "Look at this. Ain't it great?"

The apron had a plump pair of bare breasts on the front with the phrase, 'My breasts are always moist and delicious' underneath in bold letters.

"Well, there goes my boner, permanently," I said, putting the cold stuff in the fridge. "Where the hell did you get that? I'm sure they weren't selling them at the grocery store."

Roscoe slipped into the neck loop and tied the strap around his waist. "They got all kinds o' neat little novelty shops around town, and I've been looking for a new apron."

"And *that's* the one you settled on?"

"It was the breast one there was." The werewolf cracked up at his own pun, while Austin and I rolled our eyes.

"You didn't happen to see any places to buy kuus, did you?"

Roscoe opened a cabinet and lined the shelves with dry pasta. "Nah. We didn't walk through the whole town. Why do you wanna know that?"

"I found something that I'd like to have appraised by someone who knows a thing or two about magic rocks," I said, digging the opal out of my pocket. "Look at this."

"That's pretty. Where'd you find it?"

"In the woods."

I deliberately chose to be careful with my words, not because I worried everyone would think I was nuts, but because I wanted a secret of my own. Maybe I'd let them in on it later.

"I bet you could sell it for a lot," Austin said, giving the gem a closer look. "We could use the money."

I closed my hand and put the opal back in my pocket. "I think we've got plenty of money."

"Hardly," Austin grunted. "Those government checks aren't enough to tide us over."

"I'm sure there's extra money just lying around here somewhere," I said, shoving cheap cuts of meat into the freezer. "This house is pretty old, so who knows what's under it? Could be buried treasure."

That caught Austin's attention but he remained quiet.

"Wouldn't that be sweet," Roscoe said as he pulled a pan out from under the cabinet.

"Heh, yeah." Austin's eyes shifted before he made his way outside. A few minutes later, I heard him drilling screws into the porch from where I'd found the money earlier.

"He sure likes fixing things. Listen to him out there. Happy as a clam."

"He sure does," I said through my teeth, leaning against the counter. "You never told me what you guys talked about."

Roscoe filled a large pot with water before setting it on the old gas stove. "I know he's a little rough but think of him like a wet lump of clay that was dropped on the ground and stepped on a few times. It's got dirt and grass and all kinds of shit in it, but it can still be cleaned and made into something nice."

"So, Austin's a piece of shit. That's not news."

"Cody," Roscoe scolded as he threw a handful of salt into the water. "He ain't that much older than you. He's still a kid."

I raised a brow.

"Yeah, I know. Yer an old man trapped in a twink's body."

I balled my fist. "I told you not to call me that!"

"You know what I mean," he finished, flinching. "Anyway, I see through him. He's not as tough as he pretends to be, but he's in a place where you gotta be delicate or you lose him." Roscoe leaned against the counter on the other side of the kitchen, intentionally puffing out his chest to show off that ridiculous apron. "He's testing you. He's testing all of us to see where he fits in, and right now, I think he's confused."

"You make it sound like they're going to be here for a while. Adam's been acting weird lately, so he's probably about to turn. Once that happens, they're both going to be climbing over themselves to leave this place."

"You're makin' a lot of assumptions. We don't know what's gonna happen when Adam goes full-turn. They might leave, or we might have us a pack."

"I hope they leave."

Roscoe shook his head. "I'm hopin' they stay. You've gotta admit, it's been a lot more interesting with those two."

"If by interesting you mean frustrating, then yes."

"Are you and Adam still arguing?"

"The guy's hot one second then cold the next, so I don't have a clue. I keep trying to be his friend, and when I feel like we're getting somewhere, he gets all pissy about something stupid."

"What's he pissed off about this time?"

"Let's just say, the twerp doth protest too much."

"I—don't know what that means," he said, checking the pot as it roared to a boil.

"It's not a big deal. It's just funny," I said, packing the rest of the groceries away in the cupboard. "I mean, I understand why he is the way he is, but it still doesn't make it any less annoying." I closed the cabinet door and sighed. "I really miss Darryl. I wish he were here."

Roscoe ran a finger under my chin. "Who knows? Maybe he'll get sick of the ocean one day and make his way up."

"You know that's never going to happen."

"Not a chance," Roscoe said, moving away to pour the dry pasta into the pot.

"I didn't know you were supposed to boil it if you're gonna bake it."

Roscoe looked like someone punched him in the gut. "How the hell did you manage to survive all these years by yerself without starvin' to death?"

"I don't know what the big deal is. It's just pasta, sauce, and cheese."

"And somehow you managed fuck it up," Roscoe growled. "I still see that burnt atrocity in my nightmares. All that wasted food because you didn't want to pull yer head outta yer ass."

"I still don't know what I did wrong."

"See what I'm doin' here?" Roscoe asked, pointing to the pot. "Dry pasta only works if you're combining everything in a Dutch oven or something like that, but that ain't what you did. Second, you can't just dump everything into a glass pan and throw some cheese on top. You gotta layer it. And your third sin was using glass bakeware on higher heat. Nothing's gonna cook evenly, which is one of the many reasons everything was burned on the top and raw in the middle."

"Well, I know now. It's easy enough to fix."

"I'm only scratchin' the surface."

"All right! I never learned how to cook, okay?"

"Cooking and common sense go hand-in-hand. You didn't bother to read the back of the pasta box before you dove in?"

"Oh my God, you're actually angry with me, aren't you?" I chuckled slightly as Roscoe's ears went from pressed against his head to relaxed and pointed off to the side.

"Naw, I never get angry."

"Then let me cook tonight."

His ears pressed against his head again. "Get yer ass out of my kitchen."

I laughed and jumped up on the counter while watching him give the pot a stir. After a moment, he looked back and pressed his nose into the crook of my neck.

"You smell good."

"I'm guessing I smell *skunky*?"

He backed away. "I think you better go shower. Don't make me choose between sex and overcooking my pasta."

"Why is this so good?" Adam asked while shoveling in more. "What did you lace this with?"

"Love," Roscoe said, looking rather proud of himself. "And homemade tomato sauce."

Austin didn't say a word but didn't stop eating either. I couldn't blame him. This was the best thing Roscoe had made so far.

"This was your plan all along, wasn't it?" I said, scooping more onto my plate, the cheese so gooey it fell on the table in strands. "You want to make me fat."

The old werewolf said nothing while flashing his brows.

"What else can you cook?" Austin asked.

"It's easier to list what I can't."

"I've been in the mood for venison." Austin shoved another forkful into his maw, smacking loudly. I wasn't looking forward to eating like that when I finally made the shift. "I'll hunt it, you cook it. Deal?"

"I get to cook deer, and I don't have to catch it? Shit. Sign me up."

I looked over at Adam and we silently chuckled. Roscoe was hands-down the laziest bastard I'd ever met, but when it came to cooking, he didn't cut corners. Austin offering to hunt was a bit of a curveball though.

"Oh!" Roscoe said, reaching behind him to grab an envelope off the counter. "Look. Our first piece of mail."

I snatched the letter out of his hand. "Is that my check?"

"I dunno. It's from the courthouse here in Norwich."

"Oh yeah. The orientation." I tore open the envelope and read the letter. "We need to go to city hall tomorrow."

"All of us?" Adam asked.

"That's what it says."

Austin's eyes went wide. "I'll pass."

"It's mandatory, Austin," I said, pointing to the bold lettering.

"I'm not going into a government building. They'll have to come find me first."

"Maybe the three of us can go up there without him," Roscoe said.

"I don't think that's gonna fly." I handed the paper to Austin. "But it's your choice. I'd rather us not draw too much attention to ourselves though."

"I don't like this," he whispered, reading over the document.

"It's a small town in the middle of nowhere. There aren't any black helicopters," Adam said sarcastically.

Austin slammed the letter onto the table. "You think this is funny?"

"No, I think it's stupid. No one's after you. The military probably doesn't even give a fuck where you are."

"You just want them to take me. That's what you've always wanted." Austin stood and backed away from the table. "I bet you've been tipping them off this whole time, pretending to be on my side. Now they're always watching me."

"Austin," Roscoe said calmly, "if Adam had done that, you'd already be gone."

"Maybe all this is a lie. Maybe I'm still there hooked up to some machine, and this is all just a—a drug-induced hallucination!"

The far-away expression, the dilated pupils, the heavy breathing. The poor guy was having a full-blown panic attack. Roscoe stood and carefully approached the snarling werewolf.

"Why don't you come with me to the bedroom," he said, reaching for the larger werewolf's hand.

Austin wildly scanned the room, his breathing turning to panting. Roscoe was able to grab his hand before gently leading the other werewolf toward the hallway.

"Everything's gonna be fine," Roscoe assured, putting one careful step in front of the other. One wrong move could have sent Austin right over the edge. The larger werewolf trembled, drool roping from his maw onto Roscoe's arm. "They really fucked you up there, didn't they?"

The other werewolf didn't say anything, but he did allow Roscoe to lead him into the bedroom. The door clicked closed, leaving Adam and me in stifling silence.

"I hate it when he gets like that," Adam said, continuing to eat as if nothing happened. "You guys get to see what I've been dealing with for over a year."

"Dude! That was not some casual acting out. That was full-blown PTSD! He needs help."

"Good luck convincing him to get any," Adam said coldly before setting his fork down. "No one can force him to do anything, but he's too afraid of change. So he just stays in his own little hell."

"Why aren't you more concerned?"

"Because I'm not. I'm past that. I learned a while ago that I can't do a damn thing anyways. I tried everything, but now I'm just tired. Once I turn, I'm outta here and he can be you guys' problem. I don't want to spend the rest of my life babysitting someone who doesn't want to help himself."

"I guess," I said, trying not to show how annoyed I was, but I kind of understood. It was emotional fatigue, and it could happen to even the most giving person—which Adam was not. He was still a kid, and this was too much for him to handle.

"You were right. There's more to Roscoe than I give him credit for," Adam said before pulling away from the table. "Maybe a really, really small part of me finds that kind of a turn-on."

I smiled. "Mmhmm."

"It's a really small part of me, Cody. Almost microscopic," he added.

"Whatever you say."

# Chapter 12

# The Mayor

"Maybe we should have sex," Adam said, breaking the silence. He stared blankly at the ceiling while lying next to me, the faint glow of the hall night light slicing into the room. "Fuck me, Cody. Call me your pretty little princess."

"Tempting," I said, looking over at him. Though he was trying to lighten the mood, his expression remained concerned.

"What do you think they're doing in there? It's been two hours."

"Your guess is as good as mine." I sat up and fluffed the pillow behind me before lying down again. "Has Austin always been like that? I mean, you said he was fucked in the head when you first met, but like *that*?"

"Not this bad. There's a sweet side to him, but I haven't seen that person in a while. He's always moody, and no one likes to be around him. I don't even think he likes to be around himself."

"This is really upsetting."

"I'm not good with this stuff. I didn't even know what was wrong with him for the longest time. It's not like I can just break up with him and leave, either. I'm literally stuck in a position I can't get out of without some awful, lifelong consequence."

"Suppose the kuu didn't exist. Could you really leave him like this?"

Adam didn't respond.

"I'm not saying you should stay in an abusive relationship, but if there's a chance we can help him, it might be worth sticking around. Especially since you're not dealing with this alone anymore." I rolled out of bed and stumbled over Adam's pants.

"Where are you going?"

"This is about to drive me crazy. I'm going to see what they're doing."

"I'm coming with." Adam threw off the covers and followed close.

We crept toward the other bedroom, the loose floorboards in the hallway giving us away. I pressed my ear to the door but didn't hear anything. When I opened it a crack, I could see Roscoe sitting up against the headboard, sound asleep. Austin's head was in his lap while the rest of his body was in the fetal position, his huge, clawed feet dangling over the mattress.

Adam pushed the door all the way open so he could see before backing away. I followed, turning off the light and shutting the door carefully behind me.

"I didn't expect that," I said, walking back into the bedroom, relieved Roscoe had successfully defused what could have been a terrible situation. I climbed back into bed. "We should get some sleep. It's almost twelve."

Adam stood in the middle of the room, staring pensively at the floor before walking over to the bed.

"You okay?"

"I never did that. He's so big that I probably wouldn't have been able to, anyway." He pulled down the covers and shuffled next to me. "He was so calm, and he wasn't crying in his sleep."

"Roscoe told me werewolves should have a pack. He said we do better when we're in families, just like wolves. Austin's been isolating himself for a while, and you're the only one he's been around."

"Well gee, that makes me feel better."

"That's not what I meant. You're a half-turn. He hasn't been around other werewolves since the military, right?"

Adam nodded. "He said he didn't want any more friends. I just thought he liked being alone."

"Think about it. He lost the people closest to him with no warning. One day, he had a family and the next, he was alone. I think he's closing himself off because he doesn't want to experience something like that again."

"You sound like you're speaking from experience."

I shook my head. "Not really, but I can think about how I'd feel if something like that happened to me, and I know what it feels like to be abandoned and alone. Human or werewolf, we're social creatures. If we're alone for too long, it fucks us up. I'd imagine it's probably worse for him."

Adam nodded, his watery eyes shimmering in the dim glow. "It was nice to see him like that."

"Maybe tomorrow he'll be easier to talk to. You should try."

"Maybe," Adam said before turning away. "I guess Roscoe's pretty amazing."

"Hands off my werewolf," I said jokingly, but Adam didn't react.

The scent of bacon wafting into my nostrils woke me up, but my eyes didn't fully open until I felt another presence in the room. Austin was leaning against the wall with his arms folded, leering at Adam and I. He wore his torn army fatigue pants, which he never seemed to take off.

"What are you doing?" I whispered.

"Waiting," he grunted. "I'm horny."

"You've got a hand. You can either use it or wait longer. Adam's asleep."

He unzipped his pants, letting his huge cock land with a thud between his thighs. Werewolf dicks were always a mystery. They either stayed neatly behind a patch of fur on the rare occasions they weren't being used, or they'd hang limp and exposed before getting hard. "You do it."

I was too groggy to register what was happening at first, but I snapped out of it, irritation setting in.

"Austin," I said, my voice throaty. "It's seven in the morning. I just woke up, and I haven't had coffee. You don't want me anywhere near your dick right now."

He stepped closer. "You smell like you need it."

"I can get it from Roscoe," I replied, baring my teeth. The instinctual aggression surprised us both.

"God dammit, what are you doing?" Adam asked, his voice slurred as he rubbed his eyes.

"You've got a duty to perform, soldier."

"I don't feel like role playing right now," Adam responded.

"I'm not playing," he growled, stuffing his half-hard dick back into his pants before leaving the room.

Adam rubbed his forehead.

"Well, looks like he's back to his shitty old self," I muttered, letting out a yawn before throwing off the covers.

Adam stood and removed his tight underwear and folded them neatly on my nightstand.

"What are you doing?"

"These are the only pair Austin hasn't destroyed, and he doesn't look like he wants to gently slide them off of me."

"Roscoe does that with his teeth sometimes."

Adam clicked his tongue. "Roscoe's a sex god. I get it." He scrutinized my face for a moment. "I think you're lying to me. You're just trying to make me jealous over nothing."

I pointed to the door. "I believe you have duties to perform, soldier," I said, struggling to keep a straight face. This was petty, but the way he ragged on Roscoe's age irritated me. For human guys, questioning their virility made sense, but for werewolves? They aged like wine. Even Darryl was incredibly hot for being sixty-years old. "Maybe when you're done, he might be willing to talk a little."

"Doubt it," Adam muttered, sliding his feet apprehensively.

"Just humor me. Try to strike up a conversation and see where it leads."

We both stepped out into the hall, and I went straight while he turned off toward their bedroom, taking a deep breath before stepping inside. Guilt soon set in. The look he gave made me wonder what the hell Austin did to make sex so terrible.

After stumbling exhausted through the living room, I stood at the entrance of the kitchen, watching Roscoe flip pancakes while humming to a pop song playing through my phone.

"Made you coffee," he said without looking back. He knew I wasn't the most cheerful being on the planet this early, so he would graciously give me time to caffeinate before the relentless teasing. This morning, however, I was in a different mood.

"Good morning," I said, wrapping my arms around him from behind.

His tail wagged, tickling my abdomen.

"Uh oh. What did I do?"

I let out a soft laugh as I buried my face in his back fur. "You didn't take a shower yet."

"I was gonna last night, but you know." He gave the frying pan a toss, flipping another pancake. "You hungry?"

"That depends. Are you going to sing all of Katy Perry's greatest hits while I eat?" I let him go and backed toward the coffee pot. "How did you calm him down?"

Roscoe slid a spatula under the pancake and stacked it on top of the others before pulling the frying pan off the flame.

"In the mood for a little story?"

"Sure, why not?"

"I was a full werewolf when the second world war started, and in those days, humans didn't take too well to us—for good reason. I didn't have that many werewolf friends either, but I got to know a lot of human veterans while on the streets. These were the badasses that ran into a hail of bullets, explosions, and almost four million Nazi landmines on the beaches of Normandy. They also had to deal with the werewolves ol' Hitler had. It's a big reason why they don't use us in the military anymore. The shit they saw and what they experienced that day, I couldn't even imagine. You hear stories and see the movies, but it's like trying to take the perfect picture of a mountain. The photo don't look nothing like the real thing when yer standing at the foot of it."

I hopped up on the counter like I normally did and continued listening.

"The guys that were the unlucky ones couldn't cope, and they had a lot in common with our grumpy friend in there. Austin didn't go into battle, but he experienced shit that I don't think I'd have been able to handle very well, either. When yer own country does those things to you, it's more than just betrayal. You lose yer self-worth, yer security, and yer trust. When I was out on the streets, I wanted to help these guys, and I'd end up calling some of them my best friends. I learned what shell shock was; we call it PTSD now. I asked if there was anything I could do, and nine times out of ten, they just wanted someone who would listen. They needed to talk to someone, even if they didn't admit it at first.

"I learned the signs and triggers, and what to do when I'd see 'em lose their shit. It probably wasn't the best thing, but I'd sometimes help 'em get drugs to deal with it. It's kinda how I fell down that path myself." Roscoe paused and drew in a deep breath through his nose. "Then the nineteen sixties happened, and a whole new generation this country used up and forgot ended up in my circle of friends. That's why I'm careful with him, Cody. It's always different from person to person, and when you put that kind of trauma in a werewolf, especially one as big as Austin, things get dicey. He's the first for me. It's always been humans."

I stared at him, not really knowing what to say.

"You okay?"

"Yeah," I whispered, taking another sip of coffee. "Why don't you ever tell me more about your life?"

"Well, one, I can't remember a lot of it, and two, I didn't think you cared."

"Of course I care," I said, still shocked by how deep Roscoe actually was. "Did you convince him to come with us today?"

"Noooo-ooo," Roscoe said, his ears falling flat against his head. "And don't you dare bring it up, okay? We'll go up there and explain things. I'm sure they'll understand."

"And if they don't?"

"Then we should probably look for somewhere else to live."

"I don't think Darryl's house is big enough for all of us."

Roscoe shook his head. "He's a last resort. Sure, he offered, but you could tell he wanted his house back to himself. I overstepped enough by dropping in on him like that."

"Who the hell are you and what have you done with Roscoe?"

He grinned sharply and moved in closer. "Wanna eat first, or fuck?"

"What do you think?"

Downtown was busy for a Sunday. People scrambled in and out of shops, and cars packed the parking spots along the street. Adam was unusually contemplative, only giving one-word responses, so I left him alone, but it was weird that Roscoe didn't have much to say either.

"Oh, I almost forgot. What fake name did you give the bureau for Austin?" I gave Adam a slight tap on the shoulder. "I don't want to slip up in there."

"Oh, you're gonna love this," he answered with a mischievous grin. "Bernie Blödmann"

Roscoe snorted but didn't say anything.

"You named him Bernie?" I said, the volume of my voice rising. "He's going to kill you!"

"The last name's the best. I was looking up the word for 'dumbass' in a translator, and German was the most unassuming."

"Adam, you idiot! You gave that name to a government agency. Are you insane?"

"He never told me what name he wanted, so I gave him a suitable one."

I shook my head but tried to keep a straight face. "Did you guys talk at all this morning?"

"What do you think?" he responded with an eye roll. "He said 'clean yourself up, soldier,' rolled over, and that was the last coherent thing that came out of his mouth. Whenever I'd try to talk to him, he'd grunt at me. Like usual."

"What did you say to him?" Roscoe asked.

"Well, I was angry because he finished too fast and didn't get me off—"

"That's yer problem right there," Roscoe interrupted. "Even if he sucks at it, why don't you try strokin' his ego a bit?"

Adam glared at Roscoe.

"Hey, just giving you a helpful tip here. I've done it all, and I've been with more werewolves, humans, and half-turns than I can count. Not all of 'em knew what the hell they were doing, but I learned how to get what I wanted while making 'em feel like they were the best lay I'd ever had."

"How the heck do you do that?" Adam asked.

"Well, when it's over, you tell him how amazing he was, then ask if he'd be up for tryin' something new. This way, you can teach him what you want while buttering him up. That could lead to more conversation—and better sex. It's a win-win."

I stopped in the middle of the sidewalk, the skin on my face so hot it could have boiled water.

"You okay, Cody?" Roscoe asked.

"That was exactly what you said to me after our first night together."

"Oooo." Roscoe cringed, his ears folding against his head. "That wasn't what you think. You were amazing." He went to wrap his arm around my waist, but I shoved him away.

"Just shut the hell up."

Adam burst into laughter.

"Oh, like you're any better," I snapped.

"How many guys have you been with?" Adam asked, walking a little closer. "You wanna have a fuck-off? I'll invite every werewolf in town and we'll see who's better."

"You're the biggest slut I've ever met in my life."

"And that's why I'm better," he responded, turning away with his nose up.

The robotic navigation voice on my phone alerted me that I had arrived at my destination. All three of us looked around.

"Where the hell is it?" Adam asked.

I looked at my phone. "Here, I guess."

In front of us stood a single-floored, red brick building with blacked out windows. It was like all the others, except plain with a rusty drop box out front.

"Even I'll admit this is kinda janky," Roscoe said as he strolled up to the entrance. "Probably don't get much tax revenue here." He opened the door and waved us through.

I stepped inside with Adam and Roscoe following. The interior was just as plain as the outside, with seventies-style terrazzo floors and harsh fluorescent lighting. An antique-looking marquee pointed the way to a few key areas of the building, but all I was concerned with was the arrow pointing at the mayor's office.

"I guess we go this way," I said, leading the other two down the eerily quiet hall. "Where the hell is everyone? Even the city hall in Darryl's town had a guard and metal detector at least."

"I'm not complaining. There won't be a line," Roscoe said.

We stopped at a heavy oak door with a blank bronze name plate screwed into it. "Was he just elected or something?" I asked, giving the door a firm tug.

The warm glow of floor lamps lit the way into a windowless office. It had only a larger-than-normal desk, and an imposing office chair turned toward a television in the corner with Fox News muted on screen. A large, clawed hand snatched the remote from the desk, and the television went dark.

"Welcome to Norwich," a deep voice said.

"Yer shittin' me. A werewolf mayor?" Roscoe said, bounding toward the desk. "How the hell'd you manage that?"

The chair turned, revealing an unusually neat-looking werewolf. He was a dark brown color with a stylishly trimmed ashy mane and well-manicured claws, but the weirdest thing was what he was wearing. It was a black suit tailored to fit his larger inhuman frame, giving him more of a mob boss appearance than a public servant. When he stood, he was only a few inches taller than Roscoe, but he had a lot of muscle and an icy stare that made me want to slink away. His tail had a slight upward curl as it hung from a hole in the black slacks he wore. As handsome as Darryl was, this guy was on the same level.

"Where's the fourth?" he asked.

I opened my mouth to speak, but the clank of the door cut me off. A muscled blond half-turn trudged into the office, swimming in a pair of torn army fatigues barely held up by a belt several sizes too large. In contrast, he also wore a black tank top that was a couple of sizes too small.

"Looks like Bernie made it," Roscoe said with a snicker. "Little Bernie Blödmann."

"The fuck?" Austin snapped, baring his teeth which seemed a little too large for his mouth.

"You're... here," Adam said, sounding just as stunned as the rest of us. I had no idea werewolves could take that form again.

"I was told Mr. Blödmann was a werewolf." Though it was slight, the dark mayor slipped in and out of an accent. It sounded almost middle-eastern.

"Bl—Blödmann." Austin growled, his face turning an alarming shade of red as he grinded his teeth, staring Adam down. "Well, guess there was a fuck-up somewhere."

The mayor studied Austin. "Sure. It must have been a *clerical* error."

"Why are we here?" I asked, pulling the older werewolf's suspicions off Austin, at least for now. "Does everyone get such a personal welcome?"

He pointed to the hard, wooden chairs around the office before sitting down and crossing one leg over his knee. Despite how intimidating he appeared, the bare clawed feet sticking out of his fancy slacks seemed hilariously out of place.

Each of us took a seat, except for Austin.

"Just blow, you old windbag, so I can leave. I got shit to do," Austin said, growing antsier by the second. What was going on with him?

"Hmm," the mayor said, pausing for a full, uncomfortable minute, a menacing grin exposing his exceptionally white canines. "You look rather uncomfortable, Mr. Blödmann. It is not good for a *half-turn* to be so anxious."

Whatever Austin was trying to pull was obviously not working on this guy, but the mayor continued to play along, almost as if he enjoyed watching Austin's discomfort.

"It is not a coincidence you have ended up in this town. I am sure you have heard about the disturbing federal laws that were passed a couple weeks ago."

The four of us looked at one another. With everything that had been going on, the last thing I'd thought about was keeping tabs on the news.

"We've been kinda busy," Roscoe responded, pointing to the mayor's oversized blazer. "Aren't you hot in all that shit?"

The older werewolf exposed the rest of his sharp, white teeth. "Absolutely. Ask your half-turn."

Roscoe's ears fell to the sides and his tail slowly slid between his legs. I'd been around werewolves enough lately to know the body language of embarrassment and arousal, and he displayed both.

Roscoe and the others were overly submissive to this stranger, and it didn't make much sense to me. Austin and Roscoe had no respect for authority, and Adam was always ready to bend over for any werewolf that showed even the slightest bit of dominance. Not this time. He sat straight up, frozen.

The brown werewolf narrowed his eyes. "Responsible citizens keep up with important current events." He tapped a clawed finger on his knee. "To put this simply, every state in the country has until the end of next year to get werewolves off the streets."

"That sounds like it's a good thing," I said. "Everyone gets a place to live, and maybe they'll relax the ordinances against half-turns."

"No. This is *not* a good thing. The law doesn't go into detail, and it is left to states to interpret. Do you honestly think they are going to resolve the homeless problem by putting werewolves in cute little houses with white picket fences? This law all but wipes out werewolf-friendly state policies some of us have worked tirelessly to get passed for decades."

The four of us remained quiet as he continued to look us over, his eyes piercing through me as though he were looking for something hidden. Then he relaxed his glare and turned his attention back to Roscoe.

"Now, let's get personal. How old are you? The state has gotten sloppy with their records."

"Don't really know."

The mayor tilted his head upward. "Forgetting vital information like that is dangerous." He leaned in and sniffed Roscoe. "You stink like the wilds."

Though I couldn't understand what the mayor was talking about, Roscoe's eyes widened.

"And you?" He stood and took a slow step toward Adam, who shot up out of his chair in a wide-eyed panic. "What is your age?"

"Nineteen, sir."

The mayor smiled before glancing at Austin. "Interesting," he whispered, seductively slipping a finger under Adam's chin. He slid his large finger under the kuu necklace. "If there are three half-turns and one werewolf, who gave you this?"

Adam stiffened even more.

The mayor put up a hand as if to stop him from answering. He strode meticulously toward Austin, his claws tapping a dull rhythm against the wooden floor. "This is quite the riddle. There are two half-turns in my office wearing kuus, and one who is not." The mayor leaned in closer, his teeth inches from Austin's face. "What is your age?"

"Twenty-four," he said, puffing out his chest as he always did when he felt threatened, but his forced confidence shattered in seconds after he gave that answer. "I—I mean nineteen."

I had expected the mayor to grin at the obvious lie, but he continued to play along. "Which is it? Twenty-four or nineteen?"

Austin swallowed hard. "Nineteen."

"What exactly are you doing?" I asked, once again trying to pull the older werewolf's attention. The way things were going, Austin was moments from another meltdown. "You're the mayor of a flyover town, not the duke of Fenrich."

He stepped over to me, and his overbearing presence softened. "You're quite the interesting half-turn. How old are *you*?"

"Twenty-two," I answered. "Why are you so interested in our ages?"

The mayor rubbed the neat patch of fur under his chin. "I am trying to suss out the details being kept from me. I do not like it when people try to deceive me. It does not give a good first impression." He tossed a glance at Austin again. "But it is not like you all are deceiving me, right?"

How long was he going to play with his food? He'd obviously figured everything out, but Austin wasn't all that bright.

"Hey, I told you what you wanted. Is that it?" Austin asked, his legs trembling as if he were carrying a ton of weight.

"Not quite." He turned his attention back to me. "How long have you been a half-turn?"

"A couple of months."

The mayor's reaction was immediate and unexpected. His eyes glowed silver as he moved closer, and a deep voice resonated in my head, speaking a language I couldn't understand. As quickly as it started, the voice faded and the mayor backed away, loosening his tie.

"On to business," he said, sitting back down in his chair. The rest of us, including Austin, took our seats. "The elder council is overlooking the construction of werewolf-only towns across the country, but that doesn't solve the underlying issue. Norwich is an experiment, and because of this, every policymaker in the country is watching what happens here."

"Ah, that's why we're here." Roscoe's familiar cocky grin returned as his tone shifted back to his usual self. "You wanna make sure we're on our best behavior."

"Yes," the mayor replied, pointing to his nose. "Let me familiarize you with some of our laws. Werewolves are not allowed to drink alcohol, and you reek of it."

Roscoe's expression quickly shifted to horror. "What?"

"No alcohol. No drugs. No exceptions."

"Are humans still allowed to drink?" I asked. "Because that would be quite the double-standard."

"The council gave specific orders before I took this position. We are not going to risk this opportunity to make the best impression."

I went to say something else, but Roscoe put up his hand and whined in defeat. "All right. No booze or drugs. Anything else, yer majesty?"

The older werewolf turned to me for a moment. "No fighting with the humans, and stay away from the woods," he said, shuffling the papers on his desk. "That last one is the most important."

"Uh, all right. No woods and no fights. Got it." Roscoe shuffled toward the door.

"Oh, and two more things," the mayor said in a deeper voice, stopping Roscoe cold. "Do not ever insult me by taking me for a fool with such pathetic lies and ridiculous false names. And you"—he pointed at me—"I want to see you here tomorrow. Alone."

"Why?" I asked.

The werewolf turned his chair toward the television, turning it back on before shooing us away.

"No more questions. It is taking all my self-control to not lose my temper at you fools."

As I opened my mouth, Roscoe grabbed my shirt and shoved me out the door, the rest filing behind.

"Why'd you do that?" I asked, jerking away.

"Don't fuck with that guy," he said, shoving me forward. "Yer in there talkin' to an elder like yer the fuckin' leader or something."

"Elder?" My stomach dropped as I remembered some of the lore I read in Darryl's book.

Roscoe rested his hand on my shoulder. "You've got a mouth, and I'll admit, that's a big reason I like you. But a wise-ass attitude ain't gonna do you much good if you ain't got the strength to back it up."

As much as I wanted to argue, I decided to let it go. Austin sped ahead of us before turning back to stare at Adam.

"Enough about Cody being stupid. I've got a funny story. Wanna hear it?"

"Uh, sure," Adam responded with a slight upward inflection.

"Back when I was in the marines, they sent me out of the country for a little while. You wanna know what country they sent me to?"

Austin's teeth grew sharper, and his fur thickened as he shifted back into his werewolf form.

"Germany!" he barked, leaning close to Adam's face. "That better not be the fucking name you gave to the bureau!"

"What's wrong with the name?" Adam asked, feigning ignorance. "You're blond and you look kind of German."

Austin growled.

"I heard Germans fuck real good, and Adam was tellin' us earlier how good you are in the sack," Roscoe interjected.

Austin's hackles lowered as he regained some of his composure. "That better not be sarcasm old man."

"Course not. Sex and food are the two things I don't bullshit about. Remember?"

After a minute of what seemed like deliberation, Austin's angry expression gave way to a cocky grin. "Damn right I'm good."

"Yeah, you are just... so good," Adam cut in, his tone unconvincing. If Austin wasn't so dense, he would have picked up on it. "I was thinking, maybe we could try something different tonight." He gave an occasional glance to Roscoe, who discreetly nodded in approval.

"What's wrong with what I usually do?"

"Nothing! Buuuut I think we could switch it up. Maybe... go a little slower?"

Austin glared for a moment, but he eventually relented. "What else do you want me to do?"

Holy hell. It actually worked. I didn't know whether to be super annoyed or impressed.

"Well, you could try using your tongue more."

"What do you want me to do with my tongue?"

"When we get home, I'll show you. Deal?"

"Hmm," he said, slipping his arm around Adam's waist in what at first seemed like a sweet gesture. "Deal."

"Ow!" Adam shouted.

"That's right. Don't think I'm letting you off the hook for that name, you little shit."

# Reservoir Wolves

I sat on the couch watching a video on my phone while Adam kept flipping through the channels on the TV, never sticking to one show for very long. I would have said something, but from the wily glances he occasionally threw at me, that was precisely the reaction he was aiming for. While I didn't take the bait, I was also growing more irritated by the second, especially when he started increasing the volume.

Roscoe walked into the living room and paced silently for a moment, shakily holding a huge mug in one hand.

"Are you okay?" I asked. When he turned, the size of his dilated pupils freaked me out. He looked like a giant kitten trying to get adopted.

"Yeah," he replied, taking a few more sips from the mug. "Need to borrow yer phone."

My stare narrowed. "Why?"

"How much space you got on it?"

"I don't know. Sixty-or-so gigs. Again, why?"

Roscoe's ears shot up as he disappeared into the hall. Adam and I looked at one another while listening to something scrape against the wall in the bedroom. The werewolf reemerged wearing a pair of fake rounded spectacles and a square academic cap a size too small.

"Well? What do ya think?"

"I don't know what to think. You haven't explained anything!" I sat my phone on the arm of the couch and stood up. "Give me the coffee, Roscoe."

He poured the rest of the mug into his mouth. "This shit's kinda good. Could use a little Baileys to balance it out." His excitement turned to a wide-eyed panic. "I'm 'bout to go insane!"

"How much have you had to drink?"

"We ran out of beans. I—I don't think werewolves are supposed to drink so much of this stuff."

"Then why the hell do you keep drinking it?" I paused as what he said sank in. "Roscoe, that was two-and-a-half pounds of Robusta coffee! What should I do? Do I take you to the vet?"

"Listen to my idea," he said, talking much faster than before. "Sex Ed by Roscoe." He stepped closer and nudged me with his elbow. "Eh? Whaddya think?"

"I think I'm going to start hiding my coffee from now on."

"C'mon. It's a great idea for porn. I'm the big bad wolf that shows up to teach you all about sex, and you pretend to be all doe-eyed and innocent."

"Heh, yeah. *Pretend*," Adam muttered under his breath.

The room flashed red for a second.

"Think about it, Cody. We gotta have an angle that's kinda unique or we'll get buried. You know how much half-turn-on-werewolf porn there is?"

I shook my head.

"A lot. A LOT a lot." He rubbed his head. "Shouldn't be surprised, I guess."

"What about the costume idea?"

"It wasn't as unique as I thought." He took my hands in his and gave me that wide-eyed, watery stare, only this time, his wired pupils made it creepy rather than cute. "It could be really fun."

"You're not using my phone for this."

"But I don't got nothin' to record us."

"Use mine," Adam said with a smirk before fishing his phone out of his pocket and tossing it to Roscoe. "Cody's phone is a cheap piece of shit. This one's got some great camera features."

"My phone's cheap because I'm not an idiot that spends over a grand on something I barely use to make phone calls."

Adam ignored me and hurried over to Roscoe. "You can record in 4k, and you can even use the slo-mo feature for when things really get rough. It's even waterproof."

"Hmm," Roscoe said, stroking the thicker fur around his chin. "That could come in handy. I got a great idea." He looked back at me. "Don't leave or nothin'."

"Wasn't planning on it, but I might now," I mumbled, sitting back on the couch to resume the video I was watching earlier.

Roscoe had been in our bedroom for over an hour with the door closed, though occasionally stepped out the back door. Austin kept to himself in the garage working on something with his power tools. Adam and I finally settled on a show but had to crank up the volume to drown out all the drilling and hammering.

"What the hell is he doing in there? I'm about to say something."

"Don't you dare," Adam said, kicking his feet up on the couch to block me. "He's leaving me alone. That's all that matters."

"I thought you guys were getting along better. Did he do any of that stuff you wanted?"

The half-turn ground his teeth.

"I take that as a no."

"He was so close. So close, but then he got all weird because I was on top and was 'telling him what to do.' So, it was business as usual. Austin's specialty: hard and fast with no foreplay." He muted the television. "You don't seem like you're all that interested in Roscoe's idea. Why don't you let me do it?"

A slight pang sent a warm flash through my face. "Don't subject yourself to Roscoe's perversions."

"I think it'll be fun, and if he's as good as you say he is, it could be what I need."

The entire room turned red again, and the annoyance from earlier quickly manifested into something I didn't expect. "Really. It's not necessary."

"You're just going to bore everyone and kill boners."

"Like anyone will find your gaping asshole convincing enough to be an innocent high school boy."

Adam jumped up from the couch. "You're a huge pussy."

"Well, yeah. Gaping, ground hamburger anuses are gross."

"You're afraid Roscoe would prefer me over you."

"You know there's like forty other werewolves in this town, right? If you're that thirsty for attention, go set up a lemonade stand outside with a glory hole."

"I'm gonna ask him," he said in a playful tone before turning toward the hallway.

A low growl left my throat, and everything got darker. "If you step into that room, I will throw you through every window in this fucking house."

The red hue disappeared when I realized Adam was actually winning.

"Why are you so weird about this?" Adam asked, his tone a little less teasing. "You were fine when Darryl was with him, and it's not like you're serious about him. You even said that yourself."

"Just drop it."

The bedroom door opened, and Roscoe strolled into the living room with a grin so obnoxious that I began to reconsider Adam's request.

"You ready?" he asked, handing me a wrinkled sheet of paper.

"What's this?"

"It's yer script."

I looked down at his terrible handwriting, reading through each of my lines. "This is... surprisingly tame."

"And you were worried."

"I still am. This just makes me more suspicious." I folded the paper as Roscoe handed me a dirty white T-shirt with a smiley emoji on it and a red and white baseball hat. "Oh, come on."

"It's yer costume. It's what a high school kid would wear."

"Dude, I'm one giant lollipop shy of this being pedo bait. I'll just wear what I'm wearing."

"Nah. It's gotta be that." He licked his lips. "Only that. No pants."

"That doesn't make any sense either—"

"It's porn, Cody! Fucking hell. You're getting people off, not making a cinematic masterpiece," Adam interrupted, looking up at Roscoe. "Let me do it."

Roscoe's ears perked up. "Really?"

The hair on the back of my neck stood straight up, and I reluctantly put on the baseball cap. "Tell me what you want me to do," I muttered, slipping into the T-shirt.

The perverted old werewolf rubbed his hands together. "Oh boy. When we get to the room, take off yer pants and underwear, then sit at the desk."

"What desk?" I asked, then darted into the bedroom. A little wooden table and chair sat in front of a chalkboard Roscoe had hastily screwed into the wall. It was slightly crooked with 'Sex Ed with Roscoe' scribbled in pink chalk in the middle. "How? How did you get all this in here without me noticing?"

Roscoe's tail wagged, and he pointed to Adam's phone, which was tied to the handle of our vacuum cleaner. "You said the phone was waterproof, right?"

Adam nodded.

"Are we taking this into the shower or something? Because you need one."

"Uh, yeah. A shower," he said with that same devious expression from earlier.

I unfolded the sheet of paper. "I didn't see it in the script."

Roscoe snatched the paper away. "It's more fun to improvise, don't you think?"

"I don't like the way you're looking at me right now."

"If Cody doesn't want to, I'll volun—"

I shoved Adam out of the bedroom before slamming the door shut.

"It would have been more fun with the two of you," he said, straightening the camera phone. "Coulda been a real classroom."

I remained silent but didn't take my heated gaze off him.

"I know. You don't like threesomes." He snatched the cap off my head, putting it back on my head the other way. "All right kiddo. Pants off."

"Do NOT call me that on camera," I said, slipping off my pants. "This is creepy enough as it is."

"Underwear too," he added.

"I'm in a classroom. Why would I sit at a desk with a shirt and nothing else?"

Roscoe swiped his finger across the phone screen and tapped once. "You didn't read the syllabus, did you?" He walked to the front of the desk, pointing at the seat. "Now yer in detention."

I cleared my throat, stiffening up a bit as my nerves set in. The camera and I never got along, and as a half-turn, I was even more self-conscious.

"Sorry, *sir*. I forgot my homework." I plopped down onto the little wooden chair, which was cold against my bare skin.

"How 'bout we start with some easy lessons?" He wrote something on the board, then moved out of the way so he could point to it with a yardstick. "Now read this."

"I'm not reading that out loud."

He let out a nervous laugh and looked over at the phone. "We're live."

"What?" I hissed through my teeth. "This wasn't supposed to—"

"Do you want another hour of detention young man, or do you wanna read the word for the rest of the class?"

I let out a sigh, half covering my face with my hand. "Bussy."

"What was that?"

"Bussy, you fucking—" I said louder, deliberating the pros and cons of committing murder on a live stream. "Mr. Roscoe."

He put both palms on the desk and leaned in. "Now, show me where it is," he demanded, then licked the drool from his chops before turning to the camera, adjusting his fake spectacles. "Half-turn twinks, just like humans, have cute little boy pussies."

I wanted to die. In fact, if this continued for much longer, I'd probably end up doing just that.

"Why don't *you* show me?" I asked, making my tone sound as threatening as possible.

"Well, all right." He pulled the desk toward him and lifted me up before turning my bare ass toward the camera.

"Put me down!"

"As you can see," he said, struggling to hold me still while slapping the yardstick against my rear end, "this is half-turn boy pussy, and it don't ever get too loose neither, no matter what you put in there. It's a scientific anomaly, baffling scholars for generations."

"I'm gonna kill you, I swear to God!" I shouted, punching his back as hard as I could. His other arm locked my lower half in place as he parted my ass with his fingers.

"I could shove my entire arm up there and he'd walk away like nothing happened. Isn't that amazin'?" He finally sat me down, and I threw a punch at his stomach, which didn't even make him flinch. "Ooh! Looks like we got some viewers," he said, looking over at my phone, which was tuned into the stream.

"When the hell did you get my phone, Roscoe?"

Instead of acknowledging me, he scrolled through the fan chat messages.

"That ain't a bad suggestion, uh—monsterfucker47."

"Are we even bothering staying in character anymore, or has your goldfish brain already moved onto something else?"

Roscoe turned back toward me. "We got any grapefruit?"

"Can we try to keep this somewhat normal?"

"Dude, we're up to fifteen viewers," he whispered, still reading through the chat. "They really like you. I got a great idea."

"Oh God. Let's just fuck or something so we can end this."

Roscoe grabbed an old USB phone charging cable and pointed to the chair. "Have a seat. The real lesson's about to start."

"What are you doing with that?"

"Trust me," he whispered with a look I definitely didn't trust. "We got twenty viewers now, so we need to take this up a notch."

Holding the cord, he grabbed my arms and held them behind my back, forcing me into the seat. The more I struggled, the stronger his grip became.

"All right, I don't want to do this anymore."

He looked at the camera and laughed nervously. "Half-turns like Cody love to play hard to get, but they're all kinky little monkeys." Roscoe slipped the wire around one wrist and tied it to the arm of the chair before working on the other end. As much as I tried, I couldn't loosen it.

"When I get out of this—"

He grabbed my face with one hand and shoved a cheek retractor into my mouth.

"I assure no half-turn will be harmed in the making of this video," Roscoe said as he turned the chair toward the camera and got down on one knee. "Rosebud798, thanks fer the twenty. This one's fer you." He ran his long tongue up and down my shaft, soaking everything in his spit.

My eyes rolled back as he went to work, and all I could do was moan incoherent words while spittle roped down my chin, as the device he used made it impossible to close my mouth or swallow properly. This wasn't at all what he usually did during foreplay; instead, it was as if his goal was getting me off as fast as possible, even going as far as slipping a finger into my ass. Thankfully, he had trimmed and smoothed out his claws earlier today.

I jerked, tilting my head back as I got closer, grateful that Roscoe was putting a quick end to this. With one final shudder, I moaned out, fully expecting release, but instead, he pulled away at the last second. The red haze returned as I realized what he was doing.

"Oooo, he's all riled up now," Roscoe said, giving a concerned look toward the camera. The fake sentiment didn't last long as a wicked smile snaked up his maw. "Want me to do it again? You know these guys get dangerous when you tease 'em too much." He squinted at my phone. "Hell yeah. Fifty viewers."

He started sucking my dick again, and I got this strange feeling, like sandpaper rubbing beneath my skin. Predictably, I was on the brink and Roscoe pulled away. This time, a warbling howl left my throat. The rage coursing through my body was so intense I could hear my own pulse in my ears.

"Yer doin' great. They love it," he whispered, and licked the crook of my neck. Standing again, he turned back toward the camera. "Ah shit, that's a good idea, ThisIsAdamCodylol420. I never met a half-turn that didn't love a bit of piss play. You guys wanna see that?"

My eyes went wide, and I rapidly shook my head at Roscoe. It seemed Adam wanted a war, and once this was over, that was exactly what he was going to get. How was he even watching the stream? His phone was in here.

"He wants it. Don't you want it, you frustrated little monkey?" He held up a finger and got even more excited. "Oh! I know what'll make this better." He trotted over to my laptop and pulled up my PearTunes account. "Ever heard this song before?"

An acoustic guitar started playing in a familiar tune, before a bass guitar layered in with clapping. Roscoe gripped his dick with one hand as he shuffled playfully around the chair to the beat. Then he started singing the lyrics to *Stuck in the Middle with You.*

I let out a shrieking yell I'm sure the neighbors could hear as I struggled in vain to loosen the cords.

As he continued singing, Roscoe swung left, letting loose a stream of urine that soaked my chest. He was actually doing it. Of all the shit he'd pulled. Once I killed him, Adam was next.

The stream of piss went the other way when he belted more of the lyrics, this time getting into my mouth. I let out a gurgled scream of rage, the room almost blood-red as the sandpapery feeling on my skin got worse. He kept his cock pointed at my chest, pissing while thrusting his hips in time with the music.

*"Here I am, stuck in the—"*

With an ear-splitting snap, the arm of the chair separated, and I pounced upward, breaking the other arm while holding the detached piece of wood in my hand. Before Roscoe could react, I leapt onto his back and began beating him repeatedly over the head.

"Shit! Cody, I'm sorry!"

There were only flashes of light and a few grunts and words, but it was all so hazy. The detached chair arm finally broke, but that didn't deter me from clinging to him with my claws as I punched him over and over again. He hobbled to the camera and gave a shaky thumbs up.

"That's all the time we have for today—ow—and, uh hopefully you come back and watch us again," Roscoe said before ending the stream. He was able to reach the nape of my neck and give it a squeeze, which made my entire body go limp.

"Calm down, Cody." He held my arms in place, and the angry haze subsided. "Damn, I didn't think you'd get that upset."

I didn't respond at first, my head swimming as though I'd just gotten off a Tilt-a-Whirl.

"What the hell just happened?"

He let me go and sat on our mattress while rubbing his head, which was bleeding a little. "I guess I went a bit too far. Next time, I'll have to make sure to tie you up better."

I limped over to the bedroom door, my dripping shirt leaving a beaded trail. "Do werewolves grow things back?"

It took Roscoe a few seconds to respond. "Whhyyy?"

"Let's say that tonight, when you fall asleep, I cut something off with a chef's knife. Will it grow back?"

"Okay, Cody. I know yer upset, but... man, I'm feelin' kind of woozy."

I turned around, grimacing. "You should go to sleep," I growled before walking into the hall toward the bathroom, holding the broken chair arm. "I've got a half-turn to beat the shit out of."

I sat on the couch in a bathrobe, scrolling through social media while Roscoe was either giving me space or sleeping off a mild concussion. Adam had hightailed it out of the house before I could get to him, and Austin was gone too. The quiet was a wonderful change of pace from the rushing blood through my ears earlier.

Taking in a deep breath, I looked down at the thicker, fur-like hair covering my arms and chest. It wasn't far along like Adam's, but my body had definitely undergone some kind of change. Even my teeth felt a little sharper.

Cautious footfalls crept through the hallway, stopping at the bathroom as the door shut.

"You better clean all the piss off that floor," I shouted from the couch to no response.

The toilet flushed, and the bathroom door opened. Sluggish footsteps grew louder until a regretful-looking werewolf poked his head out from around the corner.

"We uh... we got like a thousand followers off that," he said, his ears sinking off to the side. "I'm sorry."

"You're not sorry! You'd do it again, wouldn't you?"

"We just made five grand! You bet I would!"

"Wait, what? Are you for real?"

"People loved it."

"You were reenacting that scene in *Reservoir Dogs* while pissing on me. How the hell did that get a thousand followers?"

"Maybe it was the dynamic," he said, plopping down next to me. I snarled, and he scooted a little farther away. "The angrier you got, the more people loved it. Comedy and porn. That's somethin' ya don't see every day."

"I don't care how much money we made. If you ever do something like that again, I may hold true to my threat earlier."

Roscoe grinned.

"I'm not joking."

"Look, I'm genuinely sorry. I thought you'd find it funny. Hell, I'll let you pee on me next time. How's that sound?"

"Why are these words still coming out of your mouth right now? I don't want to talk about it. I don't want to think about it. I don't even want to remember it. As far as we're concerned, it never happened."

He opened his mouth, but I cut him off.

"You're also going to give me two-thirds of that money."

"Wait a minute! That's not what we agreed on."

There was a dim orange reflection on Roscoe's face from my glowing eyes. This was happening way too frequently, and with all that had just transpired, I was starting to worry.

The front door slammed open, and Adam and Austin stomped inside, yelling at one another.

"It's because your little ass is mine. Kuu rules."

"I'm over your bullshit, Austin."

"I fuck you, what? Ten times a day? That's still not enough for you?"

I rubbed my head, wishing I could go back to the quiet house moments ago. "What's wrong with you guys now?"

"Let me ask you something," Austin said, standing in front of the couch. "Would you go out and fuck half the town, or stay true to your kuu mate?"

I cast a glance at Roscoe. "Right now, I don't want to fuck anyone. At all. Probably ever again."

Austin sniffed the air. "Did someone piss in here?"

Adam let out a laugh but quickly slunk away once I settled my glare on him.

*The next day*

It was breezy and cool, and the air had a sweet smell to it. The first day of fall had been a week ago, but it hadn't felt like it until now. I walked barefoot through the yard, stopping short of the woods. The last encounter I'd had out there replayed in my head, and I kept that gem in my pocket. I still didn't understand what it was, and there was only one werewolf in town that likely knew the answer.

All the blood rushed from my face when I realized I'd forgotten to go back to see the mayor yesterday. In a panic, I rushed inside to throw on a fresh shirt before slipping into a pair of shoes.

"What's wrong with you?" Roscoe asked, holding another mug of coffee.

"I'll be back later." I stopped and examined the half-empty pot of coffee on the counter. "That's your last cup. I mean it."

"Yer killin' me here. I can't drink, I can't smoke weed, and now I can't have coffee."

"That's because you have no self-control." I grabbed his wrist, checking his pulse. "You're shaking. How much did you drink?"

"We may need more coffee beans again."

"That's it. I'm cutting you off. For real this time."

"I'm maybe a hundred freakin' years old. You can't tell me what to do." Roscoe spoke so fast his tongue could barely keep up with his words. He then let out a rapid bout of laughter before taking another sip.

"Yeah," Adam cut in, snaking his way next to Roscoe. He took the werewolf's broad arms in his and leaned his head against him.

"You know what? Go ahead and drink the rest. And after that, why don't you take Adam to the bedroom." I leaned in and whispered in Roscoe's ear. "Do to him what you did to me yesterday. For the fans."

Adam grinned. "Giving up already?" He looked up at Roscoe. "So, what are we doing, big daddy? I mean, Professor Roscoe."

"Oh boy, yer gonna love it. Go grab a chair from the dining room and uh, I need to get somethin' from the garage."

I opened the door, grinning as I stepped outside.

Being a half-turn had its perks, despite the numerous drawbacks, one of them being stamina. Whether it was hours cleaning the house or a ten-minute sprint to town without having to stop to catch my breath, I couldn't deny how much more physically capable I was now.

I slowed to a light jog upon reaching the city hall building. There weren't many people around except for a man in a black suit sitting outside on the bench smoking a cigar. He had ashy dark-brown hair and a black five o'clock shadow, kind of contrasting one another. He looked both old and young, mature eyes and graying hair combined with smooth brown skin. I'd never see a middle-aged man so gorgeous in my life. I nearly tripped over the unevenly set sidewalk while trying to check him out without him noticing.

As I approached the door, I gave it a tug, but it held tight.

"It is locked," the man on the bench said in a slightly familiar accent. "It was open yesterday, though."

"Thanks," I replied, taking a few steps back before turning around. The trip wasn't a complete waste, because I still had to replace the coffee Roscoe used up. I started back the way I'd come when I heard the man behind me stand.

"The next time I tell you to meet at a certain time, I expect you to show up."

I froze. A warm breath pulsed against the back of my neck, and with it came the scent of strong tobacco and rich, spicy cologne. The man had somehow appeared only a few inches away from me. When I turned, a quick flash of silver in his irises betrayed who he was.

"Mayor?"

He grinned and took a few quick puffs of his cigar, blowing the smoke away from us. "Have a seat." The man gave me a stern look. "I have important matters to discuss with you, Mr. Schultz."

# Chapter 14

# Mysterious Motives

The mayor sat uncomfortably close, enjoying his cigar without a word for what seemed like minutes. The situation was so awkward that I wanted to stand and run, but I kind of knew what he was doing. It was the same thing he'd done the other day. His furrowed bushy eyebrows and glacial scowl had everyone cowering. His human form was no less intimidating, just smaller.

I began drumming a nervous rhythm onto my lap, and a cigar appeared in front of my face.

"Put this in your mouth."

"Usually, I get to know a guy a little better first," I said with a short-lived burst of anxious laughter, which was met with a silent, stony glare. I stopped smiling and cleared my throat. "I don't smoke."

"These are not cigarettes." He leaned in closer, his mouth inches from my ear. "Put it in your mouth, draw in the smoke, but don't inhale."

His powerful werewolf musk pulled at my nostrils, hidden just beneath the fabric of his suit, mixing with the rich tobacco and expensive cologne. It was hard to breathe him in without the accompanying half-turn arousal. The low growl in his voice didn't make things easier.

As his hand made its way to the back of my neck, I reluctantly took the cigar and placed the moistened end between my lips before slowly sucking in the smoke. Following his instructions, I didn't inhale, but I also hated the taste—at first. What followed after was a clean, peppery, almost chocolaty flavor.

"Oh," I said, taking in another draw and then blowing the smoke away. The mayor gently massaged the back of my neck with his thumb as I handed back the cigar. Even though it was a friendly gesture, I couldn't help but feel as though one wrong move could mean having the life choked out of me. "That's pretty good."

He examined the cigar for a moment. "We didn't have these in the old country. Our kind was regarded as the offspring of Iblīs, and our condition was Allah's punishment for the sins our families committed. Whether there was merit to the myth or not, werewolves had to learn to live together or die alone in the howling sands." He took a drag, held it in his mouth for a few moments before blowing the smoke away from me. "The taste sometimes reawakens memories I thought I'd forgotten. I can remember the circles around the fire, the stories. We would sing—and even satisfy our uncontrollable carnal desires. We understood we were different from humans, but many of us would feel shame nevertheless. Despite the harsh reality of living the way we did, the pack was strong, and that was how we survived."

He carefully snuffed out the end of the cigar against the metal frame of the bench, exposing a smooth, silver band on his ring finger.

"A long life is a blessing, but it is not without its challenges. We are still mortal, and so too are our brains. There is only so much we can remember before memories fade and important lessons are forgotten. When we were in the desert, it was difficult to hold on to ourselves and not become the beasts the humans believed we were. Without leadership and order, our pack fell into disarray, losing its humanity altogether. Eventually we split into two sects: the Whasha and the Midna. This marked the end of civility and unity among our kind."

His eyes pierced me in silence for a moment as if waiting for me to respond.

"Why are you telling me this?"

"Werewolves living in society are Midna." He pointed away from the buildings, toward the imposing forest in the distance. "In the wilds, we become animals. If we go there, we lose all of who we are, and we fall prey to the malevolence always hidden from sight. We forget things we should not, like your friend did. Roscoe, was it?"

"What does this have to do with me?"

"I cannot have unruly and undisciplined werewolves roving about the town. Such behavior makes us susceptible to the Whasha and the witches." He pulled something out of his pocket before placing it into my palm. It was a heavy antique flip lighter made of solid gold. "Your kuu mate reeks of the Whasha."

"What's this?" I asked, flipping the lid of the lighter, which had no fuel in it.

"A gift," he said softly before a growl returned. "It is also a warning."

I looked up at him, swallowing the lump in my throat.

"I have eyes and ears everywhere. You have a half-wit Whasha with no sense of decency, and a half-turn brat that has not learned to keep his emotions in check." He bared his sharper human teeth at me and growled. "And that... *half-turn... Bernie Blödmann*, is maladjusted and mentally unstable, but it is you I am most concerned about."

"Excuse me? I'm the most responsible person in that house!"

"Responsibility has nothing to do with it." His eyes glowed silver for a moment, and the sunlight turned almost unbearably bright, everything flashing before settling back into a normal hue. "You possess potent vironoct, and half-turns like you are exceedingly rare. There are rituals in place to detect and find those suspected of having it before it awakens. We found you first. Did you think your assignment to Norwich was mere happenstance?"

"So that guy I was talking to—"

"Was on my secret payroll," Mosavi finished, grinning.

"How do you know I'm so special?"

"I wasn't all the way sure until our meeting the other day. Plus, how many werewolves do you know that were half-turns in their twenties?"

"Well, there's a werewolf back in White Dunes—"

"I am well aware of him," the mayor interrupted, baring his teeth. "Wasted potential."

"So, I'm gonna be like Darryl?" Just the thought made me feel so much better about my condition.

"I surely hope not," the mayor muttered, his eyes narrowing again. "I expect much more from you. I had planned on keeping you locked away in my residence, but I was... advised against it. So instead, I am forced to take a more hands-off approach."

"Why the hell would you lock me up? What did I do?"

"You have no idea how dangerous you are. Inexperienced half-turns that possess the kind of power you do could abuse it—or attract those that wish to control you to the detriment of werewolf kind."

I sat in silence while watching a few humans stroll by, talking and laughing amongst themselves, none of them seeming to mind a half-turn sitting just a few steps away. I tried to absorb Mosavi's words, but most of them were rather hard to believe. When I'd lost myself to rage yesterday after Roscoe's little stunt, I kind of understood the dangerous part, but this whole alpha thing? All I had to do was look in the mirror to call bullshit on that.

"So you're... human," I said, steering the topic of discussion away from me. "How do you do it?"

"The same way *Bernie* was able to revert to half-turn form, but reverting all the way to human is something unique to elders of the vironoct."

"I should have known you'd figured that out."

"I am not a moron." He pointed to the lighter in my hand. "Myth, religion, superstition—they all have one thing in common: ignorance. Reality is much more enigmatic, and so are the magics we possess. The same enchantments that bind half-turns to werewolves also allow some of us to take on the human visage, but it has limits."

I flipped the lighter onto its other side, noting an inscription in Arabic. "Why is this a warning?"

The mayor grinned again, exposing all his now-sharper teeth, which looked more disturbing in his human form. "That is now a part of you. You will carry it at all times."

"You didn't—" I stiffened as a growl rumbled from his throat, much deeper than his human voice should have been able to produce.

"That is your answer," he continued, his teeth growing longer as he shifted uncomfortably on the bench. "I will give you two months to learn to get your pack under control. Think of it as a test of dominance."

"They're not my pack. We barely know each other."

The mayor's sclera darkened as his irises burned orange. "Anything they do from now on will be a reflection of your leadership—or lack thereof." He stood and stretched. "Now, if you'll excuse me, I am reaching those limitations I mentioned earlier. I don't want to ruin such an expensive Italian suit."

"I'm a half-turn. How am I supposed to get them to listen, especially Roscoe?"

"There are ways to force werewolves into submission using the vironoct." He leaned in uncomfortably close, his eyes turning silver.

"I could teach you, but I would have to keep you. Would you consent to that?"

The scenery around me brightened to a blinding blue, but I snapped my gaze downward, away from his. "No. And forcing people to do what you want isn't leadership."

He grabbed my chin and turned my head until I made eye contact with him again. His eyes were back to their normal orange. "Did you know that hiding Austin and lying to the bureau is a serious federal offense?"

My pulse quickened, and my palms began to sweat.

"It would be a shame if the proper authorities were alerted."

I chucked the lighter a few yards away into the grass. "You can't threaten to spill a secret after revealing one of your own. You really think these *proper authorities* would approve of a werewolf running a town?"

The mayor studied me carefully before turning away, stiffly pacing himself toward the city hall entrance. "Who would believe a half-turn?"

"What is this game you're playing with me?"

Using the keys he pulled from his pocket, he unlocked the door and pushed it open. When he turned back around, thick fur covered his human face. "I am not asking for the impossible. Simply keep your pack in check, and if you cannot do that, I will need to explore more intrusive options." Without another word, he stepped inside and closed the door.

As I turned away, a loud rip pulled my attention.

"Shit! My new suit!" he shouted from inside.

I couldn't help but laugh at the bit of karma.

Mechanical noises whirred from the closed-off garage as I approached the house. Austin had spent most of his time there, and while it was nice he'd found something to keep him occupied, that much isolation couldn't have been good for him.

The mayor's warning was still fresh, despite the unintentionally hilarious way the meeting ended. As I walked into the house, I was greeted by a suspicious scene. Adam and Roscoe were sitting together at the dining room table, laughing.

"Welcome home, buddy," Adam said, his expression infuriatingly sly—or was it content? Either way, I could feel my anger reaching the boiling point.

"What's going on?"

Roscoe held up a bottle of water. "Had to rehydrate."

I turned to Adam and wrinkled my nose. "You... actually let him do that? God, you're disgusting. You're all disgusting!"

"Why are you making a big deal about it? It was nice to just get fucked the right way for a change."

"What?" I flushed as blood angrily pulsed in my ears. "What do you mean, fucked?"

Roscoe's ears fell as he rubbed the back of his head. "Well, you see... the pee stuff kinda works better with you, 'cause you don't enjoy it."

"I hate you both," I muttered before stomping into the kitchen to put the bag of coffee beans in the cabinet.

Roscoe jumped up from his chair and shuffled behind me. "Ooo," he said, sniffing the air. "Those smell good."

"Don't touch my beans." I slapped him away. "And don't touch me either."

"He was too into it, so I didn't go all the way with the original script," Roscoe whispered in my ear. "They didn't like him as much as they liked you."

"If that's supposed to make me feel better, it doesn't." I shut the cabinet door as a sheet of paper slowly slid in front of me on the counter. It had a lopsided drawing of a werewolf with big, teary eyes holding a heart out with the word 'Sowwy' written on it.

"I'm quite the arteest."

"You're quite the asshole." I picked up the paper and examined it before folding it neatly into my pocket. "You gave yourself abs. Now that's hilarious."

Roscoe sniffed me and backed away. "Kinda expected you to smell like sex."

"You really don't know me, do you?"

"Shit. I'd have done it if I was alone with that guy."

I turned around and folded my arms. "When I read about the elders in Darryl's book, I thought they would be these gross, ratty-looking wolfmen that could barely walk. That guy has to be at least two hundred years old, and he could probably take Austin like he's nothing."

"Oh, he definitely could," Roscoe replied. "They ain't considered alphas for nothing. When we get older, we get stronger and smarter."

"I guess you're the exception?"

Roscoe smiled. "See? This is why we work. I do shit that pisses you off, and you throw insults."

"What are you guys doing in there?" Adam called out from the living room in a teasing tone. "Is Roscoe talking about how amazing I was?"

"He's just bein' a kid. Don't tell him what I said about people liking you more," Roscoe whispered.

"Yeah. You were amazing, Adam. Congrats," I said loud enough so Adam could hear before lowering my voice again. "I've got some bad news."

"What did he say?"

"He knows about Austin, and he said some pretty disturbing shit. I think we should go back to Darryl."

Roscoe leaned back against the counter. "Still have the moving truck. I can put everything back into storage, but I don't know about Darryl."

"But he said—"

"We can't," Roscoe interrupted sharply. "We need to find a way without runnin' back to him."

"I know what you did was awful, but we're in a bind. This place hasn't sat right with me since we got here, and having an elder watching our every move makes it worse."

"So, what does he want, exactly?"

"I think he's holding something back, or he's not being completely honest. He gave me some kind of ultimatum. I have to make sure you guys act normal and follow the rules."

"That's it?" Roscoe asked, looking a little puzzled. "Easy."

"Yeah. Sure it is. I bet that room smells like piss still, doesn't it?"

"Actually, it's in their bedroom. Austin might be a little mad about that later, but that's future Roscoe's problem."

"He threatened to lock me away in his house."

"Pfft. He ain't gonna make good on that if he ain't already done it."

"And how the hell do you know? He sounded pretty serious to me."

Roscoe's tail swayed. "Just seems kinda silly if he's always gonna be watching ya anyways. Plus, this all sounds like he's just tryin' to get under yer skin."

"Can we please just go? I won't be able to sleep at night if we stay here."

He grabbed the keys from a hook screwed into the wall above the light switch. "How about we take a nice little drive? We didn't get to see all that much when we got here."

"Really? A drive? After what I just said?"

"It'll calm you down, and there ain't no real police around here to pull me over—well, there are, but I think they're all werewolves, so don't gotta worry about bein' tased."

"Yeah, you're right. Now when you piss the cops off, they can actually beat the shit out of you."

Roscoe's tail wagged faster. "You ever driven?"

"No."

He tossed me the keys.

"Are you crazy? That truck doesn't belong to us."

"I'll teach you," he said, grabbing my hand as he led me out of the kitchen. "We'll be back later, Adam. Gonna go fer a drive."

Adam scrambled to his feet. "I wanna come."

"We want some alone time, and Roscoe needs an ass that doesn't look like Gruta Casa de Pedra," I snapped, pointing at the door leading to the garage. "Plus you need to make sure he's okay."

"He's fine." The half-turn's expression went from excited to angry. "I want to go with Roscoe."

I now understood what was happening. He wasn't trying to make me jealous, and he wanted another werewolf to cling to since Darryl was hundreds of miles away. Roscoe was his new distraction from Austin's neglect. Once again, I had to weigh feeling sorry for him while also keeping him from monopolizing Roscoe's time.

"I said no." I held up the keys. "I'm learning to drive, and I don't want you distracting me."

Roscoe said nothing.

"Let's get one thing straight. You might be a couple years older, but you are *not* the head of this household! If Roscoe doesn't want me to go, he can tell me himself." Adam brushed up against the old werewolf, gently running his fingers along Roscoe's stomach. "It'll be more fun."

"Never had two half-turns fightin' over me before."

I bared my teeth, staring directly into Roscoe's eyes.

"Uh… listen, Adam. I gotta side with Cody here." He leaned in and whispered something in Adam's ear.

The disappointed half-turn nodded. "Promise?"

"Sure," Roscoe responded.

The edges of Adam's mouth lifted slightly, giving him the obnoxious, imp-like appearance from earlier. "Have fun," he said before lifting his gaze to Roscoe. "I'll see *you* later."

A bubble of resentment turned my vision red once again for a moment, but I couldn't show Adam it was bothering me. Over the last few days, the two of us had stoked up the most unusual rivalry—over Roscoe. Roscoe! My plan to make Adam jealous had backfired horribly, and while this was mostly my fault, all I could fantasize about lately was chucking him into the crater of an active volcano, or at the very least, giving him a firm, back-handed slap.

"You ready?"

"Yeeeah," I responded through my teeth as Roscoe held the door open. After unlocking the driver's side, I climbed in the moving truck and unlocked the passenger door. As soon as we were both inside, I put on my seatbelt and shoved the key into the ignition. "What did you promise him?"

"Nothin' big."

I gripped the steering wheel tighter but didn't respond.

"I swear, it's no big deal. Start her up."

"I really shouldn't be doing this. It's illegal and dangerous."

"Cody, let me ask you something," he said, rolling his window down so he could lay his arm against the door. "When's the last time you took a risk—just did somethin' you normally don't do?"

"Never. My luck's shitty enough as it is. I don't need to tempt fate, either."

"Think about it. You wouldn't be here with me right now if you hadn't taken some risks. Hell, you'd probably still be in Kansas."

"Montana," I corrected. "And everything I've done, I had to because my back was against the wall."

"So, you only do anything when you have to?"

"That's not what I mean. Don't twist my words."

"All right. I think I know what I need to do," Roscoe said, his tail rubbing against the vinyl seat. "Start the truck, put her in reverse—"

He put one hand over my seat belt release. "I forgot to take a piss before I came out here."

"Excuse me?"

"Maybe you can drive us a little ways out of town so I can find a nice tree."

"Go use the bathroom, Roscoe!"

The wicked grin he gave exposed every sharp tooth in his mouth. "It's gettin' hard to hold it."

"Why are you doing this to me again?" I shouted, starting the vehicle. I tried to pull the shifter down to reverse, but it wouldn't budge. "It doesn't work."

"You gotta push the brake in first, silly."

I hit the gas pedal by mistake, revving the engine.

"That ain't the brake," he said calmly.

"I know that now, thanks," I said, pushing the brake before putting the truck in reverse.

"You might wanna put it back in park," Roscoe said. "You forgot to adjust yer mirrors first."

"Oh, you'll have to excuse me. I don't know what the hell I'm doing and you are stressing me out more!"

Roscoe shuffled uncomfortably in his seat.

"Please, go to the bathroom. I can't deal with this and drive at the same time."

"I told ya. You gotta find me a suitable tree outside of town."

"Hopefully, I find one with a thick enough branch to hang you from."

"You might wanna hurry but stay calm."

"You are so lucky I'm not a werewolf." My hands trembled as I adjusted the rearview mirror so I could see behind me. Then I moved the little knob for the side mirrors.

"Make sure you move them so that you can see behind, but you can't see none of the truck. It'll help with the blind spots."

I did as he said and quickly shifted the truck in reverse, this time able to see behind me.

"Slowly take yer foot off the brake and back out of the yard. Don't need to hit the gas, just keep yer foot close to the brake."

The truck slowly moved out of the yard, and I turned the wheel enough that I was able to get it all the way onto the asphalt. I wasn't paying attention, and my foot hit the gas.

"Whoa!" Roscoe shouted as I slammed on the brake, the force pushing us back against the seats.

The scent of pee caught my nose, and I looked over. "Roscoe."

"That scared me a little."

"This is only going to get worse. Please, I'm begging you."

"I guess you better drive more carefully then." He gave another sharp grin. "Think of me as a box of unprotected wine glasses. If you slam on the brakes, turn too hard, hit the gas unexpectedly—there's gonna be a mess."

"You've made your point. Come on, man. Don't do this to me."

He shuffled in his seat some more. "I shouldn't have had all that coffee."

"Fuck," I said, putting the car in drive.

"Just tap the gas a bit, no need to floor it. Try to stay in the middle of the road."

"I hate you so much."

We made it five miles outside of town, and luckily there were hardly any cars on the road, which made an already harrowing situation a little less so. The longer I drove, the easier the truck was to handle, but Roscoe swayed faster in his seat.

"All right. This is good," he said, holding his crotch. "That's a nice tree over there. Go ahead and pull over."

I did as he said, and before the car could come to a complete stop, he leaped out and ran into the woods. With a steady exhale, I shifted the vehicle into park and turned it off, my legs still shaking from the adrenaline. This was the first time I'd ever driven anything, and I had to admit, it was a little more fun than I thought.

After what seemed like five minutes, Roscoe strode up to the truck and playfully hopped back into the passenger's seat.

"Muuuch better," he said, patting me on the back. "Perfect tree. Not bad, kiddo."

"Don't ever call me that." I smiled at him. "And I still hate you."

"These are the best years of yer life. We don't stay young forever—well, I mean, I guess we kinda do, but still. Bein' young means you get to try new shit and fuck up, and then try more shit and fuck that up, too." He rested his padded hand on my leg. "I kinda wish I could do it again, but I know too much now."

"I find that hard to believe."

"You know what's funny? Darryl was kinda like you. The difference between you and him is, he knew when to take risks, and he also knew when to have fun. Yer too afraid to do either, and that's why yer so crabby all the time."

"That doesn't make any sense. I'm comfortable not taking risks, and I'll have fun when we're not running from someone or trying not to be homeless."

"Did you have fun driving?" he asked.

"It was okay."

Roscoe raised an eyebrow.

"It was a little fun, yes. I can't believe I did it."

"You said you only take risks when yer back's against a wall. Think about how much better this experience would have been if you made the choice on yer own terms instead of me forcing you? Think about all the times life forced you to take action, and now imagine doing those things because you wanted to experience something new. Yeah, maybe your life would have turned out the same, but the journey would have been fun instead of traumatic."

"It's never fun, Roscoe. I'm always worried. Even when I make big choices, there are so many awful scenarios that play out in my head."

"You got me for now," Roscoe said, leaning in, but stopping shy of my lips. "No one goes it alone forever. Sometimes, the biggest risk we take is trusting someone else to do the worryin' for us."

"You'd do that?" I asked. "Why?"

"Why not?"

"You're like, four times my age. Why did you even follow me home?"

"Because you act like yer four times my age, and that's kinda hot."

Our lips met as we slipped into a longer kiss. I was always comfortable with him. I even started sleeping better at night, wrapped up in his arms.

I pulled away. "You know that's bullshit. You pretend to be all stupid and immature, but then you say stuff like this."

"That's why we work."

"I thought that was just because you piss me off and I insult you."

His eyes shifted to the right. "Wanna do something else risky?"

I opened my mouth to protest, but all that came out was a sigh. "That depends."

"Let's take a walk on the wild side," he said, hopping out of the truck. He took a few steps toward the woods and waved me toward him. "C'mon."

I climbed out of the driver's seat and followed. "We're not supposed to go in there."

"Who's gonna know?" He looked around. "There's trees on both sides of the road, and there hasn't been a single car since we pulled over. Let's be real werewolves and fuck in the woods."

Some of the mayor's warning echoed strongly. Roscoe was Whasha at one point in his life, and he had seemed more interested in the woods when I'd brought up Norwich at Darryl's.

"There are pine needles everywhere. Sand was one thing, but pine needles are where I draw the line."

"I'll let you be on top."

"Are you suggesting—"

"We ain't tried that yet." He grabbed my hand, pulling me toward the trees. "Think yer man enough?"

"That's the problem. I'm still basically human. This is going to be awkward."

"You've got a big dick fer a human, though. Kinda scary thinkin' about what that monster might look like when you turn."

"You're sure laying that flattery on thick, aren't you?"

"I'm serious. You've got a bigger hog than I did when I was half-turn."

"Christ, seriously? How big am I gonna get?"

Roscoe shrugged. "Well, that part all depends. Sometimes we get huge, sometimes we don't. I'm kinda curious about what Adam's gonna look like. If he ends up being bigger than Austin, I just may lose it, cause that's gonna be the funniest shit."

"How much longer do you think he's got?"

"Hard to say." Roscoe pushed a few low-hanging branches out of the way so I could pass. "It'll be soon, though. The poor guy's really going through it. The weeks leading up to the big event are some of the worst. He's gonna get really moody, and I may have to step in to keep him in line. Austin don't know what the fuck he's doin'."

"That just killed my mood."

Roscoe looked over at me, but I kept my focus ahead.

"You must really hate Adam or somethin'."

"I don't hate him. I just... hate the thought of you with him." I rubbed my forehead. "God, it sounded even more ridiculous saying it out loud."

Roscoe wrapped an arm around my waist, and pulled me closer to him. "I didn't know it bothered you." He radiated smugness. "You really like me, don't ya?"

"Let's change the subject."

"I did promise I'd make him feel good tonight."

"Good, you didn't specify. Tuck him in and tell him a bedtime story," I muttered.

"I was thinkin' of the old proverb 'teach a man to fish.'" Roscoe stroked his chin. "Austin needs to learn how to be a werewolf because obviously the guy's so fucked up he's ignoring instinct."

"What are you thinking, exactly?"

"Well, I have a classroom all set up in his room now," he said, his tail wagging enough that it was slapping my lower back. "This is a job for Professor Roscoe."

"Oh, you've gotten promoted to professor, now?"

"Spent over eight decades on my degree." He paused and turned to me. "Yer okay with that?"

"You and Austin screwing around isn't the same as you and Adam. I don't—" I let out a frustrated groan. "I don't know why it feels different, but it does. It doesn't bother me when you're with other werewolves."

Roscoe gave my earlobe a slight flick. "It's a half-turn thing."

"I don't like all this weird magic shit," I said. "Did you know the mayor can turn all the way human?"

"For real? I can't even do that. Explains how the guy got to be mayor, though."

I reached into my pocket. "You should take a picture of when I'm fucking you so I can send it to Adam." My fingers brushed against something familiar, but it wasn't my phone. I stopped cold and pulled out the gold lighter I thought I'd thrown away. "Roscoe..."

"What's wrong?"

"I think we need to get out of the woods now."

# The Fission Reactor

**N**o matter how many times I tossed it away, the lighter found its way back to me, polished to a shine and engraved with another threatening message. I didn't know how it worked, but I started to understand its purpose. The last message that appeared had been cryptic, but it made my hair stand up. Mosavi wanted me to know he was monitoring my every move.

He put on quite a show of dominance, but was Roscoe right about him? What exactly did anyone know about the elders that ran werewolf society from the shadows, and did anyone really understand the vironoct? Was any of this kuu stuff necessary, or was it a convenient way to control an entire population? The conspiracy theories piled up in my mind as I sat in silence on the loveseat, flipping the lid of the lighter over and over.

"I'm going to rip your hands off," Austin grumbled from the other couch. He had been so quiet while watching television that I'd kind of forgotten he was in the room with me.

"Sounds like you're in a better mood." I clicked the lighter closed before tossing it onto the coffee table. Roscoe and I agreed to keep what the mayor said quiet until we figured out what his motives were. The last thing I needed to worry about was Austin melting down again.

"I could tear you apart right now."

"You won't," I said dismissively, kicking my feet up on the couch while scrolling through the messages on my phone.

He gave another glare before turning back to the television screen.

"Adam and Roscoe won't be back for a couple days, so either learn to get along with me or go hide in your garage."

Without another word, Austin tossed the remote onto the coffee table and stood.

"Hold on."

"What?"

"That was more of an invitation to converse. I wasn't actually telling you to leave."

The werewolf let out a short hiss through his teeth and opened the door.

"Come on, I'm trying to—"

The door clicked shut, with Austin now on the other side of it. These planned couple of days were already off to a *great* start. Roscoe's 'buddy' had reneged on his promise to pick up the moving truck, so we needed to get it back to the city. Since Roscoe was the only one that really knew how to drive, he had to be the one to do it. I would have gone with him, but Adam was about as persistent as a Jack Russell Terrier waiting by the front door. Instead of telling him no, I'd reluctantly stood aside.

Having Adam out of the picture for a little while allowed me some precious alone time with Austin without having to deal with both of them arguing about everything. It was hard enough to find a moment Austin wasn't pissed off, but Adam always exacerbated his bad mood. If I was going to have any chance in hell of getting control of the situation, I needed to win Austin over—or at the very least, get him to hate me less.

The squirming and rumbling of my stomach reminded me I hadn't yet eaten lunch. Being cranky and hungry wasn't going to help, so I'd leave him alone while I got a snack. Maybe I'd also watch a movie and get some chores done. It wasn't like I had to get this done today, right?

The mayor's expectations of me seemed egregious. Roscoe was the oldest and the one actually holding everyone together. His cooking was what lured Austin out of his hole, and his jokes kept the conversations light when they'd veer off into dangerous territory. Not only that, he seemed to know exactly what to say or what advice to give when the situation called for it.

Those redeeming qualities were also fused to an infuriating lack of motivation, like a Cronenberg monster of sage-like stupidity.

What was I thinking? I couldn't trust Roscoe to lead a buffet line, let alone this family.

I rummaged through the pantry, trying to find something I wouldn't need to cook. Roscoe bought a lot of sweets, which, oddly enough, hadn't added more to his waistline. I hated to admit it, but even with his gut, the werewolf was naturally handsome. It made me wonder what he'd look like as a human if he had the mayor's ability. Could he at least take on half-turn form like Austin?

As I shifted around a bunch of cream-filled snacks with nothing I wanted in sight, I almost considered tearing open a package of saltines. However, something in the far corner caught my eye. It was a black, unopened bag of pre-popped popcorn that looked like it had been purposely hidden.

After grabbing the snack, I headed back into the living room and planted myself on the sofa before turning up the television volume. The bag crackled as I tore it open. I then snatched a handful, shoveling it into my mouth.

The door leading to the garage creaked open, and Austin emerged, sniffing the air.

"Is that white cheddar popcorn?"

I examined the front of the bag. "Yeah," I said, a bit puzzled as he padded toward the couch. "Do you want some?"

He plopped down on the sofa, stuck his nose in the bag and began to salivate. "Yes."

I passed the popcorn, and he tilted the bag above his mouth, scarfing down nearly half of its contents. Bits fell into his lap as he chomped away, licking his fingers afterward before shoving his slobbery hand in.

"Keep it, I guess," I said. Austin wasn't even listening to me anymore. It was as though nothing else mattered but that popcorn. "If you're hungry, I could make you something."

He stopped chewing, and his eyes went wide. "Roscoe told me to keep you away from the stove. He was like, serious about it."

"For fuck's sake, I'm not a child! I know what I'm doing now."

Austin licked his fingers again, his expression pensive. "I could go for a sandwich."

I gave the almost empty bag of popcorn a glance. "You like grilled cheese?"

His tail thudded against the cushions, and I could barely hold back a smile. Roscoe might have unintentionally saved the day with his junk food habit.

"Got any canned tomato soup?"

"I don't know. Let me look." I jumped off the couch and hurried into the kitchen. "Is that really what you want?"

"If we got any," he responded, crinkling the empty bag into a ball. "You never had grilled cheese with tomato soup before?"

"I don't like tomatoes," I said, moving the canned goods around. "Bad news, there's no soup." I walked over to the fridge and pulled out a block of cheddar wrapped in cellophane.

"What are you doing with that?" Austin asked, creeping up behind me.

"I told you. I'm making grilled cheese."

"That's not the right cheese," he snapped, looking at the loaf of multigrain bread I'd pulled out. "Where's the white bread?"

"This is all we've got. Does it really matter?"

He flashed a disgusted look and turned away before heading back toward the garage. "Never mind. I'll eat something later."

"Wait..." I was going to lose him again. "Why don't we go to the store and you can pick out what we need?"

He stopped, seeming to give my request some consideration.

"Nah," he grunted before disappearing back into the garage.

This was going to be much harder than I'd thought, but at least we were getting somewhere.

The usual clanking and drilling from the garage was oddly absent as I walked up to the house carrying ingredients for Austin's lunch—plus more of that white cheddar popcorn to lure him out again. If I was going to get Austin to tear down his walls, this seemed like a decent first step. After all, food worked great at gaining the trust of stray dogs.

I headed toward the kitchen and unloaded the groceries. Two packs of American cheese, a loaf of white bread, butter, and several cans of tomato soup lay before me on the counter. I set to work washing my hands, then placed the frying pan on the burner before turning the stove on high.

A stick of butter softened for a few seconds in the microwave, which I then slathered on the bread before putting the cheese on the other side. Everything was going much better than it usually did. Then again, who could mess up a fried sandwich?

While the pan heated, I mixed the condensed soup with some milk in a saucepan, then placed it on the back burner. A glint of light caught my eye next to the microwave, hidden behind the toaster. There sat that strange opal I'd forgotten to put back on my dresser the other day. I grabbed the gem, slipped it into my pocket, then plopped the buttery cheese sandwich onto the pan with an alarmingly harsh sizzle. The directions said to leave it on one side for about three minutes, then flip it over.

Simple enough...

"What the hell are you doing?" Austin shouted over the smoke alarm as he dashed into the kitchen.

"Everything's fine," I said calmly, trying not to cough as I poured a cup of water over the smoldering remains of lunch. More smoke and steam billowed to the ceiling and spread throughout the house. "It's just a little well-done."

Austin disappeared, running from room-to-room, opening windows while I chiseled the sandwich onto a plate before cooling the pan under running tap water. It hissed and made an odd pinging noise, and when I placed it back onto the burner, it wobbled, no longer able to make full contact.

"Damn it. I forgot to turn the burner back down," I said, twisting the knob to five. I had destroyed Roscoe's good frying pan and would have to use one of his smaller ones to try again.

Austin stomped back into the kitchen and picked up the plate to slide the solid black briquette that was once a sandwich into the trash. "A little well-done? Are you from Venus?" he asked, grabbing my wrist as I spread more butter on another slice of bread. "You're not going to be satisfied until you burn the whole fucking house down, are you?"

"It was an accident. I let the frying pan get too hot and kind of wasn't paying attention. I'll have your lunch ready in a couple minutes," I said, pointing to the pot. "I think the soup's almost done."

The werewolf gasped, turning the burner off before lifting the lid. The once watery mixture had gotten so thick that it splattered instead of boiled. He gave it a quick sniff. "How the hell did you burn soup? It's SOUP!"

"I didn't burn it," I said, examining the pale red concoction. "Looks fine to me."

Austin grabbed a spoon and dipped it into the pot before scooping something thick from the bottom. He pulled up the utensil to reveal a clump of char.

"How did that happen?"

"Out," Austin barked, pointing toward the direction of the living room.

"At least let me clean—"

"Get the hell out of here!" he shouted again, giving me a hard shove away from the stove.

"I was just trying to make you lunch," I said, my voice a bit quivery as I exited the kitchen. My attempt at garnering some civility between us had gone up in smoke. Literally. After sauntering into the bedroom, I sat down on the mattress and glanced at the clock. It read five minutes past three, which I found odd. Either the time was wrong, or I had been cooking for about forty-five minutes.

That had been happening to me a lot. The time skips would always start with me doing something mundane like watching TV or listening to music by myself, but then my mind would wander. An hour would pass in almost a blink, and sometimes I'd rest my eyes only to wake up several hours later.

I lay back on the pillows and stared at the hazy ceiling, thinking about what else I could do to salvage this day.

A giant hand shook my shoulder, startling me awake. Austin looked down at me with the usual grimace.

"When did I fall asleep?"

"Time to eat," he grunted before leaving the bedroom.

It took a moment to reorient as I got out of bed and stumbled into the dining room. Austin was scarfing down one of his seven grilled cheese sandwiches, and next to him was a neatly placed saucer stacked with two sandwiches, a spoon on a folded napkin, and a steaming bowl of pale red soup with some oregano flakes.

"I didn't know you could cook," I said before pulling my chair up to the table.

"I can't. It's canned soup and grilled cheese. Eight-year-olds know how to make it." He frowned and narrowed his eyes. "Aren't you supposed to be smart or something?"

"I don't know why everyone thinks that's so special." I took a bite of the sandwich, which was perfectly fried.

"You're the only one here that went to college. Maybe that's what's wrong with you. You learned so much useless crap that you ended up pushing out all the important stuff."

"Yeah, maybe," I said, silently grinding my teeth. I wasn't angry because he was rude, I was more embarrassed because it might have been true. Four years of thinking I was better than my parents because I was supposedly more educated, only to find out I hadn't learned anything useful. Now that I was a half-turn, I couldn't even put the *useful* stuff to any use.

The werewolf folded one of the sandwiches and dipped it into the bowl before taking a bite.

"Ew."

"Try it," he said with his mouth full.

I pushed the bowl away from me. "You eat it. I don't like tomatoes."

"What are you talking about? You eat tomatoes all the damn time."

"That's different. They're usually *in* something. Not *the* something."

"Have you ever tasted it?"

I shook my head.

"You can't say you don't like something if you haven't even tried it."

"I've never eaten pussy either, but I'm quite sure I wouldn't enjoy it," I muttered, picking up the spoon. "It sure smells... tomato-y." After dipping the spoon into the bowl, I held it to my lips and gave it a taste. My mind wanted to reject it immediately, but my mouth didn't. There was a sweetness that complemented the savory, and the milk gave everything a creamy mouthfeel. "Hmm..."

"Kinda makes you want to try pussy now, huh?" Austin smirked. "Now, dip your sandwich in it."

"I'm gonna have to draw the line there."

"Suit yourself," he said, going back to his meal.

I let out another contemplative hum, hesitated a moment before finally dipping the tip of my sandwich into the soup. Maybe if I pretended it was delicious, it would lighten him up a little.

I took a bite and started to put on a show. "Mmm—this is..." The flavor hit me, and there was no longer a reason to pretend. "Why have I never known about this?"

Austin stuffed the last sandwich into his mouth. "When I was little, my grams used to make this for us."

"Us?"

He finished chewing but sat still on the chair. The look in his eyes was terrifyingly similar to the other night.

"You don't have to say anything else."

His breath quickened, and he scooted away, gripping the fur on the sides of his head while rocking back and forth.

I shot up and tried to put my arm around him, but he smacked me so hard with the back of his hand that I went airborne, slamming into the wall before falling to the floor. Ignoring the pain in my head, I stumbled to my feet and tried to console him again.

Austin let out a horrible snarl and lunged for me in a panic, knocking the table upward. Soup splashed the walls as one of the bowls shattered. He wrapped his right hand around my neck, lifting me from the ground and squeezing. Blood pooled in my head, and I could no longer breathe.

"Don't touch me," he shouted while staring at nothing before tossing me aside like a doll. "Don't hurt him!"

I writhed on the floor, rubbing my neck and gasping. It was pointless. I wasn't strong enough to restrain him, and he was too far gone to soothe with words. He would definitely kill me if I tried that again.

The werewolf paced the room, howling, his eyes distant and glowing bright orange. The more I tried to think about what Roscoe would do, the less feasible it was.

Then I had an idea.

The longer fur-like hair on the back of my neck stuck straight up, and I stomped one foot, catching his gaze.

"Get a hold of yourself, soldier!" I barked, the tone of my voice harsh and unnaturally low. It was then the room began to turn silver.

Austin froze, his eyes widening as their color faded from orange to light blue.

"Attention!"

It was as though his body was on autopilot as he gave a salute, standing up straight and puffing out his chest.

"Yes sir!"

With my hands behind my back, I strode with as much confidence as I could muster, not breaking eye contact as he awaited with a doll-like emptiness. Inside I was trembling, my heart racing.

"At ease."

The blue in his eyes faded, and his breathing slowed. He stumbled forward as if whatever demons were gripping his mind let go.

"Austin?"

"I'm gonna lay down," he said, his gait meticulous as he crept through the living room toward the hallway. He looked back at me, his now watery eyes silently pleading, but not before his usual scowl returned. He disappeared through the door, closing it gently behind him.

If I read this wrong, I risked knocking down a delicate house of cards, but I also couldn't leave him alone after that. The safest thing was to at least check on him without being pushy.

I tiptoed toward his bedroom door, turned the knob, and peeked inside. He was lying on his back with both hands folded behind his head.

"Are you okay?"

He didn't respond, so I slipped into the room, keeping my eyes peeled for any change in his body language. If he showed even the slightest anger or discomfort, I'd take that as my cue to leave. However, he remained emotionless, except for the tip of his tail slightly patting the mattress between his legs.

I scooted next to him, cautiously put both feet up on the mattress, then leaned back against the headboard.

"You ever wonder why we exist?" Austin asked without looking at me.

The question was so unexpected it took me a moment to respond.

"Sometimes, especially when things get bad."

"I should've never been born," he said, his tone turning to more of a whisper.

"We don't really get a choice in that," I replied. "Think of existence as... a giant fission reactor, but instead of atoms colliding, it's how we interact with other people that creates the chain reaction. Every meeting changes the course of a person's life, and then they change the lives of others. It could be for the best or for the worst, but in the end, we all end up where we need to be with the people we're meant to be with."

Austin glared at me. "A fission reactor?"

"I suck at metaphors, okay. Did it at least make sense?"

The anger that held him hostage began to lift, and he let out a laugh that shook the bed.

"You're a fuckin' nerd."

I got flashbacks to that night with Roscoe.

"It wasn't meant to be funny."

Austin's laughter faded to a light chuckle, and he shoved me with his elbow. "Uh oh, I think you might go supercritical now."

"You're an ass," I said, but paused. "You're obviously smarter than you let people think. Why in the hell do you hide it?"

"It's easier to be stupid."

"Well, yeah, to a certain extent," I said, choosing my next words carefully. "I'm worried about you."

"Yeah, right."

"If I wasn't, I wouldn't be in here right now."

"Why?" he asked, more serious this time. "What do you get out of it? Does playing shrink make you feel better about yourself?"

"That's not what this is."

"Then what is it? I've gone out of my way to treat you like shit, but you're like a gnat that I can't get out of my face." He turned toward me again. "Now that's a metaphor."

"It's actually a simile."

Austin growled. "You can't even make a fucking sandwich. Pathetic."

"Maybe I did that on purpose, so you'd make *me* the sandwich."

We both went quiet, save for the steady breeze whistling into the room through the window screen.

"Well played," he finally said, his hand brushing mine. "What you said earlier—I never thought about it that way before."

"I wish I could say I came up with it, but I heard it from some BluTube video a while ago."

"Even the fission part?"

"I ad-libbed a little."

It was risky, but I wanted to see how far I could go with him. Maybe I could hold his hand, since he was too big to lay in my lap like he had with Roscoe. I kind of expected him to swat me away, but he didn't. Instead, his massive hand enveloped mine.

"My old man had a lot of mental problems. When he took his meds, he was fine, but if he missed a dose, he got really crazy. The last time he took his medicine, he forgot to take it again and was convinced it was mind-control. I was eight and my brother was five when my mom woke us up in the middle of the night and drove us to Gram's house."

His breathing was shallow and quick, but I kept a tight hold on his hand.

"That night, Dad showed up ranting about how we weren't really his family—that we were all replacements sending information back to some secret government agency to track him. Mama called the cops, but he broke in and shot her in the head with Grandpa's revolver." He tensed, his shaky grip on my hand tightening. "Grams was screaming, but he shot her too. My brother and I ran into the bedroom, but he followed us. Another shot, and my brother let go of my hand and fell to the floor. All I remembered after that was two more shots, and a loud high-pitched ringing in my ears. I woke up in the hospital, in an empty room with a bunch of machines. I felt like the only one on the planet, all alone. Scared and confused."

My mouth hung open as tears filled my eyes, turning the room into a glass bowl. I didn't know how to react to something so unbelievably tragic.

Austin sniffed. "He shot me point blank in the back of the head, and I remembered not being able to move my arms and legs. I couldn't speak—all I could do was lie there and listen to them talking about me and my family. They thought I couldn't understand them, but I did. Have you ever been scared of living and scared of dying at the same time?"

I wiped my eyes and shook my head.

"No one," he said with a slight whimper. "There was no one to tell me I was gonna be okay. They thought I was gonna be like that until I died, but little by little, I started moving again. The doctors couldn't believe I could move my arms, but I still couldn't walk or talk, and I wouldn't be able to until I turned fifteen—and you know what comes after that. Being a half-turn didn't heal everything."

He let out the most gut-wrenching cry.

"I shoulda died that night with my family. I shoulda died with the rest of my pack on that test site in the marines." He howled, tears soaking his face. "Why am I still here? It doesn't make sense."

"Austin," I said, wiping my face as I climbed closer to him. "You're where you need to be now. Right next to me." I pressed against the side of his face with my other palm, not letting go of his hand as I maneuvered over him. "You're safe."

The werewolf sobbed again, and I leaned into him, touching his forehead with mine.

"You're safe," I whispered again, wrapping my arms around his neck. "You're my family now."

He nodded, his breathing returning to normal. When I pulled away, his hand caught my back, holding me against him.

"Stay with me," he said softly, our mouths almost touching. His voice had a child-like meekness to it, even though it was much deeper than mine. "Will you stay with me?"

"I'll stay as long as you need me to."

We were so close that his scent mixed with mine. Instinctively, my lips met his and he reciprocated the emotion. It wasn't quite sexual, but not innocent either. It was worlds different from what I experienced with Roscoe, because I was the one in control, keeping him tame. Was this the vironoct the mayor told me about?

His army fatigues brushed against my leg, but they were slightly damp from arousal. What radiated from my own groin was painful. Everything I'd been told about half-turns led me to believe we needed to be claimed in order to control our rage, but that wasn't what I wanted.

Our lips broke apart, and I pulled away.

"I'm sorry," I whispered.

From the look on his face, he was just as bewildered as I was.

"For what?"

"This doesn't make you uncomfortable?"

"No," he said, his tone a little deeper than before. "Do you need it?"

"What?"

"Roscoe's not here. Do you want me to—"

"Oh!" I said, scrambling off him. "No, I'm—I'm good for now, thanks."

His ears fell off to the side. "All right."

"Do you still want me to stay with you?"

"Yeah," he whispered, his downward inflection tinged with what I could only assume was disappointment.

I grabbed his hand again and the tenseness from earlier melted as we stared at one another, his eyes still glimmering like tiny orange pools.

"I never told anyone before," he said. "I never could."

"I won't tell anyone. And if you ever feel overwhelmed, come lay down with me. Okay?"

"Cody." He swallowed hard, opening his mouth to say something else, but instead cleared his throat. "Okay."

"What is it?"

"Thanks for getting that stuff at the store, and for trying to make me lunch. No one's ever done that."

"What about Adam?"

Austin's eyes narrowed, and his sad smile disappeared. "Adam's just a kuu bond, nothing more. He's made that perfectly clear. He doesn't care about me."

I shook my head. "He's just young and kinda selfish. He needs someone holding his hand otherwise he doesn't know what to do with himself."

"I hate that," he grunted. "Sometimes I just want to be—" He paused and let out a sigh before turning away. "God, I hate this."

Seeing his increased frustration, I let it go. It was safer that way, even though a part of me wanted to keep prying. However, this was Adam's place, not mine. It didn't feel right to go any further with him, especially since he was so emotionally vulnerable.

"All right," I whispered, wrapping my arm part of the way around him. He was so huge, trying to be the big spoon was awkward. But it seemed to have a positive effect as his tail gently thudded against my leg. "Let's take a nap."

# Chapter 16

# We've Got Trouble

I lay next to Austin, my eyes wide while I brushed the tips of my fingers through his thick mane before slipping over a divot at the base of his skull. Being a werewolf meant being able to heal from just about any injury, but this reminder of a mangled childhood stood defiant.

God's existence was always such a dubious claim. My grandparents on both sides held fast to their religions. One side was Orthodox Jew and the other was Catholic, and I often wondered how such staunchly religious people could produce children that would grow up to be terrible adults. As bad as my childhood was, the blinders of privilege disappear quickly when you see just how bad it could have been.

*Why am I still here?*

I couldn't let go of the terror in his voice. Time had frozen for him all those years ago. He had to grow up in an instant, depending on only himself for strength. And while a single pillar could support a simple structure, it can't hold up the weight of a skyscraper.

After today, I wasn't going to let him hide in that garage alone anymore.

*The Next Morning*

The other side of the bed was empty when I woke up. At first, I thought Austin had retreated to his usual sanctuary, but when I wandered the hall, I noticed the bathroom door was closed.

He was actually showering.

Roscoe would sometimes go a week or more without bathing, and Austin hadn't so much as looked at a bathtub since I'd met him. While they didn't smell awful, their fur would attract twigs and dirt from outside, which would build up and get on the furniture.

The old floorboards groaned as I padded through the house to make breakfast, but I stopped when a sheet of paper on the dining room table caught my attention. The word *microwave* had been written in thick black marker, and under that were the words *don't touch the stove* scribbled with a ballpoint pen.

The house had a residual scent of burned bacon, and in the kitchen, a wrapped plate full of scrambled eggs and pancakes greeted me. I smiled at the unusually thoughtful gesture. To think I had a junk food loving werewolf to thank for this breakthrough. I'd need to remember to buy more white cheddar popcorn in the future.

After heating the meal, I drenched the pancakes in syrup and sat at the table. The eggs were slightly overdone, and the pancakes were broken, but it was a solid five stars compared to anything I could do. I usually just ate a bowl of marshmallow cereal if Roscoe wasn't around.

Christ, Roscoe was right. I did eat like a child.

The bathroom door opened and clawed footsteps trudged through the hall until a hilariously fluffy Austin appeared in the entryway.

"Holy shit," I said, nearly choking on my breakfast. "What happened?"

He grunted but said nothing else as he made his way into the kitchen.

"Want me to brush you?"

He poked his head out from around the corner and raised a brow.

"I'll get the deshedder I use for Roscoe—whenever he lets me," I continued, making my voice sound enticing.

"You brush Roscoe?"

"Well, yeah. Doesn't Adam brush you?"

He huffed sharply through his nose and disappeared around the corner again. "No."

"Have you ever asked him to?"

"Did Roscoe ask you?" he asked, while shuffling around the refrigerator.

I let out a laugh and thought back to those first weeks of trying to improve Roscoe's hygiene. "No, I kind of forced it on him."

"I'll pass."

"Your fur is going to get knotted like that. Oh, and for future reference, this won't happen if you keep the blow-dryer on low."

Austin didn't reply.

"C'mon, let me brush you," I said, standing from the table. Only half my plate was gone, but I was too stuffed to keep eating. I stepped into the kitchen and pulled the box of cellophane from the drawer. "I mean, unless you want to go out in public looking like a stuffed animal."

"I'll brush myself." His eyes lowered again. The first time he'd given me that look, I hadn't thought much of it. This time, it was harder to ignore.

"What's wrong?"

"Nothing," he muttered, pouring himself a glass of water. Werewolves were kind of funny when they drank anything out of a glass. They would do this half-lapping, half-sipping thing because their lips were too thin and their teeth were too long to not dribble water all over the place.

"I'm getting the brush." I wrapped the plate in plastic wrap before placing it in the fridge for later.

"I don't want you to brush me!"

With the incident from yesterday fresh in my mind, I winced and shook my head. "Fine. I'll leave you alone."

"God damn it, can't you take a hint?"

"I told you I'd leave you alone, damn."

"That's not—" He let out a frustrated sigh. "Never mind."

"Austin, tell me what you want. If you're my friend, then just tell me what's bothering you, and I'll try to fix it."

"It's not you," Austin said, sauntering back into the living room with me following. He grabbed the deshedder that was lying on one of the end tables before plopping down face-first onto the couch. "Fine. Brush me."

"Are you sure?"

He groaned in response. This wasn't his usual moodiness; instead, this took on an almost child-like petulance. I supposed it was better than him nearly choking me to death, so I grabbed the brush and set to work on fluffy, damaged fur.

"Jeez. I need to bring out the big guns."

Austin's ears lowered. "Big guns?"

"I live in a house with two werewolves. I like to be prepared for these types of emergencies. Plus, spray conditioner is the only way I can get Roscoe to not smell like a garbage can."

Austin looked pretty handsome in his newer fatigues that didn't have holes in them, and I had done a bang-up job on taming that mess he made with his mane. In the short time I'd known him, he'd never changed those pants. Even when he shifted into his half-turn form, he didn't remove them.

After Austin assured me he was okay, I allowed him time in his garage alone, but I gave him a hard limit. He could only stay there for an hour, then he had to come back out and sit with me. When I laid down the rules, he tucked his tail between his legs and nodded without protest. He seemed to respond positively to military-like discipline, and I kind of got a kick out of giving him commands.

My phone rang, the caller ID displaying *Brat* along with a picture of a crying baby. It had been a while since I'd received a call from Adam, and I'd forgotten about the Carmina Burana ringtone I'd set for him.

"What's up?" I answered.

"Roscoe and I are halfway there. We're on a bus." He growled at that last part.

"Everything okay?"

"I hate Roscoe. Why did you let me go with him?"

I could barely stifle a laugh. Though I hadn't known for sure when it would happen, I'd known it would eventually. Being stuck in a car for twelve hours with the world's most annoying werewolf took patience and finesse not a lot of people had. Hell, I barely had it.

"Oh no," I said, my tone purposely feigning concern. "What happened?"

"I can hear you smiling, you prick."

"Where's Roscoe right now?"

"Laying against the window, snoring. God, he's got morning wood and everyone's looking at him."

"Isn't he just the cutest?" I asked, still trying to restrain a laugh. "How was Darryl?"

"Amazing as ever." His tone had a bitter bite to it again. "At least he gave me a *swimming lesson* before I left. That'll tide me over until I either turn or go on a horny, bloodthirsty rampage."

"I take it sex with Roscoe isn't doing it for you anymore?"

"He hasn't done anything to me the entire time I've been with him! I was expecting him to pull over whenever I was in the mood, but he just kept singing boomer songs and torturing me with puns and awful dad jokes."

He didn't do it. I had expected Roscoe to jump at the chance of screwing Adam up and down the interstate, but he'd actually taken what I said to heart. Roscoe was going to get the best hummer I could manage when he got home.

"Sorry you had to go through that."

"Well, sorry you had to deal with Austin's shit. So I guess we're even."

"Not quite." I grinned again. "Austin and I have been having a great time. He actually made me breakfast this morning because I destroyed Roscoe's pan and nearly caught the house on fire."

Another low growl came through the speaker. "What do you mean he made you breakfast?"

"Pancakes and eggs. It was more out of pity than anything." I had to dial that back a bit. The goal was to annoy him, not drive a bigger wedge between him and Austin—and me. Hopefully, when Adam got back, they would sit down and talk things out with one another. I'd already laid the groundwork; all Adam had to do was not be insufferable for once.

"Ha!" There was that shitty tone I'd missed. "At least he didn't let you starve. Have you guys been fighting?"

"No, he's been in the garage, mostly. Probably missing you."

"Did he actually say he missed me?"

"Of course he did. He's been a wreck without you."

The garage door opened, and Austin walked into the living room. "Cody, hour's done. Wanna go for a walk?"

"What was that?" Adam asked. "Was that Austin?"

"Yeah. You want to talk to him?"

There was a moment of tense silence.

"Who's on the phone?" Austin asked.

"It's Adam," I said, holding the cell phone out.

His shoulders slumped a bit before grabbing it away from me.

"Hey," he said, his tone returning to its usual grouchiness. That wasn't at all what I'd hoped for.

Adam's voice came through the speaker but was muffled enough that I couldn't understand.

"Sounds boring, but funny." He stood there, examining his claws, nodding and grunting one-word responses before finally cutting Adam off. "Listen, I'm gonna go for a walk with Cody. I'll see you when you get home." He disconnected the call and handed the phone back to me.

"Dude! Did you just hang up on him?"

"No. I told him what I was going to do and ended the call."

"Yeah, that's called hanging up on someone."

The phone rang again, and the ringtone somehow sounded angrier.

"Come on. They're gonna be here later, and I just want to walk with someone."

"Why don't you walk with Adam when he gets back?" I asked, pressing the button to silence the phone.

"Yeah, maybe when he gets here, but you're here now. So let's go."

The phone rang again.

"Hold on," I said, holding the phone to my ear. "Adam?"

"What the fuck?" he screamed, his voice a slightly higher pitch than before. I held the phone away from my ear as he continued yelling. "The asshole hung up on me!"

"He's just missing you." I glared at Austin, who rolled his eyes.

"He sure has a funny way of showing it."

Austin pulled me toward the door, and I hurried Adam off the line. "I need to go. I'll talk to you later."

The other end went dead silent.

"Okay?" I asked, expecting some kind of answer, but the connection went dead. "Austin."

"What?"

"When he gets back, you need to try to get along better with him. He may just be your kuu mate, but he also cares about you."

"Whatever," he grunted, letting out a heavy breath.

"Where are we going?"

"There's a barbeque restaurant where I saw a bunch of werewolves last time. I thought maybe I'd take you there for lunch after we browse the town a bit. I need to pick up some things from the hardware store."

"Oh, Roscoe's been wanting to go to that barbeque place since we got here," I said, locking the door behind me. "Are you sure you're okay going into public? I don't want you to feel uncomfortable."

"It's fine." He kept his eyes forward. I could tell he was forcing himself into this situation, and while I was elated he was trying, I didn't want him to be a mess of anxiety.

"If you start to get nervous, tell me and we'll leave."

Austin nodded without another word.

*Later that afternoon*

"Oh God, I'm so stuffed," I muttered before a loud belch left my throat. "I don't think I've ever eaten that much in my life."

Austin was sitting on the couch next to me with his feet up on the coffee table and a contented look on his face. He hadn't said much since we got back; in fact, most of our walk and time at the restaurant had been spent in silence. It wasn't uncomfortable, and I didn't expect him to turn into a chatty Cathy after just one day. This was going to take some time, but at least he made the effort.

Muffled angry chatter from outside grew louder, and Austin's ears pointed upward before turning toward the door. He didn't react at all; instead, he turned up the television volume.

"Sounds like they're home," I said right as the door swung open.

"Hold on, I got another one fer ya," Roscoe said as he followed a very irate Adam inside. "Did you hear about the dairy cow that jumped over the barbed wire fence?"

"Make him stop. Now," Adam said as he walked into the living room, throwing his backpack on the other loveseat. He eyed Austin and me. "You guys look comfortable."

I patted my stomach. "We ate a big lunch."

Roscoe sniffed the air and furrowed his brows. "You went to the barbeque place without me? You know how much I wanted to go, but you got all pissy about money."

Adam sat on the loveseat, glaring daggers at me. "You guys went out to eat? Together?"

"It was just lunch." I looked over at Roscoe. "And I didn't buy, but the prices are pretty good. Maybe I'll take you there this week."

"All right. I'll forgive ya," Roscoe said with a grin, his tail wagging.

Adam stood up and walked over to us before burying his nose in Austin's mane. "You actually took a bath?"

"Yup," Austin replied, tearing away from the tv show.

"You smell good."

"*You* smell like Darryl." There was a slight annoyance in his tone.

"Oh, come on, don't give me that look," Adam said, crawling onto Austin's lap. "I heard you missed me."

The werewolf tossed me a sideways glance, and I nodded for him to respond.

"Yeah."

I started to understand what was wrong with their dynamic. When Austin and I were together, I didn't keep trying to talk to him; instead, I waited for him to initiate the conversation. Roscoe did the same thing, which was why Austin had preferred being around him the last week or so. Adam, on the other hand, had this loose party mentality where he was always the center of attention. He was good-looking and outgoing, so he never had an issue picking up human guys or werewolves, but his extroverted personality clashed hard with how reserved and nervous Austin was.

"How about we have some fun?" Adam gave the werewolf another sniff. "How'd you get your fur so soft?"

"Cody brushed me and used the *big guns*."

He turned to me. "You brushed him?"

"He was really poofy."

"Hah," Roscoe cut in. "Turned it on high, huh?"

Austin nodded.

Adam slid off Austin's lap and walked into the hallway without saying anything, rather turned left toward the back door.

I got up and started after him but stopped to give Roscoe a kiss. "Meet me in the bedroom in a bit."

"Oh boy," Roscoe said, scrambling off the loveseat. "I'll go clean myself up just fer you."

Austin remained where he was, his attention back on the TV show as if oblivious to what was going on. Part of me wondered if he was doing it on purpose, or if his lack of concern was unintentional. For now, I needed to find a way to get them talking.

I pushed the back door open just as Adam sat on one of the lawn chairs surrounding the fire pit.

"Hey," I said, sitting in the chair across from him. "Sorry about Roscoe."

"Is there something wrong with me?"

"What are you talking about?"

"Roscoe didn't touch me the whole time we were gone and now..." He trailed off, looking down at his hands. "Am I ugly or something?"

"For fuck's sake," I said, crossing one leg over my knee. "You're probably one of the hottest guys I've ever met."

Adam smiled. "You think so?"

I nodded. "The reason Roscoe didn't do anything is... well, I kind of got jealous and made a stink about it."

"What's the big deal? We fuck werewolves. That's our thing."

"How would you feel if Austin and I slept together?"

"I'd feel sorry for you."

"Well, we did, and I kind of liked it," I lied, gauging his reaction. Sure enough, had his skin been lighter, it would have flushed as he bit down hard on his upper lip.

"Are you going to fuck both of them now at the same time, you fucking slut?"

"Whoa, calm down!"

"I'm not going to calm down! You fucked my kuu mate," he shouted, shooting up from the chair, which flipped backward. "He's bathing, and he's making you breakfast and taking you out to eat! What the fuck, man? He doesn't do any of that shit for me!"

"We didn't actually have sex."

"You're a lying, back-stabbing fa—"

"I'm proving a point," I interrupted before Adam could finish that slur.

Adam paused and took a deep breath before setting his chair upright. "Sorry, I don't know why I snapped like that."

"It's because you feel the same way about Austin that I do about Roscoe."

Adam's gaze shifted to the ground as he sat on the chair.

"Austin's in a very vulnerable state of mind right now, but he's trying, even if it seems like he's not. When you go back in, just sit next to him quietly and see what happens."

"Just what exactly are you implying?"

"Nothing! It's just, after being with him alone for a day, I learned things are going to take time. The guy's been trying to isolate himself for a while, and it's hard to get him in the mood to talk. If he starts to feel comfortable, he'll start talking."

Adam leaned forward, eyeing me suspiciously. "What exactly do you know?"

"Not more than you do." I lied again. It wasn't my place to tell Austin's story. "Just trust me on this."

"I think I need a break from werewolves. Roscoe was—" He paused and ground his teeth. "I don't know how you do it."

"He grows on you." I gave the half-turn a sly smile. "Like a fungus. To be honest, I think that's what keeps things interesting between us. We're so opposite that somehow it just works."

Adam stood and stretched. "Let's go out somewhere. I found a bar downtown that doesn't look too bad."

"We're not allowed to drink, remember? And you're not even old enough."

Adam grabbed my arm and pulled me out of the chair. "The mayor said it was illegal to sell alcohol to *werewolves*. I saw a half-turn in town earlier sucking down a frozen margarita, and goddamn it, Cody, I want a drink after all this." He held up a fake ID. "You're buying."

I shot him an uneasy glance but thought about it a little more. Another opportunity was about to fall into my lap, and with how tense things had been between us lately, a guy's night out at a bar might work in my favor.

"Fine. I've got a little extra money, and we don't get to spend nearly enough time together. Roscoe's going to be disappointed. He's kind of sitting in the bedroom waiting."

"Good. He can experience what he put me through."

"That was fun," Adam slurred, holding onto me for balance as we made our way to the front door. "But that music suuuucked."

My phone vibrated, and I took it out to examine the caller ID. It was unknown, so I tapped reject and dropped the phone back into my pocket.

"At least the booze was cheap." I couldn't help but grumble at how little Adam was able to pace himself. It was all or nothing with that half-turn, and since I was buying, he didn't mind running up the tab.

"Did you even drink?"

   

"Of course, I just know what moderation means," I said, trying to turn the knob, which was locked. "Huh. I guess they went out somewhere."

"Doubt it." Adam hiccupped before letting out a squeaky belch. "Austin's probably in the garage."

"You need to go to bed." I fumbled with my keys before unlocking the door.

"I'll go to bed when I'm damn ready," he said, stumbling forward. I caught him just in time. "I think I'm ready."

I led the unstable half-turn to his room, set him on the bed, and then removed his sandals.

"Good night," I said, turning to leave, but not before he caught my arm. "What?"

"Thanks for the drinks." He let go and collapsed onto his pillows.

"Yeah," I muttered as I left the bedroom. *Disappointed* was an understatement. Every time I tried to carry on a conversation with him, he'd get another cocktail and disappear. Adam had no issues working the room, dancing and flirting with at least half the guys there, all the while leaving me to fend off every person with a thing for half-turns—which was just about everyone. Oddly enough, I was more popular with the women, and one of them in particular had creeped me out.

I checked each room of the house, but it was empty.

"Austin?" I called out. "Roscoe?"

No response.

After flipping on the light switch to the dining room, I eyed the door leading into the garage. Since Austin had taken over that space and made it clear he didn't want anyone in there, we all obliged him. Tonight, though, I let curiosity get the best of me.

Upon opening the door, I noticed a large, conical tarp-covered device sitting in the middle of the workshop. Austin's tools and raw materials were placed neatly on hooks and shelves, and several work benches lined the walls. He really took pride in this area; I smiled at the thought of him sitting on one of his benches, tinkering with something.

Tight straps secured the tarp to whatever was under it, so I carefully undid them and let the cover fall. The smile on my face shifted the opposite direction. My jaw clenched with rage.

"What the fuck, Austin?" It was a copper still surrounded by jars of what looked like moonshine. So *this* was what he had been doing this whole time? Running an illegal booze operation?

My cell phone vibrated again, and I took it out to see the same unknown number. Shortly after I rejected it, the phone rang again, and I grew concerned. I accepted the call and held the phone up to my ear.

"Hello?"

A moment of silence before a very familiar and angry voice lashed my ears through the speaker. "Good evening, Dakota," the mayor said with cheerful howling in the background. Was that Roscoe?

"Oh! I—I'm sorry. I didn't know who it was."

"I've got a question for you."

"Um, okay."

"Do you know where your werewolves right now?"

"They're not my—"

"Answer the question," he interrupted.

"I don't know. I came home, and they were gone."

"Meet me at 728 North Avenue. The gate will open upon your arrival."

"Are they with you?"

The line went dead.

# Chapter 17

# The Slammer

A quick search of the address led me to the county jail, which honestly shouldn't have been a surprise, but I thought we were finally getting ahead. Austin was opening up, Adam was kind of being less annoying, and Roscoe was—well, I still had a lot of work to do on him, but I thought he'd at least not try to sabotage our one shot at living a halfway decent rural life.

What bothered me most was Austin's new hobby. He wasn't just making things—he was making illegal things. Illegal things in our house. In all the time I'd known him, he'd never once appeared drunk or under the influence, but he also kept to himself so much that I could have missed the signs. A secret still in the garage was one part of a larger problem.

Every time I opened the kitchen pantry, junk food fell out. Some was intentionally hidden in adjacent drawers or cabinets. Roscoe's eating was beyond out of control and our grocery bills along with it. Aside from the drugs and dubious stories of his lineage, I didn't really know much about his past. Being that he was likely over a hundred years old, there was a lot to uncover.

Then there was Adam. The half-turn often sat alone on the couch for hours while on his phone, playing gacha games while mindlessly scrolling through brain rot. As much as I wanted to point my fingers at all of them, I had my own issues to work through. My meticulous cleaning wasn't just to keep everything in order—it had become almost compulsive. There were times I'd wake up in the middle of the night because I'd left a cup out of place earlier, only to spend nearly an hour rearranging things.

Then there was the daydreaming and losing time. That was something new, and it hadn't really started until after I'd gone into those woods. Mosavi's words were like angry crows, pecking at me every time I'd try to put two and two together. Were there really witches? Was I under some kind of Whasha spell? As much as I feared him, Mosavi was the only person who likely had the answers, but how would I even bring it up without getting into serious trouble? That was, if he didn't already know.

"I just need to get through tonight," I said to myself as I turned down North Avenue. Despite the jail, this side of town was quiet and pleasant. All the streetlights worked, the grass was freshly cut, the houses were older but well-maintained, and the few government buildings were dim and unassuming. Whatever I thought about him personally, the mayor knew how to keep the place in order. Humans, half-turns and werewolves living together in harmony was something no one had thought possible. Somehow, though, this worked.

I thought the gate Mosavi mentioned would be a high razor wire-topped chain link fence, but before me stood a rather elegant black iron barrier. It was sleek and it automatically rolled to the side when I stepped forward, allowing just enough space for me to walk through. There wasn't a sound except for the whir of rotating security cameras overhead, each of their red dots trained on me like sniper sights. Blinding fluorescent light poured out of the barred glass door ahead, and as I reached for the handle, I took a deep breath and stepped inside.

Two brawny werewolves in forest green sheriff's deputy uniforms stood behind the desk, both half-grinning, their sharp stares making my standing neck hairs prick at my skin.

"Here to pick up your werewolves?" the black one said, handing me a sheet of paper with a bail amount typed in bold at the bottom.

"Fifteen hundred? What the hell did they do, beat up an old lady?"

"They're in some serious trouble," the lighter furred one replied. He kind of reminded me of Austin, just a bit shorter. "They were caught drinking and making rude gestures while exposing themselves behind a dumpster near The Waffle Hut. Do you know how long it took for us to get rid of that stereotype?"

"I'm gonna kill him," I muttered under my breath.

"We'd look the other way if you did," the black one said with a snorted laugh. "Anyway, the mayor figured you wouldn't be coming here with the bail money, so he's waiting inside." He pressed a button, and the door slid open.

I hesitated, my hands shaking as I made my way to the entrance of the now-exposed hallway of smooth, off-white cinderblock walls.

"Hey," the blond werewolf called out. "He's harsh but fair. If those two get life, you can tell your other half-turn roomie that we'd be happy to make the nights a little less lonely for both of you."

I looked down at the ring on his finger and then back up at him.

"Hey, don't get all judgy. It's open. Half-turns are always welcome in the boudoir," he continued with the flirty grin from earlier.

"Can't speak for Adam, but I'm good, thanks."

They waved me off as I stepped into the hallway. The door clanked shut behind me, echoing through thick silence. I walked until the walkway turned right and the jail cells appeared. After passing by three that were empty, I finally got to the culprits, who were lying on the floor against one another, snoring and reeking of booze.

"First strike."

I jumped, clutching my chest at the deep, angry voice from behind. The mayor was in his werewolf form lighting a cigar while sitting on the bench in an open cellblock with one leg crossed over his knee. "It is a big one, too," he added.

"I'm so sorry. I had a very long day, and I just wanted to go out and enjoy myself."

His irises glowed silver as he took a few puffs of tobacco.

"You honestly can't expect me to babysit full grown adult werewolves twenty-four seven," I continued.

"Did you drink tonight?" he asked, his tone less threatening than before.

"Y—yes, but I didn't break the law."

He unlatched his briefcase and pulled out two crystal-cut glasses and a fancy bottle of what looked like whiskey.

"Have another drink with me."

"Isn't this the reason those idiots are in that cell?"

"The general public as a collective is generally stupid." He glanced at the two slumbering werewolves as I sat next to him and took one of the heavy glasses. "We have this law specifically to prevent what these two did. I drink for pleasure and taste, not to make an embarrassment of myself and the town."

He uncorked the bottle before filling both glasses halfway.

"I thought you'd be threatening me again, not drinking with me."

"Why would you think that?"

"Maybe it has to do with the cursed lighter that keeps appearing in my pocket."

"You have to admit, it is rather effective," he said casually, half-lapping at the alcohol in his glass. "And don't think you're innocent here. Driving without a license and then going into the woods. I expected more from you."

I dug into my pocket to pull out the lighter. "So you have been watching me with this thing."

"Yes and no." He pointed to my glass. "You'll really like that. It's over a hundred years old and worth around two grand."

My eyes went wide. "Hopefully it's not taxpayer money." I was only half-joking there.

"Please. You think Norwich has the kind of revenue to satisfy my lifestyle?"

I shrugged and took a sip. It was so smooth, the flavor so complex I couldn't quite place it. "I don't know. It's a nice town for being out in the middle of nowhere."

"When you've got a healthy population of happy citizens, things get done. Buildings get remodeled, roads repaved, water pipes and sewage lines maintained. We have good schools, clinics, and services. Not a dime is wasted on frivolous bureaucratic nonsense. The failures of society start from the bottom but are facilitated by failures at the top."

We sat in silence for a moment, me sipping on the whiskey while the mayor stared as if expecting me to say something.

"Um... so, am I going to be allowed to take them home?"

"Not a chance."

"What's going to happen to them?"

"That's up to you," he said, finally glancing at the unconscious werewolves. "I can't have drunk werewolves with no self-control breaking the laws. So I will give you one last ultimatum, and I'm going to break my word to someone in order to tell you some useful things."

"You're still gonna force me to live in your dungeon?" I asked, finishing off the glass.

Mosavi snorted. "That possibility isn't off the table. Neither is me kicking those two out of town. They can live among the Whasha like wild animals."

"Norwich isn't Pleasantville. Austin is—"

"Your problem that you've allowed to be my problem," the mayor interrupted. "That know-it-all wife of mine will eat her words when she hears of this." His grimace warmed to a slight smile. "That lighter I gave you—it's a little more than just a means of surveillance. In the half-turn state, you are prone to uncontrollable outbursts. The kind of power you possess, however small, becomes dangerous and unwieldy, as I've already mentioned." He clenched his jaw while baring his teeth. "And it is exploitable."

"Is that why *you* lured me here? To exploit me?"

"I tried a soft-handed approach in the past, but all that resulted was wasted potential." He swallowed the remaining scotch in his glass. "I will not be as lenient with you."

"You did this to someone else?"

"I'd prefer not to discuss my failures." He shifted, turning his attention all the way back to me. "There are as few as three million werewolves in the entire world, and those with the vironoct make up a tiny fraction of a percent of that. When an elder dies, their power manifests in a random human male in early adulthood. It changes us. Turns us into leaders."

"Like alphas?"

Mosavi wrinkled his snout. "Never use that word again."

"O-kay," I said, nervously clearing my throat, not wanting to anger him further by asking why.

He pointed to the lighter in my hand. "You are already familiar with the kuu. They are not just enchanted jewelry to bond werewolves. They can be much more than that."

"You gave me a kuu?" I dropped the lighter onto the ground. "I have two of them now?"

"You only have one. The trinkets in your ears are powerless."

"So I'm not *bonded* to Roscoe?"

Mosavi laughed. "I can't even imagine." He shook his head. "Your bond belongs to me. If you try to leave town, I will find you. If you try to throw the kuu away, it will come back." The lighter suddenly appeared heavier in my hand. "You are mine until your full transformation."

The room began to turn lighter as I grew angrier. "I just want to be—"

"There it is," he interrupted, grabbing my lower jaw with his huge hand, holding my head in place as his eyes glowed.

Everything narrowed to a point. My body felt weightless, like I was dreaming. In another flash, a fancy room with marble pillars and deep red and gold-patterned carpet appeared around me. Lit candelabras stood tall in four far corners while flaming chandeliers hung from the ceiling. Before me were two werewolves. As the flames flickered brighter, I saw their faces.

"Roscoe?" I asked as the werewolf stood there with blank, light blue eyes. Austin stood next to him, his own irises the same color. He gave an army salute.

"What the hell is going on?"

"I'm seizing an opportunity while it presents itself," the mayor said from behind, slipping his clawed hands over my shoulders. "You're in control now. I want to see what you do."

Roscoe's face looked familiar. It was the same expression he'd worn when Darryl brutalized him.

"Is this some kind of mind control?"

"No, not quite. You can give suggestions, but whether or not they listen depends on your strength of will. Werewolves will happily follow someone who takes the lead, but they will also just as easily run over one who does not. Train them to be obedient."

"They're not dogs. I don't like this at all."

He squeezed my shoulders until they hurt.

"You either train them, or they leave town. Your choice."

Something warm buzzed in my pocket, and Mosavi was forced back by a white light. The strange room shattered into millions of pieces as the jail cell reappeared, but Roscoe and Austin were still standing, their eyes completely blank. The mayor grabbed me by the neck before pushing me to the floor.

"You went into the woods before, didn't you?" His eyes burned like liquid metal as he pulled the other two werewolves out of whatever trance they were in. Roscoe stumbled back before falling on his ass, Austin remained in place, bewildered.

"I was going to tell you, but I—"

Mosavi shut the cell door, locking the werewolves on the other side again. "Get out before I do something I'll regret."

     

I swallowed hard, my hands shaking again. "What about them?"

"They stay."

"For how long?"

He slammed his fist against the bars and snapped back, making me wince. "Days! Months! Years! However damn long I want to keep them for!"

"I'll get the bail money."

"No bail!"

"You can't just decide—" I pulled back when he stepped closer, leaning in until his wet snout touched my face.

"I can do what I please in this town," he whispered. "I will collect you later."

My stomach sank as I realized there was no bargaining with him while he was like this. He seemed almost feral, his eyes wide and pupils constricted. This wasn't the same calm and confident werewolf he'd been moments ago.

"I just went to get firewood. Why is this such a big deal?"

When he removed his suit jacket and his hackles stood straight, I didn't wait. I ran as fast as I could down the hall.

The walk home was hazy, dim streetlamps casting strange shadows just outside of my vision, turning every small tree into Mosavi, waiting to snatch me up. He'd almost come across as reasonable earlier, but I'd never seen or felt that kind of aggression in my life. I was worried about Austin and Roscoe, as well as Adam, who was likely still sleeping off his poor choices. If we lost our werewolves, and if Mosavi locked me up, too, what was Adam going to do?

I couldn't blame them for this one. They weren't the only ones that broke the law. Before meeting Roscoe, I had never even stepped foot in a jail before. Back in the city after changing, I was treated like a criminal, and it seemed nothing was all that different in Norwich.

As I approached the driveway, I looked out at the woods behind the house. Part of me wanted to just run away and disappear, but the rest was terrified by what else might be out there. Those werewolves seemed really friendly, but there was something wrong with them. They were more wolf than man. Was Mosavi scared of them, or were they scared of Mosavi? There was obviously a lot more to this than I was being told.

The door clicked open and I sauntered inside, my stomach still twisted. What made me sicker was not knowing when I'd be dragged away. Would he do it himself or would he send the deputies?

I stopped by Adam's room to check on him, but his bed was empty. "Adam?"

No answer. I looked over at the wall clock. Seven past three, so he couldn't have gone back out to the bar. My steps quickened down the hall. I glanced into mine and Roscoe's bedroom, but there was no one. However, I did see an orange glow behind the closed curtain coming from outside.

I pulled open the back door and stepped out into the yard as Adam poked at the fire in the pit.

"What are you doing?"

"Everyone was gone." He quickly wiped his face with his shirt and looked away. "So I decided to make a fire."

"Are you okay?" I sat on the chair next to him, but he didn't look at me. "Were you crying?"

"No!" He pushed me away. "I don't cry."

It was obviously a lie, but I nodded anyway. "Okay. Should I get some marshmallows?"

"Roscoe ate them yesterday."

"Of course he did." I leaned back in the chair. A chilly breeze buffeted the flames before calming. "I had fun tonight."

"No, you didn't. You couldn't wait to get out of there."

"That's not true."

He finally looked back at me, his eyes watering.

"It wasn't you, okay? I don't like bars, and I was really just hoping we could talk. Alone."

He sniffed once more before narrowing his eyes. "Why?"

"Because we don't talk. At all. We just argue and ignore each other. I feel like I'm always in some weird competition with you, and I don't even want to be."

"Where's Austin and Roscoe?"

"Jail."

Adam jumped to his feet. "What did they do?"

"It seems Austin has a lot of secret skills. They got piss drunk and did some... stuff."

"Did you get them out? Are they inside?"

"No. The mayor's pretty pissed, so I can't even steal Austin's stash of cash to make bail."

Adam sat back down. "How long do you think they'll be in there?"

I looked over at Adam and shrugged. "I don't know. I don't know anything, really. I keep trying to hold us together, but you guys keep doing everything you can to pull us apart. I just wanted us all to live a quiet, normal life."

"And be boring like you?" He smiled at me with his longer canines. "Why do you want to be boring like a human?"

"Because I don't like feeling like this. I don't like all the attention I'm getting. Maybe you do, but I don't."

He didn't respond. We both stared at the fire, listening to the popping embers as leaves rustled in the breeze.

"I've been wanting to ask you something, but you get all pissy when I bring it up," Adam said before tossing another small log on the flames.

"Ask about what?"

"Why are you such a neat freak?"

"Because unlike you and Roscoe, I don't want to live like a pig."

"That's not what I mean. I've seen you wash a dish like five times, put it away, and wash it again. Sometimes you'll sweep the floor, walk over it, and then grab the broom again and sweep the same place. You do it all the time when you think no one's watching."

Adam was probably the last person I wanted to talk to about this, but there wasn't anyone else. "I don't like feeling dirty."

"Dude, you have no more natural oils in your skin because you take like four showers a day. You're not dirty."

"It's different. When I came out as gay, I was told I was dirty. Now I'm half monster, and I'm going to end up smelling like Roscoe. So, I just keep cleaning so I don't feel so dirty."

"Cody..." Adam put his hand on my arm.

"It's like a stain on my soul that I can't clean. I hate that I need to have sex."

"Sex is pretty nasty." He shoved me. "That's what makes it so fun. That's what makes it feel good." He paused and his expression turned more serious. "Do you ever feel good?"

"Sometimes, but it's hard. Even when Roscoe and I are together, I always feel disappointed in myself after it's over. Sorry. It's been a night."

"Nah. I'm sorry. I didn't know you wanted to hang out with me. I did kinda ignore you and steal the spotlight."

"And you ran up the tab."

In a cocky show of defiance, Adam placed his hands behind his head and leaned back. "You can take it out of that huge chunk of money you withhold from me every month."

"Why were you crying?"

"I wasn't—"

"Cut the shit, Adam. I just spilled my guts to you."

The cocky expression faded. "I woke up, and no one was in the house."

"You could've called me."

"I did. It kept going to voicemail."

I pulled out my phone, which I had forgotten would automatically set to 'do not disturb' after two. "Oops."

"I just figured you all went back out without me. Everyone likes you more."

"Well, even if that was true—which it's not—you don't exactly make being around you a pleasant experience most of the time."

He didn't respond.

"I don't mean that to be rude. You're just such a grouch."

"So are you! You're always nagging like you're this bitter old lady who runs the house."

"I am not like a bitter old lady!"

Adam scrunched his nose. "'Adam, stop eating on the couch. You're getting crumbs everywhere. Roscoe, you didn't wash your dick with bleach before fucking me. No, we can't go out to eat because we have to save money for the impending apocalypse I've conjured up in my head!'"

"You know damn well we're on thin ice when it comes to money!"

"No, we're not! We don't even pay rent! The biggest expense we have is Roscoe's bottomless fucking appetite!"

"And that alone is all the more reason to save what we have."

I was losing this argument.

"Why are you like this?"

"What do you mean?" I asked, trying to calm down.

"We've got money. We've got a place to live. We're getting laid every day by monsters that know how to fuck really good—well, one of them does. Still really annoyed with that, by the way."

"Well, it's not just wisdom that comes with age, I guess."

"See? You've actually got a sense of humor. Why don't you ever lighten the hell up?"

"I don't know how to make you understand this. I'm used to always being a few dollars shy of being on the streets. There were some days I'd just have to go without food, or heat, or electricity. Poverty just follows me, you know? It's just like when I was a kid, and my parents— never mind."

"We're fine, Cody."

"You call this fine? We've got two werewolves in jail, and I'm probably next."

Adam laughed. "What did *you* do? Clean someone's house without permission?"

"Apparently walking in the woods is a punishable offense in Mosavi's authoritarian regime."

"Are you for real?"

"The guy doesn't fuck around, and he's threatening us. He knows about Austin. He knows everything." I picked up a stick and tossed it onto the fire. "I wonder who his wife is and if I could talk to her."

"Damn, he's married to a *woman*?" Adam chewed on his lower lip. "I bet I can change him."

I rolled my eyes.

"What? He's really hot."

"Did you hear what I said, or has the constant state of being a slut caused the last drop of blood to leave your brain?"

"Okay, so things are looking bleak, but if you guys are gone, I get the house and all the money to myself."

"You're forgetting something kind of important. See, you need to live with a werewolf to keep collecting that money, and Mosavi will likely report it and kick you out of the house."

Adam let out a sharp gasp. "We can't let him get away with this. I've got an idea!"

"Glad to see that strong sense of selfishness paying off. What's this idea?"

"So, he's married right?"

"We've established that."

"You and I need to get him really drunk, and then I'll have the nastiest, hottest sex with him, and you get his wife to walk in right as he's about to blow his load in my ass."

I stood and walked to the backdoor. "Good night, Adam. You're a fucking idiot."

"What? It's foolproof! He's a werewolf, and no one can resist this hot, nubile body."

"You don't even know what that word means." I gave him one last groan before disappearing inside.

# Aftermath

A trembling, window-shaped beam of light sat low on the wall. I'd finally gotten to sleep at around four in the morning, but the maple scent of breakfast lured me all the way awake as dishes clanked down the hall.

I threw off the covers and hurried toward the kitchen, only to be stopped by Adam, who sat at the dining room table, his eyes wide as if he'd just seen a dead body.

"And then, the key to a perfect flapjack is to flip it in the pan," Roscoe instructed as metal gently clapped against metal.

"Are you teaching Austin to up his pancake game?" I asked, strutting into the kitchen, only to lock up when I saw the mayor glaring at the other werewolf with his arms crossed.

Roscoe removed the pan from the stove and turned around with a huge grin. "G'mornin' sweetheart. Was just teachin' yer majesty here how to make a good southern breakfast."

Mosavi groaned in disgust as he made his way out of the kitchen, brushing past me. It looked like he hadn't changed his clothes since last night, but his jacket was missing and his nice white dress shirt had been ripped in multiple places. After a moment, the back door opened before clicking shut.

"Someone explain what the hell is going on," I said, turning back to Roscoe who was pouring more batter onto the pan. "I thought you guys were in jail. Where's Austin?"

"Sleepin'. We had a rough night."

"Yeah, so did I, and I'm way too exhausted to start yelling at you right now, by the way. I'll save that for later."

"Aw, don't be mad. I'm makin' us all a good old-fashioned breakfast." He pointed to the fluffy biscuits cooling in a rectangular pan. "I had to use all the Crisco for those, so we'll have to postpone the ass play."

"Funny." I picked up one of the biscuits. It weighed a lot more than it should have. "Dude. You used an entire can of shortening? There are only eight of these things."

"Yup. Gramma used to say they'd give you 'the itis' if you ate more than one." He tossed a quick glance at the entrance before lowering his voice. "Make sure 'ol grumpy ass gets two."

"What is he doing here, anyway?" I whispered.

Roscoe shrugged. "All I know is I ain't behind bars, and he's not doin' angry kinky shit to me anymore."

"What are you talking about?"

"Oh boy, when you left, that's when the weird shit happened. You know, if I was into bondage, it might have been fun." He let out a high-pitched whimper. "I ain't gonna be havin' sex for a day or two. Hope you don't mind."

"What the hell did he do to you guys?"

"It's kinda embarrassing." He grabbed my hand and moved it over something metallic hidden in his crotch fluff. "Austin's got one, too. And he said we ain't allowed out of our cages until we behave. Not like I can argue with an elder."

I couldn't help but give Mosavi props. This was a rather effective way to get a werewolf under control rather than keeping him in jail.

"Did you just smile?" Roscoe asked. "This ain't fuckin' funny."

"Of course not. This is just awful," I replied, feigning concern.

"This affects you too, ya know."

"Well, it's a good thing there are plenty of other werewolves in town that don't have their junk locked away."

Roscoe didn't respond. He just stood there, mouth wide open and glaring at me.

The coffee caught my eye, and I grabbed a mug before changing the subject. "Something tells me I'm gonna need the whole pot." I glanced at the microwave clock. "Damn, it's almost noon? I thought it was ten."

Roscoe resumed his cooking, pouring scrambled eggs into the frying pan. "He don't like talking to me. It freaks me out when he just stands there starin', so I got nervous and started explaining how to cook breakfast."

"Well, I'm never doing the OnlyStans thing again, so you could always start a cooking channel."

"Aww, for real? We got a lot of followers. You really wanna let 'em all down?"

"Absolutely," I muttered while walking out of the kitchen. Adam was now scrolling on his phone, but instead of ignoring me, he smiled and looked up.

"We can still put that plan into motion."

"You just want to have sex with him."

"Well, yes. But I'll be saving you at the same time. I can multitask," he said, swiping through his phone again before going silent.

I let out an annoyed hiss and made the dreaded walk down the hallway toward the back door. As I stepped outside, a cool breeze washed over me, carrying hints of tobacco smoke. Mosavi sat still on one of our chairs, staring into the woods.

"You may as well not draw it out," I said, sitting across from him. "I'll pack my things."

His ears pressed firmly against his head, but he didn't respond. He wouldn't even look in my direction.

"Nothing? Not going to yell at me like you did last night?"

It took him a moment, but he finally turned back around.

"I may have let my anger get a bit out of control."

The chilly breeze picked up again, the piles of dead leaves tousled by short-lived whirlwinds as they danced through the yard. Mosavi took another puff of his cigar before exhaling loudly, his eyes half closed.

"What made you change your mind about those two?"

"That is a personal matter. Plus, it seems I don't need to keep them in jail as punishment."

"Yeah, I'm going to eventually need what you locked away, so maybe we can work out community service or something."

He reached into his pocket and dangled a pair of keys in front of me.

"I'll have these delivered to you in a few days. I think you'll find your werewolves a little less unruly now. You will need to use the vironoct for the tall one, by the way. I'm putting that in your hands."

"I still don't understand what happened last night. What did you do to me?"

"That was you, not me. All I did was guide you along until something stopped me." He paused and eyed my pants. "What's in your pocket?"

"Your lighter."

"Your other pocket."

I was confused at first, but when I reached in, my fingers were met with the smooth opal-like stone.

"Damn. When did this get in there?" I pulled it out and handed it to Mosavi. "I was going to bring this up because you're the only person who probably knows what this is, but..."

Mosavi examined the shiny stone, his nose wrinkling in disgust before he handed it back.

"Well, the damage has been done," he said with a growl. "As soon as I am allowed back home, I will rub this revelation in her face."

"Ahhh," I said slyly as the elder werewolf's ears folded back. "You're in the doghouse."

"I would choose my words a little more carefully."

"Sorry," I corrected, clearing my throat. "So, what is this thing?"

"I am not sure, but it is Whashan, which means you should get rid of it immediately."

The way he said that caught my suspicions. "I don't think I will."

"Excuse me?"

"It limits your control, doesn't it?"

Mosavi said nothing.

"That's why you got so pissed off last night. You couldn't have your way, and this is the reason. Isn't it?"

"If you want to become a filthy beast, then do so away from my town."

"No. I like it here. I'll stay." I closely examined him to gauge his reaction—rage followed immediately by a reluctant resolve. "I'm not getting rid of this if it keeps me safe from you."

"Safe from *me*?" He drew in another puff of smoke. "I am the one trying to keep you safe while teaching you how to lead effectively. That item prevents me from helping you."

He didn't seem like he was lying, but there was still an air of dishonesty in his eyes. A low buzz vibrated from his pants pocket, and he reached in to pull out his phone.

"Yes," he said lowly, clearing his throat. Someone spoke on the line, but the words were too muffled to understand. "We can discuss this later—if you will allow me back." He muttered that last part. More muffled chatter came through the speaker as Mosavi turned his head away from me, whispering something into the phone before hanging up. "It seems I'll be taking my leave. Thank God."

"Was that the wife?"

"It is none of your business," he snapped, baring his sharp teeth. "I would highly advise against keeping that trinket in the house if you want my help."

"Why would I want your help?"

He dangled the keys in front of me, before dropping them onto the ground. "I'll let you come to that conclusion yourself." Mosavi stood, letting out a chuckle before striding toward the road where a black Mercedes SUV pulled up.

Once he and the vehicle were gone, I picked up the keys and put them in my pocket. At least he wasn't going to make me wait a few days. I thought about giving the other key to Adam, but with how much animosity was brewing between those two, I decided it wasn't a good idea to give him that much power.

Adam and I sat on the couch while Roscoe finished cooking, both of us staring at our phones instead of each other. Once the bedroom door opened, it shattered the awkward mood.

Austin crept through the hallway, letting out little whimpers with each step until the bathroom door clicked shut.

"That didn't look good," I said, scooting to the edge of the couch and setting my phone on the end table.

"That didn't sound good either," Adam added with a smile. "I wonder if Mosavi beat the shit out of him."

"I hope not. The poor guy was just starting to open up—" I caught myself as Adam's attention snapped back to me.

"What do you mean?"

"Nothing. He was just starting to talk is all."

He stood, keeping his narrow glare on me while coming closer. "I can tell when you lie, by the way."

"I am not lying!"

The bathroom door opened, and Austin limped out of the hallway.

"You look like shit," Adam said in a teasing tone before eyeing the dry fur on the werewolf's hands. "We're about to eat breakfast. You should wash up."

Austin didn't respond. Instead, he ignored Adam completely as he made his way to the kitchen.

"Don't be gross," I said, pulling his attention to me. Our eyes locked for a moment, and the room brightened to silver as Austin's eyes went wide.

"Yes, sir," he shouted before disappearing back into the hallway, the sudden reaction startling me.

"What the hell was that? Adam asked. "Why did he call you sir?"

I held up my hands in defense. "I'm just as confused as you are."

"What did you guys really do while I was gone?"

"We didn't do anything!"

"All clean, sir," Austin said, showing me his wet hands as he stepped around the corner. I would have thought he was toying with me if it wasn't for the empty blue glow of his irises.

"Soooo... did something happen?" I asked.

"Do you want something to happen, sir?" His tail wagged and an anticipatory smile flashed every tooth in his mouth. "I can make things happen."

"All right, you've made your point," Adam snapped, looping his arm around Austin's. "I'll be nicer to you. Wanna go have some fun?"

Austin's irises faded back to amber. "I'm hungry."

"Well, I'm horny," Adam said, trying in vain to pull the werewolf toward the bedroom. "We can eat breakfast after."

"Can't. Not in the mood," Austin said dismissively before brushing past the half-turn before disappearing into the kitchen.

"I thought we talked about this." Adam grabbed my shirt, giving it a hard tug. "We agreed to leave each other's kuu mates alone."

"We didn't do anything! I swear."

Austin poked his head into the dining room. "Sir, Roscoe wants to know if you want your eggs sunny-side up."

"Stop calling me sir. It's weird," I said, turning away from Adam's increasingly angry stare. "And I don't like runny yolks. I like them scrambled with a little bit of ketchup."

A loud, overexaggerated groan echoed through the kitchen behind Austin.

The werewolf turned around. "Cody wants—"

"Yeah, I heard. Ask him if he wants me to defrost some chicken nuggies and tater tots instead."

"Roscoe said—"

"We can hear each other just fine, Austin," I interrupted as the werewolf shrugged and stepped back into the kitchen. "I think Mosavi did something to him."

"Yeah, sure he did. He's being all weird around *you* because *Mosavi* did something." Adam pushed me away before sitting at the table. "I guess one werewolf wasn't enough for your gaping ass, huh?"

I stood speechless as Adam picked up his phone and started scrolling like usual. So much for our truce. Mosavi's cryptic warnings earlier started to make a little more sense, but I still didn't understand what he'd done or how I was going to fix it.

Austin walked into the dining room holding two plates. He sat one gently in front of me while almost dropping the other in front of Adam before walking back into the kitchen. I looked down at my plate, which had the scrambled eggs covered with ketchup that had been squirted in the shape of a dick.

"Real mature, Roscoe."

"I coulda just drawn an ass, considering that's what it's gonna taste like."

I rolled my eyes before shoving away the pancakes and bacon with my fork that had gotten a little too close to one another. Unfortunately, some syrup had run into the eggs, which I then moved over into a napkin.

"What are you doing?" Adam asked.

"Separating everything."

The two werewolves followed one other, each holding their own plates. The eggs in my napkin caught Roscoe's attention as he sat next to me, the chair groaning under his weight.

"Yer seriously gonna throw away perfectly good eggs because of a little syrup."

"Syrup doesn't belong on eggs."

"Neither does ketchup," Roscoe muttered before biting into a biscuit.

"I like ketchup on my eggs. I don't like the crust on my sandwiches or pizza, and food can't touch."

"Maybe you should have taken him up on the chicken nuggies offer," Adam said with a snort, shoveling some pancakes into his mouth as Austin slapped the back of his head.

"Don't tease him," Austin said before sitting next to Adam.

"All right, I want to know the truth. Did you guys do something?" Adam asked, turning to Austin.

The blond werewolf scratched his head. "Hmm. Don't remember."

"Austin! You know damn well we didn't do anything."

"If you say so, sir. I mean Cody."

Adam shot up and slammed his chair under the table. "I see what's going on. You're threatened because I'm hotter than you. You wanna be the only half-turn in this house, so you're turning everyone against me!"

"Adam, for fuck's sake."

"Fine. You can have him."

As he turned to leave, Austin caught his arm, but the half-turn pulled away and stormed off to their bedroom before slamming the door. The werewolf shrugged before finishing the food on his plate.

"You had better go talk to him."

"He doesn't wanna talk," Austin said, pushing the plate away.

"Then you should probably do what he wanted you to do earlier—ooh." I suddenly remembered why Austin turned him down. I reached into my pocket and pulled out a small pair of keys. "Uh, let's get that cage off."

"Hey!" Roscoe dropped his fork on the plate. "You have the keys?"

"Forget it. You're on notice."

"C'mon Cody. Yer gonna get all cranky like Adam if I don't do my duty."

"I'm a sex camel. I can go without for weeks if I wanted."

"Oh?" Roscoe picked up his fork again before stuffing bacon into his mouth, intentionally talking with it full to irritate me more. "We'll see about that."

As I stood to lead Austin to the bathroom, he pulled my plate over and slid my food onto his.

"Hey! I wasn't done eating yet."

"There's cereal in the pantry." He picked up an entire pancake and shoved it into his mouth. "Ya might like that better anyways."

As irritated as I was with him, I was worried he might actually be right, and admitting when I was wrong to Roscoe was like ripping duct tape off my chest.

A crash rattled the walls behind a closed bedroom door as we made our way to the bathroom.

"I suppose I better fuck the little twerp before he destroys the house," Austin said, a little more concerned than earlier.

Even though it was awkward, I pulled aside Austin's extra fluff to find the cage firmly attached. I wasn't even sure how it stayed on or how any of these things worked.

"I didn't know Mosavi had a kinky side." I moved the cage around, trying to find where to put the key. "You know, I was thinking... why don't you try something different with Adam? You know, spice it up?"

"Like what?"

"How do you normally do it?" I asked, examining the cage closer. There were different holes, but nothing that would fit the keys the mayor had given me.

"Well, he's usually always ready, so I just fuck him hard til I'm done."

"Yeah, how about some foreplay?"

"What's that?"

I looked up at him, thinking he was pulling my leg, but his expression was genuinely intrigued.

"Austin... how many guys were you with before Adam?"

"As a werewolf? No one. When I was a half-turn I just got fucked and that was it."

"Let me figure out how to get this damn thing off of you, and I'll fill you in on what Roscoe does to me."

The keys didn't actually do anything; it was the inscription on the ring that I should have looked at. After letting out an annoyed groan, I tossed the key ring into the garbage and grabbed a box of off-brand marshmallow cereal from the pantry. The mayor was punishing me in his own twisted way, but with the punishment came the lessons.

The only way to unlock those cages was to use the vironoct, which also meant messing with an already vulnerable mind. I did ask permission before doing it, but that didn't seem to matter much to

Austin. He was almost *too* eager to obey any command. The scene played out in my head from earlier.

*"All right, private. You've got an angry half-turn in there and one mission: neutralize the target. You've been trained for this, soldier, and I want to see a smile on that half-turn's face when you're done! Is that understood?"*

*"Yes sir!"*

His wagging tail betrayed his serious expression. For whatever reason, he responded well to the military roleplay, his eyes turning baby blue as his stare became glassy and distant. Maybe this kind of stuff was fine for Mosavi who was a borderline tyrant, but it made me feel kind of wrong.

As I ate breakfast, I had to turn up the volume on the television to drown out the moaning and banging coming from the second bedroom. Perhaps I shouldn't have used the word *neutralize* in that command. After nearly twenty minutes, Austin still hadn't finished, and I was done with breakfast. The longer I sat in the living room listening to them, the more worried I got.

While I was trying to figure out the cage earlier, I thought about Roscoe. It wasn't like him to get that upset. Hell, there was still a half-eaten plate of his breakfast sitting in the refrigerator. That alone meant there was something really wrong.

I slipped into a light jacket and stepped out into the backyard, hoping I'd be able to escape the increasingly aggressive noice. After shutting the door, I made my way toward Roscoe, who was sat cross-legged next to the lit firepit. His slight gut hung over the band of the borrowed fatigues he wore, which were several sizes too small. He stared pensively at the growing flames, not bothering to acknowledge me as I sat on one of the plastic lawn chairs.

"You didn't clean your plate."

"Not really hungry."

"Are you okay?"

"Can you please take this thing off of me?" He looked up from the fire, his sad amber eyes piercing mine. "I fucked up. I'm sorry."

"That's really all I wanted to hear." I smiled at him. "Sometimes your antics are annoying, and sometimes they cross the line. This could have ended badly if the mayor went through with his threats."

"The guy's a real piece of work. I'm glad he left. He scares the shit out of me."

     

"I don't know. I keep getting this feeling like he's overcompensating."

"Well it sure ain't his dick he's overcompensating for." Roscoe stood from the ground before sitting in one of the lawn chairs while letting out a slight whimper. "Not sure why he didn't do to me what he did to Austin."

"What did he do?"

"Just mind-fucked the guy. Austin was bein' his normal shitty self, thinkin' since he's bigger than everyone else, he can backtalk an elder. Ever since Mosavi did that eye thing, the poor guy's been weird." Roscoe caught himself. "Well, weird*er*. Austin just rolled over like a puppy with that creepy smile."

"Out of morbid curiosity, what *did* Mosavi do to you?"

Roscoe narrowed his eyes. "Why do you wanna know?"

"For science."

"I ain't giving *you* any of his ideas. The only thing I'll say is he brutalized my ass and put this fuckin' cage on me." He rubbed at his crotch. "I don't know why bein' so embarrassed kinda turns me on, but I really want this thing off, too."

"Well, apparently the keys don't work, so I've got to do something a little different."

"Oh?" Roscoe grinned. "Is it sexy?"

"Well... that depends on what you consider sexy. Remember when you said Austin got all creepy after Mosavi did the eye thing?"

Roscoe raised an eyebrow.

"Well, I have to do the eye thing to you to get it off."

"Dude. You can do that?" Roscoe's tail stopped mid-wag. "I really don't like this," he said, his tone turning serious again. "That mayor ain't right at all. And that eye thing? I think it happened to me before."

"Yeah, Darryl used it on you. Remember?"

"Nah." Roscoe opened his mouth, speechless for a moment. "Darryl didn't do that."

"Yes, he did. Your eyes went all blue and creepy before he dragged you into the bedroom."

"That son of a—" Roscoe snorted. "I guess I deserved it."

"So did this happen before Darryl?"

"I don't really remember. Always thought it was because of the drugs, but now I ain't so sure. I get these flashes in my head, and all I can see is woods and glowin' eyes everywhere. I think the reason Mosavi couldn't get me was because of whatever happened when I was younger, but if Darryl did it, then maybe those memories are wrong." He tried to say something else but stopped himself, his tail hanging limp between the gap of the folding chair.

"Well, for whatever reason, Mosavi changed his mind about forcing me to live with him and keeping you guys locked up, and I think I know that reason."

His ears fell to the sides of his head. "It's kinda weird. Never really gave a shit about what anyone thought of me, but now yer here and he's giving you a taste of the finer things."

"He's married, by the way."

"So? He's a rich alpha. He can have as many mates as he wants, and no one ain't gonna say shit. Christ, you ever seen the size of that guy's balls? It's obscene."

"Well, he's not exactly my type," I said, giving Roscoe a sly smile.

"What is your type?" Roscoe sat up a little higher, his tail beginning to sway.

"Well, let's see. I think if I were to settle down with anyone, he'd have to make me laugh. He'd have to know how to cook, because I'll starve. I've got to feel comfortable in his arms, and the sexual chemistry's got to be there."

"Sounds like you know what you want."

"Maybe, but it's too early to know for sure," I said, half-teasingly. "You know, this is the first time in my life I've been able to actually put into words what I want. I never really thought about it before."

"Me neither," Roscoe said, confidently folding one leg over his knee. When he did that, a loud rip came from under him. "Uh oh. Austin's gonna be pissed. I kinda borrowed these without asking."

"They're pretty ripped up as it is. I'm sure he won't even notice."

Roscoe stood, and the seam from the top to the bottom had been torn open, the only thing keeping the fabric on was the waistband and button.

"Okay. That's bad," I said. "Maybe hide them until we can get them tailored or something."

Roscoe sat back down. "Well, we're not gonna be able to ignore the mayor, so we need to figure out how to get on his good side or get out of town. I don't wanna end up like Austin." Roscoe pointed toward the woods. "Every now and then, I can smell 'em out there, and it kinda brings back good memories, but it scares me too."

"Smell who?"

"Ferals. They've been close but always keepin' outta sight."

"When I was out getting firewood, I ran into a few of them."

Roscoe's ears perked up. "For real? Why didn't you tell me?"

I shrugged. "It hasn't exactly been at the top of my mind lately. Remember that opal I showed you?"

Roscoe nodded.

"They gave it to me, and I think it fucks with Mosavi's vironoct or whatever."

"Now that's some good news!" Roscoe jumped to his feet, lifting me up with him. This time, Austin's fatigues ripped completely before falling off. "So, where'd you put it?"

"In the top drawer with my underwear."

"Ah, that's why I never saw it. I'm only interested in the ones in the hamper."

I rubbed my forehead.

"I'm the yin to your yang," he said, leading me back inside the house. "Get this cage off me so we can yin-yang all night."

"Nah," I said, teasingly.

Roscoe stopped in the doorway, his ears dropping.

"C'mon Cody. It was hot at first, but now I'm gettin' frustrated."

"I think that's the point of this thing."

He leaned in, and I expected him to give me a quick kiss, but then his tongue slipped into my mouth and one of his large hands squeezed my ass.

"I've gotta get that thing off you," I said, defeated as I ran inside ahead of him.

Soaked in sweat, I straddled Roscoe as he howled, and things felt somewhat normal. His chest had this spicy aroma, which was slightly different from the usual. It was nice enough that I collapsed into him, burying my face.

"I guess I needed that," I whispered. "How in the hell do you keep doing this?"

"Doin' what?"

As soon as we separated, I rolled over onto my side of the bed. "How do you make me come just by fucking me?"

"Oh that." He grinned. "It's easy. Gotta angle myself juuuust right. When I feel you clench up, I know I hit the right spot."

A black bag caught my eye in the corner of the room. "That's new."

Roscoe looked over and shrugged. "It ain't mine. I thought it was yours."

I climbed out of bed and knelt next to the heavy bag before unzipping it. "Whoa."

"What is it?"

It was an entire bondage kit, some of it glowing different colors when I touched them. I pulled out several items, including a cat o' nine tails, several metal cock rings, heavy shackles, nipple clamps wired up to some kind of small battery, and several other things I couldn't recognize.

"Oh, hell no! Throw all that magic shit out," Roscoe said in a panic while scrambling out of bed. "That stuff's got witchcraft all over it."

"Witchcraft?" I turned back toward him, wanting to dismiss what he said, but with everything I'd seen, it wasn't too far out in left field. Even the cages didn't unlock without me using the vironoct. "I wonder why he left this stuff here."

"Don't care. Throw that shit away."

"I'm keeping the cages."

Roscoe shifted his eyes away from me. "Why?"

"Insurance."

"I'm sorry I got drunk. It won't happen again, I swear."

I packed everything back into the bag before making my way over to the dresser. "You're damn right it won't happen again." After shuffling through the drawer for a minute, the glint of a large opal caught my eye. "Here," I said, tossing the stone to Roscoe.

He sat up and caught it with one hand. "Sure is pretty."

"They didn't speak at all when they gave it to me."

"That's just 'cause you can't understand 'em."

"And you can?"

He gave me an uneasy look. "With the right drugs, yeah."

"Roscoe!" I yelled, slipping back into my clothes. "Did you learn anything last night? *That* was Mosavi letting us off easy. I don't even want to think about what he'd do if you're caught using drugs."

"It's natural. That's how they talk to people who ain't in their pack."

"He was very clear about us not going back into the woods." I picked up the gold lighter that had been sitting on the dresser. "He'll



*Aeron Dusk*

know the moment I go out there. He knows where I am at all times because of this stupid thing."

"Just throw it away."

"You honestly think that wasn't the first thing I did? Every time I throw it away, it ends up back in my pocket."

Roscoe hummed contemplatively as he got out of bed and toweled off.

"Take a damn shower," I said, snatching the towel away.

Roscoe gave himself a few sniffs. "I'm fine. I had one yesterday, remember? Got myself all prettied up fer you, and you left me hangin'."

I pointed to the cock cage. "Take a shower, or I'm putting that back on you."

"I'd like to see you try."

I folded my arms. "You have to sleep sometime."

The werewolf stood quiet for a moment.

"I'm throwin' that thing away," he said, rushing for the cage, but I snatched it before he reached it.

"I don't think so."

"Yer not strong enough, you little half-turn twerp," he mocked, easily prying my hand open with his large, clawed fingers, but as he touched the metal on the cage, a blinding bolt sent him flying across the room and into the wall. There was a slight indentation where he impacted.

I ran over to him. "Whoa! Are you okay?"

Roscoe rubbed his head. "See what I mean? Throw it away, Cody."

"After what you just did? I don't think so."

"I was just joking."

"You were challenging me." The room started to turn a familiar silver, the tone of my voice growing deeper. "Don't challenge me again."

"Cody!" Roscoe's irises lightened to blue, but he squeezed his eyes shut and turned away.

The intense emotions taking over my body only grew, and I grabbed the scruff of Roscoe's neck, forcing him to look at me.

"Tell me who your leader is," I said with a snarl, and his eyes snapped wide open. "Tell me."

"It's you," he whispered, his countenance now distant. "What do you want me to do?"

I snatched the opal out of his hand and pointed at the bed, but not before a jolt of electricity shot through me in waves, causing me to stumble backward. The sensation intensified so much that I was thrown to the floor as the room darkened back to normal.

Roscoe crawled toward me, his eyes returning to their usual honey amber.

"God damn! What the hell's goin' on?"

"I don't know," I groaned, still shaking as I sat upright before examining the *opal* that now lay shattered on the floor. "Aw shit." I picked through the pieces, shaking my head. "There goes our protection."

"Look at that," Roscoe said, pointing at the gold lighter that had fallen to the floor. It glowed a molten orange for a moment before turning black. I tried to pick it up, but it crumbled like soot.

"It's gone."

"I kinda had a hunch," Roscoe said, picking up a piece of the broken gem. "I think I remember something. They protect against witchcraft. There aren't that many things that'll scare a feral werewolf, but witches sure do."

"How the hell is a werewolf using witchcraft?"

Roscoe shook his head. "He ain't. Witches can't be male the same way werewolves can't be female. And witches sure as hell can't be werewolves." He went silent for a moment. "I bet there's a witch in this town." He scrambled to his feet. "Hell, it's in the town's name. Nor-WITCH. Why didn't I see it?"

"Okay, now you're going all tinfoil hat on me."

"You don't know, Cody."

"And you don't remember. So, let's calm down and try to get some answers."

The door to our bedroom flung open, and Austin strode in, wearing nothing but a wet boner and an earnest expression.

"Fuck dude! You scared the shit outta me," Roscoe yelled, holding his chest.

Austin greeted us with a salute. "The target's been neutralized and is safely asleep, sir!"

"Oh, what the hell now?" Roscoe whispered under his breath.

"Uh... good work, soldier," I said with a bit of hesitation as his creepy blue eyes locked with mine.

"Awaiting your next command, sir."

"Damn, Mosavi really fucked him up good, didn't he?"

"This one may have been my fault. He does anything he's told, and... I kinda didn't know it would last this long."

The older werewolf cracked a sly grin. "Seriously? He'll do anything he's told?" He walked up to Austin, eyeing the larger werewolf's empty blue stare. "Oh boy."

"Leave him alone," I said, before turning back to the other werewolf. "Austin, why don't you—"

"Clean my dick with yer tongue. That's an order, soldier!"

"Roscoe, stop!"

"What? This shit's funny as hell."

Austin's eyes dimmed to a familiar blood orange, his brows furrowing as his large fingers wrapped around Roscoe's neck.

"What did you just tell me to do, fatty?"

"I—is that how you talk to yer superior officer, sold—"

The larger werewolf shoved Roscoe against the wall, leaving another head-sized dent in it. "You ever speak to me like that again and you'll be eating through a straw until your teeth grow back!" He released the older werewolf and looked over at me. "I'm going to my garage."

"Take the still apart," I called back to him.

Austin groaned but didn't respond as he disappeared into the hallway.

"Thought you said he did what he was told?" Roscoe said, rubbing his neck. "Goddamn, he dug his claws in and everything."

"I still don't know exactly what triggers it." I stood up and walked over to the door. "I'm going to go check on Adam."

"What's wrong with him now?"

"He's been getting meaner lately."

We both crept down the hall to see Adam sleeping naked, spread eagle on the bed with the biggest smile on his face. Roscoe went to say something, but I caught his mouth with my hand and led him away from the door.

"Okay, maybe this isn't as bad as I thought," I whispered, letting go of Roscoe. "Adam's happy. Austin's... happy—ish, and we're okay, right?"

"I dunno. If there's a witch—"

"Then we'll deal with that later. Right now this might be working in our favor."

Austin walked out of the garage carrying about five bottles of homemade moonshine.

"Uh, whatcha doin' with those, buddy?" Roscoe asked, slinking across the room and licking his lips.

"Dumping them," he replied.

"I got an idea!"

I grabbed a magazine Adam had been reading earlier, rolled it tightly, and smacked Roscoe over the head with it. "No!"

"Now hold on, I ain't talkin' about the booze. We could trade something to the ferals to get them talkin'. I happen to know for a fact those fuckers love white cheddar popcorn and soda. Hell, they'd suck yer dick dry for a Little Debbie Swiss roll."

Austin rolled his eyes and continued to the kitchen.

"You know for a fact?" I crossed my arms. "Are you sure you're talking about the ferals or yourself, because Little Debbie owns half the real estate in our pantry right now."

Roscoe didn't respond as Austin sauntered back out of the kitchen.

"Yer not gonna dump the beer too, are ya?"

"Beer?" I asked. "Where the hell did you get beer?"

"Made it," Austin replied, his ears slowly drooping and his eyes changing color again. "I'll dump it all, sir."

"Now, hold on, let's not get too hasty. That beer was amazing." Roscoe placed his hand on my shoulder. "Yer really gonna make Austin dump all his hard work down the drain? Yer gonna crush him. Just look at his face!"

We both turned toward the blonde werewolf staring at us with the same stern, emotionless expression he often wore.

"The guy obviously has his heart on his sleeve. Would you really want to hurt his feelings?"

"Dump the beer," I said without hesitating.

"Wait a minute! C'mon. You gotta taste it first. Please."

"Roscoe, I'm putting my foot down."

His eyes grew wide and watery as he leaned in, his pupils dilating much larger than they should have been able to. I still didn't know how the hell he got them to do that.

"That hasn't worked since we met."

"Pwease..."

"It's hard to believe someone as pathetic as you is over a century old."

His tail wagged faster. "If you don't take at least one sip, I'll do my Andy Dick impression every time we have sex."

"Bring me a goddamn beer," I demanded, to which Austin replied with a salute before disappearing into the garage. "One sip, and then it's going down the drain."

Roscoe knew I didn't really like beer, so I was kind of confused as to what he hoped to accomplish with this. Drinking foamy homemade bread-water wasn't exactly going to change my mind.

Austin returned holding a recycled brown bottle with a faded label.

"You did wash these, right?"

"Of course I did. I'm not gross like Roscoe. I didn't get these from the dumpster," Austin said with a snarl, pushing the bottle into my hand.

"I ain't dumpster-dove since I left the city, but I bet they throw away a lot of cool shit around here."

"Don't bring any garbage into this house," I said, holding the bottle to my lips. The flavor was unexpected—like beer, but with an interesting aftertaste.

Roscoe smirked as I took another, larger gulp.

The beer became a malted chocolate with a hint of heat, like either ginger or cayenne pepper.

"What the hell is this?"

"It's beer," Austin replied, matter-of-factly.

"No, I mean, what did you put in it?"

"It's a secret."

I gulped down more of it.

"You wouldn't want to know, anyway," he added.

I stopped mid-swallow and slowly spat back into the bottle. "Okay, now I want to know what the fuck I just ingested."

"Nope." Austin turned and walked back into the garage.

"So?" Roscoe asked, his expression more eager than before. "What do you think?"

"It's good, but—"

"Then let's take some bottles out in the woods, have a little fun and see if we come across any ferals to trade with."

"This is a stupid idea."

"Without that lighter, Mussolini ain't gonna know nothin'."

Austin ambled back through the dining room holding an entire box of beer, but I grabbed his arm. "I changed my mind. Don't dump those."

Though he didn't smile, the werewolf's eyes lit up, and his tail wagged.

"All right," he replied, setting the box on the table before taking a bottle out for himself. I snatched it out of his hand before he could open it.

"Don't even think about it," I said, placing the bottle back into the box.

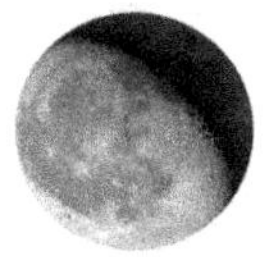

# Chapter 19

# A Feral High

Furious pounding shook the front door, tearing Roscoe and me from a stupid argument about which Star Trek was the best. At first, I thought Austin had locked himself out of the house again. He'd already lost his house key four times, so he'd gotten a brilliant idea. Instead of having the key on his person, he'd decided to hide it in a rock-shaped lockbox among hundreds of other rocks that he'd dumped around the front porch. That turned into a fun evening.

I reached for the knob as the pounding continued louder, but the moment tobacco wafted in through the poorly insulated door, I stopped.

"Shit," I whispered, peeking through the front window curtains. Mosavi was in human form, but his teeth were bare and eyes glowing that angry silver. "Well, he looks like he's in a fantastic mood."

"He always looks like that," Roscoe replied from behind, leaning over my shoulder to get a look.

"Answer the door, Dakota!" He snapped his attention to the window, his furious gaze settling on me before I jumped back.

"Well, we need to disappear." I glanced back at the dining room table, which held the large cardboard box of booze and junk food. "That lighter was his connection to me."

"He ain't gonna get in unless he goes all wolfy and breaks down the door. He's human for a reason, so he probably don't want anyone seein' what he really is." Roscoe slid the box off the table and picked it up. "This is gonna be fun!"

The sound of a key slipping into the lock made me break into a cold sweat.

"He's got keys?"

"Everyone's probably got a key now thanks to Austin," Roscoe muttered before flipping the hinge bar lock the absent-minded werewolf had installed after varnishing the door.

As soon as the knob turned, the door met resistance. Mosavi put all his weight onto it. He growled a few harsh words in Farsi before continuing his assault.

"You better hope those ferals have some answers," I whispered, grabbing a light coat from the rack and the backpack of supplies I packed earlier. Taking care to stay hidden this time, I peeked through the curtains again as the angry mayor pressed his cell phone against his ear. He turned away from the house and spoke quietly. This was our chance, and I followed Roscoe into the hallway toward the back door. "We are gonna be so fucked."

"We ain't fucked." Roscoe opened the door, and we both slipped outside. "He's bluffing. He probably don't even know yer home. And if he's in human form, he probably can't smell you—" He gave himself a sniff. "He probably smells me, though."

"We will be discussing your hygiene later. Again," I whispered, gently shutting the door behind me. "I'm cutting you off unless you start taking more showers."

Roscoe let out a quiet snigger, pushing away a few tree branches as we made our way into the woods. "I can be as gross as I want, and you'd still ride me like a horse."

"Is that so?"

Roscoe shrugged. "Let's test my theory."

"That's cute. Roscoe has a theory."

"You wouldn't last a day."

"Well, Austin's been kind of sweet on me lately. I'm sure you've noticed."

His grin faded quickly.

"Now *yer* bluffing."

"Do you really wanna call it?"

"It's Austin. The guy has the personality of a rotten pineapple, and I know you ain't gonna let him do that. Yer too much of a prude."

I bit my lower lip as we got deeper into the dense trees. The late afternoon was fading fast, and in about an hour, it would be too dark to see anything. We'd both have to rely solely on Roscoe's night vision and heightened senses.

"There's a lot more to Austin than you think. The poor guy's been through some awful things."

"Yeah, I know."

"You know some of it, but it gets so much worse."

Roscoe turned to me, the bottles in the box rattling as we quickened our pace.

"There's more than just the military fuckin' with his head?"

I nodded. "Can't talk about it, though. He confided in me." Cracking a smug expression, I met Roscoe's eyes. "He's told me things he won't even tell Adam, so that rotten pineapple's actually pretty sweet inside. He also showers more now. Still gonna call my bluff?"

Roscoe said nothing.

"That's what I thought," I continued, knowing deep down I wasn't going to do anything. No way would I break the promise I made to Adam, even if he stomped on my last nerve at times. "Do you even know where we're going?"

"Nope. If they wanna be seen, they'll find us. Ever open a piece of cheese around a dog?"

"Yeah."

"Well, that's kinda what we're gonna do, only the dogs are eight-foot-tall and really territorial."

"Well, when you put it like that, I'd rather go back and take my chances with Mosavi." I tugged at Roscoe's ratty, black, sleeveless shirt that didn't go past his midriff. This was the first time I'd ever seen him wear it, and it had the word *cum* written in the style of a popular video game title on the chest. "Where the hell did you find this?"

"Would you believe someone just threw it away?"

"Yes, I would."

We walked in silence for only a moment before Roscoe's tone slipped into something more concerning. "I haven't been able to find my orange hoodie. You wouldn't happen to know where it is, would you?"

I was hoping I could get that thing clean before he noticed it was gone.

"I put it in with the load of laundry earlier. You're lucky I didn't throw it away."

His ears pressed angrily against his head. "You washed it after I told you not to?"

"It was filthy, and I got tired of smelling it."

"You know how long it took me to get it smellin' like that?"

"Dude. Nothing should smell like that."

Roscoe huffed, looking away. "You don't understand. Smells mean everything to a werewolf. That hoodie was comfortable and familiar, and someone special gave it to me."

"It's just in the washing machine. It's not like I threw it in the fire pit."

"You may as well have. It's gonna take months to get it smellin' the way it did."

"I swear to God—"

"Don't go changin' everything," he snapped, which startled me. "It's bad enough yer makin' me take showers all the time. It's hard on my skin, you know? We ain't like humans. Gotta have them natural oils or we start to itch all the damn time."

"Then why don't you and Austin just shift into your half-turn form when you shower? My skin doesn't itch."

Roscoe gritted his teeth, glaring straight ahead.

"Don't wash my hoodie no more."

"Whoa, you're really upset."

"Just a little." He forced a smile. "Yer gonna learn to love that smell one day. Nothin' really stinks to a werewolf. Certain smells just makes us think about things."

"What do you mean?"

"Well, see that pile of deer shit over there?" He turned to the right and nudged me. Sure enough, there were deer droppings not far from where we were walking. "I can tell you almost anything about that deer just from smellin' it's shit."

"Ew. Are you fucking with me right now?"

"Ain't gonna lie about that, otherwise you'd probably think I was into it."

I squinted at him. "You better not be. The pee was gross enough."

"I'm just sayin' that smells ain't good or bad to us. They just tell us what we need to know, and sometimes they make us feel comfortable." He glared at me again. "Like my hoodie."

"I'm sorry, okay? I won't wash it again." I shoved my hands into my pockets. "What was so comforting about it? You just like your BO or something?"

"Our BO," he corrected.

"Excuse me?"

"I just like the way *we* smell... together. That hoodie had a lot of us in it, and I liked that."

As frustrating as it was arguing with him, that was unexpectedly sweet—in a strange, gross way. "Now I feel like shit."

"Good. Maybe you won't be such a hard ass about me takin' showers now."

"Oh no, I'm not changing my mind on that. The deal is I won't wash your hoodie, but I'll make damn sure you shower."

He huffed but didn't say anything more. We continued along an invisible path that only Roscoe could see, and as the last of the sunlight faded, I grew more concerned.

"How long are we going to stay out here?"

"You got yer supplies, right?"

I shuffled under the light weight of my backpack. "We're not spending the night in the woods. I didn't pack enough stuff for that."

"Yer a goddamn half-turned werewolf. This is where we should be, anyway." He inhaled deeply through his nose. "Smell that clean air. Mmm, all them pines and maples."

"You're smelling deer shit right now, aren't you?"

"Yeah, that's in there, too."

Once again, we laughed it off, but this time, I could admit being at fault and overstepping. It wasn't like Roscoe to get angry, and he had a point. Everything was changing enough as it was, but I was forcing him into this mold he didn't fit. Roscoe was older and set in his ways, and he wasn't going to change his gross habits overnight—even if one of those habits turned out to be something really thoughtful.

"You know a lot about the ferals, and Mosavi thinks you used to be one. Did you?"

One of Roscoe's ears fell as he shrugged. "I get bits and pieces of when I was younger, and I can remember runnin' through the woods a lot."

I elbowed his arm. "Run? I don't believe it."

"I run when I have to. Just ain't had to do it in a while." He shoved me back playfully. "Maybe I was a hyper little scamp, but I really don't remember my time with the ferals if I was there."

"You really don't know? We could be walking into death right now because you have a hunch."

"Well, there's a tiny chance it could've just been a really good LSD trip, but this is a different feeling. I *know* I was out there, but I just don't *know*—you know?"

"Have you been sneaking sips of beer?"

"Maaaybe."

Roscoe stepped on a loud branch, which startled me enough that I almost ran into him.

"I can't see anything. You'd... protect me if anything tried to eat me, right?" I asked.

"Uh... sure."

"That didn't exactly instill confidence, Roscoe."

"There ain't nothing in these woods that can eat you, so chill out. Plus, ferals would rather fuck you than eat you."

"Depending on the circumstances, that could be worse." I decided to change the subject. "What about your parents? Do you remember anything that's not some made-up origin story about the Italian mafia?"

"I didn't make that up. My grandpa was a big ol' Sicilian alpha."

I stopped and folded my arms, and Roscoe turned around.

"All right, I made that up, but it could be true." He grabbed my arm and pulled me next to him as we continued walking. "I can't even remember what my parents looked like. I mean, they're good and dead by now."

"It's still kind of sad. I mean, they were your parents."

"You miss yer parents?"

"Not really," I said. Sometimes a lie made reality a little less painful. "They were so strung out on drugs that my grandparents had to take care of me when DCF stepped in. Then they got all weird and mean when they stopped drinking and doing drugs. All they did was just trade one addiction for another, but they're still terrible people." I forced a laugh, trying to silence the painful memories that crept in. "Who knows? If they saw me with a werewolf old enough to be my grandfather, that could be the final stake through their hearts."

"Speaking of..."

"Not in the woods."

"Hey, food ain't the only thing that draws 'em out. They get a whiff of us doin' what we do best, and every feral will come runnin'."

"We brought food and booze. You're not going to use my ass as bait."

"It ain't that bad. You could handle it easy."

I shot Roscoe a disgusted look. "What the hell is that supposed to mean?"

"I'm just sayin'. We could solve two problems at the same time."

"I don't have a problem," I shouted before lowering my voice again. "I'm not letting a bunch of wild werewolves run a train on me, you pervert. Would you really want to see that?"

"Hell, I'd sit back and jerk to it."

I bit my lower lip again, this time a little more hurt than annoyed.

"Oh, come on, Cody. You gotta loosen up a little. You get real cranky when you try to go against nature."

"This is not natural, and I'm not some animal."

Roscoe stopped and set the box down on the ground. "I didn't say you were."

"It's implied, like I'm this insatiable sex addict that can't control his instincts and is only good at one thing."

"Cody." The werewolf pulled me into a hug. "I think you're like this because yer a little too old to be going through this half-turn stuff, and I don't know what you need," he pulled away. "Something's off about you, but that's why we're out here."

"What if Mosavi was right, and this is dangerous?"

"That guy's got issues, too. You wanna end up like him?"

"You mean rich, handsome, powerful"—I shot a glare at Roscoe—"and clean? Sounds like a dream."

"Nah. That ain't what I see. That guy's strugglin' with what he is, and he's angry that he has to fight it every day. It must be hell forcin' himself to stay in that human body while keepin' up appearances he can't even hold onto for that long without going back into hiding."

"That reminds me. We saw Austin's half-turn form. Can you do it too?"

"Yeah, but I ain't gonna. It hurts like hell, and I'm surprised Austin was able to hold it for that long. The guy's got a really good pain threshold." Roscoe rubbed his hands together. "We should probably set up camp here. It's too dark to look for these guys right now."

Our drunken laughter echoed through the forest, which was otherwise eerily quiet aside from the crackling fire.

"And that's not even the funniest part. He kept tryin' to get with me, but every time I'd kill the mood with another dad joke. I thought he was gonna turn right then and there, the way he bared his teeth and the little bristles on his neck shot up. I think Adam actually wanted to kill me."

"You do have that effect on people."

Who'd have thought beer, junk food, and a warm campfire was all we needed to make what should have been an uncomfortable night fun? I leaned into Roscoe with one arm against his thigh, warmth flushing my skin even though the air had a frigid bite to it.

"I'm not gonna lie. As annoying as he is sometimes, I feel bad for him," I said, a little more serious this time.

"I would have fixed that, but you told me not to do anything."

"Not that. I definitely didn't want you doing that. I just feel bad that he and Austin have such a shitty relationship. If Adam found out that the only reason Austin was paying him any attention was because he was under some kind of weird spell and obeying my commands, he'd probably lose it."

"Once he turns, they might end up leavin', and we'll get the house all to ourselves."

"You sound happy about that."

Roscoe cocked his head. "Not really, but ain't that what you wanted?"

I thought about it for a moment. A few weeks ago I would have definitely said yes, but I had grown attached to their mayhem. Plus, I didn't want Austin to end up alone, and that's what would likely happen if both he and Adam left.

"It's kinda weird. Just the thought of them leaving makes me anxious," I said.

"That's pack envy."

"What the hell is that?"

"Another fun werewolf thing," Roscoe said. "We all get pack envy when we're livin' with other werewolves. At first, it's just a bunch of chaos, and then everyone kinda falls into their roles. I'm obviously the leader everyone looks up to."

I looked at him and put the bottle of beer to my lips. "You're very drunk and delusional right now."

"You guys'd be lost without me."

"All right. Tell me what the leader does?"

"Easy. The leader keeps his pack fed, gives emotional support, is someone everyone comes to depend on, is responsible—"

Roscoe stopped talking, and I watched his expression go from oblivious to a sudden, uncomfortable realization.

"Go on."

"Well, fuck," he muttered, taking another gulp of beer. "Ain't that a switch?"

"What?"

"Ain't never seen a half-turn leadin' a pack before."

I took another drink. "Even Mosavi figured it out before you did."

Roscoe reached into the box and pulled out a package of cakes.

"How many of those have you had?"

"Uhh," he sifted through a few empty wrappers.

"Damn it, we're not going to have enough to trade if your fat ass keeps eating!"

"But they're so goooood."

"Put it back."

"Yes, alpha Cody," Roscoe replied sarcastically.

"You know, it's kinda cringe, but I could get used to everyone calling me that."

Roscoe belted out a laugh. "The only one that's gonna do that is probably Austin. Adam would probably punch you in the face."

"You're joking, right? Adam is the puniest half-turn I know."

"He's the *only* half-turn you know, and he could take you down with how far along he is."

"I guess he is getting a little beefier."

A rustle from the trees all around us stifled our conversation. An occasional shadow shot between the trees, but I couldn't make out what they were.

"They're here," Roscoe whispered. "Hopefully they're friendly."

"Well, they seemed friendly last time. I think."

Despite what I said, Roscoe still seemed uneasy.

"What's wrong? I thought this was what we wanted."

More branches snapped, and leaves rustled above us as well.

"They ain't bein' friendly right now," Roscoe whispered, holding me closer to him. "Shit."

"How do you know?"

"I kinda remember this. It's to rile up their prey before they attack."

I swallowed hard. "Goddamn it. Why do I let you talk me into shit like this?"

"Let's just stay calm and stay low. They want us to start runnin' so they can chase us, and that's the last thing we want." Roscoe reached into the box and pulled out a bag of unopened white cheddar popcorn, opening it with a shake. "Peace offering." As another branch broke, Roscoe wrinkled the bag closed and tossed it in the direction of the commotion.

We both glanced at each other, waiting. Several minutes passed; sweat beaded on my forehead before dripping onto my arms.

A single set of footsteps crunched toward our camp as a large, shadowy figure with glowing red eyes stepped out of the woods. He cautiously knelt to pick up the bag while keeping a suspicious glare trained on us. This one wore the same garb as the one from my first encounter but had a shorter mane and no braids. He also wore a leather harness decorated with raven feathers and bones. A rope-like belt loosely adorned his waist, two small leather sacks on both sides.

I marveled at how different this werewolf looked compared to what I usually saw. He had a slumped posture and longer arms, but he didn't have pawed feet like the others did. I opened my mouth to greet him, but Roscoe squeezed my arm.

"Don't say nothin'. Let 'em come to us and give us a sniff. We don't wanna make any weird noises or movements. We gotta submit to them when they get close."

"What do you mean?"

"I mean, you gotta lay on yer back to show 'em respect."

The feral werewolf opened the bag, furiously sniffing the contents.

"What if they kill us?"

"Nah. They'd have done that already."

The werewolf started grunting something incoherent before grabbing a handful of popcorn and shoving it into his slobbery maw. The other werewolves emerged, another four of them. Two looked older, but it was hard to tell for sure. Older werewolves weren't just more masculine—there was something in their eyes that always seemed more attentive. As the others stepped into the fire's light, their strange, paw-like feet became visible.

"Oh, we got their attention now. Lay on yer back. Slowly."

Both of us carefully stretched out along the ground, me squeezing my eyes shut as one stepped closer. His hot breath pulsed against my face and neck as he knelt next to me, his nose probing my body. The rest made their way over, sniffing both of us while making grunting noises at each other.

After another minute, I felt a tap on my shoulder and snapped my eyes open. Roscoe hovered over me.

"Looks like we're in," he said with a relieved smile as I sat up.

The five ferals sat in a semi-circle around the fire, each one staring at us expectantly.

"So, what now?"

"I guess we'll see if they wanna talk." Roscoe reached into the box and grabbed a bottle of beer before holding it out in front of him. "You guys, uh... wanna trade?"

The wild werewolves turned to each other before looking back at Roscoe with blank stares.

"This might be tougher than I thought," he said, setting the beer on the ground next to his leg.

"I thought you knew what you were doing."

"Well, they didn't kill us, so I guess I didn't fuck that up."

"This is just instilling all kinds of confidence," I whispered, eyeing the ferals as they sat rigid, their glowing eyes following our movements. "I'm getting creeped out."

One finally stood and reached into a pouch that hung from a crude rope belt he wore. He pulled out a small bundle of herbs wrapped in some kind of frayed fiber and offered it to Roscoe while pointing to the bottle.

"Oh! I think I remember this stuff," he said excitedly, his tail patting the ground as he flicked the cap off the bottle and exchanged it for the herbs.

"What the hell are we going to do with that?"

"Smoke it," Roscoe answered, wetting his lips with his tongue while untying the twine. "Ah, damn. Don't have a pipe, though." He sat the herbs on the ground next to him, then reached into the box again for the package of Swiss Rolls.

Roscoe waited as each of the wolfmen took turns drinking from the same bottle. They didn't seal their lips around the end; instead, poured the contents directly onto their tongues. Their neck fur pricked up as the beverage fizzed and foamed, filling their mouths while dripping from the corners of their thin black lips.

Roscoe held up the cakes, and another feral stood and eagerly walked over, thick saliva starting to rope from his mouth. Roscoe made a gesture as though he were smoking, and the feral picked up on it right away, reaching into his own pouch before pulling out a long pipe decorated with colorful gems.

In a friendly exchange, Roscoe took the pipe, and the wild werewolf grabbed the snacks before rejoining the others.

"This is goin' great." He held the pipe in one hand, pinched off some of the herbs, then stuffed it into the bowl. "Yer gonna love this shit."

"I'm not smoking some strange weed from these guys. I don't trust them."

"All the more reason to get high," Roscoe said, picking up a small stick and poking the end into the campfire. "Trust me. I've done this a lot."

"You don't even remember your last name. How would you even remember that?"

Roscoe pulled the flaming stick out of the fire and put it up to the pipe to light the herbs. He drew in deep then coughed before turning to me, his pupils tiny as each eye stared in slightly different directions.

"That's some goooood shit," he said with another cough, his voice pitching a bit higher. He held the pipe in front of me. "You like weed, don't you?"

"I know what weed is."

"This is just like that, kinda." He shoved the pipe into my hand. "C'mon. Stop bein' such a mud in the stick," he said, his words slurring to the point where I could barely understand him.

"This could be dangerous."

"Pipe the smoke, ya nerd."

"Christ," I muttered, grabbing the pipe. This was a terrible idea, but Roscoe wasn't going to let up. Plus, he wasn't making sense anymore. After a moment of hesitation, I took a draw, which was a lot more potent than anything I'd breathed in before. The smoke tasted like burnt sage mixed with nutmeg. It irritated my lungs, sending me into a similar coughing fit Roscoe experienced earlier. "Oh my God, I can't…"

The world started to melt into brilliant colors all around, and time slowed to a crawl as Roscoe waved his hand in front of me in a slow motion trail.

"Feels great, doesn't it?" Though Roscoe just spoke to me, that wasn't his accent. That wasn't even his voice. "It's always quite riveting the first time, but you start to grow accustomed to the feeling. It reminds me of DMT, but better."

"What the fuck's you talkin' about?" I said, barely able to control my tongue. "What's wrong with me?"

"Nothing," Roscoe replied, his words becoming clearer and more astute than they'd ever been. "Sit back and enjoy the trip, buddy."

"More bubbles," a voice from across the fire spoke. "What to trade to get more bubbles?" It was one of the ferals. Though his English was broken, I understood him perfectly.

Roscoe grabbed a few more bottles from the box, holding them by the necks in front of the salivating werewolves, some still gnawing on the sweet cakes.

"Perhaps this will persuade you to take us to your alpha?"

"Damn, dude. When'd you learn to talk so good?" I asked, my brain seemingly sinking more into a mire of numb stupidity.

"I've always talked *good*," Roscoe replied, patting me hard on the back before turning his attention to the ferals who were quietly discussing amongst themselves.

"No," one of them said. They were harder to tell apart now, despite earlier having different fur colors and patterns. "Have other things for trading." He pulled out a few glimmering opals. "Shiny rocks for bubbles? Keep dangerous witches away."

"Y'all got witches out here?" This accent seemed to get thicker and even more ridiculous the longer I spoke.

"Many witches. Alpha say to stay away. Some of us not come back after they find us." He eyed the bottles, licking his chops. "Bubbles for rocks?"

Roscoe sighed.

"I suppose it's a start." He handed the bottles to the wild werewolf in exchange for the entire bag. "One of you gave my friend here a shiny rock a little while ago. Can any of you tell me who that was?"

The ferals slurped down the beer, each one belching loudly in different pitches while chuckling amongst themselves.

"They ain't sayin' nothin'," I said, watching in awe as a few neon butterflies flitted by my face. "Jeez that's purdy. How long's this last?"

"Ooooh, boy. You're in for one hell of a night."

"Roscoe..." I tried to get angry, but uncontrollable laughter was all I could manage. Anger made me laugh, and Roscoe sounded intelligent, while I could barely form a coherent sentence. The flames of the fire were now purple and bugs around us sparkled in brilliant colors. This wasn't just some weed—it was as though my entire perception of reality shifted. Was this the way the ferals saw the world all the time?

"You know, sex is phenomenal while on this stuff," Roscoe said, reaching into my pants. "Every sense is heightened, and the orgasms don't stop."

I looked over. The feral werewolves stopped talking, each one staring eagerly.

"Naw, man. We ain't doin' this in front of them."

"Trade licks for more sweet things," one of them said, inching closer to me. "You smell like thick smoke."

"What's he talkin' about?"

"He wants to suck your dick," Roscoe said with a grin. "I told you. They'll do anything you want for sweets."

"No need for trade," the feral said, his nose buried in my crotch. "Do this for no trade."

"Well, hot damn! We might be able to convince them to take us to their pack after all. Good thing you're so delicious."

"Roscoe—"

"Just let it happen," he cut in, licking my neck. "They aren't going to bring us anywhere near their pack unless they gain our trust. This is a shortcut to that."

"This seems kinda wrong." My cock disappeared into the feral's mouth, his rough tongue lapping at everything while his lips sealed around me. It felt like every pleasure sensor in my body went straight into overdrive. "Holy..."

As the werewolf went to work on me, Roscoe gently prodded my head downward until my face was against his crotch. He smelled different. Everything smelled and felt alien, like I wasn't even in my own body anymore.

The heat of the moment made me forget about the other werewolves who were watching us while pleasuring themselves around the fire. It didn't matter if they were feral or like us; they were still perverts. I

   *Aeron Dusk*

wondered if they were ever human like us once, or if they had been born werewolves. Was that even possible?

While jerking Roscoe off, I stared at his midsection, and I noticed a slight bump on each side of his bellybutton.

"What the fuck is this?" I asked, trying to maneuver my body carefully as the werewolf below continued pleasuring me. "What the hell are these?"

"You know what nipples are."

"What?" I shuddered as the blowjob got more intense. "Fuck, he's really goin' to town down there."

"That's because you're just delectable." He leaned in and whispered into my ear. "By the way, we all have eight nipples."

"What?" I asked, pushing the feral werewolf away and climbing to my knees to lift Roscoe's shirt. Sure enough, as I pulled his fur aside, they started appearing one-by-one. "H—how the hell'd I not notice?"

"When's the last time you were down there?"

"I'm always down there. I just never saw 'em!"

"Well, you're looking into the future, bud. We all get eight of them when we turn."

"Oh, this is awful," I muttered, running my fingers over each one. "This is a real boner-killer. You know that right?"

"More licks?" the werewolf below me asked, salivating some more as he stared at my crotch.

"Uh, yeah. Go fer it," I said, still eyeing Roscoe's belly, slightly confused about whether or not I actually found this hot. I kind of expected the high to mellow, but everything just kept getting weirder. The woods weren't even dark anymore, just all different colors.

It was scary, but I'd never seen anything more beautiful.

My head pounded as I struggled to open my eyes. Though my mouth was bone dry, I could still taste the smoke and booze. My memories were hazy—I could barely recollect what happened after the more intense effects of the drug had taken hold. The odor of wild werewolves assaulted my nose with every movement against the crush of fur and muscle all around me.

The ferals never left, and from the contented look on their faces, I might have let them do a lot more to me than oral. Nausea hit the pit of my stomach as I moved away, and a thickness filling my ass slid out with a wet thud. Thankfully, it was only Roscoe. I looked up at his face, and another horrible memory hit as I frantically felt around his abdomen.

"Oh thank God," I whispered, sliding my hand against his fur. No rogue nipples. "I'm never doing that shit again."

# Chapter 20

# Self Discovery

**T**he early morning brought the usual chill, a thick fog settling around camp. Raven calls replaced the mourning doves high in the thick canopy of pines and oaks. I sat fully clothed on a log away from the smelly werewolf pile I'd been a part of earlier, all of them snoring and twitching next to smoldering embers.

My mind was a jumbled mess. Being out in the middle of the forest with no amenities terrified me, but not for the expected reasons. There were no modern world distractions, and there was nothing to clean. All I had to occupy myself was my mind, which I was too ashamed to face.

I looked down at my bare feet. A few weeks ago, I could have sworn they were normal. Everything happened so gradually that my brain hadn't kept up with all the changes—it adapted naturally. Shoes had been impossible to wear over the last few days because of the claws that had grown in place of my toenails. They were longer and hooked, and the calluses on my soles had thickened and turned a darker color like the pads on fully turned werewolf feet.

I teetered on the edge of embarrassment as I tried to remember last night, but the images in my head didn't make any sense sober. It was almost like those memories were encrypted and the only way to unlock them was to smoke more of whatever herb that was. Seeing how Roscoe had been so eager to trade for drugs instead of information only disappointed me further. I never expected him to change completely, but I'd at least thought he'd show a little more interest in helping me instead of getting high.

A rough hand landed on my shoulder, startling me. I jumped off the log and turned toward the taller of the wild werewolves wearing his leather harness and sacks. He hadn't made a sound, and his gray fur made him look more like a specter floating through the fog.

"Uh…" I tried to think of something to say, but I doubted he would understand me now. "Good morning?"

He smiled and gestured to the log before sitting. His expression and body language were different from last night. Taking the place of narrow suspiciousness was wide-eyed curiosity, his tail gently scraping against the bark as I sat next to him.

The werewolf reached into his leather pouch and pulled out a pinch of the herb before placing it in front of my face.

"No," I said, pushing it away. "No trade." After last night, I didn't want to risk doing anything more. The high had lasted so long I probably wouldn't be able to get home.

His tail swayed a little more as he held the herb in front of my face again. This time, he pretended to take a pinch of the stuff before dropping it into his mouth. He wanted me to eat it?

I shook my head, but he insisted again, this time with a more impatient grimace. There was no way to avoid this without making him angry, and I still wasn't sure what terms we were on. Taking in a deep breath, I took a pinch of the herb and placed it on my tongue. The werewolf caught my cheeks, holding my mouth open.

Confused, I tried to pull away, but his grip was too tight. He scooped the substance out of my mouth with his thick, clawed fingers before placing the stuff under my tongue. Every gland in my mouth seemed to open at once, and the trickle of morning sunlight beaming through the fog turned into a wobbly prism of pastels.

"Do not chew," he said, letting go of my face. "Hold under tongue so that the effect only last until you spit."

The world grew brighter and a deluge of memories flooded my brain. The scenery around us darkened to exactly how it was last night, and the hallucinations turned to visions of events that actually played out.

"How the hell did I not notice?" asked a blurry version of me while parting the fur along Roscoe's stomach to reveal a couple sets of extra nipples. Of all the scenes that could have played out, it was the most disturbing.

"When's the last time you were down there?" Roscoe asked in that strange, stilted accent.

"I'm always down there. I just never saw 'em!"

"Well, you're looking into the future, bud—"

The scenery melted into a bunch of flaming blobs before reforming into an all-out orgy. The tall one in the harness was behind one of the younger ones, thrusting while the other three gathered together in front of me.

"Fuck me!" I demanded, my features turning wild as the half-turn temper boiled to the surface, causing the werewolves around me to grow excited and impatient. My face grew hot with embarrassment as I turned into everything I despised. This wasn't me. This couldn't be me, right?

Watching from a third person perspective really brought to light the half-turn state I couldn't escape, but it also made me remember everything Mosavi had warned me about. This wasn't just me wanting sex—it was something more akin to eating or drinking. It was vital to my survival, and it was the Whasha that awakened it.

The feral in the middle lost himself in the moment, grabbing me by the hips, fully intending to give me exactly what I wanted, but Roscoe shot up and faced the wild werewolf head-on.

"No," he growled, pulling me into his arms. The feral bared his teeth, and he stood roughly a foot taller. Roscoe was not a confrontational person, especially when the physical odds weren't in his favor, but he firmly held his ground. Before either of them could scuffle, the larger, harnessed werewolf pulled away from his mate and stood between the two, shoving away the frustrated feral before nodding to both of us.

The vision faded, except for a rippling haze as my eyes watered. Roscoe had lied when he said he'd get off on watching them have their way with me. He was ready to fight to keep that from happening, and the disappointment from earlier melted into the rest of the colors.

"He didn't let them do it."

"Good mate you have," the feral said, placing his finger close to his mouth. "No chewing. No swallow, only spit."

I nodded as I repositioned the small wad of slobbery herbs to the other side of my mouth before spitting the excess saliva.

"I need to ask you a question," I said, turning to face him again.

He nodded.

"Were you with the ones I met the first time in the forest?"

He nodded again.

"Then why did you guys almost attack us last night?"

"We test the fat one there to see if he remembers what to do." He pointed at Roscoe's ankle bracelets. "Those were given to him by Whasha." His speech seemed to sync more with his lips, his words less broken. "You should be feeling the full effects by now."

"I—damn. What the hell is going on?"

"It is a lot to explain, but I am sure you've been told some of it by that elder who pretends."

"Mosavi?"

"So that is the name he has chosen."

"That's not his name?"

The feral slowly cracked a knowing smile. "He consorts with witches and pretends to be the opposite of what he is. He is a living contradiction, and the reason I stay in these woods so close to town."

"Why?"

His eyes flashed a brilliant silver before fading as he looked down at me. "What do you feel?"

I shrugged. "I don't understand the question."

His irises flashed again, this time remaining pure silver, just as Mosavi's had that night he'd taken control of Roscoe.

"What are you doing?"

Once again, his eyes faded to their original amber. "That is why he chose you."

"The vironoct?" His face nearly touched mine, so I pushed him back. "I just want to be left alone so I can try to put my life back together. I need to know what to do about Mosavi."

The werewolf cocked his head. "Is your life broken?"

"Yes!" I shouted, nearly swallowing the herbs by accident. "Ever since *this* happened." I pointed to my sharp teeth and pointed ears. "I can't start the career I want. I'm slowly turning into a monster. I can't seem to catch a break, and now Mosavi is threatening me."

The feral's warm stare turned to ice. He wrinkled his nose.

"What?" I asked.

"Go back to the Midna."

"I need your help." My tone was nicer this time, and I grabbed his arm. "Take me to your alpha... or chief or whatever. I think he knows how to counter Mosavi's magic with those stones."

"The stones break a witch's enchantments. What Mosavi gave you was not our magic. It is not our way."

The hair on my arms stood straight as a familiar scent caught my nose. It was irresistibly potent, just like Mosavi's.

"You're like him, aren't you?"

He said nothing before reaching into his pouch.

"What is the life you want, Cody?"

The question surprised me, and the answer caught in my throat before spilling out like vomit.

"I want everything to go back to the way it was before I went half-turn. I want my career and a lot of money so I can have a future." Though I was passionate in my response, there was something in my chest that ached.

The werewolf snarled this time. "Go back to the Midna."

"You keep saying that, but it doesn't help me!"

"You do not want our help. You should seek his."

I balled my fists and slammed them hard into the log. "That's the entire reason we're here!"

"And what is it you want *me* to do?"

"I..." The words I really wanted to say disappeared as quickly as I could think of them, so I shook my head. "I just need something to keep Mosavi away from me so we can go back to the city."

The werewolf stood and looked over at his pack before giving a grunted yip. The others in camp stirred awake, pushing a still-sound-asleep Roscoe to the side.

"You're really not going to help me, are you?" I asked. "Just tell me what I need to do."

He took my hand and pressed a bundle of herbs firmly against my palm.

"You and this—Mosavi are more alike than you care to admit. The life you want is the life he struggles to hold onto, and you will chase it like he does. You will grow bitter like he is. You will always chase but never obtain." The other werewolves disappeared into the woods, but the elder stayed behind. "You are at the precipice of self-discovery." He glanced down at Roscoe. "Some know who they were meant to be, but for others, it could take centuries to figure it out. You may be special in many ways, but at your core, you are only one part of something bigger." His thin black lips pulled into a smile one last time, and then he turned toward where the others had disappeared into the fog. "When you were in the city, did you ever see happiness among our kind?"

At that, he dashed into the brush with surprising speed before vanishing like smoke. Moments later, a distant howl echoed a farewell through the trees.

I spat the herb onto the ground, and the colors of morning shifted back to normal. My thoughts raced, and I remembered my time as a human in that city. Werewolves had just been pathetic nuisances I'd never given the time of day. When I started showing signs of my condition, the misery manifested as desperate resumes, like playing the lottery just so they wouldn't have to live one more cold and humiliating night on the streets. Those that weren't begging for scraps ended up like how Roscoe had been before I met him.

The werewolf's snoring drowned out the caws of ravens hidden in the leaves. They eventually scattered in all directions, but not before swooping to give a swift peck at Roscoe's head.

Adam and Austin were likely wondering where we were, if Mosavi hadn't drilled them for answers already. The less they knew, the better off they were. All it would take is one of those bewitched items strapped to any of us, and the mayor wouldn't need to ask. He wanted control—at least, that's how it seemed to me.

That elder feral resembled Mosavi in many ways, but he had a peace about him that I couldn't quite comprehend.

*"He is a living contradiction, and the reason I stay in these woods so close to town."*

Was he trying to protect Mosavi or protect others from him? He also mentioned witches. I had been hearing so much about how dangerous they were, but I didn't really know anything more than what I was told.

The forest was different than when I'd first walked through it. Instead of it being eerie and dangerous, there was a lingering peace that blanketed the atmosphere as the fog began to lift. I considered staying one more night under the stars, laughing with Roscoe, but a nagging inside wanted to get away from all these other dreadful thoughts.

I knelt next to Roscoe, ran my fingers through his messy mane before climbing onto his wide torso, to straddle his hips. He was like a warm mattress with lumps in all the right places, and as I lay on top of him, it was hard to keep my eyes open with the rhythm of his breaths.

Remembering how protective he was of me in that vision, I wanted to kiss him awake. At first, I planted a peck on his wet nose before trailing kisses to the sides of his open mouth, disregarding his frightful morning breath. It was difficult to get a decent angle when his tongue was hanging out, so I gave him another kiss on the nose. When I leaned back in to tackle his mouth, he sneezed in my face.

"Ew fuck!" I shouted, scrambling off him, screaming in disgust as I tried to wipe away the snot. "Oh God, it's in my mouth!"

Roscoe sat up and rubbed his eyes. "What happened? You okay, buddy?"

"I am never kissing you again," I choked out. I had to use my light jacket to wipe most of it away, but some of it stubbornly lingered on my face. "I'm gonna throw up."

"It's just a little snot, jeez. You know how many loads you swallowed last night?"

"That's not the same!" After I finished wiping my face, I nudged Roscoe with my foot. "Let's go."

"Where're the ferals?" Roscoe asked, jumping to his feet. "Shit! Did you see 'em leave?"

"Yeah, but we're not getting any help from them," I muttered, hooking my arms through the straps of my backpack. I gathered all the plastic wrappers and beer bottles scattered around camp and threw them in the empty box. "This was such a waste of time, and now Mosavi's going to know I was out here. I have to face the guy at some point."

"I'll go with ya," Roscoe said and grabbed the box. "He's not gonna know we were in the woods, anyway."

"Not unless he uses the *cursed nipple clamps of truth*, or whatever perverted fucked up shit he has lying around for fun."

"He'd be a blast if he wasn't so damn scary," Roscoe said in a stuffed-up tone, walking next to me as we headed in the direction that seemed both familiar and unfamiliar at the same time.

"Do you remember which way we came?"

"Uh, I thought you did."

I slapped my forehead. "You're the werewolf, Roscoe! You're supposed to be able to sniff us back home."

Roscoe gurgled as he inhaled the remaining mucus before spitting it onto the ground.

"I'm feelin' a little under the weather."

"That makes no sense. You told me werewolves don't get sick."

"Yeah, about that," Roscoe said, his ears folding back against his head. "That stuff we smoked kinda messes up the senses fer a day er two, but it's worth it."

I stopped and glared at him.

"Naw, come on. Don't look at me like that. It was the only way we could talk to 'em."

"Really? There was no other way?"

Roscoe scrutinized my face and sighed. "I guess you figured that out, huh? Smoking makes everything better, and you had fun, right?"

"Damn it, Roscoe," I sneered while examining our surroundings. "Okay, let's see... we walked west to get here, and the sun is coming up that way." I pointed toward the heavier brush. "If we just walk in that direction, we're bound to get to somewhere familiar."

"You sure about that?"

"No," I snapped. "I have no sense of direction. You know this!"

"All right, calm down. Goin' east is a good idea." Roscoe snorted again, spitting more snot onto the ground.

"That's so hot," I said sarcastically while snapping branches and pushing brush out of the way. Before letting go of the dense flora, I noticed something. "Hmm..."

"What's wrong?"

"I don't know. There's something about these bushes," I said, stumbling through the leaves. "I think we walked by these on the way here."

"Nah." Roscoe picked up a branch I snapped off, sneezing again. "We woulda already broken through this place if we had," he continued, wiping his nose with the back of his arm.

After a few minutes of walking, something tickled the back of my neck.

"There's a huge spider on you," Roscoe shouted.

I screamed, flailing my arms and spinning backward. Instead of a spider, I ended up with a face full of leaves courtesy of Roscoe.

"I ain't never heard a grown man scream like that in my life." Roscoe shook with laughter, choking on snot as he sneezed again. "Goddamn, I can't breathe."

"You're going in the cage tonight." I snatched the thin branch away, whipping him with it once before tossing it to the side.

"I thought we agreed that those things were too dangerous to use."

"I'll happily make you take that risk," I said, scratching at my arm, which was starting to burn a little. "There aren't supposed to be any mosquitoes this time of the year."

Roscoe's face went from a squinty grin to wide-eyed horror in less than a second.

"What?"

"Oh shit," he said, pointing at my face.

"I'm not falling for that again."

"I'm bein' serious. Yer face don't look right."

Similar to my arms, a burning and itching sensation spread from my forehead down to my cheeks.

"Uh oh," I said, my heart racing as I picked up the thin branch I'd tossed away. The leaves were turning a red color, which was typical for fall, but when I counted the three leaflets on each stem, all the blood drained from my face. "Oh my God. This is poison oak." I dropped the branch and gripped Roscoe's chest mane with both fists. "You rubbed this all over my face, you idiot! I'm going to kill you!"

Roscoe stood in the middle of the bedroom with his tail tucked between his legs, his hands bound, and his maw wrapped in an enchanted leather strap. The most satisfying part of all of this was how snug that cage was, since it perfectly molded to Roscoe's size. After that, it shrank uncomfortably small. If this was witchcraft, then I could see why Mosavi got a kick out of it.

It wasn't that hard to get all this stuff on him. Once I snuck the magic cuffs around his wrists, that was it. His body locked up, and I could do whatever I wanted.

"I'm taking a shower," I slurred, my face still swollen. I was confused as to why the reaction to the poison oak was so quick and intense. Perhaps the rapid healing had something to do with it, but I didn't know for sure. "Don't go anywhere."

Roscoe whined like an injured dog, snot still oozing from his nose. The strap securing his muzzle wasn't on that tight, so he could still breathe through his mouth.

I walked out of the room before closing the door behind me as Adam crept through the hallway.

"Ew! What the hell happened to you?"

"Bad life choices," I muttered, scratching my arms before stepping into the bathroom. "What do you want?"

"I want to know what you did to Austin."

"What are you talking about?" I stammered, trying to choose my words very carefully. "I just told him to give you more attention."

"You fucked him, didn't you?"

"I most certainly did not!"

Adam pulled me into a hug, which wouldn't have bothered me had my skin not been licked by the leafy tongue of Satan himself.

"Ow," I said, trying to push him off me.

"Stop lying." He pulled away and smiled. "Whatever you taught him, teach him more of it." He turned and walked out of the bathroom with a slight limp, but not before looking back at me with a flirty stare. "Maybe teach me too, sometime? If you're up for it."

He closed the door, and I stood there for a solid minute with my mouth hanging open.

What exactly did Austin do to him while I was gone?

I dried off and examined my face in the mirror. Everything had gone back to normal now that I had washed the irritating oils from my skin. This was one of the few times being a half-turn came in handy. As useless as I was, the rapid healing sure was nice.

I often wondered how many lovers Roscoe had had over the many years. He said he'd had a girlfriend before he met me, but I couldn't see how she or any other human would survive one night with a werewolf's endless libido. Darryl had also mentioned he'd been with a few human guys on the beach, and I remembered my first night with Roscoe. I hadn't been a half-turn then, but somehow, I was fine. This was all so baffling.

I slipped into a pair of loose boxer briefs and a black tank top before wandering back into the bedroom. When I opened the door, I found Austin and Adam gathered around a whining Roscoe, poking playfully at him.

"Do it again. This is hilarious," Adam said to Austin, who nodded in agreement before licking one finger and then shoving it into Roscoe's ear. The old werewolf let out muffled screams as he tried to move away from what amounted to the worst wet-Willie ever conceived, but the magic cuffs kept his entire body stiff.

Adam looked up at me. "Is it my birthday? You wrapped him so nicely."

"What are you guys doing?"

Austin pulled back before slipping both clawed pinky fingers back into Roscoe's ears. The werewolf let out another muffled whine.

"Having some fun." He looked up at me, his irises slowly changing color from amber to baby blue. "Can I fuck him?"

Roscoe's eyes went wide as his head snapped up to look at me.

"You know what? Knock yourself out."

"Yes sir," Austin responded, balling his fist. It took a second before I realized what I had inadvertently told him to do as he reared back, preparing to punch himself in the face.

"I didn't mean literally!" I shouted, grabbing Austin's arm. "I meant you can fuck Roscoe." With a hard shove, the old werewolf fell onto the mattress with his ass in the air. "And don't be gentle."

Roscoe struggled to protest, but Austin was already on top of him. It was rather disturbing how fast he was about to go in without any preparation.

"Stop. I'm just joking."

Austin looked back at me, frozen as he waited for the next command. Whatever control the vironoct had over him was starting to make me uneasy.

"I've got a better idea. Why don't you tell Roscoe all about carpentry? And don't leave anything out."

"Yes sir."

"Oh!" I opened the black bag of magic shit Mosavi had left and pulled out the nipple clamps. They were connected to some kind of tiny electrical box, but it didn't turn on when I pressed the buttons. "Here." I tossed the clamps to Austin as he rolled Roscoe onto his back. "If he looks bored, just give him a nice jolt."

With no ounce of hesitation, Austin attached each clamp to a squirming Roscoe, who arched his back in either pain or pleasure.

"What's this do?" Austin asked, haphazardly mashing buttons on the powerbox. "Doesn't look like it works."

"Uh, maybe don't mess with that too much, just in case," I said, turning toward Adam, who had been eyeing me suspiciously the entire time. We both walked out right as a sharp doglike yelp had me rushing back toward our bedroom.

Adam tugged at my arm. "What the hell is going on?" he asked, shutting the bedroom door. Roscoe's muffled whines and Austin's monotone explanation of different types of wood faded to background noise. "He's doing everything you tell him. Do you have some magic bussy or something?"

"Don't ever use that word again, or Roscoe won't be the only one getting tortured."

"Bussy bussy bussy," he shouted, stomping behind me like a child. "Tell me what you did, or it's going to be in every sentence."

"I didn't do anything."

"I don't bussy-lieve you."

"I swear to God, Adam." As we walked into the living room, I snatched the remote off the coffee table and turned on the television. "Can we talk about it later?"

Adam and I snapped our attention to the hallway as a loud thud rocked the house.

"I think Roscoe fell off the bed," Adam said, scratching his head.

"Did Mosavi come by while Roscoe and I were out by chance?"

He shook his head. "Who's Mosavi?"

"The mayor. How could you forget his name?"

Adam shrugged. "I'm not good with names." He hummed to himself while biting his lower lip. "God, he's the hottest werewolf I've ever seen. What I wouldn't give..."

"He's really dangerous."

"That's even better."

"Do you ever think about anything else?"

Adam let out a frustrated growl. "No."

"Are you okay?"

"I've been in pain for a week now, and no one seems to give a shit."

When he said that, I hit the power button on the television remote and turned toward him. "What are you talking about? What pain?"

"It's hard to explain."

Another loud thud came from our bedroom.

"Okay, I'm getting a little worried," I said, jumping from the couch, but Adam caught my hand before jerking me back.

"How about telling me what the hell is going on? Austin's been acting really weird, and now you and Roscoe are into bondage?"

I let out a sigh and sat back down. It was all going to come out eventually, only how Adam would react seemed to depend on how the stars were aligned.

"Apparently your kuu mate has been making moonshine in the garage. That's why they were in jail."

"That bastard!"

"I know. I also got in trouble because of him."

"He made all that booze, and he didn't share anything with me!"

I closed my eyes and rubbed my temples, which caught Adam's attention. He turned, tossing me a forced sympathetic look.

"Sorry. Why did *you* get into trouble."

"Because apparently Mosavi thinks I'm capable of leading you morons, but I can't get anyone to listen or clean up or not break the law. You don't think about anyone but yourself. Austin flies into unbridled rage, and Roscoe—well—you're well aware of his antics."

"I do not only think about myself."

"Yes, you do! You were celebrating having all the money to yourself that night if I went to jail, too. You didn't even get upset until I reminded you that you're just as fucked." I paused for a moment, trying to ease the conversation forward. "Plus, yeah. It would have been nice to talk to you when we were at the bar."

"This again?"

Another opportunity presented itself, and I'd wanted to get this off my chest.

"I tried talking to you all night at the club, but you kept ignoring me and running up my tab." He didn't respond, and for the first time he actually seemed embarrassed. "I was hoping we could hang out as friends, but you don't treat me like a friend. You treat me like a doormat. I wish I could say the bad was the first time, but hell, you even put me in an impossible situation before we moved without even talking to me first."

"I—" He opened his mouth to continue but shook his head and looked at the floor. "I'm sorry."

"Apology accepted, of course," I replied. "I don't hate you or anything, but you're just too much sometimes." I studied the look on his face, which seemed remorseful enough for me to bring up the other big topic. "I know this is going to be difficult for you, but you need to try harder with Austin."

"What I did to you was really bad, but don't tell me to be nice to a guy that treats me like shit all the time."

"You said he didn't always treat you like this. What happened?"

"What do you mean, what happened? He showed his real self."

"Have you guys ever talked?"

Adam stared at me pensively. "I guess. A long time ago."

"What did you talk about?"

"Dude, I don't fucking remember. He was always whining about something when I wanted to have fun. I told him to stop bumming me out all the time and loosen up. That seemed to help for a while, but then he started getting really aggressive."

"And you don't see a problem with anything you just said?"

"Not with me!"

"How are you this dense?" I looked toward the hallway, everything having gone very quiet since I'd left a helpless Roscoe alone with a werewolf following my orders. I had absolutely no room to talk about Adam being a bad kuu mate. Rosco and I had a dynamic where he would piss me off and I'd get some kind of revenge, but none of it felt right this time.

Then I thought about how Roscoe protected me last night, and that was when the guilt crushed me. I finally hopped off the couch and walked into the hallway.

"What are you doing?" Adam asked, following me.

"I just realized I'm just as shitty as you are." I slammed open the door to see Austin lying with both hands folded under his head while a semi-conscious Roscoe lay drooling next to him.

"Interesting conversation?" I asked.

"Yeah," Austin said, his irises back to their usual amber. He smiled and looked over at the motionless werewolf. "It's great. He can't escape, and I was just getting to varnishes."

With a bit of smug satisfaction, I looked down at the old werewolf but couldn't shake that something was off with his blank expression.

"Oh, by the way," Austin added, "I accidentally turned that thing on high. Was wondering why he kept throwing himself off the bed."

"Oh my God," I shouted, frantically searching for the key to the cuffs before dashing toward the bed. "How long was he like that?"

After I slipped the key into the hole, the enchantment Roscoe was under disappeared. I then began removing everything attached to him.

"I dunno. Maybe five minutes. It was kinda funny watching him flop around like a trout on the floor."

Roscoe didn't move, and I started to really worry. He'd warned me that this stuff was dangerous, and now I'd probably messed him up.

"Well, fun's over. Everyone out!"

"Aww." Austin climbed out of bed, eyeing Adam dismissively.

After undoing the strap on his muzzle, I gave the cock cage a tap with the magic key, and it expanded before falling off him.

"I'm so sorry, Roscoe. I didn't know."

The werewolf remained silent and turned toward the wall.

"Guess I'll leave you two alone," Austin said, walking out of the room, but not before shoving Adam to the side. The half-turn scoffed at me before walking in the opposite direction, toward the back door. I'd have to take care of that later.

"I went too far."

Roscoe still didn't say anything, and tears welled in my eyes. There was a slight wiggle from below where his tail was, but I was more concerned with the possibility that I'd just destroyed things between us.

"I'm so sorry Roscoe. Please talk to me," I said through tears. There was that wiggle again. "What can I do to make it up to you? I'll do whatever you want."

His ears stuck straight, and I grew suspicious immediately.

"I could go for some barbeque," he said, sniffling.

"Oh—okay," I said, pulling away as his tail thudded the mattress. "I'll go pick some up. Anything else?"

"Could really go fer some snacks, too. We traded all the ones we had in the cupboard."

"Fine. I'll stop by the store and get some."

I shuffled off the bed, and Roscoe still didn't look back at me.

"Are we good?"

The older werewolf sniffled again.

"I dunno."

I sighed and stopped at the bedroom door.

"I'm really *really* sorry, Roscoe." With that, I shut the door and started toward the living room, but not before I remembered I hadn't asked him what kind of barbeque he wanted.

When I opened the door, Roscoe was grinning and dancing around like a fool before freezing the moment I walked in. My remorse completely dissolved as I crossed my arms.

"What do you want from the restaurant?" I asked through clenched teeth.

Roscoe's tail dropped between his legs and his ears fell to the sides of his head.

"Uh... I could really go fer some pulled pork."

"You were fucking with me, weren't you?"

Roscoe's pupils dilated, and he gave me the saddest expression he could muster.

"It was so awful. Can't believe you did that to me. That was the most bored I'd ever been in my life."

My eyes narrowed as his tail betrayed him.

"You actually enjoyed it, didn't you?"

"I did not!" Roscoe snapped. "That was embarrassing, and I couldn't do nothin'."

His tail continued to wag, and I was actually thankful werewolves couldn't control it. It was like a long, furry lie detector, but I decided to let him have this round. Even if he was pretending to be that upset, I still felt awful.

I picked the cuffs, cage, and strap off the floor, tossed them into the bag then zipped it shut. "I'm throwing these away. You're right. They're probably too dangerous to mess around with."

Roscoe grabbed my arm.

"Let's not get too hasty," he said, pulling the bag away from me. "There's no harm in keepin' the stuff fer a little while longer."

"But you said—"

"I'm sure it's fine," he interrupted, tossing the bag into the closet before pulling the folding doors closed. He turned back and smirked. "Make sure to get sweet sauce."

"Fine."

"Oh, and horseradish if they have it."

"For pulled pork?"

Roscoe licked his lips. "Get me some roast beef, too."

"Anything else, your majesty?" I asked, my tone descending into a deeper annoyance.

"Nah. That should make up fer what you did."

"You might actually wake up bald tomorrow," I muttered under my breath while walking out of the bedroom.

"Get some spicy sauce, too!"

# Chapter 21

# The Nor-Witch

**H**owling laughter erupted from the werewolves eating at the wooden tables outside the barbeque joint. When I was here with Austin, we'd stayed outside. The building was nothing much to look at—and there wasn't even a name on signage out front.

The standing chalkboard to the entrance's right displayed the menu in beautiful cursive, which kind of clashed with the rugged rural theme. If there *was* a theme.

All the werewolves went quiet, turning to look at me in unison as I approached the entrance. This was also a common occurrence; being a half-turn, the attention was just part of daily life. It wasn't terrible, but I still found it unsettling at times.

"Hey, new guy," a smaller black werewolf called as I reached for the door handle. "Wanna sit with us?"

"I have some hungry guys back at home, sorry." The werewolves here were different compared to the city. There was no underlying desperation, no belligerent drunk shouting, no creepy advances. They all had this calmness in their demeanor, happy and sober—for the most part, their tails wagging and ears up. "I'll take you guys up on the offer next time though."

"We will hold you to it," said a larger, gray one sitting across from the black. "Bring the pack next time. They look like a fun bunch."

"There's definitely never a dull moment," I said with a smile before stepping inside the warm restaurant. The atmosphere shifted instantaneously from a cozy hole-in-the-wall to something right out of a haunted house. Barbeque usually meant open, well-lit foyers and dining areas lined with wooden seats and western décor, but this was the opposite, leaning in hard on the whole 'Halloween Town' reputation. Upside-down cast iron pentagram candle holders lined the walls of the entryway. All the windows were covered with thick black drapes, and the walls were burgundy, with fake cobwebs along the corners. At least I assumed they were fake.

A woman greeted me as I walked through the foyer, the candlelight too dim to see her face clearly.

"I was wondering when you would wander into my web." The low and seductive way she spoke gave her voice a cat-like purr. She wore a black gown so long it hid her shoes, and her upper body remained still as if she were floating across the floor toward me. The alabaster makeup was perfectly contoured, giving her slender cheeks more depth, and the whole ensemble popped with her ruby lipstick, long lashes and black eyeliner. The woman was stunning, with her long, straight hair as dark as a raven's feathers. She had a confidence in her posture that made her seem much older than she probably was. "It's nice to see you again, gorgeous."

Even though she was a woman, the sensual timbre of her voice made me blush. "Have we met?"

"Briefly." She traced the backs of her slender fingers along my cheeks before combing my thick sideburns with her nails. Her touch made me freeze. "I bought you a drink the other night."

She leaned in and kissed me on the forehead, her lips feeling soft ice before she pulled away and glided back to the counter. The concept of personal space seemed almost offensive to her, like she owned everything and everyone that walked through the door.

"Sorry, I don't remember. There were a lot of people trying to buy me drinks that night." She must have been one of the women I thought was flirting with me. "I hope I didn't seem rude."

"You were direct," she said with a sharp smile. "Your friend seemed rude to you though."

"You picked up on that?" I asked, grabbing a plastic menu from a large, fake skull shaped like a bowl. "I had a bad night."

"Well, let me make this evening more pleasurable," she said, leaning over the counter, purposely letting her cleavage heave forward. "And by that, I mean the food is on the house. Half-turns always eat free when they come inside. So do new werewolves."

"For real?"

"It's my way of welcoming your pack to our town." Her stare ravaged me the longer I stood there.

"You won't get in trouble, will you?" I held up the menu and started reading, but she pulled it down and wagged her finger.

"I guess I'll have to reprimand myself later. You'll get the howler's special feast, and when it's done, I'll have our driver deliver it."

"Oh—okay." I started backing toward the door.

"I'll have him deliver *you*, too." She waved me through the lobby toward a corner booth in the back adorned with two lit candles and two glasses of iced tea. I followed at a distance. "Get cozy. I'll bring some appetizers."

There wasn't another soul in the dining area, as if I was the only one expected. The last time Austin and I were here, we never came inside to order. Was she here then?

A tightness swelled in my chest the further I went inside. The surrounding air turned thick, and it was hard to catch my breath. As if by instinct, I stopped and backed away. The intensity of the fear was so primal. The werewolf side of me screamed a warning I didn't quite understand.

"Who are you?"

"Willa," she said, her sanguine lips pulling upward into a bewitching smile. "Willa Mosavi."

"Shit," I whispered, taking a shaky step backward, but it was like walking through tar. So she was the mayor's wife.

Her seductive smile softened into something less threatening as she grabbed my arm.

"Oh, come on." She pulled me along and pointed to the booth. "The food will be done in about twenty minutes, but I've been wanting to talk."

"Are you going to put another charm on me like your husband did?"

"That naughty beast," she whispered, sliding into the booth and pointing to the other seat across from her. "I told him to leave you alone from now on." She lifted a glass of tea to her mouth and sucked it through the plastic straw, leaving a thin film of red behind. "I won't force you to stay, but I would like to talk about what happened. My husband can be brash and heavy-handed. It's a wonder he's made it this far into politics."

"Your husband's sick."

Her eyes rolled back, and she wet her lips. "Oh, I know."

"I didn't mean it in a good way," I muttered through my teeth, reluctantly taking a seat.

She pursed her lips, seeming to feign disappointment.

"I guess since I'm here, you can answer some questions as well."

"I often have the answers." She placed the glass back on the table, stirring the floating ice cubes with her sharp, manicured finger before sucking the liquid away.

"You know I'm completely gay, right?"

"Of course I know. That's why this is so much fun. You and my Darius have so much in common, you know?"

"I wish people would stop saying that. I am nothing like your husband."

"You're still a baby compared to him but give it a couple hundred years."

Why was her presence so terrifying? It wasn't just because she was Mosavi's wife. She had this suffocating aura that made me remember the warnings of the Whasha ferals.

"Are you a witch?"

She sat up straighter, seemingly uneasy. "What a dreadful question."

"Sorry. I've just heard some rumors."

"I'm not a witch, Cody."

I let out a relieved sigh.

"I am *the* witch. The Nor-witch." The woman let out a shriek of maniacal laughter, weaving her fingers through the air like spindly wands. She stopped and snorted a real laugh before taking another sip of tea.

"You could have just told me no," I said, relaxing my clenched fists under the booth, trying to come across as nonchalant. I still wasn't sure if she was lying or telling the truth.

"Any other questions?" she asked. "Do you want to know where I keep all of the human children I eat?"

"Ha ha. I'm gullible, okay?" Of all the personalities Mosavi's wife could have had, this was actually not as terrible as I imagined. She almost seemed like a smart, female version of Roscoe. "Why is your husband so interested in me?"

"Well, look at yourself," she said, pulling an ornate compact mirror from a hidden pocket against her right breast.

"Yes, I'm a cutie. We've established that."

"No, I mean, *actually* look at yourself," she said more seriously, sliding the mirror across the table. "See what Darius sees."

I gave her a bit of side-eye and grabbed the mirror before unfolding it and giving my reflection a careful look.

"Is this supposed to be some kind of lesson of self-confidence?"

The image in the mirror rippled before going still again, and my irises took on a silver glow similar to Mosavi's. My face morphed and broadened into someone older and much more masculine, but I could still tell it was me. I'd never looked so handsome, so refined. When I smiled, my sharp teeth glistened with an ivory sheen in the dancing glow of candlelight.

The more I stared, the more wolf-like I became, my face now warping into a full lycanthropic visage. Gray streaks gave my neat mane a distinguished appearance. I was massive.

"What is this?" I asked, enamored. "Another one of Mosavi's enchanted toys?"

"*That* is your potential," Willa said, pulling the mirror away. She snapped it shut and stuffed it back into her brassiere. "Normally, you'd be too old for this stage of lycanthropy, but you're the special case."

"So, I've been told." I picked up my glass and took a sip. "This wasn't supposed to be my life."

She patted my hand. "You can't change it, Cody. Trying to hide it away will only cause you distress and bitterness. It was something I wish I'd have been around to help my husband with when he was much younger, but I didn't know him then."

"That's easy for you to say. It doesn't happen to women. You don't have your entire life and future upended by whatever the hell this curse is."

"Curse?" She shook her head. "When you were looking at your future self in my mirror, what did you feel?" she asked, pulling her hand away.

"What do you mean?"

"It's not a hard question. Were you satisfied?"

"I... don't know."

"A human life is so banal. You were a nobody living in a bare studio apartment living paycheck to paycheck. You didn't even have enough money for mayonnaise."

Another chill shook me.

"How did you know that?"

She ignored my question.

"You want to be more than some boring human with little chance of succeeding in a life they've designed to enslave you. You want to be like my husband." Though her words stung, she said them with such understanding. Flashbacks to what that feral elder told me raced through my head. "Darius seems like a cruel beast, and he is not well-adjusted, but he's more complex than that. He wants to protect you, but he also delights in depravity—a lingering side effect of his repressive religious upbringing."

"Are you really trying to paint him as being a good person?"

Willa chuckled. "Do I look like the type of woman who marries a *good* person?"

"I don't know what type of woman you are. I don't even know why we're talking." I rubbed my forehead. "And what do you mean he's trying to protect me?"

"Because you're dangerous."

I laughed at that. "*I'm* dangerous? Your husband assaulted my pack, and he's using his position to threaten all of us."

"Trust me. Your very existence is dangerous. All elders still alive started out this way, but not all become leaders. If they do, they become the most potent and powerful creatures on this planet." She reached for my hand and gently grazed her red painted fingernail over my skin. "Your presence attracts a lot of attention from those that crave the power you might possess, but it's still too early to tell how you'll end up."

"Why does any of this matter to him?"

"It matters to both of us, as we both have equal interest in your future." She chuckled and shook her head. "Now that I've met you, I see his usual methods of getting his way aren't going to work. I know you hate hearing it, but you're too similar."

I opened my mouth to protest again, but she cut me off.

"You want to be him."

"I want to be better," I snapped, looking away from her. "I'd like to be rich and handsome, but the other stuff—"

"Makes him who *he* is," Willa interrupted. "But his methods are driving you closer to the ones he's trying to shield you from." She sighed and examined my face. "You don't want to be caught by a witch."

"Are witches evil or something?"

"No," she replied sternly. "But they're not exactly good either. They don't bother humans because humans are worthless, but werewolves with the vironoct…" Her eyes narrowed with intensity. "It's a font of immortality, power, and endless insatiable sex. It's like a drug."

A person from the kitchen staff poked his head out from behind one of the doors and nodded at Willa.

She caught her breath and her countenance returned to normal. "Your food is done." She slid out of the seat. "You should have leftovers for a few days."

"You've never seen Roscoe eat," I said, following her to the counter. "Why are werewolves all that to witches? What do they do to them?"

She stopped at the counter and gave me a nod.

"That's a lengthy conversation, and unfortunately my time is short today." Willa placed her dainty hand on my shoulder. "If what my husband has is what you want, don't fall in with the Whasha. But unlike what my husband thinks, the Whasha path is not necessarily a wrong one to take. It just leads to a different future." She started to turn but caught herself, squeezing my shoulder tighter. "Also, if you don't want to end up a mindless husk, don't chance an encounter with a witch of the wilds." She let go and walked the rest of the way behind the counter. "In other words, stay the hell out of the woods. Darius owns everyone he encounters, human or werewolf, but like I said earlier, you're a special case. He knows he can't have his way with you."

"He did. When I was in the jail with him. I was in this place—"

"Really?" she asked. "You think *he* did that?"

"I didn't feel in control. I think the lighter he gave me did something."

She waved me closer, so I took a few steps toward the counter and leaned in.

"I'll let you in on a little secret."

"I'm listening."

"Whatever trinket he gave you does nothing but track your location. What you did the other night was all you, honey."

"That's not a secret. He told me the same thing."

The kitchen staff brought out bag after bag of food and setting them on the counter. There's no way they could have prepared all of this in the short time I was here.

"What is it you really want from me?" I asked.

She said nothing for a moment, then looked up at me expectantly.

"You said earlier that you didn't know me."

I looked at the full counter, the kitchen staff placing more bags on top of bags.

"Is this a bribe?"

"All I want is for you to come by again. I *really* want to get to know you better. Plus, if you want to get back at Darius, I know his secrets and weaknesses." The way she said that was almost tantalizing.

"Wait. You *want* me to get back at him?"

"Well, someone besides me has got to knock him down a notch every now and then, and after watching you handle yourself the other night, I think you might be able to use what you have to really get under his skin."

My eyes widened. "What do you mean you *watched* me?"

"Honey, it's a jail. There are cameras everywhere."

"Oh..."

The driver stepped into the lobby, and the kitchen staff silently carried the food out to the car. Willa slid across the floor toward a darkened hallway, then stopped and looked back.

"I'll keep my husband away from you for now, but don't go back into the woods again. It took everything I had to hold Darius back from tracking you down the other night. It's hard to get an angry alpha under control, and even I have my limits." She winked before disappearing into the shadows, her rose-scented perfume lingering in the air.

The four of us stood around a loaded table, the scent of mesquite and rubbing spices filling the house. Austin and Roscoe gawked at the buffet, drooling, while Adam turned to me with a suspicious squint.

"Well well well," he said with a sharp-toothed smirk.

"What?"

He slapped my ass hard. "I've done my share of *favors* for things, but there's like a thousand dollars' worth of meat here, and I know you can't afford it."

"Just what the hell are you insinuating—"

"Hell yeah," Roscoe interrupted as he shifted through the paper bags. "If yer gettin' fucked for this much free food, we gotta capitalize on that."

"I am NOT—" I paused and shot him a disgusted glance. "Did you really suggest I whore myself out just so you can have free brisket?"

Roscoe took in a deep sniff, closing his eyes. "Brisket's soooo good."

My disgust turned to something more threatening.

"I'm just jokin'," he said, nervously scratching his head. "I hid that bag after you left, so don't get any funny ideas."

"If you didn't screw some werewolf chef, how did you get all this?" Austin asked, pulling out a chicken quarter and tossing it into his mouth, bone and all.

"Mosavi's wife."

Roscoe and Austin froze, but Adam kept rummaging through the food.

"Getting kind of chummy with the mayor, are we?" the half-turn asked jokingly as he piled food onto his plate. "What's wrong with everyone?"

"Nothing. Let's eat," I said, grabbing a paper plate.

"There's something weird going on here." He flashed his sharper teeth for a second. "If we're all going to be this *family*, don't keep treating me like I'm on the outside."

"I'll talk to him," Austin said, with an unusually compassionate tone, "after dinner."

The werewolf's dark, orange stare widened before turning baby blue as if waiting for my approval. I nodded, which prompted an immediate tail-wagging response. Part of me wished I could turn off the vironoct effect, but for whatever reason, I couldn't with Austin. He was either way too willing or Mosavi's magic was permanent.

"How 'bout you guys talk in the living room, and Cody and I'll eat in the bedroom," Roscoe said, balancing a ridiculously high pile of food on his flimsy paper plate.

"The food's not going anywhere, Roscoe. You can always come back for more," I said, handing him another plate to reinforce what he was carrying. "And we're not eating this mess in my bed."

"Didn't say nothin' about the bed." He gave me a familiar mischievous grin before padding toward the hallway. "I got a surprise fer ya."

"Oh fuck me," I muttered.

Roscoe and his surprises. I followed him into the bedroom. The first thing I noticed was a curtain of hanging beads in the doorway followed by a musty smell, like cloth that had been left out in the rain and then left out in the sun—for a month.

"What. The. Hell. Did you do?" I asked, looking around the room, though most of my attention focused on an old loveseat pushed against our bedroom wall. It was a vintage dark brown, orange, and tawny flower pattern I hadn't seen since childhood. The fabric was faded, and the cushions had a thin layer of what I assumed was either mildew or dirt. There were also slight tears along the tops and sides, like they had been clawed by a housecat.

"Would you believe someone was just throwin' this treasure away?"

"Of course I would!" I shouted, causing the larger werewolf to slink backward, his ears falling. "It's disgusting. What the hell is wrong with you? Why do you keep bringing other peoples' garbage into my house?"

"Yer gettin' all bent out of shape, and you haven't even tried it out," he said before pushing a loud switch on an old nineteen-inch CRT television that had been in our closet since we moved here. It sat atop the dresser with aluminum foil capped rabbit ear antennas that weren't actually hooked to anything. They wouldn't have worked anyway since the stations were digital now. Next to it lay an ugly faux wood-paneled VCR and a stack of VHS tapes, their labels stained brown with writing in faded blue ink.

"This whole room needs to be doused in bleach." I stared at the boxy television and shook my head. "Why do you even still have this?"

"Cause it's comfy," he said, setting his plate of food on one of the two foldable TV trays in front of the couch.

It was like our bedroom had become a portal into the past, though I wasn't exactly sure what decade. A red lava lamp bubbled away on our nightstand, and an Art Deco-styled three-tiered lamp with red, black, and green bulbs brightened the corner next to a few creased posters with tie-dye colors and peace signs.

"I knew you had the TV, but where were you keeping this other crap?"

"The shed," he said, smiling. "You really don't like it?"

"I hate it," I muttered, setting my plate on the other TV table. "If you brought bugs and rats into this house—"

"Nah, I checked it all before bringing it in," he said, popping in one of the VHS tapes. "Just some roaches, but a few bugs ain't gonna kill us."

I froze. "We just got rid of the roaches, and you brought more in?"

Roscoe's ears folded downward. "I'll get it clean tomorrow."

*The Last Starfighter* theme song whined and warbled through the speaker as Roscoe adjusted the tracking. The faded, staticky picture of the standard definition screen cleared.

"Ever see this?" he asked.

"When I was a kid." I hesitated to sit on the dirty sofa, but Roscoe plopped down and patted the space next to him.

"What day is it today?"

"Sunday," I replied, checking the cushion thoroughly for any critters before sitting. "Why?"

"This'll be our old movie night," he said, squirting a packet of barbecue sauce onto a pile of pulled pork and brisket.

Once again, Roscoe's disgusting antics took on a sweet sentimentalism. My mood shifted from annoyance to comfortable and nostalgic as I leaned against him while watching the old television. The opening credits of the movie faded, and I stared at Roscoe while he watched. He was genuinely happy at that moment.

"I promise I'll clean it tomorrow," he said, turning to me after catching me staring, his lips coated in grease and sauce.

"It's gross, but... really sweet," I said, leaning against him while biting down on a forkful of shredded meat.

The tip of Roscoe's tail thudded into the space between us as he leaned in and kissed my cheek, leaving behind a thick, sticky mark.

After the movie, I got up and collected our trash before heading into the dining room to put away the leftovers. Austin sat alone on the living room sofa, blankly staring at the television.

"Where's Adam?"

"The backyard," he grunted, changing the channel.

"Did you talk to him?"

"Mmhmm."

"And?"

Austin shrugged. "And he went outside. What else do you want me to say?"

I chewed on my lower lip and headed into the kitchen to throw the garbage away before sprinting to the back door. Adam was already in a very temperamental state, but I wondered if Austin had managed to push a little too far. If they had fought, Roscoe and I would have heard them from the bedroom, but there hadn't been anything out of the ordinary.

The back door creaked open, and I stepped out into the cool, smokey air. Adam sat next to the lit fire pit, poking the flames with a stick.

"Uh oh," I said, sitting next to him. "Are you angry with me?"

"Huh?" he looked up, tilting his head.

"Never mind. I thought you were upset."

"No," he replied. "It's a pretty night, and I wanted to make a fire."

"Okay..."

"Austin said he'd come out, but he never did." He shifted one of the flaming logs, letting it fall against another one, sending tiny orange embers fluttering through the air before they disappeared into the blackness. "I wish I could make him do stuff like you can. Maybe I can convince Mosavi to let me in on this big secret."

"What exactly did Austin tell you?"

"Not much. He wasn't making sense, but apparently, you're alpha now." He flashed me a lascivious glance. "You've really changed since we got here."

"Well, yeah. I'm getting hairier."

"That's not what I mean. You're just... different. I can't explain it. You walk around like you own the world, and Roscoe and Austin do anything you say. I'm the one that has to beg for attention now." He looked back up at me, and while he smiled, his eyes shimmered. "It's like you're sucking away all the air in the room, and you're not even trying."

I wanted to reply, but instead, I stared at the fire.

"Go ahead and brag now," Adam snapped. "You've won."

"This is my fault. I've been trying to push you guys closer together so that you both don't move away after you turn."

The furry half-turn's face softened in the flickering glow.

"Wait. I thought you didn't want us here? I thought you couldn't wait to get us out of your hair, especially since I put you in an *impossible situation without talking to you first*."

"I still stand by that, but I love having both of you here. You're like family, and family can be annoying, but it's hard to picture this place without you guys."

"Then teach me," Adam insisted.

"Teach you what?"

"If you don't want Austin and me to leave each other, then teach me what you did to get him to listen to you. Darryl can do the same thing but won't let me in on the secret. He said it's none of my business, and that it was stupid of me to try. He apologized for what he said when I went with Roscoe to visit him, but I still think about it, and it pisses me off."

"He probably told you that because forcing someone to obey you doesn't exactly make for a healthy relationship."

"And you think it's healthy now?"

I let out a frustrated sigh. "Adam, I don't understand what I did. Mosavi never explained it, and he's kind of forcing me into doing things I don't feel comfortable doing. I think his wife might be more helpful though."

"Perfect," he said, shooting up from the lawn chair. "Can you take me to her tomorrow?"

"I didn't mean we should go asking her how to control werewolves."

"Then I'm gone once I shift and the kuu breaks. There are a lot of werewolves out there that would love to have me—"

"As a half-turn, yes. Do you think you'll have the same luck as a full werewolf?"

"Are you saying that werewolves aren't interested in other werewolves?" He crossed his arms. "Because that's bullshit."

"I'm saying, I don't know if you're going to have the same mass appeal you do now. I don't know enough about any of this, but I do know that turning Austin into a thrall isn't going to make either of you happy."

"He sure seems happy when he's obeying you."

"Is he really happy, or is that just some fucked-up side effect from what Mosavi did to him? I'm hoping this isn't a permanent thing, and if it does wear off, I'm not doing it again. Austin's got a lot of problems." I shook my head. "I can't force him to open up to you. He's gotta make that choice, and he'll only do it if he feels comfortable talking to you."

"So he feels more comfortable talking to you," Adam muttered. "He tells you stuff he won't tell me, and you still want us to be together?"

"You know why he tells me stuff? Because when he's a traumatized mess, I don't tell him to stop bumming me out."

"Are you saying this is my fault?"

"Yes," I snapped. "You don't know how to listen to people. You just want everyone to listen to you. It's the whole reason you want this shortcut. You don't want to work on a relationship—you just want someone you can talk at while they do anything you tell them. Grow up, Adam."

His eyes flashed. "How dare you."

"If you want to leave, I won't stop you, but I'm also not going to teach you how to fuck up Austin even more than he already is. You probably can't do it anyways."

Adam didn't respond. He stomped toward the back door before nearly yanking it off its hinges. When he disappeared inside, he slammed it shut.

I sat back down on the lawn chair and slumped forward, staring at the fire. It was time to stop playing counselor. They didn't want to be together, and I seemed to be the only one invested in making their relationship work. I just wanted a family so badly that I was willing to throw what was essentially a cat and dog into a small box, expecting them to learn to be friends.

I might not have been able to work with Adam, but I wouldn't give up on Austin.

# The Road to Recovery

Roscoe breathed heavily, still in a food coma from repeatedly going back for leftovers. He and Austin kept turning the kitchen light on and off, and I dreaded what kind of mess I'd end up walking into.

Since my side of the bed was against the wall, and Roscoe had junk piled on the floor at the other end, I had to climb over him. His gut protruded further than usual, but werewolf bodies burned a surprising amount of calories, even while doing absolutely nothing. Which was fortunate, considering Roscoe would spend the majority of his days doing as little as possible if I let him.

When werewolves put on weight, muscles overcompensated to keep them somewhat fit. This resulted in a much higher metabolic rate, and instead of that rate rising or falling over months, the effect happened in hours.

That bit of useful knowledge was the result of my frequent descents into multiple rabbit holes of internet videos on werewolf physiology. I was still disappointed by how little information there was about what we are. Aside from that bizarre book I read at Darryl's about our possible origins, there hadn't been nearly enough research.

Or maybe there had been, but that thought led me deep into conspiracies.

Roscoe snorted as I straddled him for a moment. I wanted to stay like that, my naked body against his silky mane as I drifted back to sleep, but I couldn't remain in bed all day.

I climbed off and slipped on a pair of shorts and a shirt. It wasn't unusual for me to go commando, especially since my dick had gotten thicker after going half-turn. I couldn't wear the comfy briefs I had when human, and boxers felt weird. It was easier to just let it hang, which I admit often got me quite a bit of attention.

That ugly couch seemed to stink up the room worse than last night, which meant I hadn't dreamt Roscoe's romantic dumpster diving for our vintage movie date night. He still enjoyed digging around in garbage for things he considered treasures, even though between the four of us, we had enough money to just buy things we needed.

In the hallway, Adam brushed by me before stomping into the bathroom.

"Good morning," I said.

"Fuck off."

The door closed and locked before the light flicked on, casting a wide beam across the floor from underneath. I'd need at least two cups of coffee before dealing with him. I might have screwed things up so much that a simple apology likely wouldn't suffice this time. Even though I understood why he was so easily irritable, our conversation yesterday shouldn't have happened—at least, not the way it did.

The kitchen looked exactly how I expected. Empty bags were strewn about, and paper plates full of chicken and rib bones just left there for the few lucky house flies that managed to find their way inside, but that wasn't what really bothered me. All the meticulous cleaning and extermination I'd done might as well have been for nothing—five roaches skittered about before disappearing between the stove and counter.

This was going to require four cups of coffee at the very least.

Whirring and banging rattled the divide between the dining room and Austin's garage, and since the other side of the thin wall in the kitchen was the bathroom, I could hear every off-key note Adam belted while in the shower.

"Someone is gonna die today," I muttered, filling the entire coffee pot with water before scooping triple the amount of cheap ground coffee into the filter. As that brewed, I set to work on cleaning the mess.

The kitchen sparkled as I sipped on my seventh cup, pretending to solve Goldbach's conjecture in my head while getting to work scrubbing burnt food off the stove drip pans. After I was done dusting and the sweeping in the living room, I got on all fours and cleaned the grout in the bathroom with an old toothbrush, all the while shaking like a heroin addict in withdrawal.

Roscoe crept into the doorway, before sitting on our oversized toilet with a loud groan.

"Gotta poop," he said, holding open a two-decade old Reader's Digest he brought in with him.

"At least wait for me to finish!" I threw the toothbrush into the sink then ran out of the bathroom, slamming the door behind me just in time.

I stepped back into the living room while Adam ate potato chips on the couch, him mindlessly scrolling through his phone. When he'd shove a handful into his mouth, smaller bits of chip would fall in between the cushions

"C'mon, man. I just cleaned this place."

He glared up at me, then down at his sleeveless shirt before dusting the crumbs that had accumulated onto the floor.

"Missed a spot," he muttered before scrolling again.

Not wanting to make things worse, I turned around and walked through the hallway toward the back door. Now wasn't the time for a heartfelt apology, especially since all I could think about was choking him.

As I opened the door, Austin stood at the edge of the woods, staring at nothing in particular. His tail swayed gently, so I knew he was in a somewhat decent mood. My bare feet lightly padded over the frosty lawn until I was standing next to him.

"You okay?"

"Mmhmm," he grunted, still staring straight ahead. I tried to get a sense of what he was looking at, but aside from a few birds, there wasn't anything of note.

Turning back toward the house, I walked over to the cold fire pit and sat on one of the lawn chairs, my heart rate finally dropping to a steady, less concerning rhythm as the caffeine started to wear off. Austin followed and took the seat next to me but didn't say anything. Instead, we listened to the calm wind whisper through all the trees.

"Ever feel like taking a walk in the woods?" he asked, finally breaking the silence.

"When Roscoe and I were out there, it was nice. I kinda thought about just staying there, but that notion faded quickly when I got poison oak all over my face."

He smiled at that.

"Are you having those thoughts again?" I asked.

"They haven't come back since that night."

"I think that thing with Mosavi made everything worse."

His ears stood straight. "I haven't been able to stop thinking about it."

"I'm sorry, Austin. I wish I could've stopped him."

"Why? I liked it," he said pensively.

"What?"

"I liked it," he repeated, this time looking down at me. "I think about it all the time. I also like it when you boss me around. I dunno. It just feels right."

The words in my head were an incomprehensible mess, and once again, I had no idea where to take the conversation.

"When I saw what you did to Roscoe last night, I got kinda jealous and fried his nips."

"I guess I'm a little confused."

"You can add that to the list of messed up shit about me." He chortled and looked away. "When I joined the marines, it did something to me. When sergeants would shout commands, it was a turn-on. I didn't have to make the decisions or think too much. All I had to do was follow orders." He shifted and crossed one leg over his knee. "I wanted to be told what to do."

"Dude, that stuff's fine in the bedroom, but you can't let people do that to you in real life. Is that why you neglect Adam?"

"He wants me to take control and make the decisions all the time. I can't deal with it." The hackles on his neck stuck straight. "When you told me to fuck him, that was hottest thing anyone's ever done. When I was... *neutralizing the target*, all I kept thinkin' about was you on top of me, shouting in my ear. Sometimes you'd lock me up, or I'd picture you beating the shit out of me while strapped to a St. Andrew's cross."

"Dude—"

"I know," he said, his expression returning to normal as he pulled nervously at his mane. "That's why I've been thinking about paying the

     *Aeron Dusk*

mayor a visit. I was gonna ask him when he was here, but I didn't want to deal with Adam messing it up."

"Don't do that. That guy fucked you up pretty bad last time."

Austin shook his head. "No one gets me, and Adam's never gonna understand. That big-dicked piece of shit sitting in that office does though."

"Just tell Adam what you want and stay away from Mosavi. I mean it. I'll let you guys have that bag of weird sex shit, if you want it—if I can find where Roscoe hid it."

"It's not the same if you have to tell someone." He snorted and shook his head. "I used to get really rough with him, and I wanted him so pissed off that he'd do that stuff to me as revenge. But all it did was make him more whiny. It's why I haven't been in the mood to do anything with him lately, but when you tell me what to do—" His ears folded backward. "Maybe I really am more fucked up than I thought."

"Austin, I'm not a shrink," I said, placing my hand on his leg. "I haven't exactly been patient or understanding with Adam either. He's been in pain, and you should tell him what you want him to do. See how he responds. I'll mediate if you want."

"What do you mean, he's in pain?"

"The whole shifting thing. I think he needs a lot more attention than I can give him."

Austin's eyes widened. "Aw, jeez," he whispered. "I forgot about that."

"About what?"

He jumped up from the chair and hurried back to the house, not responding. The door shut behind him, and I stared out into the woods. If anyone understood what Adam was going through, it would be another werewolf.

A bird let out a cackle high in one of the trees, but I couldn't see what it looked like. I could only hear its creepy call, which echoed farther away. After a few minutes, more birds sang, their calls seeming to echo and reverberate through my head in a deafening chant.

"*Cody. So sweet,*" a soft, feminine voice whispered in my ear. "*We would love to meet you.*"

Tens of red, beady eyes stared unblinking from the shady pines. A familiar, hot and heavy sensation pressed in from all around, more intense than when Willa had escorted me through her restaurant. It was the same primal screaming from the wolf to take cover, and this time, I wouldn't ignore it.

Trying to stay calm, I stood and made my way to the door. When the knob clicked, the woods fell silent and the voices vanished.

Adam and Austin's bedroom door was closed, but there weren't any sounds coming from the other side. The bathroom door was also shut, and I assumed Roscoe was still working off an impacted bowel from all the meat he'd consumed. As I approached the kitchen, however, I found Roscoe at the dining room table, nodding to music while peeling potatoes.

"I thought you were still in the bathroom," I said, sitting in the chair next to him. "Why are you making more food?"

Roscoe turned down the small bluetooth radio next to him. "These are gonna go bad soon if I don't cook 'em now." He looked over at me. "You hungry?"

"Not at the moment." I turned the radio all the way off. "What you did last night was really sweet."

"I knew you'd like it. You always pretend like you hate somethin' until you actually give it a chance." He smiled and dropped a peeled potato in the bowl, pointing to himself with the dull side of his paring knife. "Like me."

"That all depends on if you're going to clean that nasty couch today. I saw roaches in the kitchen this morning."

"A little more protein wouldn't hurt ya," Roscoe said, picking up another potato before noticing the disgust on my face. "Ya know I'm kidding. I'll clean it."

"Am I an asshole?" I asked, gauging Roscoe's shifty eyes.

"Uh..." He set the knife on the other side of the table. "That depends. Do you know where I hid that bag?"

"I guess that's my answer."

"Listen. Ever since that night with the mayor, you've been a little short."

"I'm on edge," I responded, resting my head against my knuckles.

"You gotta learn how to deal with that stuff in a constructive way instead of takin' it out on the pack." He nudged my arm. "You should take it out on me in bed."

"It's always about sex, isn't it?"

"Naw. I'm just telling you to start using me the way yer supposed to. That's why we're kuu mates. You think all this is just to get free housing? All half-turns need a trusty werewolf that'll be there when they need to blow off steam."

"I thought the whole kuu thing was a recent policy."

Roscoe nodded. "Yeah, but this stuff's been happening well before that."

"Then why do we even need these?" I pointed at my earrings, which I found out from Mosavi didn't really work for me. "If half-turns and werewolves end up together anyway, why do we need some kind of magical bond?"

Roscoe paused for a moment and shrugged. "I ain't an elder, so I don't know what the purpose is for any of this shit. I just know that we'll get a free ride when it's over."

"And you know this, how?"

"Because—" He paused again, stumbling over his words. "Because that's what we've been told."

"Have you actually seen any of these places? Do you know anyone who's reached the end of the contract?"

"No, I guess not," he muttered. "You think it's all a lie?"

"I don't know what to think anymore. Just some of the shit Mosavi said makes me wonder. He mentioned kuu-bound werewolves being easier to control. You were passed out drunk, so you didn't hear it, but that's been bothering me a lot." I unclasped one of the golden hoop earrings, and it came out effortlessly. "These don't work on me, by the way."

"Whoa! Shit, Cody you broke our kuu?" His wide eyes teared up.

"No. It never worked to begin with. Whatever makes me different nullifies this stuff." I quickly put the earring back in before the hole closed. "They've grown on me, though."

"That's cause you look good in 'em." Roscoe's sad eyes turned squinty when a smile pinched the sides of his maw. "So this whole time we weren't kuu-bonded, but you stayed anyway."

I slipped my arms around him. "I guess I did. You're just too damn comfortable, even if you are a slob." I pushed him away. "That feral elder in the woods was the only one that didn't seem to have some kind of agenda. When I was around him, I was more comfortable than when I was around Mosavi or his wife."

"Ooo, I meant to ask. What was she like?" he asked, picking up another potato.

"She's definitely a witch—I think."

Roscoe fumbled as he sliced, letting the knife fall into the bowl.

"What makes you think that?"

"A feeling," I responded. "There's weird shit going on in the woods now, too. The confusing thing is, she warned me not to go out there because of the witches. If she's a witch herself, she's either a good one who protects werewolves from other witches, or she's really greedy. Both explanations would make sense seeing how Norwich has such a huge werewolf population."

"If yer right, the mayor ain't the one running the town. Witches are bad news, man."

"'I'm still not one hundred percent sure." I looked back up at Roscoe. "You know something, don't you?"

He scratched his head. "I wish I could remember. Don't know why I'm so scared of 'em, but I know something happened when I was younger. It wasn't good though."

The bathroom door opened, and Austin crept into the dining room, his eyes wide as he stared at me.

"I need you to... do that thing you do."

"What?" I asked as he got closer to the table.

"I can't get in the mood, and Adam's waiting for me."

"Ain't never seen that happen before," Roscoe said. "I bet I can get it nice and hard for ya."

"That's a good way for you to die," he muttered before turning back to me. "I tried everything. *You* know what I need."

"All right. Fine." I stood and pointed to the bedroom. "Get in there and fuck your mate, soldier!"

Austin stood still, his eyes not changing color like they usually did when I gave him a command.

"Uh oh," he said.

"I don't know how to do this on the fly," I said, trying to stare directly into his yellow eyes. It seemed Mosavi's vironoct effect had worn off. "Do you feel any different?"

"No," he whispered. "Try slapping me around."

"What the fuck?" Roscoe asked. "Did I miss something really funny?"

"You could say that," I said, shakily gripping the back of Austin's neck as he got down on one knee. "This doesn't feel right."

Austin turned to Roscoe. "Can you fuck my kuu mate?"

"You don't have to ask me twice," Roscoe said eagerly as he stood from the table.

A shot of jealousy made the room turn silver.

"Sit the hell down, Roscoe," I growled and turned back to Austin, my hand now clamped tightly on the loose skin of his neck. I leaned in, baring my teeth, and his eyes began to lighten. "Get in there. I want you to fuck him so hard that he begs you to stop, and when he does, you fuck him more. Understand?"

"Yes... sir..." Austin whispered, his tone breathless as he stumbled to his feet, now uncomfortably erect. He ran to the bedroom and slammed the door behind him, and my vision returned to a normal hue as I took a deep, calming breath.

"I thought you weren't gonna do that no more," Roscoe said, sitting back down. He sounded disappointed.

"He needed it."

Adam shouted something unintelligible as their headboard slammed repeatedly against the wall.

"Goddamn," I added. "I'll sort out Austin's problem later, but this might be something I can't fix."

Roscoe started drooling.

"When I'm done with these potatoes, you want me to do that to you?"

As the sounds from Austin and Adam's room ramped up, I hastily removed my shirt, and unbuttoned my pants, which fell to the floor.

"The potatoes can wait," I said, rushing to our bedroom with Roscoe running to catch up.

Hours had passed, and it was mid-afternoon. The way Roscoe made love to me earlier was unusually rough, which I decided I didn't really like. However, I certainly wasn't going to complain since it was good exercise for him.

He lay asleep, and I rolled over him out of bed for the second time that day. I needed to check on Austin, because I remembered the command I'd given him hadn't exactly told him to stop. Would he have continued, even when he probably should have passed out? After all, the guy had been willing to punch himself in the face last night. If Austin took something a bit *too* literally, this could end up being dangerous.

I threw on my discarded clothes and rushed into their bedroom. Adam was sound asleep with a smile on his face. The sight was a relief. Even though he was probably still pissed at me, it was nice to see him happy.

Now I needed to find where Austin had wandered off to. He wasn't in the living room, and the garage was empty when I opened the door. Perhaps he was outside, staring out into the woods again. A sudden sick feeling hit my stomach as I thought the worst, and I tore off toward the back door.

Austin sat cross-legged on a lawn chair in front of a lit fire pit, his attention snapping to me as he jumped up.

"What's wrong? Did you catch the house on fire again?"

I held my chest and ambled toward another chair across the pit.

"No," I replied with a glare before sitting. "Nothing's wrong. You and Adam okay?"

He grinned and sat back down in his chair without a response.

"We really need to talk about this."

"What's there to talk about?"

"Something's wrong, Austin. I don't like you relying on this shit so much."

"I disagree."

"So I'm just supposed to keep doing this for the rest of your life?" I shook my head. "We need to find another solution. Also, if Adam finds out about this—he already resents me enough, and if you're thinking about me while fucking him..." I trailed off. "You're not still thinking that, are you?"

"I don't know what the big deal is. It's not like we're sleeping together."

"It's a huge deal. He's insecure, and he's about to go through a change that might devastate him. Do you really not understand, or do you not care?"

"I told you already. I'm not a good guy."

"Nah, you're just being a dipshit."

"How about this," Austin said, throwing a stick into the fire. "You keep doing that thing to me until Adam shifts, then I'll talk to him about what I want him to do—if he even stays with me. Deal?"

I let out a sigh and stroked my fuzzy chin. This was obviously so wrong, and we both knew it. However, Adam wasn't going to be a half-turn for much longer either. I wondered if he would even be willing to do what Austin wanted, but no one really knew how anyone would end up after the change. Adam was showing a lot of aggression, and while that was irritating, it might actually work in his favor to keep the two together.

"We do it in secret without Adam knowing. I'll give you commands, but after all this is over, no more. I don't know the long-term effects of this."

Austin smiled again. "I know you care about me, which is why it feels better when you do it. It's like a fog lifts, and I can see things clearer. I think it helps."

"I don't know enough about any of this stuff to fully trust it. It almost sounds like addiction."

"Maybe. Drugs aren't all bad, you know?"

I stared at him for a moment, gauging his expression. He did seem a little less blank, but I still didn't like any of this.

"You're a good friend, Cody."

"You are too, and that's why I'm worried," I said. "Also, don't let what Adam said back then stop you from trying to talk to him. He's older now, and he's going through enough that I think he'll listen. You should tell him everything about yourself."

"Not yet. I wanna wait and see what happens after he shifts. If we're still together, I'll tell him."

The back door opened, and Adam limped outside before catching sight of me. He turned around, about to walk back inside.

"C'mere," Austin shouted.

Adam froze. "What?"

Austin gave me a nod, and I stood before walking back to the house.

"Let's, uh… hang out," he said, prompting a very confused expression from the half-turn. "If you want."

"What's going on?" He looked at me, but I shrugged. His little tail wagged. "What did you say to him?"

"Nothing. Must have been some really good sex," I replied before walking through the back door.

*The next day*

I walked alone on the road near our neighborhood, staying clear of the town. The streets on the outskirts of Norwich were less traveled, and I ended up near the place where Roscoe taught me how to drive. The woods were on one side of the road, but there was a hilly field on the other. It was nice to have some alone time for once.

As I made my way through the tall, golden grass, I climbed to the top of the hill. I lay on my back, staring up at the cloudless blue sky. It was around sixty degrees, but the wind made it feel much colder. I closed my eyes and let the sun warm me as I relaxed. Norwich was so rural that there weren't any other noises aside from birds. The tranquility actually made me drift off, but I jolted awake as footsteps grew near.

A dark man in a black suit looked down at me.

"What a coincidence," Mosavi growled out, kneeling, his eyes glowing silver as he grinned, the sharper canines peeking from his lips. I tried to sit up, but he pressed his large hand into my chest, pinning me to the ground. "It is a beautiful day. We should stay here and enjoy it."

# The Call of the Wild

**M**osavi sat on the grass next to me, staring out into the pasture seemingly without a care about his expensive clothing. He stayed quiet for a while, his expression uncharacteristically mellow.

"Your wife said you'd leave me alone."

"No one controls me. Not even her." His phone buzzed, and when he pulled it out of his in his front pocket and looked at the name, his eyes shifted sideways. "One moment." He held the phone to the side of his head and lowered his voice. "Yes, *azizam?*"

Though I couldn't understand the word, I assumed it was a term of endearment from the way he said it. Willa was obviously on the line. I crossed my arms, giving the mayor a half-cocked smile.

"Of course," he said softly before hanging up the phone.

"You should have ended the call with the same confidence you showed a minute ago," I said, wondering how short a leash Willa actually had him on.

He bared his teeth; however, it wasn't quite as intimidating in human form. "You are walking a thin line with me."

"And what are you going to do about it? This is a free county, and I'll say what I want."

"Are you asking for me to punish you the way I did your werewolves?"

"I don't think your wife would appreciate that." I gave him a smug grin, but when he grinned back, my stomach sank.

"You definitely do not know Willa." He adjusted the gold chain around his neck.

"Is she a witch?"

He nodded. "She and I go back about a hundred years, and I would trust no one the way I trust her."

"A hundred years? How long do witches live?"

"It depends. Without the vironoct, they wither away in a few years. With a steady source, they can live for as long as they desire," Mosavi replied.

"So I'm guessing your relationship with her is more symbiotic than anything."

"Do not speak ill of her, and never belittle our bond," he shouted, the seams of his shirt popping as he held back his werewolf form.

"I'm sorry, I didn't mean that the way it came out. I actually like her, but she kinda scares the hell out of me."

Mosavi placed a hand on my shoulder. "Instinct. Sometimes it's useful. When you feel that kind of impending dread, that is when you run. Willa may be a witch, but she renounced her coven long ago—after saving my life."

"Did you meet her in Iran?"

He shook his head. "There are no witches in the old country." He turned to me. "How much do you know of our history?"

"Nothing concrete. I've been looking everywhere, but there's hardly anything about us."

"Admirable curiosity. Stories of our origin have been passed down by word of mouth for thousands of years. Would you like to hear it?"

"Yes!" I pulled back my excitement the moment his eyes narrowed. "I mean, of course."

He grunted with a nod and leaned back on his hands while staring at the sky. "Long ago, a powerful demon seduced twenty of the most beautiful women, bringing them together between the banks of the two rivers of life. The cradle of civilization."

"The Garden of Eden?"

"It is called many things, and every myth has an ounce of truth," he replied. "Human civilization had risen and fallen many times throughout the eons, and the last cataclysm happened around seven thousand years ago. Those that hadn't died off settled in the last habitable areas on earth. One such place was Mesopotamia; the other was central America. It is why many know the latter as the Garden of Eden, but it wasn't where humanity started. It was where humanity restarted."

"How do you know this?"

"The demon I mentioned earlier? In exchange for their eternal loyalty, he granted them forbidden knowledge and power—knowledge that was passed to me. They were the first coven, and they drew from one of the earth's few places of power where the line between realms was weakest. This area would grow to become Babylon, and the witches ruled in the shadow of kings. Their reign wouldn't last forever, and when Cyrus the Great conquered the empire, the witches were exposed. Those that did not escape were stoned to death or burned alive, and those that did used the ancient power one last time to cast a curse so powerful that it severed the connection between this world and hell itself. This meant that their ties to the demon were also destroyed, and without a source of power, they died off within a few years. But that was not the end.

"It is said that one out of every fifty thousand males will develop lycanthropy, and one out of every two hundred thousand females will become a witch. The curse was a last-ditch effort to ensure the witches would still be able to serve the prince of hell that granted them such blessings for eons to come. The places of power no longer exist in the earth, but"—he touched my chest with his finger—"all of that magic had to go somewhere. It cannot disappear now that the weakness between realms has been destroyed. Werewolves contain fragments of that magic, like batteries used to store electricity. Instead of sacred ley lines, the witches use us, and they know how to draw it out."

He turned toward the woods.

"When a new werewolf moves to this town, I meet with them and establish the rules. The reason towns like this do not exist is because they draw a lot of attention not only from humans in power, but from the witches in the wild and the Whasha looking to bolster their numbers. We can keep them away, but once we venture into the woods, they have the upper hand. They will lure the most potent of us to their rituals, drain us of our will, and keep us as thralls. They use our essence for their magic and longevity."

"Then how do they and the Whasha coexist in the woods?" I asked. "I met a few of them out there, and they seem to be fine."

"Do they appear fine to you?" he snapped. "The woods have always belonged to the witches, and the very trees are cursed. They call us to them, and once the wilderness has us, we start to change into something they deem more desirable. Our bodies transform and we become more bestial, losing our ability to speak. The reason the Whasha did not fall to the witches is because they learned to tap into the magic within using sacred herbs. They make their little trinkets to keep them safe, but they live as disgraceful beasts."

"They seem happy," I said, catching more of Mosavi's disapproval. "When I was out there, it felt kind of nice."

"Just because something *feels* nice does not mean that it is. Alcohol feels nice when you imbibe, but drink too much and it will destroy you."

"That's rich coming from a guy that uses his jail as a sex dungeon," I muttered, turning away. "If you and Willa can work together in harmony, why couldn't we work out some kind of way to live together with the witches and the ferals?"

Mosavi rubbed his forehead. "What you're suggesting would damn us. When I arrived in this country, I had never met a witch before, but I was lured into their clutches. All my memories from that time are gone, and I lived only to be used as a never-ending font of magic and pleasure. The pleasure was all theirs, and all I can recall from then was a blue, formless mental torment. Whether it was because she was greedy or she fell in love, Willa broke her ties to the coven and pulled me back into the conscious world. She told me what I really was and where I should go, but I also owed her my life. She would grow old and die being away from her kind, so we made a pact. I would learn the secrets of the elders, enhancing what I was, and in return, I would also give her what she needed."

He turned to me and grabbed my chin.

"There is no *living together* with witches of the wild. Most have been driven mad by their magic, and they would not hesitate to pull werewolves into their webs, making eternal meals of us."

Mosavi's shirt started to tear again, and he scrambled to his feet before mashing out a quick text on his phone. Like last time, he could only maintain human form for so long, and from the painful expression on his face, he was struggling to hold it back.

"Why do you have to keep hiding behind a human face?" I asked, standing to meet his eyes. "Are you ashamed to be a werewolf?"

"Far from it," he said. I followed him to the road as a black Mercedes drove by before pulling over. "I've explained this before, and I have my reasons." The seams of his blazer popped as muscles grew thicker. "I hadn't intended to use this time for a history lesson, but I did want to tell you that you handled your werewolves nicely. You need to learn how to tap into the vironoct's true power, and that is only something you can learn from an elder."

"I don't like your methods," I said nervously. "You really messed up Austin."

"Maladjusted werewolves have been culled throughout history or have had their wills stripped using vironoct rituals. He is lucky I decided to leave his fate to you," he said in a deeper voice. "You unlocked something the other night that you need to learn to control. If you want to be stubborn, I'll let you learn the hard way—Willa's way."

He climbed into the back of his car and shut the door. The window tint was so dark, but I saw a silhouette of Mosavi growing larger, his head morphing into that of a beast as the vehicle sped away.

The house was surprisingly cleaner than when I left, the strong scent of pine cleaner stinging my nostrils as I hung my coat next to Roscoe's orange hoodie. The television was streaming a movie, but the volume was too low to hear anything. A heavy snore drew my attention to a pair of huge furry legs dangling from the arm of the sofa.

Adam lay on top of Austin with his eyes closed and a comfortable smile in place of his usual discomfort. The scene had me scrambling for my phone so I could snap a picture. The flash went off and a shutter sound woke Adam as he gently pulled away, careful not to wake his kuu mate.

"You're a light sleeper," I whispered, motioning to the hallway. "Wanna sit outside?"

Adam nodded and tiptoed behind me until we passed my bedroom. Roscoe was also taking a nap with the windows open. Fresh air and pine replaced the musty smell that usually overpowered this part of the house. What universe had I just fallen into? Mosavi wasn't behaving like a psychopath, Austin and Adam were getting along, and Roscoe had actually cleaned something. If this was a dream, I'd be happy to never wake up again.

We stepped outside, and I gently closed the door behind me.

"It's a pretty day," I said, following the other half-turn to the fire pit and sitting across from him. "This town may be creepy sometimes, but this area sure is quiet."

"Cut the shit," Adam muttered. "Austin's eyes were blue when we were in the bedroom. They turn blue when you tell him to do something. I want to know if any of this is real, or if you're doing something fucky again."

"Were his eyes blue when he was holding you?"

"Well, no. But they are most of the time. I get this feeling everyone's doing what they're doing out of pity." He glared at me. "Or guilt."

"Didn't you guys talk?"

"Making small talk about the weather and asking me how I'm feeling isn't exactly talking," he said with a sigh. "But it's better than nothing, I guess."

"Give him some time, and he'll open up."

"Like he opened up to you?" Adam leaned in, staring wide-eyed at me. Even though we'd talked about this many times, he was never going to let it go. "You seem like you know more about him than anyone. He's obviously fallen in love with you."

"Not exactly," I said, turning away. "I don't know how many times I have to go over this. He's got a lot of issues he's trying to work through, and you know he won't talk to a shrink, so I've been trying to help him the best I can. I don't think he's in love with me, but we do have a weird thing going on."

"I knew it!" Adam shouted.

"No, you don't," I said calmly. "It's nothing like what you're thinking. That night, Mosavi did something to Austin, which I think was an indirect lesson for me. It changed everything. Austin's become dependent on—"

"Magic?" Adam interrupted, raising an eyebrow and leaning closer.

"Yeah, but that's only part of it. Once you guys talk about this, you'll understand—maybe. It's weird, but I don't want to judge."

Adam folded his arms.

"Okay, I don't judge all the time." I sighed. There was no point in making this conversation easily digestible, especially to Adam. "You know what? Fuck it. Austin likes to be told what to do. I'm not going to get into the details, but this could be something you could use."

"So you're going to teach me how to do it?" His little tail wagged behind him.

"Do what? Tell him what to do? You can do that yourself."

"You know what I'm talking about. I want to know how to make his eyes turn blue. You said he likes that, right?"

"Adam, this is a kink of his—I think. You can do this without the other stuff. He wants someone to take control."

"How the hell is a five-foot-eight half-turn supposed to 'take control' of a nine-foot monster?" Adam rolled his eyes. "Plus, nothing's going to ruin the moment faster than him being all submissive and whiny."

"Get creative. Put a collar on him and command him to be an aggressive service top—or whatever. See what happens."

He seemed to give that some serious thought, leaning forward and rubbing the side of his head. "It's been nice. He's attentive and gentle, and when you tell him what to do, he's rough and wild, but he's not sadistic like he used to be. I want him to be like that because of me, not because of you."

"That's why I told him after you turn, I'm not doing it anymore."

"The only way he'll get in the mood is if you do that magic shit to him." He examined his arms and the thin layer of black fur covering them. "Am I that unattractive now?"

"Stop. We've been through this how many times now?"

"My kuu mate doesn't want me," he muttered. "He's the only one I want right now. I talk a big game, but lately I haven't wanted to be with anyone else. I need him to want me. I feel like my body is screaming, and I *need* him."

"I wish I could tell you that he'll be receptive without my help, but I don't know what the fuck I'm doing. Let's just get you through the change first, and then you both can work on yourselves after."

"And what happens if this doesn't go away? Do you plan on shouting commands at him for the rest of his life? Do you know how fucked up that would be?"

"Maybe Mosavi or his wife will know what to do. I'll go to them tomorrow and ask."

"It really is the least you could do," Adam said, his posture stiff as he chewed on his lower lip. "Since you won't teach me."

"Adam, for fuck's sake—"

"And I guess I should thank you for using your powers for good and not evil," he interrupted, seeming a little less annoyed.

"I think he's really trying, and he does care about you. When I told him you were in pain, he panicked and ran inside."

"You really need to stop lying for him."

"This time I'm telling the truth. Just be there for him, and he'll be there for you." I stood up and pushed the chair back. "I'm going to properly reward Roscoe for cleaning. Let me know if you start feeling those urges, and I'll do my thing, okay?"

"I'm not going to get over how weird this is, but this has been Darryl-level sex. I never thought I'd say that in a million years."

"Is Darryl really that good?"

"Out of everyone I've been with, no one ever came close to Darryl—except blue-eyed Austin." He let out an annoyed sigh. "And that one time I was with Roscoe. Goddamn it, Roscoe was really good, but I'm not counting that!"

That gave me an odd sense of pride. "I might have to pay that beach wolf another visit some time," I said jokingly, but Adam's eyes lit up. "What?"

"Roscoe didn't tell you?"

"Tell me what?"

"Darryl's coming up here for a few days on Halloween."

"Why the hell am I just hearing about this now? That's in three weeks!"

"I don't know. Go yell at Roscoe about it," he responded, waving me off with the back of his hand.

I turned toward the back door, but when I opened it, I gave Adam one last glance.

"Adam?"

He didn't respond, just stared at the woods.

"Hello?"

"What?" he asked, finally looking back.

"Just thought I'd say I'm really sorry about the other day. I didn't mean what I said."

"Yes, you did, but apology accepted anyway."

"You know we need to stop doing this, right? It seems like every other day we're having to apologize to each other."

Adam smiled. "Yeah, well, we're just really different people. The fact that we're still friends at all is kind of a miracle."

     Aeron Dusk

The metal frame of the bed bent as Roscoe tried to move his arms, but the restraints didn't break. They had come from Mosavi's black bag, and Roscoe had intentionally left them lying on the floor in the closet.

He howled as I rocked my hips slowly, not giving him time to recover. This always felt so good, and Roscoe's slight gut was a little softer than the rest of him, which made this feel even better. Thinking back on when I was human, I'd have never dated a guy with Roscoe's body type. With werewolves, though, it definitely worked in their favor.

"Ready for round four?"

"Babe, I don't got nothin' left."

"We'll see," I said, leaning in to kiss him when the bedroom door slammed open.

"Adam's gone," Austin said, his tone frantic.

"What?"

"I thought he was in the backyard, but I can't find him. I can't even find his scent."

I hopped off Roscoe and grabbed the keys to let him out.

"He's probably downtown." Roscoe rubbed his wrists. "He likes that bar."

"I checked. No one's seen him."

"Maybe he went out in the woods." Roscoe scooted out of bed and grabbed his hoodie from the closet. I threw on the clothes I'd discarded earlier. "I'll go out there and check."

"He was looking at the woods earlier." I leaned in to whisper in Roscoe's ear. "You don't think—"

"They don't really mess with half-turns," he replied, grabbing a few of the enchanted stones from the dresser. "I'm sure he's fine. Probably havin' some fun with the ferals."

"He's out there all alone," Austin said, frantic, starting to tear up. "What if he's lost?"

Noting the other werewolf's distress, Roscoe patted him on the back. "He's a half-turn. He's in his element. Trust me, you ain't got nothin' to worry about."

As Austin and Roscoe hurried to the back door, the front door opened and Adam strutted inside before noticing the frantic mood.

"What's going on?" Adam asked. " Did something happen?"

"We were gonna go look for you," Austin said. "Where the hell have you been?"

"I just took a walk. Calm down." He threw his coat on the stand and made his way to the couch with a slight skip in his step. "Wait, were you actually worried?"

"Well, you left without saying anything," I said. "And Austin was looking for you in town."

"Everyone in this house leaves without saying anything," he rebutted before flipping on the television. "Come sit with me, Austin."

"Don't really wanna watch TV," he said before walking into the kitchen.

"Sit with me now! That's an order," he shouted. Austin's ears stood straight, and his tail swayed a bit.

"Yes sir," he said with a confused upward inflection before taking his place next to Adam.

"We'll uh, give you guys some privacy," Roscoe said, pulling me back into the bedroom before shutting the door. "That scared the piss outta me. Is everyone gonna start shouting orders at the guy now?"

"I honestly didn't expect him to do that," I said, turning the knob on Roscoe's old TV. "Wanna watch a movie?"

"Hell yeah! Whatcha in the mood for?"

"I don't know. You pick. I'll probably end up falling asleep anyway," I said plopping down on the old couch. "This thing smells so much better."

"Just wait until we start havin' some fun on it."

"I'm not having sex on this thing." I gave it a second thought. With how heavy Roscoe was, there was a really good chance he'd end up breaking it. "Actually, let's do it. Right now."

Roscoe's eyes narrowed as he slipped a VHS tape out of its cover.

"What? You told me to loosen up, remember?"

"Since when do you listen to me? Yer up to something." In a panic, he looked around the room. "You found the bag, didn't you?"

"Maybe," I said, hoping he'd get worked up enough to lead me to its location.

Sure enough, Roscoe darted out of the bedroom, and I crept into the hallway only to run into him around the corner.

"Nice try. I may be stupid, but I ain't *that* stupid."

Austin cracked open our bedroom door and peeked inside

"Cody, I need you," he whispered, looking back toward his bedroom. "Adam's waiting."

I carefully stood from the couch and followed the large werewolf into the bathroom.

"I thought Adam—"

"It doesn't work like it does with you," he said, slipping his fatigues off. "Just give me the order. He thinks what he did worked, and that I'm getting ready in the bathroom."

"All right. I—"

The door opened, and a disappointed Adam stood on the other side.

"I thought so," he muttered. "Hurry up." Adam looked at the floor before walking away.

"This is it, Austin. I mean it this time," I said, pulling Austin's chest mane until he was eye level. "Go make love to your kuu mate," I said, the bathroom light turning silver as Austin's eyes lightened to blue.

"Yes sir."

As he ran out of the bathroom, I turned toward the mirror. Was this really helping them? That look on Adam's face broke me a little, and I felt even more like a piece of shit. Austin was still dependent on the vironoct, and there was nothing anyone could do.

This was my canary in the coal mine. Today, he would need me for a quick fix in order to get in the mood, but like with any addiction, one day he might need more. Mosavi might have had a point, and I didn't want to find this out the hard way.

My eyes wouldn't fade back to their original color like they usually did; instead, the half-turn staring back at me had an almost malicious look to him. The room faded until my reflection was all I could see.

*You want to be him, don't you?*

Willa's words echoed in my mind as my reflection began to morph like it had when she'd handed me her enchanted mirror. I grew muscular and refined until I was barely recognizable. My body grew taller as the visage morphed into a formidable werewolf wearing a black expensive suit. The way I held myself seemed larger than life, but my eyes were empty as though the facade could shatter at any moment.

My irises finally dimmed to their normal color, and the reflection rippled until it was back to normal. This wasn't some hallucination—it was a warning. I could have everything I want but it would cost me my soul. I turned away to catch my breath before hobbling back into the room.

"Let's go to bed," I whispered, pulling at Roscoe.

"This couch is so comfortable," he said, standing and stretching before turning off the television. "Aren't you glad I found it?"

"We should really have sex on it." I crawled into bed, waiting for Roscoe to hop in next to me, but he stood still and his ears rotated toward the hallway. "What?"

"They never sound right when they're doin' it," Roscoe said before slipping next to me. "You did that thing again to him, didn't you?"

"Adam needs Austin, and Austin needs me. What can I do?"

"I just hope you know what yer doing." He wrapped me in his arms and pulled me close.

"I don't." I let out a sigh and looked back at him. "I might need Mosavi's help. There's something wrong with me."

# Chapter 24

# The Vision

I awoke much earlier than usual, the blue digital display of the VCR flashing two thirty in the morning, which meant it was two hours later since no one in the house actually knew how to set the clock. Sleep had mostly eluded me, and I lay next to Roscoe while staring at the psychedelic posters he'd crookedly tacked to the walls. The black light on the other side of the room gave everything this hippie-nightclub vibe that was starting to grow on me.

I threw off the covers and scooted toward the end of the bed, not really worried about disturbing Roscoe, since nothing short of an asteroid impact could wake him this early. The sheets and mattress had the werewolf's signature smell, but I was tired of harping on about it. Even Darryl, as clean as he was from swimming in the ocean all day, had a rather interesting funk to him when we stayed in his little beach house. Actually, it was similar in some ways to Mosavi. That kind of smell was just something that wouldn't wash off, but with Roscoe, it was always worse to my human nose.

When the smell came directly from the source, it didn't seem to bother me that much; when it rubbed off onto fabric, it was awful. Roscoe's hoodie was almost back to its original state, and I couldn't get near him when he had it on. Adam didn't seem to mind at all; in fact, I'd catch him sniffing that ragged orange thing after Roscoe put it on the coat rack. Since he was so close to turning, he probably had a much different sense of smell than I did.

Today was the half-turn's twentieth birthday, and I wondered if Austin would forget, even after all the not-so-subtle hints Adam had scattered around the house from notes to hand-drawn posters. Roscoe was actually excited because a birthday meant cake and booze. Since I knew Willa had Mosavi pretty much under control, I'd let them drink a little bit.

Who was I kidding? Neither werewolf understood the concept of 'a little bit.'

The floorboards made their usual light creaking sounds as I tiptoed through the hall and stopped at Adam and Austin's bedroom door, which was cracked open. Adam was sprawled out on the bed with Austin lying next to him. Even here, I couldn't escape the smells.

I gently closed the door and made my way into the kitchen to begin my coffee-making ritual. I was going to need to be properly caffeinated for what my day would entail.

After making sure I hadn't been followed, I grabbed a step stool and placed it in front of the stove to open a high cabinet. Powdered spirulina, dried vegetables, and jars of Marmite were like scarecrows to curious werewolves, keeping them away from what was hidden behind it. My gourmet coffee sat undisturbed in the corner, and I grabbed it, sniffing the contents while climbing down. This really was the best part of waking up.

Four large scoops of black gold landed into the filter, and I filled up the chamber with filtered water. Eventually Roscoe was going to grow suspicious of all the untouched gross shit in that cabinet, and I'd need to find another place to hide my precious. No one could be trusted.

While scrolling through my phone, I made my way into the dining room and plopped down on a chair. Willa had texted me her number, even though I'd never given her mine. It didn't surprise me anymore considering they knew everything about us anyways. I finally set the number as a contact and laid the phone off to the side while staring into the darkened living room, which was lit only by a nightlight from the hall and the incandescent glow from above the range in the kitchen. Between Austin and me—and maybe a little bit of Roscoe and Adam—we had somehow managed to turn this place into a home.

While Roscoe's taste clashed with the rest of the house, I wasn't allowed to change anything. Not that I would have. After so many decades of living on the streets, he'd finally made a place where he felt comfortable and safe. Even though the room was ours, it was his little den. A part of me loved it—mostly because I loved sitting next to him on that couch.

It was hard to imagine not wanting this to happen months ago—that I'd fall for someone who had begged me for spare change. Roscoe wasn't going away anytime soon, at least not while I was half-turn.

Then there was Adam. Austin had fallen into his role in the pack, but Adam was a wild card. With the way we clashed, he felt more like an annoying little brother than a friend, and that wasn't necessarily a bad thing. Though I'd grown to think of him as family, I couldn't shake the feeling that all this was temporary for him. He'd never really cared to make our house a home. This was all transitory. A means to an end before the change.

I dozed off right as the coffee maker beeped, startling me back awake. Before grabbing a cup, I opened the living room window, letting in the crispness of autumn as it mixed with the rich brew from the kitchen. If anything, the cold air and coffee would keep me awake.

I sat back down with a full mug and grabbed the phone as it vibrated once against the table.

*what r u doing up?*

I guess I hadn't been as quiet as I thought I was, but I also wasn't the only one not able to get a full night's sleep.

*Coffee. Want some?*

There was a five-minute lull between that last message and the door to Adam's bedroom slowly squealing open. The half-turn crept into the hall and closed the door before stumbling to the kitchen.

"Rough night?" I asked, talking over his loud rummaging through the cabinet.

Adam grunted in response. Several spoonfuls of sugar and creamer later, he slowly made his way to the dining room table, spilling some on the floor.

"You just ruined that coffee, and we're gonna get ants," I muttered as he sat across from me.

"I'll clean it later," he said, taking a sip that was likely lukewarm.

"Are you okay?"

"I guess." He took another sip before setting his mug on the table. "I just want this to be over with."

"The transformation or your birthday?" That question prompted an immediate look of annoyance. "Happy birthday, by the way."

"Thanks." He took another sip and stared into his cup. "I'm just tired of being like this. I want to be bigger and stronger, and I want to be the one to tell Austin what to do."

"You can still—"

"I want whatever you have," he snapped. "Sorry, I can't let this go. It's been driving me crazy all night."

"Why are you so hung up on this? You can't use the vironoct, and you're going to need to get over it."

Adam's sharper, white canines slipped from behind his upper lip as he put the mug up to his mouth again.

"I'm visiting Mosavi this morning, like I said I would. I haven't been able to sleep right lately." Adam still didn't respond, so I softened my tone a little more. "I just want to help."

"By stealing my kuu mate?"

"Dude, come on."

"That's what this feels like!" Adam scooted back from the table and folded his arms. "You might not have done it intentionally, but you did it." He looked down at his hands. "I was going to leave him the moment I changed, but now I'm having second thoughts."

"What do you mean?"

"Exactly what I said. He's gotten softer, and he's all I think about lately. I'm scared of being alone, and fuck... I think I've actually got feelings for him."

"You're never going to be alone, Adam. Just because you turn doesn't mean you have to leave here. I don't want you to leave."

"That's not what I mean." He tugged at the choker around his neck. "I'm afraid that if Austin rejects me, I won't be able to find anyone else. If I can't give him what he wants, he's not gonna stay with me."

"Listen, I want you guys to stay together, but not like this. You shouldn't want to be with him out of some obligation or fear. If it doesn't work, there are plenty of other werewolves and half-turns."

"You're not understanding this."

"Then explain it in simpler terms."

He slammed his hand against the table but stifled his voice. "I don't know, either. I've never felt this before." His eyes changed to a lighter color before dimming back to blood orange. "I have to stay with Austin. So I have to learn what you did, and if you and Darryl won't teach it to me, I'll learn it from someone else."

"How did you find out about Darryl?"

"I've known for a while. He hardly ever does it, but I have seen him use it to break up fights. Before we moved, I tried to get him to teach it to me so I could punish Austin, but he gave me the same excuse you did. It's *dangerous*, and I'd just fuck it up if I had it."

I stood up from the table. "You don't want whatever this is. No one should have it, not even me, and I'm not using it anymore after you turn. When you become a werewolf, you'll be big enough to give him what he wants. But that's not going to work if you both want the same thing."

"I don't," he muttered. "I hate being small." The half-turn glared at me. "And I hate being treated like some kid."

"I wouldn't treat you like one if you didn't act like one."

"Okay, so I'm not a sixty-year-old geezer trapped in a twenty-three-year-old's body, and I don't have some ancient alpha mojo. But I'm twenty now, and I expect you to treat me like that."

I looked down at the floor. "A mature adult would have cleaned up what he spilled earlier."

"It's just driving you nuts, isn't it?" Adam said with a smug grin. "I left it there to prove a point. You keep staring at that spill. The ants aren't going to infest the house after a few minutes, Cody."

"That doesn't really make the case you think it does. You never help out more around the house, and you keep asking me to teach you how to brainwash Austin. I apologized for what I said last time, but you also need to think about these things. You're so quick to act on emotion that you could end up really hurting someone, especially when you turn into a full werewolf."

Adam rolled his eyes as he stood.

"I'm not saying this to piss you off. Don't you see the issue here?" I asked, standing up to place a hand on his shoulder.

"The issue is that my kuu mate can't even touch me without you telling him to. That's a big problem." He pulled away from me. "Ever since I went with Roscoe to return that truck, Austin changed. He went from taking his anger out on me to treating me with indifference, and I don't know what's worse."

"Is he still treating you that way?"

"Only because you told him not to."

"The only thing I tell him to do is what you do in the bedroom. How he treats you outside of that is him trying to fix what *he* broke."

His expression softened again. "You're not lying to me about this, are you?"

"Why the hell would I risk making things worse by lying?"

"Because none of my friends ever do anything nice for me without stabbing me in the back." He took a deep breath and looked out the open living room window as dawn broke through the orange maples. "Every time I've ever had friends, they never actually cared. They just used me because I told them I had money. When I started to go half-turn, and I left home, I realized how it all really worked. All those people I thought I was tight with didn't give a shit."

"And you think I'm like that?"

"Why not? I met you in a café and you didn't seem to like me. I have one of the hottest werewolves for a kuu mate, and he treats you like a prince. Even Darryl wouldn't shut up about you when I went back to visit him. That night at the bar? Everyone kept coming up to you, and you didn't even want their attention. I had to keep working the place, and I still didn't have any fun." He looked back at me. "So yeah, forgive me if I'm a little suspicious of your motives."

"How many times do I have to tell you this. That night at the bar, all I wanted was to spend time with you," I said as he looked away again. "I wanted us to talk and get closer, but I guess now I know why you kept avoiding me. You're trying too hard for all the wrong reasons, and that's what's driving people away. Darryl and I had common ground with Roscoe, so we became friends. And the only reason I didn't like you when I first met you is because you were a jerk."

"I'm just tired of being used and thrown away," Adam said. "I try so hard to get attention because Austin sure as hell isn't doing that much these days—aside from lately." His glare softened. "I guess I should be thanking you, but I keep wanting to rip your head off."

I held out my arms, and Adam smiled before leaning in for a hug.

"Well, I know exactly how much money you have, so that's obviously not the reason I'm friends with you," I said with a laugh.

Adam pulled away and smiled.

"And Austin's really trying. We just have to get through this rough patch. To be honest, I can't wait to see what you're gonna look like as a werewolf."

"Think I'll be hot?"

"I'm sure you don't have to worry about that," I said as Adam turned and walked into the kitchen. "What are you doing?"

"Cleaning up my mess." He turned back around and cringed. "I just saw an ant."

"Damn it! I told you!"

The walk downtown gave me time to dread what was coming. Being around Mosavi always made me uncomfortable.

Willa's barbeque restaurant stood empty; most of the werewolves in town were likely still asleep or working. I had never really taken the time to learn what they all did here. Obviously, they weren't all police officers and firefighters, though every law enforcement officer and rescue worker was a werewolf, which kind of made sense. They didn't seem the type to work office jobs, but there were a lot of farms on the opposite side of town, away from the forested areas. If there was one thing everyone wanted a werewolf for, it was manual labor.

Perhaps when I turned, that would be the only thing anyone would ever hire me for. What a dreadful thought. Then again, if I took the path Mosavi had laid out for me, I could live a life of prestige. How had he gotten it all? Was it even his, or did his symbiosis with a witch have something to do with it?

As I passed the building, a strange gust of wind hit me from the front. When I took a few more steps, a dainty hand fell onto my shoulder, causing me to jump and let out the most embarrassing yelp.

"Jesus Christ," I whispered, holding my chest before turning toward a smiling woman. "Where the hell did you come from?"

"You're so adorable," Willa said, taking me by the hand. She wore a maroon gown rather than black this time. "Did you come by to see me?"

"Your husband, actually."

"Ooooo."

"Not for *that* reason."

"No one ever visits my husband for much of anything else," she said. "He's very good at what he does."

"Shouldn't he be running the town instead of a sex dungeon?"

"Powerful people multitask, Cody," she said, dragging me closer to the restaurant. "Come. Stay with me for a while."

"I really need to talk to Mosavi."

"About Austin?"

I nodded.

Willa led me into the restaurant, which was a lot brighter than last time. Red curtains had replaced the black fabric that had previously covered the windows, and were drawn to let light stream inside. "Unfortunately, Darius is going to be tied up for most of the day."

My shoulders slumped forward. "If he's going to be in meetings all the time, why bother offering to give me advice?"

"Oh, you misunderstand. He had to be punished for seeking you out yesterday after I told him not to."

I tossed her a narrowed glance.

"Don't look at me like that. He loves it when I demoralize him."

"Did I wander into some kind of vortex of depravity when I moved here?"

"Once you get to know him better, you'll see beyond that alpha male veneer, and you may even find some common ground with him."

"I doubt that," I said as we slid into the same booth as last time. "What do you know about Austin?"

"What you are doing to him is something he needs," Willa said in a gentle, less teasing tone. Sometimes she could sound almost... motherly if she wanted. "Some werewolves rely on it to work through past trauma. I don't know what your friend has been through, but when I saw him in person after you moved here, I felt something dreadful around him. It has since dulled."

"I can't do this for the rest of his life. This isn't going to fix him permanently."

"You won't need to. Think of this as a form of therapy that only works on werewolves. When you give him commands and use that magic within you, it rips away the scar and allows him to heal the way he should have from the start."

"So, this is normal?"

"Is it normal for a half-turn to possess such an ability? No. But this is a normal technique all leaders can do for their pack. You may not understand how you're doing it, but sometimes you don't need to." She took a sip of hot tea with a slice of ginger floating on top. "This is going to sound really corny, but as long as you're doing this out of a place of compassion and not control, he will get better, and one day he won't need it anymore."

"So, I'm not screwing him up?"

"Hardly," she replied, shaking her head. "I think I may have been wrong in our meeting last time."

"What do you mean?"

She frowned. "You're nothing like my Darius."

"Sorry to disappoint." I waited for her to respond, but she sat silently before giving into a soft smile. "What?"

"You came seeking his guidance, but he just may turn to you one day."

"And pigs will start to grow wings."

Her eyes seemed to shimmer as she gazed into mine.

"Your husband's motives are clear, but yours aren't. Why are *you* so interested in me?"

"Why do you think?"

"You're a witch."

She flashed her brows before taking another sip of her tea.

"I don't know if I should trust you."

"You shouldn't," she said without hesitation. "You shouldn't trust any witch. I didn't save Darius all those years ago out of love. I wanted a constant source of power at my fingertips, and with him, I would never go hungry again."

"At least you're honest. If I shouldn't trust you, why am I here?"

"Do you often place your trust in people you barely know?" she asked.

"Well, no."

"I say this because I know the hearts of witches in the woods. Since you arrived, they know what you possess. They feel it—they smell it. You being here even awakens something in me that has lain dormant for over a century."

The uneasy feeling returned, and the softness of her face went rigid.

"Why are you protecting the town from them? Are you doing this out of kindness or because you want more power?" I asked, half knowing the answer.

She let out a sigh, waving to one of the male kitchen staff who peeked through the door. He gave her a nod and scurried to the back.

"Neither. I fell in love," she admitted.

"I thought you said—"

"Things change," she interrupted. "When witches join a coven, we give up all emotions that would anger our prince. Compassion, empathy, kindness—even love was forbidden, and we were forced to lock it all away with the vilest magic that was nearly impossible to reverse. Darius knew my intentions. He wasn't a fool. At first, I thought the beast simply craved what his instincts desired, and being a witch,

I wanted his essence." She reached into her cleavage for the intricate, folded mirror, then handed it to me.

"I don't want to look at this again," I said, handing it back to her, but she held up her hands.

"Words can deceive, and memories fail." The waiter placed two cocktails in clear glasses on the table before hurrying away. "But visions don't use gentle words or white lies. They tell painful truths. If you really want to know if you can trust me, that mirror can do more than what mere words can."

I narrowed my eyes before taking a sip of what tasted like sangria. "How do I know the visions are true?"

She shrugged. "I'll let you come to that conclusion. In order to know for sure, you should experience what I did on the first night Darius and I were together, and the events that happened years after."

I held up the mirror. "This can do that?"

"Honey, I'm a witch. If you think this is amazing, you should see what I have in my cellar." She looked at the clock and back at me. "Which reminds me. I haven't fed Darius yet. Why don't you take that home, and we'll meet again tomorrow?"

After slipping the mirror into my pocket, I slid out of the booth. Willa held up my drink.

"For the walk home," she said, standing to meet my gaze. "I meant what I said about Austin. You're doing what instinct leads you to do. It's what any pack leader would do, and I've been around enough werewolves to understand this. Have more trust in yourself, and trust in others will come naturally."

The smell of fried chicken lured me into the house as I took one final sip of the drink I'd been nursing. I thought I'd only been gone for an hour, but when I looked at my phone, I saw it was nearly noon. I was losing time again, often when I was hyper focused.

"Ooo, yer in for some good shit," Roscoe called from the kitchen. "The colonel's got nothin' on these herbs and spices."

As I walked in, Roscoe lowered another batch of chicken into the dutch oven with a huge container of peanut oil on the counter next to him. On the other side stood a beautiful chocolate cake with whipped buttercream icing and a couple candles in the shape of a twenty.

     

"You already made his cake?"

"Sure did. I sent those two out for some errands, and Adam didn't put up much of a fight. Austin wasn't too keen on it, though."

"Well, that's Austin for you." A large, familiar fruit caught the corner of my eye. "How the hell did you manage to get a watermelon? It's almost October!"

"Dude, they sell all kinds of out-of-season stuff at the farmer's market. It's all grown here, too." Roscoe leaned against the counter as the chicken sizzled. "They say all the produce is magically delicious. I didn't ask questions, and I wanted a couple watermelons."

I looked back at the far counter again. "Where's the other one?"

Roscoe cleared his throat and patted his stomach. "Well, I wanted to test to see if it was as good as they said."

"I didn't really know what to get Adam, so I just put five hundred dollars into a card."

"Jeez, Cody. That's a lot of money. You sure about that?"

"It's his money. I've been telling him that I'm holding onto it for rent, but I've really been putting most of it away in a safe for him later so he won't spend it."

Roscoe rubbed my head. "Yer just so stinkin' good. Ya know?"

"Tell that to Adam. He still thinks I'm trying to backstab him and take Austin away."

"Those two are so confusing. One day they hate each other and the next they're fine."

I walked over to the refrigerator and opened the door, noting the two-gallon jugs full of purple liquid. "Apparently, we don't know as much as we did. Is this Kool-aid?"

"Yeah. I ain't had this shit since I was a kid... I think."

"Roscoe, I don't think Adam's going to like having kiddie drinks at his birthday party."

"Well, that's why it's half vodka."

"Roscoe!"

"What? You said we were allowed to drink."

"A little bit!" I opened the trash can lid, and sure enough there were two empty bottles of cheap vodka. "How did you even buy this? They aren't allowed to sell to werewolves."

"Adam got 'em yesterday."

"That fake ID has sure been getting a lot of use."

Roscoe removed the chicken and drained it in a wire basket over a paper towel, his stomach growling.

"Try to control yourself. We do want Adam to have some food left for his own party."

"I ain't gonna eat nothin' yet."

"I don't trust anyone who eats an entire watermelon in one sitting." It was then that something dawned on me, and all the blood from my face drained. "Oh my God."

"What's wrong?"

"Roscoe… what the fuck, man?" I ran to the fridge, grabbing both jugs of grape Kool-aid before placing them next to the watermelon. "Are you intentionally trying to piss him off? I've gotta pour this shit out."

"What? No! That's all the booze! And what the hell are you talkin' about? When I was in Arkansas—"

"Do not finish that sentence, for the love of God. We need to get this shit out of here. The fried chicken is one thing—"

The front door slammed open, and Austin walked inside with a growl as Adam followed, berating him.

"It's *my* birthday, and I don't want to spend it in the goddamn hardware store!"

"Well, I didn't wanna go to some stupid bar."

Adam froze before sniffing the air. "Is that fried chicken?" His little tail began to wag. "And it's southern style!" He ran into the kitchen with the biggest grin on his face.

I gave Roscoe an uneasy stare before looking back at Adam, trying to use my body to block the cluelessly racist items on the far counter.

"Look at the cake!" Adam glared at Austin. "See? Roscoe gets it."

Austin walked behind the counter and picked up the watermelon. "Yup. He sure does. Where the hell did you get a watermelon in October?"

"Oh shit, is that grape Kool-aid?" Again, Adam's little tail wagged as he picked up a jug.

"Uh—yeah," Roscoe said, now fully understanding what he'd done. "It's got half a bottle of vodka in it."

"I don't know how that's gonna taste, but I'm down for getting shit-faced."

Roscoe and I looked at one another again, this time a little more relieved, but that was short-lived as Adam took it all in and grew quieter.

"Oh! I've got your gift," I said as his once gleeful expression turned to a wide-eyed anger. "This was all Roscoe's fault! He's a redneck. A very stupid one."

"I didn't think nothin' of it. I just thought about what I'd like to eat on my birthday. And back in Arkansas—"

"See?" I interrupted. "He's stupid. Very, very stupid."

Adam let out a sigh and smiled. "Well, I mean... it's the thought that counts, I guess. But this is the most racist shit I've ever seen in my life."

"Well, just wait until you try my chicken." Roscoe held up a drumstick in front of Adam's face, but the half-turn glared at him. "You know you want to."

Adam snatched the chicken away and took a huge bite. "You're a fucking stupid hick."

Roscoe grinned and leaned in, flashing his brows. "Well?"

The half-turn closed his eyes and let out the longest sigh. "It's good. It's the best fucking thing I've ever eaten in my life."

"Happy birthday, ya little scamp."

"Happy birthday, Adam," I said, handing him the card.

The half-turn held the envelope up his nose. "I smell cash!" He kissed me on the cheek. "If this card has a watermelon on it, I'm going to punch you through the wall."

"It does not." I looked around for Austin, but he had slipped unnoticed out of the kitchen during the commotion. "Where's Austin?"

"Probably hiding in his garage," Adam said with more resentment. "He never remembers my birthday, and he never gets me anything."

"Do you ever get him anything?" I asked.

Adam didn't respond.

"You know, someone's got to make the effort here. Do you even know when Austin's birthday is?"

"Uh... April, I think? Maybe it's May."

"It's August first," the large werewolf said as he walked back into the kitchen holding a sloppily wrapped box before placing it on the counter. He leaned into Adam and grabbed both of his arms. "I'm not the easiest person to live with, and I'm sorry."

Adam looked away for a moment, almost as if embarrassed. "I guess... I'm not that easy to live with either."

The werewolf locked lips with Adam for a few seconds before pulling away and walking out toward the dining room. He looked back for a moment and disappeared into the garage.

After examining the box, Adam started to unwrap it. "This is the first gift he's ever given me." He opened it and let out a childlike laugh before pulling out a stuffed white bear wearing armor. "How the hell did he get this?"

"What is that?"

"It's Pawlibear! He's my favorite champion in—it's one of my games."

"I hope he don't stay in there all day. We got grape Kool-Aid booze out here."

The door to the garage slammed open and Austin peeked out, his ears perking all the way up. "Booze?"

"Only a little bit!" I shouted, blocking the way to the jugs as all three ganged up on me.

Roscoe snatched one of them and began pouring the liquid into plastic cups.

"I mean it!"

"Oh, lighten up, Cody," Adam said. "It's my birthday. Mosavi's not going to know anything as long as no one's stupid enough to walk around drunk downtown." He shot a narrow stare at the both werewolves.

As they guzzled what was essentially vodka and sugar, a knock sounded at the door. I hadn't expected anyone else since I kind of wanted to keep Adam's party on the downlow. When I opened the door, my stomach dropped.

"I was instructed to bring a gift," Mosavi growled out. He was in human form wearing his usual suit, but above his shirt was a thick, spiked collar strapped uncomfortably tight. He brushed me aside before stepping into the house. The three in the kitchen scrambled to spit out the alcohol and hide the evidence.

He cocked one of his bushy brows before setting a small gift on the table, eyeing everyone with that piercing, accusatory gaze he often wore. It was so quiet that we could hear Roscoe's stomach growling.

"Uh... hey yer majesty," Roscoe said seriously with an awkward head bow. "Want some chicken?"

"I do not," he replied, keeping unusually calm.

"I was drinking, sir! I admit it," Austin said, eagerly stepping forward, his tail wagging. "I should be punished for it. Severely."

"What the fuck? Shut the hell up," Adam whispered, just barely audible.

Mosavi bared his teeth before taking another calming breath, adjusting the thick collar around his neck.

"I have only come to—" He was obviously struggling to hold his form as his words began to sound shaky and angry. "Give a gift and say..." Mosavi paused, exhaling through his teeth again. "Happy birthday." He growled that last part as if someone was nudging him.

"Ooh! What did ya get me? I bet it's expensive," Adam said, dashing over to the table.

Mosavi caught his hand and gave it a hard squeeze. "How about a thank you," he said slowly through his sharp teeth again, still obviously trying to keep himself from shifting. "You little—" He groaned and tugged at the collar. "Adam."

"Uh, thank you," the half-turn said nervously as Mosavi let him go.

The mayor started back to the front door.

"You're not going to stay?" I asked, regretting that question when Adam elbowed me in the ribs.

"No. I need to get back." And with that, he stepped outside, but not before saying, "I would strongly advise pouring out the evidence before the police get here."

Once he disappeared, I snatched both jugs away from Austin and scrambled to dump them down the sink.

*Trust in yourself...*

Willa's words repeated as I lay in bed, trying to take a late-afternoon nap to catch up on sleep I hadn't been getting much of lately. Austin was in his garage, and Adam spent the remainder of his birthday outside tending to the yard. Our conversation earlier had made a deeper impact than usual, and he was actually doing something other than watching TV or playing on his phone. Maybe Austin's gift had softened him a little more. I didn't even know he liked plants.

Roscoe was in the kitchen, already starting on dinner. He was making his baked ziti, and that was something we were all looking forward to. The sauce was homemade and took seven hours to cook for some reason. One thing Roscoe loved more than food was cooking for other people. He would always anticipate our faces when we took our bites. The way his tail would wag with every satisfied moan always put me in a better mood. His passion for cooking even surpassed his terrible hygiene. When he was in the kitchen, he actually cleaned himself up.

The mirror Willa handed to me felt warm in my palm as I held it against my chest. She said not to trust her, but her words contradicted her actions. Perhaps that was the point. Showing rather than telling. Still, I'd take whatever vision I saw in this mirror with a grain of salt, especially knowing the type of control she had over Mosavi. I'd actually felt kind of sorry for him earlier as he struggled under that collar like a beaten dog. Of course, after the police paid us a visit, the sympathy went away.

I cracked open the mirror and peered into its clean reflection. Aside from a brief flash of light, nothing more happened. I stared into it longer before finally snapping it shut and laying it on the nightstand. Perhaps I'd try again after I woke up.

*When I opened my eyes, a large brown werewolf lay next to me on a strange bed. He stared at me with silver eyes, using a giant clawed finger to gently brush away the strands of black hair in my face. My body didn't obey nor did my mouth.*

*"Beast," I said in Willa's voice, as if compelled. It sounded so cold and devoid of emotion. "Are you that insatiable?"*

*"Yes," Mosavi said in a low whisper. "I could take you again and again. Fill you with my seed until you beg me to stop, but you would still be empty."*

*I rolled over, looking up at the log ceiling. We were in a small cabin, the hearth glowing bright orange on the other side of the room.*

*"Again with this. You would fill me with power, per our agreement."*

*His rough hand cupped one of my breasts, and he rolled closer, his thin lips caressing my neck.*

*"Your soul is worth more than a bit of power. What if I could help you get it back?"*

*"What does one need with a soul?" I asked, sitting up. "Such a useless concept."*

*"Perhaps not in the literal sense." He moved close enough that I could feel his breath. "Do you really feel nothing?"*

 *Aeron Dusk*

"I feel the warmth of the fire and a pain in my loins. I want to feel that pain again, beast."

"Darius. You have not told me your name."

I pushed him down and climbed on top, guiding his half-hard cock to the aching space that desired to be filled.

"I have no name, and your name means nothing to me."

The vision faded, and this time we were in a different place. The cabin was slightly larger, and I lay naked in the bed as Mosavi stepped into the room. He wore a white dress shirt and black slacks. He was human, though he looked much younger.

"Why do you take that ridiculous form? The other elders are supposed to teach you potency and strength. Humans have neither of those things."

"It is a new skill, and one that may prove useful. I thought this would please you."

I grew hot with annoyance. "You thought wrong. I only hunger for the wolf, not—whatever this is."

"This is who I was, Willa."

"I told you not to call me that," I said, pointing sharp nails at his body. His new clothes tore away from him, leaving his dark, handsome figure naked in the middle of the room. "At least that is still the same size."

"You will not tell me your name, so Willa is your name now," he growled impatiently before climbing into bed. "And I will not be your beast tonight. My name is Darius."

"Does your cock still work?" I asked. "Or has it been crippled by this new form?"

"Do you really feel nothing at all for me?"

"I only feel hunger."

The room faded again and morphed into a larger house. Mosavi stepped into the bedroom in his human form before removing his shirt, his thick chest hair giving him a wilder look.

"I am on the council," he said, but his voice lacked any enthusiasm. "I made the proposal for the enchantments to keep werewolves from being drawn into the woods. The others agreed."

"Why do you care?" I asked. "Witches need that power. Why do you disrupt the natural order?"

"Why did you?" he rebutted.

"I told you already."

"And you lied." He removed his pants and shoes before his body began to transform back into huge werewolf. "You do not know why you lied, but you did."

"This again. Why can you just not be content with lust?"

"This is our sanctuary," Mosavi shouted, his voice shaky as he grabbed my arms. "You broke your coven, Willa. He no longer has any hold over you."

"You tread dangerously."

"I do not care. I know you will not enslave me, or you would have done it when you helped me escape." His eyes glowed silver again. "I always sense the real you with the vironoct. His influence has been slipping year-by-year, and yet you still fight to keep it."

Despite the lack of emotion, I could feel tears trickle down my face. I dabbed one with the tip of my finger.

"Weakness," I said, wiping another tear away. "I hate this."

His smile grew warmer as he gently took my face in his hands.

"You are mistaken. This is your strength."

The room went dark and brightened until I was lying in a canopy bed surrounded by high ceilings and lavish décor, but I wasn't naked. Darius walked into the room in his suit, but as a werewolf.

"Are you not hungry for the wolf, Willa?" he asked, loosening his tie before rubbing the long, thick bulge running down the inseam of his pants.

"Perhaps later," I said as he climbed into bed, still fully clothed. This time, he smelled like he usually did. Spicy cologne mixed with tobacco.

"You do not seem well lately."

"I feel like a fool," I whispered.

"Why?"

"Why do you care so much for me?"

Darius gently caressed my cheek, his eyes glowing silver again. "This is what I am. I have taken you for my mate, and I cannot stop what I feel."

The room faded until all I could see was Mosavi on the ground in the middle of the woods, blood pouring from a hole in his chest. I knelt next to him, tears reluctantly streaming from my eyes despite still feeling empty.

"They know about you," he gasped out, his words slurred as he lost more blood. "You need to leave this place."

"Beast," I said, covering the fist-sized hole with my hand. "We had an agreement."

"One that I must regretfully break," he whispered. "Rescue another, and maybe you will grow to love him. I am sorry."

I shuddered, running my fingers along the fatal wound. It didn't seem to be made by any weapon I knew of, and his rapid healing had not kicked in.

"Stupid beast," I whispered as heat traveled from my chest, down my arms and into his body.

"What are you doing?"

"Something foolish. Something selfish," I whispered, keeping my hand over the pulsing wound as more of myself flowed into him. It felt as though my life drained, and it became harder to breathe. "Darius."

His eyes widened.

As the rest of my essence faded, something flowed back into the void in my chest, coming up from my arm. An overwhelming sensation had me sobbing as I fell against the werewolf.

"Willa," he whispered. "You can have me. Even my soul."

His voice echoed in my mind as everything faded to white.

A large hand shook me awake, and I snapped my eyes open to see Roscoe standing over me with a concerned look.

"Dinner's ready," he said calmly, leaning in for a kiss. "Wanna eat now, or have some fun?"

"Can you lay with me for a little while?"

"You okay?" he asked, slipping in beside me under the covers.

"I just had a bad dream, and I could use the company."

# Chapter 25

# Beer and Brats

It was like I'd blinked and a few weeks had passed. Darryl would be arriving soon, so I wanted the house looking good, but keeping it clean was an uphill battle with Roscoe and Adam simply existing in the same space.

"Damn it, Adam," I muttered while sweeping, lifting the cushions to find more crumbs while dishes clanked in the kitchen. "No cooking!"

"I'm hungry," Roscoe said, peeking into the dining area.

"You just ate breakfast." I lowered the dustpan and swept the rest of the mess away. "It hasn't even been an hour."

"It's second breakfast," he said with a grin.

"This isn't the fucking Shire. Darryl is going to be here this afternoon, and I don't want this place to look like slobs live here."

"You know what you need?" He held up his new frying pan. "Some French toast."

"The grocery bill is getting out of control again," I said, brushing by him to dump the contents of the dustpan into the garbage. "We're up to five hundred dollars a week now, and that's on the cheap."

"Werewolves gotta eat good." He pulled out the eggs and milk. "We'd make more money if you'd just let me pee on you in front of the camera again."

"I hate you," I whispered, placing the broom in the closet. "I saw some farms outside of town. You should look into employment that doesn't involve torturing me."

"You—you want *me* to be a farmer?" he asked, his ears lowering. "That's hard work."

"See what the other werewolves are doing for work. You can't just stay in the house eating all the time."

Roscoe patted his stomach. "I sure can," he said, skillfully cracking six eggs into a bowl one-handed and whisking with the other.

"What about a restaurant?"

"I'm a walking health code violation, Cody. I can't be in a commercial kitchen."

"Then shower more."

"That's not what I mean. I got too much fur. It gets in everything."

"Wear a full-body hairnet."

Not fully appreciating the joke, his eyes narrowed.

"We live in a town with a bunch of hungry werewolves. You think they care? I bet you can start your own business if you talk to the mayor."

"That guy hates everyone," Roscoe said, dropping a pad of butter into the pan. "My ass still has phantom pains."

"You're such a baby. You're like double my size, and I manage." I hopped up on the countertop, letting my legs dangle over the side. "If there's one thing I know about Mosavi, it's that he respects hard-working and motivated werewolves who actually contribute. If you want to get on his good side, show some initiative and ask him what it would take to start a business here. And if all else fails, I could pull some strings with Willa."

"I dunno," he said, flipping the bread. "Do we really want to get on the guy's good side? I still get a bad feeling when I'm around him. Plus, he did get the police on us during Adam's party."

Austin walked into the kitchen to refill his coffee mug without saying anything.

"See, Austin's a grouch, but at least he's all subby and soft."

The larger werewolf quietly took a sip of his coffee before punching Roscoe hard in the gut. As the smaller werewolf coughed and sputtered, Austin looked back at me.

"Lawn's done. Need anything done here?"

"Nah, I think we're good. Thanks for doing that."

"Mhmm," he grunted before taking another sip of coffee and walking out of the kitchen.

I looked over at Roscoe who was still holding his stomach. "What a great guy."

"Damn, is he gettin' stronger? Jeez."

"Back to the topic at hand. Do you want to stay on Mosavi's bad side? Because I sure as hell don't. We've already got targets on our backs after the shit you and Austin pulled that night, and we can't exactly leave this town to live somewhere else. Hell, it was hard enough finding this place, and it was only because Mosavi intervened."

Roscoe looked back at me and slipped a piece of French toast on a little plate, squirting some syrup on it before scooting it toward me.

"Plus," I sighed and picked up the plate and fork, setting it in my lap, "I don't think he's a bad person, and I think I really like Willa."

"I ain't lettin' my guard down." The werewolf placed more battered bread into the pan.

"You just got the wind knocked out of you by a *subby and soft* werewolf. I didn't even know you had a guard to put up."

"You know what I mean. We don't know what his motives really are, and anyone who hates ferals ain't someone I want to get to know better."

"He told me that the woods and the ferals are cursed. That's why they look so different. He's protecting us from that and the witches."

Roscoe didn't seem all that concerned as he fried the other side of the bread.

"Considering how freaked out you are about curses, I kind of expected you to care about cursed woods."

"They didn't seem cursed to me." Roscoe flipped the French toast and caught it in his mouth. "They seemed happy."

"They couldn't even talk. That's not normal."

"How do you know?" he asked with his mouth full. "How do you know that any of *this* is normal, and that's not the way we're supposed to live?"

"Because we were human," I answered, taking a last bite before setting the empty plate next to me. "We were born human, Roscoe."

He flipped another piece of toast into his mouth.

"Can you use a plate, please?"

"Better like this," he said, barely chewing before swallowing. "Plus, that's more dishes for you to do."

"Me?" I jumped off the counter. "I'm not cleaning this up!"

"I cooked the food, and you ate it. Now you gotta work it off."

The room turned silver, but I remembered something that calmed me back down.

"I found something in the shed the other day."

Roscoe's eyes shifted to the hallway, and he braced himself to run.

"Don't bother," I said, pushing him back. "I already moved it to a place you'll never find. I'd imagine Darryl would have a field day using all that stuff on you when he gets here."

"All right, I'll clean," he responded with a slight whine. "I knew I shoulda just thrown all that magic shit away."

"That was the laziest hiding place. It was literally sitting on the top shelf. What, did you think I wouldn't be able to see it?"

"I didn't think you'd actually go in there," he answered.

"Use the Fabuloso." I pulled the spray bottle and a washcloth from under the kitchen sink and set them next to the stove. "I want this place to smell like Sunday at Abuela's," I added, before walking out.

Adam had been on a warpath for nearly twenty minutes, screaming at Roscoe and Austin for eating his chips. After they allegedly proved their innocence, he turned his sights onto me.

"All right, asshole. Where are my white cheddar popcorn chips?"

"You've lost your chip privileges," I said, glancing out the window for the third time in the last twenty minutes.

"You knew the whole time I was yelling at them, and you didn't say anything! You have ten seconds to tell me where they are or so help me."

I ignored him as a white van pulled over to the side of the road. The sliding door opened and a huge, brown werewolf hopped out while holding a duffel bag in one hand and a guitar case in the other.

"He's here," I said excitedly as I dashed to the front door. Just seeing Darryl again was a relief. Even though I'd only stayed with him for a month, he was the most level-headed and responsible person I'd encountered, especially among the werewolves. It was going to be nice to have someone else to rein in Roscoe and Adam for a little while.

Adam leaned forward against the window sill, his little tail wagging in anticipation. It didn't take a genius to know what he was thinking. Austin had been doing his best lately, but the half-turn was a lot more demanding. So much for only wanting to be with his kuu mate.

I opened the door as Darryl waved to the driver and the van pulled off.

"You're late," I shouted, running up to the huge werewolf and grabbing his bag. "Finally decided to visit, huh?"

"Damn. Nice place," he said, giving me a one-armed hug. "Could use an ocean view, though."

"This has got to drive you nuts." I led him up onto the porch, and we both stepped into the house. "All forests and hills as far as the eye can see."

"It's a good change of scenery." The werewolf eyed an anxious Adam near the hallway. "You gonna give me some time to unpack?"

"No," Adam replied impatiently, before darting into the bedroom.

"How's he been?"

"He's been Adam. We're all waiting with bated breath for him to finally change."

"It's gonna happen pretty soon, and his attitude will get better. All half-turns get moody before they turn." He flashed me a smile as he sat his guitar on the floor next to the bag. "It's something you get to look forward to, eventually."

"Can't wait," I muttered.

Drilling noises rumbled the walls from Austin's garage, and we both turned toward the door.

"I take it Austin's been Austin?" He wrinkled his nose and turned away.

"He's been doing better, actually. He and Adam have been working through some things."

"Darryl," Adam shouted from the bedroom.

"It's been a long drive," the werewolf said, slipping off his shorts. Seeing him wear anything more than a life buoy strapped to his back was kind of weird, but it was common courtesy for werewolves to put something on while taking a taxi. "Where's Roscoe?"

"The grocery store, hopefully figuring out how employment works."

"Does he need straightening out?" Darryl's eyes flashed from orange to silver.

"I've been keeping him on a short leash. When you're done with Adam, you mind if we talk a bit?"

"I know that look," he said. "If this is important—"

"Darryl, my ass is literally in the air right now," Adam shouted from the bedroom.

"That can't wait much longer." I chuckled and pushed the werewolf toward the hall. "We've got a fire pit outside, and it'd be good to have some music later." I looked at his guitar.

"Maybe you and Roscoe can sing along."

"I'll leave that to Roscoe."

It was late evening, and the sun was already behind the trees as I stacked firewood neatly into the pit. I'd been collecting and chopping it all week, so we'd be able to have a fire every night while Darryl was visiting. Roscoe was in the kitchen, and Adam and Darryl were still going at it so loudly that even being outside did little to dampen the noise.

Austin hadn't come out of his garage, and I'd need to check on him a little later. Knowing how much bad blood was between him and Darryl, I wasn't going to force him to be social.

After pouring half a tin of lighter fluid on the logs and tinder, I lit a match and threw it in. I kept the flames stoked with the dried Spanish moss I'd gathered from the oaks on the outskirts of the forest.

The back door opened, and Roscoe trotted outside while holding a bottle of beer.

"Let's have a barbeque!"

"Where the hell did you get beer, Roscoe?" I sprinted toward him to snatch it away, but he kept it out of reach.

"Relax. It's only one beer. I'm gonna cook with it." He put it to his lips and gulped half of it down. "Don't need the whole bottle, and I wouldn't want it to go to waste."

"You're so full of shit," I said, sitting back down on the lawn chair and using a poker on the burning logs. "I'm the one that's going to get in trouble."

"The mayor ain't gonna do nothin' to you while Darryl's here. Two alphas cancel each other out."

"Mosavi's an elder, Roscoe."

"So? I'd like to see that fancy ol' sourpuss scrap with someone like Darryl."

"I don't think that'll go as well as you think, especially since his wife's a witch."

"Ooo, I forgot about her," he muttered, setting the beer on one of the plastic tables before plopping down next to me. "If I just use it fer flavoring, I don't think he'll have a problem with it."

The door opened again, and this time, Austin stepped outside, looking at both of us before turning away.

"Get yer ass out here," Roscoe called out jokingly.

Austin let out a huff of air and slowly backed outside again. He turned and sniffed.

"How did you find that beer?"

"That beer?" I asked, eyeing him suspiciously.

His ears flattened and he looked away.

"I mean, beer, you know? It's illegal and stuff."

"Mmhmm." I grabbed the bottle and dumped it on the ground.

"Hey!"

"Cooking with it, my ass." I tossed the bottle into the metal trash can next to the shed.

Austin sat across from Roscoe on the other side of the pit.

"This is gonna be a long week," he growled out. "Why did you invite Darryl of all people?"

"Ask yer kuu mate," Roscoe replied. "Darryl's a good friend, and I didn't mind."

"Why don't you two get along?" I asked.

"Don't wanna talk about it."

"Maybe you should, especially if it has to do with Adam." I sat next to Roscoe again, turning toward their bedroom window as the moans grew louder. "Have they always done this?"

"The sex shit doesn't bother me," he said. "It's the guy's better-than-you attitude. Every time they're together, Adam won't shut up comparing me to him. Plus, I know there's more going on. I'm not stupid, I just ignore it."

"The kid's not too bright when it comes to, you know, anyone else but himself," Roscoe said.

"That's the problem. He's twenty years old and still acts like a kid, and he doesn't listen. It's not gonna work out when this is over, and I don't think he's worth hanging on to."

"You don't know how he's going to end up after—"

"We're not right for each other," Austin said louder, holding up his hand. "I'm too fucked up, and he's too selfish."

"He told me he wants to stay with you after this is over."

"He's only saying that because he's afraid he'll be alone. I'm just his sure thing." The moans from the bedroom died, and Austin wrinkled his nose. "Okay, the sex bothers me a little, but I can't exactly tell him to stop, especially since I can't even get it up without being told to." He pulled at the mane on his head. "Why am I so pathetic? Even Roscoe's geriatric dick still works."

"I'll... take that as a compliment," Roscoe grunted, patting the other werewolf on the back. "Don't be too upset. At least it does work."

"I was talking with"—I paused, carefully choosing my words—"*someone* who understands more than I do about your condition, and the good news is, it's temporary. The bad news is, I have to keep doing what I'm doing until you get better."

"I visited the mayor," Austin said, catching both of us off guard. "I couldn't help myself."

"When the heck did you do that?" Roscoe asked.

"A couple days ago, and again yesterday," he admitted, his ears drooping. "He's a monster, and he uses all kinds of weird shit on me, but he knows what I like. I hate myself after it's over, but it feels good when he's doing it. The physical pain makes me forget all the other pain, and I'll beg him to beat the shit outta me, choke me, or dry fuck me."

Roscoe and I eyed one another.

"You both think I'm nuts, don't you?"

"Does it help?" I asked.

"I want to say yes, but I never feel like it's okay. It's like my brain knows this is wrong, but at the same time, I won't think twice about going back."

"I, uh, kinda get what yer sayin'," Roscoe said. "He's got a weird way about him. It's an elder thing."

"It's just another reason to keep Adam away," Austin said. "He's never going to understand. I'm huge, and that's the whole reason he chose me. He wants me to be—"

The back door opened again, and Darryl stepped outside naked, of course. The timing couldn't have been worse. Austin grimaced and stood before walking toward the house.

"Austin," I called out, but the werewolf didn't turn around.

He brushed past the brown werewolf, shoving him lightly with his shoulder before disappearing. Even though they were roughly the same in size and similar in physical appearance, they couldn't have held themselves more differently. Darryl had a natural and comfortable confidence while Austin was rigid, like he was a ceramic vase that would shatter if someone accidentally knocked him over.

"Looks like I'm not helping," Darryl said, walking toward the fire. "I was under the impression Austin couldn't handle this alone."

"He can't," I said. "But maybe next time you and Adam should go somewhere more private."

"I'd rather not do this at all." He sat on the chair next to me, crossing one leg over his knee. "I'm starving," he added.

"Ooo!" Roscoe shot up out of the chair. "I got yer favorite brats, and I was gonna baste 'em with beer but..." He shot me a glare.

Darryl looked around. "Where's the cooler?"

"Werewolves aren't allowed to drink in Norwich," I said. "It's the law."

"What kind of authoritarian bullshit is this?" Darryl uncrossed his legs and stood up. "You can't have a cookout without beer."

"You'd have to take it up with Saddam Hussein in city hall," Roscoe muttered as he made his way to the back door. "He's a werewolf, by the way."

"You serious? How the hell did he manage that?"

I threw another log onto the fire. "He can turn human, so I think only the werewolves here know."

"Interesting. Only elders can do that."

"Consider yerself lucky you haven't met him yet," Roscoe muttered before walking into the house.

"Now I really wanna meet this guy if he's got Roscoe riled up." He looked around, eyeing the edge of the woods. "It's pretty out here—a little too quiet and creepy for my taste, though." Darryl settled a hand on my leg. "What did you want to talk to me about earlier? Need a swimming lesson?"

I laughed. "Tempting, but the water level might be a little low after Adam." He smiled at me, his sharp teeth glistening in the flickering flames of the pit. He hadn't trimmed the thicker fur on his face into the usual soul patch; instead, he let it grow out a bit more into a full furry beard. He still had that old-wolf surfer look about him. "I know you can do the whole vironoct thing. Are you an elder, too?" I asked.

"Christ, I'm not that old." His brows furrowed in frustration. "I'm way younger than Roscoe, you know."

"You smell like the mayor. Plus..." I turned toward him, trying to channel the emotions whenever I'd give Austin a command. My vision brightened as the firelight turned a bluish silver. "I can do it, too."

"I know," he said. "And you'd better keep that a secret, or they'll be after you like they were me."

"The mayor is the only one who knows, and I think he may be hiding as well."

"What makes you say that?"

"His wife's a witch, and she showed me some visions from their past. From what I could see, I think they tried to kill him because of it."

"Aw fuck. I know exactly who you're talking about." Darryl rubbed the sides of his head in frustration. "So Darius is the fucking mayor."

"You know him?"

"Not personally. He tried to get me to join his little revolution, but I didn't want any part of it. I know oppression when I see it, and his was just another version of the bullshit that already exists. I don't like politics. I don't like living in the shadows while pretending to be human. And I really don't like witches, even if she claims to be a good one."

"They keep the town safe from the witches in the woods. At least, that's what they claim."

"So, you met her?"

"Yeah," I said. "She's actually kinda cool."

He looked around and took a deep breath through his nose. "When I arrived, I got a bad feeling. Maybe as soon as Adam turns, you guys should come back to White Dunes. I'll build an addition to my house."

"Austin's not going to agree to that."

"Then leave him here. He can be just as miserable by himself as he is with everyone else."

"It's not that simple," I said, catching myself. "Never mind."

"There's nothing you can say that would excuse the way he treated Adam."

"There are a lot of really awful things he's working through."

"Self-inflicted, most likely," Darryl added. "He made the choice to join the military after I warned him not to."

"Remember when we were eating that marlin you and Roscoe caught?"

"What about it?"

"You said you knew Austin when he was a half-turn. How much did you know about him back then?"

"Not as much as I probably should have. Just knew he was the kinkiest half-turn I'd ever met. You wouldn't know it by looking at him now what he was into. There were times I thought things were going too far when they weren't going far enough. I drew the line in the sand when he started asking me to tie him up and make him bleed. I'll happily do that shit to Roscoe, but not half-turns."

"Can you keep a secret?"

Darryl's ears perked up. "Do you even have to ask?"

He had a point.

"When Austin was a child, his father killed his grandmother, mother, and brother in front of him, shot him in the back of the head, and then killed himself."

"Jesus fucking christ," Darryl shouted.

"Shh," I whispered. "He told me that in confidence, and I wouldn't have said anything if I didn't think you might be able to help him, too. The shit he said he went through—then the whole military thing."

"Does Adam know?"

"No, and I don't think he'll ever say anything to him. After Adam turns, Austin's going to let him go."

"That's probably for the best," Darryl said, with more sympathy in his tone. "Adam doesn't seem like the kind of guy who's good with this kind of stuff."

"I think everyone's writing Adam off a little too early. Who knows how he'll end up after this is over, or what type of person he'll be in a couple of years. We'd know if Austin would just open up more to him, but the issues go deeper than that. Adam might not be able to take up the role Austin wants filled."

"So he's still like that, huh?" Darryl asked. "Even now? The guy's as big as I am."

"And that's the problem. He's trying to be someone he's not, which is one of the reasons why he treated Adam the way he did. I'm not excusing this, but this kuu bullshit is making everyone desperate. Poor Adam's caught in the middle, and he doesn't really know what the hell is going on."

Roscoe walked back outside, holding a huge tray of raw sausages in one hand and a long sausage fork in the other. Adam followed, rubbing his hands together.

"Sausage overload tonight," the half-turn said, eyeing Darryl and me.

Austin was likely in his garage, so I made my way to the back door. "I'll be right back," I said.

"Could you grab my guitar while you're in there?" Darryl asked.

"You bet."

Austin sat on one of his workbench chairs, staring blankly at his collection of tools lining the wall.

"I don't want you in here alone," I said. "Come outside with me."

"I don't want to look at either of them." He turned to face me, his eyes glassy. "I bet Adam hasn't even noticed I'm not out there."

I grabbed his huge hand with both of mine, giving him a tug until he stood up. Instead of following, he pulled me back and wrapped his arms around me.

"Austin?" I asked, looking up at his face. His eyes watered even more, and he squeezed me tighter.

"In a perfect world, you'd be my kuu mate." He pulled away and wiped his eyes. "Roscoe's more Adam's type, and you're mine."

"You're only saying that because I'm the only one you've actually talked to."

"You're the only one I trust who's still alive. I wouldn't have to go to Mosavi if you'd... It wouldn't feel wrong with you."

"Why are you telling me this right now? Is it because of Darryl?"

"Adam's in love with him, and I want you."

My heart sank, and my stomach knotted. It wasn't like I hadn't suspected this, but I also hadn't thought he would actually say it.

"Roscoe and I—"

"Are just kuu mates," he interrupted. "You're the only one that makes me feel better."

"Because you've isolated yourself, Austin. You knew Darryl for years before you met Adam, and you never once told him anything. You don't open up to Adam, either. You need to socialize, and you can start by having fun tonight."

"So you don't feel the same way about me?"

"You're one of my closest friends, and I love you, but not like that."

Austin pressed his ears against his head and looked away.

"C'mon, don't be upset." I reached for his snout and turned him back to me. "We don't have to be lovers to be family. There's no telling what's going to happen in a few months, let alone a couple of years from now. Mosavi's wife told me that what I'm doing to you is werewolf therapy or something. Let's take this one day at a time." I took him by the hand and led him toward the door.

"I'm not gonna like this," he muttered. "It's too awkward out there with him."

I stopped and looked back into the garage at the extra refrigerator.

"I'm going to regret this. Go grab a case of beer."

"Uh, what beer?" Austin asked, his tail tucked between his legs.

"I'm not blind, you dumbass. I know you made more because Roscoe's a complete idiot," I said, punching his arm. "Where else would he have gotten that bottle from earlier?"

"What about Mosavi?"

"His wife is the ace up my sleeve—at least I hope so. Plus, Darryl's here."

He backed away and turned toward the fridge. "All right. I'll be out with my newest batch."

Despite what happened earlier, the weirdness faded between Austin and me. Alcohol helped, and Darryl took advantage of the relaxed atmosphere, pulling out his guitar.

"This is one of Roscoe's favorites," Darryl said, strumming a horrifyingly familiar tune.

Roscoe snapped over to me with a huge smile, raising his brows. I immediately had a Pavlovian reaction as horrifying memories of that day flashed with piss-colored clarity.

"Nope," I shouted, throwing up a time-out signal with my arms. Darryl stopped playing, and Roscoe pouted, now a half a foot away from me. "Any other song, but that one."

# Chapter 26

# Halloween — Part One

"Thanks for walking me," Austin said, his eyes baby blue and somehow ever more devoid of emotion. The collar he wore was one of those thicker, studded ones often seen on Dobermans; the leash I led him with was hot pink.

"Where do you need to go next?" I asked, ignoring the weird stares from passersby.

"I'm good. Let's go home. Gotta get to work."

"What are you working on now?"

"A house. Wanna put something nice in the backyard."

"You—you want a doghouse?"

"Sure do. I bet you could teach me all kinds of tricks."

"Austin, you're not a dog."

He stopped and got on both knees, laying his head against my stomach as he looked up at me with those sad eyes.

"Come on, man. Everyone's looking at us."

"I wanna be your loyal, obedient dog, Cody."

"Oh God!" I jerked awake and sat up in bed next to Roscoe. The dreams I'd been having lately kept getting more bizarre and awkward. While the vironoct may have been good for Austin's mental health, it was driving me to the brink.

I rubbed my eyes and pushed away the blanket before scooting toward the end of the bed. While keeping as quiet as I could, I tiptoed out into the hallway. Deep snoring vibrated the walls in surround sound as I made my way through the house, Austin in bed with Adam and Darryl on the couch.

I'd offered to sleep in the living room and let him and Roscoe sort things out in our bed, but he insisted he didn't want to put me out. The guy barely fit, his legs hanging off the arm of the sofa and his arm dragging on the floor, half of his body teetering over the edge.

I knelt next to him and lightly shook him awake.

"Darryl, go sleep in my bed," I whispered. "You're gonna break the couch."

The huge werewolf sat up, the sofa complaining under his weight as he rubbed the gunk from the corners of his eyes.

"What are you doing up?"

"Trust me, I don't wanna be."

"Want a swimming lesson?" he whispered in a slurred voice, his eyes half open. Even when tired, it was all werewolves thought about.

"Darryl." I shoved him and sat back against the cushions. "Happy Halloween, by the way."

"Can't believe the luck. It's a full moon, too."

"What did you bring for the costume party?"

Darryl stood up and stretched. "Oh, you're gonna love this."

He unzipped his large duffel bag and fished around before pulling out a smooth, gray sheet of fabric. After he firmly shook away the creases, he slipped it over his head and pulled it about halfway down.

"What do you think?" he asked.

It was the cutest shark costume I'd ever seen. The head was like a hoodie with spaced rows of little plastic pointed teeth and large eyes with big, black pupils. Darryl poked his head out from the mouth; the rest of the costume covered him like a snug-fitting armless jacket. It even had a long shark tail with enough space for the werewolf to tuck his own tail into.

"I honestly was not expecting it to be this adorable."

"Right? A surfer buddy's wife made it custom for me. What are you gonna wear?"

"I don't know. Roscoe said he wanted to go with a theme, so I'm leaving it up to him."

"You sure you wanna do that?" Darryl slipped out of his shark costume, folding it neatly before stuffing it back into his bag.

"Well, I was sure at first, but you just made me concerned.'"

"Roscoe's *themes* are always... interesting. He really likes to get into character, too."

"Of course I should know this by now."

"It actually turned into a fun tradition. Roscoe would dress up as something elaborate, get piss drunk and get into character. I remember one time, the host of the party bent over to grab something out of the cooler and he shouted 'this is Sparta' before kicking him head-first into the pool." Darryl rubbed his chin. "He did that about three times before people got fed up with his shit and booted him out."

"Oh God," I muttered under my breath. "At least he won't be drunk."

"Sounds boring, though." He folded his arms. "Maybe I should have a little one-on-one with Darius."

"I'm trying to keep the peace, so I don't think that's a good idea."

"I'm surprised he hasn't tried to keep you locked away," Darryl said, sitting back on the couch. "That's what he tried to do to me. Indoctrinate me into his cult of stuffy creeps."

"Well, he probably wanted to do that to me, too, but his wife keeps him in check."

"We're pretty rare, Cody. All werewolves have small amounts of the vironoct, but only a few can tap into it like we can. A huge sign is usually when a half-turn shifts later in life, or that's what I'm told. It's why I kinda knew about you."

"I remember you telling me you were a late bloomer."

Darryl nodded. "Yeah, but when Darius found me, I had to lie low. I can't prove it, but I think he's the reason the organization never found me. I remember he was angry with me when I turned him down, but he also left me alone. That was about the time I met Roscoe. Say what you will about the guy, but he knows things that he has no business knowing."

"I think I know what you mean."

"I don't know whether the guy plays dumb, or if he really can't remember certain things, but he has this innate sense I can't figure out. Like, he's really wise, but he's also an idiot." He eyed me and smirked. "Confused yet?"

"Not really." I stood and headed into the hallway. "I'll be right back."

I tiptoed into the room and opened our top drawer before pulling out a leather sack one of the feral werewolves had traded us that night we were in the woods. I crept back out and gently shut the door behind me, then also shut Adam and Austin's door for good measure.

"Here," I said, tossing the bag onto Darryl's lap. "He knew what this was, and a lot of other stuff. I think Roscoe used to be feral, and Mosavi seems sure of it."

He opened the bag and pulled out a pinch of herb. "What the hell is this?"

"Some kind of psychedelic the ferals use. Roscoe and I got high off it that night, but while we were using it, we could understand what they were saying."

"Cody," he said, dropping the herb into the bag. "You can't go out into the woods like that, dude."

"I know that now."

"Roscoe should have known better, but he probably just wanted to get high." He eyed the bag. "So, uh… what's it like?"

"Incredible," I said, sitting down, scooting up next to Darryl in anticipation. "Roscoe and I use it sometimes when we're fucking, and oh my God, it enhances everything."

Darryl glanced toward the hallway.

"Can it help you get to sleep?"

"If I smoke it, yeah, but the high lasts longer. It sucks to use in the house, so Roscoe and I usually smoke it next to the fire. The last time we did it in the house, that ugly couch in our bedroom started chasing me." I grinned mischievously. "Wanna get high?"

Darryl scrambled to his feet. "I'll race ya outside."

The morning birds echoed through the woods as dawn painted the sky an orangey-blue. Darryl and I lay next to each other on the grass, having spent most of the night tripping. We had also done a little more than talk, but I didn't really feel weird about it. It was less like a gross one-night stand and more like spending a really nice evening with a good friend who really knew how to fuck.

"That was incredible," Darryl mumbled in a nasal tone, still not able to move much. "These butterflies won't leave me alone."

I turned toward him. "Are you still high?"

"I may have taken a little too much." He sneezed. "Ugh, I feel like my head is full of snot."

"Yeah, that happens to Roscoe, too."

He sneezed again, and the back door opened. I slowly turned to watch as a smirking Roscoe stepped outside.

"I knew I heard something last night," he said, walking over to us and picking up the sack of herbs.

"Goddamn Roscoe, your head is huge," Darryl said, still lying flat on his back. "You look like a Funko pop. Dude, are those nipples?"

"Still high, huh?"

Darryl sneezed again and groaned, closing his eyes.

"What'chu guys want fer breakfast?" Roscoe asked, giving me an unusual look as I sat up and rubbed my eyes. "Got lots of eggs. One of the guys at the end of the street raises chickens." His stomach gurgled. "Man, I'd love to raise some chickens."

"You'd raise chickens?" I asked.

"Nah, I'd end up eatin' 'em before they'd lay any eggs," Roscoe said with a laugh. "But I am thinkin' about it."

"The answer's no. I'd be the one taking care of them."

"But think of all the eggs!"

I stumbled to my feet and reached for Darryl's hand, but he brushed me away.

"I'm gonna lay here for a little while longer. I feel nauseous."

"Are you going to be okay?" I let out a stifled laugh as Darryl swatted at something invisible before closing his eyes again.

"If this shit ever wears off."

"I'll get ya some hair of the dog," Roscoe said as he stepped into the house.

I ran in behind him and closed the back door. "We don't have any gin."

"Don't need any for my recipe."

I followed him into the kitchen, and he reached into the cabinet for a lowball glass before gathering a bunch of different ingredients in bottles.

"Is that the ghost pepper sauce you tricked Adam into eating?"

Roscoe didn't say anything as he squeezed a fresh lemon into the glass before dumping in a tablespoon of the hot sauce.

"What's wrong?" I asked.

"Huh?" His smile seemed forced. "Nothin's wrong." He reached into the fridge for a couple of eggs before cracking them into the glass.

"God, Roscoe, that looks really gross."

"Yeah, but it'll work," he said, scooping some horseradish sauce into the cup with finely grated ginger.

"You're going to kill him."

"Nah, he'll love it." Roscoe cracked open a can of vegetable juice and poured it in before stirring vigorously. "Now for the hair of the dog." Roscoe pulled some loose fur from his armpit and sprinkled it on top.

"Are you fucking serious?"

"It works, I swear!" He trotted out of the kitchen and made his way down the hall, his tail wagging.

I eyed him suspiciously as he disappeared but shrugged it off and reached into the fridge for sparkling water.

"What the fuck?" Darryl shouted before gagging loudly. Coughing and choking were all I could hear for a few seconds before the spigot connected to the water hose outside the kitchen window squealed. The backdoor opened and Roscoe trotted proudly back inside holding an empty glass.

"It worked," he said, pulling out ingredients for breakfast.

"He drank all of it?"

"Sure did. Drank it all in one gulp." He didn't look at me as he pulled down a mixing bowl. "Gonna make us one big-ass omelet."

More coughing fits from outside pulled my attention before ending in a finale of retching.

"Jesus Christ," I said, running to the door. "That sounds bad."

Before I could grab the knob, the door flew open, and Darryl stormed inside.

"Where is that bastard!"

Rapid footsteps shook the house as the front door opened and slammed shut.

Adam burst from his bedroom and ran into the hallway, looking both ways in a panic. "What's going on?"

"Why did you drink that shit?" I asked.

"I didn't," he said. "He poured it into my mouth while I was lying on my back." His eyes went wide as he grabbed my shoulders. "I'm sorry, Cody. He had a good run, but I'm gonna have to put him down."

Roscoe peeked in through the living room window, and Darryl snarled, about to run outside before I pulled him back.

"I give you full permission to kill him after he makes breakfast."

"Don't know why yer so upset. Look at how spry you are," Roscoe said after shoveling in a forkful of eggs. "My remedy works every time."

Darryl said nothing, rather glared at Roscoe while he chewed on a piece of leftover sausage.

"You stopped hallucinatin' right?"

The larger werewolf held another sausage to his mouth before meticulously biting off the end of it. It didn't take a genius to figure out the symbolism.

"Oh yeah," I said, remembering something from earlier. "What's the theme of our costume?"

"Oh yer gonna love it. It's a surprise."

"Every time you string those two sentences together, I know it's going to be stupid," I muttered. "I'm not going to the party looking like a mix of dirty shit you pulled out of the trash."

"It's Halloween. We're all gonna look like idiots," he said, his tail wagging through the gap in the oversized dining room chair. "Plus, I didn't get anything from the trash. It'll be great, I swear."

"He did a good job on ours," Adam said. "I didn't know you played video games."

"I don't. Got my inspiration from some porn I saw online, and that little stuffed animal Austin gave ya."

"All right," I said, standing from the table. "I want to know what you've done."

"Nope. It's a surprise."

"Then I'm not going."

"Oh, yer going. I'll drag you kickin' and screamin' if I have to. The costumes don't work unless both of us wear them."

"Roscoe, I swear—"

"I'm gonna make you have fun," Roscoe said, eyeing Darryl again. "Y—you excited, bud?"

"Oh, I'm not your bud," Darryl said lowly, cracking his knuckles. "You should hurry and finish your breakfast."

"My polar bear costume looks dumb," Austin muttered.

"It's cute. Ain't it, Adam?"

"It's perfect. His personality matches the character's, too," Adam said.

Austin pouted over his plate. "I don't play stupid video games."

"He shoots lightning from his claws." Adam patted Austin on the back. "He's the coolest champion!"

"What the hell kind of porn are you watching that has polar bears?"
I asked. "How are you even finding all this stuff? You barely know how
to use a smartphone."

"I needed some inspiration, so I borrowed yer laptop."

"That's not mine, you idiot! Mosavi let me borrow it until I can
afford one. If there's monitoring software on that thing, and I have to
explain to him why there's polar bear porn—"

"Uh..." Roscoe interrupted, his ears low. "There ain't no monitoring
software on it."

"How the hell would you know that?"

"Cause... there ain't nothin' on it no more. I got sidetracked and was
jerkin' to something hot, then I got some kinda weird warning telling
me I had to pay six hundred dollars. Then it just stopped workin'."

Both Darryl and I glared at Roscoe.

"Aw, c'mon guys. It's Halloween. Best day of the year! Turn those
frowns the other way."

I turned to Darryl. "Destroy him."

The werewolf cracked his knuckles again.

Later that evening, Adam emerged from his bedroom wearing a shiny
leather thong, a wide-brimmed hat, and boots wide enough to fit his
larger feet. Draped across his chest was a bandolier of fake bullets
with a realistic-looking AK-47 strapped to his back.

"What the hell are you even supposed to be? Carl Weathers on a
pride float?"

"Isn't it obvious? I'm Jason from *Leagues and Losers*. I just had
Roscoe make it more my style."

Austin moped, dragging himself into the living room wearing an
actual polar bear suit with gold-painted armor.

"This is humiliating," he said. "I look stupid."

"No way," Adam said, wrapping his arms around Austin while
shoving his face into the bear costume. "I've always had a thing for
Pawlibear."

I tried my best to hold back laughter, but a snort escaped and
Austin snapped toward me.

"It looks great!" I said.

"Nope. Not doing it." Austin unzipped the costume.

   

"Cody, you idiot," Adam said, trying to stop Austin from practically tearing off the suit. "Come on, please. I wanna ride you into battle."

"No," he grumbled, and Adam turned to me.

"This is your fault," he whispered. "Fix it. Do that thing."

"I just find the name kinda funny, Austin," I called out. "The costume looks fine!"

Austin disappeared into the room, and Adam folded his arms.

"Damn it," I muttered, following the lumbering bear-wolf. "Austin."

He turned around, and the hue of the room turned a silvery-blue.

"You're going to the costume party dressed as..." I took in a deep breath through my nose, trying to keep a straight face. "Pawlibear. Understand?"

Austin's eyes turned light blue, and he nodded. "All right."

"God, that's handy," Adam said excitedly. "Can I tell him what to do now, or does it just have to be you?"

"Don't even think about it, Adam. I mean it."

He frowned. "Fine."

"Cody, yer costume's ready," Roscoe shouted from the bedroom.

"And here we go," I said under my breath as I walked toward the hallway. Roscoe snorted like a bull, scuffing his foot against the floor, pretending he was about to charge. The *costume* was him completely nude, with thick leather and gold bands around his wrists and ankles. There were also a pair of horns tied to his head, and a large gold septum ring hanging from his snout.

"You are going to wear something to cover up, aren't you?"

"There ain't no clothes in the labyrinth." Roscoe tossed a leather belt with a sword and hilt onto the bed with a few other thin leather straps. There were also two gold-colored shin and arm guards.

"Who am I supposed to be?"

"You ain't never read about Theseus and the Minotaur?"

I sorted through the *costume*, trying to figure out what went where. "Where's the rest of it?"

"Yer lookin' at it."

"Where's the leather gladiator kilt thing?"

"Budget ran a little over due to the bear, so I had to improvise." His smirk returned. "It's completely in character."

"That bear costume had to have cost at least a couple hundred dollars, Roscoe! I'm supposed to just go out in my underwear?"

"Nah," Roscoe said, pulling my shorts down around my ankles. "Let me put it on ya."

After running a strap from my shoulder down to my abdomen, he attached it to the thinner strap around my waist. He then fastened the thicker belt with the sword hilt and began snapping on the arm and shin guards. He coiled some thin gold-painted rope and tied it in place to the other side of the belt with a buttoned hoop, then took a few steps back and ogled me.

"This is a joke, right?" I said, looking down at my junk swinging freely between my legs, the belt partially covering my groin.

"Oh yeah," Roscoe said, biting his lower lip. "I wanna be slayed by you, babe."

"Careful what you wish for," I said through my teeth while reaching into the drawer for a pair of boxer shorts.

"Yer gonna ruin the theme." Roscoe stopped my hands, but I pulled away and slipped into the shorts. "Theseus fucks that minotaur, ya know."

"Yeah, I don't remember that being a part of the myth," I said, sifting through my top drawer. "Find me something decent, or I'm just going to wear normal clothes."

"Adam," Roscoe shouted. A few moments later, our bedroom door opened and the half-turn walked in.

"Hey! Theseus and the Minotaur," Adam said. "Lose the boxers, Cody. They're clashing with the theme."

"See? Adam gets it."

"I loathe you both right now," I said, still shuffling through the drawers for anything that would come close to matching. With no luck, I thought back to something I'd seen in one of the compartments of Mosavi's bag of magic sex.

The autumn air clashed brutally against my bare skin, and I didn't have nearly the amount of half-turn fur Adam did to buffer it. What a strange feeling. I should have been more embarrassed, but this look really flattered me. Roscoe may have been a complete idiot, but costume wasn't his worst idea.

Even though it looked a little too modern, the studded leather thong pulled from the case was the perfect addition. Part of me was a little worried there were magical tricks to this thing, but after scrutinizing it for nearly a half an hour, I'd taken a gamble that it was just a normal piece of kinky clothing.

"Kinda impressed," Roscoe said, pulling at Darryl's shark tail. "This is really well made."

"If there's one good thing I learned from you, it's how to pick a good costume." The shark tail wagged. "Plus, it suits me. Always wanted to be a shark."

A hand slapped my ass, and the taut thong amplified the sound.

"Ow, jeez!"

"Where the hell did you get this? I want to borrow it when you're done," Adam said. "Goddamn, I'm kinda jealous now." He looked up at Austin happily lumbering along in his bear suit, his eyes still that empty blue. "It may not be as sexy as Roscoe's costume, but I still love it." He hugged Austin again. "He's so soft."

"That should have partially worn off by now," I said, eyeing the werewolf with concern. "You okay, buddy?"

"I'm great," he said with a creepy smile and an odd, cheerful tone. "I'm a... pawlibear. Rawr."

"Hmm." I examined him and scratched my head. "Keep a close eye on him tonight, just in case."

"Of course," Adam said, hooking his arm through Austin's.

I didn't like how careless Adam was being, but this was helping—or at least I had to trust the word of a witch that it was. Austin would have never relaxed enough to have fun tonight anyway, so it couldn't hurt, right? Then again, he'd never been out in public while under the effects of the vironoct.

We entered the center lobby of town hall, which ceased to look like any kind of plain government building. The décor was lavishly over-the-top. Fog machines and multicolored lights illuminated a path of cobwebs and realistic-looking dead trees with red eyes that leered at us from the darkness. The main area was just ahead, but to get in there, we had to pass through a narrow entryway. There were two figures standing on the other side, just visible to make out.

"Oh yeah. I remember that smell," Darryl said, sniffing the air. "Dude loves his cigars."

We approached, and I smiled nervously at Willa, who was dressed in a flowing red gown with a lace cape and hood draped over her head. I had to do a double take when I saw what was in the wicker basket she carried. Fun-sized dildos and buttplugs, a cat-o'-nine-tails, and travel-sized bottles of flavored lube.

"I didn't know it was that kind of party." I glanced at Mosavi, who eerily wore the same collar and leash I dreamt about earlier. He also wore a black cloak and held a scythe. This was quite the odd take on Little Red Riding Hood.

"I had to make a little detour with the wolf on the way to grandmother's house," Willa said, holding up the basket before looking me over. "I am genuinely impressed." She ran her fingers over the thong. "Careful with that. It could make a beast out of you."

"What?" My eyes widened. "Is it dangerous? Should I take it off?"

"Maybe later, when the party really starts." She licked her lips, but her expression turned to concern when she looked up at Darryl. "Oh, you're new."

"You must be the witch," he said, extending his hand, but Mosavi snarled, slapping it away.

"I thought I smelled weed and failure," Mosavi said threateningly.

"Relax dear," she said, grabbing Darryl's hand. "You are absolutely adorable."

"I'm just here to spend Halloween with my friends," Darryl said, further examining them. "I'm only staying a few days, so don't get any ideas."

"You should make your stay shorter," Mosavi growled out, now visibly shaken. The only other time I'd seen him like that had been in the vision of Willa's mirror.

"That's not a very gentlemanly way to welcome a guest. I thought you were all about not being a beast," Darryl said, patting the mayor on the shoulder. His touch had an immediate effect of causing Mosavi's hackles to stick straight out. We all filed in behind Darryl, but Willa caught my hand.

"I hoped we could talk a bit in a more relaxed atmosphere." She watched on as Darryl made his way to the bar.

"I thought drinking was illegal."

"All rules are suspended on Halloween," Mosavi said calmly, his disturbed demeanor returning to normal. "Humans know the risks, but if they join us, that's their choice. We've never had too much of an incident at these events."

"You guys really like Halloween." I looked around the room, and if I hadn't known we'd stepped into a building, I'd have sworn we were still



Aeron Dusk

outside. Humans, werewolves, and a few half-turns danced together in the middle of the room, their bodies gyrating and rubbing against one another.

"It's a night of magic," Willa said, weaving her fingers through the air, leaving behind a winding trail of glittering blue light. "The town-wide Halloween party in Norwich is a fairly new tradition that came along with the new leadership."

I turned to Mosavi. "I really didn't expect to see you here as a werewolf. Aren't you afraid of being found out?"

"No human will recognize me." He seemed a lot warmer than usual. "This is one of the few nights I get to be myself in public."

"How is Austin?" Willa asked.

"He's doing okay. I think." We turned toward the dance floor, and the bear suit stuck out in the most hilarious way. Adam guided Austin's arms around him as they danced to the steady rhythm of the Halloween-themed house music pounding through the speakers. "I hope you're right."

"Of course I'm right," she said, tracing her icy fingers along my bare back. "You're always so tense. I'm beginning to think Austin's not the only one in need of therapy."

"My dungeon is always open," Mosavi said with a grunt.

"I'll pass on *that* kind of therapy, thanks."

"I'm gentler with half-turns." He reached into the basket and pulled out a darker, small bottle of what I thought was lube. "If you change your mind, bring this along. You'll need it." He pressed the bottle into my hand.

"What is it?"

"I have a hard time believing you're gay sometimes," Willa said, slipping her arm around my waist before leading me to the middle of the room. "You're like an innocent little boy. Little Red Riding Whore is going to corrupt the shit out of you."

# Chapter 27

# Halloween — Part Two

I watched from the corner as Willa pressed against Mosavi, her arms wrapped in red lace as she held his hands to her plump, pale breasts. This was the first time I'd seen her dance, and everything about her body language screamed confidence. She flowed like water over the floor.

"She's showing real emotion," Darryl said, sliding into the seat next to me. "Didn't expect that."

"Mosavi changed her."

"How do you know?"

"I uh... saw it in a dream," I said, trying to speak over the volume of the music.

He tilted his head and narrowed his eyes.

"Don't look at me like that. I know it was one of her visions. She wanted me to see their history."

"I wouldn't trust it."

The music shifted to something with a tango beat, and the two came alive, commanding the dance floor. Her lithe body twirled and contorted to the seductive music, all while leaving a trail of lace and mist. Mosavi was just as graceful, but more masculine and rigid as he handled her, leading her around the black-lit tiles.

He was so refined, but grabbed her with bestial passion, both of them matching every movement as though they had rehearsed this dance all their lives.

"If she's controlling him, this could be really bad."

"She's not." I walked back my confidence as I'd found myself asking that same question not long ago. "Just talk to her for a little while, and you'll see. She's not like that witch I saw in that vision. If you've met one, then you know what I'm talking about."

Darryl stared pensively at the woman, stroking the thicker fur on his chin. "She's the first witch I've ever met."

"Then how do you know how they are?"

"I read a lot, Cody." He patted my back and looked around the room. "Where the hell did Roscoe go?"

"He heard something about tacos and that was the last I saw of him."

"I swear he never stops eating."

"I worry about him." I turned toward Darryl, breaking brief but uncomfortable eye contact with the mayor. "It's almost like he can't control himself."

"He's always had a couple screws loose. He didn't eat this much when he was using. Have you tried talking to him about it?"

"I've tried, but he shuts me down in the typical Roscoe way. Plus, if he can't remember his past, therapy's kind of pointless."

Darryl let out a slight hum. "I think he still remembers on a subconscious level. No one just forgets the entire first half of their lives unless something really bad happened. I mean, Austin was shot, and he hasn't forgotten." Darryl shook his head. "I wish he could forget that, though."

We both turned our attention to a bewildered-looking armored bear with Adam clinging to his back like a child. His eyes were still blue, but they were slowly fading back to normal.

"He looks really cute in that. It's funny. You're both the biggest werewolves here and you both have the cutest costumes."

"There's only so many things a werewolf can dress up as. A great white shark man and a—" Darryl glanced at Austin again. "Whatever-the-hell that is."

"I think Adam called it a Pawlibear."

The half-turn that was once clinging to the back of the costume slid down to the floor. He rubbed his head while slowly making his way to the punch bowl.

"I wonder if he's sick."

"Nah. I have a feeling. It's kinda why I'm here."

"You think he's going to finally turn tonight?"

Darryl shrugged. "The odds are good. It's a full moon, and he looks like he's ready, but it could happen next week, for all I know."

The music stopped, and the crowd cheered. Willa sent the mayor away, and her eyes connected with Darryl's as she flitted across the room to our table.

"Why in the world are you two just sitting here?" she asked, sliding into the seat before turning her attention to me. "Where's Roscoe?"

"Tacos," Darryl and I said in unison.

She stared at Darryl again. "*You* don't seem to be having fun. Is Norwich a little too festive?"

"Festive? This is on a different level. Does the entire town shut down for Halloween?"

"Shut down? No. The town comes alive! Have you ever dreamed of living in a place where werewolves and humans not only coexist but thrive together?" She lifted her hand in the air, pointing to the mix of hundreds of people in the giant hall. Werewolves, humans, and half-turns laughed and danced, some sitting at tables while playing games. "This is what Norwich is really about, but we're aware of the rumors."

"What are you?" Darryl asked, his ears pressing against his head.

"I'm the Nor-witch." She let out a fake cackle but quickly dialed it back when Darryl didn't respond. "Eh, that joke is getting old anyway."

Mosavi noticed Darryl's hostility from across the room and rushed to the table, sliding a drink in front of Willa before sitting in the seat next to her. He said nothing, but his ears pulled tightly against his head in the same angry gesture.

"I want you out of my town."

"Dear," Willa said, tracing her fingers over his. "This is a night to relax and enjoy. You don't do that enough lately." After a moment, Mosavi's ears shifted slowly upward as Willa turned back to us. "You both should be enjoying the night. These festivities aren't just for fun." She looked around and lowered her voice. "This celebration belies the danger. We are besieged from all sides every day, but on this particular day, the shields have to go up." Her eyes flashed blood red. "And yes, I am siphoning magic from every werewolf gathered here, even you, Darryl." She pointed to the disco ball on the ceiling. "Without that, and enough werewolves to feed it, the coven would descend upon this place."

"How do I know you aren't feeding our essence to coven right now?" Daryl asked.

"You—" Mosavi paused and took in a deep breath through his teeth before quieting his voice. "Willa is the reason Norwich exists, and why werewolves have a real refuge—not just a refuge, a modern life with all the amenities of civilization instead of being forced to live as animals in the woods or on the streets begging for food. Our kind continues to fall, and the organization has done nothing but watch."

"The organization?" I asked, prompting Mosavi to let out an exhausted sigh.

"The... Administration of Werewolf Oversight and Opportunities."

Willa smirked and Darryl let out a snort. At first, I didn't get what was so funny until I put together the acronym. I'd received correspondence from them before, but it wasn't until now that I put it all together.

"Is that really what they're called?"

"It was created by a human who hated werewolves. He had an unfortunate accident not long after," Mosavi replied, grinding his teeth. "But you know how bureaucracy is. They've been sitting on that name change for about ten years."

"I'm confused. I thought witches couldn't survive long without a coven," Darryl interjected.

"It is possible, obviously. I haven't had one in over a century," she said, holding Mosavi's hand. When she looked at him, it was as though nothing else in the world mattered.

"If this is an act, it's pretty damn convincing," Darryl said, almost swallowing his words as if enthralled by the display.

"We saved each other, and we've been saving werewolves since we took control of this place two years ago. Cody and his pack didn't end up here by chance." She smiled at me again. "I never did get around to apologizing for how long that took. Committing federal offenses while not getting caught takes a bit of time."

"What?" I asked, dropping my voice to a whisper. "Was this illegal?"

"None of you are in government records anymore," Mosavi said, glaring at Darryl. "Unlike you. Still in your hovel with all the rotten fish?"

"You mean my beach house on prime real estate worth over ten million today?" The larger werewolf flashed a grin. "Yes. I'm still there."

The darker werewolf crossed his arms. "Are you working for them?"

"AWOO? No. They tried, but like you, they weren't able to make me an offer I wanted."

"At least you are not a total fool."

"Hold on a minute. Where the hell has our money been coming from?" I asked.

The mayor raised his brows and cocked a half-grin but didn't respond. Willa, on the other hand, occasionally glanced up at the glowing disco ball while fidgeting with the straps of her gown.

"Are you okay?" I asked, catching her attention.

"Of course." Her eyes brightened. "We should enjoy the rest of the night."

"Why do you need the shields? Why not just commune with your kin?" Darryl asked, also likely noticing Willa's unease.

"My kin? They are not my sisters. The witches of the woods are vengeful, and they will stop at nothing to drain me of my magic and enslave my Darius. We are going to win this fight, though. As more werewolves arrive, my wards grow stronger, and the town can expand. Humans and werewolves, they're all welcome. It is Darius' dream, and I will do all I can to make it come true."

Mosavi smiled warmly as they pressed their foreheads together, Willa kissing him on the nose.

"Draining werewolves to protect werewolves from being drained." Darryl looked up at the disco ball, now glowing a pastel yellow. "I don't like this at all."

"It's completely safe," Willa said. "The werewolves will be weakened for a day or two before they're back to normal. This building is quite literally the center of town, so the barrier extends all the way to the woods on all sides. We've got more werewolves now, so it's a lot stronger than last year."

"Everyone knows to stay out of the woods, right?" Darryl asked.

"It's one of the laws," Mosavi replied before glaring at me. "When they aren't being broken by undisciplined half-turns."

"Cody broke a law." Darryl choked out a loud laugh. "If it were any other situation, that would be more unbelievable than a lucid witch."

Roscoe appeared in the doorway holding several tacos while being shoved into the room by two other werewolves. He looked around until he found me, then trotted over while shoving one of the tacos into his mouth.

"Want one?" he asked with his mouth full, holding one of the meat-filled shells in front of my face.

"Well, that's up to you." I held up the bottle of poppers Willa gave me earlier. I'd always thought poppers were pills, but apparently, I'd had it all wrong for years. "It's either sex or tacos. It can't be both for obvious reasons."

Roscoe shoved the rest of the tacos into his mouth before grabbing my hand. "Oooo!"

Werewolves. If there was one thing Roscoe loved more than food... As we walked out of the center, I caught a glimpse of Austin stripping off his costume while Adam ran away, the werewolf's eyes glowing a furious yellow. It seemed the vironoct had worn off faster than usual.

He looked down at the floor before finally disappearing after Adam.

"I think I should see what's going on."

"Nah, let them handle things for once. Let's have fun!"

I wasn't entirely sure when I'd lost my thong, but I was drunk enough that my embarrassment vanished in a sea of propositions and catcalls. I never thought I was ugly, but I was so self-conscious that I also never found myself particularly attractive either. My history with men wouldn't have been enough to write a one-page report on, and the few terrible experiences I'd had made it hard to think of myself as worthy of affection.

Before I'd met Roscoe, I'd been a pretender. I worked at a gay bar, but I secretly despised the culture and every man I served. Forcing myself into the thick of what I hated had only isolated me further, because I never felt like I belonged. None of it had helped me accept who I was, but my gradual evolution into lycanthropy was changing that. While human Cody could hide in the shadows, avoiding confrontation and heartbreak, half-turn Cody couldn't hide from anyone.

"Let's fuck in the hay maze," I said, pulling on the golden cord tied around Roscoe's neck, leading him through the haunted labyrinth. "Always kind of wanted to be railed by a minotaur."

"Yer bein' unusually nasty," Roscoe said with a grunt, straightening the horns on his head that had come loose. "Wish it was a full moon every night."

We approached the stacked hay bales but were beaten to the action by a few other partygoers who had the same idea. A human man, a werewolf, and a woman. The only one who noticed us in the dark entryway was the werewolf, and when he silently beckoned us over, Roscoe looked back over at me for approval. It might have been a night of debauchery, but I wasn't that loose. With a shake of my head and smile, I pulled a reluctant Roscoe out of that part of the maze.

As we stepped out of the shrubs, I stopped and gazed at the moon. If I had to describe the sensation, it was like being plugged into an outlet after being completely drained.

"I sure am glad there are no trick-or-treaters in Norwich, because everyone has lost their minds."

"Wasn't expectin' the town to turn into one big orgy," Roscoe said, his voice almost a whisper.

"You almost sound disappointed."

"Don't get me wrong, it's hot, but there's somethin' missing. Halloween ain't the same without kids dressing up and lookin' fer handouts. Makes me all nostalgic."

"You remember trick-or-treating as a child?"

"Naw, I'm talkin' about when I was living in the city, looking for hand-outs." He nudged me with his elbow. "Every Halloween, I'd get lots of candy to hand out to the kiddos, but I'd always run out too soon."

"You ate it, didn't you?"

He wrapped an arm around my waist and laughed in response.

"Willa said that the kids here get a whole area of the town sectioned off with bumper cars, laser tag, ice cream, taco stands—"

"Goddamn it! We're on the wrong side of town," Roscoe shouted. "I want some more tacos and ice cream."

"I can make you some tacos when we get home if you want."

"Uh," Roscoe stumbled through his words.

"How hard could it be?"

"Five, Cody," Roscoe said, holding up his hand.

"Excuse me?"

"That's how many times you've said that and nearly burned the house down." One ear dropped sideways. "I really don't get how someone can be so bad at somethin' so easy."

"Maybe you could teach me how to cook. That might be fun."

He gave me a squeeze. "You really wanna learn?"

"We can make it a night, like movie night. It's just another thing we could do together."

Roscoe tensed a bit, and I looked at his face, expecting a smile. Instead, he looked like he was on the verge of tears.

"Fine, I won't make you eat what I cook."

He let out a quiet chuckle but didn't respond.

"You've been acting kind of weird today. Are you upset with me?"

"Of course not. It's just, uh—" He stopped walking and looked away. "No one's ever wanted to spend time with me like this. You know, doin' regular stuff. It's always been sex, drugs, or drinkin', or all three. Never really just sat on an old, ugly couch and watched old movies with someone who enjoyed it."

"I knew it!" I shouted, trying to lighten the mood. "You think that couch is ugly, too!"

"Oh, it's hideous, and I love it."

"Fair," I said, continuing to walk alongside him. "You never did any of that with your *many* girlfriends?"

"I lied. You think any woman would live with a dumpster diving monster that sucks dick fer smack?"

"Why are you always so secretive about your life? It's not like lying about having girlfriends made you more appealing."

"Habit," Roscoe said, his eyes still averted. "I haven't exactly been the romantic type, so I like to put on an act." He turned and gave me a deep sniff. "You smell good. Is that a new cologne?"

"It is, actually. I thought you'd hate it."

"Well, I do like yer regular smell. You know, that skunky, weed smell."

"I do not smell like that!" I snapped. "Since you got into my head, I've been asking just about everyone I meet if I smell okay, and not one person said I smelled skunky."

Roscoe raised a brow. "They're lyin'. You smell like the dankest weed. It's incredible. I just wanna bury my nose in yer crotch."

"Every human I've talked to said I smell like cologne, but..." I thought back to a few weeks ago when I'd gone with Austin to the barbeque place. "Every werewolf has a different take. One said I smelled like gasoline, another said I smelled like Londonport roast beef, and two thought I smelled like one of those rubber kong dog toys."

"Ya know, that kinda makes sense, actually."

"I don't smell like any of that!"

"You smell like all of it, cause that's what half-turns smell like to us. Every half-turn I've been around smells like you, so maybe you just give off a scent that reminds us of things we love smellin'."

I looked down at my naked body. "Everything about me is so weird now."

We walked further along the road in silence, but Roscoe pulled his arm back and started fidgeting with his chest mane.

"There's something else bothering you, isn't there?"

"Eh. Just thinkin' about the day I met you. I was about to do something that I was gonna regret."

His tone became somber, and I turned toward him, studying his face. He looked at me for only a second before staring straight ahead.

"That day, I spent my last thousand dollars on Fentanyl, Xanax, Adderall, and weed, and I was gonna take that bus outta town, find a nice tree to sit under, and get higher than ever. Nothin' killed me yet, so I was ready fer anything. My pockets were full, and I was about to end two years of sobriety.

"Never believed in fate, but the moment I saw you, I felt somethin' weird. I knew you was gonna be a half-turn soon, 'cause you had that smell. So, I sold that synthetic shit back to the dealer at a discount and kept the weed. That was the baggie I gave you that night. I didn't have a job, but I started doing odd things fer people to make money so I could stay with you." He turned and locked eyes with me for much longer this time. "I keep thinkin' I'm gonna screw something up again, like I did with Darryl—like it's all temporary."

It was like someone knocked all the air out of me. This was the Roscoe that would often come out when I least expected it, and it was why he had me so hooked.

"You're not going to screw it up, and even if you did, I'd help you through it." We continued along the narrow road until we were just outside of town next to one of the corn fields that had just been harvested. I took his giant hands in mine. "You're one of the most talented and interesting guys I've ever met. You can cook me a three Michelin star meal and serenade me as I eat it. How did someone like you end up on the streets?"

"It started out with me tryin' to get back those missing years. I thought there had to be some drug that would help me remember, but all that happened was I became a junkie. That story I told about me havin' sex with all them guys and blackmailin' them fer money to move to the city was a tall tale too. The truth is, I don't remember how I got to the city. It's like decades of my life just disappeared fer some reason."

"You should talk to me more about this stuff, you know?" I pointed to the kuu earrings dangling from my lobes. "When I thought I couldn't leave, you could have slipped right back into the drugs, using me and treating me like shit, but instead, you treat me like a best friend—when you're not peeing on me."

We both broke into hushed laughter.

"Can I tell you somethin' without you gettin' upset?"

I arched my brow. "That depends…"

"Seein' you with Darryl this morning made me real angry, and I've been thinkin' about stuff." Roscoe rubbed his head. "I hate thinkin' about stuff."

"Angry? Seriously? Dude, you were talking about how hot it would be to see those ferals run a train on me."

"I actually thought it would have been, but when they tried, I got real protective. It was weird. That's never happened before." He shook his head. "Cody, I'm not used to feelin' like this. Don't know what to make of it." He smiled softly and pulled me close. "Nearly killed Darryl with that *remedy* but seein' him get a bit of payback after fuckin' you was worth him tearin' up my ass after breakfast."

"We didn't even go all the way."

"Wait, you didn't?" Roscoe's eyes went wide. "It's Darryl. No one goes just halfway with Darryl."

"Have we met? He and I had a little fun jerking each other off, and maybe a little oral here and there when we got high off that shit. That's the extent of it. He's a good friend, but he's not you."

His eyes watered again.

"Why you gotta say shit like that?"

"Because for some stupid reason, I really like you." A pile of fallen cornstalks caught my eye. "Wanna fuck on that?"

"Hell yeah. Maybe we'll get lucky and find a good ear or two."

"That's gross, Roscoe."

"What? Wasn't gonna do sex stuff or nothin'. I was gonna eat 'em."

Roscoe was mid-thrust when he froze and looked up at the moon.

"Why did you stop?" I asked, catching my breath. He didn't respond, seeming almost entranced. "Roscoe?"



Aeron Dusk

"Oooo... Someone just turned," he said, sliding the rest of the way out of me before rolling onto his back. "It's gotta be Adam."

"Thank God!" I shouted, climbing on top of the spent werewolf. "Hopefully he'll be less of a bitch now. You're done already?"

"That feeling kinda kills the mood a little. We should go find him. Austin's probably gonna need some company, too."

"How do you know all this?"

Roscoe shrugged. "Dunno. Every werewolf knows when it happens, though." One lonely howl from the north started a cascade of howls that erupted from town in the south. Roscoe's ears fell. "Aw, shit no..."

"What's the matter with you?"

He covered his ears and shook his head. "Nope, not gonna do it..."

"You're scaring me right now."

More werewolves joined in the chorus, and Roscoe whined, holding his head tighter.

"Jesus fuck," he muttered, gently sliding me off him. He sat up and pointed his nose to the sky before belting out the most hilarious howl I'd ever heard. It kind of warbled, like he was trying to clear his throat. "I hate this," he shouted before howling again. "Can't stop. It's like throwin' up."

"This is the first time I've ever heard you do that," I said, trying not to laugh, but I was failing with every high-pitched yip and yowl. They always seemed so human in personality that I'd sometimes forget werewolves did stuff like this.

"Don't get used to it." He let out one final howl that was a lot cleaner than his first few. "Don't look at me. I'm a freak," he said jokingly, covering his face.

"Well, I learned something new tonight. Werewolves can feel when half-turns change, and they howl uncontrollably."

"Would you believe some werewolves do it 'cause they like it?" Roscoe scoffed and stumbled to his feet. "It actually makes me cringe."

"It's kinda hot—when you don't sound asthmatic."

"I ain't done that in years. A little dust on the vocal cords." He reached down and grabbed my arm. "I bet Adam and Austin are havin' the roughest sex of their lives right now. I remember my first night under the moon. You won't ever feel something like that again, and yer body just wants to release everything it's got."

"You think I'll be bigger than you when I turn?" I asked, walking alongside Roscoe, who broke into a light jog as we got closer to the woods.

"Dunno. It's all random."

"I can't wait to see what Adam looks like."

Roscoe stopped and tried to pick up more scents, but the look on his face turned from intrigue to worry.

"What's wrong?"

Roscoe lifted his leg and reached down to pull off one of the anklets. It was threaded through one of the colorful stones the ferals gave us weeks ago.

"Aw, no. Those dummies went into the woods."

"Are you sure?"

"It's a fresh scent trail."

Eerie cackles called from the trees, the same songs I'd hear from behind our property. I turned to Roscoe who kept his stare alert and his hackles raised.

"We should get Willa," I said, pulling Roscoe toward the direction of town.

"I... can't leave 'em. Not again." He took more shaky steps to the forest's edge before locking up, like he was standing on a cliff several thousand feet in the air.

"Again? What are you talking about?"

Roscoe didn't respond. Instead, he kept his intense stare on the blackened trees. I pulled him back.

"Run to get help. You're faster than me."

"You can't go in there."

"I'm not a werewolf," I said, grabbing the stone out of his hand. "Added insurance though, just in case."

"Please don't go." His almost trance-like tone cracked into a high-pitched whine as he held onto my right arm, his grip so tight it hurt.

"Roscoe, calm down." The world around me faded to silver as the glow of my eyes reflected in his. The vironoct wasn't as effective on Roscoe for some reason, but it would last long enough for him to do this one task. "Run to town and get Willa. She'll know what to do."

His irises looked like two morning glories, blue around a yellow center. He fought it for almost a full minute before both eyes turned solid. Roscoe nodded and bolted toward town, faster than I'd ever seen him run.

*"Cody..."*

A young woman's voice whispered in my ears, but it didn't come from any one direction. I held my breath and stepped into the blackness of the forest's edge, my bare feet stumbling over gnarled roots. I was still mostly naked, save for the leather belt and hilted fake sword swinging from my hip and the golden rope dangling from the other.

"Okay, I was a lot braver a few minutes ago," I whispered to myself before turning toward the light of town, but there was nothing but trees. I had only just entered the woods, but now I was in the middle of a forest, the clearing up ahead illuminated by the moon. The world around me transformed into a labyrinth of shadow, and there was no way to find my way back.

If only I had been the real Theseus.

*"Lunam matris potestate..."*

The whispers echoed as I pushed my way through the trees, the suffocating stale air overwhelming me. It was like running through a basement as a child, trying to get to the light before the monsters got me—only there was no light, and the monsters were everywhere.

"Austin? Adam?" I called out, but the only answer I received was more incoherent chanting, a little louder than before. The singsong feminine voice transitioned to a demonic timbre.

*"Odiosa diaboli amplexus..."*

"Where are you guys?" I shouted, but it was hard to hear my own voice over the flood of hissing, haggard screams stabbing at my mind.

*"Lupus venit ut impleatur!"*

I stumbled backward when flames burst from the ground all around me, culminating to the center of the clearing before giving form to a crooked wooden cross jammed into the ground. Austin's body was sprawled along its planks, tied with thick rope by the wrists and ankles, his weepy blue eyes following me as I stumbled closer.

How were his eyes blue? The vironoct had worn off before he left.

Another werewolf stood in front of him, holding Austin's dogtags in the air like a trophy. The werewolf was short and slender, his fur lighter black like fresh coffee grounds with a wiry mane that had grown out considerably. The Anubian-looking creature turned to face me, his eyes blood-red as he grinned.

"Adam?" I called out while inching closer.

"*Vasa nostra esurientes*," he said, but that wasn't Adam's voice. The voice was a multitude of otherworldly tones. "Join the feast."

# Chapter 28

# Halloween — Part Three

"**W**hat did you do?"

Those words barely slipped out before every primal instinct bubbling just below my consciousness pulled at me to run, just as Mosavi had warned. It didn't matter where, but running was all I could think about as the terrible aura smothered me from all directions.

"You came. It's my big night," he said, his voice now normal again, though much deeper. "I can do what you do now, but I can do it better." He turned to Austin, gently raking his claws down the werewolf's chest. "Tell me what I want to hear."

Instead of glowing silver, his eyes turned solid white. Austin cried out in pain. He tried to speak but only managed a whine.

"Oh well. I guess he doesn't need to talk anymore."

"You're hurting him!" I shouted, stepping closer.

"What are you talking about? I'm making him happy. This is what he wanted you to do to him. Remember?"

"Not like this. Have you lost you're fucking mind?" I pointed to the huge werewolf, now hanging sprawled on the cross. "Get him down from there!"

"He likes the pain." He looked up at Austin. "Don't you?"

Austin nodded reluctantly before turning away.

"We need to go," I whispered as rustling danced from tree-to-tree beyond the light of the fire. I held out a trembling hand to Adam. "Please."

"It's so peaceful out here." His voice was no longer his own, rather the multitude of crone-like chanting I'd heard earlier. "Do you not feel at peace?"

I took a step back, but the werewolf took two steps forward until I felt the heat from his body.

"They want this," the voices said. "One wants power and the other wants to be free from the prison of his past. We're not evil, Cody. We only want to give those gifted with our master's essence a life of bliss."

"That's not how this works, and I'm not stupid enough to believe in a life of bliss. It always comes at a price." I clutched the stone I'd taken from Roscoe earlier and cautiously stepped toward the cross, hoping whatever this was could protect me.

"Don't touch him," Adam shouted in his own voice as he lunged forward, pinning me to the ground. "They want to help us."

"No, they don't. They don't care about us. They just want to use us."

He traced his hand down my arm until sharp claws scraped against my numb fingers. "They can't welcome us when you're holding that."

So that's why they hadn't come out of the shadows. It seemed as though Adam's body acted as a barrier protecting them from whatever magic was in this stone.

"Get off me," I shouted, struggling, but werewolf Adam was a lot stronger.

"Come on," he whispered in my ear, his tongue sliding along my neck as he tried to pry my fingers open. He was no longer gentle, claws stabbing into the flesh of my hand. I cried out, but that didn't faze him. He seemed almost hollow—like a doll. "They just want to meet you."

It didn't matter how much this hurt—I couldn't let go. Even though he spoke in his own voice, he was obviously under their control. I struggled to calm my thoughts, but the vironoct was harder to use under pain and distress. No matter how much I tried, I couldn't clear my mind.

"I could rip your hand off, Cody," Adam said with a sickening smile. "I could do it easily now."

"Then don't," I pleaded, still struggling for control. "Do you really hate me that much?"

There was a momentary flash of amber in his eyes, and his ears flattened against his head. It didn't last; his eyes regained their bloody appearance.

"I despise you," he snapped, removing his hand from mine before raking his claws across my face, slicing into my left cheek. "Everyone loves Cody, and everyone treats me like the kid who's in the way."

"I've tried to be your friend, but you're the one that always fucks it up!"

"You didn't even want me to live with you. I'm just a pest, aren't I?" He leaned in until his snout touched my nose, his sharper teeth grazing my skin. "I'm not pesky little Adam anymore. I bet I could make you my pet, too."

Adam jerked as the witches tried to wrest control.

"Stop telling me what to do," he shouted at nothing, his eyes turning pure white like they did earlier. "Be my pet, Cody."

An obvious weakness opened up, and I was finally angry enough to exploit it. Whatever magic he gave off did the opposite of what he expected. It only heightened my senses and resolve. The world around me turned silver as the vironoct finally surfaced. Adam was a werewolf now, and even with whatever power they'd given him, he had no defense against it.

A death-like chill rushed in from the wind around me, and screams echoed through the trees, as Adam's eyes faded to an empty blue.

"*Ingratus! Wretched!*"

"Untie Austin," I said calmly, pushing Adam away.

"*We won't let you leave.*"

The crow-like voices screamed louder in my head and all around.

"*You'll never find your way without us. These woods are ours.*"

"Shut up!" I screamed, grabbing handfuls of hair as Adam freed each of Austin's limbs.

"*Let us help. Let us please you. Any wish we will grant.*"

Though I held tightly to the stone, it did little to silence what had taken residence in my head. The brush rustled even louder from all around us where the light of the flames couldn't reach, and all the sounds melded into a familiar voice I hadn't heard in years.

"*A real mother would never abandon her child to a cold and heartless world.*"

Though my own mother would have never used those words, the way she spoke was so convincing, like a knife through the heart. There was nothing I could do but bear the full brunt of their manipulation while struggling to hold onto my resolve.

"*My sweet baby boy. I know I've made mistakes, but nothing you could ever do would make me love you less.*"

Tears streamed down my cheeks as Adam and Austin stared, eager for my next order.

"Come on," I said, waving them after me. "Stay close."

"*I watched you grow into a handsome young man. I'm so proud of you.*"

The more she spoke, the more everything around me dissolved into a dream-like void. That voice wasn't my mother's, but I wanted it to be.

We wandered farther from the fire before the embers disappeared. The trees heaved as though they were breathing, but I put one trembling leg in front of the other. As long as I held the stone, the witches couldn't get me, and if the vironoct didn't break, they couldn't manipulate Adam. That was what I was most afraid of, and I kept glancing back to make sure he was still following.

"*I'd never let the world hurt you. You're safe in my arms.*"

Every step was like walking through a waist-deep mire, the ground sapping what little strength I had. Ahead, a gentle purple glow caught my eye. It flitted and sparkled, and a slender, womanly figure emerged from it.

"*Stay with me, Cody. Don't leave me all alone in the cold forest. Don't abandon me.*"

There was genuine terror in her voice as I drew closer to the source of the light. She didn't want me to see it, or was this a trick? I slowed my pace and looked back at the blackness. The trees had morphed, reshaping and melting as though made of liquid.

"Cody," Willa's voice called out from the light.

"*Come home.*"

The woods took the shape of a cozy cottage I didn't recognize and the silhouette of a woman with flowing hair welcomed me with open arms.

"*Come home, Cody.*"

A hand fell on my shoulder, and I screamed.

"It's me, dear," Willa whispered, taking my hand. "We need to get to the beacon now before it disappears."

"*Our fallen sister will lead you to destruction.*"

My feet didn't move. It became harder for me to trust my own senses. Was this really her, or was it another hallucination?

"What do you see?" Willa asked.

"My mother," I said, wiping away the tears.

"Throw the stone at the vision."

"They'll get me."

"Not if we run," she said, shaking me out of my stupor. "But I can't pull you all out of here while you hold it. It affects me just as much as it does the coven." She looked back at Adam and Austin. "Tell them to run to the light, and when you throw the stone, follow them and don't look back, no matter what you hear."

I nodded, pointing to the way ahead. "Both of you run."

Without a word, they sprinted ahead, and I reared back, ready to throw the stone.

"*Cody...*"

The voice let out a heartbreaking cry.

"*I'm so sorry for everything.*"

"Throw it!" Willa shouted. "You have to throw it!"

I squeezed my eyes shut and tossed the magic stone at the vision, and I heard my mother scream before the forest collapsed inward.

"Come with me, quickly." Willa's voice brought me back, and she pushed me forward. I nearly tripped over my feet as I scrambled toward the fading purple beacon in the distance.

"*You're hurting me. Please look at me.*"

I started to turn, but Willa pushed me again.

"Don't look back," she shouted while more of the forest collapsed inward, hounding our steps like a crumbling bridge. As the light grew brighter, I flew into nothing. Time froze, and I floated through a formless, silent void.

Everything returned to normal when I hit the ground hard, the impact knocking the wind out of me.

"Aw shit," Roscoe said, pulling me to my feet with his massive hands. "Are you okay?"

After catching my breath, I nodded. "Where's Willa?"

"Right here," she said from behind without even a hint of breathlessness. "That was impressive control."

"What do you mean?"

"The way you resisted their calls. Not many can do that, especially on the full moon."

"They almost got me," I said, my breathing returning to normal. "They're in my head."

"Not anymore." Willa tapped against something invisible at first, but it rippled with violet light similar to a rock falling into a pond.

"Cody?" Adam said, touching his face with his hands, almost shocked that he was a werewolf now.

"We're okay," I said, turning to Austin, who hadn't returned to normal. "I'm letting you go. We're not doing this to you anymore."

He didn't respond.

"Come on, Austin. Snap out of it."

A little bit of life returned to his face, and his ears fell to the sides of his head. His irises remained baby blue as tears soaked his fur.

"Austin?"

He remained silent, but he stared at Adam like a terrified dog backed into a cage.

"What's wrong with him?" Adam asked. He tried to reach for Austin's hand, but the werewolf cowered away.

"Do you remember what happened?" I asked, noticing the dog tags now around Adam's neck. "Why do you have those?"

"That's what she told me to do." Adam looked down at his chest. "She said that when I turned, I could do what you did if I put them around my neck while I was on top of him. That was when everything got fuzzy."

"What are they, exactly?" Willa asked. "They must hold a lot of significance if the coven could use them for control."

"They belonged to his pack he lost in the military," I said, watching as Adam's expression turned to horror.

He quickly unlatched the chain and fastened it around non-responsive Austin's neck.

"I didn't know," he said. "He never told me that. He just said they made him look tough."

"This sets us back considerably," Willa said. "You did something you shouldn't have, Adam. This ability would never come naturally to you."

"No," Adam cried out. "I didn't want *this*."

Willa slid her finger under the chain Austin wore. "This represented something close to his broken heart, and you took that from him." She looked back at the remorseful werewolf. "You may not have realized it at the time, but this may have damaged him more than we know."

"Can it be undone?" I asked.

"I don't know," Willa responded. "This is a fusion of witchcraft and the vironoct. Adam should have never been able to use it, but when the coven took control of his body, they tapped into the power all werewolves possess." She shook her head. "They would have never been able to do this if Adam hadn't been willing."

"So, it's my fault," Adam said, wrapping his arms around Austin who stood straight, still staring at nothing while tears fell from his eyes. "I'm sorry. Please come back."

He didn't respond. He didn't even look at the smaller werewolf.

"We should get him home," I said, both sad and furious, but this was just as much my fault as it was Adam's. I should have taken his anger more seriously, but I'd mostly ignored him, thinking it would all go away when he transformed.

"I'll need to discuss this with Darius. He may be able to fix what was broken, or perhaps even your friend Darryl." She held her finger to her lips. "But let's keep what I did here between us. I don't want him knowing the risk I took to bring you back to safety, and I may have locked them both in the building."

"Why would you do that?" I asked.

"They would have gone into the woods after you, and I would rather risk myself than the town. If something happened to Darius, I could not continue living. He is not only my love—he is my lifeforce."

"He's gonna be pissed," I said, as Adam led his catatonic kuu mate by the hand toward the town without looking back. "I don't know what we're gonna do. He was so close to being okay, but now—"

"We'll have somethin' good to eat, and we'll sleep on it," Roscoe said.

"I don't think anyone's gonna be hungry after this."

Roscoe slid his arm around me. "I'll make somethin' anyway."

"Aw come on," Adam shouted from his bedroom, startling Roscoe and me awake. "It's everywhere."

I jumped out of bed, Roscoe following. When I burst through the door into their room, the strong smell of urine hit me.

"What happened?" I asked while Adam grabbed an armful of towels from their closet. Austin was sitting up, but like last night, was unresponsive.

"He wet the bed." Adam stood over the werewolf and snapped his fingers. "Get up, I need to get the sheets."

Like a marionette, the blond werewolf turned and lifted himself from the damp mattress.

Roscoe hummed contemplatively as he scratched his head. "He's still doin' what he's told, but ain't doin' nothing else. You probably gotta tell him when to go to the bathroom now."

"Are you kidding me?" Adam asked, ripping the sheets off the bed. "How am I going to know that? He's not saying anything."

Roscoe shrugged. "Dunno, but you better figure it out before he takes a big steamy shit on the floor."

Adam's eyes widened. "Austin, go to the toilet and do your business."

The huge werewolf cocked his head.

"Uh, I think you need to be more specific," I said, pulling Roscoe out the door. "Make sure he's actually on the toilet, please. I'd rather not have any surprises like that."

Adam sighed, grabbed Austin's hand, and led him toward the bathroom; Roscoe and I walked outside to the chairs around the pit. Darryl was already out there, stoking the fire.

"Darryl?" I asked, but he didn't turn toward me.

"Why are you two up?" he asked, his tone licking at my ears like the angry flames he stoked.

"Austin pissed all over Adam's bed," Roscoe said. He normally would have laughed at such a silly statement, but not this time. The werewolf plopped down on one of the larger plastic chairs and leaned his head back, looking up at the sky. "He ain't gonna be able to do anything anymore without Adam."

"I want to know exactly what happened last night," Darryl demanded as I sat.

"Adam lured Austin into the woods before he turned, and then he did some kind of vironoct ritual on him. Now Austin's broken," I said, tossing a piece of wood into the fire. "After all that progress, it's all fucked now."

Darryl let out a sigh. "I should have forced you all to stay. If I'd have known what kind of town Norwich was—"

"It's a great town," Roscoe interrupted. "Full of good people, and Willa ain't a normal witch. This is just as much my fault, but bein' out here was the best thing for us."

"Tell that to Austin," Darryl snapped. We all sat quietly as he calmed down. "I'm sorry," he said. "I think I'm taking my own guilt out on you both."

"What do you mean?" I asked.

"I kinda always wished something bad would happen to Austin, but knowing what I know now... and with what just happened—"

"Well, thankfully wishes don't come true," I said, cutting him off. "What happened was a consequence of neglect, not wishful thinking. We can each blame ourselves, but what's done is done. Austin's gone."

"Let's not jump to conclusions," Darryl said. "It's the vironoct, not some kind of curse. There's always a way to undo it."

"So, you know how?" I asked.

"No. I never wanted to follow in the footsteps of the elders. If there's a way, Darius would probably know."

"That's what Willa said." I rubbed the crust out of the corner of my left eye. Neither Roscoe nor I had gotten a decent night's sleep. "If he can't fix him, we'll have to find an elder that can."

"I got an idea," Roscoe said. "We still got them herbs. If Mosavi can't get through to him, I bet the ferals can."

"That's a terrible idea," Darryl said. "After what happened last night, you want to take the chance of going back into the woods?"

"You got a better idea?" Roscoe replied, unusually calm given how on edge Darryl was. "Cause if not, them ferals probably have more answers than anyone here. Hell, they live out there with the witches, and they're just fine. You think we should go to the A-W-O-O?"

Darryl sighed. "I'd rather us not get involved with them."

"Ya almost make it seem like they're some kinda werewolf mafia," Roscoe said jokingly, but Darryl didn't even crack a smile. "They, uh, ain't the mafia, right?"

The larger werewolf shrugged.

"Shit!" Adam shouted from inside the house. We all turned in unison.

"I hope he didn't mean that literally," I muttered, prodding Roscoe. "Go see what's wrong."

"I ain't goin' in there."

"I'll check on them," Darryl said, standing and stretching his arms. "Cody, can you put on some coffee?"

"I was just thinking that."

We all sat around the table, everyone eating in silence except for Austin, who continued staring at Adam.

"Please stop looking at me like that and eat your food," Adam said, exhausted, but Austin didn't respond. "Eat, damn it!"

"Tell him what to eat first," I said, pointing to Austin's plate. "You have to be specific."

"Eat your eggs," Adam said. Austin picked up his fork and began eating. "I can't keep doing this. I'm going to go insane."

"You have to," Darryl muttered. "He's solely dependent on you now. Stupid actions have consequences, Adam."

"I feel awful enough as it is. You don't have to keep reminding me." Adam took a bite of bacon, noticing Austin staring at him again. He had already finished off his eggs but hadn't touched anything else. "Eat your bacon next."

The werewolf did as he was told.

"Willa texted that Mosavi will be here before noon," I said.

"I hope he can fix him." Adam grabbed a biscuit from Austin's plate and held it up. "Eat."

"Has he had anything to drink?" I asked, noticing there wasn't a glass of water in front of him.

"Damn it," Adam said, running to the kitchen.

"He's kinda like a pet now," Roscoe said, scratching a rigid Austin behind the ears.

"Yeah. A pet rock that pisses everywhere," Adam said, walking back into the dining room with a tall glass. He handed it to Austin. "Drink your water."

He grabbed the glass and began lapping at it.

"I need to head back home tomorrow," Darryl said, pushing his empty plate away. "There're only three lifeguards, and I don't want to overwork the others. I wish I could stay longer."

"You gotta do what you gotta do," Roscoe said. "It was nice havin' you here, though. Like old times."

"I don't remember you trying to kill me with a bogus hangover remedy in the old times," Darryl said, taking a drink.

"It wasn't bogus!"

Darryl's eyes narrowed, but he didn't respond.

"Maybe I went a little overboard with the horseradish." Roscoe looked down. "Sorry."

"At least the reason was noble." Darryl smiled. "I'd have never believed it twenty years ago."

Roscoe let out a belch that rattled the walls.

"That's hot," I muttered, clearing the table. "Are you going to do your mid-morning fart at the table too?"

"Got nothin' in the tank," he said, pulling my hand. "You didn't kiss the cook yet." Roscoe pointed to his apron. "Sure wish I knew what happened to the one with tits on it."

"Oh, you lost it?" I asked and gave him a quick kiss on his thin lips.

"It's the darndest thing," Roscoe said, scratching his head. "Can't remember where the hell I put it."

"That's a shame," I said, knowing exactly where it was as I'd thrown that ugly thing away the week after he bought it. "Hopefully it turns up somewhere."

"Went down to the store to buy another one, but would you believe they don't sell 'em no more?"

"Unbelievable," I said, grabbing Roscoe's empty plate and stacking it on top of the others.

"I've been rackin' my brain trying to figure out what I did with it. I remember you was standin' in the kitchen talking to me, and I folded it and put it in the drawer." He shot me an intense stare. "Kinda strange, ain't it?"

"Well, you know how things sorta vanish around here," I said, stumbling over my words as I walked into the kitchen with him now uncomfortably close behind. "Are you actually gonna help me do the dishes?"

He folded his arms but didn't say anything.

"You know, don't you?"

"Yup," he replied. "When I figured it out, I spent all day at the landfill tryin' to find another one." He leaned in closer to my ear. "Where do ya think that couch came from?"

And that was when I figured out something interesting about Roscoe. He could smile in your face while deviously plotting his revenge, and I had been clueless the entire time.

Mosavi knelt in front of Austin, who sat on the sofa, completely rigid from his ears to his feet. His eyes glowed silver as he tried to break through whatever enchanted wall was keeping Austin from full consciousness.

He wasn't wearing his usual suit, nor had he arrived in his blacked-out Mercedes. He looked like any other werewolf with a torn T-shirt and frayed jeans that fit him perfectly.

"Pay attention," Mosavi demanded. Instead of doing what he was told, Austin glanced at Adam first.

"Look at him, Austin," Adam said, and the werewolf obeyed.

His irises went from blue to dark amber, and for a moment, whatever Mosavi was doing appeared to work. Adam's tail started to wag as he witnessed Austin's expression change from empty to something I couldn't quite place.

The mayor shook his head, and Austin's eyes faded back to blue.

"This only works if the werewolf wants to be brought back," he said, turning to Adam. "You're an idiot. Do you realize the severity of this?"

"He does," I said, pulling Mosavi's ire away. "What can we do?"

Mosavi got to his feet and let out an annoyed hiss of air through his teeth. "Hope it doesn't last."

"That's it?" Adam asked. "That's your answer?"

"That's my answer." He pulled a chain out of his jeans pocket and tossed it at Adam. "Put it on."

With a nervous swallow, Adam slipped the gold chain around his neck.

"You will now know when his basic needs are not met, and you will tend to him until what you've done wears off." Mosavi paused. "If it does."

"This doesn't help me at all!" Adam shouted, his frustration manifesting as a snarl. "I can't keep telling him what to do."

"Willa worked her fingers to the bone enchanting that," Mosavi shouted, causing Adam to slink backward. "If you're going to be an ungrateful little shit, I'll take it back."

Adam held the chain against his chest and shook his head. "Thank you."

"If you can't help him, then we'll need to find other avenues," Darryl said. "The ferals may know—"

"What would they know? How to rub sticks together?"

"They know more than you think," Roscoe chimed in. "It ain't like they don't got no sense. They use magic, and they got elders too."

The mayor scoffed. "If I cannot undo this, then those animals surely won't be able to help."

"What has he got to lose?" Darryl asked.

"His will. His mind. His body. And it really will be permanent," Mosavi snapped.

"The witches are weaker now, and we have these rocks," I said.

Mosavi laughed. "Rocks. Of course. The answer to holding back immense demonic forces are obviously rocks. Let me guess, you also have magic plants and beaded jewelry."

Roscoe and I glanced at one another. He might have been sarcastic, but he also wasn't far from the truth. I pulled one of the smooth stones out of my pocket and handed it to him.

"This is what shattered the spell I was under. The ferals gave them to us."

Mosavi rolled his eyes. "You're going to do what you want and put your trust in dirt-covered trinkets. I won't stand in your way. It is not like I have been able to since you arrived."

"I know you don't like it, but it's either this or we get the organization involved," Darryl said.

Mosavi grabbed a tuft of Darryl's mane and pulled. "You are now threatening my town."

The larger werewolf snatched Mosavi's hand and squeezed. "I'll do what needs to be done, so let's hope it doesn't come to that. Austin may have been an insufferable prick for years, but he doesn't deserve this."

Both werewolves pulled away, lowering their hackles.

"Let me discuss things with my wife. If the ferals cannot help, and you involve them… we will have no choice but to leave this place."

"Like I said, it's a last resort. I—" Darryl paused and shook his head. "I don't want to cause you and your wife any trouble. This town is something I didn't think was possible."

Mosavi took a step back and blinked in surprise. "It is my dream come to fruition. I may not be the nicest person to be around, but I care deeply for our kind and for the humans that welcome us." He eyed Darryl again. "How do I know I can trust you to not tell anyone what you have seen here?"

"You don't," Darryl responded, looking at me. "You can trust him, though."

Mosavi turned to meet my gaze.

"He is a lifeguard," I said. "If you can't trust one of those, who can you trust?"

"I suppose," Mosavi said before walking to the door.

"You're not going to shift back to your human form?" I asked.

"No one would recognize me in this pauper's outfit, and the shifting back and forth has been taking a mental toll on me lately." He turned back to me after pushing the door open. "At your *earliest* convenience, I'll meet with you alone at city hall."

"What time?"

"Earliest. Convenience. Cody," he repeated and shut the door behind him.

"Mayor Douchebag has left the building," Roscoe whispered with a snicker, not realizing the living room window was wide open.

The doorknob clicked, and the entrance creaked open. Roscoe winced, cowering behind Darryl as Mosavi pointed at him. "I'll see you at the jail later, Roscoe." The door slammed shut, and we all stood silently, waiting for him to walk out to the road.

"What's he gonna do, have me arrested?" He looked out the window at Mosavi as he held his cell phone to his ear.

"I don't know why you keep doing this. You know he's got a short fuse, and you're always trolling the wrong people. Need I remind you about the taser incident?"

A patrol car pulled into the driveway, and we all looked at one another in silence.

"Oh come on." Roscoe watched with a stunned expression as two werewolves in uniform strutted up to the porch. I recognized one of them from the barbeque restaurant.

The cops opened the door without knocking, and the one I recognized stepped inside, twirling a pair of cuffs around his finger.

"We got us a repeat offender."

"Now I know for a fact this ain't legal!" Roscoe shouted as the officer jerked his arm behind his back. "I know my rights!"

"That's great, Roscoe. I won't have to tell you about the one to shut the hell up." The other officer held the door open as the cop behind Roscoe shoved him outside. He flashed me his teeth and tipped his hat. "You all have a pleasant day. You should come by the restaurant again, Cody. Everyone misses you."

I thought back to the other day when I brought Roscoe and took them up on their offer. "It was fun, wasn't it?" I said, prompting Roscoe to look back at me, his mouth agape with a furrowed look of betrayal. "Will I at least get conjugal visits?"

The officer looked back at me without answering. "He'll be ready for you to pick him up in a few hours."

He shut the door, and they dragged Roscoe away. His protests soon silenced as the car door slammed shut and the patrol vehicle sped off.

"Roscoe's making friends wherever he goes," Darryl said. "Now I'm in the mood for barbeque before I leave."

"Darryl, Roscoe just got arrested," I said. "I should go talk to the mayor again."

"You can't fight city hall," Adam said, touching the necklace he wore. "Plus, Austin wants barbeque."

"You can tell that?" I asked.

Adam nodded. "I guess this necklace is pretty handy after all."

# Chapter 29

# Lazy Day

**"T**hanks for rescuin' me," Roscoe mumbled with half of a pulled-pork sandwich in his mouth. The weather was beautiful and clear, but the air had a harsh bite to it when the wind picked up. Still, everyone insisted on sitting outside. Since I was the only one without any fur, I wore a few layers.

"You're lucky I'm good at what I do," I replied, suggestively wiping the barbeque sauce from my lips.

Roscoe stopped chewing. "You sucked both of 'em off at the same time?"

"Sure did. You owe me now."

"Austin, eat your brisket," Adam said, taking a bite of a burger. The werewolf did as instructed, tears still lingering in his eyes. It was strange behavior because he didn't seem to be crying, but the tears never stopped. "I'm having a hard time believing any of what you just said."

"I'll have you know, my oral skills are legendary."

A black Mercedes pulled up along the curb, and Willa emerged from the back. Roscoe and I grew tense as we waited for Mosavi to join her, but the car pulled away instead. A gust of wind kicked up fallen leaves on the sidewalk, tousling her straightened hair while nearly lifting her surprisingly cheerful mauve dress.

"It's my favorite half-turn," she said, seeming genuinely surprised to see me, even though we'd been coming here more often lately. "It's a gorgeous day."

"Where is everybody?" I asked, noting the empty tables around the patio. Austin's head hit his empty plate, and he began snoring.

"Still asleep. I'm surprised you werewolves have the strength to be out and about."

"I feel fine," Adam said, poking Austin, but the werewolf didn't react.

"I'm exhausted," Darryl muttered. "How long does this last? I don't wanna feel like shit the entire trip back home tomorrow."

"Barely a day." Willa hiked her dress and climbed over the bench, sitting next to me. She eyed Roscoe, who was still furiously stuffing his face in between yawns. "What a healthy appetite."

"Why's everyone so exhausted?" Adam asked.

"The ward I used last night drains a bit of energy from each werewolf to keep the witches away. It merely feels like a mild hangover."

Roscoe's head drooped mid-chew before jerking back up again.

"Why don't you make yourself some *hair of the dog*, Roscoe?" Darryl flicked a potato wedge at the older werewolf's face. "It'll wake ya right up," he continued, mocking Roscoe's accent.

Roscoe snatched the wedge and popped it into his mouth. "Don't waste food."

"Darius told me to stop off at the station and let Roscoe out, but he mysteriously vanished." She turned to me. "No one knew he was even there to begin with."

My face grew hot as I felt the others' eyes on me.

"Legendary blowjobs. Right," Adam said smugly, lifting Austin's head before sliding the dinner plate out from under him.

"Okay fine. I did a little vironoct manipulation." I punched Roscoe's arm. "Stop antagonizing the mayor. Dumbass."

"How is Austin?" Willa asked, her demeanor growing more serious.

"He's still not able to go to the bathroom on his own," Adam responded, petting his sleeping kuu mate's head. "I'm such an awful person."

I shook my head. "If you were, you would have left him like that instead of taking care of him."

"But I don't want to take care of him, and that's why I feel terrible." He folded his arms on the table and rested his head. "I'm a werewolf now, but I can't even enjoy it."

"He might be able to do basic tasks on his own as soon as the drain wears off," Willa said. "But he'll still not be able to do much more than that without you. Darius mentioned you were going to pursue a wilder alternative to curing Austin."

"And I bet he sent you here to talk us out of it," Darryl said.

"He did, but I don't agree with my husband all the time. The truth is this magic isn't binary. There are many ways to tap into it, and the one who knows everything about elder magic would be the very being responsible for it." Willa paused. "But summoning a prince of hell to get those answers would be a rather bad idea."

"What do you think about the ferals?" I asked. "We've had a few encounters, but we still don't know much about them."

"That's outside of my knowledge as well, I'm afraid. Everything I do for Austin from here on out will only be temporary. The magic Adam used should have never had this effect, even with the corrupting influence of the coven. Magic was the catalyst but not the cause of all of it, nor will it be the solution. Austin has locked himself behind his own source of power, and he refuses to resurface, so no amount of therapy will work either." She sighed and reached across the table to rub the sleeping werewolf's ears. "This is beyond anything we know, but I'm not ruling out the ferals. There's also the risk to think about."

"We know how to ward against those witches," I said. "The ferals gave us those stones I used last night."

"The witches aren't the risk. If Austin stays too long, he'll become feral and won't return. There's also a chance that whatever pack finds him out there will prevent him from going back. Not only that, werewolves feel at home in the woods, more so than they do in civilization. If Austin is reluctant to break through this spell, it might be impossible for him to come back once he's out there and can forget his past."

"They can do that?" I glanced at Roscoe who had fallen asleep sitting up, drool dripping from his hanging tongue. "Can they actually make you forget your past?"

"It's very common, and it's why ferals rarely return. The moment they come back to their old life, there's always an emptiness that can never be filled. They would never fully adjust to life in the town, but I don't think that's necessarily a bad thing. They keep the coven from becoming too unruly with their own unique knowledge. It's why I'm not averse to you seeking them out, but it will be up to you all whether you want to take the risk. He's *your* packmate."

"Would he be happier out there for good?" Adam asked.

We all turned toward him in unison, Darryl and me shooting him glares.

"Maybe it wouldn't be such a bad thing to leave him with the ferals," he continued.

"This isn't a get out of jail free card, Adam," Darryl said. "You won't be able to just leave him out there."

"Why's that?" he asked.

"You're a werewolf now, and you get all of the weird shit that comes along with it." Darryl yawned again, barely able to keep his eyes open. "If you do decide to dump him there, Austin's gonna have to be aware enough to agree to leave the pack, or he'll just follow you back home."

"Do you still really want to leave him?" I asked. "I know you planned on it before, but you guys seemed to be getting closer lately."

"I don't know what I want anymore." Adam's ears fell. "I just want to be happy. I don't think I've ever felt happy."

"Then this might be good for you and Austin in the long run, if this all works out," Willa said. "You both may learn new ways to cope with your problems."

"No way," Adam said. "I'm not going out there. What if they don't let me come back?"

"I'd take him, but he's not listening to me anymore," I said. "You're the only one that can do it."

"But—"

"Or have a mindless werewolf following you every minute of every day, for the rest of your life," Darryl interrupted, his tone growing more impatient. "You decide."

"You don't need to decide right now," Willa said. "Give it time and see if the problem resolves itself."

Adam averted eye contact, his posture submissive. When he'd been a half-turn, it had been hard to pick up on his feelings, but now his emotions were much harder to hide.

Darryl's scornful gaze softened, and he wrapped one arm around Adam, pulling him close.

"Maybe I've been too hard on you. Sorry," he said softly, rocking the smaller werewolf from side to side. "We all fuck up, and we'll keep fucking up for the rest of our lives. You seem like you don't care, but I know you do."

Adam didn't respond, laying his head against Darryl's chest with his eyes closed.

I stood and stretched before shaking Roscoe awake. "Let's go home."

### The Next Day

Darryl's ride pulled into the driveway, and the werewolf slipped a burly arm through one of the straps of his bag while holding his guitar case.

"I wish you could stay," I said, wrapping my arms around him.

"And I wish you guys would move back to the beach. Being away from the ocean is stressing me out."

"You have been a tightass lately. Kinda wish you would go back to being a beach bum that gets high all the time," Roscoe said, smooshing me between him and Darryl. "Is Adam gonna say goodbye?"

"We had a long talk last night, and it's going to be rough for a while." Darryl pulled away and stepped out onto the porch, nodding to me. "You're gonna need to give him some extra attention."

"He's really upset with me, isn't he?"

"Kind of, but you guys will get through it. When he wakes up, I think the two of you should go somewhere to talk alone." Darryl rubbed his hands together as he turned toward the car. "The first thing I'm gonna do when I get back is get stoned and lay on the beach—and maybe wreck some human's ass. We'll see how the day goes."

"Call us when you get there," I said, giving Darryl one last hug.

"I will."

The werewolf trotted across the yard, then tossed his bags and guitar case in the backseat before opening the SUV's passenger side. He gave the man driving a flirty smile before saying something I couldn't hear. The human's eyes widened when Darryl shut the door.

"Hope he's got lube in his bags," Roscoe said, standing next to me.

"I'm sure Darryl doesn't fuck everyone he meets."

"He has this weird way of talking people into it without sayin' much. I knew a human guy once who was straight as a board. After an hour surfing with Darryl, they disappeared somewhere, and later on he was limpin' back to his hotel with one of Darryl's towels around his waist."

"I'm calling bullshit."

"I swear, it's true! Surfers go to the beach to ride the waves, but they always end up ridin' Darryl."

"Was he really as carefree as you said he was earlier? That doesn't seem like him at all."

"Yeah, he was a lot more fun before... Well, you know."

I opened the door and we stepped back inside. The toilet flushed and Austin crept through the hallway toward the living room.

"Austin?" I asked, waiting for Adam to emerge, but he didn't follow. "Did you go to the bathroom all by yourself?"

He didn't respond, tears welling in his emotionless eyes as usual. After staring at nothing for a solid minute, he finally sat down on the sofa.

"Maybe he's getting better," I said, turning to Roscoe who grabbed a plate of cold bacon from the table. "What are you doing?"

"A little test," he said, holding the plate in front of Austin's nose. "Ya hungry big guy?"

The blond werewolf's stomach growled, and Roscoe sat the plate in his lap before backing away. We observed him for about five minutes, hoping he'd start eating, but he showed no interest.

"Nope. He's still fucked. No werewolf I know can resist a plate of bacon."

"Well, he's going to the bathroom on his own. That's a start." I stood behind the sofa, rubbing Austin's ears. "I sure hope they can help him."

"He'll either snap out of it, or he'll end up stayin' out there. Nothing we can really do."

"We were just starting to get close."

"That's somethin' I've been wondering about. How close did you guys end up gettin'?" Roscoe eyed me from the side.

"He was opening up about everything, showing some real emotion." I let out a slight chuckle. "He even said he was in love with me. That's something you'd never expect to hear from Austin."

"Ahh," Roscoe said in his usual tone. "I figured as much." With a smile, he padded toward the kitchen. I followed, watched as he opened the cabinet and grabbed the half-empty bottle of habanero sauce. "I'm gonna make him something special fer breakfast."

"Roscoe, no," I shouted. "We had a long talk about it, and we came to an understanding." I snatched the bottle out of his hands. "Can you just say what's on your mind instead of trying to kill people with hot sauce?"

"I'm makin' breakfast."

"You already made breakfast."

"Second breakfast." He grabbed the bacon grease-covered frying pan and a large bowl. "I'm in the mood for hoecakes. Ever have those?"

I pushed myself between him and the stove. "I've noticed a pattern here. Every time you're upset, you eat."

"Yer wrong. I ain't upset." His stomach growled as he gently pushed me aside. "I'm hungry."

"Do you love me?"

Roscoe's eyes shifted, but he kept his face forward. "That's a loaded question."

"Really? Seems pretty straightforward to me."

"We should just enjoy the day," he said, turning the burner to medium. "It's real pretty outside."

My face grew hot. That had come off a bit forced, and I kind of understood why he avoided answering. Things would get awkward regardless, and I wasn't sure how I'd react to it. To lighten the mood, I quickly changed the subject.

"So... What the hell is a hoecake?"

Later that evening we all gathered around the fire pit, and Austin gazed silently into the flames with Adam in the chair next to him.

"I can't take this anymore," Adam said, breaking the silence. "I want to get him to the ferals tomorrow, but I don't know where they are."

"Neither do we," I said, looking over at Roscoe. "We still have Austin's beer in the garage refrigerator. We might be able to attract them."

"Uhh..."

"You drank all the beer, didn't you?"

"Darryl helped!"

"What else do they like?" Adam asked. "We've got those porterhouse steaks in the freezer."

Roscoe slinked forward in his seat, showing all the signs of a dog that had just chewed up an expensive duvet. Adam and I glared at him.

"Sorry! I get hungry when I'm stressed."

"And happy. And sad. And horny," Adam added. "Maybe you could talk Willa into another barbeque discount."

Roscoe's ears perked up.

"You're getting nothing," I said. "In fact, you're not even allowed to help us carry it into the woods."

"What if we don't find them tomorrow, and we have to sleep out there?" Adam asked. "And Boss Hog decides to have a midnight snack?"

"I ain't gonna eat any of it." Roscoe gritted his teeth. "Could I at least eat the French fries? They don't keep well."

"We're not ordering fries," I said.

"They come with the meal. Yer gettin' the meal, ain't ya?"

"We are getting meat."

"No soda?" Roscoe asked. "Remember how much they liked the bubbles?"

"It'll go flat by the time we find them. We'll pick up some two liters at the store." The bit of drool hanging from Austin's mouth made me remember something else. "We should get a few bags of white cheddar popcorn, too."

"We've got like five bags of that stuff in the pantry," Adam said.

Roscoe's eyes widened as he turned to the smaller werewolf and shook his head.

"What?"

"We do?" I asked. "I didn't see any."

"Roscoe hides them, but I smelled one of the open bags on the top shelf behind the oatmeal."

I shot Roscoe another glare.

"I know we talked about my junk food problem, but it's just popcorn. Plus, you hide shit all the time. You think I don't know about yer coffee?"

"What about all the cupcake snacks in your closet behind those old-people discs?" Adam asked.

"I don't know what yer talkin' about." Roscoe nervously cleared his throat. "And they're called records. Why were you in our closet?"

"Because you have that weird sex stuff, and I was curious."

"All right," I said, clapping my hands together. "We'll have barbeque, and all of Roscoe's junk food to trade. That'll save us a trip to the store."

Roscoe let out a dog-like whine.

"And you're no longer allowed to go grocery shopping without me."

"I am four times yer age, young man!" Roscoe protested.

"We can't be blowing our budget on food we don't need. I know werewolves are pretty resilient, but eating all this stuff can't be good for you."

"I'm as healthy as a horse!"

"And you weigh about as much as one," Adam chimed in, looking down at the lawn chair Roscoe sat in. "Every time you sit out here, those legs bow so much that Darryl and I were taking bets on when they'd give out."

Lately, I hadn't been noticing as much weight gain since I was around him all the time, but now that it was front and center, it was all I could see. It wasn't like I was grossed out or anything—in fact, his extra girth was really nice to cuddle with at night.

Roscoe looked down at his gut and gave it a pat with both hands. "Almost ready for winter."

"Do werewolves hibernate?" I asked.

"This one does," Roscoe answered. "Mmm, I can't wait. Hot chocolate. Turkey. Cookies. Oh!" He stood and gave a wide, toothy grin. "I just got an idea you might enjoy, Cody."

"Where are you going?" I asked.

"I'm feelin' festive all of a sudden."

He opened the door and disappeared inside.

"I guess that's my cue," I said, about to stand and follow Roscoe, but Adam put up his hands.

"Wait. Can we talk for a little bit?"

"Sure." I lowered myself back into the seat.

"I haven't been able to sleep. Every time I close my eyes, I remember what I did to him. He was acting so sweet, and I don't know what came over me."

"What happened, exactly? How did you end up in the woods?"

Adam's ears fell. "When Austin took off his costume, I got annoyed and left the party. I was already feeling like crap, but I'd just been wanting to go into the woods lately, like something was calling me. I think Austin knew I was about to turn. That's why he followed. Have you ever had swollen gums?"

I nodded, remembering my first night as a half-turn.

"The only thing that helped ease the pain was sex. It was kind of weird the way he changed, like he was doing this stuff out of instinct. Our bodies were completely in sync with one another, and after I finished turning, I heard a woman. She asked if I wanted to do what you could do, and she told me how to do it. Everything after that was fuzzy except the moment I grabbed Austin's dog tags and everything went white. He screamed, Cody. It was like I'd stabbed him or something, but the voice kept telling me this was what he wanted."

Adam patted Austin's head, and the larger werewolf's tail swayed a bit. That was the first reaction I'd seen in a while.

"Do you remember anything after that?"

He shook his head. "Just fragments of what seemed like a dream. Fire. Crosses. Voices. Then when I was out of the woods, I realized it wasn't a nightmare." Adam looked up at me and wiped his eyes. "Darryl told me what you did. I never had a friend that would let me borrow his shirt, let alone risk his life for me."

"You're like my little brother," I said, scooting my chair next to him. "You can be a real pain in the ass, but I still love you. I don't want you to leave, and I don't want anything bad to happen to you. Either of you."

"I always thought you were this lame nag, always bossing us around."

I smiled, waiting for him to finish, but he just looked at me.

"But?"

"But what?" he asked. "You're a lame nag, always bossing us around." I let out an annoyed groan, and he wrapped his thicker arm around me. "But I still love you, and I don't want anything bad to happen to you either." He pulled away and scratched his head. "Would you even be considered a big brother now that I'm taller than you? You're the new pipsqueak of the house."

"Thanks," I muttered, then jumped out of the chair when Roscoe yelled something incomprehensible from inside.

He screamed again, and I dashed through the door, nearly colliding with him as he frantically flailed about.

"What the hell is wrong with you?" I asked, trying to grab his arm, but he kept running in circles, covering his crotch.

"Bad idea! Baaaad idea!" He ran into the bathroom and turned on the tap before shoving his dick under the faucet. It looked like he had painted it with red and white stripes using gel food coloring. "Oh my God! That's worse!" He pulled away and ran back into the bedroom, leaving behind a strong scent trail of peppermint.

"What did you do, Roscoe?"

"I wanted to make ya a candy caa-aane."

"Did you pour peppermint oil on yourself?"

Roscoe nodded with a whine.

"You really are an idiot."

"Ye-e-e-eees!" Roscoe cried out with tears in his eyes. "It won't stop burnin'! Help!"

"Good thing it's just oil. Get in the shower, I'll go grab the dish soap."

# Chapter 30

# Hunger

The weather couldn't have been more perfect for November. The air was crisp but not frigid, and the sky was a solid sapphire blue whenever we'd step into a clearing. The forest was thick in some places and thinning into small, grassy meadows in others. Austin and Roscoe carried supplies for trade on their backs while Adam and I brought along all our necessities. We each wore an enchanted stone just in case of unwanted encounters, but there hadn't been a trace of anyone for hours. No witches, no werewolves. Even the birds were quiet. The only sounds were our heavy footsteps and the wind rustling through the colorful canopy.

"Maybe they only come out at night, like last time," I said, turning to Roscoe in time to see him lick drool away from the corners of his mouth. "Don't even think about it."

"It's all I *can* think about. Maybe a little snack cake'll tide me over." He gave the air a sniff and reached for Austin's bag. The larger werewolf growled and jerked away. "C'mon, just one."

"No. One turns into ten with you." I patted Austin on the back. The one good thing to come of this magic was how well he obeyed the command to not allow Roscoe near his bag.

"Ugh. Blood sugar's so low. I'm gonna pass out."

"Oh, stop with the theatrics. You ate an hour ago. If you're that hungry, go hunt a deer or something. You know, like a werewolf *should* be able to do."

"Then I'd have to skin it, butcher it, build a fire—" Roscoe let out a sigh. "I didn't bring my spices."

"Can't you just eat it the way it is?" I asked. Roscoe wrinkled his nose, pretending to gag. "You're supposed to be a bloodthirsty monster."

"In the bedroom," Roscoe added. "I ain't killing and eating a whole deer without cookin' it. I ain't *that* hungry."

"That's gross, Cody," Adam said from behind.

"What the hell—"

"Yeah," Roscoe interrupted. "You go kill a deer and eat it like an animal if that's what gets you goin'."

"Oh, come on!"

"Would that count as being racist?" Adam said to Roscoe, speaking over me. "Or species-ist?"

"I'm a half-turn, you idiots," I shouted. "And this is the dumbest conversation."

"Definitely," Roscoe said, ignoring me. "And I bet he wants us to do all that while he gets to eat all the human snacks."

Adam and Roscoe cracked smiles at one another, while I became more frustrated.

"One cake," I muttered.

"Get me one too," Adam said. "Better make that two more. I'm sure Austin's a little hungry."

"If we run out of things to trade, that's on you guys."

"We brought most of the pantry with us," Roscoe said, reaching for the bag on Austin's back, prompting another snarl. "Uh, you better say the magic words."

Adam ran in front of Austin, looking him in the eye. "Let Roscoe into your bag just this once."

The other werewolf nodded, and Roscoe reached into the backpack, snatching several cakes before slowly backing away.

"Better make it one more," I said, holding out my hand.

"Couldn't resist, huh?" He slapped one of them into my palm.

"Well, they are the Christmas tree-shaped ones," I said, then tore open the package with my teeth. "They don't make them all year, and they taste better for some reason."

Adam popped one of the cakes into his mouth and chewed. "I haven't celebrated the holidays in years."

"It's been a while for me too," I said, thinking back on the last six years I'd spent alone, watching festive movies while eating turkey TV dinners.

"I used to get high under that big Christmas tree on Main Street until the cops would kick me out," Roscoe said with his usual grin, though this one seemed more forced than usual. "I haven't cooked a huge Thanksgiving dinner in years. Maybe when all this is over, I'll cook us all a holiday meal."

"If we can get Austin back," Adam muttered.

A sniffle broke the chatter, and we turned toward Austin as he began crying. At first, I thought he was responding to Adam's concern, but his expression was blank, as usual.

We all stared into the dancing flames of the campfire. On one side of me was Roscoe who gave off so much heat I had to slip halfway out of my jacket, and on the other side was Adam, who kept dozing off and drooling on my shoulder. Austin sat up straight, his blue eyes remaining locked onto the flames as his ears pulled back into an almost fearful position. I wondered what was going through his mind—if anything.

We wanted to stay up, hoping the fire would attract the ferals, but the later it got, the more I doubted they were interested. After my last conversation with that elder, the prospects were grim.

*Go back to the Midna.*

My answers to the feral's questions that day only seemed to annoy him.

"I think it's time we get some shut eye," Roscoe said, pulling me closer to him. "I got my hoodie, and it's big enough that I can zip you up in it, too."

"Did you wash it?"

"It's got all my good stink in it. I told you that last time."

"Pass," I muttered. Roscoe laid next to me as Adam dozed off on my shoulder again. "Hey," I said, giving the smaller werewolf a shake. "Don't forget to tell Austin to go to sleep."

He nodded and whispered a command. After a moment of shuffling, Adam fell asleep in Austin's embrace, both of them starting to snore. This would have been cuter had they both done this voluntarily.

"They're not going to come," I whispered to Roscoe. "They probably don't want to get involved with the Midna any more than they have to."

"Aw shucks. Guess we'll have to eat that barbecue then."

I lay next to him and rubbed his stomach while kissing him on the nose. "Maybe. I know *you'll* be happy."

"Talking about the holidays got me thinkin'."

"About the food?" I asked, giving him a slight shove.

Roscoe smiled and sniffed my head. "Nah. I'm thinkin' about how nice it'll be to spend it with you."

That made me smile. "When's the last time you spent it with anyone?"

"Sober?" he asked. "Don't remember. What about you?"

"The last holiday I spent with anyone was when I lived with my aunt for a few months. After I graduated, I left that town and started a life by myself." I turned all the way toward him. "Remember when we first met and you said I had a loose ass?"

Roscoe chuckled. "I just said that to get under yer skin."

"There weren't that many guys before—well, none that ever wanted to stick around. I didn't even expect you to stick around, but two enchanted earrings and a bunch of amazing sex later, here we are."

"You regret it?"

I shook my head. "That's the weird thing. I don't."

"I knew it was only a matter of time before the seeds of my charming personality would grow on ya."

"More like the spores of a particularly smelly fungus," I added, my thoughts shifting to something else. "I wonder if Austin celebrated the holidays after everything that happened to him."

"Sometimes I just wanna give the guy a hug and not let go," Roscoe whispered. "I wonder why life can be so nasty to some and so good to others. It's like there's only so much goodness in the world to go around, and those with everything suck the rest of it away, and they don't even know it. They just go about their lives ignorant, thinkin' their petty problems are the end of the world when they don't even know what real problems are."

"This year, we're gonna take some of that goodness for ourselves," I said, snuggling against Roscoe's chest. "We deserve at least that much."

The ground was unbearably cold. I shivered, struggling to open my eyes. The others were gone and so was the campfire. With a groan, I pushed myself upright and looked up at an unfamiliar canopy as waning moonlight streamed in through the mist. My hand grazed a small leather sack on the ground, and I picked it up, the familiar scent of psychedelic herbs stinging my nostrils.

A pair of eyes glowing amber stared at me from the shadows, waiting.

"Where am I?" I called out. No response, which was not surprising. The feral wasn't going to emerge until I'd taken the herbs, so I reached into the bag and pinched a small amount, tucking it between my gums and cheek like last time.

In an instant, the moonlight brightened into a multitude of colors, glowing moths and neon-like lines flitting around me. Though I knew it was still dark, I could see the feral clearly as he watched from the trees.

He was gigantic and black with braids and feathers in his mane. He wore a leather harness with about six small sacks hanging from it as well as a frayed belt with two larger sacks on both sides. The werewolf ambled languidly on his pawed feet before sitting on a hollow log next to me, his heft causing it to creak a bit. It wasn't often that I saw werewolves bigger than Austin, but this one would have towered at least a foot over him.

"Hello," I said, my voice sounding as it had while under the effects of this drug.

"Cody..." He growled my name so deeply it vibrated the ground. He reached for my chest and gently lifted the enchanted stone Roscoe had made into a necklace for me. "Come home?"

"We came here for help."

"Help?" He looked around. "No witches."

"A friend of mine did something he shouldn't have done using the vironoct. He was under the influence of witches, and now another friend can't break the magic."

"Hmm," the feral mumbled, scratching his head. "Under witch's control?"

"It's not witchcraft."

The feral stood and waved me forward before walking toward the scent of smoke. Keeping the herbs in my mouth, I followed him as the colorful path brightened even more. I tapped the werewolf on the arm and pointed to Austin lying next to the fire.

"He needs your help."

The elder didn't respond as he approached, rather knelt next to the blond werewolf and placed a hand softly on Austin's head. He stayed like that for about five minutes before looking back at me.

"What do you think?" I asked.

His irises brightened to a brilliant silver, and the colors around me turned solid white.

"Sleep," a deep voice whispered inside of my head.

*Austin*

Every day was the same. I didn't care what Adam did to my body as long as I couldn't feel. Since I'd been here, locked in my blue box, there had been no more sleepless nights. There had been no more waking nightmares.

I was unlovable. If the kuu didn't exist, I wouldn't have anyone, and there were times I wondered if that would have been so bad. I let my guard down with Adam. When we met, I felt something for him, but he ended up being like everyone else. If he was going to hurt me, I'd hurt him. It made me feel better to make him hurt, but he set me free by putting me here. My comfortable blue box where people can't hurt me anymore.

With a wave of my hand, the handle of a cleaver materialized, and it was heavy against my palm. I swung the blade, hewing my left arm until it lay lifeless on the blue floor. I couldn't feel anything; the arm turned human and faded away before reappearing back on my body.

The person who hurt me most was me, and I couldn't stop crying. Hurting this body brought me short-lived vindication. Whenever I'd want to feel it again, I'd remove another limb. They always grew back.

I didn't know reality anymore, and I would see faces and hear voices. Most of the time, the only face that came through was Cody's, so I'd claw out my eyes. I'd opened myself, and he'd rejected me.

I lopped off a leg, and it fell with a muffled thud. As expected, the limb turned fleshy before disappearing and reappearing on my body.

This place was like purgatory. Terrifying but comfortable.

Every so often I'd come to the realization that this may have been death, but the moment I started to feel anything, another dismemberment would make me forget about it. When I'd see the blood drip from my wounds, I didn't feel relieved. I kept reliving that horror over and over again until I wasn't afraid anymore.

When Adam put me in my blue box, my mother came, and the gun I remembered from then appeared in my hand. I aimed, and she fell lifeless to the floor, disappearing and reappearing. I'd scream each time I relived it until the tears stopped. Then another phantom would surface. My brother—still frozen as a child. Again, I'd pull the trigger, and again I'd scream.

Over and over, people I'd once loved would visit only to die, and now all that was left was me. I knew it was only a matter of time before I'd finally be able to put an end to this, but something kept me from doing it. No matter how many times I tried to stop crying, I couldn't.

Why couldn't I stop?

*Cody*

I woke once more in front of a fire. The four of us lay in a row next to one another, but we weren't at our campsite. Above me was a rocky ceiling partially obscured by smoke; toward the entrance of the small cavern, dappled sunlight danced its way along the smooth floor.

"Roscoe," I said, trying to shake the werewolf awake. He didn't respond. I turned to Adam, who was lying on his stomach, and rolled him onto his back. He was like a breathing corpse, not waking no matter what I did. I gently pried one of his eyelids open with my thumbs, revealing a pale, blue glow.

The scent of herbs mixed with morning breath hit me as I separated Adam's jaws and discovered a wad of saliva-soaked greens along his black gum line. A small sack fell to my side, and I turned toward the elder I'd encountered last night sitting in the shadow of a rocky pillar.

Eager for an explanation, I pinched the herbs and tucked them between my cheek. Reality morphed into a burst of colors, and heightening senses enough that I saw more feral werewolves sitting along the back wall of the cavern.

"Where did you bring us?" I asked, resting against the warm cave wall.

"Home," the elder said, his giant maw slowly forming a grin. He was so huge, it was almost unsettling. We were warned they might not let us leave, but it was too early to jump to that conclusion.

"We didn't come here to live. We came here for help."

"If you have come here for help, that means you are helpless. The Whasha are your family and your salvation. Why would you not want to stay?"

I gave that question a lot more scrutiny, careful with my response.

"It's not the right time. I'm not ready to give up my memories or my way of life."

"That all depends on you," he said, his speech meticulous. "When everything is complete, I will know."

"When what is?"

The giant werewolf pointed to the other three lying unconscious on the floor. "I have reached in and pulled to the surface each of your pasts." He slowly climbed to his feet, taking care not to hit his head on the rocky ceiling. With a few strides, he sat directly in front of me and pointed at Roscoe. "Starting with him."

"How is this going to help Austin?"

"You are all corrupted, and no amount of barriers or wards will prevent the inevitable." He ran his fingers over Austin's leg. "This one is lucky, but you all have heard the voices. The coven knows when they see weakness, and they will come for you again. You will endure the ritual. Whether you fail or succeed, time will tell."

"What happens if it fails?"

"Then each of your memories will be sealed, and your pack will remain with us."

A feral sitting quietly out of sight padded over and handed the elder a smoking pipe. The giant werewolf drew in deep and exhaled a puff of pastels that sparked like a damaged electric wire.

"I do not know what past has been locked away in your friend's mind, but whatever is there, you must help him heal. You are the leader of your pack, and your strength is their strength. If they fail, you fail."

"Wait a minute—"

With a deep draw, he exhaled into my face. The last thing I remembered were two silver irises turning a deep shade of red.

*If they fail, you fail. Your fate is their fate.*

The muggy, stale air wrapped around my body like a still damp blanket that had been in the dryer, my bedsheets drenched in sweat. I examined my surroundings. Sluggish mosquitos made their way in and out of the screenless window of a run-down bedroom. A tan teenaged boy in faded overalls stood in front of a dusty dresser mirror, brushing the knots out of his unruly brown hair. He looked to be about fifteen and was a few inches shorter than me.

He stopped brushing and examined his chin, picking at the darker bits of facial hair that stood out among the peach fuzz. The most striking things about him were his eyes. One was hazel, the other a golden amber color. His appearance must have been unusual to him as well considering how long he stared at himself.

"Yer gonna be late," came a female voice from down the hall.

"Why do I gotta go to school, Ma?" the boy asked, dropping the brush onto the scratched-up wood of the dresser as he walked out of the bedroom.

Confused, I jumped from the bed and made my way through the old, wooden house until I was in a small kitchen with a rusty, cast-iron wood-burning stove. The boy sat at a crooked table, and a young woman with long, red hair and fair skin walked over to him while holding a plate. It held a single hoe cake with a tiny dab of butter.

"Hello?" I asked, trying to get their attention, but neither seemed aware of my presence. I walked up to the woman and waved a hand in front of her face, but she walked through me as though I were made of mist before setting the plate in front of the boy.

"You should be lucky," she said, turning back to the stove. "Your pa left us just enough to get by, and you should finish yer education."

"Ain't no point. You can be an educated war hero in this country and still die not havin' enough food."

The woman dropped a bowl in a wooden tub filled with dingy water. "We may be hungry, but we ain't starvin'. Yer pa's parents came to this country from real poverty, and even the worst times here don't compare to other places. We're free here."

"Free to starve." The boy quickly devoured the fried dough and stood from his chair. "If this is the best there is, then I don't want to be a part of it no more."

"Roscoe!" the woman shouted as the boy darted from the house, letting the door slam behind him. Even though I'd heard *Roscoe*, she'd uttered something else. Roscoe wasn't his real name, but I couldn't understand what it was.

He was so different, not just physically, but in the way he spoke. There was this anger as well as hopelessness. It was as though I could feel his every emotion. The room faded and I followed the boy along a dirt road with a dried-up cornfield on one side and dying rows of sorghum on the other.

The sun blazed overhead. Roscoe wandered off the path toward the shade of a huge oak, the Spanish moss hanging from each branch like graying wizard beards. There was no wind and hardly any clouds to provide relief from the sweltering heat.

The boy's stomach rumbled as he sat on a knobby root and folded his arms over his knees, laying his head against them. It was odd to see Roscoe so thin—way too thin. I could feel his hunger as a dull but persistent pain.

I sat next to him as he softly cried, and gently placed a hand on his back. This time, I was able to touch him. He was so emaciated that I could feel the bumps along his spine. The overwhelming misery coupled with the hunger and heat made me want to do anything to put an end to it. This memory faded as though I were in a play, and I was once again in Roscoe's bedroom.

He stood in front of the mirror, a little older but just as lanky, his darker and thicker facial hair taking over the prepubescent lighter hair from before. Both eyes were now a deep gold, and he brushed the frizzy knots from his longer brown hair.

There were no sounds from the kitchen or any other part of the old house, only the incessant buzzing of cicadas from outside. Roscoe laid the brush on the dresser and slowly walked into the kitchen, me following close behind. The wood stove looked like it hadn't been used in a while, and the young man leaned over the wooden tub. He stared out the kitchen window to a clearing in the yard at two piles of stones. As if following a path of habit, he sat at the table with an empty plate, pretending to eat.

"I ain't goin' to school no more, Ma." Roscoe pushed the plate away and looked up at no one. "I don't look right, do I?"

As I went to say something, he spoke again.

"This don't feel like home no more. I always get this feelin' like maybe I ain't supposed to be here. I know you didn't mean to leave me, Mama. You didn't wanna leave me." Tears fell from his face, pattering against the rough wood of the small table. "I sure miss you."

My eyes watered as I approached him.

"Roscoe," I whispered, placing my hand on his head. "Can you hear me?"

He smiled through the tears but still didn't acknowledge me. The room faded away and another memory played out. This time, I was in a strange rural area, surrounded by flat, dry land, the sky choked with brown dust. Roscoe was older and slightly thicker as he walked along a dirt path, his upper body and head covered in a ratty coat that almost resembled a hoodie. Dirty cloth covered his nose and mouth, but he couldn't hide his eyes. Two irises glowed a dark orange and the whites had darkened to black, giving his shrouded silhouette a demon-like appearance.

Though he seemed less starved than before, I could still feel his hunger as he pushed onward with no destination in mind. He was looking for something, but he didn't know what. It was close, and that was all he knew. That was what kept him going even when he wanted to stop.

The poverty and desolation coupled with the suffocating dust storms made me realize what time period we were in. Roscoe must have been around seventeen or eighteen, given the fact that he was approaching the final stages of his transformation.

He pushed on, but his legs trembled with each step through the howling winds. Ahead was a billowing wall of brown dust as a strong haboob sandblasted the plains. Visibility soon dropped to nothing, but Roscoe kept going, taking one trembling step after another before finally falling to the ground.

"Roscoe," I shouted, kneeling next to him. I tried grabbing his arm, but he wouldn't budge. Hunger, dehydration, and exhaustion overwhelmed me as I tried to speak, getting a mouthful of sand. I understood the spell I was under. Everything he felt during these memories, I also felt. Hopelessness nearly engulfed me until a large figure appeared feet away.

It was hard to make out at first, but as the figure approached, it took on the form of a feral werewolf clad in leather harnesses and feathers, his paw-like feet making easy work of the sandy terrain. He knelt next to Roscoe, holding a bladder of water to his mouth.

The young half-turn gulped it down and looked up at the startlingly huge creature, knowing he had finally found what he had come all this way for. The memory went dark, but another soon took its place. Roscoe was underneath the feral who had rescued him, barely lit by the moon.

He writhed in pain and pleasure as they both mated, and I could feel Roscoe's transformation. It didn't last long, and when it was over, two werewolves licked at each other. The face of a newly turned Roscoe looked more familiar now, but his fur was dark brown, and his feet were large paws. They spoke to each other in a series of familiar grunts, growls, and whines as they stared up at the sky.

These visions had one thing in common: they were tragic. As Roscoe grabbed the feral's hand, I knew this wasn't going to have a happy ending.

"I don't want to do this anymore," I shouted. "I can't."

The scene faded to a cold and grainy black.

# Chapter 31

# Head Hopping

*Adam*

I froze, terrified, huddling in a small doorway. The man who just murdered two children put the revolver to his own head and pulled the trigger, sending blood and fragments of bone against the adjacent wall.

More blood than I'd ever seen soaked the old carpet of the single-wide trailer I'd somehow ended up inside. I wanted to throw up and look away, but the blond child was still alive, twitching and taking rapid, shallow breaths. I dashed to his side, though I was afraid to touch something so fragile. There was no way someone could survive something like that, right?

Sirens called from down the road, and the front door exploded inward as men in uniform stormed the place, their guns raised.

They crept through the small, cramped space toward the room I was in. I threw up my hands. However, they didn't seem to notice me. Two officers stepped inside the room and examined the scene, one covering his mouth as if about to vomit.

"Multiple homicide victims," he said into the radio, barely keeping his composure. He knelt next to the man still clutching the gun. "Possible murder-suicide but keep an eye out for anyone else in the vicinity."

The blond boy moved again, and both officers knelt beside him, one of them checking for a pulse. He held the radio to his mouth again.

"Dispatch, we need an eleven forty-one."

The room disappeared, and I was left sick and confused by what I'd just witnessed, not sure whether to burst into tears or run. This wasn't some kind of bad trip or nightmare. This felt real. I even smelled the blood, the gunpowder, and the stale cigarette smoke. All I could do was go along with whatever this was.

An invisible force dragged me through the darkness until I was in a cold fluorescent-lit room full of medical equipment. The child I'd seen earlier lay unconscious in a hospital bed, kept alive by countless tubes and machines. The ventilator whooshed in time with the steady beep of his weak vital signs.

Keeping my distance, I looked around the room for a nurse or family member, but there was no one. The kid was in a coma all alone. The hands of the clock on the wall quickened as the light outside disappeared. Two nurses entered, both trying not to look at the boy too much.

"Thanks for helping," the younger brunette nurse said, clearing her throat. She looked to be in her mid-thirties; the other one was much older. "I keep thinking about my kids. Every time I leave this place, I go home and tell them how much I love them." She laughed and wiped her nose with a tissue. "They're getting really sick of it."

"Why don't you check room 102 and see if Mrs. Allen needs anything."

The younger woman nodded and quickly left, not looking back. The older nurse stoically changed the empty bag of saline for another before holding onto the child's hand.

"You may not have any family, but we love you little Austin—"

It felt like a huge needle was being jabbed into my chest as I stepped closer to the child. This couldn't have been my Austin. He was so small.

"You're not alone, so come back to us." The woman kissed his forehead and slowly walked out of the room, letting the door come to a soft rest against the frame.

"Austin?" I whispered, my face close to his. I could deny all I wanted, but I began to understand what I was experiencing. I was being punished in the worst way.

With a trembling, padded hand, I slipped it over his tiny one as I sat on the chair next to the bed. He was so cold, and if it weren't for the machine saying otherwise, I would have thought he died hours ago. "Why didn't you tell me?"

"I *tried*," Austin's adult voice whispered in my head.

Tears soaked my face as I leaned further into him. "You were just a little kid. This shouldn't happen to little kids."

His eyes snapped open, startling me enough that I jumped out of the chair. He stayed still, but the intensity and terror on his face drilled into me as the room and everything in it faded away. The hands on the clock spun so rapidly they lost form, time speeding along. People popped in and out of existence.

Finally, the clock slowed to normal, and I was in another room. The once little boy was a few years older now, his eyes open but not a lot behind them as he lay at an incline, a bit of dried crust along the corners of his cracked lips.

"How's our patient today?" a middle-aged male doctor asked, looking through the charts. "I feel sorry for you. It's been three years, you're still in PVS, and we're legally obligated to keep you alive." The doctor's tone was ice as he checked Austin's vitals. The child was unresponsive. "Not even the worst people in the world should have to live like this, let alone a child."

The doctor left the room, and I sat next to Austin, holding his slightly warmer hand again. Though he seemed awake, he wasn't *there*, letting out quiet moans every so often. This was agony.

"I'm so sorry, Austin."

The child moaned again but continued to stare at the wall.

"Is this really what happened to you, or is this my guilt eating me alive?"

He turned until his eyes locked with mine, and all consciousness seemed to flood into him as he opened his mouth to speak.

*Roscoe*

This was weird. Don't remember gettin' high before going to bed, but as I sat in a pew surrounded by crazy motherfuckers screamin' nonsense, I started having my doubts. Only the strongest shit would've made me comfortable being there. Still, no one seemed to notice a huge werewolf stinkin' up the place. Then they brought out the snakes...

Why the hell did they have snakes in a church? Wasn't that like inviting Satan or somethin'?

"'Scuse me," I said, clearing my throat as I scooted between the pew down a burgundy carpet. Still no one paid me mind as they hooted and hollered, jumping around while shaking cabasas and banging bead drums. Last time I'd seen something this insane, Darryl and I'd overdid it on the peyote tea in Sedona. That was sure a *one-and-done* experience, especially when we threw up all over each other.

As I neared the doors, a little boy near the altar, probably not more than seven, caught my gaze. He had thick, dark brown hair, neatly combed back while wearin' his Sunday best. Just a plain white dress shirt with what looked like an oil stain, and a red tie with black slacks and those shiny dress shoes that always sounded squeaky when people would walk in 'em. He was scared and crying, and I immediately noticed the bruises over his eyes and on his arms.

"The Holy Spirit keeps me safe, so too can it cast out demons of disobedience."

The kid was shakin' like a leaf, but he didn't say nothin' as the man approached him.

"In the name of the holy spirit, I cast you out." The back of his hand slammed into the kid's face, and he fell to the floor without a sound.

"Hey!" I shouted, runnin' to the stage. I didn't often get violent, but if I saw a grown man lay his hands on a child, all bets were off.

My fist went through him like he was made of air.

So I *was* high. Never had a hallucination so real before.

The kid groaned and rubbed his head, and I knelt next to him to pick him up. For some reason, I could touch him. "You okay, kid?"

He shuffled away and wiped the tears from his eyes before looking up at me. "Roscoe?"

With a gasp, I let him go, and the whole room went dark and quiet. The way he said my name gave me chills. It was higher pitched, and he was holding back tears, but that was definitely Cody's voice.

"No way," I whispered as another hallucination appeared. I tried pinching myself, and it hurt, but it didn't do nothin' to snap me out of this.

Before I could blink, the church disappeared and a run-down mobile home just poofed into existence with me on the front lawn. There was trash everywhere, and the grass was overgrown. A rusted old Thunderbird sat under a big oak tree, its tires flat and windows broken, weeds and vines growin' out of it. I'd seen neighborhoods like this before, and the kids that grew up in 'em never had good childhood stories.

A man and woman were yellin' at each other inside the old, run-down home, glass shattering. Bein' the nosy SOB I was, I couldn't resist a good domestic disturbance. I'd lived on the streets near a few trailer parks, and it was always entertaining for days—when there weren't no children involved.

When I opened the door, the smell of meth, weed, and alcohol hit me, really taking me back. The man looked like an older version of Cody, except he was sickly thin with messy long brown hair and a few missin' front teeth and the rest of the teeth startin' to rot. The woman had fairer skin and blond hair with bags under her sunken-in eyes. These were hallmark junkies, and just by lookin' at the yellow tinge in the man's sclera, he wasn't long for this world.

As the fighting grew violent, my attention fell to a little boy peeking out from his cracked bedroom door. There weren't no tears in his eyes, just wide-eyed fear. This was the childhood Cody never wanted to talk about, and all I wanted to do was block out the noise for him.

Just walking through the house was kinda hard. It was like wanderin' a landfill of old pizza boxes, trash bags, ripped up papers, makeshift pipes made from coke bottles. And then there were the needles. A crooked, single-tiered birthday cake sat on a wobbling dining room table with nine candles shoved in it that had been freshly blown out. It was the poor kid's birthday, and I'm sure I knew what he wished for.

Things were really startin' to make a lot of sense. I walked into his bedroom—the only clean area in the house, but there was only so much he could do with what he had. His arms were bruised with bed bug bites, and an occasional roach scurried across the floor before disappearing into another crack in the wall.

"Hey, little Cody," I said as a loud thud hit the wall in the living room. I shut the door all the way. "Happy birthday buddy."

He didn't look at me. He didn't say nothin'. He just stared at the door as if he was waiting for something, and that something came barreling in screaming at him.

Before I could react, I ended up outside watchin' two boys sit under a run-down shed in the middle of bumfuck nowhere, looking out across the ugliest plains I'd ever seen. There weren't hardly no trees, just some nasty-looking storm clouds in the distance.

"I'm not allowed to hang out with you anymore," a boy said to the older kid who looked like Cody. He was taller with black hair and a jock-like physique. "It was fun though."

Cody didn't say nothin'.

"We knew this wasn't going to work, and we told each other that if one of us got found out, we'd stop."

"Things change. All those things you said. I actually believed them. You were never going to run away with me."

"And do what? Drop out of school and give up my scholarship? Hitchhike and be homeless?"

Cody looked at the gravel, his eyes almost empty.

"I'm not ruining my life just to have a fling with some guy from high school." He stood up from the bench and took a few steps outta the shelter into the sun. "I shouldn't even be here, but I wanted to make sure you understood that this is it. I don't even want you looking at me when we're in school."

Cody took a deep breath and closed his eyes.

"I'm sorry," the other kid added.

"Just go away."

The other boy cleared his throat and turned, hopping into an old pickup truck before speeding off.

Cody stayed on the bench, watching the truck disappear over a hill. As devastated as he looked, he didn't cry. He picked his backpack off the ground and set it next to him before giving the zipper a tug. He reached inside and grabbed a flimsy plastic bakery container. It held a colorful birthday cake with a candle and the number seventeen on it, and it was small enough for two people. Watching him hold onto it while lookin' like he'd lost everything nearly broke me.

"I'm not going to make it one more year if I stay," Cody whispered before opening the container and lighting the candle. "I wish... I hope I never have to spend another birthday alone." He blew out the flame and threw the cake in the trashcan next to him. That was when everything went black.

"You won't," I whispered, reaching for the place Cody was sitting as I wiped my eyes. Why hadn't he ever told me about any of this? "You just wait, little Cody. I'm gonna make you the best birthday cake you ever had, and you won't ever be alone again."

My little blue box disappeared right as I was about to take a nap. I heard something I didn't want to hear. Someone else's voice.

"Mom! Adam won't play with me," shouted a little girl materializing inside of a huge house.

A lean, black woman in a gray fitted business dress pulled her cell phone away from her ear before shouting up the stairs.

"Adam, play with your sister."

"She's not my sister! She keeps dressing me in girly stuff."

The woman put the phone back up to her ear and sighed. "The sitter's running late. Can you have them postpone the board meeting until I get there?" The voice on the other end was barely audible. "Stephen's already gone. I need you—" The voice interrupted her as a little boy stomped down the stairs. He was a puny little shit, skinny with a high-pitched voice and short cornrows held in place by rubber bands. They had little yellow butterflies at the end. I could barely hold back a chuckle at the bright pink Barbie T-shirt he had slightly covered with the top half of his denim overalls.

"I don't wanna play with her," the boy said. "I want Dad."

"Hold on a moment," she pulled the phone away from her ear again. "I am on the phone. Go back upstairs."

No one seemed to care that I was there, like they didn't notice me. Why was I having a dream about Adam being a kid? I ran over to the stairs, and lifted my arms over my head, making sure my claws were visible. Adam liked bears, so I tried to roar like one.

"You're a cute little shit," I said as Adam huffed and stomped back up the stairs, but he stopped and slowly turned his head—like he suddenly realized I was there.

"Look at the bear," he said, pointing at me.

The people in the room disappeared, and the house decor turned festive. Gold and silver garland wrapped the beams holding the stair rails, cotton towns lit up tables and hutches, and Christmas lights of all colors had been hung along the ceilings. A giant twelve-foot Christmas tree stood in the large living room, casting a warm, incandescent glow that beamed through the frosted windows to the darkened snow-covered deck outside behind it. Despite its size, there weren't many presents under it.

A teenaged Adam sat alone, cross-legged on the floor, staring at his cell phone. This place was a mansion. Why in the world did we never have any money when his parents were this loaded? I crept through the house until I was standing next to him. Kid Adam didn't seem to notice my presence this time, so I took the opportunity to sneak a peek at his texts.

He was wearing normal boy clothes, and the cornrows he'd had as a child had been shaved into a shorter, faded style that made him seem older. As a teenager, he had a very distinct appearance about him, and anyone could have probably figured him out. He wore a stylish tight black shirt with that stupid Pawlibear character on it and black track pants with two white stripes on both legs.

He sat there, staring at the message he sent, waiting for something to happen.

*U said you'd be home. Where r u?*

His cell phone vibrated, and a soft Christmas carol hummed through the speaker. Adam put the phone to his ear and answered.

"You were supposed to be here."

A soft, male voice spoke through the phone, and I could hear it clearly with my sensitive ears.

"My flight got canceled. I'm sorry, Adam. I'm not going to make it home for Christmas."

"Maya and Alyssa aren't here. No one's here."

"I can't control the weather, and I wish you'd stop calling her Maya."

"Why? She's not my mother. She hates me."

"She doesn't hate you."

"Bullshit. Even you don't care. Every time you're here, you're always comparing me to Alyssa." He lowered his voice. "'Alyssa's on the honor roll, why aren't you? Alyssa has friends to hang out with, why don't you have any? Alyssa got accepted to Yale, and you haven't even considered community college.'" His voice went back to normal. "Every time I've tried to talk to you, you always brush me off and tell me to be more like her."

"That's because you're not taking your future seriously. You're not getting good grades—"

"That's because I'm always looking over my shoulder. The teachers don't like me, and everyone makes fun of me."

"That's high school. It may be hard, but you're pretty lucky. I grew up—"

"In the hood, yeah I've heard the story," Adam interrupted. "And with all that rags-to-riches success, you can't even come home for Christmas."

The phone went silent for a moment. "I'll do what I can to get home, I promise."

"You shouldn't have left. It's the last three years all over again."

"I'm a bad father, I know. Sometimes you have to take opportunities when they're presented, and I couldn't pass up this client. You'll understand when you're older."

"I'll see you whenever you get here," Adam said, defeated as he ended the call. He crawled over to the tree and picked through the presents until he saw one with his name on it from his dad. He pulled it to the front and rested the package against another before scooting away.

The scene unfolded like a tragedy as Adam sat next to the tree clutching the unopened present, sobbing alone in the living room. It was daylight, but there was no one else around.

"Dad," he sobbed. "You should have been here."

Before he could finish, an all-too-familiar school bell rang, and I found myself in a colonial-looking hallway with pillars and tall ceilings, windows overhead casting natural sunlight on tall, red lockers. A commotion echoed through the empty building, just around the corner. I walked along the waxed, tile flooring, approaching a rattling, standing locker.

"Let me out!"

That was Adam's voice. I tried to pull the combination padlock, but my hand went through it. These visions were strange. Sometimes I could touch things, but other times I couldn't. I stuck my head through the solid metal like a ghost until I could see Adam fumbling with his phone in the darkness.

Over-and-over again, he tried calling multiple people, but no one answered. Eventually he stopped trying and slid down against the back of the locker, folding his knees. He was small enough not to get stuck like that, but just sticking my head in there made me claustrophobic.

"Guess I'm spending the night here," he squeaked out with a sniffle, laying his head against his knees. Then his eyes glowed yellow and he let out an angry shriek, pounding his fist against the steel so hard, it dented. With another growled scream, he stood and shoved both fists into the door, bending it with a groan before it exploded open.

I backed away as he looked down at his hands, which were a little fuzzier than normal. This must have been the start of his half-turn, though he still could pass as human—for now. The fear in his eyes told me he knew what was happening, but that was quickly replaced with a vengeful grimace.

He took off toward the door of the main building, and I trailed him, curious. Tirelessly, he sprinted through a gated suburb before approaching a group of three larger teenage boys, each wearing red and white letterman jackets.

"Who let the fag out," the larger of the three sang out, making five woofing sounds. Adam didn't slow his pace, rather tackled the boy to the ground. Someone as small as him shouldn't have been able to have such an impact, but his leg muscles propelled him with enough force to do the impossible. Adam sent his right fist into the kid's face again and again as the others tried to pull him off. With one final slam of Adam's fist, the boy lay unconscious, but the enraged half-turn wasn't finished. He allowed himself to be dragged off before grabbing another by his throat. The bully's friend tried pulling Adam off, hitting the half-turn repeatedly with his own fists, but it had no effect.

"I'm calling the cops," he shouted, pulling out his phone. Adam snatched it away and shattered it against the ground before sending one last fist into the kid's jaw. All three lay sprawled out along the sidewalk, and Adam walked away, still balling his fists as if daring anyone to challenge him. The teenage boys were still breathing, thankfully, but the larger kid was the worst off.

"Hell yeah," I said, following Adam closely. The only other time I saw him take charge like this was the night he turned. He continued for several blocks until he passed the entrance of a cemetery. The boy stopped and looked back at the gates.

Finally, his shoulders slumped and he turned, making his way inside. His pace slowed to the point where he was barely walking anymore, as though he was trying to stop himself. Eventually, he froze in front of a large headstone. There was a line of scripture etched in it along with the name Stephen Campbell.

"I guess this was something else you didn't tell me," he whispered, kneeling next to the grave. "Our house is empty. Maya told me she doesn't want me around. Alyssa's away at school. Now I'm turning into a freak. You left me alone, Dad. I don't have anyone left in my corner."

With that, he climbed to his feet and started toward the road.

I'd always assumed both of his parents were alive and cared about him, and he was just this spoiled brat. He never talked to me about this stuff. I watched him slowly disappear, his defeated expression all too familiar.

I looked back at the grave, and a chill washed over me as I remembered my mother in happier times. He had a dad, and I had a mom. They were the only ones who loved us, but we both lost that. I understood what he felt then, because I felt it more times than I ever wanted to. All those moments Adam and I had shared together, and I could have made them better, but I hadn't. I had been indifferent to him, just like everyone had been in his early life. I didn't know him.

"I'm sorry," I whispered, pulling at the fur on my head.

### Cody

I watched helplessly as red-eyed crows surrounded the werewolves, cackling and mocking. Roscoe and his mate clutched one another, their ears pressed against their heads. The murder turned to mist before reappearing as four young naked women with white hair.

"Aren't they precious, sisters?" one of them asked, brushing her blood-red nails against Roscoe's face. "So frightened, but you shouldn't be. You're safe with us."

The werewolves' eyes turned white as their fearful expressions went hollow. All four witches ran their hands over the enthralled beasts, writhing with lust as they each took turns gripping their cocks, forcing them to arousal.

"The pack is waiting. Let's prepare the feast," they all said in unison, two of the witches wrapping frayed collars of rope around their necks before leading them through the woods.

I followed at a distance as they made their way to three moss-covered cabins, a bonfire in the center. Several werewolves were tied to crosses, their eyes just as white and cloudy as Roscoe's. It was like their souls were gone, because they weren't even struggling out of the restraints. More young women emerged from the cabins, encircling the fire as they chanted. Roscoe and his mate stood still as a bluish mist pulled from their chests, joining the mist collected from the others over the fire.

The coven reached into the flames in unison with their bare hands, skin charring before healing almost instantly. They seemed to derive pleasure from the experience, each one trembling. The fire went from orange to elder blue, and they breathed in deep, the rising flames arching into their lungs.

So this was how they'd taken the vironoct, just as Mosavi said.

A few of the witches took their places in front of a different bound werewolf. They knelt until their crimson lips wrapped around throbbing erections. The witches ritualistically sucked and stroked until the beasts howled in release, shooting their seed into hungry mouths, only for it to be spat into opaque jars at the base of the crosses. Without giving the werewolves reprieve, they'd begin again.

Two witches led Roscoe and the other to their own wooden crosses, and night suddenly turned to morning. The werewolves were no longer bound, each one sitting on dead leaves, staring into nothing like empty husks.

Roscoe, however, seemed almost coherent. The witches were gone, and after another few moments, Roscoe's eyes darkened to their usual reddish orange. He looked around, obviously confused at first, but quickly jumped to his feet, making nonsensical grunts and whines while pulling at the others, trying to get them to move.

They remained rigid and unresponsive, and Roscoe turned to his mate, his ears drooping as if he finally realized the futility. He pressed his forehead against the other werewolf's forehead and cried out, trembling against the emotionless creature. Using both hands, he reached down toward his mate's ankles, sliding off the colorful bands he wore. They looked like Roscoe's beaded anklets.

After removing the hand-made jewelry, he wiped his face and slowly padded away, once again leaving another family behind.

# Chapter 32

# Roscoe's Purpose

*Cody*

The beat of bass thumped through the poorly lit alley, and a door opened and slammed shut. The sound was followed by a heavy crash into plastic bags as someone fell into them, scattering bottles and cans while sending screaming rats scurrying into the streets.

Though I knew everything was a vision of the past, the realism was startling. I might not have been able to interact with most of the people and objects, but sights, smells, and sounds were vivid. Especially the smells. There was one smell in particular attached to a snoring lump I knew well.

Though he looked a lot younger and thinner, the werewolf sprawled out over plastic bags was Roscoe. He was drunk, of course, but there was also something different about his body, like he had gone completely numb from the neck down. There was no way to know how much time had passed between the last vision and now. However, judging from the blocky Pontiac GTO parked on the other side of the street and the tie-dye Volkswagen minibus behind it, it was safe to assume the decade.

The door to the club opened again, and another werewolf hobbled out, followed by an irate human man.

"You're both fired," the human shouted in a thick Italio-American accent, pouring a pitcher of ice water onto Roscoe's head. "Get the hell outta here, or I'm calling Vince."

"C'mon man," the tall, black werewolf said as Roscoe gasped and moaned. "He's having a gnarly trip. I told you he hadn't done this stuff before."

"He shagged my girl. If we didn't go way back, I wouldn't think twice about having him tied up and thrown in the lake."

The partially sober werewolf grabbed Roscoe's arm before lifting it over his shoulders. With a series of half-aware grunts, Roscoe leaned into him as they disappeared around the corner. The scene faded and reappeared, Bon Jovi blaring through the speakers in a small room full of colorful lights. There were two werewolves, including Roscoe and one dark-skinned half-turn lying naked on a sturdy coffee table with lines of cocaine trailing down his chest. He looked to be close to turning because he was hairier and had a small tail jutting from his lower back.

Roscoe knelt next to the half-turn, his snout inches away from the white powder, but a clawed hand caught his nose.

"Hold it," the half-turn said with an impatient scowl. "One hundred for the blow, one hundred and fifty for the blow job. Two hundred for a full fuck."

"Aw man. I only got a hundred." Roscoe backed away, reaching into the pocket of his orange, discarded hoodie pocket that had been lying on the ripped couch.

The half-turn gawked at Roscoe's thick cock and licked his lips. "Maybe I'll give *you* a discount," he said, grabbing Roscoe's slick shaft while pointing to one of the lines. "You get that one"—he pointed to the other black werewolf from the alley—"and you get the other."

Both of them turned into beasts and pressed their snouts into the cocaine, the stimulant mixing with half-turn pheromones making them snarl with ecstasy. When they were done, Roscoe was barely able to slow himself enough to allow the guy time to prepare. His dick sank into the needy half-turn's ass, eliciting a low gasp as the other werewolf positioned himself at the other end.

Part of me was a little jealous, but the other part of me knew where this was headed. A human man walked into the room, younger-looking with light brown hair fashioned into a mullet, his thick facial hair trimmed into long sideburns and a soul patch. The black-furred werewolf immediately caught his scent and grabbed the man's arm in a fit of lust.

"Darryl," the half-turn shouted as Roscoe thrusted harder. "Get the hell outta here." He grabbed the other werewolf by the dick and pulled. "He's a human. Leave him alone."

The black werewolf yelped and turned his attention back to the half-turn on the coffee table. Human Darryl slowly backed out of the door. So that's what he looked like. I'd have never guessed aside from the facial hair, considering he was about four inches shorter than me.

The vision progressed until it was just Roscoe sitting on a stained carpet, leaning against the corner as he slowly came down from another state of mixed inebriation and stimulant abuse.

"You look pathetic," came a young man's voice.

I turned toward Darryl who sat on a wooden chair while plucking a guitar string, twisting the tuning knobs at the top. It was a beautiful instrument, hand-carved and lovingly polished.

"I wish you'd stop coming around here," he continued, staring in disgust.

"Don't like me?" Roscoe slurred. "Join the club."

"The only reason Ramón keeps you around is because he's about to turn."

"Guess I'm the only one that can make his eyes roll back, huh?" He looked up at Darryl. "Ever been fucked by a werewolf before?"

"None of your business." Darryl held up a hand. "Also, I know where this is going, and no. I'd rather dive head-first into a sewer."

"Eh. I'm too tired anyway."

Darryl gave the guitar one final test strum before playing something sounding like flamenco. Roscoe smiled, his tail swaying in time with the rhythm.

"Shit, dude. You're good," Roscoe said. "Like *really* good. Who taught you to play?"

"My dad," Darryl responded, his eyes closed as he focused on the music.

"Is yer old man famous or somethin'?"

Darryl stopped mid-strum before opening his eyes again. He gently placed the guitar on a stand before reaching for an ashtray with a pre-rolled joint pressed between the divots lining the center.

"You want a hit?" he asked, positioning the joint between his lips.

"Can't turn down free weed." Roscoe pushed himself off the floor and sat on the other chair at the table.

After taking two hits, Darryl passed it to Roscoe. He took in a deep drag, holding it in and exhaling loudly.

"I want to get out of this place," Darryl said, taking the joint back from Roscoe. "You ever been to the beach?"

"A few times. White Dunes is a three-hour bus ride."

"I wanna go there, but I'm scared. I don't have the money to leave, and Ramón wants me to take over this shitheap."

"He's got cash. Ask him for some money to get you started."

Darryl laughed. "You don't just ask Ramón to give you money with no strings attached. He's been guilting me into working under him since he gave me a place to stay. I want to repay him, but I don't want to live here anymore." He looked up at Roscoe. "I'll end up like you if I stay."

Roscoe coughed and snorted, seemingly hurt. Strange considering he seemed to revel in his lifestyle when I first met him.

"Yeah, you don't want that."

"What's your deal, anyway?"

The werewolf shrugged. "Don't know. Can't remember nothin', but I know that's probably for the best." He reached into his hoodie pocket and pulled out a fat wad of cash before casually dropping it on the table. "Was gonna use this for something harder, but I think you should go to the beach."

Darryl's eyes widened. "What are you doing?"

"Makin' sure you don't end up like me. There's five hundred. It should be enough to get you there. It's gonna be hard for you." He sniffed the air before turning to Darryl. "That ain't weed. It's you..."

"What do you mean? You don't know me." Darryl pushed the money away. "What do you want?"

Roscoe picked up the stack and pressed it into Darryl's hand, then stood. He walked over to the front door and slipped outside before looking back. "I want you to find what makes you happy, and you got the talent to do something good. Don't waste it here. And when you change, don't let it ruin yer life." With that, he disappeared into the night, closing the door behind him.

The scene shifted to outdoors. Rows of blue tarps over refrigerator boxes lined the sidewalk of the city's outskirts. Trash bags full of belongings were stacked in grocery carts, discarded needles and balled-up aluminum foil were scattered along the street. Roscoe walked along the encampment with bags of hot food next to a one-legged middle-aged man who hobbled along using a rusty walker.

"Here ya go sweetheart," Roscoe said, handing an old lady a plastic container, giving her a wink. "Made yer favorite."

She blushed and graciously took the food from his hands. "Thank you, handsome."

"You sober now?" the man asked as they walked by another tent. Roscoe set the last bag in front of it.

"Nope," he replied as they continued toward a wooden bench. The man sat and Roscoe joined him, crossing one leg over the other. "You better be, though."

"I am, I swear."

They both took deep breaths through their noses.

"I just love the smell of piss in the morning," the man said, leaning back and pointing at all the tents. "Behold. The foundation of the richest country in the world, and everyone ignores it. We get used up, and when they're done—" A gunshot in the distance made the man scream as he held his face in his hands. "It would have been less of an insult to die in the war."

Roscoe slipped an arm over the man's shoulder. "Lean into me. Don't worry. No one's gonna do nothin' with a big scary monster around."

The veteran cried out, grabbing tufts of Roscoe's fur and burying his face in it. The episode went on for a few minutes before he pulled away.

"You've got some powerful pits, dude." He wiped his face with the dirty collar of his coat.

"They're good fer what ails ya." Roscoe patted the man on the back. "Sometimes we all need someone to hold onto. I ain't got the answers for ya, but I do got a soft shoulder."

"You're a damn saint."

"Eddy, I'd burst into flames if I ever walked into a church," Roscoe said before both let out stifled laughter. "I ain't a saint; I just like people. I like hearin' their stories." He pointed to the old woman from earlier. She was slowly eating the pasta Roscoe had given her. "Mrs. Thompson had a son out of wedlock a long time ago. She never got married, but she'd do anything for her kid. Worked three jobs when women workin' wasn't a thing. He went off to fight in 'Nam, but he didn't come back. Good moms are—" Roscoe cleared his throat, holding back a surge of repressed emotion. "It's good to listen, but I wish I could do more."

"If there is a God and heaven exists, I hope you'll look me up if I make it."

"How 'bout you settle for keepin' me company while yer alive?"

"Deal."

The sun disappeared and Roscoe knelt in the flickering light of a burning barrel. He was next to a tent holding onto an arm that had a rubber tourniquet tied to it. Roscoe held the man's hand with both of his and looked up at the sky, tears soaking the fur on his face.

"Wait fer me, buddy. If we both make it to heaven, wait fer me." He removed the tourniquet and gently placed the lifeless arm inside the tent before covering Eddy's face with his jacket. After patting the man's chest, Rosco stood and ambled along the tents as if in a trance, disappearing into the black alleyway.

His memories were becoming even more painful to watch as I followed him into the darkness, only to end up on the beach in the middle of the day. The warm sea breeze of this familiar place lightened the mood. Roscoe sang while Darryl—now a full werewolf—played his guitar as they both sat on the sand. People walked by, tossing money into the guitar case, cheering and clapping after each performance.

"We're gonna take a break, but we'll do some more tonight," Roscoe said, turning from the dispersing crowd. "Can't believe how big you got."

"Can't believe how fat you got," Darryl said, poking Roscoe's stomach with his finger. "You have an incredible voice."

"Why thank ya, sir. How much more do you need to start building yer house?"

"More than I can get doing street performances." He looked at his tent in the distance. It was in the same place his house would be in the future. "That's all mine. I own that little part of the beach, and I get to surf and play my guitar every day. It's like a dream."

"I knew you'd make somethin' of yerself."

"All because you gave me that chance." He pulled the guitar case close, looking at the impressive amount of cash they'd received. "It's yours."

"I didn't come here to collect a debt."

"Then why'd you leave the city?"

"It was time," he said, his ears off to the side. "I needed some sun and fresh air." He smiled at Darryl. "And a friend."

"Ever surf before?"

"No, and I ain't about to start."

Darryl pulled out a plastic ziplock bag with some weed in it. "I think I could persuade you to give it a try... *dude.*"

"You just smoke this shit out in the open?"

"It's legal here," he said, pulling a thin sheet of cigarette paper from a metal case.

"No shit. When did that happen?"

"Midterms. It was on the ballot."

"Ah. I don't pay no attention to politics."

"I do when weed's on the line." Darryl twisted the ends of the joint and handed it to Roscoe. "I also noticed something weird. Werewolves are in the government now. They have their own branch and everything. There's talk about social programs that can benefit us."

"Sounds like a trap." Roscoe grabbed a lighter and lit the end of the joint before inhaling deeply. After taking another one, he passed it back to Darryl. "Can't trust the government. They ain't gave a shit about us for as long as I remember, so it's a little suspicious they start carin' now."

"You're half right. They probably wouldn't have cared if there weren't so many homeless werewolves causing problems. They're trying to get the human and werewolf bums off the streets."

Roscoe gritted his teeth but didn't say anything.

"I don't think it'll benefit us. Plus, it's not gonna happen for a few years at least." Darryl looked out over the ocean as the sun disappeared behind a passing cloud. "Thanks, Roscoe."

"For what?"

He pointed to the ocean. "For all this."

"I believe you end a thank you prayer with an amen, seein' as I created the ocean an' all."

"You know what I mean, jackass."

"All I did was get you here. You did the rest."

A child's cry broke through the sound of waves crashing against the shore, catching everyone's attention.

Roscoe's head snapped toward the commotion. "Ah shit. Ain't no lifeguards here?"

Darryl jumped to his feet and ran into the ocean before gliding across the rip current like a fish. It was just as I remembered from our time at the beach when Roscoe and I showed up a few months ago. The way he swam defied his nature, and I almost believed he was a shark in a past life.

It took less than thirty seconds for Darryl to reach the bobbing child. He lifted the boy onto his back and swam parallel to the shore, where the kid's frantic parents ran to meet up with the werewolf. Before long, they were safely on the beach, and after the mother hugged the child, she threw her arms around Darryl, thanking him.

He walked back to where Roscoe was with a huge smile on his face.

"Damn. Ain't never seen a werewolf swim like that. I just sort of float on the surface of the water like a buoy."

"I think that's the tenth person I've pulled out of the water in the last two weeks. This place is getting packed."

"Where are the lifeguards?" Roscoe asked.

"There aren't any. They're all further up the coast near Crooked Palm, but now this place is seeing more action. Maybe they'll put a station here soon."

"Maybe you should take the job."

Darryl snatched the joint out of Roscoe's hand. "I'd never pass a drug test."

Roscoe shrugged. "Well, you've been lookin' for another job for extra money, and you seem to be pretty good at it even when yer stoned. Couldn't hurt to try."

"Maybe." The larger werewolf let out a heavy laugh. "Could you imagine me wearing those dorky red shorts with that red dildo strapped to my back?"

"Why not just be naked? Ain't like people can see nothin' most of the time."

"Tried that. Had a run-in with the fuzz because of it. I'm petitioning to have this part of the beach clothing optional... well, for werewolves, anyway." He looked down at Roscoe's bare crotch. "How do you get away with it?"

Roscoe shoved his arm into Darryl's. "Get this. A cop tried to get me for that indecent exposure bullshit, so I went to a thrift store and got the tightest speedo I could get my hands on. You could see every vein and outline, and I technically was following the law. I looked more indecent in that thing than I did wearin' nothing at all. They eventually told me to just take 'em off after a lot of people started complaining."

They laughed, but as that died, a more somber atmosphere took its place.

"What about you?" Darryl asked. "What do you want to do for the rest of your life? Cuz it's a long one."

Roscoe stared out at the waves as the sun peeked back out from behind the clouds, seeming to give the question more scrutiny than usual.

"I dunno. Didn't expect to live this long."

"Werewolves live for hundreds of years, dude. What did you expect?"

Roscoe shrugged. "I didn't know that. Just thought all the drugs and booze were pickling me or something. I look damn good for—however the hell old I am now."

"You don't know your age?"

"Hell, I don't even know if Roscoe's my real name anymore." He tapped his head. "The ol' memory's a little fuzzy when it comes to anything more than a few decades ago."

"This place is better than the city. Why don't you look for a job around here and stay with me?"

"A job might interfere with the pickling process."

"How about you stop with the hard drugs?" Darryl tossed the plastic baggie into Roscoe's lap. "We've got cheap weed and light beer. Don't need anything more than that."

Roscoe shuffled the bag around in his hands. "This certainly sweetens the pot. All right. I'll see if I can find a shitty job."

"Don't you have anything you wanna do? Ramón said something about you being able to turn tasteless leftovers and expired food into the most delicious meals he's ever eaten."

Roscoe frowned. "Naw. I don't wanna cook food fer people no more. Too many painful memories."

"Sorry."

Roscoe playfully shoved Darryl. "It's all good. I'll go be a bouncer or somethin'. That's an easy job. You just stand there and scare the shit out of people so they don't bother causing problems. I've been thrown out of bars more than I've had to throw anyone out."

"How much does that pay?"

"Enough to get by. Could help you get yer house built faster." He held his hand out. "Wanna let me stay on that little strip of sand you got?"

Darryl grabbed his hand and shook. "You got it."

The beach scene shifted, and a half-built house stood behind two tents close to the water. Darryl was seated up on a high lifeguard chair surveying the crowded waters, but Roscoe was nowhere to be found.

"Ready for a shift change?" a male, human lifeguard called up to him.

"Yup," Darryl replied, jumping down from the chair. "I'm gonna get baked. Anyone seen Roscoe around?"

"He's out of jail?"

"For now. We'll see if he stays that way." He gripped the handle of his lifebuoy and made his way to the tents. The leftmost one had a pair of furry legs sticking out of it. Darryl bent over to grab Roscoe's ankles and pulled the unconscious werewolf across the sand toward the water. The moment a wave crashed into them, Roscoe yowled.

"Oh shit! The tide's too high!"

"The tide's not high. You are," Darryl said, slapping Roscoe's face a few times. "You can't keep doing this, dude. Every time you say you're gonna get clean, I find another bottle of pills. You said you'd help me with the house, but even *my* money keeps going missing."

Roscoe spat out water, a strand of seaweed dangling from his bottom canine.

"Everything's fine. Just need a little something to help me sleep at night."

"A half a bottle of hydrocodone is not a little something. This is getting serious, and I don't know if I can keep this up. I love you like a brother, Roscoe, but I can't handle this."

"Everything's under control." He reached into the tent and pulled out a bottle of pills, then poured them into his hand and tossed them into the water. "Ain't gonna take those no more."

"Great. Now the sharkmen are going to have an opioid problem."

"You still on about that? There ain't no sharkmen."

"I saw one!" Darryl's eyes went wide as he held out his arms. "He was about as big as I was! I tried to wave him down, but he panicked and disappeared into the water."

Roscoe narrowed his eyes. "He panicked, you say. Huge muscley monster with two rows of teeth ran away from a werewolf?"

"Who is also huge with one row of equally sharp teeth and glowing eyes. Hell, I'd be scared of me."

"Yer crazy."

"He was hot. If I see him again, I'm gonna swim after him."

Roscoe yawned and crawled back into his tent. "Good luck with that."

"You're gonna sleep all damn day?"

"It was a late night. Gotta get up in five hours fer work."

The daylight faded. I stepped forward only to end up in a pawn shop. Roscoe pacing outside with a guitar case in his hands, and Darryl's story played out in real time. He froze in the entrance, his eyes wide and body trembling.

He looked around the empty shop before making his way to the counter. The pudgy balding man behind it eying Roscoe suspiciously.

"Need a loan," he said, sliding the guitar across the counter.

The man opened the case and shook his head. "Where did you get this?" he asked in a hushed tone before shutting the case.

"My dad left it for me, but times are tough."

"Whoever you stole this from, you better make sure it gets back to them. This is a legitimate business, sir."

"It ain't—" Roscoe drew in a deep breath before lifting the guitar off the counter. "All right." He sauntered out of the building, growing more anxious as he passed under streetlights toward a much seedier side of town. Two scantily clad women sitting on a curb while sharing a crack pipe caught Roscoe's eye.

"You ladies know where I can... do some tradin'?"

"Depends on whatcha want in return, good lookin'," one of the ladies said in a thick, high-pitched Brooklyn accent. "Ben down the road deals in antiques. Vinny on Peachtree Lane's got a more... modern inventory you might be interested in."

Roscoe put up his hood and nodded. "Thank ya."

"If ya go to Vinny, tell 'im Sasha sends her best."

"No, Roscoe," I whispered, following him close. He told Darryl he sold the guitar to a pawn shop, but of course Darryl knew it was a lie. They never would have sold a stolen, priceless guitar that fast.

The vision finally faded, and I dreaded what came next, but instead I ended up in a black room with one uncovered lightbulb overhead and Roscoe rocking back and forth on the floor, his head in his hands, crying.

I knelt in front of him, placing a hand on his shoulder. "Roscoe?"

He looked up and nodded before bursting into tears again.

"I'm a baaaad guy, Cody. I manipulated you into keepin' me around, and I destroyed the only friendship that ever meant anything—and I left my pack and my mate. It was a mercy mama died young so she didn't have to see her screw-up boy turn out like this."

"Roscoe, look at me," I said, holding the underside of his jaw in my hand. The pain in his eyes broke me; he'd been hiding this for as long as I'd known him. Every funny antic, lighthearted jab, the way he'd shrug off my criticisms—it was all a mask. He hurt every time, and I'd been unknowingly making it worse. "You're the most wonderful person I've ever met."

"Yer lyin'," Roscoe said, wiping his face. "You were right to be suspicious of me when we met. I was gonna get high, remember?"

"But you didn't. You followed me home, where you belonged."

Roscoe's watery eyes grew wider, his voice cracking. "Home..."

"I couldn't call that place home without you. You brought adventure and fun into my sad, boring life. You make me smile every day, even when you're being an ass. I love that about you."

Roscoe wiped his face and looked down. "I thought... even with the kuu, there'd be no way someone like you could stand to be around someone like me. I always expected you to leave, but you didn't."

"You're stuck with me."

"I don't deserve you."

"You grew up hungry and alone. Somehow you had the strength to keep on living. Then you met someone and fell in love, but you couldn't help what happened. If you stayed, they'd have finished what they started. When no one else cared, you cooked delicious meals for all those homeless people and you helped a veteran through the worst time of his life. You helped a strange human you didn't even know make his dreams come true." I shook Roscoe's shoulder, forcing him to look up, and that was when I couldn't stop crying. "Terrible people don't do that stuff, Roscoe. You touched so many lives, and while you think it didn't matter in the end, it did, and it made you a better person. You made mistakes. Everyone has. But we're not defined by them."

I wrapped my arms around his neck and fell into him. We stayed like that for several minutes, me stroking his head while he held me.

"Thank you," Roscoe whispered. "Thank you, Cody."

The room turned white as the visage of a broken Roscoe shattered under me, leaving me alone in silence.

# It's a Beautiful Life

*Roscoe*

The stench of the city made me reel. It wasn't just the smell, it was what they brought with them. Everything came flooding back to me, things I'd long forgotten. There was a calmness to it, though, somethin' I never experienced with these memories, like someone wrapped me in a big hug.

It didn't last.

I was in a messy dorm room with really good art of hot monsters taped to the walls. Cody sat on a twin-sized bed next to a guy with a shaved head. He was shorter, but he did have an interestin' mid-western accent. He handed Cody a drawing of a huge werewolf standing under a solar eclipse, gettin' a blowjob from a smaller werewolf.

"Happy birthday," he said before kissing Cody on the cheek. "It's how I see us."

"You really like werewolves," he said. "I love it."

"We should take a road trip and see the eclipse."

"That's kinda far. Can your car even make it?"

These visions hadn't been happy, but this one was deceptively sweet. I remembered somethin' Cody said a while ago about being hurt—this must've been the guy that did it.

"Only one way to find out." He shoved Cody with his arm. "Stop always worrying so much."

"Jim…"

"I mean it. We'll be fine. It'll be awesome. I'll bring my vape pen, and we'll get high on the way."

"I don't think you've ever not been high the whole time we've been dating." Even though he said it in a joking way, his tone had this underlyin' hint of seriousness.

The scene shifted to a hotel parking lot as Cody and the other guy walked around. The area was flat and dry, kinda reminded me of the southwest. The one he'd called Jim was crying, and Cody looked confused.

"I'm a terrible person," he said, wiping his face.

"You're not a terrible person. Where did this come from all of a sudden?"

"I just... think we should chill."

"We're a thousand miles away from home. Are you breaking up with me?"

"I don't know. Maybe we need to take some time. You're still precious to me, though."

The sun disappeared and Cody sat alone in a small room, holdin' the drawing in his hands.

"You were a terrible person," he whispered, tossin' his cell phone onto the bed next to him. The last few messages made me angry.

*We don't even talk anymore. I just want a friend.*

*Sorry. I can't give you what you need, Cody. Find some other friends.*

He balled up the drawing and threw it into the trash before turning out the lights.

The vision shifted into a mostly empty studio. There wasn't a TV or a couch, just a twin air mattress on the floor with some neatly made-up sheets. The dining area consisted of a small table decorated with jarred candles, and even though the place looked a bit run-down, it had Cody's charm. He always kept everything neat no matter where he was. Everything was meticulously placed, folded, vacuumed, dusted, and smellin' fresh.

Before we met, I never did care that much about neatness. I came crashing into his sterilized world like an out of control dump truck. After this was over, I was gonna start carin' a lot more.

I understood these visions. Cody must've found the ferals, and they were giving us a test. Never knew whether this was their doing or if the magic they used had a life of its own. I did remember some pretty strict rules about who could use it and when, and I wasn't too keen on going through this again considering what it did to me last time I failed.

A little rainbow-colored cupcake sat in the middle of a saucer with one unlit candle in it. A plastic bag crinkling from the kitchen caught my ear as I watched Cody pour boxed wine into a red Solo cup. It might have been cheap, but I always did like the taste of that stuff. Hell, I used to carry those around with huge bendy straws sticking out of 'em.

He put the box back into a mostly empty fridge and dragged himself to the table, set the wine next to the cupcake, then plopped onto his chair, exhausted.

"Was this the right move?" he asked himself, grabbing a red lighter from his pocket. He was wearin' a skimpy bar uniform and a pair of ragged running shoes. "Nothing ever feels like home. I'll never have a real home."

His eyes were red, and his lashes were damp. I took my place behind him, restin' my hands on his shoulders. He didn't acknowledge me, but I could actually feel him in this vision. I could even smell him. Cody always made me feel like I was home, and I'd have given anything to make him feel the same way at that moment. But it was just a vision, and I had no choice but to let it play out.

He lit the candle and closed his eyes. "This is stupid." With that, he blew out the candle and pushed the cupcake away, then looked over at his cell phone with a sigh. "I hate this day. I was such a mistake."

"Don't even. Yer an incredible guy," I said to him, sitting on the only other chair in the room. "Workin' full-time while goin' to school. You went through hell just like I did, but I gave up before I even started. Here you are. You just don't see what I see."

He ate half the cupcake then took the remainder into the kitchen and wrapped it in cellophane. I looked down at his phone so I could see the date. March first, five years ago. He never told me when his birthday was, but I'd also never asked. We were both swept up in desperation for a few months. I'd needed to secure him as a kuu mate before anyone else got a whiff of what he was, and he needed someone to feed him and help him through this tough phase of his new life.

The room exploded in fast beats and lights, drunk gay men singing off-key into the microphone while everyone else either danced or talked over the music. Cody zoomed from table-to-table, taking orders while dropping off food and drinks. He did a bang-up job keeping up with everything, but every five minutes, he'd step into the back and shake off some anxiety.

"Cody?" A full-figured drag queen stepped into the back. He was wearin' a comically huge blonde wig in the shape of a bouffant, a pair of white gloves, red kitten heels, and a tight red dress with sequins. I couldn't tell how old he was under all that makeup, but he looked on the younger side. "Are you okay, sweetheart?"

"Had too much caffeine."

"I've told you to go easier on those energy drinks."

"I've gotta get through the night without passing out," Cody replied, looking over the guy's outfit. "That looks good on you."

"Of course it does. I make all my clothes custom to fit every lump, nook and cranny."

"When you're up on stage, how do you stay so relaxed and fun?"

"A little booze, and a lot of not giving a fuck what people think." He brushed a lock of stray hair from Cody's face with his manicured fingers. "I was young and shy like you, but one day I put on a dress and some makeup and pretended to be someone else for one night. I did it for a while, and I could be anyone I wanted. But then one day I realized I wasn't being someone else, I was just being me without all the guard rails. All those friends I made as the classy Lanja Ray were the same friends who liked me whenever I was Robert."

"So, all I have to do is get drunk and put on a dress."

"Well, since you're not twenty-one yet, you'll just have to settle for the dress."

"I'll settle for these embarrassing daisy dukes for now." Cody gave Rob a sideways glance. "None of the other people working here have to wear this *uniform*. Why do I?"

"You're the only one that actually wore it." Rob let out a laugh. "I just give these out to my hottest employees. You're the only one that's actually come to work dressed like this."

"Oh my God."

"Hey, you keep 'em coming back. Speaking of..." He cracked open the door while pointing to a handsome man in a leisure suit. "That guy was asking about you."

"*That* guy? You're joking."

"Not your type?"

"Not in his league," Cody said, grabbing the door to close it.

"You're single, you're young, you're hot, and you're hung. You're in everyone's league. Go talk to him."

"How do you know—"

"Honey, everyone knows." I grinned as Rob pointed to the bulge in Cody's shorts. "Why do you think you get so many good tips?"

"I can't do this while I'm working."

"Then get his number." Rob reached for a pen and his order pad before shoving them into Cody's chest. "Do it, or else."

"Or else what?"

"I have a show in thirty minutes." He leaned in. "And Lanja Ray needs a new assistant."

"This is harassment!"

"Take it up with HR," he said, tossing a tiny red handbag over his shoulder. "You're not in Kansas anymore, Toto. Stop acting like you're still in the closet."

"All right, I'll get his number."

"I'll be watching." Rob tripped over his feet as he stumbled through the door. "These damn heels."

"Yeah. The heels," Cody muttered. "The jello shots had nothing to do with it."

Rob smiled and clopped back into the bar. "Get his number, I mean it." He closed the door behind him.

Cody hesitated, fumblin' with the pen and pad and gritting his teeth. After pushing open the door, he grabbed a tray of drinks from the counter and headed past a few people walking by, slower this time. Never seen the guy so pale as he grabbed the order before taking it to the table next to the man eyeing him.

"Hey," he said, grabbing Cody's attention. "When you're done, you mind if I buy you a drink?"

It looked like the poor guy was gonna fall over, and he let out a nervous, high-pitched giggle. It was kinda cute seein' Cody like this.

"Sure!" His excitement soon faded as he caught himself. "I mean, no. I can't. I'm not old enough."

The man's expression took on a creepier vibe.

"How old are you?"

"Twenty."

His eyes widened. "What's your name?"

"Cody, yours?"

"Michael." He reached out his hand to shake, but Cody immediately caught sight of the gold band around his finger.

"Oh..." He stopped and pulled his hand back. "I didn't know you were—"

"It's an open marriage," he interrupted. "We've been looking for a younger third."

"A third?"

"You know. Nothing serious, just some fun in the bedroom." He grabbed his phone. "I have a picture of my husband if you're interested."

Cody forced a smile and shook his head. "Sorry. I'm looking for something more serious."

"You shouldn't be settling down. You should be hooking up." He grabbed Cody's arm. He was pretty well-built, about a half a foot taller, and probably in his early thirties. "I know how guys like you are."

"Guys like me?"

He looked down at Cody's outfit. "You're the hot guy that loves attention from the right kinds of guys." He pulled a wallet from his jacket pocket. "Good dick also comes with benefits."

That shouldn't have been the first interaction with an interested guy after that last breakup; I wasn't sure how I would have reacted, either. Eh, fuck it. I knew exactly what I'd do. I had been a huge, desperate slut back in my half-turn days. Cody didn't look so good, and I could tell by his rosy cheeks he was mortified.

"Excuse me." Cody turned away and walked by the bar, waving at Rob. "I'll see you tomorrow."

"Cody—" Rob called out, but he was already out the back door, running to the bus stop with me followin' close behind.

"I hate being gay," Cody said, sitting on the bench just as the bus rounded the corner. The poor guy looked like he was about to throw up. "Guess I'm just an easy faggot to everyone, huh?"

The vision shifted to him sitting at home on his air mattress, scrolling through a dating app on his phone. Each time he'd go to swipe right on someone he found attractive, he'd freeze and give the picture more scrutiny. Then he'd click on the profile and read every word.

"What is FWB?" He opened his browser and typed in the acronym before letting out a heavy sigh. He swiped left and started reading another guy's profile. "What the hell is a service top? Into bears and chubs? Like teddy bears?" He typed that in and squinted. "These shit apps should just come with a dictionary."

He swiped left again. "Ooo, he looks promising." Cody read through the profile. "A lawyer, loves dogs, twenty-five, monogamous..." His eyes narrowed as he continued reading. "Too perfect. Vers—at least

I know what that means." His shoulders slumped forward as he got to the last part. "He has a kid. Well..." He swiped left and turned off the screen before laying back onto his pillow.

"I'm going to die alone." Cody stared up at the ceiling as the air conditioning kicked on. "I guess that's the way it is."

His phone chirped, but he ignored it.

"Maybe there's something wrong with me."

The studio apartment changed to something a lot more familiar, and instead of an air mattress, he had a real mattress on a wooden frame. The dining room table was the same, but now he had a flat screen TV and a beanbag chair in front of it. Cody sat at the table shuffling through a stack of papers, pushing some to the side and throwing others into a small garbage bin.

"Well, these internships are out," he muttered, tossing another small stack into the trash. He held up another sheet of paper and shook his head. "Too risky."

His phone buzzed against the table, and his face turned an off-shade of pale when he read the unnamed number. He pressed the side button to silence it, his focus shifting from the paperwork to the voicemail alert that soon followed.

Cody picked up the phone and swiped away the home screen, looking like he was struggling with something. He eventually navigated the menu to the voicemail.

"Hey Cody, this is Aunt Sandy. Your father died a few days ago. I won't speak ill of the dead, but this was a wake-up call for your mom. Anyway, I know you've cut ties with this place, and I'm not saying you should come to his funeral, but if you want to come visit me, I'd love to hear all the wonderful things happening in your life. I love you. You're my favorite nephew, you know."

He pressed the callback button and held the phone to his ear. The dial tone clicked.

"So, what finally did the fucker in?"

"Hepatitis C."

"Rest in piss, you piece of shit." Cody's tone was ice cold as he picked up another paper. "I don't mind speaking ill of the dead. Speaking of horrible people, how's Mom? Still on the pills?"

"She may not be the best person in the world, but she's still my family. She's made a lot of unforgivable mistakes with everyone, especially you."

"She was an awful mother. They weren't just mistakes. She kept me in that shithole, hungry and dirty just so she and Dad could get another fix."

"Will you come visit me?"

Cody went quiet, dropping a paper before rubbing his forehead. "As long as I'm not pressured to give the eulogy, because what I'd say wouldn't exactly be church-worthy."

"You don't even have to go to the funeral."

"No, I want to make sure the man is really dead. And I want it to be an open casket." Cody paused. "If Mom's had this huge awakening, why didn't she call me?"

"You changed your number and told me not to give it to anyone, remember?"

"See, this is why you're my favorite aunt."

"I'm your only aunt," the woman added. "I'll buy the plane tickets for next week and get the guest room ready. We have a lot to catch up on, and I want to hear everything. Do you have a boyfriend yet?"

Cody cringed.

"I'm more interested in a career."

"You're still in your shell, aren't you?"

"Aunt Sandy—"

"Dating is hard for everyone, not just gay men. Ask any woman over forty. You've always been kind of a golden child, despite what your parents did. You're smart, handsome, driven, but you're too damn judgmental and closed off."

"I'm not—"

"Cody, the way you talked about others borderlined being a cynical asshole, and you're gonna hate me for saying this, but that's how your father used to talk."

Damn, that hurt even me, but I was likin' this Aunt Sandy. Wonder if Cody'll ever go visit her and let me tag along.

"Ouch," Cody muttered, briefly pulling the phone away from his ear.

"You hold yourself and others to impossible standards, and that's only going to make you more miserable the older you get. I know a lot of this falls on bad parenting, but you're an adult now. It's up to you to decide how to live your life, and if you're not happy, you have the power to change it."

"It's hard," Cody said, leaning back in his chair. "I keep trying to put myself out there, but I've already been hurt. And I don't want to be a fucking stereotype."

"Everyone gets hurt, sweetie, and you don't have to be a stereotype. There's no right or wrong way to be who you are, but don't let that state of mind stop you from letting yourself have fun, even if you end up being a *stereotype*. You should probably start with changing that attitude as well."

"You're being spicy today."

"Well, I've been on the phone with your hysterical mother for a few hours, trying to drum up some sympathy, so I'm a little wound up." She paused. "So, I'll see you next week?"

"See you next week."

"Oh, Dakota?"

"I hate that name. You know this."

I could almost hear that woman smile over the phone.

"Happy twentieth birthday. I'd have sent you something, but you never gave me your address."

His studio faded until the ceiling turned to blue sky as far as the eye could see. The sun was brutal, and I watched the scene unfold, the funeral playing out the way funerals often did with one exception— Cody's resentful face. He stood in the back wearin' a baseball cap and sunglasses, dressed in a bright salmon shirt and white basketball shorts.

A preacher led everyone in prayer as the casket was lowered, and Cody took that moment to slink away toward the line of cars parked along the winding cemetery road. He opened the door of a small red sedan and slid into the passenger seat while scrollin' through his phone.

The car felt hot to the touch, and I realized I could interact with it, so I opened the door and crammed myself into the small back seat. I had to leave the door open since half my body wouldn't fit.

A blond woman in her early forties climbed into the driver's seat. She was heavy-set, wearin' a plain black dress and a little bit of makeup.

"Well, you made your statement loud and clear, and you didn't even say a word."

Cody set his phone in his lap. "This place is just as depressing as I remember."

"Have you said anything to your mom?"

"Nope, and I don't plan to. If she wants to talk, she can start with an apology and work from there." He turned to his aunt. "Just being in this town brings back shitty memories. Whenever I'm alone, I'm depressed. Whenever I'm around people, I panic. Whenever I even think of dating a man, I can't shake away years of abuse."

"Have you considered therapy?"

"Therapy takes years, and I can't afford it." Cody let out an angry groan. "It seems you can move all the way across the country, but your problems follow like a shadow."

Another woman made her way to the car, also wearing black. I knew right away she was Cody's mom, thinner with darker blonde hair pulled back into a straight ponytail. She looked so different and much older compared to the first vision of her. She wasn't wearing makeup or jewelry, and her eyes were bloodshot from crying.

"Great," Cody muttered as she approached the open door.

"You could have worn something a little more respectful."

"That would have required some sort of respect. What the hell do you want?"

"You haven't spoken to me in years, and your father—"

"Was a piece of shit junky and so are you." Cody cleared his throat, shaking out words that seemed to stick them both like knives. "If they were burying your remains as well, I'd be just as indifferent."

"Cody," his aunt cut in. "That's crossing a line."

"Let me tell you about lines that run deeper than the meth marks on her face. The line was crossed when they almost let me die of pneumonia, or when they constantly beat the shit out of me, or when we lived in filth and garbage, or when I couldn't even have a birthday without them breaking into a fight." He turned back to his mom. "You never should have been a mother. I should have never been born, because you fucked me up more than anyone."

The woman broke as tears filled her eyes, but Cody was like ice.

"'The child who is not embraced by the village will burn it down to feel its warmth.' If I ever have any real power one day, I'll burn this whole place to the ground." He slammed the door and fastened his seatbelt. "I'll get my stuff ready to go back home."

His mother slowly walked away, back toward the gravesite, and Cody started to cry for the first time. The car disappeared leaving him sitting on the floor of a black room, holding his head in his hands.

"I'm a terrible person," he whispered. "I'm a hateful, judgmental piece of shit. I still hate them. I still hate you, Jim. I keep letting you hurt me, and you're not even here."

I sat next to him, pulling him into my lap, my arms wrapped around his chest.

"Listen to me babe. We can't change what happened to us. Good or bad, it becomes a part of who we are."

"I hate this world. I never belonged here."

"Nah, you belong right here with me," I said, holding his back against my chest and kissing his head. "You've shut yerself away for too long, but the world ain't all bad. Yer the best thing that's ever happened to me, and if I believed in God, I'd thank him every day that I found ya. You made me a better person, you got Austin to open up to you, and you saved him and Adam. What kind of a terrible person does that?"

"I'm always nagging you, and I treated Adam horribly. He reminded me of everything I hated about myself."

"Adam knows you don't hate him, and you nagging me got me on the right track. You could've turned into a real psycho like yer dad, but you broke that cycle. Yer responsible and you care. You say you hate yer mother, but I didn't feel that. You said the opposite of what you felt because you was hurtin'. Yer gonna be one hell of a good leader one day. I'll be right there with ya, picking you up when you fall, making you laugh when yer sad, and I'll keep makin' you good food. I make the best meals for people that mean the most."

Cody turned and looked me in the eye, a sad smile inching up his face.

"Thank you, Roscoe."

He shattered into a million pieces then disappeared, and the black room brightened to a blue sky with beautiful green hills. Cody stood in the middle of it, and we ran to one another.

"Roscoe?" Cody asked, throwing his arms around me. "Is this really you?"

"Yeah," I replied. "Looks like we passed."

"You know about the ritual?"

"I remember doin' something like this when I joined the ferals a long time ago. You got me my memories back." I held him tight as we stood in the middle of the warm field together. "One hundred and seven."

"Huh?"

"That's how old I am. I was born in rural Arkansas on December 21st, 1916. My dad died when I was about seven, so I don't remember much about the guy other than what mama told me. He was a Sardinian immigrant. He did teach me a little Italian, though. All these years the memories were never really gone, just fuzzy."

"Did you mean what you said?" Cody asked. "Will you keep making me delicious food?"

"You never have to ask. You and I will sit together on that ugly couch and eat it while watchin' old movies." A new memory popped into my head from the trial we just went through. "You said I was the most wonderful person you ever met. No one's ever said that to me before."

"I meant it. No one comes close."

"Damn," I said. I was about to choke up, and I held him tighter. I couldn't picture myself holdin' anyone else. "Yer makin' me gross."

"You were gross before we met." We both laughed, but Cody looked worried.

"What's the matter?"

"I can't imagine what Adam's looking at right now."

"It's gotta happen, though. The only one who's gonna break him out is the one who put him there."

"The elder told me what would happen if they don't make it. I don't want to lose my memories."

"They'll be fine. There's more to Adam than he lets us see, and Austin's got a lot to work through. It's gonna take time, so let's enjoy all this. It's pretty here."

"It's like a thousand pounds has been lifted," Cody said, walking alongside me. "I really do think you should become a chef."

Gettin' my memories back meant remembering all those meals I cooked for my friends in the camps. They used to be painful, but not anymore. My old friends aren't broken, dirty, or miserable. They're smiling while enjoying the meals I made.

"I like the people in Norwich, and I can make food for people I like."

Out of the corner of my eye, Cody cracked a smile while starin' at me.

"I love you—r cooking," he said, studying my reaction.

"And I love... yer voice. We should sing together more."

They weren't quite the words we meant. It wasn't the right time, and I wasn't sure when it would be. There were some things from the past that didn't heal. The last time I'd said those words, I lost everything. If something were to ever happen to Cody—

"We can sing together while you're teaching me to cook."

"We can sing that Aqua song you love so much."

"I swear I will intentionally burn the house down if you put me through that again."

"You got no taste. Nineties Europop was the best."

"How about I meet you halfway with 'Beautiful Life' by Ace of Base?"

I couldn't help but smile. His past might have made him cold in some ways, but he hadn't become that person who hated the world. He was so much stronger than he ever gave himself credit for.

"Perfect."

# Chapter 34

# Rough Waters

*Austin*

I wanted out of whatever this was. I wanted to go back to my little blue box, but an invisible hand kept pulling along through the past. One moment I was standing in a cemetery, the next, I was in an alley, watching a scrawny teenager pick through a garbage can. He turned and looked right through me. Aside from the stench of old food, there was a brininess to the breeze that overtook the stagnant air.

Adam grabbed what looked like a half-eaten hoagie and gave it a sniff. He could still pass as human, but there were obvious signs. Slightly pointed ears, dark gray taking over the whites of his eyes, the dim glow of his orange irises, even his once smooth forearms looked a little hairier. This must have been at least a year before I met him, but I'd had no idea he was living like this.

"Still good," he growled before furiously scarfing down the sandwich like he hadn't eaten in days. He smelled like he hadn't bathed in a while either. Taking another bite, he stepped out of the alley, looking both ways then darted toward the sound of waves crashing. Now that I could see my surroundings in the light of the full moon, I recognized this place.

Like a frantic shadow, Adam dashed between the streetlamps until he was finally on the beach. There was a bonfire in the distance and the sound of a guitar, but Adam stayed in the darkness, sitting on the sand while watching the moon's reflection on the ocean. I'd never been here at night during a full moon, but it was pretty to see.

"What are you doing?" I asked, sitting next to him. I knew he wasn't going to answer, but if I didn't say something, I was gonna pop. "Living like a bum when you have a nice house waiting for you. It might not have been perfect, but it beats eating out of the trash. Dumbshit."

A car door shut behind us, and I turned toward a police officer holding a flashlight. Adam jumped up and ran to the water, narrowly evading a beam of white light. Why were the police looking for him?

A couple walked by, and the officer flagged them down.

"Excuse me, I'm looking for a teenager. Black male, about seventeen, showing signs of lycanthropy. He was last seen in this area."

"We just got here," the man said. "We haven't seen anyone like that, just a werewolf up the beach."

"All right, thanks." He turned off the flashlight and grabbed the radio from his shoulder. "He's not here, and the lifeguard hasn't seen him."

"Ten-four," came a staticky male voice from the speaker.

As the officer got back into his car, frantic splashing came from farther out in the water. In the moonlight, I watched helplessly as Adam struggled to stay on the surface.

"Adam!" I shouted, jumping into the turbulent blackness. This was just a vision, but it was real to me. He was screaming and choking, and I had to do something. He was the only thing I could touch, so I could pull him out. But it was too late. He'd already been swallowed by the waves. It wasn't long before I was pulled into the undertow as well. Could I drown in this?

I held my breath until I couldn't anymore, struggling to get to the surface. No matter what I did, though, something pulled me further down. This was it. Reflexively I gasped, and it was still air. I was breathing air in the ocean.

Looking around, I tried to find any sign of Adam. The moonlight was just bright enough to illuminate the area ahead, and I saw him. He was still, lifeless, just buoyant enough not to sink further, but not enough to surface. A large, dark figure several feet below me grew larger, frantically trying to get to the boy.

The shadow would go up, sink, come up, reach for Adam, then sink again. It doggy-paddled and flailed, but I couldn't make out what it was until it got closer. The shadow morphed into a huge man with a shark head, a shark tail and a dorsal fin. Despite all that, he couldn't swim worth a damn.

With a final jump, he grabbed Adam, pulling the boy as he seemed to skip along the bottom of the shallower part of the ocean shelf. He was hydrodynamic enough to run like he was on the surface of the moon, his tail propelling him forward as he finally emerged, carrying Adam in his arms.

The fucker was as big as me, but he had this wide, sad stare. The shark man wore what looked like a pair of Darryl's red shorts, and a necklace made from bone and driftwood with a seashell in the middle.

"Oh no, oh no," he said in a high-pitched panicked voice, pacing back and forth along the sand. "What do I do, what do I do?" He turned toward the bonfire and the sound of a guitar, then took off toward it like a ghost crab.

"Darryl, Darryl," he shouted. He had a strange way of speaking, always repeating himself, his tone alternating between high and low.

In the distance, Darryl threw his guitar aside and ran over to examine the commotion.

"What happened?"

"I don't know, I don't know. He was in the water, but he's not breathing. He's not breathing."

"Calm down, Bobby. Lay him on the ground."

*Bobby* did as he was told, and Darryl went to work administering CPR. After a few chest compressions, he sealed his mouth around Adam's, breathing into him. It went on like this for another minute before Adam coughed up a mouthful of water. Darryl turned him on his side, pounded his back to get the last of the fluid from his lungs.

"That was close," he whispered, checking Adam's pulse. "It's a little weak, but I think he'll be okay. I need to call an ambulance, though."

I had assumed these visions were Adam's memories, but he never would have remembered something like this while unconscious. Maybe Darryl wasn't making this sharkman shit up after all.

"Oh good, oh good. I was scared," Bobby said, holding his hand to his chest.

Though he terrified the shit out of me, that monster was kinda cute in a weird way. From the sing-songy way he spoke to his slightly higher pitched voice, he was the opposite of his appearance.

"You saved his life, Bobby. Lucky you were there to find him."

Bobby's face brightened, and he grinned, rows of sharp teeth glistening in the moonlight. "I was out looking for pretty shells, and I saw him and got scared. I got scared. I was going to leave him alone, but he wasn't moving. He wasn't moving."

"Did you swim?"

"I tried. I tried. I ran though. I ran through the water."

Darryl patted the huge creature on the back. "You tried. That's what matters. We'll keep working on it." He looked down at Adam who was still unconscious. "This is the kid the police were looking for." Darryl knelt again, slipping a finger behind his slightly pointed ears. "Ah, shit. Poor kid."

"What's wrong, what's wrong?"

"He's a half-turn."

"What's that?"

"He's gonna turn into a wolf man, like me one day."

"You mean, people can turn into wolf men?" His eyes went wide and glassy. "Could I... turn into a wolf man? Could I?"

"It doesn't work like that," Darryl said, prompting a teary response from Bobby. "You're perfect just the way you are."

"I'm useless. What kind of shark can't swim?"

"The kind of shark I like." Darryl gave a flirty grin before turning his attention back to Adam. "I don't have to worry about taking him to the hospital. Whatever damage was done will heal. I don't want to risk anything until I know why they're looking for him."

"Are they like the humans looking for me? They have harpoons!"

"You need to stay away from those boats," Darryl scolded. "And no, they're not the same."

Bobby's eyes darted from side to side as he heard people talking farther up the beach.

"They'll see, they'll see. I need to go." He turned toward the water, but Darryl wrapped his arms around him from behind.

"Come to my house tomorrow night."

"I can't, I can't. Family's been suspicious. Gotta spend the day with the family."

"Well come back soon, okay?" Darryl kissed the sharkman on the nose, and even though it was dark, Bobby's face darkened like he was blushing. Was it even possible for a shark to do that?

"I will, I will. I promise." He ran to the ocean before disappearing into the black water.

This vision was so off-the-wall bizarre that I started to question what I was seeing. Considering what had happened to Adam, I had my doubts this even took place. It could have been brain damage caused by his near-death experience.

Darryl scooped the teenager up off the ground and carried him back to his shack.

Night turned to day, and I was inside, watching Adam sleep on Darryl's oversized bed while the werewolf lay on a tall inflatable mattress, reading a book next to an open window. This place always had a calming effect, but I never allowed myself a moment's peace whenever Adam and I visited. There was still a lot of unresolved animosity between me and Darryl, and all of it was my fault.

A groan came from the bed, and Adam slowly sat up, rubbing his eyes.

"Good morning," Darryl said, licking his index finger before flipping the page of his book. "How are you feeling?"

"Like I was run over. Who the hell are you?"

"Well let's see. For some reason you were in the ocean and you nearly drowned. Oh, and the police are looking for you." He looked up at the teenager's widened expression. "I'm Darryl."

"Please don't tell anyone I'm here. I'll do anything you want."

"First tell me why they're looking for you, then I'll decide what to do."

Adam jumped out of the bed and sprinted for the door, prompting Darryl to drop his book. With a few steps, he easily caught the boy, grabbing him by the nape of his neck.

"Don't be stupid, kid. You can't run from a werewolf."

"Let me go!"

"How 'bout you sit back down and start talking?" He dragged Adam to the bed and forced him onto the mattress. He glared, arms crossed for a few minutes before the teenager started to speak.

"My... stepmother tried to put me in Stonebrook."

"Did you hurt anyone?"

"Kind of." Adam looked down at the floor. "They had it coming."

"Well, the law doesn't see it that way. I don't have to tell you how fucked you are, considering you're on the run." Darryl sighed, sitting on the bed next to Adam. "The only way out of this is to find a kuu mate. Once you do, you're no longer in the human's jurisdiction."

"What the hell's that?"

"You gotta find a werewolf to shack up with."

"Fuck that. You guys are gross."

Darryl laughed. "Boy, do I have some bad news for you, kid. You know what you are, right?"

Adam nodded before looking down at the floor again.

"You don't have a lot of time to be picky, either. You can hide out here until you start showing more signs, then they'll start to sniff you out. Once you get a piece of paper from a werewolf you like, get your kuu and I'll pull some strings to get you out of the human's database."

The vision grew hazy until I was in a familiar building. My fur stood up on the back of my neck when I saw myself sitting alone at a table, drinking from an entire pitcher of beer. This was The Boozy Beast on Ruskin Street, a place I'd visit often while trying to... self-medicate.

I remembered catching Adam's scent, and I didn't have long to make my move. I'd been carrying that stupid resume around for months without any luck. Every time I'd smell a fresh half-turn, I was too late. But that night, I was in the right place at the right time.

Like an out of body experience, I watched myself leer at him, now a whole year older and a lot hairier than before. I reached into the pocket of my army fatigues, grabbing a wrinkled, folded sheet of paper before walking up to the popular half-turn. Every werewolf within three blocks was in that bar that night, each one peacocking, trying to outdo the other. It was ridiculous, like watching one of those nature documentaries.

I remembered what I felt that night, not wanting to be just another animal competing for mating rites. It didn't really take much to get his attention, the perks of being the biggest thing in that bar. He was turned on the moment he laid eyes on me. I knew I had him.

"Here," I said with a grunt, placing the paper in his hand before walking away. The bait was set, and there was nothing more I needed to say. All I had to do was wait at my table with an extra pitcher of beer on hand.

He stared at me and then read my resume. With a smile, he walked over to my table. It was startling how accurate it all was, even insignificant things like what was on tap that night. No one would have remembered these details.

Then I had a terrifying revelation. What if this really was the afterlife? Had I died and was now being punished?

"You spelled demonstration wrong," Adam said, sitting across from past me.

"Does this place look like a school to you? Do you want to hop on my dick or not?"

"You must not want a kuu mate with that attitude."

"Look at me. Does it look like I'm desperate?" I was such a prick, but I sure knew how to play it cool. The truth was this entire interaction was a bluff. No one liked me, but I had to make myself look like I was out of reach. The bad boy act worked with the younger, less experienced guys, so Adam was my chance to try it out. "Come on. I can smell how turned on you are." I grabbed his hand, placing it on my crotch. "I bet I've got a bigger dick than all the werewolves here."

Adam huffed and pulled back his hand. "You're gross."

I knew I had to dial that back.

"Yeah, but I can get you off every day. Doesn't that sound good?"

"How about that *demonstration* in the back room?"

I stood and grabbed his hand, pulling him along to the back of the bar.

The scene disappeared, and all the depression came rushing back as the stained, bare walls of our old, tiny one-room apartment appeared. Adam sat on the couch, fidgeting with his kuu necklace while I watched TV. I wasn't really watching anything, just staring while pushing back memories triggered by the smell of burnt food from the kitchen. This was the first time Adam had used the oven, and I was trying to hold it together while not giving myself away.

"Are you still mad? I forgot, okay," Adam said, poking me in the arm. "I'll just order something."

My memories of this day were fuzzy, but I had a terrible feeling.

"Austin? Hey!" He shoved my shoulder, and in an instant, I had a hand wrapped around his neck, pushing him into the sofa. Seeing it secondhand made me want to throw up. I tried to grab past me by the arm, but as expected, I phased through.

Adam burned a roast, which was close to the smell of burning flesh I remembered during the weapons tests in the military.

"I'm on fire," I screamed, squeezing Adam's throat tighter.

"Please..." Adam squeaked out, and I jerked away, snapping out of the episode. Adam jumped off the sofa and ran to the corner of the room, trembling. "What the hell is wrong with you?"

"Don't touch me when I don't wanna be touched," I growled out. Though I looked remorseful, I never apologized. It wasn't Adam's fault, but I blamed him anyway. I always needed someone to blame, and he was there.

"I'm sorry. I didn't mean to burn the food. Why are you treating me like this?"

"It's not the food. I—" I ran my fingers through my mane before grabbing a fistful of fur. "The smell—don't cook anymore if you're gonna burn it!"

"I don't wanna wear this anymore," Adam said, pulling the chain around his neck, but the magic made it tighten until he let go. "I'm stuck with you, aren't I?"

"Until you're a werewolf, yeah." Tears welled in Adam's eyes, which broke my heart. Past me didn't show any emotion at all. "Listen. If I start to go blank, stay away. And don't burn food. I can't handle the smell."

"Are you gonna tell me what the hell is wrong with you?"

"Military fucked me up, okay? Did all kinds of things to me. You couldn't even imagine the pain." I looked up at a terrified Adam. "Don't. Burn. Food."

With that threat fresh in his head, Adam tore out of the house, leaving me alone as I turned back to the TV. These memories had always been so fuzzy, but now I could see myself for what I truly was. These weren't just visions of the past. I was reliving all of Adam's trauma, and I'd played a role in a lot of it.

"I don't wanna see anymore," I cried out, but everything continued as it did.

Past me flew back against the wall as Darryl sent another fist at my face, breaking my jaw with a snap.

"I didn't know *you* were the one he made the kuu with," Darryl roared, pinning me to the floor. "You ever do that to him again, and I'll hold your head underwater until you stop moving."

I'd forgotten this. I was so out of my mind, I couldn't remember the beating Darryl had given me that day. We were about the same size, but there was no contest in strength.

He looked over at Adam. "You should stay with me for a few weeks."

"Wait—" I whined, holding my broken jaw, which would take an hour or so to completely heal.

"I don't know what's happened to you, but you're not going to take your issues out on him. If you want someone to spar with, I'll be more than happy to break your face again."

He and Adam walked out of the apartment, leaving me alone in pain on the floor. Darryl had never hated anyone, but he hated me. I made sure of that.

Another day passed in a blink, and I was in bed with Adam. He was drenched in sweat and I was panting, the room filled with the scent of sex. After it was over, we never looked at one another. He would turn to the wall and I'd stare at the ceiling. Until then, I had only considered Adam a necessary nuisance. This was never about love, rather a means to an end, but that wasn't what I saw in Adam's eyes as tears filled them.

"Why do you hate me?" he asked, his voice a gentle whisper.

"You have to give enough of a damn about someone to hate them."

God, this hurt. What the fuck was wrong with me? This wasn't who I really was.

"I just don't understand. I thought you liked me. We used to talk. What did I do wrong?"

I examined myself closely, watching for any facial tic, any outward sign of what I felt inside. When I turned toward the window, I saw it—the sign of the emotions I was hiding. Though I tried to fight back the tears, they came anyway.

"You didn't care," I said. "I tried to tell you, but you didn't care."

The moment I said it, I remembered what set this off. Why didn't that memory play out?

"What are you talking about?"

"You won't be a half-turn forever, so when this is over, you'll be free. Use me for sex, but I don't want anything more from you."

"Fine. If this is what you want, I don't care anymore."

I watched on as Adam drifted to sleep, and past me continued to stare out the window as the sun dipped below the skyline of that awful city. He kept his word, and that was the last time he tried to talk to me.

"As long as you hate me, you're safe," the past me whispered, eyes half-closed.

I didn't remember saying that.

His eyes snapped open, and we both stared at one another.

"That's what you felt, right?" past me asked. "As long as people hate you, they won't die. But what could you possibly gain from living like that?"

The scene faded. This was no longer a look into what I thought I remembered, but what actually was. I was… talking to myself. That was the real me.

"I should have tried harder to understand you, Austin." Adam sat on the floor of a black room with his head in his hands. "I should have told my dad I loved him, instead of hanging up on him. I should have owned up to what I did to those bullies instead of running away."

Instead of a blue box, we were both the only light in what looked like an endless void. Maybe this was the last time I could make amends. If I really was dead, I wanted to pass. I wanted to make it right, if it was still possible.

"Hey," I said, sitting next to him. "You know you didn't do anything wrong, right?"

"I didn't listen. I didn't care. You tried to tell me, and I didn't care."

"It's not that you didn't. You couldn't." I hesitated, steeled myself with a deep breath, and slipped my arm around him. He was so warm, which was nice in such a cold place. "Adam, I don't know how to make this right. I used my past as a crutch to keep myself from hurting anymore, but all I did was hurt myself by hurting you. I never gave you a chance to care, even when I tried to tell you what happened to me. You were eighteen, and I should've known better than to dump all my issues onto a kid. What could you do?"

Adam didn't look up.

"I'm a terrible person. I resented Cody for being the one everyone loves, even you. I resented Darryl for not making the kuu bond with me. I resented Roscoe because he treated Cody so much better. And I resent you for putting me through hell. I hate you, and I hate hating you."

No physical pain I'd ever experienced hurt as much as those words did.

"It's okay to hate me. I never made it easy, but you're not a terrible person. You were thrown into things you shouldn't have been thrown into. Your dad knew you loved him. I could hear it in his voice when he was talking to you. Darryl saved your life, and he protected you, especially from me. He was too old for you to make that kind of bond with him, and I think deep down you knew that. Darryl was more like a father you were missing. Always protecting you."

"Do you hate me?" Adam asked, wiping his eyes.

"I never hated you for a moment. Not for one moment, Adam. I swear."

He wrapped his arms around me, and the vision of him shifted to a full werewolf as he looked into my eyes again.

"Thank you."

The sound of shattering glass filled the room as his image crumbled, and the black room turned to blue sky and green, rolling hills. The cool wind blew, and the sun warmed my face.

Had I made it to heaven? Had I truly made amends for what I did?

No...

Inside still felt hollow. Around me was paradise, but I couldn't feel joy or peace. Something terrible was still happening, but what that was, I couldn't place. Something with me had changed, though.

My face was dry, and I didn't want to go back to my blue box anymore.

# Chapter 35

# You're Safe in My Arms

*Adam*

The visions tossed me through months and years before I could even blink. Standing before me was an older teenager, maybe around fifteen. His hair was dirty blond and he was a lot less frail than before. All his hair had grown back, his muscles had thickened, and the once vacant pupils now burned with furious determination.

His steps were uneven, and he still needed to hold things for balance, but every day he pushed himself a little further. When the doctors would praise him for reaching another milestone, he didn't smile. He barely spoke, and when he did, it was usually a one or two word response.

This day, he walked with a metal crutch instead of the cane or walker the rehab center had provided. He carried it most of the time instead of using it for support, but when he'd grow tired, he'd put it under his arm and keep walking.

A brunette girl around his age caught up to him. She was missing one of her legs from the knee down, the fresh amputation scars partially hidden under bandages. She was very lean as though she had been an athlete before ending up here, but she also wore a smile that seemed to warm everything around her.

"Hey," she said, walking next to the teenage boy, who was only slightly taller. Austin must have been around five feet, five or six inches, barely as tall as I was when I was human. She handed him a chocolate pudding cup. "I saved it for you."

"Thanks," he grunted.

"You're always walking alone. Where are your parents?"

Austin's face remained oddly stoic, but he squeezed the pudding cup hard enough that the foil popped and the contents fell to the floor.

"I don't need anyone's help." He dropped the half-empty container and hurried out the door of the facility, balancing on his crutch. I followed him until he stopped close to the edge of the woods surrounding the rehab building.

This place wasn't familiar, and I wasn't even sure what state I was in. Huge laurel oak branches sprawled outward, Spanish moss hanging like old rags. The weather was humid and hot, and the shade barely made a difference.

Austin slowed his steps and carefully sat on the ground, using his crutch for leverage. He stared at the trees for a moment before closing his eyes to breathe in deep through his nostrils. When they opened again, they glowed a pale orange.

"I'm gonna run one day. I'm gonna run into the woods and never come back. I don't wanna come back." His cheeks were wet as he wiped his tears with the collar of his white T-shirt. "Why am I still here?"

The scene faded, and a short, blond half-turn made his way through fallen leaves as he sprinted along the forest floor. For the first time, Austin smiled. It was only for a moment as he leapt from the ground to the branches, swinging to the next before deftly landing on his feet. These woods were different from the others. In the place of massive, sprawling oaks were tall, skinny pines, and the air was crisp and dry. In the distance, mountains with light snow patches towered several thousand feet into a cloudless sky.

Austin leapt up into the thin branches of a yellow poplar tree, holding himself steady with one hand while shielding the sun from his face with the other. I jumped into the tree as well, which was much easier now that I was a full werewolf.

Getting a closer look at the teenager, I could see he made good on his word. His T-shirt was ragged and dirty, the blond, fur-like hair covering his body had flecks of dander and sand, and whatever skin was uncovered was just as filthy as the rest of him. He likely hadn't been back to civilization in a while.

His eyes darted to what he was after in the distance. It was a deer with large ears and white on its face and underside. Austin studied it carefully before letting himself fall to the ground. He had grown a lot bulkier than before, muscles I'd never seen on a half-turn rippled with his every careful movement.

He focused his glowing, orange stare on the clearing ahead, making sure he moved into the wind. I could smell the deer, and though I'd never hunted a day in my life, the scent seemed to bring out something I often repressed. Austin didn't repress the wolf. It was like he didn't want to be human anymore.

As soon as he was within sprinting distance, he prepared himself to lunge, but froze when another werewolf leapt onto the deer, instantly severing its spine with his massive jaws.

"Better be a lot quicker than that if you wanna eat," the werewolf said in a mocking tone, looking up from his fresh kill. He was pure black with a few specs of gray on his muzzle and completely nude but had a lot more fur than most of the werewolves I'd seen.

"I did what you said." Austin ran over to the kill, clenching his fists. "You said to track, stay downwind and be patient. I'd have killed it myself."

The werewolf patted Austin on the back. "Not bad at all for a half-turn."

"I didn't want your help," Austin hissed.

The werewolf slung the carcass over his broad shoulder. He was about as big as Austin would end up, though there was something off about him physically. His arms were a little longer and he was almost standing on his toes. They weren't quite paws, but he wasn't flat-footed either.

"You don't have the strength or the ability to kill one of these yet, but when you go full-turn, nothing's gonna stop you."

"How long do I have to stay like this? I hate this body."

"Depends. Everyone's different. Sometimes it takes years, sometimes a few months, but you're the strongest half-turn I've ever met. If something were to happen to me, you'd survive no problem out here on your own."

"What do you mean if something were to happen? Nothin's gonna do you."

The werewolf started walking toward a hill in the distance as Austin trailed close.

"I dunno. Things happen. We're resilient, not immortal."

"You're never gonna tell me your story, are you?" Austin asked.

"Not 'til you do."

Austin didn't respond, instead he kept his eyes on the werewolf. They approached a small opening in the side of the craggy cliff with an ashy fire pit out front.

"You don't have to cook it. We can just eat it like that, right? That's what werewolves do," Austin said, stopping as his elder dropped the buck to the ground.

"It's what *werewolves* do, yeah." He gave a sharp-toothed grin and pulled off one of the deer's legs with a nauseating snapping sound before dropping it into Austin's arms. "Wanna eat like a werewolf? Here ya go."

The eager half-turn held the leg to his mouth and used his smaller canines to break the flesh, but he couldn't seem to tear the meat away. Again, he tried, this time shaking his head, but his teeth just weren't long enough to sheer anything.

"May as well be human," he mumbled, tossing the leg to the ground.

"Stop being hard on yourself. Everyone has their limitations. Deal with it." The older werewolf pulled a large, sharp blade sticking from the trunk of a scarred pine, paring the skin of the animal like a delicate fruit before ripping the rest of the hide away with his massive hands. "You get angry over the stupidest shit."

"It's not stupid!" Austin kicked the leg out of the way. "I'm sick of being helpless!"

"Well, good thing you're not. I'm not usually in the habit of helping the helpless."

"But I—"

"Can't eat meat directly off a carcass. Who the hell cares? Humans can't do that either, but they managed to eat meat just fine for thousands of years. You gotta brain, so use it. It's not only about brute strength. You gotta be smart enough to use what you've been given to survive out here."

Austin sat on a small, flat boulder, staring at the ground. "I'm not smart. I want to be strong."

"Why do you say you're not smart?"

"Never finished school."

The black werewolf let out a growly chuckle. "Obviously. You're out here with me instead." With his index finger, he lifted Austin's chin. "Got some news for ya, kid. School doesn't make you smart. It makes you obedient." He let go and continued skinning the carcass.

"Do you ever get lonely?" Austin asked.

The older werewolf stopped what he was doing and sat on the boulder.

"Yeah. There's not a lot like us. They're like domesticated dogs stayin' in their miserable cities, barely living miserable lives. The humans hate us, but the werewolves just stay there like strays. Those that leave that shit-hole end up in Colorado Springs, joining the military. I feel sorry for 'em."

"Why? I've been thinking about it myself."

The older werewolf shook his head. "Don't ever trust the military. Don't ever trust humans."

"My parents and brother are dead," Austin said, changing the subject, prompting the werewolf to turn toward him. "My father killed everyone, even put a bullet in my head, but I'm still here. I don't know what to do. I thought I could find my purpose out here, but this doesn't feel right either."

"Damn, kid." He slipped his arm around Austin's back, but the half-turn pushed him away.

"I don't want sympathy," he snapped, but his snarl softened. "I want to know why you're here."

"I killed people," the werewolf responded without hesitation. Austin's face turned pallid. "I tore five men to shreds, and I don't regret any of it."

"So you're a killer, like my dad."

"No. I'm just a killer. I'm not your dad. Those five men raped and murdered my daughter." His voice trembled. "My only child. Humans took her from me. I'd probably kill more of 'em in a rage if I didn't come out here."

"I—" Austin paused, letting out a sigh. "Shit. I'm sorry. I think about what I would do if my dad didn't kill himself, and every scenario leads back to my hands around his neck, letting him breathe for a second before choking him again until he slowly dies, all while looking at my face. I'd be a killer, too."

"That's why you're out here with me, kid. You may not be mine, but we're a lot alike."

The woods around me went dark, the light of the moon overhead illuminating a slightly older Austin sitting alone on his boulder, looking out into the woods as if waiting. Night soon turned to day, and the half-turn lay on the ground, staring at the sky, not moving as the light faded again. Three days passed, and Austin finally started to cry. It was the first time I'd seen him cry in this vision.

"He's gone," he whispered as if he had been expecting this day to come. Sluggishly, he pushed himself from the rocky ground and made his way east, toward the orange light of dawn blanketing the cold valley. I stood there, confused as I looked around for the other werewolf. What had happened?

Familiar cackling overhead and smoke from a chimney filled the air that sent an all-too-familiar chill racing through me. Even in the remote wilds of this beautiful place, the witches hunted their prey. Austin made his way through the forest, keeping as quiet as he could, but it didn't make a difference. Malformed, shadowy ravens with red eyes flew from branch-to-branch, almost hungrily watching as the half-turn ran through fetishes of teeth, bone and feathers dangling from bare aspen branches.

The scene soon turned to a familiar beach, and the ravens turned to screeching gulls overhead as the frothy ocean lapped against the sand. Austin sat on a dune as the sun dipped halfway below the horizon, its distorted reflection zigzagging along the water's surface. In the distance, a werewolf on a surfboard rode the waves with perfect balance and grace. I smiled when I realized it was Darryl. Sometimes I really missed this place.

The half-turn was covered in thicker body hair, and a small tail jutted from his lower back between the cleft of his ass. I remembered how uncomfortable that thing was. It had been too short to push off to the side when I'd sit, and too long and stiff to not accidentally bend it the wrong way if I wasn't paying attention.

Darryl hopped off the board, sinking waist-high into the rough waters before tucking the surfboard under his arm. He sloshed his way onto the beach, then sat next to Austin.

"You feeling okay?" Darryl asked, eyeing the older half-turn. "Need some extra attention?"

Austin shook his head.

"I'm getting a little worried. You're obviously in pain, but you keep holding back. The only way you're going to get over this phase faster is by letting me help you."

"I don't need help. A little pain never killed anyone."

"No, but it could kill other people," Darryl said. "It's dangerous for a half-turn to go this long."

"It's only dangerous if you're weak."

The werewolf sighed and turned to the ocean. "It's not a weakness to depend on others once in a while. At least sleep in the house."

"I don't like sleeping inside."

"Is there anything you like?"

Austin looked up at Darryl, his brows furrowed. "No."

Without another word, Darryl stood up and brushed the sand from his fur before walking over to his house. His deck was only partially finished with stacks of wood lining the parameter of his property. Austin watched on curiously as the werewolf flipped on a floodlight and set to work measuring and sawing.

The half-turn slowly made his way over as Darryl hammered a couple nails into the board, securing it to the deck frame.

"Did you build this house?" Austin asked.

"Kind of. I had some contractor friends help me out." Darryl smiled and handed the hammer to Austin. "Want to help me?"

Austin gripped the heavy tool tightly, pounding a half-driven nail into the deck so hard the head sank into the board with a crack.

"Too hard," Darryl said, his tone a lot more patient than I would have expected after Austin ruined the plank he'd just measured and cut. The werewolf rocked the loosened wood back and forth before pulling it loose from the foundation and tossing it to the side. "I'll save that piece for something else." He grabbed another board and handed Austin the measuring tape. "I want this cut to six feet. Measure it and then mark it. After that, use the saw and put that strength to good use."

The half-turned nodded and did as Darryl told him, seeming to enjoy the process. He measured, marked, and then began cutting. For using a handsaw, he cut the edge surprisingly straight.

"Damn, kid. That's some good work."

"Don't call me that. I'm not a kid."

"You're a kid compared to me." Darryl grabbed the plank and began hammering it to the frame. "Cut six more pieces, the same length and we'll call it a night."

They faded as the darkness gave way to mid-day. Darryl was sitting on his lifeguard chair, watching over a crowd of swimmers while Austin hammered away, adding a railing and steps to the deck. I hadn't known Austin was the one that built this, and he seemed content doing it, losing himself to the sounds of construction.

Day soon turned to evening, and Austin had disappeared, but the deck was finished. Darryl approached, climbing the sturdy steps while holding onto the railing.

"Damn," he whispered to himself, cautiously padding across the newly built structure, feeling for any loose planks. He turned, looking out toward the ocean to see Austin lying near the water, partially obscured by one of the white sand dunes the beach was famous for. "The kid's a little rough, but I think he'll be okay."

"Attention, mongrel squad!"

The sudden shift in scene made me jump, as Austin, now a full werewolf, stood rigid next to three other werewolves in a line as a human man in camouflage slowly paced in front of them. Despite the insult, the mood seemed unusually upbeat.

"Because of your excellent latrine-cleaning, you've all been officially promoted to..." The man paused, folding his arms. "Grout." He pulled out four toothbrushes and slipped each into their pants pockets. "Make the country proud boys. Dismissed!"

The werewolves scampered out of the barracks, leaving a line of humans behind still at attention.

"The rest of you, hit the course!"

"Yes sir," they all shouted in unison, filing out behind the werewolves. I phased through the soldiers, easily catching up to the others as they bantered, but Austin remained quiet, trailing them at a short distance.

"I think sergeant has the hots for you, Steve," a shorter, brown werewolf said, jiggling the toothbrush in the light gray werewolf's pocket. "Did you feel how slowly he slid it in?"

"I'm actually fucking him, but don't tell anyone or we'll be court-martialed."

Austin quickly caught up, his ears pulled back and his eyes wide. "Are you dumb? That's, like, six rules broken!"

The others howled with laughter, and the larger werewolf recoiled, falling behind the others again.

"I wonder what they're gonna make us do next," the brown werewolf said. "You remember last week when they had us prepare dinner after cleaning the toilets?"

"Sergeant was extra spicy that day," Steve replied.

"I didn't wash my hands, and I fondled all the Hawaiian rolls."

The black and silver werewolf gagged, wrinkling his nose. He was about as tall as Austin, but a lot lankier.

"You fucking—" He gagged again. "I ate six of those, you piece of shit! I wondered why they were all squished."

"Oh, come on, Randall. You've eaten worse things in survival training," the brown werewolf replied. "Besides, we were the only ones that didn't get sick. Everyone was puking and shitting everywhere. What a fun night. I bet they won't let us touch any more food after that."

"This is why they hate us, you know?" Austin pulled open the door to the communal showers. "And why we're stuck scrubbing grout with toothbrushes instead of training."

"We were scrubbing shit with toothbrushes before you got here," the black werewolf said with a defeated sigh. "I keep thinking they're saving us for something fun like tactical warfare, but it's like they don't have any use for us. We're twenty soldiers in one, and they treat us like we're army pets."

"That's kinda weird," Steve said. He reminded me of a leaner and better-spoken version of Roscoe. "I didn't even think they'd accept me because I didn't have my GED. Who knows. Maybe they're saving us for some super-secret mission. Did you hear about the werewolf sect of al Qaeda."

"Wait, terrorist groups have werewolves?" Austin asked, his eyes widening.

"Yeah. They're called al-Betas."

Three of them snorted laughter, but Austin rolled his eyes and groaned.

"That was a good one." Randall got down on his knees and began scrubbing furiously. "They probably do have werewolves, though. Someone like Austin wouldn't hesitate to reach into their asses and pull out their colons. He's the biggest motherfucker I've ever seen."

"When I was a half-turn, I knew a guy just as big. He was a lifeguard," Austin said, joining the others on the tiled floor.

"A werewolf lifeguard?" the brown werewolf said with a chuckle. "How the hell did he manage that?"

"Never asked. I thought werewolves just had normal jobs like that. What did you do before you ended up here, Blake?"

"Probably the same thing we all did," the black werewolf grumbled. "The only reason I signed up for this shit was because I'd actually get paid a real salary so I wouldn't have to sleep on the sidewalk."

"Me too," Steve said.

"Same," Randall added.

"I just want to get stronger," Austin muttered, looking at his toothbrush. "This is a stupid waste of time."

Blake dipped his toothbrush in a small bowl of soapy water and continued scrubbing. "You're already huge. How much stronger do you want to get?"

"That's not what I mean. I just—" He looked around at the others and slumped forward. "Never mind. I guess this is fine being told what to do. I can turn my brain off and just keep myself focused on the task."

"You've only been here five days," Steve said. "Another couple weeks of this you'll be singing a different tune." He dropped his brush and knelt next to Austin. "At least we're not alone. Like it or not, you're a part of our pack now. Werewolves gotta stick together."

"A pack?"

"Never had one?"

Austin shook his head.

"It's like a family, but closer. How long have you been a werewolf?"

"A couple weeks. Right when I turned, I came back home to the mountains. Didn't sit well with that lifeguard friend I had, and we had a falling out. I needed to do this. Joining the military would make me stronger, and having more structure could help me forget some things."

"You've seen some shit, haven't you?" Steve asked, and the others gathered around.

Austin gritted his teeth and looked down at the drain on the floor. "Something like that."

"You don't have to talk about it. The pack's got your back. Ain't that right, boys?"

"Yes sir," the other two barked in unison.

Austin went stiff as the three wrapped him in a group hug, their tails wagging. Eventually he closed his eyes, a slight, contented smile replacing his normal rigidity, his arms now resting on the backs of his new friends.

Those names...

I remembered seeing those names etched on his dogtags. Even though it hadn't happened yet, I knew what was coming. Now that I could put faces to the names, my heart broke at seeing just how eager they were to bring Austin into their little family. This was the moment he'd felt like he belonged somewhere, but even that would be taken away.

All that time I spent resenting him, thinking he was a cold, heartless asshole. I never wanted to know what he went through because I didn't care. I had my own problems to deal with, and I wanted him to support me.

The scenes played out like the sad montage to a coming tragedy. The four became inseparable, and eventually did get to do something more than basic training or cleaning buildings. Now they sat in oversized seats of a civilian jumbo jet, the other three excitedly looking out the window like dogs, their tails wagging and ears perked. There were other military personnel in the surrounding seats, many watching movies or listening to music, but Austin remained serious, his nose buried in a yellow *German for Dummies* book. Over the intercom, the pilot mentioned the weather in Saarbrücken, and Austin soon joined the others in looking out the window.

"You gonna order for us at restaurants when we're allowed off base, Austin?" Randall asked, shoving the larger werewolf's arm.

"Someone's gotta learn the language. You guys are way too dumb."

"Guilty," Steve said. "Never thought I'd get to go to another country. I'm gonna eat so many sausages."

Blake grabbed the straps of his backpack and pulled it into his lap. "Glad they sent us together. I thought for sure they were going to split us up this time."

"All right boys," Steve belted out. "When we land, let's take it all in. Who knows when they'll let us do this again."

Thunder crashed as the scene shifted quickly, four of the werewolves huddled in a tent as hail pelted the trees and ground around them.

"Welcome back to the front range," Randall shouted, joining the others in keeping the tent upright. "It's like war, but the weather edition."

"If the hail gets any bigger, it's gonna rip through," Austin shouted.

With that said, a larger hailstone tore into the top of the tent, hitting Austin in the head. The three of them shielded the larger werewolf, covering their own heads while the ice pelted their backs. The storm only lasted for another five minutes before the wind and rain died, the only sounds remaining were groans from the injured werewolves as they emerged from their tattered tent.

"Well, that was fun," Randall said, soaking wet and breathing in deep. "I love the smell after all hell breaks loose."

"Didn't anyone catch the weather report?" Austin asked, rubbing his head.

"Oops. Knew I forgot something," Blake said, shuffling around his backpack. "Left the weather radio back in the barracks."

Austin slapped the back of Blake's head.

"Hey! At least we brought the tent this time."

"Should've just bivouacked for all the good this did," Austin said, picking through ripped-up nylon and bent, flimsy metal rods.

Randall knelt next to Austin, looking for his bag. "You said you used to live in the woods. How did you deal with the storms?"

"You don't get storms like this at higher elevations. Just gotta worry about the blizzards burying you in the winter."

"We should take a trip to the mountains and spend a week in the real forest."

"No!" Austin shouted loud enough for the others to snap their heads toward him. "No," he repeated, softer. "We—we can't go in those woods."

The other three nodded, not pressing Austin any further. They seemed to understand how to handle his fragile mental state. Instead of arguing, they went along with it.

"If you say we shouldn't, then we won't," Steve said.

Austin's ears fell to the sides of his head. "Bad stuff happened out there when I was half-turn. The day I left the forest, I didn't stop running until I got through some of the most fucked-up demonic shit I'd ever seen. I lost a good friend that day, and I don't wanna lose you guys."

"We're not going anywhere," Blake said softly. "You're stuck with us."

The scene darkened, and the smell of chemicals burned my nose as Austin sat alone on the floor in a concrete room, his fur falling out in clumps only to regrow. He shook violently, occasionally choking on bloody vomit he spat onto the floor.

Several humans wearing protective masks and yellow hazmat suits filed into the room, one holding a rapidly clicking Geiger counter.

"Can I please go back to my pack?" Austin asked, his voice weak. "It's been almost a month."

"This is the last test, Austin," one of the men said, his voice muffled. "Once the levels go down, you can leave quarantine."

"When's that gonna be?"

"Another couple days," the man said. "You're doing good. You're a part of something really important that's gonna save a lot of lives."

"No one will tell me what's going on."

"That's because we can't. We'll check up on you in three days."

The scene faded until it was just Austin sitting on the lower bunk of a bed, rocking back and forth. There was no one else in the barracks and it was midday. The door opened, and Austin jumped to attention, his tail wagging slightly before falling limp as a man in uniform entered.

"You should be sleeping. We're going to need you rested up for some more tests."

"More? I thought that was it." He looked at the door. "Where are the others?"

"In isolation."

"Why do we have to do this? I don't understand."

"You're not privy to those answers," the man snapped. Every human in these visions seemed out of focus, and sometimes they were featureless shadows like this guy. "You're to report to sector R by twenty-one hundred."

Austin swallowed hard before squeaking out a, "Yes, sir." When the man disappeared, the werewolf ran to the bathroom before vomiting into the sink.

"I can't do that again. I won't do that again," he whispered to himself, his eyes wide and shaky. "I gotta find my pack."

Day quickly turned to night, and Austin dashed from wall-to-wall, staying out of sight as he moved to an area guarded by two shades in fatigues holding M4s. He took in several rapid, shaky breaths before sneaking by, leaping high over a wall packed with curled razor wire, then disappeared on the other side.

I phased through and followed until he leaned up against the side of a large building, careful to stay out of sight as two men in yellow suits exited, one holding something that reflected a bit of the blue halogen lighting surrounding the yard.

They didn't say anything, and one of the men pushed up his mask, appearing to stare at the things in his hand. As with the other humans, his face lacked any features as he dropped what he held into a nearby trash can.

"That was fucked up," he said, turning away.

The other man pointed to the discarded mask. "We need to get to decontamination."

The tone was somber as they slowly walked out of sight. After a few minutes, Austin dashed over to the garbage can and slowly pulled the tangled chains from the bin. The all-too-familiar thousand yard stare returned as he dropped his arms, still clutching the discarded dog tags.

He let out a worried whine and ran to the building the men emerged from, trying desperately to pull open the door, but it was locked and solid. Upon hearing commotion return to the yard, he disappeared, leaping over the wall.

The scene turned to a black room with Austin standing alone, staring at the dogtags in his hand. He didn't cry, move, or blink. It was almost as though time had frozen for him. I grabbed a tuft of fur on my chest, squeezing as I slowly approached. His dark orange eyes faded to blue as I stood in front of him, and his ears folded back.

"Austin?"

He didn't respond.

"Please talk to me."

"You gotta tell me what to do," he said in the robotic tone I'd become accustomed to over the last week. "Tell me what to do. Please."

"No," I choked out. "This isn't the way it's supposed to be."

He didn't respond. Instead, a long sword-like blade appeared in my hand. I held it up, and that's when the tears began to soak his face.

"What is this?"

"I can't do it myself. Everything goes back to the way it was," he whispered. "Maybe it'll work if you do it."

"Do what?"

"Kill me."

I stepped back, the blade falling with a metallic clank to the black floor as I lost what composure I had. My stomach turned as I tried to find any sign of the Austin I'd seen when he was with his pack, but there was no emotion, just tears filling empty, blue eyes.

"I won't."

"Please," he repeated, this time his voice went from monotone to bursting with anguish. "It hurts so much to live. You can make it stop."

I fell into him, wrapping my arms around his waist and crying into the thicker fur on his chest.

"I'm so sorry," I whispered.

"Why am I still here?" he asked. I remembered him saying that as a limping little teenage boy sitting under the oak tree. How many times had he asked himself that while all alone?

"So we could have this moment." I pulled back just as his eyes faded to their usual orange. "So you could find a family."

"No!" he shouted. "Don't say that. You'll all die, just like them." He gripped my upper arms, his claws sinking into my flesh. "You have to hate me!"

"I only hated you because that's what I thought you wanted! I know you don't want that! You never wanted anyone to hate you."

He let out the saddest whine as he let go and dropped to his knees.

"Don't hate me anymore," he cried out as he fell onto his hands, tears steadily dripping onto the floor. "I don't wanna be alone."

Trying to hold onto what emotional strength I still had, I knelt in front of him, pushing his heavy upper body from the floor.

"I can't make promises about the future. I can't say everyone will be around forever, but right now," I pulled him into a firm embrace, "you're safe in my arms. I swear."

He looked up and locked eyes with me.

"When I was really little, my mom used to sing this song—I can't remember it, but the lyrics promised I'd be safe in her arms."

His words brought back a memory I'd forgotten until now, but I no longer believed any of this was coincidence. A week after Dad's funeral, I'd heard the song he mentioned, and I remembered the lyrics like they were sung to me yesterday.

My voice cracked and trembled as I struggled to sing while stroking the back of his neck. I sang until I got to the last part of the chorus. "... you will be safe in my arms."

We sat like that for several minutes in almost deafening silence.

"I'll never hate you, Austin. Don't ever think about dying again because our family wouldn't be complete without you."

His tears stopped, and he pulled back with a smile.

"Thank you," he whispered, before the image shattered into millions of pieces, giving way to blue sky and rolling, green hills. Austin sat under a laurel oak tree with his back turned to me, but he was wearing something that made me laugh and cry at the same time. As my heavy footsteps fell beside him, he turned and grinned before scrambling to his feet.

"How did you get that Pawlibear costume?"

"I learned it from when I was in my blue box. You gotta want something bad enough, and it'll happen."

"And this is what you wanted?"

He pulled me into a hug, and everything around us turned a blinding white.

"No. I just wanted to see you smile again."

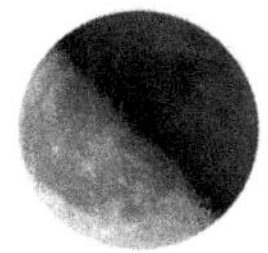

# Chapter 36

# Flowers and Family

*Cody*

The sunlight grew brighter until it bleached the green hills and purple wildflowers. Colors bled into the ground, and everything around was featureless. Roscoe disappeared, and tribal drumbeats filled my mind, the rhythm speeding up as they beckoned me to the surface.

When I felt like I was falling, my eyes snapped open, and I choked on herbs that had been tucked into my cheek. I spat the psychedelic mixture onto the cavern floor, and the neon butterflies and multi-colored specs disappeared.

Roscoe, Austin, and Adam each jolted awake, spitting out what had been placed into their mouths, and the drums outside of the cave grew to a crescendo before softening back to a steady rhythm. Yipping and howling commenced before a different beat took control of the feral tribe.

"Memories are intact," I said, looking over at the huge elder sitting cross-legged by the fire. "I guess we passed?"

He nodded, now seeming to understand me, even without being under the effects of the herb.

"My head," Austin whimpered while rubbing his temples. "Where the hell are we?"

"Did you come back to us?" Adam asked, scrambling across the stony floor toward the larger werewolf until he was on his knees before him, holding Austin's face. "You're talking."

"Had this weird dream," Austin said, "and you were in it."

We all turned toward the sound of a giant tail thudding a joyful tempo.

"That was no dream," the elder grunted. "I did not expect any of you to pass, and my pack would add four more this day, but I misjudged." He turned to Roscoe before reaching into his pouch to grab a large handful of white powder.

"How are we understanding you?" I asked.

He threw what he had into the fire. "Breathe deep."

We looked at one another, and Roscoe nodded, taking in a deep snort through his nose as smoke filled the cavern. Each of us joined in, and the vibrant colors of the high returned, but different this time. The fire shifted to a pale blue before taking on the shape of a familiar scene. A younger Roscoe slid a wad of money across the table toward a bewildered Darryl.

"This small act of selflessness changed everything." The elder sprinkled more of the dust over the fire, and the scenes shifted. Older Darryl stood proudly on the beach, folding his arms as he smiled and gazed out over the water. "If you had not given young Darryl his chance"—the scene shifted to a large werewolf sitting slumped over on a street corner, unconscious—"he would have gone down a familiar path. And you, Roscoe..." The fire showed the older werewolf lying under a tree eerily still, empty pill bottles scattered around. "This was to be your fate on the day you should have met Cody."

Seeing him lying lifeless and alone like that was too much. I looked away. The visions of his past alone had been painful enough. I squeezed Roscoe's hand, and he looked down at me with an unfazed grin. Even seeing himself like that didn't do much to dampen him.

"I guess you saved me, Cody."

"He did, and had you not started a new path, such tragedies would have befallen all of you."

The fire roared as Adam gasped for air, trying to swim. Inevitably, though, he was dragged under the rough waters where his eyes remained locked in terror as he took a final desperate gasp of sea water.

"Darryl wasn't there to breathe life back into you, and neither was the one who pulled you from the water." The elder blew another handful of herbs onto the fire. The flames lapped violently as more smoke filled the cave. A hazy vision appeared of Austin falling into a fit of traumatic rage while running toward three police officers, each firing several rounds into the werewolf. He would make quick work of the humans before coming to his senses, clutching the lifeless body of a young woman in uniform while sobbing and rocking her back and forth.

"Why am I here?" he cried, looking down at the gun that had fallen to the asphalt. He held it to his head, and with a deafening crack, the flames grew brighter.

"Adam wasn't around to pull you off the streets. Every day, the sounds of the city, and the stress of being alone and uncared for ate away at your already fragile state of mind."

The fire turned a darker sapphire, and there I was a half-turn, wandering a cold facility in a drugged-up stupor. My body dragged itself like a husk along the halls until I passed beveled, silver lettering that read Stonebrook—the facility where the most desperate half-turns ended up. The vision shifted again to a mangy brown werewolf sitting at the same bus stop where I had found Roscoe, his fur matted and sticky with flies gathering on damp, bloody spots. His stare was empty and defeated, and he didn't seem to pay any attention to the humans walking by, eyeing him with disgust. He didn't beg or speak— he just stared at nothing.

"Without Roscoe to pull you from this life, the moment you realized that all the debt and hard work meant nothing, you fell into despair believing you were worth nothing. Why try to live a good life when there is no good in the world? Why go on with no one to care?"

The vision suddenly turned into a violent whirlwind of flames, startling the elder as I reappeared in a windowless building, my eyes blank and white, a shadowy figure approaching. The white smoke from the fire cycled upward before the vision evaporated into nothing.

"That was something I did not expect," he said, holding up his hand. The drums outside fell silent, and the fire dimmed to a softer orange.

The elder might not have known what was happening in that vision, but I did. I'd seen it happen to Roscoe's pack, and to a young Mosavi. The huge werewolf's silver stare lingered on me for a moment before turning back to the others.

"Amazing, is it not?" he continued. "Had that one event not occurred all those years ago, none of you would have found the right path. We never know in the present the lives we touch, each of us nudging ourselves and others along fate's narrow paths. It was not merely coincidence. You were all meant to find one another."

A younger feral wandered into the cave holding three packages of Little Debbie snacks, with one torn open. He smacked loudly before sitting on a makeshift pallet of leaves and straw.

"Ooo!" Roscoe jumped up and walked over to the feral, his ears off to the sides. "Forgot we brought these. I'll take that Christmas tree one—"

The feral snarled, turning his back to Roscoe and cramming more of the cakes into his mouth like a starving dog.

"Aw, come on, guy. I haven't eaten in days."

"You have only been here a few hours," the elder said with a deep, throaty laugh. "You should begin your journey home while the sun is still high. With Samhain passed, the witches are weak, but they can still be dangerous the closer to midnight it is."

"Thank you," I said, standing to meet the huge elder next to the fire. I held out my hand, and his hands engulfed mine, a small, smooth stone pressing into my palm.

"You and your pack did all the work. All I did was observe. Take this to your elder and tell him to meet me on the solstice. I have been watching over him for years, and he may need real Whasha guidance as you all did. And perhaps, I would need him."

*Austin*

We didn't talk much on the way back home, and we didn't say anything before going to sleep. What could we say that hadn't been said already? Part of me wanted to know what Cody and Roscoe had experienced, but I'd seen enough sadness for a lifetime. Awful things might have happened to me, but everyone was struggling with their own demons, even Adam.

I would have loved to say I was cured, but even with this weird werewolf magic, ya can't snap a finger and make over a decade of hurt disappear. The elder pulled me aside before we left, and I knew what he would ask. It was something I'd given careful consideration.

*"If it meant forgetting those you loved and lost, would you abandon those memories for a cure?"*

Knowing he could erase my past was a relief, but that was the coward's way out. I'd forget my mom, my little brother, my grandma...

I grabbed the dog tags jingling together against my chest fur.

Everything I had gone through would disappear, and everyone I'd met along the way would as well, even Adam. I wouldn't be the same anymore—I'd be feral. What we go through in life shapes the person we become, even the worst of it. I'd wanted nothing more in life than to be stronger so I wouldn't need a family.

What was I thinking?

Here in our cozy little home, I had a real family. This was all I ever wanted. I'd spent most of my life on the edge of death, but there was always something inside that pushed me a little further. A gut feeling that told me there was a better life waiting. Keep going. Don't give up. Maybe it was hope or instinct—it didn't matter what it was called. It saved me.

I stared out the window while sitting on the bed I shared with Adam—my once kuu mate. Would he leave now? I didn't want him to go. There were times I could've surfaced from the spell he put me under, but if I'd done that, there wouldn't have been a reason for him to stay.

Now, I would let him decide. There wasn't a kuu or weird magic. Just us, and everything we'd seen.

The door to the bedroom creaked open, and I turned toward Adam, who held something behind his back.

"Hey," I said. Smiling like this was strange, but I did it involuntarily when I saw him now. When we were together in that beautiful place, I could see who he really was for the first time. "What'cha got there?"

"Don't laugh. Just humor me, okay?"

"Okay," I said, catching a glimpse of a reddish-pink petal sticking out from behind his back.

"Close your eyes."

The room darkened as I waited, then I felt something drape over the top of my head, leafy protrusions falling to the side.

"Okay," he said, taking my hand and pulling me off the bed. We walked over to the dresser mirror, and I couldn't help but laugh at the sight. He had picked azaleas from the bushes outside, which shouldn't have even been in bloom, braiding them together in a floral crown. I looked like a contradiction, but as I examined closer, my face seemed softer.

"Heh. This is pretty."

"I got up early to make it. I was thinking about what I want to do here in Norwich, and since I've been tending to the plants outside in private to take my mind off things for a while, I actually started to like it. Willa gave me some stuff to grow plants in the off-season, but they'll die when the snow comes. People like pretty floral arrangements, and they always make me happy."

I looked back at the mirror, adjusting the laurel of flowers on my head.

"I like it. It's soft and pretty meets big and ugly."

"More like big and handsome," Adam corrected. "Listen, I wanted to say I'm sorry for everything. No one should have had to go through what you did."

"Don't apologize, especially since I was the one that treated you like crap. I can't go back and fix that, and I don't wanna be feral and forget who I am and who I loved. I also don't wanna forget you."

"We can start over, you know? We can get to know each other better now that there's not this wall of animosity keeping us apart. We never talked about anything, and we should have done that. I'm just as much to blame because I saw you suffering, but I ignored it."

I grabbed both of his hands, holding them to my lips. "You really wanna stay with me? After everything I did?"

"I never really wanted to leave to begin with," he replied. "I like it here, and I really want to dominate your ass in bed now."

With a sniff, I wiped away a fake tear. "That's the sweetest thing anyone's ever said to me."

"You should have told me what gets you off."

I shook my head. "You were a half-turn, and I needed to be a werewolf. But I won't object to you telling me what to do—" The look on Adam's face went from flirtatious to worry. "In the bedroom, stupid."

He put his hand over his furry chest and sighed with relief. "Yeah, *that* I can do." He looked around and held out his arms. "Well, we're in the bedroom. How about we start with a hug?"

I held out my arms, and he fell into my chest, wrapping himself around me, resting his head under my chin. With my eyes closed, I took in his comforting scent as we stayed like that for... I don't know how long. It was easy to lose myself in this moment as I remembered him singing that song, only now I didn't feel like crying.

The difference between my new pack and all the families from the past was—I actually felt safe now. Whatever happened in the future was out of my hands, but I'd hold onto what I had in the present with all my new strength.

*Roscoe*

Eggs and bacon sizzled in the skillet as I hummed to the music blasting through Cody's phone. I didn't have an account of my own, so I used his. He never said anything about all my different playlists taking over his account because I knew his little secret—he actually liked my music. He'd deny it up and down if I confronted him, so I left it alone.

Cody wandered into the kitchen with a yawn as he fumbled his way through the cabinet.

"Where's my favorite coffee cup?"

It was an involuntary reaction, but my ears fell off to the sides, catching his attention immediately.

"Roscoe!"

"I'm sorry. I was movin' stuff around a couple weeks ago and it fell. Didn't know it was yer favorite."

"It was double insulated and expensive. That cup survived four moves, but somehow couldn't survive you."

Lookin' at him so sad made me remember something I was savin' something for just such an occasion.

"How would you like a new favorite cup?"

"I can't just point to a cup and designate it my favorite. You know this about me. It has to pass a myriad of rigorous tests before I'd even consider it."

I slid my metal spatula under the eggs and bacon and onto a plate before putting more in.

"Speakin' of favorite things, I used to have a favorite frying pan and a favorite apron." I glanced back at Cody who was now looking at the floor—ah, that cute look of guilt he could never hide. "You know I ain't mad about silly things like that. *Things* don't matter."

"After everything we've been through, you'd think I'd be less of a stickler." He crept up behind me, wrapping his arms around my waist. "Fuck it. I'll drink coffee out of a bowl if it means I get my caffeine fix."

I pointed to the cabinet under the sink. "Was gonna give it to you fer Christmas, but I hate waitin'."

Cody pulled away and walked across the kitchen before reaching under the sink for a box I'd neatly wrapped in a paper grocery bag so it wouldn't be too conspicuous. He slowly peeled the tape to keep everything intact.

"Jeez, Cody. I ain't gonna use that paper again. Just rip it open."

"Sorry, habit," he said, tearing it the rest of the way, revealing a box with a picture of a double-insulated coffee mug, bigger than his other one. There was no way to put a price on his expression. "Whoa!"

"It gets better," I said. "Take it out of the box."

He impatiently ripped open the box to get at the mug before holding it to the light. Etched into the glass was his name. On the other side was that drawing I gave him a while ago to apologize with me holding up a heart.

"Roscoe, this..." He placed the cup on the counter and wiped tears from his eyes. "This is my new favorite cup."

"But you ain't tested it yet."

"It passes," he said, throwing his arms around me again. "How about we eat breakfast in bed?"

Hearing him say that made me gasp. He never let me eat in bed.

"You mean it? I can put on a movie, too?"

He rubbed my stomach before grabbing lower. "How about you eat, and I take care of something else."

"Oh shit." I hurried and scooped the rest of the food onto the plate before turning off the burner. Two of my favorite things in life, and I'd get to have 'em at the same time. Had to rush in case Cody changed his mind, but he was all too eager to get me in that bedroom. "Yer really okay with this?"

"They're just sheets." He looked back at me, raising his eyebrows as we entered the bedroom. "I know I'm going to regret this, but maybe we can, I dunno... experiment with new things?"

"You know, I've always had this fantasy of fucking on the beach and bringin' in a human third."

His grin flipped almost instantly. I shoulda known that would get me in trouble.

"You're this close to getting nothing."

"Uh... yeah forget about that. Let's eat!"

*Cody*

I lay on top of a sleeping Roscoe, his abdomen rising and falling as he snored, lulling me into and out shallow naps, but it was almost noon and there were chores that needed to be done. I also had to pay Willa a visit to discuss what happened, as well as pass along the feral elder's request. Mosavi had strong feelings about the werewolves living in the woods, but I now understood something we were all lacking.

If we were going to live better as something more than human, we would need to strike a balance between Midna and Whasha. Feral life might not have been for most, but the life of a werewolf in a human city was a miserable existence. The humans were misguided in their reasoning, but removing werewolves from cities was not the *Kristallnacht* I thought it was. It was an inevitable result.

This had me again pondering the reason the elders in charge came up with the kuu as a solution to the compounding misery. They were so secretive that all their actions did was further fuel the ideas of conspiracy Mosavi had hinted at.

It was then I had a horrifying thought. What if Willa wasn't the only powerful witch that had broken free from her coven? The idea of a malevolent rogue sorceress cohorting with a cabal of enthralled elders was a nightmare scenario.

I climbed off Roscoe, giving him a gentle kiss on the nose before heading to the bathroom. As expected, bacon grease ruined my sheets, but it no longer drove me crazy. The old me would have rolled Roscoe out of bed and meticulously hand-washed those sheets until every drop of grease had vanished. And if I couldn't do that, I'd buy new ones and put the kibosh on food in bed. It was so stupid to waste energy trying to keep everything the way I wanted when life itself was one big Roscoe-sized mess. Like it or not, I was going to be a werewolf one day, and I'd have to abide all the smells and stains and dirt that would come along with it.

Even Mosavi, as clean and prim as he was, couldn't hide his werewolf musk, nor could he hold back his primal urges. Under that custom-fitted blazer was a torn, dirty dress shirt, and behind that clean-shaven, handsome human face was the most deranged sex-addict I'd ever met.

I hated myself again for being turned on by that.

The more I thought about the dishes piled in the sink from breakfast, the less I cared. I ran the hot water and hopped into the shower.

"I'll let someone else clean today," I whispered to myself before grabbing the soap, knowing damn well the three werewolf slobs living here probably wouldn't even notice the mess, let alone clean it. Maybe that would change later on.

Willa and Mosavi sat in the opposite booth, staring curiously at me. Mosavi was in his dressed-up human form, and Willa wore a black flowing gown that fluttered dramatically, even in the stillness of the restaurant.

"That's really all there is," I said, sipping on my water before digging into my pocket to pull out a small sack of herbs and the stone. I dropped them onto the table.

Mosavi grabbed the bag, leaving the stone where it was. He gave the herbs a sniff before scattering a pinch of it into his glass of iced water.

"The elder put us through a ritual where we experienced each other's pasts. Whatever he did worked, because Austin's back and he seems normal."

"What is this, dear?" Willa asked, turning to Mosavi. "I've never seen it before."

"It is a desert poppy from my homeland," Mosavi said, dropping the small leather sack back to the table. "Once dried and infused with vironoct, they take on a psychedelic property. These were used for storytelling and healing when I was young."

"The elder said he wants to meet you on the solstice." I slid the stone closer to him.

Mosavi scowled, shaking his head. "What could there be to discuss with animals?"

"He spoke eloquently. He seemed different from the others, and he said he's been watching you for years."

"Of course he has. He is my older brother."

Willa and I turned to him in disbelief.

"Your... brother?" she asked. "Why have you not said anything about this?"

"He is my brother by blood only. He seeks to undermine me at every opportunity, tempting my werewolves into leaving this wonderful haven we've created. That beast thinks he knows what's best for us, but I know my way is the best."

"I think both of you are right," I said, prompting an angry stare. "I also think both of you are a bit misguided. There is no Midna or Whasha. Both are a part of us, and when we get too much of one and not enough of the other, we need something to balance us out. The ferals use this to forget, to keep them happy out there, but if they didn't have this, they'd end up like Roscoe, always looking for the next high because something's missing. Werewolves in the city use drugs and alcohol the same way the ferals use this herb. There's a part of them missing that they can't figure out."

"What do you know—" Mosavi said, but Willa raised her hand in front of him.

"Let him finish."

Mosavi lowered his intense glare and nodded.

"Whether you meant to or not, you found a balance. You think the werewolves are happy here because they're in civilization, but really the reason they're happy is because they are surrounded by nature while still being in civilization. They can embrace their wild side while also not losing their humanity in the process. We're human and beast, not one or the other."

"And how do you know this?" Mosavi snapped. "You haven't lived even a quarter of my lifetime, and you are not yet a werewolf, but you seem confident in this absurdity."

"Maybe I'm wrong and this is just a silly theory, but these visions gave me insight. Think about it, Darius. You were there when the Midna and Whasha parted ways. Had they stayed together, you could have created a Norwich a long time ago. Right now, both sides are susceptible to witchcraft because both sides are broken. The ferals use charms and magic to keep the witches away, but they're still vulnerable out there. One mistake and that's it for them. In the city, werewolves might be just as vulnerable—" I paused, remembering my thoughts from earlier.

"So, you've come to the same conclusion," Willa said, reaching into her exposed cleavage for that ornate mirror she let me borrow a while ago. "I knew you would."

"Am I right? Is there a witch at the top?"

"Your guess is as good as mine," she replied, holding up the mirror. "I've been scrying as often as I can, but there's a barrier of shadow I can never break through. Even though I can siphon incredible power from the werewolves in town, I'm still limited. However, I think the answer may lie within your kuu. You're the only one left in town that has one, even if it doesn't work, but I wouldn't dare tamper with them. The moment I do, they will know who I am and where Darius is. The only way to get the answers we seek is to study an active kuu charm. Yours is active and will likely remain that way even after you turn because it was never correctly fused with you."

"Do you think the witches in the woods have anything to do with this?" I asked.

"Doubtful. If there is a witch in a position of power controlling these elders, her anonymity is for her own survival. Suppose every coven in the world were to know who she is, they would descend upon her with the prince of hell himself. If she is anything like me, she is meticulous, cunning, and she knows how to stay hidden from His sight."

"Do you think she's evil?" I asked.

"I don't know," Willa responded. "She could be evil or greedy. If it's the latter, she won't last long. If it's the former, that makes her formidable."

Mosavi picked up the sack of herbs and stuffed them into his blazer pocket. "I'll give consideration to that meeting. If there's any merit to your theory, I'll know for sure. There is no trust, though. He'll try his tricks to strip me of my will and keep me in the wild where he wants me, so I will have you and Willa accompany me on the solstice." His eyes glowed silver. "You will not refuse."

"I won't refuse. Jeez," I said, holding up my hands.

His eyes faded back to their usual dark orange, but his shirt began to pop as he started to lose control over his human form. "You had better not be in on his tricks."

"I think he only wants to see you again. Maybe you'll both find a way to help each other."

His blazer tore from the back as his werewolf form exploded in a show of fury, and he slammed his growing hand on the table. I jumped as the wood cracked, and claws erupted from his fingertips.

"This pie-in-the-sky mentality is unbecoming of a leader."

"Maybe for your brand of leadership, but I like to consider every option. I think a good leader would be open to that."

Mosavi closed his eyes and took a deep breath before opening them again, a little calmer than before.

"Whether you'll admit it or not, you like me and my pack. It's something you're missing, Darius."

"You are assuming a lot."

"You know, you both are always welcome at our house."

"A prison cell has better aesthetics—"

"I would love to!" Willa interrupted, as Mosavi groaned and rolled his eyes. "And so would Darius. Especially with the holidays around the corner."

"I thought we made plans for Italy," Mosavi said with a slight whine.

"Screw Italy." She turned and smiled at me. "Family is better. And speaking of family, maybe you and your brother can share a hundred years of wisdom from different worlds." Willa kissed Mosavi on the cheek and followed it up with a light slap. "And I want to meet him since you've kept this valuable information from me." She grinned, licking her front teeth. "You know what this means, right?"

Mosavi's ears folded against his head, and he nodded, averting his eyes. "I will have the maid and butler strap me to the rack before you return."

"That's a good boy."

"You're both freaks," I muttered, blushing.

"Freaks with a strong marriage that will last for eons," Willa added. "Now, let's see about getting you guys a nice big welcome home feast."

"You're going to get Roscoe coming here every day if you don't stop."

She held up her glass. "He's good for business."

# Chapter 37

# The Future Leader

The last time we'd seen Austin or Adam had been early yesterday when they'd come out for the free barbecue. While Adam had engaged in some small talk with Roscoe, the scratched-up Austin had kept quiet, grabbing as many bags as he could carry and scurrying into the hallway like a raccoon on a nightly garbage binge. Adam snatched a whole rotisserie chicken in his mouth before following, giving us a wave as he disappeared around the corner.

Austin was obviously into whatever they were doing, and Adam's erect ears and swaying tail meant he enjoyed his new role in their relationship. Great sex was only sex, though. It didn't replace the need for further compatibility, but if Roscoe and I were any example, it was a great place to start.

Speaking of Roscoe, he was still comatose from the ungodly amount of food he'd devoured last night. He reminded me of a hibernating bear, his belly distended like he'd put on fifty pounds of fat in just a couple hours. However, I knew that when he eventually awoke midday, it would be as though he hadn't eaten anything at all. Werewolf physiology was an enigma, but perhaps I'd understand it more once my time came.

As I crept through the hallway toward the kitchen, the irresistible scent of fresh, expensive coffee caught my nose, followed up by the rush of water and clanking dishes in the sink.

"It's a damn miracle," I said, strutting into the kitchen as Adam slipped a plate into the dish drainer.

He turned and opened his mouth to speak, his new rows of sharp teeth glinting in the dim light above the stove.

"This kitchen's a mess, Cody. Aren't you supposed to be keeping it clean?"

"Nope." I brushed past him to grab my new favorite coffee cup from the cabinet. "Did you see what Roscoe gave me?"

Adam held out his larger clawed hands, and I sat the glass mug into his palm.

"This would be really cute if I didn't know the story behind it."

"What story?" I said, eyeing him intensely before snatching the mug and filling it with fresh coffee. "There is no story."

"It was just piss, Cody. If I had a dollar for every werewolf that peed on me—"

"Change of subject," I interrupted, giving him a sniff. "Someone's actually using the oatmeal shampoo I bought over two months ago."

"This stuff is amazing! My fur is so soft, and look." He rubbed the shorter fur on his arms. "No dander! Shit, I should have used it on my ashy elbows when I was a half-turn."

"You're actually strong now, so this changes things," I said, eyeing Adam with excitement. "I need your help holding Roscoe in the bathtub so I can give him a good scrub-down with that shampoo."

"I have a better idea. I bought something online that you can borrow. I'm going to use it on Austin when it arrives because he's just as bad as Roscoe." He picked up his phone and began scrolling.

"Now I'm intrigued."

"Here," he said, handing me the phone. It was a werewolf-centric website with grooming products. "The harness."

"Werewolf washing harness." I scrolled through the text and read more. "Unbreakable material with a lock to hold even the most unwilling werewolf in place. Holy shit!"

"How much do you want to bet a half-turn runs this online store?" We both laughed but stopped as the bathroom door closed. "I think Roscoe's up."

I looked over at the microwave clock. "Not for another five or six hours. It must be Austin." I leaned closer. "What did you do to him last night?"

"Oooo." His voice lowered to a whisper. "This thing right here." He looked down and grabbed the enchanted chain he wore that Willa had made for him. "I can feel everything I do to him while we're fucking.

It's like sensory overload. Whatever spell Mosavi's wife put on this, it works differently now that Austin's better."

"I think that witch should be running an adult outlet and not a restaurant."

"Make sure to thank her for me when you go to their house today."

I put the coffee cup against my lips but stopped, narrowing my eyes at Adam. "What?"

"Oh. I knew I was forgetting something. You left your cell in the living room, and she called while you were sleeping. Mosavi wants to do something to you, or something like that. I didn't catch all the details."

"Details are fucking important when it comes to Mosavi, Adam! Can you not answer my phone if you're not going to at least write this stuff down?" I muttered. "Did you happen to catch a time, or does this all fall into a vague 'at some point?'"

"Around noon." He went back to scrubbing the caked-on food from one of the plates. "You're actually gonna go?"

"It's either I go there or he shows up here. Would you rather that?"

Adam shook his head.

The toilet flushed, and the bathroom door opened. Austin's heavy footfalls creaked along the floorboards toward the dining room before stopping at the entrance to the kitchen.

"Good morning," I said enthusiastically, but wasn't met with the same energy.

"'Mornin'," he grunted, eying the coffeemaker.

"Want some coffee?" Adam asked.

"Yup."

"How do you take it?"

"Black."

Adam and I looked at one another and shrugged.

"You sure are talkative," I said, handing Adam a cup from the cabinet.

"Gonna be in the garage," he said, stepping back out of the kitchen.

"Wait a minute," Adam said sharply, setting the cup on the counter before folding his arms. "Pour your own coffee, and you're only allowed in there for an hour. I'm putting my foot down before it goes into your ass."

"An hour's not long enough," he said, turning back around. "Need at least three."

"Why?"

Austin grabbed the cup. "Just trust me. I need three hours," he said, pouring his coffee.

The smaller werewolf's glare softened when Austin gave him a reassuring smile.

"All right. You've got three hours, then I want that big, needy ass of yours in the bedroom."

Austin's tail sprang to action as he turned to leave without saying anything more.

"Never thought I'd see him so calm and happy," I said. "So, you saw everything in those visions?"

Adam nodded. "I hated him, Cody. The shit he put me through while we were kuu mates was awful, but after seeing all that..." He turned back to the sink. "He wanted people he loved to hate him, but he was also desperate for anyone to love him. If I had only known about the hell he was going through, I could have helped him."

"I don't know about that," I said, placing a hand on his shoulder. "I don't think anyone here could have helped him. You saw what happened to him when I tried. He said he loved me, and that was the start of his downward spiral."

"He said he loved you?" Adam's eyes shimmered as he gritted his teeth.

"He said a lot of things like that, but I knew he was just clinging to me because he had alienated everyone else."

The smaller werewolf's shoulders slumped forward, and I didn't want him to get the wrong idea.

"Austin's only ever had two ways of looking at people: either with complete disdain, or with devastation. The way he looked at you just now was so different from any of that. He barely even acknowledged me."

"We've got a lot to work on, but at least he doesn't resent me anymore. He listens to me now." Adam rinsed the last of the dishes and pulled the plug on the drain. "We only had sex for a couple hours last night. We spent the rest of it talking. For as long as I've known him, he was a stranger lying next to me every night. I didn't know who he was, but now it's like I get to experience getting to know him for the first time."

"And now that you know him, what do you think?"

Adam leaned back against the counter and rubbed the short fur on his chin. "I think we're gonna be okay. We're both scared of saying the L-word, but if that time does come, we'll both mean it."

"It's the same with Roscoe and me. We've come close to saying it, but the timing just seems off. It's too soon, even though I can't ever see myself leaving him. There's something about him that makes me a better person."

Adam wrapped an arm around me and squeezed.

"I think we all make each other better," he said before pulling away. "I actually feel sorry for humans."

"Why's that?"

"They'll never experience what this is like. You don't feel it yet, but when you turn, something in your brain clicks. As much as I loved my dad, you guys are closer to me than he ever was. It's like I can feel everyone right here." He grabbed the fur above his abdomen. "Sometimes it hurts."

"That I kinda get," I said. "After those visions, whenever I look at Roscoe sleeping now, my chest hurts. I never want to see him sad again."

"We need to visit Darryl." Adam stepped into the dining room, and I followed. "He doesn't have a pack, you know? He just stays on that beach all alone. I never thanked him for saving my life."

"He saved us all. All our visions had him playing a vital role in our lives according to that elder. Roscoe may have set the wheels in motion, but Darryl kept Roscoe grounded long enough for him to meet me. He gave me and Roscoe a place to live when he didn't have to."

"He let me live with him, too. He also let Austin stay at his house, and got him interested in building things," Adam added. "A part of me will always love him, even though we were never meant for each other."

"Thanksgiving," I said, stepping back. "We're going down there for Thanksgiving."

"I think he'll like that."

The mayor's mansion was just as I remembered. There was an unexpectedly mundane normalcy to the architecture, not quite gothic, but also not quite colonial. The pillars on both sides of the concrete steps leading to the oversized double doors supported a flattened overhang with granite gargoyles. It was safe to assume that those and the pointed arch windows were Mosavi's compromise to Willa for allowing him a more traditional style home.

When I reached the entrance, the doors slammed opened.

"Finally," Mosavi muttered, dragging me into the foyer by my arm. He was in his werewolf form this time, his outfit more casual than normal. He was shirtless, wearing only a pair of blue jeans with frayed bottoms and a hole for his tail. "It is thirty minutes after twelve."

"Well, I would have been here sooner had someone picked me up from the front gate, which may as well have been on the other side of town." I looked around at the huge open interior, a clash between white marble and black granite wrapped in different autumn decorations. There was even a spiraling staircase to the left of the entrance. "Who the hell needs a driveway that long?"

"Is that Cody?" came Willa's voice from the second-floor balcony. She fluttered across the floor and descended the stairs as though riding a cloud. Her outfit was even more casual than Mosavi's—a burgundy nightgown that was nearly see-through. Her breasts jostled freely on either side of the v-opening, revealing a lot more cleavage than usual.

"Am I... early or something?"

"I just said you were late," Mosavi growled. "We weren't going to spend our free time simply waiting for you to show up."

"You're always so pleasant," I said as Willa approached.

"Let's get down to business. We have things to discuss about the town and your role in it," he replied, stepping barefoot on the reflective black flooring and heading toward a room on the other side of the foyer. It had a fireplace, wooden walls, French windows, tufted leather furniture, and full bookshelves nearly two stories high. In the center stood a cherry wood table holding a glass-topped humidor, filled with a variety of expensive cigars. Next to it was a crystal bottle of some kind of alcohol and three Glencairn glasses. "Sit."

"Make yourself at home, dear," Willa corrected, glaring at her husband. "Do you like scotch, or would you prefer wine?"

"He should drink scotch." Mosavi moved quickly across the room to grab the bottle. "It's more masculine and refined."

"But our wine is older and more delicious," she argued.

"It doesn't pair well with cigars."

"How about some soda?" I asked, prompting them to look at me like I had four heads. "I mean, uh, mineral... water?"

"This was a stupid idea," Mosavi muttered, pouring a glass half-full of the oak-colored liquid before forcing it into my right hand. "You're not a toddler. Savor the taste. Appreciate the finer things."

"I grew up in a crack house with boarded up windows." I placed the glass on an end table before taking a seat. "And I currently live in a house that might have been a meth lab at some point. I can't really appreciate the finer things I've never had."

"That'll change if you spend more time here," Mosavi said, sitting in the chair opposite mine while Willa lounged on the couch, her legs up, taking her time to cover her exposed bosoms, which had slipped free.

"The girls are rather rambunctious today," Willa said, taking a sip from her glass, raising a brow as she examined my reaction.

Mosavi let out a surprising laugh. "For once, it seems you have no power here."

"Worth a try." Willa smirked and set her glass back on the table.

"I'm so confused right now," I said.

"Never mind," Mosavi continued. "How are you liking Norwich?"

"It's better than the city. Can't really complain."

"That's not exactly a flattering answer." The werewolf snipped the end of a cigar before lighting it with a thin piece of cedar. "What would you like to see change to make it the best place you've ever lived?"

"All things considered, it is the best place I've ever lived, but I can only compare it to the dumps I came from," I said as Mosavi glared at me. "That came out wrong. The town is really amazing, and I'm not just saying that because you're looking at me like you want to rip my throat out. I've never seen humans and werewolves so happy living practically on top of one another. The city was segregated, and where I grew up, werewolves were always forced to leave. I just wish—" I paused, and Mosavi stopped puffing on his cigar, cocking his eyebrow.

"Wish what?"

"I wish we could do something about the witches." I looked over at Willa, whose expression went from whimsical to dark. "We're surrounded by nature, but everyone's too afraid to enjoy it."

"Nature offers nothing of importance anyway." Mosavi snipped off the end of another cigar and handed me the lit one he was drawing from. "And nothing can currently be done about the coven. All we can do is ward against them."

"If Willa was able to break free, then couldn't others?"

"That is the million-dollar question," Willa said. "My sisters are bound to a prince of hell, and that bond is usually ironclad. The only reason I broke free was—" She sat up on the couch and looked over at her husband. "Our life forces became intermingled the day I saved Darius's life. He was like a filter. Each time I breathed into him, his body purified it before it flowed back into me again. It's careless to assume this would happen with any other witch, because my circumstances were different. Though I was not completely free from the influence of my coven, I had broken the pact many years prior."

"I saw the vision. You had already taken the first steps against your nature before any of this happened, just by saving Darius."

Willa nodded and her smile returned. "I still do not know what happened, or why His influence over me faded. I don't want to get my hopes up, but perhaps there is a slim chance my sisters can be saved."

I thought back to Roscoe and his pack. "Finding a way to save the captured werewolves should be a priority."

"Childish, wishful thinking," Mosavi said. "And dangerous. Once a thrall to the witches, there is no coming back."

"Is that so?" Willa shifted closer to the edge of the couch, eyeing her husband.

"I have the elder vironoct coursing through my veins, which makes me more resistant to their control."

"Then why not use that to break the others free?" I asked.

"Just because I am resistant does not mean they cannot entrap me, like they did before."

I looked over at Willa. "But you have your wife to protect you."

Mosavi jumped from his chair and pointed a clawed finger at my face. "I will not put her life in danger for some half-turn's idiocy!"

"Darius," Willa said calmly as she placed her index finger and thumb between his shoulder blades. His eyes rolled upward, and he fell to his knees. "That's enough. I'm not a child to be coddled, nor am I some flailing, helpless damsel. One day I will be feared by those who wish us harm, mark my words. And you..." She looked down at her husband and back at me. "You will start treating my sweet Cody better."

"I'll not let him convince you to risk exposing yourself." He turned from me, still on his knees, and lay his face in his wife's lap as she sat. She gently stroked the top of his head. "We have always been more than lovers. You are my closest friend, and without you, I have nothing. An eternity with all the pleasures in this world could never come close to just five minutes in your arms."

Willa shifted to her knees before falling into his embrace. The dramatic way they spoke and behaved toward one another reminded me of those old-timey romantic flicks. When I thought about how long they'd been alive, anything else would have likely seemed unnatural.

"You are overreacting, dear. Merely giving this consideration won't put me in danger. We've been discussing the possibility of saving the thralls. I don't for a moment believe it's permanent, even for the average werewolf." She released Mosavi and glanced at me. "We've talked through all of this, but we always come back to the same conclusion. Even with Mosavi being an elder and me being a witch, it wouldn't be enough to break such powerful magic. The only beings powerful enough to come close would be an entire council of elders like the ones we've mentioned before, but they may be compromised."

"He should leave," Mosavi said. "He's not the one I want."

"He's the one I want, Darius." Willa stood and helped Mosavi to his feet. "I want you to lead this town, Cody. We can't stay here forever, and we need an elder who can make logical and wise decisions. Despite being so young, you fit the bill."

"Uh, isn't this an elected position?" I asked.

They smirked at one another.

"Sure," Mosavi answered dismissively.

"Why did you both smile like that? What happened to the last mayor?" I asked, growing increasingly disturbed.

"Unimportant." Mosavi took another puff of his cigar. "Obviously I cannot change Willa's mind, so you need to be willing to let me groom you for this position."

"You are such a deceitful wolf," Willa said. "You have been wanting Cody since he arrived."

"I hate politics," I said. "I don't even follow the presidential elections."

"Your pack naturally looks to you for leadership," Willa said. "It's the way things work with your kind. The werewolves of Norwich will be drawn to you. Even the humans won't be able to resist your charisma if you let Darius teach you what he's learned."

"Then I'd have to live here for the rest of my life. What if I want to go somewhere else?"

"By then, there will be others to take your place," Mosavi said. "We are only just getting started, and we'll need *you* as that starting point. We have other towns to make into sanctuaries, and those towns will also need werewolf leaders. This is my purpose. I want all our kind to live freely with the same opportunities humans have. I don't care what I have to do"—the cigar crumbled as he gripped it in a balled-up fist—"or who I have to break to make my vision a reality."

"I hope you're not planning on trying to break me."

"If only I could," he muttered. "You're a stubborn little shit with a potent vironoct. Even Willa's enchanted trinkets did next to nothing." The brown werewolf snarled again. "So, with that admission out of the way, I need you as an equal to me. Obviously in your half-turned state, you're not suitable, but you can be molded when you reach your apex. After that, failure or success is in your—hopefully—capable hands."

"This has to be your choice, though," Willa said. "Once I see what you become, we may be able to work together on dealing with the witches around Norwich, but I make no promises on the outcome."

"And if anything happens to her because of your stupidity, I will destroy you," Mosavi added. "Understand?"

"You would never do such a thing," Willa said, smacking Mosavi across the maw. "Stop with this posturing. Why must you keep putting on this act?"

The elder looked at the floor.

"I don't want anything to happen to anyone," I said. "If we decide it's too dangerous, I'll call the whole thing off but not doing anything is a contradiction to what you want."

Mosave wrinkled his nose.

"You said you wanted all our kind to live freely, but there are werewolves out there that are literally slaves. You can't say that and then ignore hundreds or thousands of captured werewolves."

"A point well made," Willa said. "Even your old pack is still out there. Have you really abandoned them?"

"This is for you! All of it! I do this for us. They would have wanted a safe place to live had we had one in those days. Instead, we ended up out *there*. I'll not let that happen to anyone else."

"But werewolves are able to live out there—"

"The Whasha are fools who willingly give themselves to the wild when there is safety in our town!" Mosavi shouted. "My brother—" He took several deep, shaky breaths as he regained control of his temper.

"Is your brother," I finished, standing. "But it's not really my place to say anything. I'll let you fight it out with him on the solstice. If that's it, I need to get home before Roscoe wakes up."

"What a shamefully lazy beast," Mosavi muttered, following me into the foyer. "Just looking at him sends me into a rage. That is not a werewolf."

"Maybe if you got to know him better, he'd grow on you, too." I passed a room with a black grand piano, stopping to look inside. "Do you play the piano?"

"No," Mosavi said, his face showing a bit of excitement. "But I do collect rare and antique musical instruments. Would you like to see them?"

I really wanted to leave the unpleasantness from earlier, but at that moment, Mosavi was showing a slightly softer side. If this was going to work out in any way, and if I wanted both him and Willa to be closer to our pack, I had to figure him out. Willa wasn't always going to be there to stop him from going for my neck each time I pissed him off, which I was bound to keep doing.

"Sure," I said, allowing the mayor space to step into the room before me. As I followed, I gazed at the impossibly tall walls containing holders of different instruments. There were guitars, violins, an assortment of odd-looking woodwinds, and brass. "This is a strange collection for someone who doesn't play music."

"I never at any point said I didn't," he said, looking back at me.

"But you—"

"I said I don't play the piano." He brushed his padded fingers over the polished cover of the huge instrument. "This Bösendorfer is around one hundred and fifty years old and is probably worth half as much as this house."

"Holy shit," I whispered, closely examining the scarred, glossy wood. "How do you know it's that old?"

"I had it appraised five times to get the approximate date it was made before I bought it." He pointed to a beautifully polished violin in a glass case on the other side of the room. "*That* is the instrument I play."

I approached the glass, looking down at the curvy wood. Though the instrument was incredibly well taken care of, it looked ancient. "It's beautiful."

"You should hear it sing. Nothing less would be suited for something crafted by Antonio Stradivarius himself."

"Who's that?" I asked, looking back in time to see Mosavi's eyes glow a furious silver.

"Y—you... who's that?" he said, almost speechless. "You don't know a Stradivarius when you see one?"

"What part of *crack house* did you not understand earlier?"

Mosavi closed his eyes and drew in another calming breath. "My apologies," he said through his teeth. "Perhaps I'll entertain you one day with the history of everything in here."

"That sounds—like so much fun," I said, faking a smile as something familiar caught my eye. "Oh my God."

"What's wrong?"

I pointed to the wooden guitar in the center of the wall. "Where did you get that?"

"Ah, that was something I won at an auction in London. This is the only one of its kind, and it was played by a master." He reached for the guitar and gently lifted it from the supporting arms before flipping it to the other side. He pointed to a tiny signature along the neck. "Sebastian Shields was one of the most talented classical guitarists in history, and he was a werewolf."

Could I have been mistaken? Darryl said his father wasn't a werewolf.

"How old is it?"

"Over a hundred years for sure. I was lucky to see him perform before he vanished. No one knew what happened to him, but he did have a human son that had some talent himself. Never became as famous as his father, but he did play this guitar. I thought this was lost to history until I heard it would be up for bid. I got on a jet that night."

"I think this guitar belongs to Sebastian's grandson."

Mosavi's eyes narrowed to suspicion, but he didn't respond.

"It belongs to Darryl."

The elder laughed. "What? You can't be serious. That failure—" He recomposed himself before standing more upright. "Have you proof?"

"I—" I sighed, shaking my head. "I don't have physical proof, but I know it's his. Roscoe stole it and pawned it for drugs. It destroyed their friendship."

"If I recall from his records, Darryl's last name was Finn, not Shields."

I smirked at that. There was no way Darryl's real last name would have been that coincidental.

"Why are you smiling?"

"I doubt that's his real last name."

His eyes narrowed. "You don't know."

"I don't, but if you heard him play the guitar, I think you'd know. He's really good."

Mosavi placed the guitar back on its shelf. "A lot of people are *really good*, but no one has ever been Sebastian good. That werewolf had talent that went beyond simply playing an instrument. He transcended reality when he performed. I still get chills remembering that last performance."

"How much would it cost to buy it?" I asked, knowing it was out of my hands. There was no way any of us would be able to afford it—at least not now.

"Nothing. There is no amount of money that would be enough."

"Listen, I'll do anything to get that guitar. What do you want?"

"Why are you so persistent? *You* didn't even know who Stradiveri was."

"Because it was Darryl's father's guitar. It was the only physical thing he had left to remember him by. His father taught him to play on that instrument." I thought back to the tears in Darryl's eyes on the beach the night he'd reminisced. "You're right. There is no amount of money that would ever be enough to replace priceless memories."

Mosavi closed his eyes, seemingly giving my words consideration, but with him, there was no telling how this would end up. Unless it involved Willa, the mayor had little empathy when it came to others.

"I can't believe that piece of shit lazing around my town sold a priceless heirloom to get high!" Mosavi let out a soft growl before opening his eyes again. "As if I didn't despise him enough already... If what you are saying is true—"

"He didn't know what it was worth, and he was in a really bad place."

"You're not going to succeed in pulling at my heartstrings." Mosavi leaned in close. "If Darryl is indeed the grandson of Sebastian Shields, I'll return the guitar to him on three conditions."

"Really?" I said, almost hyperventilating. If Roscoe gave this back to Darryl, it would be enough to really mend things between them. Just the look on his face would be worth whatever Mosavi wanted in return.

"Condition one: our poor butler and maid haven't had a decent vacation in years. I'll have Roscoe take over their duties while they take a year off with pay."

My eyes went wide. "A whole year? I think he really will die if he has to actually work."

"If only I could be so fortunate," he said with a satisfied smirk. "Condition two: I'll be there to witness this exchange, and listen to Darryl play it. If I don't get that same feeling during his performance, you and Roscoe will be joining me in the dungeon two nights a week. And condition three: you will give me a solid answer of yes to being my protege, and you'll do so gladly."

"I swear I'm gonna kill Roscoe," I muttered under my breath. "All right."

"You must really like this werewolf to make such a one-sided and risky deal."

I looked directly into Mosavi's eyes, his face reflecting the silvery-blue glow. It was then he knew how serious I was.

"I wouldn't be here if it weren't for Darryl. I'd do anything to get him his guitar back."

Mosavi nodded and smiled before slipping his arm around my neck, squeezing the top of my shoulder. "I look forward to your unwavering devotion to me and this town."

Once again, I found myself in an unpleasant situation with the mayor, and again it was Roscoe's fault. At least I had Willa in my corner, and in spite of all of his blustering, she was the one who had the final say.

At least I sure as hell hoped so.

# Chapter 38

# Bringing the Music Back

*Cody*

"**I** have to do what?" Roscoe shouted while following me around the bedroom. "What the hell did you do Cody?"

"I'm getting Darryl's guitar back." I tossed an empty suitcase on the bed and started neatly folding and stacking outfits into it.

"That guy had it this whole time?" He plopped down on our ugly brown couch. "He's had it in fer me since we moved here, and now you've gone and signed my life away."

"It's light housework in a mansion, not breaking stones in a gulag. You can stand to do a little more than just eat, sleep, and fuck."

"But that's the golden trinity! That's the perfect life, and it's all I wanna do."

I grabbed more clothes from the dresser. "Well, now you can do it all in a maid's outfit."

"He ain't gonna make me wear one of them frilly black and white dresses, is he?"

I snorted involuntarily at the thought. "Dude."

"Hmm, ya know, I could make it work, with the right alterations."

I stopped packing and shot him one of my most disgusted looks. "If I ever see you in one of those, I'll probably never be able to have sex with you again."

"*You* could wear one. Shit, I'm gettin' hard just thinkin' about it."

The front door slammed open, and rapid, clawed footsteps raced through the house.

"Cody!"

"In the bedroom," I shouted as Adam ran in. "What's wrong?"

"Oh man oh man, if I'm right about this, Austin's gonna freak the fuck out." He handed his phone to me. "Look."

I scrolled through an app, looking at a bunch of pictures of three werewolves in different places. One had them posing in front of the Matterhorn in Switzerland and another had them relaxing on a beach in Fiji.

"What am I looking at?"

"It's a social media app for werewolves called 'The Fuzz.'"

I handed the phone back. "You know I hate this stuff. I never even logged into the DicTalk account you set up for me a couple months ago."

"No, look at these guys," he said, sitting on the bed and pulling me down next to him. "I think these were Austin's packmates in the marines."

"What?" I snatched the phone. "Are you sure about that? I thought they died!"

"Shhhh." Adam covered my mouth. "I don't want Austin to hear."

"You saw 'em in yer visions?" Roscoe asked.

Adam nodded. "Randall, Steve, and Blake. They're alive and apparently doing pretty well for werewolves."

"I don't understand. Why does Austin think they're dead?" I asked.

"He assumed they were. A couple soldiers threw their dog tags in the trash and kept hinting that something bad happened. But they also mentioned being contaminated, which may be why they threw the tags away—not because the werewolves were dead. Austin never saw their bodies either. He tried to break into the building, but it was too secure. He ended up assuming the worst and got the fuck out of Dodge."

Roscoe's tail thudded against the bed. "Where are they livin' now?"

"I don't know. They don't really live anywhere. They just travel to different places, stowing away or hitchhiking. They've even got a channel where they record themselves hopping on freight trains like hobos." Adam scrolled back to the top of the app and clicked his profile. "I'm going to send them a message with Austin's picture and see if they recognize him. I'm like ninety-nine percent sure it's them."

"It's been quite a few years. Hopefully they haven't forgotten him," I said, snapping my suitcase shut.

"Nah," Roscoe chimed in. "If they were as close as Austin said, they're probably searchin' the whole world for him and haven't stopped. Packmates have a really strong bond." Roscoe's tone cracked beneath his excitement.

"I sent the message," Adam said, turning off the screen before looking up. "Now we wait."

The moment he spoke, the phone vibrated again and again.

Thanksgiving was tomorrow, but today we'd begin our long road trip to White Dunes. Willa and Mosavi were coming with us, which meant we'd be traveling by limo. Roscoe sat on the living room sofa with a sour look on his face, his fur still puffy from all the blow-drying earlier.

"Don't look at me like that. Mosavi's not letting you into his limo smelling like ass."

"I didn't smell like ass," Roscoe muttered. "I like my smell. Now I look stupid."

"I'll brush you in a bit. Oh! I've got a cute bandana with a bunch of little bones on it."

"Ha ha." Roscoe looked away from me. "Puttin' me in that harness was mean, and when the hell did Adam get so strong?"

I picked up a wide wire brush and began running it through his fur. "I love this. You're so soft, you smell good, and you're handsome."

"I look like a fat Pomeranian."

"You'll look great when I'm done, and you're more Chow Chow than Pomeranian."

The bathroom door opened, and Adam pulled Austin into the living room. The huge werewolf's fur was just as puffy and unruly as Roscoe's, and he had the same disgruntled expression. His ears were low, and his tail tucked, the whites of his eyes showing as he looked away.

"Can I get that brush when you're done?" Adam wrapped his arms around Austin, his head sinking into thick chest fluff. "This is nice," he said, his voice muffled.

"He got you with the harness, didn't he?" Roscoe asked.

The sad-looking werewolf nodded.

"How'd he get you?" He shoved my arm. "This one promised me sex and breakfast in bed."

The larger werewolf let out a sigh.

"Sex and breakfast," he muttered.

"You guys are just evil." Roscoe scooted away, snatching the brush from my hand before pointing it at Austin. "Look at that face. That's a broken werewolf right there. Promised food and fuckin' and got double-crossed by two evil twinks."

"Don't call me that," Adam and I snapped in unison as I grabbed the brush again.

"I'm telling you, Roscoe, Mosavi would not let you into his limo smelling like that. It was either I give you a bath, or he does—and I can almost guarantee you wouldn't have any fur left if he did it."

Roscoe swallowed hard.

"And I only used the harness because you always put up a fight, and I'm not using the vironoct on you guys anymore."

"I am gonna get back at you one of these days." He leaned in close to my ear. "I can give you a *shower* too."

"Roscoe..." I felt my lower lip curl into my sharper canines. "If you even think about doing that again, I could have Mosavi make your life even more miserable than he's already going to."

"All right, all right." Roscoe pouted, turning away as I continued brushing him.

After I finished, I handed the brush to Adam, then leaned in close to Roscoe. "Who's my handsome boy?"

Roscoe wrinkled his nose; however, his tail gave him away as always, thudding the cushion behind him.

"Come on. Who's my handsome boy?"

"It's me," he said in a quiet, low voice. "I *really* don't like you right now."

"Is he bringing the guitar?" Austin asked, this time stringing more than a few words together.

"Yeah," I replied, looking out the window. It was a quarter to nine, and they would be outside of our house within the hour. "Mosavi insisted on hearing Darryl play it."

"Wonder what he's gonna say when he gets it back," Roscoe said. "I've been lookin' for that damn thing for years. I still don't know if it'll be enough."

I brushed a few locks of Roscoe's mane away from his eyes with my hand. "He forgave you already."

"He still doesn't like me. Nothin' will ever be the way it was between us. That wasn't just me fuckin' up, Cody. That was me burnin' a friendship to ashes, all for a high that wouldn't even last."

"Whatever happens, this is the right thing. It'll be up to Darryl after that," I said.

"He used to be so carefree. We'd get stoned, and he'd go out and ride the waves or play his guitar. He smiled all the time, but now he ain't the same. He's... cautious and downright mean and violent sometimes. Returning his dad's guitar ain't gonna bring back the old Darryl."

"You're right," Austin said as we all turned to him. "He'll never be his old self again, and that's not always a bad thing."

The stretch limo pulled to the side of the street in front of our house, and before the driver could open the door, Willa hopped out holding a pie tin wrapped in foil. Mosavi called after her, smacking his head on the frame as he emerged. The driver backed away as the old werewolf roared, cursing loudly in Farsi.

"Oh, he does not look happy," Adam said, grabbing his bag.

"When does he ever?" Roscoe cut in while opening the front door just as Willa climbed the steps. "Is that pumpkin pie?"

"It sure is," she said, patting Roscoe's stomach before handing him the dish.

He turned and glared at me. "I bet she wouldn't tie me up and force me to bathe."

"Yeah, you wouldn't tie him up, would you?" I asked, giving her a knowing grin. Roscoe was going to witness her depravity first-hand soon enough.

Roscoe froze as he was cutting a slice of pie with the claw on his index finger.

"What was that look?" he asked. "What's goin' on?"

"Enjoy the pie," Willa responded, giving Roscoe a wicked smile.

The werewolf picked up the slice and shoved the whole thing in his mouth. He chewed slowly while eyeing us with narrowed suspicion.

"Hurry up," Mosavi said, pointing to the raised trunk of the limo. "Let's not make loading the car an all-day event."

"And how are you today?" I asked, tossing my suitcase into the trunk.

"Looking forward to our two nights a week," he muttered.

"That's if you don't like Darryl's performance."

"I won't." When he climbed back into the car, Willa smacked his rear hard with the palm of her hand.

"He's not keen on road trips," she said, lowering her voice. "If I roll down the window, he'll stick his head out with his mouth open. It's really cute. He can't help it."

"Oh my God, I have to see this," I said as we both broke into more laughter.

"Let's go," Mosavi shouted from inside.

Though it was late November, the briny sea breeze blowing in from the ocean was just warm enough for us to lie on the beach, but a little too cold to swim—at least for me. Mosavi and Willa dropped Roscoe and me off at Darryl's while they and the others made their way to the Marriott further up the shore. As amazing as it would have been to stay in the presidential suite, I wanted to spend time here.

We were preparing ourselves emotionally for what was going to happen over the next day. Austin was unaware of what Adam had planned, but tonight was all about Roscoe and Darryl. I expected him to be overjoyed, but with how fragile their friendship was, this day could go in any direction. That guitar could pull the scabs off healing wounds, but I had to trust that whatever happened, things would get better.

It was around four in the afternoon, and Darryl was high on his lifeguard chair, watching the human surfers trying to ride what few larger waves there were. Roscoe gripped the handle of the black guitar case, his posture stiff as we climbed the steps of the deck.

"Relax," I said, gently stroking Roscoe's back. "It's all gonna work out."

"If he still hates me after this, then I'll know where I stand."

"Darryl is complicated, and he doesn't hate you. You know that more than anyone." I opened the door and sat my suitcase next to that awful hammock I'd fallen out of countless times during my stay here. "You weren't thinking clearly that night. That's what addiction does."



Aeron Dusk

"It was still my choice. The pills didn't buy themselves, and that guitar didn't grow legs and walk away." He looked down at the case. "I won't be able to breathe right until this thing is in his hands."

I glanced out the window at a now empty lifeguard chair.

"I think he caught our scent." I opened the front door again, scanning the shore for any sign of the beach wolf, but he was gone. "You should go find him and give it to him. I'll stay here."

"Give what to me?" Darryl asked, startling us both as he seemingly materialized on the other side of the door. For someone so huge, he sure knew how to stay hidden. "I thought I'd be spending Thanksgiving by myself this year."

I stepped out onto the deck and wrapped my arms around him. Darryl's fur always smelled so fresh, and he was slightly damp, the sea water soaking through my black shirt.

"I missed you." Those visions made me an emotional wreck. Seeing him now was even more significant than before, knowing what I knew.

"All right, what's going on? Who died?"

"Huh?" I asked, but he held his thumb to my cheek, wiping away a stray tear. "Oh, I'm just happy to see you again."

"It's been less than a month. What's going on?" He looked over at Roscoe, who was still partially hidden behind the door. "Why aren't you being belligerent right now? You're worrying me."

Roscoe cleared his throat and stepped onto the deck. "I uh... I got somethin' for ya."

"Hopefully it's a four-course meal. I'm starving."

Roscoe slowly crept out into the open before letting the door fall against the frame. He held the guitar case in his hand while locking eyes with the larger werewolf.

"I've been lookin' fer this thing for years, but Cody found it."

Darryl stiffened, his breathing growing heavy.

"I feel like I can finally apologize the right way," Roscoe whispered, tears now pouring from his eyes. His entire body crumbled into a submissive stance while gauging Darryl's reaction. "I know nothin' I ever do will make it up to you but just knowin' you got a piece of yer dad back will be enough fer me."

The huge werewolf took a few steps toward Roscoe, extending a trembling right hand to grab the handle. He set the case flat on the spool table before lifting the latches. Slowly, he pulled it open before breaking into a light sob.

"Darryl?" I asked, stepping close to him as he hovered over the instrument.

He turned and scooped me into his arms before dragging Roscoe in close, burying his nose into the crook of his neck.

"I forgave you a long time ago, Roscoe," Darryl whispered, his deep voice breaking. "I thought you didn't care about me. I was there as a way to score easy drugs, but when I cooled down, I remembered what you did all those years ago. You could have used the money you gave me, but you were trying to get clean, and you didn't want me to fall into that life. At that moment in time, I was more important to you than the drugs were."

He let us go and wiped his eyes with the back of his arm.

"You came back with Cody, and I found out you rescued someone else, just like you did me all those years ago. You made a really bad mistake, and it took me a while to understand that. I never hated you. I was angry." He pressed his forehead into Roscoe's. "I love you, dude. You'll always be my packmate." He turned to me. "And you!" His tears turned into laughter. "You're worth a lot more than this guitar ever was. I knew that when I met you."

"Now you're just being sappy," I said, sitting down on one of the plastic chairs surrounding the wooden spool table.

"Yeah, but I mean it. How did you even know what the guitar looked like?"

"It's a long story," I said, pointing to the cooler. "How about I tell you over some beers?"

"You like drinking beer now?" Darryl asked, cracking open the container before tossing me a bottle.

"Nope, it's still gross, but tonight I'll make an exception."

The beach was empty except for six of us gathered around the bonfire; Roscoe was hard at work on Thanksgiving dinner in the kitchen. All the scents of food and flames filled the air as Darryl began playing his father's guitar. There was something almost magical about the music, like he'd been holding it in for years.

The giant beach wolf swayed from side-to-side as his fingers nimbly traced the strings along the neck, the pointer and thumb claws of his other digits meticulously plucking each note. The guitar sang just as Mosavi described.

I kept glancing over at the elder, studying his face. It did little good because I could never tell his exact emotions just by looking at him. Stony indifference? Stony interest? That's all I got as he sat on the sand, his arms crossed.

With the final note, the guitar resonated far longer than it had before, filling the air as the ocean waves applauded.

Mosavi uncrossed his arms, rubbing the fur on his chest, the hackles on the back of his neck raised. "I remember this."

"Thanks for taking good care of my guitar," Darryl said with a cocky smile, knowing what he'd accomplished. "Never seen it so polished before."

"You really are his grandson. Darryl Shields." Mosavi drew in a deep breath, the intensity of his stare remaining. "If it weren't so absurd, I'd believe in reincarnation."

"Shields. I haven't gone by that name since I was human."

"It was foolish of you to change it, knowing the greatness behind such a name." Mosavi's hackles finally flattened against his smooth mane. "Perhaps I wouldn't have given up on you so easily."

"I'm glad you did. I didn't want that life." He looked around at the ocean. "Everything I've ever wanted is right here."

Even though he was annoyed at first, Mosavi's face shattered into something much softer. "Sebastian always performed with his eyes closed as well."

"I need to be in a different place when I play these pieces," Darryl said. "When I close my eyes, I can see every note as a ribbon. Each one is a different color, and I can picture where my fingers should be at just the right moment. It's my way of slowing time. Dad always told me that's the way his father played, but my dad could never see the notes like that. He kept his eyes open."

"You transcend reality," Mosavi said, a wide smile finally parting his face. "I could never replicate the feeling myself with the violin, but I've come as close as I'll ever get. You go well beyond that. It's genius, as much as I hate to admit it."

Darryl laughed. "Genius is a little too flattering for a stoner werewolf living in a shack on the beach."

"Perhaps," Mosavi said, his eyes almost glistening. "Perhaps merit shouldn't be based solely upon appearance." He turned to me. "I guess I owe you an apology."

Willa turned and gave her husband a surprised look.

"Oh?" I said, rubbing my palms in anticipation of the crow he was about to eat.

"I owe you one, but you're not getting it. We still have a lot of work ahead of us."

"You're such a—" I whispered but stopped and forced a smile when he glared at me. "So, I take it our two nights a week have been canceled?"

"Regrettably."

Austin's stomach rumbled from across the fire.

"It's two o'clock. When the hell is Roscoe gonna be finished?" he asked.

"One mustn't rush perfection," Roscoe said in a fake Italian accent as he made his way to the fire. "Everything's almost done. Just waitin' on the rest of the turkeys in the smoker. They're gonna be so juicy."

"How many turkeys did you end up getting?" Austin asked. "I counted like eight of 'em. We expecting more, or are you gonna go on a binge?"

"They're on their way." Adam had been glancing at his phone every five minutes until now. "I wanted to invite a few of my friends from the city."

"Well shit. How about some damn appetizers then?" Austin held his stomach. "I haven't eaten since last night."

"That's not the sound of hunger. The seven lobster dinners you ordered for room service and horked down on my bill are likely still digesting," Mosavi said through his teeth.

"Oh yeah. That was good shit," Austin said casually. "Thanks, Mayor Moneybags."

Mosavi was close to lunging, but Willa grabbed the sensitive area between his shoulder blades to calm him like she had the other day.

The sound of bus brakes squealed in the parking lot far behind Darryl's shack, and Adam leapt to his feet before making a mad dash toward the commotion.

"Good. Everyone's here," Austin muttered, turning to Roscoe. "Bring on the food, Emeril Lagasse."

Roscoe scooped up a handful of sand.

"Bam!" he shouted, throwing it to the ground, but a strong breeze whipped it directly into Mosavi's face. "Uh oh." Roscoe tore away from the fire before running back into Darryl's house with his tail between his legs.

"This is all a test, isn't it?" Mosavi snarled, turning to Willa. "Everyone is seeing how far they can push me before I start rampaging."

"Relax, dear," she said, brushing the sand away. "It's the beach. We're going to get sand everywhere anyway."

Out of the corner of my eye, Adam was quietly leading three werewolves to the beach, signaling for me to keep Austin distracted.

"Uh, Austin, what's in that little box you brought with you?"

His eyes brightened. "It's a surprise for Adam, but don't tell him. He thinks I was just working on the still."

"I take it things have been going alright for you two," Darryl said.

"I think so," Austin said. "I've got a lot to make up for."

"Adam doesn't see it that way," I said as the four werewolves stopped just shy of the fire. There was a short brown werewolf with a thick black mane, a silver werewolf around Roscoe's height with dark gray mane, and a taller skinnier werewolf with shaggy black fur. They each wore a dog tag and army fatigues similar to Austin's.

"The pack's got your back, ain't that right boys?" the silver werewolf said, his voice cracking and shuddering slightly.

Austin snapped his head toward them as the others shouted in unison, "Yes sir!"

"W—what?" Austin scrambled to his feet, stumbling a few times in the sand before running up to the other three. He let out a high-pitched whine. "How?"

"Where the hell have you been?" the silver werewolf said through tears as they all surrounded the larger werewolf in a group hug. "You went AWOL without saying a word to us."

"I thought you guys were dead," he shouted hysterically, pulling away before wiping the deluge of tears from his eyes. He reached for his chest and snatched the dog tags he wore before pulling them away until the chain broke. "They threw these in the trash. I thought they killed you all, and I thought I was next." He struggled to catch his breath, his legs shaking as though he would collapse at any second.

"It was all classified, and they didn't fill us in on anything until later. North Korea developed a nerve agent that can take down werewolves without having any effect on humans. They were testing ways to immunize us against it, but they weren't gonna kill us. They kept the doses really low until they found something that worked. They were protecting all of us."

Austin looked down at the tags in his hand. "All this time..." His voice was weak and shaky just like his legs.

"We've been looking for you everywhere," the taller black one said. "You have any idea what you put us through? We weren't ever gonna let you go."

"Big-little shit," the short brown one said with a chuckle. "We missed you taking everything seriously all the time."

Austin finally fell to his knees as the others held onto him, each one pressing their faces into his. Adam leaned in close to me before whispering into my ear.

"I've been chatting with them for weeks. They're gonna live in Norwich with Austin. They really were looking all over the world for him." Tears welled in his eyes as he smiled, watching the four lick at each other. "I didn't understand what I was a part of when I was a half-turn, and I don't care what our original purpose was to the witches. We're so much better."

"I can't wait until my day comes," I whispered, looking around at everyone. Darryl watched the pack's emotional reunion while cradling his father's guitar. Mosavi slipped an arm around Willa's waist as they kissed softly. Roscoe emerged from the shack and made his way back to the fire before standing by my side.

"Now that's a happy werewolf," Roscoe whispered.

I tugged at the thicker fur on his chest, and he leaned in, allowing me to wrap my arms around his neck and pull him into a kiss of my own. It didn't matter where we were or how bad things had gotten before—when our lips met, we were at home.

"We're gonna need a bigger house," I whispered to Roscoe. "I think we're about to add a few more to our pack."

"Hell yeah. More people to cook for," Roscoe said, his tail wagging.

Austin and the others pulled away, and the larger werewolf turned to Adam while reaching into his pocket. He pulled out a small, wooden box.

"I don't deserve all this," he said through tears before gently pressing the box into Adam's hand. "This doesn't even come close to what you just gave me."

     

Adam opened the gift and smiled as he looked inside. He pulled out a polished, silver chain that had two dog tags with leather wrapping, Austin's name was on one and his name was on the other.

"You looked good when you wore my chain that night you turned." He took the piece of jewelry and slipped around the smaller werewolf's neck. "It's better than any kuu, and Willa helped me make it. I think you'll like what it can do."

Adam pushed his larger mate into the sand, falling on top of him, their eyes locking for several moments. It was as though everyone else had disappeared and they were the only ones left on earth.

"You've been asking yourself for years the same question." Adam rested his head along the crook of Austin's neck. "This is why you're still here."

# Chapter 39

# Leaving the Pack

*One Month Later*

A loud bang from the roof tore me out of bed, but Roscoe remained fast asleep. An actual bomb could go off, and he'd still be drooling, face-down in his pillow. I only knew this because Steve and Blake had decided to play a little prank recently involving a pot of firecrackers under our bed. I'd nearly died of a heart attack, but Roscoe had scratched his stomach, turned over, and kept on snoring.

Another boom rattled the house followed by what sounded like a pop and hiss from the bathroom. I was wide awake now, dashing through the hallway. A torrent gushed from a hole that had been punched through the drywall exposing the plumbing.

"What the fuck is happening right now?" I shouted as Steve slipped backward before falling into the tub.

"Ah shit," he said, his ears falling back against his head as he struggled to right himself. Austin and Randall rushed in behind me. "Someone turn off the main line!"

Austin disappeared, and Randall helped Steve out of the tub, both now soaking wet as they tried to prevent the water from shooting onto the floor. I kept my distance but that didn't help, because as soon as Austin cut the main line, the two shook all the water off their outer coats like dogs.

I stood in the middle of the bathroom with my arms out in shock, water dripping from my face.

"Ooooo... sorry, Cody," Randall said before clearing his throat. "Habit."

"What happened to my shower?" I asked, growing angrier as I spoke. The entire place was turning into a construction project; I hadn't slept properly in weeks with all the noise and dust.

"Well, there was mold in the drywall, and I was gonna replace it and put in some really nice tile and a new shower." Steve's ears were still low, but the tip of his tail wagged a little. "See, we're gonna knock down this wall"—he pointed to the wall next to the bathtub with a window looking out into the back yard—"and extend the bathroom to put in a shower and a nice big jacuzzi bathtub. You're gonna love it when it's all done!"

"You're going to knock down a load-bearing wall?" I reached for a towel and began drying myself. "Need I remind you guys, I don't own this house! Did you get permits for anything?"

The gray werewolf laughed. "Pfft, permits. Blake talked to someone on the phone who gave him the go-ahead."

"You're a fucking contractor, Steve! You know damn well we need this shit in writing!"

"Blake's the one that handles all the agreements, so go yell at him."

I took a step back, my feet splashing in a puddle of water that was now making its way across the wood floors. "You knocked out the drywall to take care of the mold there, and now we're going to have mold everywhere."

"Austin was gonna replace the floor anyways," Randall said as Austin walked back into the bathroom. "Ain't that right, mate?"

"I was gonna do it *eventually*." Austin let out a sigh. "I still haven't finished the extra foundation around the garage."

"I can't handle this," I muttered before walking out into a waterlogged hallway, the planks of wood already warping under my feet. It was seven in the morning, and I hadn't had my coffee yet. As I walked through the house, I found everything caked in the usual white dust, the wall dividing what was once the garage and the dining room now missing.

There were used paper plates and beer bottles lying next to air mattresses strewn across the area, and the kitchen looked like a complete disaster. My coffee pot was still half-full of day-old java that no one cleaned out, and both sides of the sink had piles of grease-covered dishes and pans.

There were six werewolves living in this house, and I had lost control of the situation. As much as I tried to get ahead of the messes, a tsunami of fur, dust, grease and trash appeared faster than I could clean. I stood gazing in awe at the mess, and something inside of me finally snapped. It wasn't anger—it was something a lot more disturbing. The room lightened to silver.

"Uh, Roscoe was gonna clean this," Blake said. I hadn't heard him come in from outside as the pulsing in my ears had become so loud it drowned out everything else.

The room faded back to a normal hue, and I turned toward the black werewolf with a widened expression.

"I will burn this whole place to the ground." My voice was empty to match what I was feeling at that moment.

"We'll get it clean, I promise!"

"I will burn this place to the ground with everyone still inside, I swear."

"O–kay," Blake took a step back. "You need coffee. I'll make you a fresh pot."

I didn't respond. Instead, I made my way to the dining room table before sitting on the chair, looking around at the devastation. A week ago, Mosavi had insisted I live with him for a while so he could teach me elder things, but as usual, I had refused. Living with him would likely keep me on edge, but I knew now there were much worse things in life. Hell, I'd have chosen to live in the woods at the moment just to get away from all the filth and noise.

The door creaked open, and Adam trotted carelessly inside, his clawed hands covered in dirt from working in his greenhouse. Austin bought it for him using that stash of money under the porch. As he shut the door, he left a brown handprint on the wall next to it.

"Hey Cody. You mind going to the hardware store with me for some more soil? I need an extra pair of hands."

The room turned silver again. It was getting harder to control the vironoct—every day, more fur sprouted up on my arms and legs. Was it possible to bring about the transformation through unbridled rage alone?

"Oh, you're in a mood again," he said, averting his eyes. "Maybe I'll get Randall to do it."

I remained silent. If I so much as opened my mouth, I knew what would happen. Once I started yelling, it was like Castle Bravo.

Everyone seemed so happy lately, and I didn't want to ruin what we'd spent months trying to fix.

There was little choice left. I had to leave the pack for a while.

I stood and walked over to the door, the floor in the living room now covered in the water that had made its way from the bathroom. After slipping on my wet sandals, I quietly made my way outside.

The elegant double doors opened. I had expected to see Mosavi's butler, since he was the one that answered the intercom to let me into the estate. Instead, I was greeted by a grinning Darius, his sharp, white teeth glistening as if mocking me.

"You look a mess."

"Thanks," I muttered. "I wanted to ask if—" Man, this was hard. With every word, his sharp grin grew wider.

"Yes?" The way he said that made me want to punch him in the face.

"Is the offer to live here still on the table," I said quickly.

"Hmm. I don't know. You were quite adamant and rude about not accepting my gracious offer when I made it the first time."

"I was wrong, okay?" I was now speaking slowly through my teeth. "I would very much appreciate it if I could stay here for a couple months."

"I'd have to discuss this with—"

"Is that Cody?" Willa's voice echoed excitedly from inside the foyer as she descended the stairs.

"I guess you can discuss it now," I whispered as he groaned, his wife obviously ruining his plans to make me grovel.

"My dear. I thought you were still sleeping."

She strolled up behind him and smiled at me. "I was, but then I heard Cody's voice and had to come down. Are you finally ready to stay here for a while?"

"Yeah." This was so humiliating. "It's a little too hectic at home right now."

"Oh, that's right. I remember Darius on the phone discussing the construction plans."

The elder werewolf's eyes widened as he turned and shook his head.

"Oh. Was that a secret?"

"Wait," I said as Mosavi turned back to me. "What exactly were you talking about?"

"It was an over-the-phone orientation, similar to what you all had to go through. I needed to make sure they followed the law."

"Oh."

"Aren't you forgetting that you also gave them permission to remodel that old eyesore of a house?"

Everything in my vision turned silver. "It was YOU!"

"Careful, now. You don't want to do anything you'll regret," Mosavi said, holding up a hand.

"If I were a werewolf right now—"

"But you're not, so keep your temper in check." Mosavi turned and gave a slight snarl to Willa as she smirked and flashed her brows at him. At least I had *someone* on my side in this town.

If she wasn't living here, I'd have probably taken my chances in the woods.

"It's a little chilly out, but let's have some mimosas by the pool," Willa said, pulling me the rest of the way inside the house. As angry as I was, her bubbly personality always cheered me up. "Don't worry, we'll have more than enough time to get back at him," she whispered.

### Winter Solstice

Darius stood snout-to-snout with his wilder brother, both of their hackles raised as they bared every sharp tooth in their mouths. This *family reunion* was going about as well as I expected.

Willa and I glanced at one another before she finally broke the ice.

"It's nice to finally meet you," she said, pulling the larger feral's attention away from the confrontation. "You certainly look different from your brother."

"Are you the witch?" the elder asked, his tone hesitant.

"I prefer to be called a lady, but if we must be specific—yes."

The feral looked back at his brother as if gauging his body language. "No tricks. No spells. No trinkets." He turned away and began walking along a dirt path. This place was both familiar and strange. Even though I'd been here before, the forest always seemed to change, like a living maze.

Mosavi glared back at me, and I shrugged before following the feral elder.

"What a waste of time. We could be in the Caribbean," Darius muttered.

"It's almost Christmas. Wouldn't you rather try to make amends with your family?" I asked, looking back in time to see Mosavi roll his eyes.

"I would rather be on my yacht pleasing my wife with a little half-turn ass on the side."

I shuddered at that considering what had happened a few days after I moved in. Willa had been tending to her restaurant, and I'd had a little too much scotch during one of Mosavi's 'lessons.' He was every bit as rough and dominant as I'd imagined he would be.

"Just so you know, that's never going to happen again."

"Just like you would never take me up on my offer to live with me." He flashed a devious grin and I turned away. "Next time I'll have Roscoe serve us food afterward."

"Can you please not make him wear the maid's outfit anymore? It's really going to his head."

"It's hilarious. It's like having my very own court jester."

"You're such an ass."

We stepped into a clearing with several artificial caves carved into the large hills. Norwich was relatively flat, but further out into the woods were large sandstone hills. The last time we were here, everything had been gold and orange, but now even the leafiest trees had lost their foliage, and the only green remaining were the large Douglas Firs and other conifers blanketing the hills.

A small, rapid stream split the little feral village in half, a crooked log bridge connecting it. Several werewolves smoked herbs around a large bonfire while others carried freshly killed game to log butchering tables.

"This is what I always imagined hell would look like," Mosavi muttered.

"Don't be so crass. It's unbecoming," Willa scolded. "It's quaint and lovely. It's been a while since I was out in the middle of nature. There's always something so peaceful about it."

"Norwich is peaceful enough," Mosavi said. "This place offers nothing that we cannot have better."

The larger elder turned back to Darius and frowned, shaking his head. "Do you ever find joy in anything anymore, little brother?"

"I find joy in many things."

"Such as?"

"My wife."

The elder leaned in closer to him. "And?"

"I have all the money I could ever want. I have a nice house. Cars. I can go anywhere in the world I please. I live in comfort and luxury you could only dream of."

"All of those things bring you joy?"

"Are you hard of hearing?"

Mosavi's brother smiled. "My ears hear your words, but they do not hear joy when you speak them."

"It must be all the caked-in dirt."

The feral elder frowned again.

"Why have you called me here?" Mosavi asked, posturing aggressively. "Did you expect me to find joy in the oppressive stenches that settle over this place like smog?"

"I simply wanted to share the solstice with my brother." He held out a familiar leather pouch. "We should smoke."

It quickly became clear what the other elder was doing, and part of me—a very small part—wanted to warn Mosavi. The rest of me wanted to see what hilarity would ensue once that herb stripped every last bit of his smugness away.

The feral elder glanced at me and gave a half-grin.

"This looks different than I remember."

"Do you no longer smoke?" Mosavi's brother handed him a pipe carved with intricate designs. The craftsmanship seemed almost ancient.

"I smoke, yes. Only the finest tobacco."

"Would you turn down tanbaku?"

Mosavi's eyes widened. "How did *you* get something so fine?"

"We are not completely cut off from the Midna. We do make trades."

The smaller elder loosened the collar of his dress shirt before unbuttoning the top half. He'd wanted to make a statement, which was why he'd dressed up before trudging through the woods, but I could tell he regretted the decision. He wasn't wearing a blazer this time, but his nice slacks had become dusty with small tears from thorns and leafless underbrush.

"This doesn't look like tanbaku," Mosavi said suspiciously, his tone softening a little as he grabbed the pipe. "But it has been a long time. Perhaps a little couldn't hurt. It would at least mask the smell of musky animals."

And with that, the larger elder put an arm across Mosavi's shoulder and led him to the cave where we'd all had our visions.

"Do you have your phone?" I whispered, turning my attention to a bewildered Willa.

She reached into her cleavage and pulled out a diamond-studded case with her smartphone inside. "Of course. Why?"

"You're definitely gonna want to record this."

"I loooove you," Mosavi slurred while leaning against me on the long walk back out of the woods. "You smell soooo good."

"Oh God, this is the best Christmas present I've ever gotten," I said, trying to hold back laughter. Willa and I had been watching Darius's mental decline for the last three hours as he and his brother caught up. Because of the way the herb worked, he was going to remember every embarrassing detail once he was sober—but he would also remember whatever visions he had.

We had also been recording the interaction between the two, which had started out lighthearted but soon darkened into something more serious and personal. After my own experience with this, I felt it wasn't my place to stay, but Willa wanted to remain. He was her husband, and there was a lot that Mosavi had kept to himself over the centuries.

"I sincerely hope you have more of that herb," Willa said, leaning in to kiss her husband on the lips. "I don't think I've ever seen him so giddy."

"I'm horny," he blurted out, giving me another sniff.

"When we get home, dear," Willa said, looking over at me. "Would you take care of it?"

"No!"

She sighed. "But I'm so very tired."

"They're *your* wifely duties!"

Mosavi began drooling on my shoulder half-asleep, and I shoved him awake.

"Oh, I don't think he'll last once we get home." I shoved him again. "God, you're heavy. Walk, damn it."

"Who needs to walk when you can float? We're floating." He fell into me again. "Like all these butterflies."

"Damn it," I shouted, almost tripping over a root as his full weight crashed into me. "I'm tempted to leave him here."

"As hilarious as that would be, there will be hungry witches about." Willa rubbed her chin. "I wish I'd brought something to help him sober up, but I kind of like him this way."

"I looove you, too," Mosavi said with a lopsided grin as he turned to her, his eyes squinty as he stumbled. "Yer just the prettiest girl I ever done met."

"What the hell is that accent?" Willa asked, cooing like a love-struck teenager. "You're off the hook, Cody. He's mine."

"Just so we're clear, I was never on the hook to begin with."

"Mmhmm."

I groaned and continued walking toward the clearing ahead. "Oh, thank God. We're almost to the road. The car's coming to pick us up, right?"

Willa didn't respond.

"Right?" I asked a little louder as Mosavi fell into me again.

"Of course, dear." She pulled out her phone. "Just need to make a quick call."

*Christmas Eve*

"Roscoe, take it off," I said through my teeth as the excited werewolf pranced around the dinner table, setting plates in front of everyone in a very tight, black and white maid's outfit with every horrifying frill imaginable.

"Leave it on," Mosavi said with a teasing grin before shoving a wad of cash into the lacey strap around Roscoe's waist. "It pleases me."

"Hell, I didn't know I'd be paid," Roscoe said, glaring at me before doing a clumsy twirl before putting a finger in his mouth, biting it seductively. This was him getting back at me. At first, it had been just a mild irritation, but the maid outfits got more and more elaborate and harder to ignore.

Randall and Steve snickered at the other end of the table, and Blake lifted the skirt.

"Dude, are you wearing panties?"

Roscoe slapped Blake's hand away. "Sir, I am a lady." He made sure to say *lady* in a much deeper voice while looking at me.

"What would work better at blinding me right now? Bleach or chlorine?" Austin asked, looking over at Adam. "I can't believe you had sex with *that*."

"It was a dark and desperate time," Adam said, shooting me a smile. "We've all done things we regret."

"All right. I've had enough," I said, shooting up from my chair while pulling out my phone. "You know what would please me? Entertainment with dinner." I pulled up the video of Mosavi and began playing it.

"Take that stupid outfit off, Roscoe!" the mayor shouted in a panic.

I stopped the video and took a deep breath through my nose before sitting back down. "All right. Now we're going to have a nice Christmas dinner."

"I really hate you," Mosavi growled.

"No, you don't. You loooove me, remember?"

"Honey, don't poke the bear anymore," Willa whispered into my ear, sounding unusually worried. "So, how's the construction coming along?" she asked, changing the subject.

"We've got the extra foundation laid, and more support beams in place. We'll be able to start on the second floor soon," Randall said.

"Second floor?" I asked loudly as Roscoe came back into the dining room now completely nude. "I thought you guys were just adding onto the house... laterally."

"Roscoe," Mosavi said calmly, closing his eyes while letting out a low growl. "I want you in clothing."

"But I didn't bring none except for the maid's outfit."

The mayor rubbed his temples in a circular motion. "Put on a pair of my sweatpants."

"Yes, yer majesty," he said before turning back around. "Oh! Dinner's almost done."

"We're opening up the kitchen a little more, making the dining room bigger while also moving the front door to where the garage was. The house is old, but she's got some good bones," Blake said, pulling a folded sheet of paper from his pocket and sliding it toward the mayor. "Oh, and uh... we're gonna need a bit more money to finish the project."

Mosavi picked up the paper and unfolded it. "What happened to all the money I've already given you?"

"You know... inflation. Tariffs. Taxes—contractor fees."

Mosavi folded the paper and slid it back across the table. "I see."

"Yeah, so, uh... we'll need it before next month so we can finish."

I knew Mosavi too well, and the calmer he was, the more worried everyone should be. He didn't respond to the audacious request; instead, he picked up his glass of scotch and lapped at it with his tongue.

"Blake, was it?" Mosavi asked as Roscoe walked back into the elaborate dining room wearing a pair of slacks that barely fit.

"Yes sir."

As Roscoe sat down next to me, a rip broke the uncomfortable silence. I could practically feel the heat coming off Mosavi's body.

"I'll give you the money next week," he continued, not looking at Roscoe as he spoke through a tight grimace. "You'll simply need to come here to collect it."

Blake's ears perked up and he nodded with a clueless smile. "You got it, sir! What time do you want me to come by?"

"Midnight." The mayor's stare turned to ice, and Austin cleared his throat before giving Blake a concerned look.

"That's a little late, but okay."

"Well," Roscoe said loudly, shattering the suffocating aura as he stood again, the ripping growing louder. "Dinner's not gonna serve itself."

Mosavi looked at the pants Roscoe had selected, his eyes glowing silver. "Why did you wear those?"

"Ya told me to put wear yer pants."

"And you chose my two-thousand-dollar Giorgio Armani dress pants instead of the sweatpants I told you to wear!"

"Damn, two thousand dollars? I think you got—" The pants made one more tearing sound. "Ripped off."

"Dear, how about some Christmas music?" Willa said, pulling Mosavi's dangerously razor-sharp focus away from Roscoe. "It's a little too quiet."

"Yes. Yes, some music," Darius said shakily. It was odd seeing him hold back so much, but I was kind of proud of him. He handled the situation a lot better than I would have.

*Later that night*

Everyone was drunk, filing out of the mansion and leaving behind what looked like the aftermath of a frat party. An expensive one. Even though Mosavi had tried to pull the brakes, no amount of vironoct persuasion was enough to stop what had started once the werewolves found the liquor cabinet. To be fair, Mosavi had already been three sheets to the wind before everything went tits up.

"Looks like Roscoe's got his work cut out for him tomorrow," I said, slowly entering an unlit study with an exhausted Mosavi lying on one of the tufted sofas. "You look like shit."

"I apologize for everything," he said, his tone taking on an airy quality as he lapped at the whiskey in his glass. "I had no idea what you were putting up with until now."

I stepped all the way into the room, pulling the beaded cord on one of the desk lamps before sitting across from him. I didn't say anything; instead, I picked up a glass and poured some whiskey.

"How do you handle such chaos without losing your mind?"

"You know what's funny? Willa told me we had a lot in common, and I told her she was full of shit. But after tonight?" I held up the glass. "I guess I kind of see it."

"A month ago, I'd have had them all thrown in jail if they pulled then what they pulled tonight."

I took a sip and leaned back. "What's changed?"

He lapped at his whiskey again. "I feel sick when I think about my behavior in the woods. Part of me wanted to stay with my brother—a very small part, but not insignificant. That frightens me."

"It shouldn't," I said, studying Mosavi's face. Even with his short temper and pompous attitude, I'd noticed something softer about him after Thanksgiving, when Austin was reunited with his lost pack. "You never did answer your brother's question."

He didn't respond, and I knew it wasn't because he didn't want to. It was because he couldn't.

"You didn't expect me to see who you really are, did you?"

"Not exactly," he said with a sigh. "Willa is too close. We have been through hell and back together, but I have closed us off from others for her protection. Losing her scares me more than anything in this world. In all that time I thought I was protecting her by pushing away my baser instincts, but all I was doing was making us both miserable."

"Did you have a vision?"

"A painful one." He took another drink. "I can't save the world, Cody. I want to, but saving the world for our kind means destroying it for others. If I could close off my conscience and do what I feel needs to be done, I would hate what I would become."

"Well, you're not God." I slid off the couch before sitting next to the distraught elder. "Your motives are good, Darius, but what good is saving the world if you destroy it for yourself? What good is living this lavish lifestyle when you're miserable?" He went to object, but I cut him off. "Don't try to deny it. I've been living with you for a month, and you've never really smiled."

Mosavi placed his empty glass on the table. "I don't want you to become me," he said, this time with a real smile. "You seem to understand things I have long since forgotten."

"Not really. We've all gone through some terrible things. My pack. You. Willa. I wasn't happy until I met Roscoe and the rest. I could have easily been bitter and ruthless like you if I was in that state of mind when you met me."

"This was the first holiday we've spent with others in decades. Willa enjoyed every moment, even the chaos." He let out a laugh. "I think she may have encouraged the chaos. She'll always have the witch in her, after all."

"Did *you* enjoy it?"

Mosavi stopped laughing before falling into quiet contemplation for only a moment. "I did."

I grabbed the crystal bottle and filled both of our glasses. "You may not be a part of our pack, but maybe you'd consider being less distant and mean."

"Hmph," he grunted as our glasses met with a soft clink. "Let's not get ahead of ourselves."

# Chapter 40

# The Stars

*Ten Months Later*

I'd been sitting on the couch in the living room staring at a huge black television screen, my reflection barely visible. The person staring back at me was almost unrecognizable, the silver glow of his eyes like two tiny moons. Everything had gotten bigger, from my muscles to my height, but I hadn't shifted yet. The thick hair I once had turned to fur, nearly covering my lower body, and a little tail hung lower behind me.

My face was different, too. There wasn't any more hair than usual, but the surge of testosterone sharpened my features. My brows were thick, and my jaw had broadened. There was a different magic behind my eyes, beyond the physical, and beyond the vironoct. It had been locked away for so long in a prison of my own making.

With one realization, the chains inside of me shattered. The terrible memories of my old human life lightened until they floated away, leaving only contentment. Living in the past only limited me, but letting it go set me free.

I looked around at the much larger living room, the expensive leather couches and cherry wood tables freshly polished to a shine with beautiful lamps and elaborate sculptures of different animals. The walls were clean and painted an off-white color that captured and reflected the sunlight that beamed in through the huge bay windows.

In all my life, I'd never lived in such a beautiful place. Everything had either been added to or completely remodeled. Even the kitchen had brand new appliances, much to Roscoe's joy. That was his domain, and he kept it as clean as he could. I think all we needed was something nice to be proud of, which made our home worth maintaining.

Adam started his own landscaping business, and he spent most of his time transforming our yard from an unruly jungle of weeds and trash to an enchanted forest with beautiful flowers, maple and poplar saplings surrounded by the greenest sod. With Austin's help, he had designed an artificial pond and a waterfall. The others built a gazebo near our fire pit, which was the only thing that hadn't changed, aside from the new lawn furniture.

Blake, Randall, Steve, and Austin had built a successful contracting company, and Darius was all too eager to have them build up the town, giving dour government buildings much-needed facelifts. I'd never seen Austin or Adam so full of excitement and purpose. The transformation had been gradual. The bond they shared only intensified the more fulfilled they were with their roles in life and love.

The front door opened, and Roscoe trotted in holding several bags of groceries. It was all fresh produce, vegetables, meat from the butcher, wines and spices. I wasn't sure when he stopped buying junk food altogether—another gradual change.

"How were things at the restaurant?" I asked, sliding off the couch to greet him with a one-armed hug and a kiss on the nose.

"Aw man. Never seen so many tourists in my life. I'm pooped."

I grabbed the groceries out of his arms and headed into the kitchen.

"How're ya feelin'?" he asked, following me close as I sat the bags on the black granite counter.

"I don't know. It's hard to put it into words."

Roscoe smiled and leaned in for another kiss, more tongue this time. When had he gotten so fit and even more handsome? He always had a charm about him, but he was so different now. Since he owned his own restaurant, he had to stay clean. He wasn't overeating junk food anymore, so his gut had gradually disappeared and the natural werewolf muscles came through. Roscoe had gone from looking old and worn out to decades younger in just a few months.

"It's gettin' close." Roscoe reached into one of the bags to sort the produce. "Maybe you'll turn on Halloween like Adam did."

"Does it hurt?"

Roscoe shook his head. "No way. It's almost sad that you'll never feel anything like that again. Yer whole body feels like it's breakin' free from being tied down, and you just feel right after. You don't feel like a monster or nothin'. You just feel normal."

"Do I look different?" I asked, turning back to him.

"Yeah and no. Yer still the same Cody, but I can tell yer gonna be big."

"Will you still want to be with me?" That thought had been bothering me for months. What if after I turned, he lost interest?

Roscoe's eyes widened. "Aw, come on Cody."

"I know. I'm just worried."

He took me into his arms, and my face fell into his broad chest. Roscoe still had that *Roscoe* smell to him, but it was so pleasing to the nose now—like a hit of something familiar in all the change.

"Yer my everything, ya know. It don't matter what you look like when this is over, yer stuck with me." He paused and looked down at the ground. "I think I know why yer worried."

"You do?"

"We don't talk much about what we saw, but I just want you to know that I ain't anything like all those guys that hurt you." He let out a laugh through his teeth and looked back up. "That last one didn't even look like yer type."

"When you're lonely and desperate, anyone's your type. You can also fool yourself into believing you have a connection with someone who really doesn't care about you. When I think back on those years with clarity, the obvious was staring me in the face, but I didn't want to believe it." I shook my head. "He kept calling me by his ex's name, and I just thought it was normal."

"Ouch. Well, if it makes you feel any better, I can't even remember all my ex's names." We both chuckled, half-serious. "I'm not gonna leave you. You weren't meant for that last guy. He was a piece of shit, and he'll get what he deserves in time. But you know, even though he wasn't a good guy, if he hadn't done what he did, you wouldn't be here. I wouldn't be here."

"We saved each other." Tears lingered in my eyes as I remembered that vision of him under the tree. "I'm so proud of you, Roscoe."

"And I've always been proud of you. Ever since that day we met, you were someone I could never reach. A solid ten while I was barely scrapin' the surface. When I got to know you better, I wanted to be someone you could be proud of one day, too. Took me a while, but I don't think I've ever been this happy."

"You were, once."

Roscoe shook his head. "I let him go, Cody. I let that side of myself slip away because it wasn't a good life. Livin' out in the wild is hard, and yer always lookin' over yer shoulders. We were gonna get caught. It was only a matter of time."

"We'll find them one day. We'll get rid of the witches for good."

"They ain't evil, just empty. Maybe you can figure out how to Willa-fy 'em all."

"Maybe." I ran my hand playfully along Roscoe's stomach. "You actually have abs now. You match the drawing on my coffee mug."

"Ya know, one day it just hit me outta the blue. I don't need all that crap to make me feel good when I'm wakin' up next to the best drug I never wanna quit."

"Well, I've never been compared to a drug before, but I'm flattered. Speaking of the bed." I gave Roscoe a head tilt while eyeing the hallway.

"Aw, come on. I know where this is goin'."

"Can we at least get a new bed? I can live with the ugly shag carpet and eyesore loveseat but at least let me get us a new bed. We're going to need a bigger one anyways for when I turn."

"But the mattress has our smells on it."

"Yeah. That's the problem. We're going to get a nice mattress and a mattress cover to keep it that way."

Roscoe hummed in contemplation while pulling more groceries out of paper bags.

"I know. It's a big ask considering I've been changing and decorating the house, but all I want in the bedroom is a new mattress. I won't touch anything else."

"Promise?" Roscoe asked, looking back at me. "It ain't like I don't like change, but I feel like we've been changin' everything too fast."

"I promise. Plus, you don't weigh as much as you did, so we'll get rid of all those lumps you don't like."

"I like my lumps!"

"You complain about your back every time you wake up."

"Yeah, 'cause I sleep on it wrong."

When I stared at him with my arms folded, he let out a sigh.

"Okay, it's a little uncomfortable." He folded the bag and set it off to the side. "Just pick out a nice one, okay?"

I looked down at the counter. "What are you gonna make tonight?"

"I was thinkin' with all the changes lately, we could have something we ain't had in a while."

"Like what?"

Roscoe wrapped his arm around me, pulling me close. "Wanna help me make some baked ziti?"

*A Week Later*

It was going to happen soon, and my last phone call to Darryl had him scrambling to get up here in time. Halloween was just around the corner, and every day my body felt a little heavier. I kept to myself more since even the slightest noise would have me snapping at everyone. Why did I feel so empty?

Instead of a white van, a brand new black Mercedes SUV pulled into the driveway. Mosavi was actually driving it in his werewolf form. Most of the town knew about him now, but he still kept up the human facade during public events. It was strange not seeing him in a suit, and he rarely wore them as a werewolf now, opting for denim jeans and no shirt at all. The only thing adorning his upper body was a gold chain necklace with a pendant hanging off it. It was an otherworldly jagged symbol enclosed in a circle, much like a pentagram.

He walked up to the door and opened it without knocking, as he usually did. Darius and Willa would come over every other day, bringing expensive booze and cigars. I'd thought he would want nothing to do with us again after last Christmas, but he was changing as well. While he was still aloof and at times, downright mean, he'd become more social after that visit with his brother, especially with me.

Mosavi closed the door behind him and turned, holding a black felt box in his right hand.

"Willa wanted me to give you this for when it is time." His tone was the usual deep, but his inflection seemed almost sentimental.

I took the box and opened it. Inside was a similar gold chain affixed with a different jagged symbol pendant, also encircled.

"Wow, it's beautiful." I picked it up and fastened it around my neck. "Thank you. What is this symbol?"

"It's a mark of the elder. We are both eager to see what you become."

I placed the empty box on the end table and looked away. "I still feel kind of useless."

"Useless?"

"It's funny. When we first formed this dysfunctional family, I thought I was the only one that had a goal in mind, but it all disappeared. Everyone else found their success, but I'm just sitting inside this house."

Darius dropped a hand onto my shoulder, his claws digging in a bit. "When I met you, I sensed ambition. It was what drew me to you—more than the vironoct. You have not lost those parts of yourself. Your priorities are simply shifting with the times and circumstances. What was important to you as a human is changing, and that is why you feel the way you do. But those feelings will change as well."

"I don't know what I want to do with my life, Darius."

"That is not something you have allowed yourself to reach for as of yet." He walked over to a liquor cabinet and standing humidor he'd gifted us after the remodeling was complete. No one usually dared drink what was in there without Mosavi present, and I'd actually grown fond of the cigars. We were the only ones that smoked them.

He pulled out two Cuban cigars, then shifted his attention to the alcohol before letting out a snarl. "All right, who the hell polished off the scotch?"

I walked over to the cabinet, examining the empty bottle next to the other fancy liquors. "Well, your culprits are probably the usual suspects."

The scowl on his face shifted with quiet laughter. "I am proud."

"Huh?"

He turned to me, placing a cigar into my hand. "Do you really think these unruly, undisciplined, wild animals would have ever found their true potential without you guiding them?"

"I didn't have anything to do with that."

"You're not an idiot. You were living in luxury at my mansion, but you weren't content with that. You could have stayed but didn't. You came back to this dump and whipped it into shape. You were the one that worked out the deal for Roscoe's restaurant. You were the one that forced Austin and the others to get the state licensing required to start a contracting business. You were the one that encouraged Adam to actually make money off what he loves doing. And I know for a fact that none of them have the brains to keep it all running smoothly."

He had a point, though I'd never thought of it being anything more than a natural next step. All I'd done was push them while keeping the finances and clients in order. They did the rest.

"You made this house a home," Mosavi added. "You brought warmth into our home as well. Willa talks so much about you, it gets on my nerves at times."

"She's still trying to seduce me."

"Once a witch, always a witch." He grinned for a moment, but it faded. "We are close to Samhain again, and I have been giving your ambitious suggestion a lot of thought. We need to do something about the coven, because Willa and I cannot leave to start over until the threat to Norwich is gone."

"You still want to leave?"

"No. But I need to. There are other towns we will build into werewolf sanctuaries, and we have attracted a lot of unwanted attention from those who are trying to segregate us into communes."

I turned back to the window. "You can't just leave the pack, you know."

A white van pulled into the driveway.

"I am not in your pack. I am your mentor." He glanced out the window. "Speaking of potential."

"He's happy with what he has, and who knows? They might make him the mayor of White Dunes."

The large werewolf climbed out of the van before grabbing his luggage and guitar case. He and the driver talked for a little while, both nodding and waving goodbye.

"I see he brought the guitar," Mosavi said, taking a deep breath through his nose while grabbing another cigar for our guest.

I opened the door, and Darryl slipped inside, dropping his things before pulling me into a crushing hug.

"Jeez, look at you." He let go and examined me further. "You're gonna be one big fucker."

"It will be quite a sight to behold," Mosavi said, catching Darryl's attention. "The birth of a new elder."

"Darius."

"Darryl," the mayor replied, and they gave each other an approving nod. They weren't chummy by any means, but they also didn't hate each other anymore. "Smoke?"

"Can't say no to that." He took the roll of tobacco and looked around. "I thought I had the wrong address for a second. This place is huge!"

"It still doesn't feel big enough with six werewolves living here," I said, nodding to the back french doors that were now at the far end of the dining room instead of the end of the hallway. "You should see the backyard."

🕯 🕯 🕯

*Halloween Night*

"Yer not gonna wear yer costume?" Roscoe asked, adjusting himself in his tight leather thong while fanning out a gray fur cape. He wore shiny faux plate greaves and gauntlets with an overly elaborate greatsword slung over his shoulder as he examined himself in the mirror. Earlier, Austin had been all too eager to help him wax away some of his face so he could draw on realistic-looking battle scars. I don't think I'd ever heard Roscoe scream so loud.

"I think he wore a little more than that in the game," I said.

"He did?" Roscoe scratched his head. "This is exactly what he looked like when Adam was playin'."

"Adam likes to use slutty mods. You do look hot though."

"Come on, Tarnished." He held up a leather suit of armor with his other hand. "Don't you want yer... ample reward?"

"Sorry. I'm not feeling up to it. All I wanna do lately is sleep."

Roscoe leaned his fake sword against the wall before sitting next to me on our new bed. As much as he expressed his disapproval, he'd fall asleep almost instantly once he laid down.

"You don't gotta wear nothin' if ya don't want to. It's yer night, ya know."

"We don't know that yet. I've been feeling like shit for weeks now, and nothing's really changed." I looked over at him again. "I hope you don't leave."

"Now, stop that." He removed his gauntlet and slipped his arm around me. "We've been through this already." He sighed and stood, removing his costume until he was wearing nothing. "I've been thinkin' that it ain't normal for you to feel like this for so long."

"Then why am I still like this? Is there something wrong with me?"

"Yup." He pointed to my shirt. "Take off yer clothes."

"I don't wanna have sex right now."

"We ain't. Take 'em off."

I narrowed my eyes suspiciously at him before standing and removing my clothing. "Okay?"

"Let's go outside."

"It's cold."

"Dude, yer covered in fur right now. No excuses. Let's go."

"My dick is still visible."

"Yeah so? Everyone here's seen it." He picked up his cell phone and began typing out a text, then then went into the closet and pulled out a relic of his past—the old orange hoodie he'd worn when we first met. "I cleaned it."

"I thought you said—"

"I said a lot of things. I'm startin' over. It'll be our smells, and our pack's. Once you turn, you'll love that smell, because it's everyone. It's home, ya know?"

That made me smile. There was something I'd wanted to say to him for so long, but I was always too afraid. I was still afraid—after all, I'd said it once before only to have it end in pain.

Roscoe grabbed me by the arm and led me into the living room before making our way out into the back yard. Darryl was already outside standing near a newly made fire while staring up at the waxing moon. He wasn't wearing any clothing either, but that wasn't unusual.

"Man, what a night," he said before turning back to me. "Not gonna dress up—in anything?"

"I think we're gonna have us Halloween at home, and I got a surprise fer Cody."

"Okay, I'm worried," I said while following Roscoe over to the fire. Once he sat, I took the spot next to him with Darryl on the other side.

Roscoe grinned, a few of his sharper canines glistening in the light of the flames.

As the minutes passed, one-by-one, the others arrived, each removing their costumes and clothes before taking their places on the grass around the fire. Blake, Randall, and Steve playfully shoved each other a little too close to the flames, knocking over the logs causing an ember to land on Austin.

The large werewolf screamed while rolling on the ground, smothering the burning fur. With a snarl, he charged at the other three while shouting all kinds of curse words. Adam, Darryl, and

Roscoe burst into laughter as the four scuffled in the dark away from the group.

"I'm actually shocked they managed to remodel the house without destroying it," Darryl said before straightening the logs, adding a couple more to the fire. He looked up at Adam. "How's Austin doing?"

"He still has some issues, but we're working through them." He turned in time to see Austin holding Steve in a chokehold. "They've all been helping him. He hasn't had one of his episodes in a while, and whenever he does, we know how to calm him down. The terrible shit he went through isn't just gonna disappear, but he knows he's safe, and that's really all he needs."

"What about you?" I asked. "It seems like we don't ever get a chance to talk anymore."

He paused for a moment and smiled. "I'm in a good place, too." He pointed to Roscoe. "You two say the L word yet?"

That familiar pang in my stomach returned, and I looked away. Roscoe opened his mouth to say something but was cut off by a woman's voice.

Willa led the way, her bare white skin almost glowing in the moonlight as she skipped through the grass, her perfect breasts bouncing in time with her cadence. Mosavi followed closely, also naked. They both took their places by the fire.

"Okay, so why are we all naked?" I asked.

"Because it's fun and natural," Willa said, shaking her chest playfully at me. "Embrace it, you two." She glanced over at an uncomfortably annoyed Mosavi before looking back at me. "He doesn't often go out without clothes either."

"Only animals do this," he grumbled.

Willa turned back to her husband. "Do I look like an animal to you?"

He huffed in annoyance before letting out a defeated, "No."

"Well, looks like everyone's here," Roscoe said before turning back to the other four still scuffling. "You guys, get over here. I got some good stuff." He pulled out a familiar pouch and gave that signature shitty grin.

"Oh, hell no!" I shouted, starting to stand, but Roscoe snatched my arm, pulling me back down.

"I second that motion," Mosavi shouted, trying to scoot away from the fire, but it was too late. Roscoe grabbed a handful of the herb before throwing it into the pit.

The flames erupted into a deep blue as thick white smoke poured outward, engulfing us all. The effects were immediate, turning the darkness to neon day, colorful hallucinations fluttering around us.

"Mmmm," Roscoe hummed, contentedly closing his eyes while swaying from side-to-side. "Shoulda brought some music."

"I'll grab the guitar," Darryl said, attempting to stand but stumbling before falling back to the ground. He lay there, sprawled on his back for a solid minute before muttering a slurred, "Never mind."

"I hate you so much," Mosavi said through his teeth, his dangerous glare fixed on Roscoe. "I just want to..." Slowly, his facial expression went from hostile to the same squinty-eyed laughter the others were experiencing. "I just want to hug you until you stop breathing."

"I feel left out," Willa muttered, trying to inhale more of the smoke that obviously had no effect. "At least this is fun to watch."

"Hey."

The voice next to me sent a shudder through my body. It wasn't as deep, but it had the same warmth. I turned toward Roscoe, but he wasn't Roscoe. This visage of him was half-turned as he wore his now oversized orange hoodie. He had messy silvery-black hair and a scruffy beard, his thickly muscled body covered in the same colored hair that was on his head, only with visible tan skin.

His canines were still longer and sharper, but the rest of his teeth looked more human. His ears were larger and pointy, just like when Austin had reverted to his half-turn form.

"Roscoe?"

"I never showed this to nobody before." He pulled me into his lap before wrapping me in his hoodie. "Nobody's ever been worth bein' vulnerable around, but you make me feel this way every day."

"Is this the drugs? Last time it gave you an overabundance of nipples."

"Nah." He propped his scruffy chin up on my shoulder as he continued whispering in my ear. "I know why you've been holdin' back. Yer afraid of turnin' 'cause of me. Yer still afraid that once you turn, I won't like you no more."

A slight nausea turned my stomach as I tried to push those thoughts away.

"Cody... I love you. And I'll love you no matter what. That's a promise I ain't ever gonna break."

The blue flames turned a watery blur as tears distorted everything a little more.

"You been waitin' for me to say it, but I didn't know how." He hugged me tighter. "This is the way it shoulda been, so don't be afraid of it no more."

The dam inside of me crumbled as my body went completely warm. Every inch of flesh tingled, and everyone around the fire stared wide-eyed in anticipation. Roscoe was right. I felt like I wanted to pull off my old, human skin, and stand in the moonlight reborn. For the first time in my life, there was a joy in my chest that radiated in bursts so powerful that I didn't want it to end.

Roscoe pulled away as my bones popped, the sensation dropping me to the ground until all I could see was the moon overhead. This should have been painful, but there wasn't pain, just a strange sensation of growth as my body expanded over the grass. My once short tail grew longer, jutting well past my inner thighs. I held my right hand up in front of me, the now silver moon illuminating the transformation as thick, brown fur spread, the skin on my palms hardening into black pads, hooked claws growing longer.

As my arm dropped to the side of my new body, I kept my gaze up at the sky while Roscoe's werewolf face came into view, looking down at me. He smiled at first, but then his expression turned to horror.

"Oh, goddamn it."

I sat up suddenly when I heard the howls break out from the distance.

"Aw shit!" Roscoe shouted.

I understood how Roscoe felt. The others around me began howling, and Roscoe struggled to contain it. Before I could say anything, my snout pointed up to the sky and a powerful howl shook everything around us.

That was me? It sounded so clean and strong—and deep.

"Oh my God—" Roscoe's words were interrupted as a shaky, gag-like howl left his maw.

Mosavi's howl joined mine, just as strong and clean. Roscoe's intermittent cursing between howls made me want to burst out laughing, but I couldn't. The involuntary instinct continued for several more minutes before finally subsiding. Roscoe was kind of right. It was like throwing up, but at least it felt good.

Everyone huddled in close, except for Mosavi, who stood back with Willa. He was completely out of it with a goofy, distant look, his tongue hanging out as his wife stroked his head between his ears.

"I, uh—" I paused, taking in the new timbre of my voice. It was so deep, almost bestial. "I—" Speaking was a struggle with the new mouth and flatter tongue, but every wall inside of me turned to dust before disappearing into the autumn wind.

I could say it. There was nothing left to hold it back. I'd walked through fire just to end up a better person on the other side, surrounded by family while wrapped in the arms of someone who actually loved me.

As I sat up with my head higher than it had ever been before, I turned to Roscoe and pushed him to the ground under my added weight.

"I love you, too. For the rest of my life."

Roscoe never really cried that much, but he fell to pieces in my arms as if the weight of the world vanished. It really was a beautiful life—we just needed to see it for what it was so we could enjoy it.

*Only when it's darkest can we truly see the stars.*

If you enjoyed this story, please remember to give it a review.
To learn more visit www.theliteratebeast.com.